3085226

TIME

THE UNAUTHORIZED GUIDE TO
DOCTOR WHO

1985–1989

SEASONS 22 TO 26, THE TV MOVIE

TAT WOOD
with additional material by LARS PEARSON

ian Press...

asons 7 to 11) [Second Edition]

Fluid Links: The Unauthorized Guide to the Doctor Who Eighth Doctor Adventures

Available Now from Mad Norwegian Press...

THE ABOUT TIME SERIES
by Lawrence Miles and Tat Wood

About Time 1: The Unauthorized Guide to Doctor Who (Seasons 1 to 3)
About Time 2: The Unauthorized Guide to Doctor Who (Seasons 4 to 6)
About Time 4: The Unauthorized Guide to Doctor Who (Seasons 12 to 17)
About Time 5: The Unauthorized Guide to Doctor Who (Seasons 18 to 21)
About Time 6: The Unauthorized Guide to Doctor Who (Seasons 22 to 26, TVM)

DOCTOR WHO REFERENCE GUIDES
AHistory: An Unauthorized History of the Doctor Who Universe [Second Edition out now]

Doctor Who: The Completely Unofficial Encyclopedia
by Chris Howarth and Steve Lyons

OTHER SCI-FI REFERENCE GUIDES
Redeemed: The Unauthorized Guide to Angel by Lars Pearson and Christa Dickson
Dusted: The Unauthorized Guide to Buffy the Vampire Slayer by Lawrence Miles, Lars Pearson
and Christa Dickson
Now You Know: The Unauthorized Guide to G.I. Joe by Lars Pearson

FACTION PARADOX NOVELS: THE COMPLETE SERIES
Stand-alone novel series based on characters and concepts
created by Lawrence Miles

Faction Paradox: The Book of the War [#0] by Lawrence Miles, et. al.
Faction Paradox: This Town Will Never Let Us Go [#1] by Lawrence Miles
Faction Paradox: Of the City of the Saved... [#2] by Philip Purser-Hallard
Faction Paradox: Warlords of Utopia [#3] by Lance Parkin
Faction Paradox: Warring States [#4] by Mags L. Halliday
Faction Paradox: Erasing Sherlock [#5] by Kelly Hale
Dead Romance by Lawrence Miles, contains rare back-up stories

Copyright © 2007 Mad Norwegian Press (www.madnorwegian.com)

Cover art by Jim Calafiore; cover colors by Richard Martinez (www.artthug.com)
Jacket & interior design by Christa Dickson (www.christadickson.com)

ISBN: 0-9759446-5-7
Printed in Illinois. First Edition: November 2007

table of contents

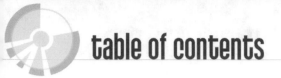

table of contents

Essays

About Time prides itself on being the most comprehensive, wide-ranging and at times almost *shockingly* detailed handbook to *Doctor Who* that you might ever conceivably need, so great pains have been taken to make sure there's a place for everything and everything's in its place. Here are the "rules"…

Every *Doctor Who* story gets its own entry, and every entry is divided up into four major sections. The first, which includes the headings **Which One is This?**, **Firsts and Lasts** and **X Things to Notice**, is designed to provide an overview of the story for newcomers to the series (and we trust there are more of you, owing to the success of the Welsh series) or relatively "lightweight" fans who aren't too clued-up on a particular era of the programme's history. We might like to *pretend* that all *Doctor Who* viewers know all parts of the series equally well, but there are an awful lot of people who - for example - know the 70s episodes by heart and don't have a clue about the 60s. This section also acts as an overall Spotters' Guide to the series, pointing out most of the memorable bits.

After that comes the **Continuity** section, which is where you'll find all the pedantic detail. Here there are notes on the Doctor (personality, props and cryptic mentions of his past), the supporting cast, the TARDIS and any major Time Lords who might happen to wander into the story. Following these are the **Non-Humans** and **Planet Notes** sections, which can best be described as "high geekery"… we're old enough to remember the *Doctor Who Monster Book*, but not too old to want a more grown-up version of our own, so expect full-length monster profiles. Next comes **History**, which includes all available data about the time in which the story's supposed to be set.

Of crucial importance: note that throughout the **Continuity** section, *everything* you read is "true" - i.e. based on what's said or seen on-screen - except for sentences in square brackets [like this], where we cross-reference the data to other stories and make some suggestions as to how all of this is supposed to fit together. You can trust us absolutely on the non-bracketed material, but the bracketed sentences are often just speculation.

The only exception to this rule is the **Additional Sources** heading, which features any off-screen information from novelisations, writer interviews, etc that might shed light on the way the story's supposed to work. (Another thing to notice here: anything written in single inverted commas - 'like this' - is a word-for-word quote from the script or something printed on screen, whereas anything in double-quote marks "like this" isn't.)

The third major section is **Analysis**. It opens with **Where Does This Come From?**, and this may need explaining. For years there's been a tendency in fandom to assume that *Doctor Who* was an "escapist" series which very rarely tackled anything particularly topical, but with hindsight this is bunk. Throughout its history, the programme reflected, reacted to and sometimes openly *discussed* the trends and talking-points of the era, although it isn't always immediately obvious to the modern eye. (Everybody knows that "The Sun Makers" was supposed to be satirical, but how many people got the subtext of "Destiny of the Daleks"?). It's our job here to put each story into the context of the time in which it was made, to explain *why* the production team thought it might have been a good idea.

Up next is **Things That Don't Make Sense**, basically a run-down of the glitches and logical flaws in the story, some of them merely curious and some entirely ridiculous. Unlike a lot of TV guidebooks, here we don't dwell on minor details like shaky camera angles and actors treading on each others' cues - at least unless they're *chronically* noticeable - since these are trivial even by our standards. We're much more concerned with whacking great story loopholes or particularly grotesque breaches of the laws of physics.

Analysis ends with **Critique**; though no consensus will ever be found on *any* story, we've not only tried to provide a balanced (or at least not-too-irrational) view but also attempted to judge each story by its own standards, *not just* the standards of the post-CGI generation.

The last of the four sections is **The Facts**, which covers ordinary, straightforward details like cast lists and viewing figures. We've also provided a run-down of the story's cliffhangers, since a lot of *Doctor Who* fans grew up thinking of the cliffhangers as the programme's defining points.

how does this book work?

This gives you a much better sense of a story's structure than a long and involved plot break-down (which we're fairly sure would interest nobody at this stage, barring perhaps those stories presently missing from the BBC archives).

The Lore is an addendum to the Facts section, which covers the off-screen anecdotes and factettes attached to the story. The word "Lore" seems fitting, since long-term fans will already know much of this material, but it needs to be included here (a) for new initiates and (b) because this is supposed to be a one-stop guide to the history of *Doctor Who*.

A lot of "issues" relating to the series are so big that they need forums all to themselves, which is why most story entries are followed by mini-essays. Here we've tried to answer all the questions that seem to demand answers, although the logic of these essays changes from case to case. Some of them are actually trying to find *definitive* answers, unravelling what's said in the TV stories and making sense of what the programme-makers had in mind. Some have more to do with the real world than the *Doctor Who* universe, and aim to explain why certain things about the series were so important at the time. Some are purely speculative, some delve into scientific theory and some are just whims, but they're *good* whims and they all seem to have a place here. Occasionally we've included footnotes on the names and events we've cited, for those who aren't old enough or British enough to follow all the references.

We should also mention the idea of "canon" here. Anybody who knows *Doctor Who* well, who's been exposed to the TV series, the novels, the comic-strips, the audio adventures and the trading-cards you used to get with Sky Ray ice-lollies, will know that there's always been some doubt about how much of *Doctor Who* counts as "real", as if the TV stories are in some way less made-up than the books or the short stories. We'll discuss this in shattering detail later on, but for now it's enough to say that *About Time* has its own specific rules about what's canonical and what isn't. In this book, we accept everything that's shown in the TV series to be the "truth" about the *Doctor Who* universe (although obviously we have to gloss over the parts where the actors fluff their

lines). Those non-TV stories which have made a serious attempt to become part of the canon, from Virgin Publishing's New Adventures to the recent audio adventures from Big Finish, aren't considered to be 100 percent "true" but do count as supporting evidence. Here they're treated as what historians call "secondary sources", not definitive enough to make us change our whole view of the way the *Doctor Who* universe works but helpful pointers if we're trying to solve any particularly fiddly continuity problems.

It's worth remembering that unlike (say) the stories written for the old *Dalek* annuals, the early Virgin novels were an honest attempt to carry on the *Doctor Who* tradition in the absence of the TV series, so it seems fair to use them to fill the gaps in the programme's folklore even if they're not exactly - so to speak - "fact".

You'll also notice that we've divided up this work according to "era", not according to Doctor. Since we're trying to tell the *story* of the series, both on- and off-screen, this makes sense. The actor playing the Main Man might be the only thing we care about when we're too young to know better, but anyone who's watched the episodes with hindsight will know that there's a vastly bigger stylistic leap between "The Horns of Nimon" and "The Leisure Hive" than there is between "Logopolis" and "Castrovalva". Volume IV covers the producerships of Philip Hinchcliffe and Graham Williams, two very distinct stories in themselves, and everything changes again - when Williams leaves the series, not when Tom Baker does - at the start of the 1980s.

There's a kind of logic here, just as there's a kind of logic to everything in this book. There's so much to *Doctor Who*, so much material to cover and so many ways to approach it, that there's a risk of our methods irritating our audience even if all the information's in the right places. So we need to be consistent, and we have been. As a result, we're confident that this is as solid a reference guide / critical study / monster book as you'll ever find. In the end, we hope you'll agree that the only realistic criticism is: "Haven't you told us *too* much here?"

And once we're finished, we can watch the *new* series and start the game all over again.

22.1: "Attack of the Cybermen"

(Serial 6T, Two Episodes. 5th - 12th January 1985.)

Which One is This? Colin Baker gets a go at beating the Cybermen, in what's a sequel to "The Tomb of the Cybermen" (5.1), "The Tenth Planet" (4.2), "The Invasion" (6.3), "Earthshock" (19.6), "An Unearthly Child" (1.1), "Resurrection of the Daleks" (21.4) and pretty much everything else.

Firsts and Lasts Officially, this is the first story deliberately tailored as forty-five minute instalments (as opposed to "Resurrection of the Daleks", which was made as a four-parter and later compressed to two). In overseas syndication, Season Twenty-Two was sometimes shown in omnibus format (meaning "Attack of the Cybermen" would have been shown all in one sitting on some US networks, but Ghana - for example - saw it as made), but more often the forty-five minute chunks were often broken into the traditional *Doctor Who* episode length. This means that the episodes on those occasions had all sorts of makeshift cliffhangers occurring at roughly 22 minutes and 30 seconds in (and see **Cliffhangers** for more). For this reason, we'll list "Four Things to Notice" for this story and the other Season Twenty-Two adventures (except 22.4, "The Two Doctors" which gets six).

It's also the first story since "Logopolis" (18.7) to first air on Saturdays at teatime and - at least for episode one - it's a triumphal return.

Four Things to Notice about
"Attack of the Cybermen"...

1. The pedigree of this story - that is to say, who precisely wrote the silly thing - has always been a subject of curiosity. It's credited to Paula Moore (a.k.a. Paula Woolsey, and see **The Lore** for more about 'Moore') but if you've read Volume V of these books, then you can probably tick off the features in "Attack" that seem like exactly what Script Editor Eric Saward would have done if he'd directly written this story. So extraneous characters, often written for benefit of celebrity guests, are bumped off without the Doctor or his companion getting a scene with them; whole scenes are lifted from *Alien*; neurotic punctilio occurs

Season 22 Cast/Crew

- Colin Baker (the Doctor)
- Nicola Bryant (Peri)

- John Nathan-Turner (Producer)
- Eric Saward (Script Editor)

with regard to continuity references; a brave character uses the gallows humour of a ten-year-old who's read *Battle Picture Weekly* just once too often, and becomes almost impatient to facilitate a noble, self-immolatory explosive finale because he's lost all hope; people with damaged hands are displayed in gory detail; and the Doctor brandishes hand-guns of various descriptions and shoots a baddie at point-blank range.

What's surprising about all this is that Saward not only fails to receive a writer's credit (although he adapted this story for Target paperbacks), but that the official account held that the accredited author was not him using a pen-name. Honest. We were told it was Saward's ex, using a pen-name, with a storyline by fan-in-excelsis Ian Levine. Saward just added the Cryons. No, really.

2. Just for a giggle, the Doctor "fixes" the chameleon circuit - thus making good on a threat that producer John Nathan-Turner had been making for ages. In press conferences and hand-outs over the past two years, publicity-mad Nathan-Turner (or JN-T as he styled himself in this phase) had announced plans to ditch the TARDIS' police box exterior (and see 21.3, "Frontios"), on the grounds that 1980s kids didn't know what it was supposed to be. (To judge by "Attack of the Cybermen", however, these 1980s kids were assumed to care about pointless references to old episodes wiped by the BBC before they were born.) It's handled like a viable running gag, so long as the programme-makers could find enough implausible objects with convenient doors that could be carted around on location shoots. Another production team might have kept this change - surely, it'd be no more drastic than the abrupt paradigm shifts unleashed in "Spearhead from Space" (7.1) or "The Deadly Assassin" (14.3) - and milked the publicity for all it was worth. But Nathan-Turner did it once, for a gimmick, and almost nobody remembers it.

3. With the mythology surrounding the "The Tomb of the Cybermen" - which at the time didn't exist in the archive, and a video-tape of which was believed able to cure warts with a single touch and convert water to butterscotch-flavoured Angel Delight (*the* special treat you had while watching *Doctor Who* in 1967) - it was inevitable that they'd try a remake. As you'll recall from Volume V, a lot of elements in mid-80s stories are there as much to get applause from convention-goers as to entertain the people paying licence fees. However, nobody seems to have told director Matthew Robinson, costume-maker Anushia Nieradzik or designer Marjorie Pratt, so they've avoided anything retro. Instead, they've built a standard 1980s *Doctor Who* marble-effect set with what look like shower doors, filled it with a couple of "Earthshock"-model Cybermen (see, of course, 19.6, "Earthshock" and 20.7, "The Five Doctors") and not even thought about stencilling the infamous "Mod" Cyberman logo from "Tomb" anywhere. They *did*, however, conduct filming in the same quarry in Gerrard's Cross, and rehire one of the key players from "Tomb"...

4. We defy you to listen to the snatch of synth-harmonica music when the Doctor pops up from the manhole, fresh from incapacitating a fake bobby, without thinking of *Teletubbies*. And once this idea has taken root, try to watch any scene with Michael Kilgarriff as the Cyber-Controller and keep a straight face.

The Continuity

The Doctor Has been a little absent-minded since his latest regeneration [21.6, "The Caves of Androzani"], and calls Peri by the names of former companions [and one other, see *Background*]. He insists his present incarnation is as stable as it will ever be, but his behaviour is somewhat erratic and downright capricious at times.

He's taken it upon himself to fix the TARDIS systems root and branch, starting with the chameleon circuit, and knows how to sabotage the TARDIS' navigation systems while the Ship is in flight. He seems more susceptible to cold than in previous incarnations, whilst his shoulders again seem very sensitive to touch. [This is apparently his vulnerable spot - see 9.3, "The Sea Devils"; 12.5, "Revenge of the Cybermen"; 13.1, "Terror of the Zygons"; X1.1, "Rose" and several others[1].] He's outraged at the implication that the

Time Lords have somehow dispatched him, as an unwitting agent, to deal with this situation. [Whether or not the Time Lords *have* done such a thing - or by what methods they might have accomplished this - is never confirmed, however. This is arguably a sign of this Doctor's intense dislike of manipulation, as he surely cannot criticise - if the Time Lords *are* involved - their ultimate goal of stopping the Cybermen from saving Mondas and mucking up what he calls the 'Web of Time'.]

Annoying verbal tics he's acquired since we last met him: when Peri says something he doesn't like, he repeats it three times, each louder than the last. He seems to think that saying, 'Wait, watch, learn', will endear him to people, and he still rubs his cat badge for luck. Most oddly, on his first meeting with passing strangers (in this case the police investigator Russell), the Doctor goes into the spiel about his being a Time Lord from Gallifrey in the Constellation of Kasterborous. [As opposed to his simply ("simply"!) saying he's a freelance investigator formerly attached to the UN. Tragically, we'll re-examine this same sort of bizarre info-dump in 27.0, "The TV Movie" - or whatever it was called.] He has also taken to saying, 'I am *known as* the Doctor'. [And we'll pick this up under 23.1, "The Mysterious Planet".]

• *Ethics.* Finding out that Lytton was working for the Cryons changes the Doctor's entire opinion of the mercenary, despite everything that has happened before. [Are we to infer that being paid by nice aliens makes Lytton morally higher than when nasty ones were outright coercing him? Possibly, but we'll further consider this under **Things That Don't Make Sense.**] Notoriously, the Doctor seems quite prepared to let Peri threaten Russell with a gun to obtain information, although this is chiefly presented as if it's just a ruse. He incapacitates one of Lytton's fake coppers in hand-to-hand combat [from 21.4, "Resurrection of the Daleks"], although this occurs off screen, so it's unclear exactly how he prevails. He seems to merely go through the motions when attempting to persuade the Cryon named Flast to find another way to detonate the explosive Vastial, and is worryingly quick in accepting her offer of suicide to wipe out the Cybermen. He also [in what was doubtless scripted as a desperate struggle for survival, but instead looks like Colin having a crack at breakdancing] guns down two Cybermen and the Cyber-

Is Continuity a Pointless Waste of Time?

To read fanzines from the 1980s, you would think that the whole point of making new *Doctor Who* was to confirm theories about the old episodes. Or to put it another way, a large constituency within fandom believed that the internal consistency of the over-arching story that had been running since 1963 was possible, desirable and an end in itself. Unfortunately, that constituency had the production team's ear, and some areas of fandom now believe that this tendency within the script is what alienated the general public, made ratings slide and caused the quality of the stories to suffer - thereby killing the series.

This rather simplistic equation ignores a *lot* of other factors that were at work, but there's a ring of truth about it. Certainly, the obsession with including items from the past for their own sake - rather than because the story needed them - led to "Shopping List" scripts such as "Time-Flight" (19.7), "Warriors of the Deep" (21.1), "The Mark of the Rani" (22.3), "The Two Doctors" (22.4) and ultimately (not to mention painfully) "Dimensions In Time" (A1 in the Appendix) and 27.0, "The TV Movie".

But let's get pragmatic for a moment. If you're the producer of a costly, strenuous and under-resourced series, then you occasionally take a gamble but you also please the crowds with reruns for things that worked. Not for nothing had the Daleks been periodically brought back since 1964, in the interests of giving ratings a bump. (All right, actually, the production team were ordered to do it by Huw Wheldon with half an eye on toy sales, but the point stands.) In fact, Innes Lloyd spent two years as producer cutting his losses and doing things that had paid off in the past. He also - like any producer - had the problem of recouping his outlay, so once he'd paid for a dozen Cybermen costumes, he was sure as hell going to use them again. Ditto the Ice Warriors.

When ratings are high and viewers are demanding novelty, you refrain from milking any one element. But when the AI readings and viewing figures are shaky, and the letters keep demanding the Gubbage Cones back, then you will probably yield to the temptation to bring the Gubbage Cones back. In the short term, such "continuity" means that Sil recognises Peri and is back while viewers remember him (22.2, "Vengeance on Varos"; 23.2, "Mindwarp"), which is just a matter of good housekeeping. And if you've got a dozen "Earthshock" model Cybermen costumes, then you don't splash out valuable resources to rebuild

1960s costumes for the scenes from "Attack of the Cybermen" in the tomb.

Well... you *would* do that sort of thing if you're *Star Trek: The Next Generation* and (say) you've got a story that requires recreating the old *Enterprise* bridge, but the expense involved for that can be offset by using it for exhibitions. Take the worst excesses of *Who* fan neurosis, multiply it by ten and you've got the Trekkies - and that's your problem right there. Thinking that *Doctor Who* is somehow like *Star Trek* is the source of several problems in the JN-T era and after (see **What's All This Stuff About Anoraks?** under 24.1, "Time and the Rani").

All of that said, let's be clear on what we're discussing. "Continuity" became a catch-all term (of abuse, eventually) for an approach to the series, but it is a basic requirement of any long-running drama. As any soap fan will tell you, it's annoying when characters get entirely new pasts to cover a recasting, or someone blithely goes about his business on a day that long-term viewers recall was the anniversary of his wife's death. Accounting for such details is a simple matter of good faith with the regular viewers, and verisimilitude. Plausibility at a plot level is a matter of taste, but it's fairly crucial on a character level when you're dealing with sequential series. Research into fan readings of TV indicates a slight gender difference on this, but it's more pronounced in the related but separate issue of canonicity: male fans are allegedly more prone to take the author's previous credits as the test of whether to "buy" a theory, female fans on average are more likely to say "But ____ wouldn't do that". This skew is less marked in *Who* fandom, as far as anyone can tell. (*Doctor Who* fans bucking the trend of gender-assignment? Hmmm, why might that be?)

That kind of continuity is more or less present in any period of *Doctor Who* you care to name, and some phases get extremely soap-ish - referring in detail to the previous story's event at the start of each new one, or having longer-term character arcs unfolding. A good example would be Season Ten's threads about Metebelis III, then Jo's marriage, and then Mike's breakdown running under Season Eleven until everything ties together with "Planet of the Spiders" (11.5). Another example: Jo's slow maturing to the point where she can fend off the Master's hypnotic powers (10.3, "Frontier in Space"). Bad examples abound in the Davison era, particularly with Turlough's whole

continued on page 11...

ABOUT TIME 1985–1989

Controller. This is while he tries to save Lytton, who is already three-quarters Cybernised and therefore probably beyond hope.

• *Inventory*. With all the odd jobs he's been doing about the Ship, it's small wonder that he's tooled up. He now has a sonic lance - a orange luminous probe with buttons along the handle, and which looks like it might be handy for lighting barbecues. With the sonic lance, the Doctor can open locked doors, tinker with the TARDIS' innards, generate enough heat to trigger explosive material and skewer Cybermen to death through their chest plates. Lytton, as part of his function as dispenser of vital information whenever the plot requires it, both identifies this item and from it immediately deduces the Doctor's proximity. [Why they couldn't just call the Lance a "sonic screwdriver" and have done with it is a puzzle.] The Doctor also has a hand-held detector that tracks distress signals, and a pen-torch that's similar to the old Hartnell model.

• *Background*. The Doctor apparently visited the Refrigerated Citadel(s) of Telos under Cryon rule, before the Cybermen adopted the planet as their home. [For a related if somewhat debatable theory, see **Whatever Happened to Planet 14?** under 6.3, "The Invasion".]

In his post-regenerative confusion, the Doctor refers to Peri by the names of some of his former companions, including Susan, Zoe, Tegan and even Jamie. He also mistakenly calls her 'the Terrible Zodin' [and see **The Supporting Cast** for where that off-handed remark takes us].

The Doctor seems to know who The Lone Ranger is.

The Supporting Cast

• *Peri*. Hasn't been to Britain before - despite her having noticably picked up traces of the accent - and confounds our stereotype of Americans by being nervous and inexperienced around guns. When the confused Doctor mistakes Peri for some of his former travelling companions, she appears to understand the references - or at least, she knows that 'Jamie' is a male name in this case. [As opposed to - say - the Doctor name-dropping Jamie Lee Curtis. However, this would almost imply that the Doctor at some point sat Peri down with his photo-album and drilled her on the names of his former shipmates. This isn't a conversation one can imagine the Fifth Doctor ever having, whereas the Sixth Doctor doing a

Powerpoint presentation - or more likely something involving a special room in the Ship with a desk and blackboard pilfered from Coal Hill - is horribly plausible. As we'll see, it's also something that would make events in "Timelash" (22.5) more sensible, if only in this one, tiny regard. Moreover, if the Terrible Zodin *was* a companion and Peri doesn't know who she is, then it's possible that the Doctor removed all of Zodin's photos and tippexed her name from the guest-list.]

The Supporting Cast
(Morally Ambiguous But Pretending To Be Evil)

• *Lytton*. Declares that he wasn't working for the Daleks ["Resurrection of the Daleks"] out of choice. [He could, of course, be fibbing. In "Resurrection", Lytton seemed like a willing Dalek servant like all the other Replicants. The overall implication - never disproved in either of his two appearances - is that he's a copy of the original Lytton, and somehow broke his Dalek programming (without, it must be said, the mental trauma endured by the Stein-double in "Resurrection").]

Here we learn that Lytton hails from Riftan V (see **Planet Notes**), and not - as he claimed to the hired muscle Griffiths - from Fulham. The Cybermen cite Lytton's people as warriors 'who fight only for money', and Lytton is here shown in the Cryons' employ. [Although what form of payment he's offered for helping them isn't stated; see **Things That Don't Make Sense.**]

Lytton has learned a fair amount of mid-80s London slang, and his efforts to emulate someone of the period are good enough to fool even Russell, an undercover policeman. During his brief time in London [since "Resurrection"], Lytton has coordinated several raids to acquire specialised electronics [probably military] and thereby constructed a distress signal. He bounces this around London via several unoccupied residences, from a source in a lock-up garage (over the entrance to the sewer). He knows a good amount regarding the Cybermen and Cryons, and has somehow detected the Cyber-ship perched on the dark side of the moon. Two of his stooges - still dressed as policemen [after "Resurrection"] - keep watch on his signal relays but are eventually captured and seemingly converted into Cybermen. [Once again, see **Things That Don't Make Sense**, this time for more on Lytton's bewildering distress signal.]

Is Continuity a Pointless Waste of Time?

...continued from page 9

storyline. (Most tellingly, he meets the Brigadier again in 20.7, "The Five Doctors", but there's no sign of recognition on either part. Not even an "ah, that's where you got to!") Treating the Doctor as a consistent character across several lives and trying to make sense of the discrepancies generated when new writers and producers came in has been an issue since the Hartnell era. (The star himself, as we saw in Volume I, would police "his" show tenaciously on behalf of younger viewers who half-believed it was all true.) Apart from soaps, no drama has ever had long-term viewers with so much invested in it until the late 1980s and the invention of "Cult" as a category.

At the very least, one needs to keep casual viewers up to speed on what has happened to such-and-such a character, or why the story begins with the TARDIS needing repair and unable to effect a quick exit. These days you can do it with a pre-credit "previously..." sequence, so it's not a big worry. Even that might not even be needed if you craft your storytelling deftly enough. To anyone whose first ever experience of *Doctor Who* was "Horror of Fang Rock" (15.1), it didn't matter that the Rutans had been mentioned before, or that the casual allusion to something called Sontarans connected up to earlier stories. The people in the story acted as though it meant something to them, so that was all that was required.

What was vexing the fanzine writers of the 1980s was whether every small detail needed a line of dialogue to explain to the casual or younger viewer who Omega was (20.1, "Arc of Infinity") or whether every new story needed some connection to a previous one. So you got very dull scenes with the Doctor talking to his companion about some point that had been raised in the *Doctor Who Monthly* nitpickers' column "Matrix Data Bank" (such as the origin of the Cybermen in 19.6, "Earthshock", and whether the thing that had the Doctor wake up as Patrick Troughton was a 'regeneration', a 'rejuvenation' or a 'renewal' - see 21.7, "The Twin Dilemma"). We got to a stage where, as usually happens, fandom started using the word to mean something else: capital-C "Continuity" means the effort to make out it was all one long story with interconnections between every minute detail, and the BBC breached that at their peril. Just as "canon" is used adjectivally in dull online discussions, so fans talk

of "the Continuity" like it was a physical object.

Soon it got personal: would you rather watch a good story that got the names of the three Silurians muddled up with regards to the novelisation "Doctor Who and the Cave Monsters", or a bad one that got everything neurotically right but didn't have any plot, characterisation, tension or mood? Did it matter if a new story, watched by seven million people (and a good chunk of them under 12), contradicted a story that got four million viewers in 1967 and no longer existed in the archive? If you thought it did, did that make you a bad person or a truer fan?

Well, said one camp, it mattered if more effort was put into that than into getting the basics of television drama right. Otherwise, if (to take a contentious example) 14.3, "The Deadly Assassin" contradicted 8.4, "Colony in Space", it was tough luck because "The Deadly Assassin" was great and "Colony in Space" wasn't. But that was because both stories (just) predate fandom and are therefore considered sacrosanct. If a newly-made story contradicted both of them and all other Time Lord stories, claiming that they weren't from Gallifrey at all but Droitwich, then the question would be whether the new story was worth watching on its own merits.

Thus "Genesis of the Daleks" (12.4) now routinely gets voted 'Best Story Ever', even though on broadcast it was scandalously out of keeping with established Dalek history. We are now given to re-thinking the previous stories and being very selective on how far we believe any of what's stated there, if the new story is good enough to overpower the old one. If not... "Attack of the Cybermen" was seen by more people than "The Tomb of the Cybermen", but is far less well remembered by even fans. A "strong" story can outweigh a "weak" one, it seems. So even today, when the "Tomb" DVD is freely available and "Attack" is only on video and from specialist shops, the reputation of "Tomb" withstands all the attempts to steal a march on it. Little of what we take from "Tomb" is affected by what took place in "Attack".

The Continuity-keeners, however, didn't see it that way. The extant stories are beyond reproach, even if they contradict one another. All new stories have to fit inside this accepted and agreed framework. The more it all slotted together, the more self-referential and "real" it was, the better. The fact that the things being brought back were all from

continued on page 13...

The Supporting Cast ('Terrible', and Possibly Associated With Furry Kangaroo Creatures)

• *Zodin*. Someone the Doctor says he hasn't thought about for some time, but here described as 'a woman of rare guile and devilish cunning'. [The last time we heard the name (20.7, "The Five Doctors"), the Second Doctor used it to denote one of his enemies, a woman who had some association with a furry race who hopped about like kangaroos. One implication - at least in the original edit of that story - is that this happened when the Second Doctor met an older Brigadier, although this has mercifully never appeared as a spin-off novel (but see 27.0, "Grace 1999" for a hair-raising near-miss). That said, the dialogue is ambiguous enough that Zodin might have nothing to do with the Brigadier whatsoever, but see 26.1, "Battlefield" for the Brigadier's future and a lot of odd UNIT developments that don't surprise the Doctor.] Even this is rather unclear, but the logical conclusion is that Zodin is a person who had an army of hirsute aliens. It's also feasible - given her apparent mention amidst a small roll call of the Doctor's companions - that Zodin is actually a former companion herself, possibly as part of a subterfuge per her 'devilish cunning'. (Although to be fair, the newly-regenerated Sixth Doctor may have simply gone a bit bonkers.) Either way, it's relevant to ask why the Doctor might be thinking of her now, and see 22.3, "The Mark of the Rani" and its accompanying essay for a possible answer.]

The TARDIS Is *still* being re-wired by the Doctor [see "The Horns of Nimon" (17.5), "Logopolis" (18.7), "Arc of Infinity" (20.1), "The Five Doctors" (20.7), plus many other stories where the console blows up but works perfectly well next episode, eg. 19.6, "Earthshock"]. Circuitry important to the TARDIS' functioning is located in head-height roundels in more than one corridor [one of them being the same corridor used in "Arc of Infinity"]. A nearby ante-room contains a table with spare parts, and a shoulder-height roundel in which a small printed-circuit board is installed - this is removed and inserted in a roundel by the console room viewing screen. Inserting the circuit leads to 'crossed wires' and sends the Ship out of control, with extreme g-forces affecting the occupants. This ends with a materialisation in the Solar System near Halley's Comet, and the Doctor is convinced that a small breach in the hull would cause the Ship's air to leak out.

These opened roundels make plinky-plonky sounds [that's the technical term] like the console these days. The console picks up local transmissions while the TARDIS is in space, including an intergalactic distress signal from 1985 London. The ante-room's roundels also affect the navigation, and permit the Doctor to send an SOS to Gallifrey. The main door control sparks violently after Russell accidentally zaps the wall with a Cyber-gun. [Whether the one is related to the other - or whether the door control was somehow shorted by the entering Cybermen - isn't clear.]

Once the Doctor 'repairs' the TARDIS' chameleon circuit, the Ship arrives in the place where the Circuit first broke: IM Foreman's scrapyard at 76, Totter's Lane, London. [We are assuming a postcode beginning E3. The TARDIS might deliberately home in on Totter's Lane owing to the chameleon circuit issue; then again, it is in walking distance of where the Doctor wants to go, and could just be a giant coincidence.] After a few moments, it then changes from its usual police box pattern to a painted wooden pedestal about ten feet high, with some sort of entrance on its backside. [The script claims that this is a kitchen range.] It changes form with a whooshing noise, which is even more attention-getting than materialisation sound.

After homing on Lytton's signal, the TARDIS relocates and becomes a church organ; the Doctor can actually play this instrument without benefit of a pump or a choirboy labouring over the bellows [and the organ *seems* to have pedal-bellows, at least]. Even the Doctor can't find the door straight off the bat. [So if a perceptual filter *is* in place (see X3.12, "The Sound of Drums"), - it's a stupidly effective one that even messes with the driver's head. We might have to attribute talk of the filter to a TARDIS upgrade as part of the Time War (see also 27.0, "The TV Movie"), since there's little evidence of such a thing before the Welsh series. Think about it: in how many classic series stories do people ask, "That's strange... what's that blue box doing there?"]

Anyone entering the organ-TARDIS has to duck behind it, but nonetheless enters the console room standing [cf 2.9, "The Time Meddler", so an atrium probably still exists between the Ship's interior and exterior].

On arriving on Telos, the Ship materialises as a brass latticework gate, as would be used on a

Is Continuity a Pointless Waste of Time?

...continued from page 11

past *Doctor Who* stories made anything you did with them like *Doctor Who*, even if it was just a board-game written up as an adventure (see 20.7, "The Five Doctors"). The thinking behind why these elements worked in the first place is irrelevant. If "The Two Doctors" had featured a new quasi-militaristic alien race, then fewer people would think that the militaristic aliens have any business being in the story. The sad fact is the Sontarans were always meant to be in the story, regardless of whether they helped the plot, whilst the decision to film it in Spain rather than New Orleans meant that the second aliens weren't needed either. All that calling the bombastic BEMs 'Sontarans' adds is a sense of a good monster being wasted. But, as we've seen already (see **Did Doctor Who Magazine Change Everything?** under 18.2, "Meglos"), there was now a constituency within fandom that thought each story's merit was directly connected to its quotient of nostalgic returns or references. Quite why they felt this way - actively preferring stories they knew would be crap to any alternative on offer - is interesting, from a pathological point of view.

Without opening the can of worms about the connection between belonging to a fan-club and obsession, it's safe to say that comfort exists in having a known order you can rely on. Investing a lot of emotional effort into anything apparently self-contained is therapeutic. Having anything alert you to the fact that you have put so much of yourself into something so *slight* can be upsetting. Of course, most of us are aware of the silliness of our fixation and playfully brandish it as a self-mocking quirk, like supporting a useless football team out of loyalty or collecting things others think are trash (stamps, matchboxes or *Doctor Who* books of various descriptions).

It's a situation everyone knows about; any record collector can identify with the need for every vinyl edition of a single, everyone who's got a dad knows about the need for every gardening implement or recipe for cakes, everyone's heard of someone with a Hornby railway set in the attic, ostensibly for the kids. Everyone who's been to a British *Doctor Who* convention has met people whose idea of conversation is listing stories that have got Cybermen in them.[2] It's only a more extreme version of something basic to all humans, to make order and sense of a chaotic world. However...

We've now crossed a line. Continuity was once something inserted into stories as a little extra, to connect the adventures and make the characters and their motives seem more solid and plausible. Now it has jeopardised this foundation. It might look cool to have the First Doctor and Tegan laying into the Master for slaughtering a dozen Cybermen, because it's a combination of favourite elements from the past that we've not seen in one place before. But in terms of the old-fashioned form of continuity, Tegan should have been helping with the massacre because the Cybermen just one season earlier had killed her friends Adric and Professor Kyle. The habit of "sampling" things from the past has become an end in itself, and entire stories are based around brandishing of elements wrenched from their context and collaged together. It's a Linus-blanket for people who want to believe *Doctor Who* is a documentary series about real time travellers, and it's the same infantile state of mind that insists on "realistic" special effects (see the essay under 10.2, "Carnival of Monsters" for more on this). The "correct" term for this rigidness is no longer "continuity" but "fanwank"[3]. And if people insisted on using terms like "Whoniverse", it might be said that they deserved to have stories like "Attack of the Cybermen" or "The Two Doctors" made for them, because nobody else does.

In any long-running story, the question of access crops up. As we'll see in a later essay (**Where Does "Canon" End?** under 26.1, "Battlefield") the ability of the average viewer, or reader, to come to a new story cold is a significant issue. As Stan Lee used to say on this very concern, "Every Marvel comic is potentially someone's first comic", meaning it was imperative to re-explain the series' fundamentals on a regular basis. With that in mind, the abrupt drop of two million viewers between the broadcast episodes of "Attack" speaks volumes. Before the spread of the term "cult TV", the impression amongst the general public had become that *Doctor Who* was made for someone else, not them. The development of *Doctor Who* as a genre in and of itself meant that the range of things that could happen next was severely curtailed. Compare the beginning of "The Crusade" (2.6) and the near-contemporary (as regards history) "The King's Demons" (20.6), and the difference is clear. What are the odds that Tegan and Turlough will go a whole story without meeting a space-being or a returning foe?

continued on page 15...

Victorian lift [see 26.2, "Ghost Light"; 15.6, "The Invasion of Time"], only more ornate, as with a pre-War department store. Afterward, the chameleon circuit packs up again and thereafter the TARDIS always manifests as a police box.

With a few keystrokes on the console, on the panel nearest the main door, the Doctor can activate a self-destruct that's apparently pre-set to twenty seconds (and aborted at nineteen). [But again, this could just be a bluff on the Doctor's part, to save Peri's life.] He de-activates the SOS signal to Gallifrey on the console panel close to the interior door.

The Non-Humans

• *Cybermen*. By appearances, these are roughly the same "make" as the Cybermen seen in "Earthshock" (19.6) and "The Five Doctors" (20.7). However, they're far less bullet-proof than on previous occasions, and prove killable by several bullets through the mouth opening, or via a glancing blow to one of their hydraulic lines. It seems easier to decapitate them than ever, and some dormant Cybermen apparently perish when the Cryons reset the tombs' thermostats. One of the entombed Cybermen contains an inbuilt distress signal in its head, under the face-plate.

The top dog among the Cybermen is formally identified as 'Cyber Controller' [as opposed to the slightly different 'Cyberman Controller' in "Tomb" or the non-anthropomorphic 'Cyber-Control' terminal in 5.7, "The Wheel In Space" and "The Invasion"]. He [and the pronoun is advisedly used] is a larger-than-usual Cyberman with a more bulbous cranium and no "handles", and his movements are more stiff and mechanical. [Presuming this *is* the same character as was electrocuted at the end of "Tomb", then it's small wonder he's feeling a bit creaky, and feeling in need of his oil can. But then it *is* 1985, and maybe he's doing Electric Boogaloo.]

In the Cybermen base in the London sewers, a detonator is clearly labelled in English, and the rest of their equipment has very conventional dials and levers [and is apparently cannibalised from human machinery]. At this stage, as the Cyberleader points out, the priority is consolidating their numbers rather than making big shows of force. [For this reason, Lytton's scouts and the sewerage workers are processed on the hoof rather than taken to Telos.] The Cybermen's conversion process doesn't always work properly, and

on Telos, rejected specimens whose "cybernisation" failed for whatever reason are put to work mining the planet's surface. They retain some of their cybernetic upgrades - robotic arms and legs, according to the prisoner Bates - but are not mentally conditioned.

There's a new category of Cybermen: namely, the Cyber Scouts. They're touted as Cybermen who have been sent to, um, scout, but on screen they're realized as a number of darker, matte-grey Cybermen who sneak up on people in sewers. [Mind, they're often not successful at this. Perhaps they've got inferior abilities, but it's rather hard to judge, as they never get any lines.]

• *Cryons*. The indigenous race of Telos, although they curiously seem to all be female. They're humanoid with bulbous heads; long, thin fingers with extensive nails; ruff-like frills around their necks [cf the Haemovores, 26.3, "The Curse of Fenric"] and very large eyes. Their skin is a metallic silver-blue, and they have walrus-like moustaches. Their voices are attenuated, as though coming over short-wave radio. All the Cryons seem to be wearing white plastic jumpsuits and high heels, and one of them - Flast - has a cape. Their speech is accompanied by exaggerated hand movements [rather like the Menoptra in 2.5, "The Web Planet"].

The Cryons built the refrigerated cities of Telos [and the so-called 'tomb of the Cybermen' was apparently one of theirs] because they are unable to survive temperatures above the freezing point of water. On being exposed to heat, they become weak and vapours sublimate from their skin. A Cryon shot by a Cyber-weapon glows for a few moments and evaporates, but is seemingly conscious and in pain as this happens.

The Cryon people - or certainly Flast - somehow know much about the Time Lords, but fail to recognize the Doctor as one on sight. [It's possible they learned of the Time Lords from Lytton, who in turn learned about them from the Daleks, but that presumes - as Lytton hasn't been to Telos before now - that they got rather chatty in their communications.] The Cryons' plight is such that they eagerly reply to Lytton's distress message, and hire him to steal the time-ship that the Cybermen procured on Telos. The Cryons claim to consider the function of bodyguard as 'noble' [suggesting a Bushido-style code of warfare]. Judging by Flast, the Cyrons are benevolent to the point of wanting to stop the Cybermen from revising history and

Is Continuity a Pointless Waste of Time?

...continued from page 13

(Admittedly, by Season Two the historicals as a sub-genre have begun to get formulaic too, and you can almost set your watch by Tutte Lemkow's appearance. We've moved from "Adventures in History" to "Historical" as a category of story.) From the point of view of casual viewers, the degree to which *Doctor Who* was something you either bought into as a whole or didn't, or instead a string of adventures you could take or leave story by story, is the degree to which the stories needed footnotes.

And however much the internal consistency of the *Doctor Who* story made the plots seem real, the contrivances required for the narrative to relay the details made for the most arch, unsayable, unlistenable dialogue ever transmitted. If - look, just go with this for a moment, please - a real space-mercenary was confronted by a real Cyberleader, their conversation would probably not be the info-dumpfest we get twenty-seven minutes into "Attack of the Cybermen". The Cyber-lieutenant would not bother telling the Leader things the Leader already knows, for starters, and the Leader would not tell Lytton all about Lytton's home planet, nor would Lytton ask where the Controller is just so the viewers at home would get to hear that the Cybermen are based on Telos. That's just one example that happened to be to hand as we reviewed "Attack of the Cybermen". It becomes the dominant factor in stories edited by Eric Saward, and the hour or so Paul McGann spent as the Movie Doctor.

As we'll discuss in a later essay, the assumption of an over-arching system, into which items like plots and mentions of old monsters can be slotted, is vexatious to anyone writing a story in a different genre to the majority. There is a set of aesthetic and cognitive boundaries that *Doctor Who* won't cross, even though it happily plunders stories from outside those boundaries. This could be why even "pure" historical yarns become part of an overall category of "Science Fiction" (see **Could It Be Magic?** under 25.4, "The Greatest Show in the Galaxy"). Now, as anyone paying attention in the 1990s knows, when you have these overall all-encompassing theories, or meta-narratives, you'll get attempts to wreck them for comic effect. Not abandon them totally, not pretend they aren't there, just ask awkward questions. Accidental errors and inconsistencies become deliberate breaches. "Incredulity towards metanarratives"

was what the philosopher Jean-Francois Lyotard said was the hallmark of what he dubbed "post-modernism". However, long before then it had been a sly rebellion practised by outsiders (see **Is** *Doctor Who* **Camp?** under 6.5, "The Seeds of Death" and **The Semiotic Thickness of** *What?* under 24.4, "Dragonfire").

Once continuity-fetish was identified as a trend in fandom, certain fans resisted this and made a big deal about wrecking it all, ignoring all continuity and being - as they called it - "free". This arguably has a pathology all its own, but they certainly had a point. The anomalies between stories may have allowed for inventive solutions that generated new ideas for stories, but tearing it all up and starting again allowed anyone to play without an A-Level in Fanboy.

From this point of view, *Doctor Who* is best thought of as an anthology series, wherein each individual story is a one-off with some characters from the hit TV show *Doctor Who* popping in. The entire point of the series was to allow stories you would never get anywhere else. So what was partly a pragmatic move, a means by which a long-running series (first on television, and then various spin-offs) could keep the story manageable and user-friendly, also allowed individual writers to come on like rebels and iconoclasts and deliberately smash things up to look cool in front of their mates.

This sort of thing happened a lot in long-running comics, and the application of 1980s comic-logic to *Doctor Who* was Andrew Cartmel's main innovation as script editor (see **Did Cartmel Have** *Any* **Plan At All?** under 25.3, "Silver Nemesis"). The spin-offs - almost entirely written by comic fans - picked up on this, but as we have seen throughout Volume V, treating the series like a traditional Superhero comic was what had been happening since 18.1, "The Leisure Hive". Attempts to make logically self-consistent chronologies of Dalek history or Earth's Empire were an entertaining parlour-game, but nobody ever came up with the same answer. The Dalek chronologies, despite seeming to have been rewritten first by time-travelling Daleks, then by the Doctor's first meeting with Davros, then by the Time War, are just about resolvable into one timeline (well, one and a half - see 9.1, "The Day of the Daleks"), but not everyone buys that. What was never attempted on screen was a clear-out of all these anomalies, a "Crisis on

continued on page 17...

saving Mondas - even though this will, by extension, guarantee that the Cybermen will arrive on Telos and conquer the Cryons.

Planet Notes

• *Telos*. As with "Tomb of the Cybermen", the planet's surface is warm enough to support humans with no protective clothing. [Obviously, the biggest issue here is how the Cryons - who can't survive in temperatures above freezing, and now require refrigerated cities - could be native to such an environment. Telos obviously has colder regions - such as the area that contains the Vastial, which explodes in temperatures above zero - so it seems odd that the Cryons wouldn't build their shelters in such a colder locale, as opposed to a region where the outside temperatures are guaranteed to kill them.

[The logical inference, it must be said, is that something fairly big has happened to this planet's environment since they evolved. It's possible that the sun around which Telos orbits has become significantly brighter in a comparatively short while, or that the planet itself has a very eccentric orbit - see 9.4, "The Mutants" and 16.1, "The Ribos Operation" (16.1) for other examples of this. Alternatively, it's been suggested that the planet has been terra-formed - obviously not by the Cryons and logically not for the benefit of the Cybermen - or more to point equipped with an environmental shield, and see **Whatever Happened to Planet 14** under "The Invasion" (6.3) for arguments on why this *could* mean that Telos is part of Earth's solar system. Even this isn't a flawless solution, however, and see **Things That Don't Make Sense** for more on this.]

Telos is the only known source of Vastial, a mineral that's very common in the planet's colder areas. It becomes unstable at ten degrees above zero [Celsius] and self-combusts at fifteen degrees or higher. Diamonds are common on Telos [so the planet theoretically had a volcanic past].

• *Mondas*. Elaborating on what was discussed in "The Tenth Planet" (4.2), the Doctor says that Mondas is presently headed toward Earth by means of a 'propulsion unit'.

• *Riftan V*. Lytton's world of origin, and described as a 'satellite' [meaning a moon of a bigger planet?] of Vita 15 in star system 690. The people there are killers for hire, and notorious around the galaxy.

History

• *Dating*. The Earth sequences manifestly take place in summer 1985. Lytton has been stuck in London for several months [after "Resurrection of the Daleks", set in 1984], and has learned enough of the local ways to pass for a native (making jokes about Council workmen and picking up phrases like 'minder', 'Old Bill' and 'wind-up').

The Telos segments are a bit harder to pin down, although "Attack of the Cybermen" is presented as a sequel to "The Tomb of the Cybermen" [a story that *probably* takes place no earlier than the 2500s], so the Telos bits presumably take place some time after. It's clearly intended [and confirmed in Saward's novelisation of this story, see page 83 in particular] that the Cyber-Controller seen here is the same character as was electrocuted and entombed at the end of "Tomb". [He's admittedly undergone a *massive* upgrade in the interim, but they've even gone and rehired Michael Kilgarriff to play the part. In itself this might be questionable - as by the same logic, David Banks would be playing the same Cyber-leader in 19.6, "Earthshock"; 20.7, "The Five Doctors"; "Attack of the Cybermen" and 25.3, "Silver Nemesis", and obviously *that* isn't right - but in a story that so blatantly paints itself as a sequel to "Tomb", it's genuinely hard to see the Cyber-Controller as anything but the same character. If he's not, it's an *astonishing* coincidence that he's another Cyberman with the title 'Controller' *and* who's affiliated with Telos *and* whom the Doctor believed destroyed - and again, see Saward's novelisation for confirmation that he certainly believed it was the same character who took a spin with Toberman. Besides, we now know that the Lumic-style Cybermen (X2.05, "Rise of the Cybermen") can upload the functions of Cyberleader to any available Cyberman, so there's no reason why this Controller can't have the "Tomb" one's memories on-stream, even if such biological bits as he has left came from another person originally. Or indeed vice versa, if you prefer.]

Moreover, it's broadly hinted that the Cybermen relocated to Telos after Mondas' destruction in 1986, then subjugated the Cryons and assumed control of their refrigerated cities. [For confirmation of this, see the novelisation, Lytton's comment that the Cybermen 'had nowhere else to go', and the Doctor's (admittedly bewildering, sometimes) conversation with Flast -

Is Continuity a Pointless Waste of Time?

...continued from page 15

Infinite Skaros". For that we had to wait until 2005. It's hinted in X1.3, "The Unquiet Dead", that the Time War has ripped up the old continuity and it's perfectly possible for Earth to have been consumed by the Sun on two mutually-exclusive dates (3.6, "The Ark"; X1.2, "The End of the World"), even though Dickens still dies in 1870 no matter which history they're in.

But there's a sting in the tale. This group of fans always justified the abandonment of long-accepted programme lore as part of a story wherein a character or characters were breaking it all up. First it was the Doctor changing the past (as he had been ordered to in "Genesis of the Daleks"), then it was down to some agency or other like Faction Paradox (in the books) or Threshold (in the comics). The BBC Books had the Doctor blow up Gallifrey, then loosely put it back together again so the Daleks could just blow it up before the televised stories resumed. So however "postmodern" these continuity-smashers are, they're usually still working within a metanarrative. Even Paul Magrs' books, where established lore is just ridiculed and cherry-picked with additional unseen adventures that couldn't be reconciled to the televised stories, posited a 'Fugue' - a parallel to the "canon", geddit? - as a justification, rather than just getting on with telling new stories. And the Fugue was then made part of BBC Books' continuity. The Doctor remembered it in later, more orthodox, stories.

Therefore, the most sensible approach to continuity is probably that taken by Terrance Dicks: continuity is what any average but attentive viewer could reasonably be expected to remember. This is about a year's worth of broadcast stories back. With the average lifespan of a companion being about a year, this is enough for the Doctor to explain things to new characters (and thus new viewers), but not tell anyone things they knew. Anything from the remote past (two years or more) needs to be reintroduced. Within that temporal "spotlight" of a year, the allusions can be as detailed or vague as required, so that the end of

"The War Games" (6.7) has foes from up to a year ago wheeled on as evidence in the trial and Claire Jenkins rehired for one line as Tanya in a rebuilt Wheel set (5.7, "The Wheel in Space"). However, the same episode recycles clips from stories eighteen months back as stock footage in a different context (see 5.5, "The Web of Fear"), and claims that Jamie comes from 1745 now. With organised fandom and video technology, an "elite" of viewers would not be happy with such discrepancies, but they were tiny compared to the majority. Unfortunately, in the 1980s, that "elite" called the shots.

Now, of course, the new series has been going for more than a year, which means that by the end of Series Two, Rose Tyler remembers things that viewers should as well. (And, if not, we now have those 'previously on…' segments and flashbacks scripted in more brazenly than even "Planet of the Spiders" or the first four Nathan-Turner seasons.) With everyone watching all more or less 'on the same page', any old item can be brought back in such a way as to re-introduce it from scratch, from the TARDIS to the Cybermen. They can pick which aspects of the previous continuity to retain or discard (so now the Macra were always space-travelling parasites, and "The Macra Terror" wasn't genocide at all, honest - see X3.3, "Gridlock" and 4.7, "The Macra Terror"). These days, their only real problem is getting right the continuity with their own episodes, like how many maroon leather jackets Martha owns, or when exactly the Judoon arrived (X3.1, "Smith and Jones" - we're supposed to think that Tish started two high-profile jobs in a week, and neglected to mention the first one at Leo's party the day before). Now, though, most of the central planks of the old series are back at the hearts of new stories, and the whole of Britain got stupidly excited at seeing UNIT, Torchwood, the Master, Gallifrey and Cybermen all in one episode (X3.12, "The Sound of Drums"). As one fanboy-turned-academic described the BBC Wales approach: "Fanwank is the new black."

in which he raises the point that saving Mondas would result in the Cybermen never having visited Telos and conquered the Cryons. That would not remotely be a concern, if the Cybermen had settled Telos prior to Mondas' destruction.

[All of that said, the fly in the ointment is that for an adventure that's obsessed with continuity,

"Attack of the Cybermen" makes an astounding hash of its internal logic. While the overall aesthetic says, "the Telos bits occur in the future", some of the details are so sloppy as to make you think they're happening concurrently with the Earth scenes in 1985. For a start, Flast claims that Halley's Comet is heading toward Earth 'at this very moment' - as if it's occurring in her time - and the Cyber-Controller (or "Fat Controller", as one of his minions - obviously a fan of *Thomas the Tank Engine* - appears to call him) monitors events in the 1985 London sewers as if they're contemporary. For someone who allegedly hails from the future, he sure seems surprised when events unfold as they do. (Then again, this could simply mean that the Cybermen lost the bulk of their records and history in the period following Mondas' destruction.)

[Another oddity: it's almost easier to assume that the Cybermen in the sewers are - like the ones on the dark side of the moon - contemporary stragglers from "The Invasion" who are now reporting back to their base commander in their own time-frame. The alternative - that the Telos Cybermen have used their all-important time vessel to travel back and set up a "recruitment" camp in the London sewers of the 1980s, when there are surely more viable prospects elsewhere in space-time - isn't impossible, but is definitely more awkward. (Then again, it's possible that the Cybermen have decided to only convert pre-1986 humans, because if their plan to save Mondas succeeds, any post-1986 recruits would - temporally speaking - be a liability. It's possibly no more paradoxical than the overall goal of altering history and saving Mondas, but it *might* be something worth avoiding.)

[Yet another oddity: Lytton's ability to communicate with the Cryons before the story opens is downright strange if "Attack" *isn't* taking place at time of broadcast. It would suggest that he has enough technical know-how to rig a temporally-active distress signal (not impossible, though, as he worked for the Daleks), and that the oppressed and desperate Cryons have the capability of signalling back to him through time. (Never mind that if they *did* have such a device, they could use it far more effectively by contacting well-armed races with an axe to grind about the Cybermen.) Besides, if Lytton is broadcasting to the *future*, who the hell is he hoping to contact? The Daleks, who stranded him on 1980s Earth? His own people, even though there's no evidence of their being time-active? It's bewildering, but...

[While we're left with some details that don't add up, most of the inconsistencies simply aren't weighty enough to overturn the notion that "Attack" is intended as a sequel to "Tomb". Completism motivates us to put as much evidence

on the table as possible, though, so for benefit of anyone *really* examining this issue... Piece of Unhelpful Evidence No. 1: the Cyberleader states 'Now we can now time-travel... set the coordinates for the planet Telos' while on board the Doctor's captured TARDIS. Fine, except it's ultimately too ambiguous as to whether the journey to Telos does entail a trip through time or not. At a pinch, the line could simply refer to the fact that they have the Doctor over a barrel: not very likely, but it's there.

[Piece of Unhelpful Evidence No. 2: comparing the design between "Tomb" (now that we have the video back in the archive) and this story does little to answer the central dating question here. It's tempting to think that the explosion which does in the Telos facility in "Attack" leads to its being buried and later uncovered in "Tomb", but in truth it's not set into a cliffside, so it's unlikely that the one would visually lead to the other. Nor does the Cybermen design tell us much, as this model or something similar will turn up on Earth in 1988 (in 25.3, "Silver Nemesis"), and seems a fairly standard type. Arguably, it's easier to inflict on the human-form than the later "Tomb" model (which, on the evidence of 4.6, "The Moonbase", is a full-on conversion). Besides, hybrid Cybermen designs crop up all over history (5.7, "The Wheel in Space"; 10.2, "Carnival of Monsters"; X1.6, "Dalek", etc). ...

[A wider point needs making here: it's only this "make" of Cyberman that knows anything about Time Lords. So do the Cryons and Lytton. So it's possible that the entire 1980s Cyber-saga is from a *revised* timeline where the Cybermen's attempts to change their past fail so spectacularly, they cause their own extinction (see "Silver Nemesis" for a genocide in 1988 that seems to preclude all later stories). Under that scenario, the time-lines "reset" themselves to the 1960s chronology, which would explain why Cybermen in "Tomb" think of Troughton as the only Doctor (and seem to believe he's simply a very clever human, not a Time Lord), and only refer to 4.6, "The Moonbase" from the History Computer. Along those lines, the Cybermen seemed too penny-ante a race to be included in the Death Zone ("The Five Doctors"), but at some point the Time Lords are taking them seriously, so they obviously represent a massive *potential* threat. Perhaps, at the end of the day, it's all this historical revision that has resulted in the gut-wrenching continuity on display here. No wonder BBC Wales junked the whole mess and started again with a parallel universe when they (re)introduced the Cybermen.

The Analysis

Where Does This Come From? As we've noted in the course of *About Time*, the fundamental nature of horror films had shifted in the mid-1970s. Specifically, concern about the loss or theft of selfhood had swung to concern the treatment of people as meat. Perhaps as was inevitable under those conditions, the concept of the Cybermen drifted from a fear of mechanisation and mood-altering drugs to being about what had happened to the bodies of those converted.

In "Earthshock", we discussed the way that action-movies had fetishised the semi-mechanised muscular body, but this is part of a wider shift in the 1980s, in which the notion of "pumping iron" went from being a fringe activity to how many people spent their leisure time. The quest for the hard body was about control, at a very basic and personal level. It was also narcissistic to the point of homoeroticism... watch any ads from this period, especially those for personal grooming, and the one word everyone seems to use is "performance". Even hair "performs better" with such-and-such a conditioner.

Since "The Tomb of the Cybermen" in 1967, the emphasis in Cyberman adventures had been that they were unstoppable baddies, tin-plated Commies and whatever, but that they hypnotised people only to remove them from conflict-zones, not as a prelude to conversion. The idea of converting humans into Cybermen is so far down in the mix that Robert Holmes (script editor on 12.5, "Revenge of the Cybermen" and not one to miss a chance for a possession sub-plot) forgot it was ever there. With "Tomb" back on the agenda (see **The Lore**), this notion was due for a return. Moreover, the success (in critical terms if not ratings or audience appreciation figures) of 21.6, "The Caves of Androzani" had emboldened Saward with regards to what was feasible on a show made for a family audience. Except that where "Caves" had largely been about suggested or threatened violence, "Attack" deals with its aftermath. (In fact, the next story - "Vengeance on Varos" - will show how the debate about violence on television had moved on from whether it should be shown at all, to how responsible broadcasters seemed to glamourise it and discuss its impact.) It must've seemed logical, therefore, to explore (or rather reintroduce) the idea that Cybermen were predatory, and had once been people themselves.

Lytton's gang are taken from the stock company of East End villains that you will find in almost any late 70s / early 80s, locally-made film or exportable TV show. Since 1981, and the unexpected success of *The Long Good Friday*, this strand of hard-edged thug-opera has kept several otherwise unemployable actors in work. After the fad died down, they went on to TV shows like *Minder* (produced by Verity Lambert), *Only Fools and Horses...* (see 13.6, "The Seeds of Doom") and inevitably *EastEnders*. Saward was a big fan of *Minder*, and attempted to get the writers to contribute story ideas to him. *Minder* and *Only Fools* were both comedies about dim-but-crafty wannabe entrepreneurs coming up against established crime-lords. Lytton looks and acts exactly like the kind of person Arthur Daley (an unscrupulous and incompetent importer-exporter in *Minder*) or Del-Boy (a wily but out-of-his-depth market trader in *Only Fools*) would run into during some dodgy deal. Likewise, Griffiths is the kind of person those characters would hire to beat up our heroes, only to be outwitted by the fast-talking patter-merchant. (We'll pick up this theme with 23.1, "The Mysterious Planet" and 24.4, "Dragonfire".)

But we're pussy-footing here around the big topic. Like "Warriors of the Deep" (21.1), "Attack" is an exercise in pick 'n' mix, taking elements that worked well before and rearranging them in the hope that it will all gel. *Doctor Who* is far from alone in this way of thinking. Remember that this is 1985, the year when sampling and scratch-mixes went from a gimmick in hip-hop to the mainstream approach to film and pop-video montage. We're not even going to try to dignify "Attack of the Cybermen" as a bricolage, as it's more like a stew made from leftovers. The point is that instead of being apologetic about it, this approach is proudly proclaimed.

Look at it this way: these days, the BBC goes in for what it calls 360-degree cross-promotion. Anything successful gets a tie-in with another outlet, such as one of their subscription channels or in your local retailers. In 1985, the overseas sales were earning more than *Doctor Who* cost, although this was put into the Drama Department's collective "pot" (a practice that meant the show couldn't always get the recognition for the income it accumulated). Capitalising on this, the merchandising outlet BBC Enterprises (later BBC Worldwide) began putting out old stories on video. By public demand (allegedly), the first story released was the Tom Baker story "Revenge of the Cybermen". A new Cyberman adventure on telly helped to push the video range, and vice versa. Similarly, as we will see, the attempts to put out an LP based on audio-recordings of "The Tomb of the Cybermen" came at around the time this story was commissioned, and the BBC released 6.5, "The Seeds of Death" on video just months after "The Two Doctors" was aired.

This is the start of the kind of thinking that led the BBC to refer to *Doctor Who* as "the property" in contract negotiations with anyone writing spin-off books. By 1999, matters were such that the narrative for the missing episodes of 2.6, "The Crusade" ("I'm Ian Chesterton, and I've just messed myself") had references to BBC Books with Ian and Barbara in, as well as other stories available on video. Prior to 2005, pretty much the only reason for showing old episodes on terrestrial television was to promote the videos, books and DVDs. The overall point - which you've hopefully gleaned - is that whatever its merits as a story in its own right, "Attack of the Cybermen" is as much as anything a sales-pitch for *Doctor Who*, the merchandising bonanza. (See **Did They Think We'd Buy Just Any Old Crap?** under 22.5, "Timelash")

Things That Don't Make Sense All right, if that's IM Foreman's of 76, Totter's Lane, then Ian and Barbara were parked in someone's front room when they spied on Susan. The other side of the road is a row of 1880s terraced houses and, while there's one small gap between two houses, it's on the wrong side and too narrow to park in.

The Cybermen need to sort out their priorities. You'd think their scheme to rewrite history and thereby save their homeworld of Mondas would take precedence over all other concerns, yet much of the story is consumed with all manner of petty side agendas, such as their letting two escaped prisoners - Stratton and Bates - wander free and behead the limited stock of Cyber-troops with a flute (all right, a stupidly flute-like digging tool), as part of what is, given the circumstances, a shockingly pointless psychology experiment.

Moreover, the notion that the Cybermen want to blow up the surface of Telos to study the effect on the atmosphere sounds like an unbelievable waste of time and resources - if their plan to save Mondas fails, then they will have destroyed the very refrigerated cities they prize so highly, and where will they go then? Conversely, if their plan to alter history succeeds, then - as the Doctor and Flast seem to believe - the Cybermen will never have visited Telos in the first place, so the entire experiment would be purged from the timeline anyway. Not to mention that the information isn't *much* use under any circumstance, unless they're to use Vastial on other planets [but as the experiment will help to eradicate the only source of the material - Telos - this doesn't seem very likely].

More importantly... consider that the Cybermen allegedly want to prevent Mondas' destruction, and deem that crashing Halley's Comet into Earth is the best means of doing so. As opposed, say, to simply just using their time machine to retroactively contact their brethren on Mondas and warn them of the danger. It's not as if the two strains of Cybermen are beyond scratching each others' tin-plated backs, or the ones on Telos wouldn't bother trying to save Mondas in the first place. [And if you favour the notion that the Telos portions of "Attack" take place in 1985 - meaning a year ahead of Mondas' destruction - then simply alerting their homeworld to the danger seems an even *more* obvious route to take, no time travel required.]

In any event, it's left entirely unstated *how* the Cybermen plan to divert Halley's Comet, or *how* precisely this will save their homeworld. Granted, it will certainly 'disrupt' Earth as intended, but Mondas perished [in "The Tenth Planet"] because it burnt out while trying to absorb Earth's energy. So will bombarding Earth with a comet allow for better absorption of our planet's energy, or is the goal to simply scare off Mondas from even making the attempt? In which case, the Mondasian Cybermen could *still* probably use a warning that, "By the way... your planet is prone to melting if fed too much energy."

Lytton's plan (such as it is) involves making contact with Bates and Stratton, and seems to take for granted that they'll have escaped from the Cyberman work detail. Besides, if the time ship is theirs - as is implied on screen - how is it that such dim bulbs were given responsibility for a time vessel in the first place? [Saward's novelisation says that Stratton and Bates hail from the planet Hatre

Sedtry, that the time vessel was a prototype and that they crashed on Telos while taking it on a test-flight - a scenario that works, just. Still, best to ignore the fact that just two stories from now, in "The Two Doctors", the Time Lords are shown moving to prevent the development of such independent time-technology. And that one reading of that story makes it highly unlikely that the Cybermen could time travel at all.] And if, as Russell claims, Lytton has made such a splash in the underworld, why has he here recruited the most inept gang since the Ant Hill Mob?

The advent of the Doctor and his TARDIS seems to have been part of the Cyberleader's plan all along, sometimes. Lytton's operation seems to do the same, sometimes. Note especially how Lytton's continued distress signal - once he's made contact with the Cryons - makes no sense unless he miraculously presumes that the Doctor and the Doctor alone will answer it, thus enabling him to hitch a ride to Telos. But if that's the case, it seems entirely more sensible for Lytton to steer clear of the Cybermen altogether and just convince the Doctor he's working for the Cryons, an oppressed people. Because otherwise, it's daft of Lytton to plot the time vessel's theft on behalf of the Cryons while simultaneously taking the risk that the Cybermen will capture the Doctor's time-active TARDIS.

Lytton and the Doctor already know a lot more about each other than they ought to. Watch "Resurrection of the Daleks" again and you'll see that they never even exchange words. They're in the same room on two (brief) occasions, and neither is conducive to small-talk: the first time Lytton is pointing out a Thing That Doesn't Make Sense about the Daleks' inability to stick to a simple plan, the second Lytton is shooting (very badly) at the Doctor. Neither instance afford the Doctor a chance to find out that Lytton is even called 'Lytton', nor that he survived the gunfight. [As is so often the case in this period, it's as if everyone in the cosmos has a programme guide readily to hand.]

Speaking of Lytton's signal, by what logic does the Doctor go from saying that it will take weeks to trace the various signals back to the primary source, to then tracking it in moments? He seems to think that Peri's idea that the sender could leg it while it's being traced is some kind of breakthrough, and concludes from this that someone must be watching the empty house - therefore, he can tap three keys on the computer and *Bingo!*

instant result. And why, after the Doctor skewers a Cyberman with his sonic lance, does he just leave the useful device buried in its chest? It seems rather wasteful, and as Lytton proves, it's easy enough to pull the Lance out.

At the end of episode one, how do the Cybermen gain entry to the TARDIS before the Doctor and Peri return? Did the Doctor foolishly forget to lock the door, or should we infer that the TARDIS' glitchy chameleon circuit has rendered the door lock inoperable? Oh, and notice how the doors magically close after the Cyberleader escorts the captured Lytton and Griffiths inside the Ship, even though the door control shorted out moments earlier.

A lot of fans mention it, but it's true... it's astoundingly inept of the Cybermen to lock the Doctor and Flast in a cell with a massive amount of explosive material, and it's even more of an oversight that the Cybermen don't frisk the Doctor beforehand and discover his sonic lance - a device that's previously been shown to slay Cybermen, and which is capable of opening locked doors and heating said explosive. The Cyber-guard outside their cell seems especially witless, trundling over and happily sticking its hand out to examine the small box placed in the corridor, even though Vastial is known to ignite on contact with warm air. What does he *think* they've just shoved out the door? [It does, we have to admit, look like it might be a portion of Pilau rice, in one of those foil containers you get from Indian Takeaways. Without a nose, this model of Cybe needs to *look* to see if the Telos Balti House got his order right. Perhaps they *do* care about well-prepared meals. They also obviously receive regular supplies of milk from a supermarket, as there are dairy trolleys all around the Tomb - see also 17.1, "Destiny of the Daleks".]

The Cybermen have finally installed CCTV, but despite this enabling the Cryons to see the Doctor in his cell, they somehow don't know that his cell-mate Flast is among the living. And the Cryons promise to pay Griffiths a fee of £2 million in uncut diamonds, but how precisely does he think he's going to receive such a (literally) weighty payment? One presumes he isn't lugging it in his backpack, and Heaven knows why Lytton's party would even *think* of returning to Telos after stealing the time-ship.

In terms of dramatic tension, why make the first overseas-only cliffhanger the Cyberman lurking behind the Doctor and Peri, when if they'd just hung on for 45 seconds more, they could have ended with the impressive first appearance of the Cyberleader and Griffiths screaming in terror? And why does Halley's Comet have the same serial number (9/12/44) as Turlough (21.5, "Planet of Fire")?

Critique Amazingly, after "Earthshock" tried to do *Alien* for eight-year-olds, this story prefigures the sequel *Aliens* by seeing how many ways the previously-unstoppable monsters can be splattered about. It's a curious irony, then, that "Attack" tries to re-acquaint the public with the idea of Cybermen being organic people turned into science-zombies, yet it's also the story that - in the eyes of the nation's kids - cements their status as robots.

To be fair, episode two entails the Cybermen being devious, the plot strands coming together and Lytton's part in all of this explained. Unfortunately, there's no real reason for anyone to stick around that long to see the resolution (as the almost three-million viewer drop-off between episodes one and two proved), mainly because the new format has made the story so top-heavy. If you're reduced to only one cliffhanger, then it *has* to be good, but the finale to episode one has no tension leading up to it, and in itself is just corny. Anyone who's seen *Doctor Who* in the last two years knows that within seconds of the next episode, the Doctor will say 'Wait!' and come up with some plan as contrived as the cliffhanger itself. Worse, in many ways the first episode is an exercise in vamping until everyone happens to congregate in the TARDIS.

Look, we'll come out and say it: in general, forty-five minute episodes are a mistake. X2.4, "The Girl in the Fireplace", springs to mind as a story that actually has three-quarters of an hour's worth of material, but on too many other occasions, matters are stretched or rushed to accommodate this length. In Season Twenty-Two, the next adventure - "Vengeance on Varos" - comes closest to using the new format well, but in "Attack of the Cybermen", the effort to make the two episodes different has resulted in a disastrously lopsided story. If we'd had any hint that Lytton was playing a different game in episode one, the revelation in episode two would have been shocking but looked less like a last-minute decision on the writers' part. Some clue early on as to who Bates and Stratton are - or why we

should care about them - would have helped, and above all, it would've opened things up to get out of those sewers before it looked like the whole story would be set there. Conceptually, this looks like a story written before 1970, when the episodes were made week-by-week, and the sewer set needed to be struck to make way for the tomb set.

And it's self-consciously retro in other ways. Next to no thought has gone into why the Cybermen are in tombs at all. It is presented as self-evident that they need a refrigerated city so badly, they'll wipe out the Cryons to get one. Yet nothing suggests that the tombs have any merit as a script idea; it's just accepted that it worked in 1967, so let's do it again. In this, it escaped the programme-makers' notice that the point to "The Tomb of the Cybermen" was that it's a Mummy's Curse story, and the traps and logic-games are obstacles in a quest-narrative. By contrast, the Tomb in "Attack of the Cybermen" is a giant barracks, and any idea of the Cryons as a last-ditch resistance movement is wasted. It's a real shame, too, because there's the potential for a really exciting story here, if only the Cryons and their situation had been introduced earlier, and in a less cumbersome manner than Peri and Griffiths asking the Doctor and Lytton for an info-dump while they're locked in a cupboard aboard the TARDIS.

Yes, that's right... the TARDIS has been hijacked! There's so much more potential here than the few minutes of backfill narrative that we get, and a lot more to excite and entertain the casual viewer than people ambling around the most hygienic sewers in TV history (until 25.2, "The Happiness Patrol" at least). In fact, as we'll see in **The Lore**, a really good version of this story, set inside Halley's Comet, got quashed to make room for the sewers and Telos. And the sewers are there because it's a Cyberman story and they did a Cyberman story in sewers in 1968 - even though the few people who might actually care about this were too busy fuming about how badly the tombs have been changed, and how little care has been put into making the story make sense.

If you're a *Doctor Who* fan of more than ten minutes' standing, then you probably know this story is something of an easy target, so let's try to be upbeat and positive here. By definition, a script like this requires stilted dialogue from many of the protagonists - so Lytton's gang are a blessing, and keeping Griffiths alive was a sensible precaution. Killing him actually was a bad move, because a character who's taken the companion's role for so much of the story needs to complete his or her narrative journey. Likewise, having Cryons with personality flaws and one with an occasional turn of phrase was smart. If this were a Big Finish CD everyone would love the Cryons, but alas we can actually see them. That is, we can see *them* but not their expressions. Why cast such experienced performers and then hide them?

Another plus: Terry Molloy (as Russell) gets a chance to come out from under the latex - at short notice and taking over a small part - and is entirely convincing. (If, as "The Twin Dilemma" seems to indicate, the idea of a cop as the male sidekick for an as-yet-uncast Doctor was kicked around, this is how to do it.) We also ought to praise Brian Glover (as Griffiths) and Maurice Colbourne, even though his portayal of Lytton is John Kline (his character on *Gangsters*) without the wit and Malcolm Clarke on incidental music - spots this and gives him a theme that's a *Gangsters* retread. Brian Glover is by now playing the usual Brian Glover character, so putting them together shouldn't have worked, but it does.

This is us *trying* to be positive, so imagine how long a bad review would be. In short, the music is a microcosm of the story. Clarke has taken the tapes of things he did that worked before, then added a few new ones, but by the end he's slapping one on top of the other regardless of whether they're in the same key or tempo. Like a lot of this story, there's a feeling that everyone's asking "will this do?"

The Facts

Ostensibly written by Paula Moore, but as **The Lore** will discuss, more accurately a fusion of Saward and Paula Woolsey, with a bit of Ian Levine thrown in. Directed by Matthew Robinson. Ratings 8.9 million (yay!), 7.2 million (oops!). That said, audience appreciation was 61% for episode one, and a more charitable 65% for episode two.

Working Titles "The Cold War"

Supporting Cast Maurice Colbourne (Lytton), Brian Glover (Griffiths), Michael Kilgarriff (Cyber Controller), David Banks (Cyber Leader), Terry Molloy (Russell), Michael Attwell (Bates), Jonathan David (Stratton), James Beckett (Payne), Brian Orrell (Cyber Lieutenant), Sarah Berger (Rost), Esther Freud (Threst), Faith Brown (Flast), Sarah Greene (Varne).

Oh, Isn't That..?

• *Maurice Colbourne*. He was a shady SAS officer Kline in Philip Martin's *Gangsters* (lots more on this in the next story and beyond), then was the eponymous Tom Howard in *Howard's Way* (see 22.3, "The Mark of the Rani" and 23.3, "Terror of the Vervoids"), an honest shipbuilder faced with competition from smarmy Londoners (played by... well, see 22.2, "Vengeance on Varos" for that). 80s kitsch doesn't come any kitschier or more 80s than this (except one gobsmackingly pointless series but we'll come to that presently under "Terror of the Vervoids"). And we assume you've read Volume V, and therefore and know about 21.4, "Resurrection of the Daleks" and *The Day of the Triffids* already.

• *Brian Glover*. Probably only known to US readers as the bloke in the pub in *An American Werewolf in London*, or as one of the early victims in *Alien*[3], or as Magersfontein Lugg (the sidekick in *Campion*, starring Peter Davison). To us, he's the voice of Tetley Tea's "Gaffer" and Allinson's Bread ("wi' nowt tekken out") but not - as is often thought - the far bigger rival loaf, Hovis. (See "The Mark of the Rani" for more on the associations between Northern-ness and brown bread.)

But really, he's so much more. To all intents and purposes, he was Yorkshire made flesh, and so very much in demand. He started out as a miner, then a wrestler (British professional wrestling was so radically unlike the US version, it's very confusing to have the same word for both), then did a spot of acting here and there. An early one is *Kes* (1969), where he's the sole funny bit in a touching but grim tale. He also was God in the Wakefield Mystery Plays in 1975 (we could explain this, but it would require a bigger book).

• *Michael Attwell*. If you've seen 5.3, "The Ice Warriors" and wondered what Isbur looked like outside his armour, now's yer chance. But by this point, Attwell had been comic thugs in things like *Turtle's Progress*, East End villains in just about everything and would soon be a regular on *EastEnders*.

• *Faith Brown*. Comedienne and mimic, often muddled up with Janet Brown (comedienne and mimic). Someone should have got them to do a stand-off for who did the better Margaret

Thatcher. Steve Nallon should have been judge (see 25.2, "The Happiness Patrol"). Faith's a better singer, tho'. British readers might vaguely recall that she was in *I'm A Celebrity - Get Me Out of Here!* in November 2006, but these things fade from the memory so quickly.

• *Sarah Greene*. Child actress turned *Blue Peter* presenter, here trying to be taken seriously as an ac-torr again. It didn't work.

Cliffhangers [For Season Twenty-Two, cliffhangers artificially inserted for overseas syndication are included in parenthesis...]

(In the sewers, a dark figure stealthily follows the Doctor and Peri); the Cybermen march into the TARDIS, kill Russell and laboriously prepare to shoot Peri; (two Cryon commandos - Varne and Rost - refuse to help rescue the Doctor).

The Lore

(NB, increasingly, there will be two or more almost mutually-exclusive accounts of behind-the-scenes events whilst Eric Saward is on board as script editor. The point of these Lore pieces is to allow the reader to get some idea of the overall "story" of the making of *Doctor Who* and provide evidence for our conjectures elsewhere. So in this volume, we're trying to get a concise account from what is - to be frank - a welter of divergent rumours, claims, counter-claims and actual documented facts.)

• Back when Eric Saward was a jobbing writer pitching a story about plague and "resting" actors (19.4, "The Visitation"), Paula Woolsey aided him in researching the period. She'd been a teacher and had written for radio herself. More to the point, she'd dated Saward. So when her story "The Cold War" came up for consideration as a *Doctor Who* adventure, Saward bore it in mind.

Meanwhile, with the audio recording of "The Tomb of the Cybermen" was being pitched to BBC Enterprises as the logical follow-up to the hit LP "Genesis of the Daleks" (see 12.4) and with Ian Levine advising the series on how to maintain continuity, Nathan-Turner found the idea of a Cyberman story set on Telos appealing. Levine came up with some ideas, as well as a number of other proposals for clearing up continuity "issues" concerning the Master, and Saward took these on board too. Eventually, a kind of shotgun wedding

between these stories was arranged. Just to add to the mix, the character of Lytton was re-examined. Saward's claim is that his only real contributions are Griffiths surviving into episode two, and the Cryons not being ghostly, but instead corporeal beings with distinct personalities. We doubt that the idea of calling the Bank "Masters and Johnson" was his (British readers can get their American friends to explain this, and then the Americans can have the rhyming-slang "merchant bankers" elucidated in return).

• However, the script of episode two as broadcast was extensively reworked, to minimise the number of sets as much as anything else. Originally, the Cryons and Lytton were attempting to lure the Cybermen to a showdown inside Halley's Comet. More filming was allocated, and so a lot more material was written for episode one to be set on the surface of Telos. Bates and Stratton were introduced, and once director Matthew Robinson had noted how 'blokey' it all was, the Cryons became a matriarchy.

• Saward had every reason to deny extensive involvement in this story's authoring, as both the BBC and the Writers' Guild took a dim view of Script Editors self-commissioning themselves (except in emergencies, see Volume IV for some examples of this). If he tried anything even slightly dodgy with Pip and Jane Baker - who were co-chairs of Guild - working on the show, he'd be in big trouble. Indeed, with the move to 45-minute episodes, it would be surprising if heavy amendments were *not* needed, especially with a credited writer new to television. These days, Saward claims that he wrote it, checked it with Levine, and then Paula Woolsey just took all the money. He doesn't talk to her any more.

• The new format was at least partly a response to the success of "Resurrection of the Daleks" the previous year. Showing two episodes a week (as was the practice in the Davison era) required viewers to have both evenings free, and covering the need for updates had resulted in some excruciatingly arch dialogue. The Dalek story had received the best ratings of the year, although attributing this to the format rather overlooks the publicity blitz for the Daleks' return to London, plus an inherited audience from the ice dancers Torvill and Dean and their record-breaking performance in the Winter Olympics. Pacing the episodes and making use of the continuous narrative - now without need to set up cliffhangers and resolve them - meant a lot of work for Saward. (As we will see, this added to the delays on "Vengeance on Varos".)

• Nathan-Turner, of course, was keen to get some publicity for the "stunt-casting", and so Rost was originally to have been photographer and actor Koo Stark. However, the Cryon costume was impractical and she had her own staff handling her publicity. (For those with short memories, Ms Stark was famous for two things - soft porn and shagging Prince Andrew. She's managed to parlay that up to some successful charity work these days and, let's face it, she *is* a pretty good photographer.)

The fall-out from that caused *more* publicity, so Robinson quietly recast Rost with an RSC player. (Sarah Berger's involvement came as a blessing for Nicola Bryant, who was still self-conscious about her lack of experience.) Prior to this, the part had been offered to Jenny Hanley, presenter of ITV's *Blue Peter*-clone *Magpie* and daughter of Chancellor Flavia (AKA Dinah Sheridan, from 20.7, "The Five Doctors"). Varne, as we've seen, was played by *Blue Peter* and *Saturday Superstore* presenter Sarah Greene. Robinson had worked with Greene before, on *The Swish of the Curtain*. Greene recalls how dehydrated she got in the costume; one can of beer made her pass out after a day's recording.

• *Saturday Superstore* was a key weapon in Nathan-Turner's publicity campaigns for the series, and he often appeared alongside his stars (once, rather bizarrely, while offering an Ian Levine record as a prize along with a Marshman mask and some Gail Bennett paintings; see 22.5, "Timelash", for more on the latter). On the day episode one aired, Baker and Bryant (plus Jacqueline Pearce from "The Two Doctors") went on the show for the second time (the first being the Saturday before 21.7, "The Twin Dilemma", the third during "The Mark of the Rani").

• Another missed casting coup - in those days there was a fad for "robotic dancing", and one pair, "Tik and Tok" (not their real names), were seldom off *Top of the Pops*. They were approached to play Cybermen, but declined (they were due to tour America at around this time, but we can't find any definite dates). At this point, we have to admit perplexity. The usually infallible historian Andrew Pixley claims that Esther Freud is the daughter of Clement Freud (former celebrity chef, weirdly cast as presenter of *Cartoon Time*, then MP, now broadcaster). Writer and broadcaster Emma Freud fits

that description. Yet other sources claim that the novelist Esther Freud, daughter of painter Lucien Freud and author of *Hideous Kinky*, is the same one who's inside the big plastic head. And the novelist (who won awards for *Gaglow*) *did* start off as part of a theatre troupe called The Norfolk Broads. But if Pixley's wrong about something, it's possible that the fabric of space-time will unravel.

• The story's opening shot was to have been a close-up of some rats in the sewers. Despite the presence of a rat-wrangler, they misbehaved and fluffed their takes. Other problems in filming were caused by a rapid flourishing of the plant-growth at the Gerrard's Cross quarry (which was desolate on the recce but verdant when they went to film there, causing a delay whist some frantic weeding took place). Trevor Raymond broke his arm early on, so the role of Stratton needed to be recast in a hurry. Yes, they went back to the same bit of quarry used in 1967, as if anyone watching at home would spot this. (The British public, spurred on by Terry Wogan, thinks that all locations for *Doctor Who*, plus desert-based things like *Tenko* and *Beau Geste* and of course *Blake's 7*, use the one quarry. This has led to an urban myth about the Foreign Legion being confronted by Servalan's troops. Sad-cases like us can spot which of the dozen or so quarries in 40 miles of Television Centre is used in any given episode.)

• Terrance Dicks likened the writing of "The Five Doctors" to a Hollywood mogul who'd cast his girlfriend and needed her to be in every shot. This curious anxiety might perhaps explain why Saward's novelisation renames "Threst" as "Thrust".

• Matthew Robinson was intended to direct the unmade story "The Nightmare Fair" (see **What Would the *Other* Season 23 Have Been Like?** under 22.6, "Revelation of the Daleks"), although a contract wrangle may have prevented this in any case. He'd previously directed "Resurrection of the Daleks," but "Attack of the Cybermen" is his last contribution to *Doctor Who*. He went on to direct the first few episodes of *EastEnders*, and was later producer of *Byker Grove* (which was like *The OC*, but with Geordie accents and plots including freak paintballing accidents), and is thus responsible for Ant and Dec.

• Cyberleader David Banks proposed several story ideas. One of them was rejected outright, while another never made the screen but became the Virgin *New Adventures* novel *Iceberg*. We can all rest easier now.

22.2: "Vengeance on Varos"

(Serial 6V, Two Episodes. 19th - 26th January 1985.)

Which One is This?   Sil the Galactic Slug and a planet where the public are kept quiet by live coverage of executions. Politics is a potentially lethal version of *X-Factor*, and a starving populace seems very well supplied for hair-care products.

Firsts and Lasts   It's the first of two appearances for Nabil Shaban as Sil, the last of three for Martin Jarvis (see 2.5, "The Web Planet"; 11.2, "Invasion of the Dinosaurs" and Volume V for comments about Peter Davison's casting). This story is the first since "Black Orchid" (19.5) not to have been offered to us as part of a longer sequence - for instance, a trilogy of some kind or the return of an established character, race or planet - or with an ending leading in to the next such story (such as 21.3, "Frontios") - although it *did* acquire a sequel, 23.2, "Mindwarp". (Indeed, "Black Orchid" was picked over at the start of the next story, 19.6, "Earthshock", making 24.2, "Paradise Towers" retrospectively the first real "stand-alone" story of the 1980s.)

Mercifully, this is the last time a story begins with the Doctor trying to fix the TARDIS console. For the rest of the 1980s, the Ship works properly and only outside influences make things go wrong. (Well, there's one more internal glitch, but it's debatable what causes it: arguably the lurch in 22.4, "The Two Doctors" is a result of an extraneous time-eddy created by either the Kartz-Reimer experiment, *or* it's the product of the recent visit by the Second Doctor's TARDIS. So we'll keep things simple and just say it ends here.)

Four Things to Notice about "Vengeance on Varos"...

1. As the Yeti were to Troughton, and the Slitheen were to Eccleston, so Sil is to Colin Baker. Except that the Yeti and the Slitheen were monsters (even though one Slitheen displayed more personality in her second appearance, X1.11, "Boom Town") and Sil is a proper character who happens to look alien. So perhaps, taking that into account, the better comparison is with Delgado's Master. Important though Sil is to the plot, he's kept in the background as a grotesque detail for much of this story, and works best as comic

underscoring to the unpleasant developments.

2. Except that there's *someone else* comically underscoring Sil, with two characters who are entirely isolated from the plot giving a running commentary on what we're watching. We keep hearing political wrangling about "the viewing public" and "the voters" (the same thing in this case), but we only see two of them: Arak and Etta, a middle-aged couple. The source of most of their bickering is the stuff they're watching on TV, which is the same stuff that *we're* watching for most of this story. Padding, a cheap method of doing crowd-scenes with only two actors, a Greek "chorus", a Brechtian *verfremdsdungeffekt* or postmodern self-referentiality? Maybe it's all of the above, or something else entirely.

3. ... but if it helps you decide, the only cliffhanger in the BBC's transmitted version is Martin Jarvis (as the Governor) in a gallery of TV monitors, directing coverage of the Doctor's apparent death. We see a monitor on which the Doctor seems to be breathing his last, and hear the Governor say 'and cut it... there!', followed by the episode credits. Then in the next episode, the revived Doctor turns to the prison chaplain and asks: 'Do you always get the priest parts?' Owing to this sort of stuff, and writer Philip Martin's previous form, many people thought there was a lot more to this story than met the eye (see **Where Does This Come From?** and **The Lore**).

4. In case this all seems like too radical a departure from conventional *Doctor Who*, normality reasserts itself with Peri and her new friends escaping through a ventilation shaft. This is, however, unusual in being the first vent-shaft big enough for six-foot security guards to walk in upright, and people to stride through three abreast.

The Continuity

The Doctor   His reaction to the latest in a string of TARDIS systems failures is unprecedented - he sits in an ugly chair and sulks about spending the next few thousand years twiddling his thumbs. He's also insensitive to Peri's potential fate as a result of the breakdown, arguing that she's "lucky" because she'll only age and die in the TARDIS but once, whereas he'll keep on regenerating. He can identify the Ship's present location - between galaxies of Cetes and Sculptor - by looking at a starfield on the scanner. [Cetes and Sculptor are actually constellations, as seen from Earth. The galaxies, if such they are, must be named by humans after their apparent direction, like Andromeda and M31.]

• *Ethics.* Upon seeing someone facing imminent threat of execution, the Doctor intervenes and saves the man's life - never considering, apparently, that the condemned might justifiably deserve to die. As part of this rescue and escape, the Doctor "delays" pursuit by swinging round a lethal laser beam that disintegrates a guard. And upon learning more about the state of affairs on Varos, he never seems to consider that perhaps Varos *doesn't* need regime-change of some kind. (Although, admittedly, this is after the authorities have been shooting at him for a while.)

Just before being tipped into an acid vat, the Doctor inadvertently causes one guard to fall in and perish, then is embroiled in a tussle that ends with a second guard meeting a similar fate. However, it's actually the dying first guard - who's flailing and trying to escape from the acid - that pulls his comrade in, not the Doctor. [Contrary to what is sometimes stated, the Doctor doesn't so much grin as wince at the fate of these doomed men, but the feeble quip he gives while leaving the scene of the crime - 'You'll pardon if I don't join you' - doesn't do him any credit.]

The Doctor *does* arrange the premeditated killing of the Chief, the torture-master Quillam and two guards with the toxic vines, but waits until Quillam has announced an intention to kill the Doctor and his party slowly and horribly.

• *Inventory.* He's carrying a ball of string and scissors. There's a horseshoe magnet in his pocket, convenient for over-riding the controls on an unstable laser gun. "Question-mark" braces (similar to those seen in 21.5, "Planet of Fire") hold up his trousers.

• *Background.* The Doctor says he tried to read the TARDIS manual 'once'. Whilst knowing about Varos and its supply of Zeiton 7, he seems to have never visited the planet before now.

The Supporting Cast

• *Peri.* Apparently thinks of herself as a little bird (ahh), as her body grows feathers - as governed by the impulses of her mind - when under the Transmogrifier. They're very colourful feathers, it must be said, so she's apparently got an idea of herself as exotic and flamboyant, as well as wanting to escape. She refers to the geejee fly blown up to giant size in the Purple Zone as 'a

creature of her worst imaginings' [which considering what she's seen lately is remarkable]. She can take readings off the TARDIS console, and she's familiar enough with the Ship's interior to know when an auxiliary storage hold has gone. [That settles it... the Doctor has made her sit an exam in Companioncraft. See 22.1, "Attack of the Cybermen" and 22.5, "Timelash".] All these corridors look alike to her.

The Supporting Cast (Evil)

• *Sil.* The plenipotentiary from Galatron Mining Corps. He has been secretly paying the Chief and [perhaps] Quillam to ensure that the Governor loses a few votes, and will therefore be more amenable to Sil's contract negotiations. The main issue is the price of Zeiton ore: the Governor (or 'Governyeuuur', as Sil calls him) wants a price of seven credits per unit, whereas Sil is holding out for a lower price. Because the Governor withstands the cellular degenerations from his losing votes better than anticipated, Sil - who is running out of time - orders a Galatron invasion force to seize control of Varos. Sil hopes that the bargain price he will secure for Zeiton - or outright command of its source - will make him powerful even among his own people and the galaxy at large.

Sil is from an aquatic world [Thoros Beta, seen in "Mindwarp"]. He finds Varos' dry air and heavy gravity unpleasant, and has two huge, muscular attendants to wheel his carriage around and attack other people if necessary. But most of the time, their job is to keep Sil moist with sprays and stock his bowl of marshminnows.

Although one of these guards can definitely speak English, nobody has told Sil that his Translator unit - a green box with a light attached to his chest - is malfunctioning (hence the aforementioned 'Governyeuuur') and producing odd statements like 'You lying liar'.

Sil is vain in the extreme, convinced that he is gorgeous while Peri is repulsive.

The TARDIS

According to Peri, the Doctor's tinkering with the Ship of late has resulted in three electrical fires, a total power failure and a near collision with a storm of asteroids. He also managed to wipe the flight computer's memory and jettisoned three-quarters of 'the storage hold' [surely one of many, whatever Peri says] by mistake. [In fact, the Doctor's "revamp" of the Ship's systems may well have damaged the bits that're contingent on Zeiton 7, inadvertently necessitating this whole adventure.]

In generating orbital energy, the TARDIS' power is routed through transitional elements that rely on Zeiton 7, and without this the TARDIS is stranded in space-time. Life-support and data-retrieval systems, however, continue functioning normally. This breakdown follows soon after the Doctor tinkers with a circuit beneath the panel [if the interior door is Twelve O'Clock, this located at Three O'Clock]. Should anyone care, the Manual says that in this phase, the orthogonal readings should be ZS+ 101 EQ [no mention of whether the Doctor's got Dolby].

The Zeiton 7 problem leaves only enough vestigial power for one short journey, and with Varos apparently nearby spatially, it becomes a matter of trying [or simply hoping] to arrive during the planet's mining period. Curiously, the possibility of liberating power by deleting interior sections [18.7, "Logopolis"; 19.1, "Castrovalva"] is not mentioned, perhaps as a result of the recent accident with the hold. [Peri may have insisted on a safety cut-out, although it's unclear why the Doctor doesn't consider switching off this failsafe.]

The TARDIS workshop is near the console room, and has an air-vent that closes unless propped open with something [in this case the Manual, last seen in 19.2, "Four to Doomsday"].

The Non-Humans

• *Sil's people.* [We'll learn more about them in "Mindwarp", and so we'll just sketch what's revealed here.] Sil's race have leathery skin, an olive colour, and are sort-of midway between a caterpillar and a mermaid. They're humanoid from the waist up, if a little stunted, and have two arms with five digits. [Sil has a habit of bunching his fists and then rapidly splaying his fingers - as though shaking off water - which is apparently his version of drumming his fingers in annoyance.] Around the face is a frill of tougher skin, and the head comes to a point. From the waist down, Sil displays a segmented tail. This waggles up and down in excitement, usually at the same time as Sil emits a guttural laugh.

Sil consumes a great many marshminnows - these are green, and kept in a pot with some bright green aspic or gel. He sits on wheeled box that contains a vat of pale green liquid and some electronics. Two large men - muscular types wearing gladiator-style helmets and tunics - accompany him. They're the only black men on Varos, and

appear to have been brought by Sil from Thoros Beta.

Planet Notes

• *Varos.* Varos orbits a red sun and is shown to have a desert surface, with the entire population living inside pressurised hemispherical concrete units. The occupied areas are designated as Zones and Domes, and the Punishment Dome is heavily-equipped with remote surveillance cameras that broadcast the sadistic events within. The guards who serve the Punishment Dome must sometimes wear anti-hallucination helmets, a means of nullifying the induced hallucinations of the Dome and its Purple Zone in particular. Such are the potency of the Zone's technically-stimulated mental effects, somatic changes are possible - imagined deserts can cause real dehydration and heatstroke.

Proximity to Zeiton 7 - or the Transmogrifier device derived from it - can physically alter the human body according to the beliefs and mental self-image of the individual victims. The effect was noticed when miners on Varos developed claws, fur and bigger hands as an aid to digging. [This perhaps lead to permanent alterations over generations, like Vega Nexos in 11.4, "The Monster of Peladon".]

All adults on Varos are required to vote YES or NO to the Governor's proposed policies, and the degree to which the "NO"s have it determines the intensity of the cellular disintegration ray under which the Governor is manacled following each vote. No Governor has ever survived four failed votes, and the concept behind this system is that a man in desperate fear for his life will find political solutions that others would not.

The Varos electorate seems to number less than two million, as the vote tabulation that we're allowed to see registers 633,156 Yeas and 987,627 Nays. Governors are randomly-selected from among the Guard Elite with the draw of a hat, but membership in the Elite seems hereditary. [The Governor speaks of his duty as being inherited, and the rebel Jondar found out about this unacknowledged caste system, hence his death-sentence.] Despite appearing to lack atmosphere breathable by humans, Varos has native life. Geejee flies, cankermoles and toxic vines are all either seen or described. [It would seem that a cankermole has a small appetite, which fits in with the desert conditions.]

Why are Elements So Weird in Space?

Throughout these books a theme has emerged: once you leave the school textbook level - and look at the more rarefied areas of pure science - *Doctor Who* is actually closer to what's happening in the real world than *Star Trek*'s make-believe engineering.

Other programmes may get the scientific terminology neurotically right, or hire people to tell you which button does what on a pretend spaceship, but the lateral thinking and overall *feel* of science is respected in *Doctor Who*, or more often just taken for granted (at least, once rehearsals start). So it should come as no surprise that Zeiton 7's magical properties can be readily resolved with the Copenhagen Interpretation of quantum physics, presuming that's what floats your boat. But that's not the point we need to make now; you can look it up for yourselves, and that *is* the point. It's not that *Doctor Who* is especially scientific, but that science - especially biology and particle physics - after a certain point starts to get like *Doctor Who*.

Think about atoms, and you think of a sort of teeny solar system (unless, that is, you're really well-informed and can conceptualise not-quite-real events). The electrons orbit the nucleus like planets around the Sun. The nucleus consists of as many protons as there are electrons, and as many neutrons as are appropriate for that element. The neutrons have neutral charge, hence the name. Electrons have negative charge. (Actually, that's a bit of a misnomer, as any electrician can tell you: they're the ones that move about causing current. The electrons, obviously, not the electricians.) So if you've got an electron and a proton, you've got the simplest possible atom: hydrogen is only *just* matter.

Yet if we get away from that "solar system" model, and think of the electron as a zone of probability of there being a particle, we're a lot closer to what's happening at this miniature level. Particles are distillations of energy, in a sense. The forces that attract them are also part entities and part tendencies. An electron is impelled to be as close as possible to an available proton, the way water is impelled to be as low down as possible, and the temperature of a gas is always tending to be the same throughout.

So you've got hydrogen - and as far as anyone's aware, most of anything that *is* matter and not energy is hydrogen. Helium is the second-simplest atom, and you can make this by adding two hydrogen atoms together and leaving the left-over fraction to return to being energy. (That's why thinking of atoms as solar systems is misleading: "solid" particles becoming pure energy because they can't do anything else is counter-intuitive.) Back in the 1950s, this was done experimentally over what soon ceased to be islands in the South Pacific. Or if you want to see it happening today, there's a large amount of hydrogen becoming helium about ninety-three million miles away, and we're orbiting it. All stars work by hydrogen fusion - get enough hydrogen together, and it starts happening once gravity gets to work forcing the atoms into one another. Basically, a galaxy is just hydrogen gone lumpy.

The electrons that aren't really orbiting their nuclei have a fixed number of spaces where they can probably be. More than two electrons means the atom gains a second "shell" (if you must, think of it as a higher orbit), which in turn has a set number of available spaces. In general, it can be up to seven (as there are eight electrons in a "full" shell, which means no spaces), but obviously helium and hydrogen are a bit different. An atom with two electrons in its outermost shell would be very likely to make a good match with an atom with two remaining spaces in its own outer shell. (Think of it like Tetris. Once the space is filled, the shell may as well not exist for all the effect it has on other atoms.) These two atoms would eventually rub into one another and make a bond.

Now you understand chemistry. That's really all there is to it, except the details. Some of these combinations (molecules) have to have a bit of energy to make the bond (heat works in most cases) or give off energy. (Again, that's usually heat but sometimes a slew of spare electrons. Put copper in a weak acid, and you can power a Walkman with what comes out.) And what's more, the number of available spaces on the outer shell is more important and more reliable a guide to an atom's properties than the total number of electrons. That's how the Periodic table works: elements are arranged horizontally by how many electron shells they have, but vertically by how many spaces there are on the outer shell. Hydrogen's number 1 (and is counted, for these purposes, as an alkali metal), and helium, at number 2, is over at the other end of the table. The ones immediately under helium are neon and argon, non-reactive gasses. Similarly, fluorine is 9 and chlorine is 17 (note the spacing, 8 away from each other and

continued on page 31...

• *Thoros Beta*. Sil's homeworld, which has less oppressive g-forces than Varos. [And again, we'll see this planet in all its lurid glory in "Mindwarp".]

History

• *Dating*. Varos has been populated for some centuries, and Peri says it's 'three hundred years' since her time. ["Mindwarp" provides a date that seems to be 3rd of July 2379, which suggests a dating slightly later than Peri's estimate.]

Varos was named after its founder, who seems to have been responsible for the surveillance network and the curious social arrangements. Originally, Varos was a "Botany Bay"-type penal planet for the criminally insane [see 3.4, "The Daleks' Master Plan"], and over the intervening two centuries the population have become accustomed to the brutality and spartan life.

Varos is the only source of Zeiton 7 - prior to the announcement that traces of the mineral have been found on 'asteroid Bio-Sculptor' - and the mineral is virtually the planet's only resource. According to Sil, at present the engineers of every known solar system are crying out for supplies of Zeiton 7 'to drive their space-time craft'. [It seems impossible to believe that this era is littered with as many time machines as we have trains, or history and politics would be way more knotted than what we're shown here. Ergo, it's probably best to assume that 'time' in this case just refers to a method of space travel, in the same fashion that ships in *Blake's 7* fly on a "time-distort" scale. We'll pick this up in "Mindwarp".]

Mining operations have been Varos' lifeblood prior to offworld interest in recordings of the Punishment Dome's torture and executions taking off. Despite this, the galaxy at large seems not to have noticed Varos, and the government there seems oblivious to the true value of Zeiton ore. Indeed, Sil - as the legate from the Galatron Mining Corporation - claims to be unaware of the planet's sideline in judicial snuff-movies. Galatron and their rival combine - Amorb - presently seem more powerful than any federation, empire or league.

The Analysis

Where Does This Come From? Philip Martin's first thought when inventing this story was to create a society and see what happened. (You'll be amazed, after hearing this, to learn that his first pitch was after seeing 19.1, "Castrovalva" in 1982.) The play *Marat / Sade* contains the idea of a prison / asylum putting on entertainments of increasing brutality, and Martin trained as an actor when this show was perpetually in production somewhere in London. There's also a hint of SF thinking, perhaps overtly influenced by Philip K Dick's *Clans of the Alphane Moon* (in which a hospital / prison has been left alone for centuries, and the various psychoses have formed nations: schizophrenics on one continent, obsessive-compulsives on another...).

Dick had just died when Martin began writing, and the publicity this event and *Blade Runner* coincidentally created meant that Dick's books were magically back in print and in supermarkets. We can't rule this out, as Martin has said that he went to legitimate SF for his background reading. A cited source is Isaac Asimov's bestseller *Extraterrestrial Civilisation* and a throwaway comment about how few aquatic life forms make it into stories, considering that they'd probably outnumber land-based ones.

Meanwhile, although Mary Whitehouse had fallen silent about *Doctor Who* several years earlier (see Volume IV, and especially 14.3, "The Deadly Assassin") she was still busying herself with clean-up TV campaigns and railing against the permissive society. By the 1980s, she had the ear of a government broadly sympathetic to her complaints and a new target: video nasties.

To explain, domestic video recorders had caught on in the late 1970s, and the first half of the 1980s saw a boom in the number of commercial titles, mostly for rental purposes (retail tapes at the time could be prohibitively expensive - "Revenge of the Cybermen" would have set you back £40 in 1983). The big studios were generally wary of the new technology, and the system of blockbuster movies reaching supermarket shelves within months was still years away. However, independent distributors found there was a ready supply of obscure, barely-seen films that they could rush onto the market. Many of these were low-budget horror, pornography or both. Also, the burgeoning video market was entirely unregulated and thus a moral panic was born.

The tabloid press coined the phrase "video nasties" and set out to demonstrate that small children were watching snuff movies. By way of proof, the best BBC news could muster was a ten-

Why are Elements So Weird in Space?

...continued from page 29

thus one under the other), very reactive gasses.

All these elements were made the same way hydrogen became helium. Well... almost. The more exciting ones higher up the table were the result of more energetic and complicated processes at the end of the star's life-cycle. A bog-standard star on its last legs will collapse into a smaller, hotter body (a white dwarf) and the majority of the elements readily available to us are made - the first thirty or so in the table. (Actually, it stops when it gets to 26, iron, because the fusion process for this element is one that takes more energy than it gives out. Sadly, this isn't the place to explain why that's the case.)

A few million years later, the star goes bang and all these rich and handy elements are scattered into space. When a new star coalesces from hydrogen and stardust, it collects together any agglomerations containing these elements by gravitational force. That's why the planets closer to the Sun - such as Earth - have things like aluminium and iron in their crusts and cores while the outer bodies like Jupiter are all hydrogen and... well, more hydrogen. They may have attracted some of the more exciting elements towards them as satellites, but they themselves do not contain more than traces of anything else. Jupiter, which is bloody enormous, has a fractional proportion of Helium-III, a groovy isotope that could be a handy power-source (and when something as big as that is involved, a "fraction" could be as big as our moon) but the Gas Giants are aptly named.

This all looks and sounds like a roundabout way of saying that "The Daleks' Master Plan" (3.4) is a load of hooey, because a hefty, handy element like Taranium couldn't get out as far as Uranus. Actually, that's not the case. Go back to your *Child's Book of Science Stuff* and look carefully at the Periodic table. Notice anything odd? There's 92 'basic' elements, and a whole bunch more someone made or predicted ought to exist. The ones from 93 to 110 are all like uranium but moreso - they're heavy, toxic and radioactive, and with half-lives all over the scale. Earlier on, you go from well-known and useful ones like iodine and barium to no-mark elements like praesodymium, dysprosium and thulium (all real, 60, 66 and 69 respectively). Then you get onto gold, lead and mercury, which ought to be rarer. There are these "sidebars" in the table for anomalous groups (the lanthanides and actinides, pretty unstable and unlikely to occur in nature anywhere, certainly not hereabouts). How do we know that the transuranic elements so far concocted in cyclotrons aren't themselves an irritating discrepancy from how the rest of the elements from 92 onwards would go if we could find them?

Well, there's a problem with making these elements. Let's assume that Zeiton 7 has atomic number 200 and is relatively stable, at least as far as lasting long enough to be mined by humans is concerned. If there is a correlation between the density of an element and the energy required to fuse it into being from lower-down elements, a star big enough to make Zeiton would not be a white dwarf on its demise. If it became a conventional black hole, then we can say goodbye to any exotic elements it may have wrought. Maybe a quasar produced it, but these are so far away that we can give up hope of such elements being found locally.

That is, presuming it was done all in one go. A big star will easily get as far up the periodic table as silicon. So, we might surmise, a star made of the detritus of a previous star might fuse medium-size elements into bigger ones. Achieving the kind of atomic numbers we're talking about would perhaps take three or four generations of stars, which - unless some rock 'n' roll stars live fast, die young and leave a good-looking cloud of heavy elements - would take several more aeons.

But in *Doctor Who*, we keep finding amazing minerals on Earth-type planets - mainly in this galaxy and not too far into the future (cosmically speaking). Once again, we can look at real astrophysics for guidance, but the marriage of this and what the stories say takes a bit of a leap of faith. But, once again, it's less of a leap than for any American show with scientific advisors. We have, in earlier volumes, explored the possibility that the Universe's expansion has at some comparatively early stage been slowed down to allow time for intelligence to evolve. Various essays have suggested that things mentioned in *Doctor Who* only really make sense if this is the case, and astronomers are coming around to the idea that maybe the Hubble Constant isn't as constant as advertised.

Ergo, under "normal" circumstances, a really seriously dense element like this notional Zeiton would only occur when stars that have themselves inherited elements from earlier generations

continued on page 33...

year-old with the 1951 version of *The Thing From Another World*, but all horror films were tarred with this brush. That "nasties" were borderline illegal and a social menace went without saying. The closest thing to snuff on the market was *Faces of Death*, a compilation of pre-existing footage of - among other gruesome things - state executions.

Police raids on newsagents and video shops became commonplace and videos as innocuous as *The Best Little Whorehouse in Texas* (the Dolly Parton musical) and *The Big Red One* (the Lee Marvin WWII flick) were referred to the Director of Public Prosecutions (DPP). The DPP drew up an official list of "nasties" supposedly in breach of the Obscene Publications Act, but in fact it was a ragbag of titles ranging from arty horror classics to ludicrous schlock that only gained cachet from being "forbidden". Not all of the side-effects of this were bad: the publicity and sales boost that this gave Sam Raimi's *The Evil Dead* paid for the sequel / remake (watch the credits at the end of *Evil Dead II* for an oblique reference to this) and thus paved the way for him to make *Spider-Man* and *Xena: Warrior Princess*.

Whitehouse was in the thick of this and - on the basis of a showreel of money shots from films such as *Zombie Flesh Eaters* and *Ilsa, She-Wolf of the SS* - persuaded Tory MP Graham Bright to sponsor a Private Members Bill to introduce video censorship. The Video Recordings Act was passed in 1984 and required that all commercially-released videos should now bear film-style certificates from British Board of Film Classification (BBFC), an industry body that until now had no official powers. This did not please Whitehouse and her followers, who'd spent the 1970s denouncing the BBFC as one of the bastions of permissiveness, and saw the Act as effectively giving government licence to the "nasties". At the same time, the *Daily Express* couldn't understand why implementation of the Act had to be delayed a year to allow 58,000 commercial videos (including early *Doctor Who* releases) to be classified.

However, Whitehouse had managed to secure a clause in the legislation requiring the BBFC to take into account the fact that videos would be seen "in the home". This kerfuffle is why the VHS copy of "The Talons of Weng-Chiang" (14.6) goes into slo-mo at one point in episode one (see also 27.0, "The One with Eric Roberts"). A lot of small distributors and retailers were forced out of business, but eventually police raids stopped (except, for

reasons far too complex to go into here, in Greater Manchester). All but a handful of the DPP's list of obscene films eventually crept out on video or DVD, more often than not uncut. Bright lost his seat. "Video nasties" still crops up as a tabloid phrase occasionally, but notably for our purposes, the period in which it was a burning issue coincides almost exactly with the period of writing and production of "Vengeance on Varos".

Martin had heard all the arguments about violence on TV before. He'd written a series called *Gangsters*, which began as a relatively earnest play about organised crime in the new, multi-ethnic Birmingham. As such it was part of a thoroughgoing effort on the part of Britain's most interesting and unloved city to reinvent itself as industry collapsed and 'Britishness' was being rethought. (The mid-1970s in the West Midlands was a time of perverse pride in the grottiness of all things Brummie, leading to such bizarre phenomena as Ozzy Osbourne, Jasper Carrott, Slade, *Tiswas* - more, much more, on that later - and the alarmingly odd Cliff Richard flick *Take Me High*. Slade's thuggishly mis-spelled records should really have been your soundtrack for Volume III, but you've heard one in both of the Christmas specials.)

Then things went a little peculiar. Martin was asked to turn the play into a series, and it entailed ex-SAS ex-con John Kline (Maurice Colbourne from "Attack of the Cybermen", as we're sure you remembered) and his colleague Khan (Ahmed Khalil - he's Latoni in 19.5, "Black Orchid" - an undercover vice cop who laid on the Peter Sellers accent when dealing with dodgy politicians) set about breaking up drug barons, people-traffickers and neo-Nazi politicos. It could easily have been a British Blaxploitation knock-off, but they did this in a manner that pilfered from 30s Jimmy Cagney films, westerns, spy dramas and comic-strips. The basic *Starsky and Hutch* audience drifted away, replaced by more discerning punters who got into the playful use of generic tropes that simply looked silly when set in the Bullring Centre or Balsall Heath.

At the same time, Martin got frustrated by "Clean-Up TV" lobbyists and the inability of the BBC's Pebble Mill studios to be quite as cinematic as he hoped. Casting some of the ethnic actors caused a problem, as people might look the part but couldn't say the lines. So Martin did that as parody too, and wrote the process of writing a hit TV show into the storyline. This, of course,

Why are Elements So Weird in Space?

...continued from page 31

of stellar debris could fuse these further into more and more massive atoms. Assuming an eight-billion year lifespan of a run-of-the-mill star like ours, we have had time for two or three generations. So out here in the cosmic suburbs we have ready access to oxygen, iron and even uranium. After a few more billion years of this high-energy composting of stars, we could expect a whole galaxy full of heavy stuff like cadmium, thorium and gold. If the time needed for a generation of stars was only two billion years or so, however, we could expect to find thumping great atoms like a 200-electron beast (our notional Zeiton) in abundance on planets fairly close to their stars. (It probably wasn't intentional, but our one glimpse of the exterior of Varos suggests that it orbits a red giant, so it could be very close to its star and not uninhabitably hot if they all stay indoors. Which the populace evidently does.)

Now, as we've seen (**How Many Significant Galaxies Are There?** under 2.5, "The Web Planet"), only a handful of the galaxies we can observe have the second-generation stars that make life possible. (At least, that's true at time of writing. Give it a few aeons, though...) This is still a gobsmackingly large number of stars, of various sizes and levels of activity. However, the period of time in which *Doctor Who* adventures tend to take place is fairly limited and all around our era, cosmically speaking. There may not have been time for all this pressure-cooking of exotic matter. This is, of course, assuming that we can extrapolate from Earth's solar system how all stars and planets might be.

There's our wild card. As we saw in "The Edge of Destruction" (1.3), at least one solar system - very possibly this one - was artificially "force-grown" by the Doctor's TARDIS ploughing back through time, possibly attracting matter together with the mysterious 'time force' (19.1, "Castrovalva"). If indeed it was *this* solar system, then the conditions here could be markedly different to those in any other region of space. Maybe our sun is the weird one. More recently, and perhaps more significantly, "The Runaway Bride" (X3.0) shows Earth coagulating around a Racnoss ship with a vast amount of the soon-to-be-outlawed Huon particles. (How do you remove fundamental particles without unsettling the whole Cosmos? Maybe this is when the change in Red Shift happened and Omega or whoever amended *all* the laws of physics.) Even though it potentially means abandoning many of the suggestions in the essay with "Inferno" (7.4), it reinforces the idea that our planet's mineral composition is inevitably a one-off.

allowed more brutal and stylised violence, as it was "just a laugh" (the second series brought in the Triads, and had Bruce Lee parodies at the "No Weh" laundry). His investigation of casual racism and the increasing lack of any common bond between people became more overtly polemical. The second series had spoof Bond titles, with a bomb going off in a Morris Minor. (If you know your British cars, this is both poignant and ludicrous. The factory that built this daft vehicle had been the city's biggest employer - if you've not seen one, hang on for 24.3, "Delta and the Bannermen".)

Martin had played the crime-boss in the pilot (in which he was drowned by Colbourne - amazingly two years before a near-identical scene in 14.3, "The Deadly Assassin" episode three, but in Bilston Canal, under Spaghetti Junction). He later returned as the White Devil, a ninja assassin who looked and sounded like WC Fields, and killed Colbourne's character halfway through the last episode. By this stage, a character called "Philip Martin" - also played by the author - was writing the scripts in cutaway scenes filmed in Pakistan, dictating to an elderly man with a portable typewriter. We're still a couple of years ahead of the word "postmodern" being coined, mind. Characters were making asides to the camera and walking off the set, Kline's funeral had tombstones for Philip Martin, and there were some even more in-jokey bits, such as people not only quoting old movies but adding citations afterwards. (If you're keen to catch a glimpse, it's all on DVD.)

You can see how people who knew Martin's work suspected that "Vengeance on Varos" might have more in it than met the eye. You can also see how we were less than impressed when *Moonlighting* - which was so pleased with itself for acknowledging its fictionality on screen - reached our screens. (But then, *Doctor Who* had been doing it since 2.9, "The Time Meddler"). As a result of *Gangsters'* curious status as a hit show that had gone weird, the Open University did a documentary about it and included an almost impenetrable essay in one of their books on media. This tome, and the essay in particular, is a masterpiece of mid-80s academic overkill, and made those fans studying media latch on to this story more than even 19.3, "Kinda". (See **The Semiotic Thickness of What**? under 24.4, "Dragonfire".)

Let's not ignore the obvious. "Varos" reached our screens towards the end of the most vindictive period of industrial unrest since the Peterloo Massacre (see 22.3, "The Mark of the Rani"). The energy lobby said that oil and gas were more economically viable for running power stations than coal (yes, that's worked out well, hasn't it?), and that coal was no longer worth mining. This made an excellent excuse to close down an industry whose unions had caused the previous Conservative government grief (see **Who's Running the Country?** under 10.5, "The Green Death" and the notes for 11.4, "The Monster of Peladon").

Miners - fighting for the preservation of communities built around coal - made a last stand despite new legislation that specifically targeted them. The police were used for political ends, as was the judiciary. The strike, despite all this, lasted for a year and has left deep scars. (Films such as *Brassed Off, Billy Elliot* and *The Full Monty* turn this into a pretext for feel-good comedies or semi-fantasies, but these have been massively popular in the US, where the anger behind such works is invisible.) You didn't have to be from a mining town to feel that destroying a generations-long tradition and entire communities for the sake of political dogma was wrong.

Mind, every other UK industry was in the same boat. As we have seen, Birmingham's manufacturing base was being crushed, and steelworking, shipbuilding and aero-industry were all allowed to perish. (Armaments manufacture survived, however, because Denis Thatcher had shares in many of these - see 25.2, "The Happiness Patrol" - and Tory-voting farmers wouldn't feel the pinch until 1997.) Basically, stories like "Varos" and "The Mark of the Rani" are as inevitable as a story about a moon rocket made in 1969 (6.5, "The Seeds of Death").

And in a 1977 edition of the science series *Horizon*, they had shown a possible future where viewers had a box with which they could order goods shown on a TV shopping service, not to mention vote in talent shows. A trial run was being conducted in America - in one of the states that ends with a vowel - and British reviewers used this as a chance for a dig at indolent Yanks. However, a couple of years earlier had witnessed the first referendum in the UK, on a matter that cut across party boundaries: membership of the EEC. The lack of party apparatus meant that the national broadcasts were significantly less slick than anything we'd seen for a generation, and most of them were - like the opposition parties' responses to the budget every year - a bloke in a suit talking to the camera and trying not to sweat. (Again, we used to look across the Atlantic and despair at the slick campaign commercials, tantamount to brainwashing, used in American politics. "We" meaning the UK public: the politicians simply kick themselves for the cross-party support for limits on what can be done, and which were set in place when ITV was created.)

Things That Don't Make Sense For a start, there's the title. Precisely who extracts vengeance from whom, and how? [If it's alliteration you want, then "Video on Varos" seems quite apt. There's also "Votes", "Vendetta", "Vile slug-like things", "VO5 Conditioning Mousse", "Vomit-inducing patchwork jacket"...]

Economics Issue No. 1: Galatron's limitation on the price of Zeiton 7 relies on the Varosians not knowing how much the mineral is worth off-world. But they conduct trade using 'credits', which suggests a currency based on an agreed standard, rather than barter. And the only reason an entire planet is being kept from starvation is that they rely on imports. You see where this is going? How could the Varosians be *so* oblivious to Zeiton's worth under such an arrangement? (For that matter, Sil seems astonishingly brazen to talk about the true demand for the Zeiton ore while the Governor appears to be floundering from a dose of the cellular-disruption beam. It would serve him right if the Governor perked up and said, "Only joking. What's this about engineers across the galaxy wanting so much of our ore?")

All right, so maybe the imports come from Galatron, and credits are a currency only useable for their goods [you have our permission to burst into a chorus of "Sixteen Tons" by Tennessee Ernie Ford]. But if so, Galatron could arbitrarily decide to make a 'credit' worth a third its previous value, then raise the cost per unit of ore to whatever the Governor asks and still come out ahead.

Fine, so maybe 'credits' is the galactic unit of currency, and somehow Galatron is unable to regulate the imports to Varos of basic foodstuffs, except to have robots deliver it and thereby not let on that Zeiton 7 is priceless. And maybe someone other than Galatron is distributing the Varos torture videos off-world, and that someone *also* wants to keep the Varosians in the dark regarding the worth of their minerals.

That's an awful lot of assumptions, and even if all of that is true, there's *still* basic economics to worry about. If the supply of food is constant, and the Varosians now have more dosh per head thanks to events in this story, then you're going to get runaway inflation. And even if they fix that, you've got a population brutalised by generations of TV violence and now rolling in cash and bored... Nice going, Doctor. [In **The Lore** we're going to argue that this might have been deliberate.]

Economics Issue No. 2: the finale seems exceptionally baffling, as we're told that off world prospectors have found a new source of Zeiton 7, and therefore... demand for Zeiton 7 has reached such an extreme that the Governor can now force a new deal out of Galatron. Do the words "supply and demand" ring a bell?

Why should Time Lord technology depend on a substance from one single solitary planet? Or assuming that Zeiton is merely the most suitable mineral in striking range of the Doctor's stricken Ship, why does he speak as if a journey of a few light years spatially is simpler than picking the right three hundred or so years temporally? Is he planning to stay in this area, travel through time and then drift towards Varos using a solar sail or something?

When, we might ask, does Quillam start working for Sil? In episode one, Sil's underlings seem to only include the Chief and possibly Bax (although the latter is just seeing how the wind blows, by the look of it). Yet in episode two, it's said that Quillam, Head of Entertainments, is also on Sil's payroll. But if that's the case, why is Sil so badly informed about the Transmogrifier and the execution and torture videos, all of which are under Quillam's purview?

Also, Quillam seems to have put a lot of thought into maximising the nasty side-effects of Zeiton exposure. He could have made more money accentuating the positive. A society that's perfected induced hallucinations doesn't really need to keep the public happy with live executions - with some research and development, they could make everyone live their dreams. Or they could use the Transmogrifier as a cheaper alternative to Botox and surgery to make rich ugly people look like they think they should. But no, Quillam seems to have voluntarily made his home planet a hell, and himself poor. There are loony scientists and there are *really* loony scientists.

And why does Quillam only recognise the Doctor once the latter has taken off his half-mask? Did the mask *really* conceal that the Doctor is a Harpo-haired man in a revolting patchwork jacket? [Perhaps the Doctor has learned the Master's talent of making people fall for really rubbish disguises - see 8.3, "The Claws of Axos" and 20.6, "The King's Demons" in particular, and unbelievably we'll revisit this issue in 22.3, "The Mark of the Rani".]

During the UK cliffhanger, Bax tells the Governyeuuur that 'there's no sign of life' as the monitor shows the Doctor apparently dying. Look at the bloody screen! He's still breathing, dagnabbit!

Not so much a problem in this story, but certainly an issue when compared with adventures such as "Frontier in Space" (10.3): when the TARDIS breaks down, why does the Doctor whitter on about how he and Peri will age to death in the Ship, when he could just call the Time Lords for help? All right, he'd have to swallow his pride after abandoning his post as Lord President (20.7, "The Five Doctors"), but it's surely preferable to repeatedly perishing and regenerating in the middle of nowhere.

Oh, and the TARDIS Manual seems to have blank pages.

Critique Say what you will about this story, it's as near as the production team gets to making the new long-form episodes work. Whereas "Revelation of the Daleks" (22.6) has performances more worth savouring - and is the only Colin Baker story in the same league as this - "Varos" has a plot that actually makes more sense each time it is watched. Yes, a few scenes look under-rehearsed or cheap (but no more so than the bulk of this season.), and it's not entirely as clever as it thinks it is, but this story gets more marks for effort than anything else this year.

One problem remains. Is Jondar a parody of the typical rebel leader we get in stories like this, or is he just badly written and poorly acted? We know that Jason Connery can do a lot better than this, but we're never sure he isn't *meant* to be this wooden. With a model-shot pilfered from *Blake's 7* at the start, isn't Jondar the kind of clichéd rebel the Doctor *should* encounter, the sort of person whose rebellion is exactly what the authorities anticipated? Or are Connery and Phillip Martin playing it for real? With hindsight, and the awful example of the rebel leader Tuza in Martin's subsequent "Mindwarp", we can't be sure. But given Martin's previous form, he could be laughing at us for not knowing any better.

Indeed, with the use of a higher authority elsewhere writing telexes (or digital signals on a TV screen in Sil's case), the words 'my patience is exhausted' (a catchphrase of both *Gangsters* and 30s dialect comic Adolf Hitler) and the cops taking bungs from Galatron, it's not too far from Philip Martin's Greatest Hits. Sil might almost be one of the grotesque lackeys in the second series of *Gangsters* (one has an electronic larynx, like Peter Hawkins in 60s Cyberman stories, and another is pretentious, cowardly and given to malapropisms). But in many ways *Gangsters* was a case of people seeing more than was intended, and we can't avoid asking if we're here indulging a sloppy production by thinking that errors are clever ruses.

Still... let's look at what's here. The Doctor is wise, curious, impulsive and entirely unpredictable. His response to a small crisis on the TARDIS is not to shout at it, but to give in - we've never seen this sort of thing, even in Hartnell's day. Otherwise, though, he's pretty much the same Doctor we've always known, and the alleged sadism of the acid-bath sequence is mainly down to people's misinterpretations (thinking the Doctor has outright committed murder) and a dodgy camera-angle or two. He also figures out the traps in the Purple Zone, and for once this Doctor's overt theatricality is an asset - Jonathan Gibbs (working the incidental music) picks up on this and plays to it, with a moment of PT Barnum calliope music after the green lights interlude. Generally speaking, this script was written for a generic Doctor, with a few odd tweaks that no other story will have, and with Baker filling in the rest.

Meanwhile, Peri does companion things and is less wet than normal. She's dangerously close to generic herself, but the detail of her "wanting" feathers adds as much as Tegan's 'garden' does to her (20.2, "Snakedance"). We've also got one rebel

couple - not in jump-suits this time, but instead crafted as the usual Season Twenty-Two characters trying to find the truth. They helpfully tell us things about this planet's odd system of government and judicial murder, even as another couple - Arak and Etta - imply a lot more by throwaway remarks about things we can't quite understand. A lot of this is just routine mid-1980s *Doctor Who*, and the ironic ending, where the Doctor seems to have removed what little meaning there was to anyone's lives, is part of Saward's overall conception of the series as being about people losing hope and getting killed, but there's more going on here than usual, and the clue is in the scenes where there isn't any music.

Whether it's Philip Martin, the director or both, this story just *feels* different to everything around it. At times it's like a 90-minute play that someone's sabotaged by dubbing on the music from a *Doctor Who* story. At others, it's like channel-zapping between a radical fringe theatre and children's television. It's lit more sombrely, with a lot of dark corners and coloured spotlights. It also *sounds* slightly different, with filtered voices not just for the alien but the hallucinations, and a fly sound that was one of Dick Mills' favourite effects. Significantly, there are silences. As we said, the fact that the wall-to-wall Radiophonica has been left to one side makes a huge difference to how we take in the dialogue.

Or to put it another way... *Doctor Who* is, by definition, melodrama. Music is supposed to be there for mood and a sense of place (especially in alien planets of historical settings), but most mid-80s stories sound like mid-80s cheap dramas the world over, using synthesisers chiefly because they can't afford an orchestra. The fanfare for the Governor's broadcasts is almost exactly like the one for BBC home videos, and the rest of the music is like the soundtrack to a BBC wildlife documentary of the period. This is a story *telling* us that it's not just a story. And in the quiet moments, with the characters just talking, it's a drama that happens to be set on another planet.

As proof of all this, look at the cut scenes on the DVD. So much of "Varos" works because the guest cast seem to believe in this planet as anything else, so the cut pair of TARDIS scenes - so like the usual beginning and ending of a Season Twenty-Two story - can only feel like a let-down. There's nothing wrong with Colin and Nicola, but having a conversation about the end of "Attack of the

Cybermen" cheapens what's going on in *this* story. Any reminder that this is "just" a *Doctor Who* story detracts from what's really important. In an odd way, the believability of this planet almost excuses the otherwise unforgivably bad car-chase and zap-gun duels - any more competent and it would all be less like theatre, and your concentration would lapse.

If anyone asks how it actually felt to be living in Britain under Thatcher, rather than go through the usual clichés ("Frankie Says" T-shirts, mullets, matte black furniture and clips of policemen beating up miners), just sit them down and ask them to watch this. Then ask them to imagine a world where this could be followed by *Jim'll Fix It*.

The Facts

Written by Philip Martin. Directed by Ron Jones. Ratings: 7.2 million, 7.0 million.

Working Titles "Domain", "Planet of Fear"

Supporting Cast Martin Jarvis (Governor); Nabil Shaban (Sil), Nicholas Chagrin (Quillam); Jason Connery (Jondar); Forbes Collins (Chief Officer); Stephen Yardley (Arak); Sheila Reid (Etta); Geraldine Alexander (Areta); Graham Cull (Bax); Owen Teale (Maldak); Hugh Martin (Priest).

Oh, Isn't That..?

• *Martin Jarvis*. Still, mysteriously, not Sir Martin. Between his last *Doctor Who* outing as Butler in 11.2, "Invasion of the Dinosaurs" he's been busy. He did a massively popular sitcom, *Rings on their Fingers*, about a couple who married after five years of cohabiting and yet still found it hard to adjust. The next few years had him trying to evade typecasting, mainly by reading things on radio or tape, and by providing so many voice-overs for ads that he and his wife set up an agency. In particular, he has made Richmal Crompton's *William* books his own, despite the famous 1970s TV version (see 23.3, "Terror of the Vervoids"). He was also still associated with classic serials, since his breakthrough role in *The Forsyte Saga*.

• *Steven Yardley*. He had, as most of you know, played the benevolent, lumbering Sevrin in "Genesis of the Daleks" (12.4), and had been the eponymous *XYY Man*. (According to a fashionable late-70s theory, a chromosomal oddity made him prone to psychotic violence. This is remembered, if at all, for introducing Detective Sergeant George Kitchener Bulman to our screens. See 24.3, "Delta and the Bannermen".) For the British Public, Yardley is the dodgy Ken Masters in *Howard's Way*, which reached our screens just after *Doctor Who* went on gardening-leave in 1985. (This was ostensibly about boat-building, but was a lamentably wrong-headed attempt at a British *Dallas*. Inevitably, Kate O'Mara turned up in later episodes - see next story.) Most of Yardley's screen-time in this seemed to be sipping cocktails, raising his glass to rivals in a curious quarter-turn manner and trying to look good in pastels and espadrilles. Long before this he'd been womanising goalkeeper Kenny Craig in *United!* (see most of Volume II), virtually the only cast-member who looked like he'd ever seen a match before the auditions.

• *Sheila Reid*. She did "Varos" soon after doing an almost identical character in Terry Gilliam's *Brazil*. She'd earlier been in the similarly dystopian (but funnier, if not deliberately) 1972 flick *ZPG*.

• *Jason Connery*. He'd been cast as Ian Fleming in a drama-documentary, but this wasn't broadcast until just before "Varos", making *Doctor Who* almost his first telly. About a year later, he took over the lead in HTV's *Robin of Sherwood* (this, of course, reminded everyone about Dick Lester's 1976 *Robin and Marian*). As with the schoolyard debates after each Doctor's regeneration, the fans of this series split on party lines, pro-Connery and pro-Praed (it didn't help that some of the writers seemed unaware of the change). These days, a whole generation of kids see him as the heroine's incredulous father in *Shoebox Zoo*, and we can finally stop talking about him as Sean Connery's son.

• *Nicholas Chagrin*. He was fresh from the first episode of *Bird of Prey*, which was a paranoid computer-age thriller, a bit like those 70s conspiracy movies like *Three Days of the Condor* but set in Surrey and with the Robert Redford role given to Richard Griffiths (and we'll have a lot more on *him* in 27.0, "The Paul McGann Disaster"). Big things were expected of Chagrin back then.

• *Owen Teale*. This story's fully-clothed blond hunk went on to appear in the fifth season of *Ballykissangel* (the year after everyone stopped watching), and he's done the rounds of almost all the cop-shows. More recently, he was the panto baddie in the *Torchwood* episode "Countrycide" (AKA "The Talfryn Chainsaw Massacre").

Cliffhangers (Maldak advances on the police box that has just arrived out of nowhere); the Doctor is seen to die and the Governor cuts the transmission; (Peri is groggy from the Transmogrifier but the guards will be arriving soon).

The Lore

• At risk of repeating ourselves, the early drafts of this story were submitted at around the time Nyssa was leaving and Turlough (still at this stage a denizen of the unmade "Space Whale") was being brought in. Martin had previously been approached, on the back of *Gangsters*, by Script Editor Christopher H Bidmead. 1980 had seen Martin writing a one-off SF drama for the BBC (*The Unborn*), whilst working as resident dramatist at Liverpool Playhouse. He had also written a play, *Thee and Me*, about near-future Lancashire, which transferred to the National Theatre. So when the early Davison stories started playing with ideas and non-naturalistic drama, Martin thought he'd have a crack at *Doctor Who*. (We note that the producer of *Gangsters*, David Rose, is kind-of a godfather of challenging drama in late-70s / early 80s BBC circles, and that as soon as Martin gets a spot on *Doctor Who*, names like David Halliwell and Jack Trevor Story start being bandied about. See **What Would the *Other* Season 23 Have Been Like?** under 22.6, "Revelation of the Daleks" for more on their possible contributions.)

• Saward was impressed by Martin's basic concept, not to mention other ideas Martin seemed able to spin almost off the top of his head, and invited him to submit a four-part breakdown. Nathan-Turner, however, was worried about it getting "too political" and insisted on vetting the storyline. Martin suggested that if he'd wanted to write a polemic, he could have got it made more easily, but this was just an idea he could only do as *Doctor Who*.

Then they changed Doctors and decided on the 45-minute format, causing Martin to rewrite and in the process accommodate requests from Saward to bring Sil and Peri to the fore. Martin was also asked to write a book called *How to Write for TV* at the time, but avoided getting haughty with the producer. He did, however, sardonically suggest to Saward that it was almost a let-down to get the story made, as the rewrite fees were the steadiest income he'd had in years.

• Saward liked the idea of the "Chorus" characters (Arak and Etta) and asked for more of this, more sympathy for the Governor and more... well, more. The scripts were under-running even with the expansions to make them long-form episodes. Indeed, Saward augmented some scenes, including the priest's dialogue. Shortly after this, Martin scored a gig as a radio drama producer at BBC Pebble Mill, Birmingham, so all subsequent commissions were in-house (see "Mindwarp" and the comments about "Mission to Magnus" in the aforementioned essay). Martin was pleased that the script was intended to be made entirely in the studio, as *Gangsters* had been affected by the switch from location film to interior VT and back.

• Martin's first thought was that Sil should be inside a fishtank. He conceded this was hard to achieve, but thought it something that hadn't been before (we might cite Arcturus in 9.2, "The Curse of Peladon" as being as near as they'd come). The producer vetoed this on grounds of practicality, but the prospect of children copying it might have also preyed on his mind. Water and electrical cables is not a good mix, as Martin himself said, and as we'll discover in "Battlefield" (26.1).

• Director Ron Jones' biggest problem was casting Sil, yet with hindsight his choice seems inevitable. Nabil Shaban had been in several TV programmes (often documentaries about his bid to act) and had been in on the launch of the Graeae theatre group. Born with osteogenesis imperfecta (a form of brittle bone disease), Shaban had spent a lot of time watching television in hospitals as a child, and had been hooked on *Doctor Who* from the moment the Daleks appeared. He had, indeed, written to Barry Letts asking if he could take over as the Master, and to Nathan-Turner wanting to succeed Tom Baker as the Doctor. He didn't get either of those parts (obviously), but was in the TV play *Walter* - shown on the first day of Channel 4 in 1982 - and almost upstaged Ian McKellen.

Now, a memo was doing the rounds at the BBC about casting actors other than the routinely able-bodied (hence a rash of minor characters in terribly positive roles in shows like *Call Me Mister*). The Graeae group were named in the memo, and in the meantime *Walter* raised Shaban's profile. Slam Dunk, you might think, although Jones actually auditioned three members of the company. The schedule was arranged so that Sil only had three studio days, and Shaban's lengthy costume and make-up sessions required him to have a "minder" (in this case Tom Watt, a former colleague of Shaban who was just about to become famous in *EastEnders* and later as a football commentator). The marshminnows were dyed peaches, which gave Shaban the runs. Originally, the latex suit was in one piece, but this proved impractical and the headpiece was detached. Shaban based the guttural laughter on snakes a friend of his owned, and suggested that Sil should have a few snakes as pets.

• It had been thought that Michael Owen Morris (21.2, "The Awakening") would direct this story; Jones joined the project slightly late, but found the 45-minute format slightly more flexible than the previous length. He'd worked with Martin Jarvis as an actor before training as a director, and decided that the Governor should be slightly younger than scripted to make his survival under the cellular-disruption beams more plausible. With such a stylised story and so much emphasis on things not being what they seem, Jones believed that an absolutely straight performance in this role would pin the story in reality. Fortunately, Jarvis - previously a giant moth in pantaloons (2.5, "The Web Planet") - could give any role gravitas. Nicholas Chagrin had just been in the curious cyber-conspiracy thriller *Bird of Prey*, which was a bit like those 70s paranoid movies like *Three Days of the Condor* but set in Surrey and with Richard Griffiths (see 27.0, "Starring Paul McGann") instead of Robert Redford.

• The title was changed, as they'd just done a story called "Planet of Fire", so "Planet of Fear" became "Vengeance on Varos". The "double-v" logo for the planet's authorities was cited as Martin's inspiration for this otherwise pointless title. Jones asked the graphics department to design something fascist but not obvious, and this logo was made a feature of the costumes. (Martin's script had the different departments colour-coded, but Jones went for muted colours, so that Baker's costume would be more noticeably "wrong" and the planet's connection with mining was kept in the viewers' minds.)

• Quillam's death was different until very late in rehearsals. Apparently the original idea was that the patrol car ploughed straight into the vine-grove, whereupon the vine would have spontaneously wrapped around his neck. This was an obvious candidate for trimming, as it would have been technically feasible with more time - but

more time was something they didn't have. Another problem was finding exactly the right stock footage of a desert - every agency contacted said that such a shot was top of their wish-list. The allusion to the then-current ad for Perrier water was, says Baker, deliberate.

• Martin, an aficionado of bad reviews, loved the *Radio Times* letter complaining about the horror "exceeding the atrocities of World War II" and claimed to have had it blown up and displayed in his toilet. He believed the ambiguous ending was deliberate, as the people of Varos didn't know any better, but the Governor was still in charge to hold things together. He also defended the violence, saying that bitter experience had shown him that showing things on screen was actually less disturbing than leaving it to the imagination.

22.3: "The Mark of the Rani"

(Serial 6X, Two Episodes. 2nd - 9th February 1985.)

Which One is This? Trouble at t'mill. Luke Ward copse a feel (geddit?) and the Master has his orchids crushed.

Firsts and Lasts Obviously, the whole point of this story is to introduce the Rani, who's a bit like the Master but played by that Kate O'Mara off the telly. More significantly, this is the debut of Pip and Jane Baker, the most prominent writers of this phase of the series. (That's "prominent", mind, not necessarily "gifted".) Listen carefully and you'll hear the word 'bugger' used for the first time in the series, as happens when the potato man is attacked by overage schoolboys. (It's really clear on the undubbed "extended scenes" on the DVD, but less audible in the broadcast version.) This story has the first 'BBC wishes to thank...' credit for a place (in this instance, the Ironbridge Gorge Museum) rather than an organisation.

Four Things to Notice about "The Mark of the Rani"...

1. The sesquipedalian Bakers have become *personae non grata* among the programme's cognoscenti through their logorrheantic obfuscation and lexical legerdemain - but, let's face it, few if any of us can forget their way with words. It's not so much the vocabulary as the indiscriminate way everyone shares the same style (except "comedy" Geordies) and the way this stilted construc-

tion leads to ridiculous pomposity. Colin Baker, a trained lawyer, manages to make it sound like his Doctor's natural speech, just about. We can just about believe that this version of the Master might say something like 'fortuitous would be a more apposite epithet', but in Pip 'n' Jane's world, space captains, "ordinary" girls like Mel and Peri, mad scientists, scaly aliens and even vegetables talk like this.

2. Yes, vegetables. We'll examine this *idée fixe* of the Bakers in lurid detail when they inflict rampaging vaginal tulips on us (23.3, "Terror of the Vervoids"). Anyone making a list of things you'd expect in a Pip 'n' Jane story will take the Rani's landmines, the collecting of Earth's greatest minds for harvest and characters suddenly talking like *Friends of the Earth* pamphlets in his or her stride. However, no amount of prior warning will quite equip the first-time viewer for the unpleasant fate of George Stephenson's assistant, Luke Ward. For that matter, nobody seeing this development a second time (and some of us have to for research, but what's *your* excuse?) can avoid thinking of the preceding hour and a quarter as little but stalling until this extraordinary "money shot". If you've not seen it, what we're trying not to say is that Luke - this story's bleached-blond hunk - treads on one of the Rani's magic landmines and is transformed into a singularly unconvincing tree. If only that were the end of it...

3. With only one cliffhanger in this story, and three quarters of an hour to build up to it, you'd think this could've been scripted a little less like a Norman Wisdom film. Actually, there's something else it looks like, and which is rather more contemporary for 1985. Being filmed in what purports to be the industrial North, and with a man in a scruffy coat strapped to a trolley careering down a picturesque hill, this story is *Last of the Summer Wine* with cheesy synths[4]. Especially galling is the way the programme-makers resolve the cliffhanger by re-editing the reprise to show us something - the wooden platform that Stephenson slots into place to save the Doctor - that we missed at the end of the first episode. So that's *Last of the Summer Wine* meets *Flash Gordon* (see **Where Does This Come From?** for another Buster Crabbe / Saturday-morning serial resemblance). But the whole adventure is set in the North-East in the Industrial Revolution, so we have men in very tight trousers and terrible Geordie accents (see **What Are the Dodgiest Accents in the**

Series? under 4.1, "The Smugglers"). So that's *Flash Gordon* meets *Last of the Summer Wine* meets Catherine Cookson's *The Mallens*. People still switched over to watch *The A-Team*, mysteriously.

4. In two "official" appearances, one breathtakingly wrong charity fundraiser (see Appendix for more on "Dimensions in Time"), one spin-off audio and a hilariously sadistic "Make Your Own Adventure" book, the Rani has developed a cult following - especially amongst a particular (not to mention rather vocal) constituency in fandom. Suffice to say that in her first appearance, in between kneeing the Master in the bollocks and flouncing around Redfern Dell like it was a catwalk in Milan, the Rani establishes her claim to be Fag Hag of the Known Universe. She recruits fit young men by running a bathhouse, then doses them with uppers and gives them gimp-masks, little leather waistcoats and hair-gel. No wonder their wives feel neglected...

The Continuity

The Doctor Has excellent peripheral vision - bordering on Spidey-Sense - when it comes to assassination attempts directed his way. In this scenario, he seems able to leap about twenty feet, quicker than the human eye. Mustard Gas is toxic to him, and he recognises the Turner reproduction that the Rani owns. The Doctor is expressly forbidden to interfere with history [tell that to Galatron Mining Corp in the previous story]. According to Peri, he frequently says that discretion is the better part of valour. [Apart from anything else, this suggests that this Doctor thinks of himself as Falstaff.]

• *Ethics.* For just a split-second, he almost seems to lose it and shoot the Master. [Even though the cause of this - Luke's dendrification - is the Rani's doing, the Doctor seems to target blame for this toward the Master. However, the Doctor's lapse admittedly comes at the end of a trying day, when the Rani has used his compassion against him twice.]

• *Inventory.* He has a weird spherical wire-dispenser, and a portable time-distortion detector. [The latter looks suspiciously like the tracker he used for Lytton's signal in 22.1, "Attack of the Cybermen".] In one of his waistcoat pockets is a jeweller's screwdriver - useful for comprehensively wrecking the Rani's navigational controls. He's wearing a different cat badge now.

• *Background.* The Doctor has met Shakespeare [but we knew that]. He quotes from three of the Brummie scribbler's plays: *Hamlet* ("There are more things in Heaven and Earth..." paraphrased), *Julius Caesar* ("Cowards die many times...") and *Henry IV part I* ("The better part of valour is discretion"), although as usual Falstaff's words are rearranged. He muses about going back to see the Bard. [It would now appear that the first time anyone has come up to Shakespeare and introduced himself as 'the Doctor' is 1599 (X3.2, "The Shakespeare Code"), but that the Fourth Doctor knew him as a boy and as a struggling actor. See also 17.2, "The City of Death"; 13.2, "Planet of Evil". That's only if you count the televised stories, of course; Shakespeare's status in the spin-off novels and audios is a lot more complicated, especially once you factor in Nev Fountain's BF audio "The Kingmaker".] The Doctor also knows "The Battle of the Baltic" (Thomas Campbell): 'There was silence deep as death' [which was from around the right time for this story]

He hasn't met George Stephenson prior to this adventure. He's run into the Rani several times before, and says she's the 'obvious culprit' regarding the personality changes - probably owing to an imbalance of body chemicals - as witnessed in Killingworth.

The Supporting Cast

• *Peri.* Has finally remembered that she's supposed to be a botany student, as per the character-notes. [It seems, from the cut scenes, to have been her idea to go to Kew Gardens.] In fact she knows a bit about herbal medicine, and identifies valerian as the plant to use in a sleeping draft [see 19.1, "Castrovalva"]. In keeping with her unorthodox fashion-sense, she thinks that shocking pink tights go with nineteenth century dresses, and has selected a [really unappealing] yellow pea-jacket that simply doesn't go with the ensemble. [She also eschews the bonnet that should be worn with any dress of that period and the parasol and clutch-bag have been left in the wardrobe too.] She seems to know a lot about Daleks and their use of Time Corridors, since she doesn't bother to ask the Doctor what he's on about, as she usually would. [The Doctor may have left a *Time-Travel Adventuring for Dummies* book in her room.] The Master's unexpected return brings her stammer back. All these mines look alike to her.

The Supporting Cast (Evil)

• *The Rani.* Exiled by the High Council after one of her biological experiments went out of control - namely, that mice were turned into monsters and ate the President's cat [see 14.3, "The Deadly Assassin"], taking 'a chunk' out of him too as the Master recalls. Now, she is Queen of the planet Miasimiah Goria, a world presently (according to the Master) in chaos. The Rani attempted to heighten the awareness of her subjects, but this lowered their ability to sleep. [Oddly, the Time Lords don't seem to mind the Rani running a planet and perhaps plotting to use it as the power-base for galactic conquest. This might suggest that anything the Rani was planning was historically doomed to failure - or that the Time Lords have already intervened on that score.] She has harvested humans undetected during times of particular conflict - she cites the Trojan War, the American War of Independence and the Dark Ages [but that's just a "top of the head" conversational list]. This is, to her, no more unethical than humans eating meat. [It seems as if the Rani has a particular axe to grind about meat, but she wears leather trousers - Kate O'Mara's well-publicised vegetarianism may have led viewers to misread this line, but see the way this issue plays out in the rest of this season.]

The Rani is a specialist in neurochemistry, and essentially sees all personality and ability as the work of enzymes. Earth's damp atmosphere gives her breathing difficulty [odd that she picks Northern England as a place to harvest, if even Troy gives her gyp]. Her scanner is able to show her anything happening anywhere nearby, without cameras [see 23.1, "The Mysterious Planet" for a possible explanation], and also allows her to relay instructions to her minions. She owns a remote-control zapper that murders her servants at the push of a button - even from a distance, when the zapper is used alongside her scanner. Her wrist-unit, as well as communications, contains vials for her lungs and knockout capsules. She's also engineered a type of worm that, when swallowed, slaves people to the command of anyone administering it.

• *The Master.* He has a magnet that can attract wood - or, at the very least, move door-bolts. He also has the Tissue Compression Eliminator [which now seems to zap people to miniscule, they become invisible - there's certainly no little gateman or guarddog doll-figures seen about the place after the Master kills them]. He also carries a small laser for cutting bolts, a bauble on a chain for hypnotising people and a pencil and pad. Later on, he confiscates the Rani's box of blue maggots and her vial of brain-juice. [Despite all this, he still seems not to have any pockets at all in his poncy velvet suit.] He can sketch police boxes with amazing accuracy.

A knee in the groin hurts the Master as much as it would a human. [This fueled years of speculation about male Time Lords' "equipment", although the fact that the Master is presently in Tremas' stolen body (18.6, "The Keeper of Traken") complicates matters. Tremas' daughter Nyssa had to come from *somewhere*, after all, and to further befuddle the issue...] The Master tells the Rani that her brain fluid is 'perfectly safe, next to my hearts - *both* of them'. [The way it's said makes one wonder if it's to remove any doubt regarding how many hearts the Master has these days, as the Rani - a fellow Time Lord - would presumably not need telling otherwise. This could well suggest that Tremas - and by extension Nyssa and all Trakenites - has two hearts too. Alternatively, it's possible that the second heart is a side-effect of the Master's exposure to the super-healing Numismaton Gas (see 21.5, "Planet of Fire" and **When Did The Doctor Get His Second Heart?** under 6.1, "The Dominators"). Or perhaps whatever he says on screen, the Master presently just has one heart and he's just really forgetful.]

For all his ranting about the Doctor always wrecking his plans, the Master on this occasion draws the Doctor's TARDIS off-course [via his own TARDIS console, one presumes] to Killingworth and embroils him in these events.

The TARDIS(es) The Doctor's Ship seems to be working perfectly - that is, if only people wouldn't keep drawing it off course. The Rani's TARDIS seems more sophisticated, and she has rigged it to operate with a Stattenheim remote control. Her ability to do this impresses the fellers. [Unsurprisingly, as it was said in "The War Games" (6.7) that use of such remote control drastically curtailed the lifespan of a TARDIS' space-time elements, yet there's no mention here of the Rani's TARDIS having such an impediment. Her success on this score may be very significant - the Rani is a bio-chemist, not an engineer, and her discovery might usher in a wholly new style of time travel. If so, this might well explain why she

was exiled from Gallifrey rather than executed. Along those lines, the next story will make clear that biology is significantly more useful in TARDIS design than we've been led to believe.]

The Rani's TARDIS has been disguised as a wardrobe and left in the bathhouse. When it dematerialises, two vertical neon lights flash [why this occurs is never made clear, although it's possibly akin to the TARDIS' lamp flashing on occasion], and the exterior does not change to suit being down a coal-mine. Inside the Ship, things are very different from the Doctor's vessel [or the Master's, judging by its interior appearance in 23.4, "The Ultimate Foe"].

The overall look of the Rani's Ship is of steel and pink lighting. Shelves in the console room contain useful knick-knacks and experiments, including the tree-metamorphosising landmines and a Tyrannosaurus embryo. In place of the traditional roundels, larger circles are embossed on the walls. The console room is entered by a small stairway, which comes off a door that is to the left of the entrance atrium. The console itself is curved, with a cylindrical base and a conic section for the controls - these are hemispheres, operated like an inverted computer mouse, rather than the traditional switches or buttons. The scanner is spring-mounted on the console itself (in a miniature of the embossed roundels) and shows a bulbous image like a crystal ball. It resumes its place by being pushed down manually. [The Doctor seems to have taken this idea on board, and has something similar in his own Ship by the new series.]

Instead of a vertically-moving "piston", the Time Rotor of the Rani's TARDIS is a revolving gyroscope with a *trompe-l'oeil* pair of steel hula-hoops set at an angle, so that they appear to move up and down as they revolve. [Like so much of 1980s *Doctor Who*, this looks like a steal from *Superman: The Movie* - specifically, the bit when the Zod squad are sent off to the Death Zone. A similar gimmick was used by the witch in *Hawk the Slayer*, see 24.4, "Dragonfire".] The console is rimmed with hemispherical bobbles, like those on a Dalek [which could, of course, mean that... no, let's not even go there.[5]]

For all its advanced design, the Rani's vessel seems remarkably easy to sabotage. The Doctor is able - in a short span of time - to poke about and affect the navigation and temporal velocity, sending the Ship when used out of control and on a one-way trip beyond most galaxies. The g-forces

Why Do Time Lords Always Meet in Sequence?

Back when repeated meetings between Time Lords was just Jon Pertwee and Roger Delgado bitching at each other, you could pretty much assume what you liked. In some ways, having the Master experience their encounters in a different sequence from that of the Doctor and the audience would make a lot more sense. UNIT dating, always a fraught issue, could suddenly fit into place if the stories' running-order was determined by how the Master thought they happened, with the Doctor and Jo thinking "Colony in Space" (8.4) happened before "The Claws of Axos" (8.3) and "The Mind of Evil" (8.2). It would need you to explain why everyone's so surprised to see someone they thought was stranded on Earth aboard Axos, and why the Doctor refuses to commit himself on whether someone he knows escaped might have got out of what was an obvious no-win situation. Of course, the immediate problem there is that the Master would be interfering with his own subjective past, and so must either do something he *knows* all along will fail, or risk setting up horrid time-paradoxes (which, at the very least, would alert the Time Lords to his location).

But then the Doctor and the Master regenerated, we got to meet more Time Lords and it became apparent that whenever the Doctor encountered one of his own people, they were his contemporaries from the Old Country. He never seemed to meet anyone from Gallifrey's future, or remote past - save for very old ones mysteriously still around, like Rassilon (20.7, "The Five Doctors") or Omega (10.1, "The Three Doctors"; 20.1, "Arc of Infinity"). And whenever he did, it seemed that as much time had passed for them as for him. (This made life on Gallifrey - a supposedly ancient, timeless and static society - seem positively frantic, with Borusa almost constantly regenerating while the Doctor and his chums hardly seemed any older.)

As part of this, twice a year we had the Doctor realising that his oddly-accented adversary is the Master, and saying "so, you escaped from Castrovalva / Xeriphas / Loompaland". The specific encounter cited was the previous one as seen on screen, and it seems that the pair of them were locked in synch. Then, in "Time and the Rani" (24.1), it's clearly stated that the Doctor and the Rani are the same age. This surely can't be a very long string of coincidences, can it?

Well, let's look for exceptions, the obvious being the One That Got Away, "Shada" (17.6). In this, two fugitives from Gallifrey's ancient past are around in 1979 Cambridge, with the Doctor and Romana interacting with them as though they were all from the same cohort. Chronotis, whom the Doctor has visited many times (although we only hear the Porter talk about those in the historical past) can call the Doctor to a specific day and city. It looks like an anomaly, but Chronotis / Salyavin had been in suspended animation for millennia, and his ancient TARDIS is so old as to have been de-registered. He would obviously keep time journeys to a minimum, and hide his presence by keeping to chronological sequence where possible.

But hang on... the Porter recognises the Fourth Doctor, so it must have been *that* incarnation who visited him. And the visits date back to the 1950s. There's obviously time travel involved here, because whenever the Fourth Doctor was "born" in "Planet of the Spiders" (11.5), it was long after that decade. Then there's Skagra, leader of a revolt against the High Council so long ago that even Romana, a historian, hadn't come across any records of it. (And if Skagra ain't *actually* a Time Lord, he certainly knows enough about their technology for the rules we're discussing here to apply.) He's not been in stasis, so he must have travelled in time.

So if "Shada" had made it to the screen, it's possible we wouldn't be having this conversation. Score one for the Canon Police (see **Where Does "Canon" End?** under 26.1, "Battlefield"). Other asynchronous meetings, usually Doctor-on-Doctor action, take place either under Time Lord supervision and sanction ("The Three Doctors") outside time altogether (Season Twenty-Three, "The Trial of a Time Lord") or both ("The Five Doctors"). "The Two Doctors" (22.4) remains a sticking point, but we could - and will - argue that the Time Lords stage-managed the whole event, which rules out all that Blinovitch-related hassle. The Second Doctor says it's just an accident, but he's obviously got good reason to deny that the Sixth Doctor has been railroaded. In each case, the Time Lords of the "present" are involved, so it's Pertwee's lot who organise "The Three Doctors", and "The Five Doctors" is supervised by the Castellan from the last Gallifrey story and the same President (played by someone else, again). Notably, they only scoop up Doctors from their past.

This is looking like the basis for a hypothesis. If a

continued on page 45...

43

involved on this trip pin the Rani and the Master to the walls, and temporal spillage accelerates the growth of the Tyrannosaurus. Indeed, the Doctor is able to enter into the Rani's TARDIS by using the key to his own Ship [so her security precautions *really* need work].

The Time Lords Like many other exiles [the Doctor, the Master, the War Chief from "The War Games", the K'anpo from 11.5, "Planet of the Spiders", the Monk from 2.9, "The Time Meddler"] the Rani uses a title rather than a name - 'Rani' being the female form of "Rajah", suggesting status. [Incidentally, it's odd that all the female Time Lords we see appear to have held higher than usual rank. Romana is clearly stated to be the Doctor's superior in every way except experience. Rodan (15.6, "The Invasion of Time") was clearly over-qualified for her job. It would almost seem that, like bees, Time Lords are mainly male and in effect neuter, with a few females running things. This raises the interesting possibility that they're born - or 'loomed', if you prefer the books' terminology - as female if they hail from higher-ranking families. More bizarrely, they may *all* be born male and only achieve - or rather be granted - femininity after they sit their exams. Romana mentions being 'a Time Tot' (17.6, "Shada"), which might indicate a "pupal" phase. The only time we see a Time Lord or other Gallifreyan who looks younger than twenty-five human years is the young Master in X3.12, "The Sound of Drums", but that alone doesn't invalidate the point we're trying to make here about Time Lord genders.

[Suffice to say, it might not be coincidence that both Romana and the Doctor are knowledgeable about bees - see, for instance, 16.6, "The Armageddon Factor"; 24.3, "Delta and the Bannermen" and 14.5, "The Robots of Death". So if they are divided into Queens and Drones, this would explain why the Rani is not executed, brain-wiped or sent to Shada, but instead was allowed to take a TARDIS and set herself up as monarch of a planetful of insomniac superbrains; why the female Time Lords are so much more patronising and assertive. This might also explain why it's *only* when they have no "superiors" that the Doctor has started noticing girls (especially in stories written by Steven Moffat), and the Master - prior to his being Prime Minister - takes a wife.]

It seems that the effect of "time spillage" on Time Lords is not the same as for T.Rex embryos.

History

• *Dating*. Good question. [It's clearly before 1829, as Sir Humphrey Davy is still alive. If it's considered safe for people like Davy, Faraday and Telford to travel, then the story is more likely to occur after Napoleon is safely exiled. If so, it's either after the Peninsula War or after Waterloo (so it could be in the nine months or so before his return from Elba in 1814-15 or after June 1815). Wartime travel restrictions would make this story impossible. Never mind being 'a nation of shop-keepers' as Napoleon said, Britain was at this time a nation of curtain-twitchers, with paranoia rising to a level rivalling McCarthyite America. A police-state of gossip and suspicion of strangers was in place, leading even Wordsworth and Coleridge to be suspected of spying - renting a cottage, going for long walks without actually getting anywhere and carrying maps and sketchbooks, all highly dodgy. (In this light, the value of one's reputation and the power of scandal in Jane Austen's works suddenly all seems a lot more sinister.)

[Ergo, if the reports of Luddites are to be taken literally, the latest probable date is 1816, but we're almost at the start of a number of other riots that will dominate Britain's culture until 1848 (see **Where Does This Come From?**). In fact, that far north, it was unlikely the followers of the fictional "Ned Ludd" would have caused any bother. 1815 is the year when Davy and Stephenson disputed the patent on the safety-lamp used in coal-mines (now called a "Davy lamp"), so for them to meet enthusiastically might mean that "Mark of the Rani" occurs before this. Marc Brunel, another of the invited guests, was declared bankrupt in 1814, and was in a debtors' prison by 1821. (He was, however, bailed out by influential friends.) If he was invited to a colloquium like Ravensworth's any time after 1814, it must have been during the brief spells when he was in favour - possibly 1818 (when he had finally got a patent for his tunnelling shield, with which he built the Thames tunnel some years later). By 1841 he was an establishment figure, but this is way too late for our use.

[There's a small snag, as you might expect, because we have real people and semi-real people mixing. As Mark Wyman pointed out in *Doctor Who Magazine* No. 343, Stephenson's writings mentioned a Lord Ravensworth, but no such person existed between 1784 and 1821. Thomas Liddell was created Baron Ravensworth - he was

Why Do Time Lords Always Meet in Sequence?

...continued from page 43

link exists between when a Time Lord leaves Gallifrey, and how long subjectively elapses between returns or meetings outside the homeworld, perhaps the Blinovitch Limitation Effect also governs dealings with other Time Lords. If they've met before, they have to meet again as many seconds later for both parties. Thus, the Fourth Doctor can pop back and meet Chronotis in 1947 or whenever, but after that can't meet him in 1720 unless both parties travel backwards in time from after 1947 - very likely as long after the first meeting for both parties. As the Doctor, the Master, the Rani and Drax all seem to have left Gallifrey at around the same time, they all meet at various times in history, but as long after each previous meeting as it seems to the Doctor. You know what this means. Behold: Gallifreyan Mean Time (GMT), a standard chronology for all Time Lords with respect to Home, regardless of when they are in the outside universe.

Curiously, whenever the Time Lords originated and wherever Gallifrey actually is, the baseline chronology seems to be linked to Earth's (and the TV show's) history, with November 1963 as a starting-point. Stories such as "The Two Doctors", "The Three Doctors" and "Colony In Space" all link time for the High Council with time for the viewers and the Doctor. It's the Time Lords of the "present" who are afflicted by a Black Hole in "The Three Doctors", at the same time as Dr Tyler detects "space lightning".

Somewhat annoyingly, this doesn't solve as many problems as it ought. For the Master to pull the Doctor from the intended appointment at Kew Gardens to Killingworth Colliery, he has to know in advance that the Doctor will - at some stage in their joint future - want to go to Kew in 1813 (or whenever the hell it is). It's the same problem we had with "Logopolis" (18.7), and positing some psychic link between the two of them opens entire cans of worms about their willingness to see each other suffer. Throwing the Rani into the mix means that her decision to travel back to 1813-ish to siphon off magic brain-juice must have occurred at the same moment (subjectively) as the Doctor thought, "I'll take Peri to Kew". Assuming, of course, that it was actually the Doctor's decision.

So if "The Mark of the Rani" episode one is Day One, then Day Minus One must have seen the Rani (possibly in ancient Troy, 1200 BC), the Master leaving Sarn in 1984 and the Doctor leaving Varos in the twenty-fourth century all having the same idea. We refer you back to "Logopolis" ('We're Time Lords - in many ways we have the same mind') and its root story "The Time Monster" (9.5). If the Master's imminent return occurs to the Pertwee Doctor in a dream, or in bad vibes requiring a mooch around in Cloisters (in "Logopolis"), it's likely that their TARDISes are sending out telepathic feelers. After all, the Ships would presumably be programmed to ask each other if they're going to the same time and place, to avoid paradoxes.

This allows the option that the sequence of meetings are locked into step, but the time between each meeting for both parties is more elastic so long as the TARDISes aren't involved. The Master could land his TARDIS on Xeriphas and wait for fifty years before the rematch in "The King's Demons" (20.6), even if just under a year has passed for the Doctor. This might allow for the apparent lapse of centuries between meetings with various Borusas (see especially 15.6, "The Invasion of Time" and 20.1, "Arc of Infinity") without having to posit a seventy-year gap between "Time-Flight" and "Arc of Infinity" during which Nyssa (now with an extended lifespan) and the Doctor did repairs on the TARDIS, got their hair done and played an awful lot of Monopoly. We then just have to find a solution to the apparent anomaly whereby the Monk's TARDIS is "generations" beyond the Doctor's, even though only fifty years have elapsed for the Monk since the Doctor left. (Whatever a 'year' means in this instance: see **The Obvious Question: How Old is He?** under 16.5, "The Power of Kroll" - but bear in mind we're now told Gallifrey only had two suns, not that this affects the chaotic orbital dynamics. Perhaps this is why they average everything out over five hundred years.) The Doctor's Ship is a museum-piece, but still... why should this be the case?

Well, what's the one thing the Time Lords can't know? Their own future. They've got blocks on their knowledge of things concerning Earth's last fugitives (21.3, "Frontios"), and they're sketchy on the consequences of the Daleks being allowed to develop unchecked (12.4, "Genesis of the Daleks"; X1.6, "Dalek" et seq). Even a detail like the as-yet-unrealised plan to cover up the leaks from the Matrix (23.4, "The Ultimate Foe") has to be discovered by an inquest taking place outside time, and

continued on page 47...

the uncle of the Liddell who co-wrote the standard Greek dictionary for Classics students. (He was therefore the great-uncle of Alice Pleasance Liddell. Yes, *that* Alice.) Born in 1775, he's way too young to be the 'Lord Ravensworth' that Terence Alexander is playing here. Yet Killingworth is where Stephenson was based at the most likely time for this story, and the future Lord Ravensworth lived in Ravensworth Castle near Gateshead (where they talk like the characters are trying to in this story).

[The final scene's conversation about Stephenson's trouble with the pressure valve suggests that the story occurs before 1813, when he devised one for his first locomotive, the *Blucher*. Whether *Blucher* looked like a 1/4 scale version of *Rocket* (as used in this story), we cannot say.]

The Analysis

Where Does This Come From The opening two minutes of Northern, folksy film - remarkable and lyrical though it is, with no dialogue and restful music - resembles two famous ads from the period (the 1980s, that is, not the early 1800s). One, more for the synthesised Delius and shots of countryside, said "One day, all towns will be like Milton Keynes". (We fear they may be right.) More overtly, and more to do with the story's appeal overall, this seems like a deliberate retread of the campaign for Hovis, the nation's favourite brown bread.

In the 1970s, most people knew full well that white, sliced processed bread wasn't doing their digestive systems any good. Some people baked their own, especially after an unexpected shortage in 1974, but the problem for manufacturers was that the alternative - brown bread - was just too old-fashioned, so the advertisers capitalised on that. "Proper" bread was associated with being from the North of England, traditionally associated with thrift, integrity and stability, so they milked that for all it was worth.

A young director, Ridley Scott (see 1.2, "The Daleks"), made a thirty-second slot that is now *the* kneejerk association people have with the North and the Industrial, and Hovis ads are the benchmark against which all deliberate attempts at nostalgia are measured. To the soundtrack of a brass band (all collieries had one, and most still do even though the coal mines have closed, by and large) playing the second movement of Dvorak's

Symphony No. 9, "From the New World", sepia soft-focus footage of people in big caps and clogs ran. A boy would push a late-nineteenth century bicycle up a steep, cobbled hill (actually in Dorset, but it *looked* like Yorkshire) to deliver groceries. The voice-over, originally by Joe Gladwin (Wally Batty from *Last of the Summer Wine*) explained how when he were nobbut a lad, his da' would make t'bread and he'd deliver it oop t'hill. (Forgive the grammar, that's how they supposedly talk.)

Blist's Hill Museum, where the bulk of the location work for this story was shot, is almost a monument to the success of that ad and others that followed. We say "almost", but it's fair to mention that the Industrial Revolution was itself revolutionised in the 1950s. Far from being a subject for school history textbooks, the legacy of music from the era and the machinery from the factories was being reassessed. It was the era when the advent of tape-recorders and the success of American archivists in documenting folk songs inspired the BBC to do something similar. In the period just before rock and roll, students in duffel-coats would protest against nuclear weapons and racial segregation (not that they had much reason to in Britain as yet), then listen to Ewan McColl records. (We are willing to bet that Pip and Jane Baker dated like that). Then came Bob sodding Dylan.

So by the 1970s, practically every teacher in the country was hell-bent on giving their pupils the "authentic" experience of the Industrial Revolution, which meant subjecting them to folk music and dragging them to canals, mines, factories and "working" museums. In place of learning detailed lists of when the Corn Laws were revised and repealed, 70s kids had actors dressed in mob-caps and hessian waistcoats talking like Brian Glover (or, if you were unlucky, Peter Childs as a Geordie). These Equity rejects would be taking them for a lesson, 1840s style or giving them a go on a cotton-mill. The Hovis ads spared the next generation this fate, but making small working townships with shops where you could buy food - or scents made by people you'd just seen making tomorrow's batch - provided years of dull days out for the nation's youth in the 70s. The overall shift from Events and Famous People to *How We Used To Live* (the name of a schools' TV series that did this in detail) was at its peak in the mid-1980s, before the National Curriculum made

Why Do Time Lords Always Meet in Sequence?

...continued from page 45

knowledge of this future plan causes a riot on Gallifrey in the Sixth Doctor's era. (Or at least, we *assume* that this is the case. It makes just as much sense for the Trial to be in some Twelfth Doctor era as far as Gallifrey is concerned, and the Master's coup is just slightly more plausible if he's come forward as a champion of the old ways against this corrupt regime from his future. It makes the Valeyeard's involvement marginally more plausible, but the Inquisitor's delight that the Doctor has won and will return to his own timeline - and rewrite the future without her in it - even more odd than it is as shown.)

If the full enormity of what we're saying hasn't sunk in yet, we'll spell it out: the TARDISes are more clued-up about the Time Lords and their dealings than the Time Lords themselves. They're not only in touch with one another from their own "cohort", but can sniff out possible futures for their users and select (or at least influence) when and where they meet. They may be using their telepathic links with the operators - say - to make the Rani think it's her idea to go to Lakertya and thereby cause the Doctor to regenerate (24.1, "Time and the Rani"), when it's actually their TARDISes making the decision. Gallifrey monitors events and patrols the consequences, but the wandering time vessels make all the moves.

Which is all a bit sinister, but it's in keeping with another part of the "story" of *Doctor Who* (see **Who Decides What Makes a Companion?** under 21.5, "Planet of Fire"). It also makes a bit more sense that - shortly before being reunited with his old college rival, the Rani - the Doctor's scrambled memories throw up thoughts of the Terrible Zodin, 'a woman of rare guile and devilish cunning' ("Attack of the Cybermen").

What it *doesn't* quite account for is the way other advanced races seem to be up to date on the Doctor's gossip. Yes, some of them have limited time-travel capability, and know the High Council's phone number, but by Season Twenty-Two it seems there's a subscription news service on the Doctor's "recent" activities, wherever in time and space the subscriber happens to be. It could, of course, be a matter of historical record that's being rewritten as history gets amended, but that's another essay (see **How Does Time Work?** under 9.1, "The Day of the Daleks"). There's also a possibility that we've overlooked: that the Second Doctor is right and these asynchronous meetings are always happening, but only one has been worth us knowing about. We refer you to 23.1, "The Mysterious Planet" and accompanying essay.

History teaching all about Henry VIII and the Nazis.

The Bakers would have been at school when the emphasis shifted from the Great Men and the role of steam-power in Our Island's Story (the last remnants of the Whig Interpretation that had the Empire as inevitable, and the rise of Britain as history's happy ending) to thinking about the poor bleeders mining the coal, being press-ganged into the Navy or losing their children in weaving accidents. For the last generation raised on Empire, it was self-evident that a nation that had sussed mass-production and crop rotation would come out on top. When thinking about a key point in History when a small intervention could have wrecked everything, the Industrial Revolution was as obvious to that generation as World War II, or Athens under Pericles.

It was also at this time that the teaching of nineteenth century history included more on the Peterloo Massacre (in which Lord Castlereigh sent troops to quell a protest rally, and women and children were slaughtered along with the allegedly armed men), the Tolpuddle Martyrs (people sent to Australia for the "crime" of demanding fairer working conditions and the vote) and the Chartists (please don't ask: if you're British you either know this or ought to, and if not it'd take ages to explain). In an odd sort of way, it was a flipside version of the Whig Interpretation, with universal suffrage and education as the "happy ending" instead of the Empire.

By 1985, the Government were trying to restore "Victorian Values" without actually coming out and saying that losing the Empire was a tragedy. (Again, see 26.2, "Ghost Light".) The fear of technology taking people's jobs was almost corny by then, and the word 'Luddite' was back in circulation during the dispute over Rupert Murdoch's use of digital compositing in newspaper printing. (This was part of an overall change, moving from Fleet Street to Wapping and risking even the Government his newspapers supported challenging his near-monopoly of media ownership - see our comments on Docklands under 21.4, "Resurrection of the Daleks" and elsewhere in this season.)

The eponymous Mark of the Rani is a slightly strange permutation of a familiar trope. Being a Rani, she might have been expected to have a sort of tilap, a reddish dot or diamond in the centre of the forehead (as she would later adopt a nose-ring for herself, in 24.1, "Time and the Rani"). As a kind of "brand" for her servants, it would tie in with the slight air of Saturday Morning Pictures in this serial. Indeed, a purple mark was the sign of the dreaded "Purple Death" in *Flash Gordon Conquers the Universe* (1940). Buster Crabbe, as Flash, overcame this every Christmas on BBC 1 from 1976 onwards, every morning in the school holidays.

The title has the slight sense of being connected with Thuggee cults, and a possible link between Indian hypnosis and nineteenth century British steadfastness can be made via novelist Wilkie Collins or *The Sign of Four*. (We might even say that the title "The Mark of the Rani" sounds suspiciously like a Sherlock Holmes pastiche. This time, though, it's Peri who comments on a dog not barking.) But for some reason, the Rani's brain-chemical is drained through the neck - something that takes us into Dracula territory. (There is indeed a 1930s Bela Lugosi flick called *The Mark of Dracula*, but in plot terms it's a long-shot.)

More than anything else, the Rani is intended to be an extreme version of reductivist science, i.e. treating people as chemicals. The Bakers claim to have been inspired by an overheard comment from a neurochemist acquaintance at a party, but again we have to remember that in the 1980s, people were constantly being reported as having isolated the gene for such-and-such. (This is not to say that they *had*, just that the reporting of it was put into mechanistic terms.) With a new openness about the use of medicines by prominent politicians in the 1950s and 1960s, people were "explaining" history through pharmacology. The Bakers, who met through politics, couldn't have failed to have come across this trend. And let's not forget how many dud decisions of the 1980s were made under the influence of cocaine.

As seasoned pros, the Bakers had written for any brief they needed, and had done a script for the Forensic Science drama *The Expert* (mentioned a lot in Volume II). It was about the pharmaceutical industry's quest for the ultimate sleep-ing pill, and included the fact that it needed the brains of thirty goats to be drained to provide enough neurotransmitter for one human to sleep. Things like that stay with you.

Things That Don't Make Sense Most of what Stephenson says, but let's not be picky. [In fact, so much of the dialogue could count as Things That Don't Make Sense we'd be here for months.] To start with the small plot-points, though...

The Rani seems unduly fooled by the Doctor's bathhouse disguise. She tells the Master, 'I saw the Doctor', but once she's gassed the man unconscious and has him on her laboratory table, she *only* shows a glimmer of recognition after she's tried to siphon off his "human" brain chemicals, taken a reading of his forehead and listened for his hearts-beat. The trousers, the poncy hairdo, and the fact that she's been in Killingworth for weeks if not months and *nobody* like him has been in the bathhouse should have been major clues, likewise his driving past her place with a hand-held electronic device making blooping noises *as she was watching from her doorstep*. He's also been going around proclaiming 'I am known as the Doctor'. Hardly a three-pipe problem.

Early on in the story, why should the absence of birdsong be introduced as a clue and then dropped entirely? Is the Rani harvesting birds as well? (If so, given her apparent attitude toward meat, she's probably not eating them.) Or maybe the Master is spectacularly more successful with his scarecrow outfit than any other disguise he's tried. Why, though, if he goes to the bother of donning such an outfit, does he remove his garb *as soon as* he's in public rather than before or after (because that's not even slightly suspicious, no) and why does he not even try to hide? There's one moment, when the gate closes, where he's plainly in the Doctor's line of sight.

Why is Peri plucking valerian leaves when it's the roots she needs? How come the Bakers, not shy of gobbledegook, have everyone saying 'the chemical that promotes sleep' instead of naming it? (Dr Science tells us that the array of symptoms displayed makes seratonin the most likely candidate, although others suggest adenosine, as it's more directly connected with drowsiness.) For that matter, it seems strange that there's only *one* chemical that promotes sleep [it could be acetylcholine for all we know]. And *only* humans produce it? Not any other mammals from this planet, or any others. If so, why come to Earth's history when there's a future with whole galaxies full of us? It's as if she really wants the Master to come along and wreck things.

Why does the Doctor - while he's choking to death - literally waste his breath naming the Rani's lethal cloud as 'dichlorodiethyl sulphate' (or near enough) instead of the three-syllable 'Mustard Gas'? Like Peri'd know what he meant anyway. Besides, Mustard Gas can cause large blisters on exposed skin, so for the Doctor and Peri to don gas masks isn't really suitable protection. [After their recent Spectrox Toxaemia incident in 21.6, "The Caves of Androzani", they - and the script editor - might be expected to know this.] Then the Doctor escapes this trap by opening a door and potentially gassing everyone in the street outside [see, for example, 6.5, "The Seeds of Death" - in which someone realises too late that this was a very silly thing to do]. According to the counter on the DVD player, it takes 39 seconds for all the gas to disperse [unless time flows *much* more slowly inside the Rani's TARDIS, in which case the stuff with the Tyrannosaurus embryo makes less sense than ever].

And why does the Rani need her TARDIS to power a gas-bomb? Wouldn't a rigged-up gas cylinder have worked just as well? If it's in any way connected with the bathhouse interior having a secret room that the filmed exterior doesn't allow the space for, then this should have vanished when she summoned her TARDIS, even though Peri was there in that room watching the cupboard dematerialise.

Then there are the "hyperactive" miners. They're very calm when waiting for the wagon carrying the machinery, aren't they? Indeed, their alleged "turmoil" begins with standing around in the bathhouse and flicking each other with towels. This is why Lord Ravensworth's men go around armed, is it? (Maybe the miners will move on to wedgies and Chinese burns soon.) Besides, if the Rani is *only* draining the miners' brains, and not surgically removing the glands that secrete the mystery sleepy-time chemical, then presumably they'd have some more of the chemical after a few days anyway. It's like milking a cow once, then selling it because it's been drained of the ability to produce milk. And if Jack Ward didn't [all together now] have the strength to lift a Toby, how is making him unable to rest going to revitalise him enough to smash a cartload of machinery? This makes no sense at all, unless there's a deleted

scene involving a can of spinach.

But it makes more sense than the fact that the Rani has a planet-load of hyperactive aliens on Miasimiah Goria. The Master and the Rani call them 'aliens', like Time Lords are native to this oddly-named planet. The only way she can have installed 'aliens' is if there's an indigenous population, otherwise they're just "colonists". So, a planet with natives *and* foreign beings with artificially-enhanced mental powers, and the woman responsible for this explosive mix just leaves them to go off and harvest human neurotransmitters. What kind of evil tyrant does this? A soon-to-be-deposed one. And what's she apparently *done* to these so-called aliens? She's made them jittery and restless and somehow extended their consciousness. It's never made clear whether this just means "made them smarter" or "made them telepathic" or what. Whatever it is, these aren't people on whom an evil queen can safely turn her back. [Then again, if they're that advanced, they should have twigged that their Queen is a bit bonkers. So perhaps they're just humouring her and are using their enhanced powers and insomnia to win big cash prizes on late-night quiz shows.]

The Master melodramatically threatens to have his thugs hurl the TARDIS down a mine-shaft, 'all the way down, to the bottom'. As opposed to, perhaps, it abruptly halting three feet from the floor and spinning around? And why does he think this would be of *any* concern or stress to the Doctor, as TARDISes have been repeatedly proven to withstand such damage? The last time we saw the Master ("Planet of Fire"), his own Ship was unscathed after being buried in rubble. 'Finito, TARDIS - how's that for style?', he says. Do we *really* need to answer?

We'll draw a veil over the Rani's landmines, except to ask how the nine she takes from her TARDIS become the about thirty or so that she seems to have planted in Redfern Dell. As there's no evidence of the villains retrieving these devices, how did they magically appear back where she got them from a later scene? The rope around the Doctor's wrists has suspiciously twentieth century sellotape on the ends and plastic coating elsewhere.

And if we're continuing to feel charitable, we might politely skip over the idea that 'genius' is a commodity you can harvest like coal or aloe vera (although next time we hear the Rani say this, we'll give her both barrels), and instead wonder if anyone knew who Michael Faraday was before

Stephenson's *Rocket* was built. Or indeed, who George Stephenson was. More importantly, we might wonder why George Stephenson is working on the engine that his son Robert designed and built. But we'll refrain from passing judgement on the line, 'I suspect thee's contribution would set a cat or two among the pigeons', as it's ju-u-ust possible that someone from the North of England (who used "thee" and "thou" in everyday speech all his life) might make such a rookie error.

It's strange that the villains believe the Doctor is 'impressed' by the Rani's scanner showing something that she's imagining, as this sort of thing has actually occurred quite often in the series. The Doctor does it himself in "The Wheel in Space" (5.7) and the Time Lords seem to do it as a matter of routine (6.7, "The War Games"). Rigging up something for humans to do the same is easy (11.5, "Planet of the Spiders"), and even the Moroks can do it (2.7, "The Space Museum"). But despite all of this, the Doctor's two rival Time Lords think he's never seen the like.

The Rani loses control of her Ship because of something the Doctor's done to the controls, so apparently her Stattenheim doo-dah that everyone goes on about is more useless as a back-up set of controls than you might think. And why is the gadget called a 'Stattenheim Remote Control' anyway? Is there a Time Lord with a German name?

Amazingly, Pip and Jane wrote a Thing That Made Sense (Sort Of) concerning how the Master might have survived being burned to a frazzle on Sarn (see "Planet of Fire") but Eric Saward cut it. It's there in the novelisation, if you're brave. Then brace yourselves for a look at the way the Rani escaped from the dinosaur, in their book of "Time and the Rani" and compare it to the Master's account in "The Ultimate Foe" (23.4) in novel form.

A big one: why does the Master go to the trouble of setting up a scheme that already requires him to joust with one rival Time Lord, and then deliberately drag the Doctor's TARDIS off course to jeopardise his plans further? Moreover, why does he hypnotise Luke into ingesting a maggot that will make him suggestible? Why not just, um, hypnotise Luke into obeying him? [We can think of a couple of reasons for this - the Master's hypnotism hasn't been rock-solid reliable in past, except that he managed to put the whammy on a whole Concorde-load of people even in this incarnation in 19.7, "Time-Flight". Or maybe the

Doctor would recognize the signs of hypnotism in someone, not that he usually does. And Luke's behaviour under the power of the magic maggot isn't even slightly suspicious, is it? It's still irritating that this rather obvious point isn't explained on screen.]

And there's still a whole bunch of Arborifying landmines over in Redfern Dell. Has everyone forgotten?

Critique   For all that we make fun of them, the Bakers have "got" this Doctor first go, and partially recaptured a lot of the feel of Hartnell historicals. For better or worse, they've put the series back in touch with its quasi-didactic roots and grounded a story in a bit of real science and a lot of real history. In case we're feeling like the fidgety kids at the back of the class, the Rani offers a sardonic commentary on proceedings, and says what we've been thinking about the Master since "Castrovalva". (Well, most of it - this is a family show, after all.) And for almost the last time, this looks like mainstream BBC drama of the time, and with a suitable amount of thought and care put into it. In fact, dammit, bits of it look better than anything we've seen since "The Talons of Weng-Chiang" (14.6, and recall how that story went over-budget). Even now, this still *looks* good.

So why isn't it more satisfying to watch? It's not that the plot's especially ropy or hard to follow. Everyone - even the comedy Geordies and the Master - seems to have reasons for their actions (at the time, at least, if not with hindsight) and there aren't any abysmal performances. Place the Conrad twins in here (21.7, "The Twin Dilemma"), and it's obvious how much better everyone else is, accents and all. All the electronic effects function, and the material before and after the tree gropes Peri is perfectly fine. So are this story's detriments really all down to one mildly embarrassing sequence and a panto tree?

Unfortunately, it's more basic than that. The whole is less than the sum of its parts, because this adventure manifestly exists to introduce a new regular villain and nothing else. Essentially, it's just there to showcase Kate O'Mara, and it has no ambition beyond doing this competently. Once the programme-makers put the character through her paces, it's a matter of filling what remains of the ninety minutes of screen time. Like "Planet of Fire" and rather too many other stories, it's not a story in its own right, but instead an incident in the wider story of *Doctor Who*. Yes, it's considerably better in overall production values, but this is - at its core - a retread of "The King's Demons" (20.6), where a picturesque bit of "heritage Britain" is used as a backdrop for Time Lords bitching at one another. The general public wants to *explore* this backdrop and meet the interesting people who live there, not watch a silly man in velvet going 'heh-heh-heh'. It's lovingly shot, but if that opening sequence had been extrapolated over two whole 45-minute episodes, most viewers would have liked it as much or more.

This alerts us to something we've been worrying at like a dog with a bone since Volume I. *Doctor Who* is occasionally amateurish, but it allows writers and directors to work out anxieties lurking below the surface. Once or twice, it's sunk below a base level of professionalism acceptable by audiences now or at the time of transmission, but it has never, *ever*, been bland. When a good story is badly-directed, or a wonky script made brilliantly, somehow there's a connection made between audiences and the programme-makers. Kate O'Mara, Pip and Jane Baker, director Sarah Hellings and everyone else involved in "The Mark of the Rani" have all made something very agreeable whilst it is being watched - save for one or two atrocious moments - but except for the tree sequences, it goes in one eye and out the other. *Doctor Who* is being treated like wallpaper.

But this is 1985, and the BBC *wants* wallpaper. In this period, so many fifty-minute filmed shows are being sold worldwide simply because they have pretty scenery and photogenic people doing things in it. It barely matters whether the characters are vets with 1930s cars, detectives with MK II jags and drink problems, or old ladies who solve crimes. Television drama presently exists to soothe, and to keep the corporation solvent enough to make news programmes. Although we know what's coming around the corner for *Doctor Who*, we should at least feel grateful that it was spared the indignity of becoming a time-travel version of *Bergerac* or *Lovejoy*. "The Mark of the Rani" is a lot edgier than the series would have become if it'd been spared in 1989. Even the tree is a gamble they wouldn't have taken in a 1990s version (see 27.0, "The McGann Movie"). Who knows? Maybe the rubber tree is the reason the series was able to return in 2005. (Certainly, the formula of "a person we know from the banknotes + alien monster + lots of location filming" seems to be trotted out in the new series once a year.)

So let's talk about the trees. On paper this all has a fairy-tale feel to it, like Omega not having a face under his mask (10.1, "The Three Doctors") or Ursula being turned into a paving-slab (X2.10, "Love and Monsters"). The idea of being made into a tree - still alive and conscious but immobile and living for centuries - is in keeping with a lot of the things we've seen over the years. However, the problem here is that the tree doesn't abruptly grow a frond to stop Peri - but instead, a whole branch bends and grabs her tits, exactly like it would if this were a man inside a rubber tree costume. At this point, we've left Hansel and Gretel far behind, and descended into *Rentaghost*. This all matters because the whole landmines issue is the one part of this enterprise that seems like someone tackling a personal demon or genuine fear. Everything else appears to have been an item on a check-list.

It would matter less if what surrounded that shot was more memorable. This is a story that has vindicated the idea of getting new blood onto the series, and whatever you might think of their dialogue and ideas, the Bakers are fast, efficient workers who can accommodate any last-minute changes. We've almost drowned it out with our laughter, but there's a vigour to their writing. Meanwhile, Sarah Hellings has embraced the challenge of this technically-demanding series and taken full advantage of serendipity (see **The Lore**). Even in languidly-paced scenes such as the opening, the shots are paced to do their job. Jonathan Gibbs also rises to the occasion, rapidly furnishing a score as unlike the previous story's as was possible in the short time allowed, and making something that has aged better (save for the DJ's old records in 22.6, "Revelation of the Daleks") than any other music from this season.

So it's rather unfortunate that in the end, despite everyone's hard work, it's all a *bit* better than just-good-enough. Even the principals fade into adequacy. The Doctor and Peri now like each other, making them almost generic. Colin Baker's zest for the part makes him able to stand comparison with his predecessors, but this only shows how inferior the story is to vintage examples. The Rani swamps the Master - even though she's supposedly lurking in the shadows - and she has a TARDIS that looks like a daytime chatshow set from the mid-80s. Thank goodness she also keeps a rubbishy rubber dinosaur, which *does* make it seem like *Doctor Who*.

The Facts

Written by Pip and Jane Baker. Directed by Sarah Hellings. Ratings: 6.3 million, 7.3 million.

Working Titles "Too Clever By Far", "Enter the Rani' (which just makes us think of Bruce Lee trying a Geordie accent).

Supporting Cast Kate O'Mara (The Rani), Anthony Ainley (The Master), Gawn Grainger (George Stephenson),. Terence Alexander (Lord Ravensworth), Peter Childs (Jack Ward), Gary Cady (Luke Ward), William Ilkley (Tim Bass), Hus Levent (Edwin Green), Kevin White (Sam Rudge).

Oh, Isn't That..?

• *Peter Childs*. He was all over the cop shows like a rash, but at this point would have been most familiar to *Doctor Who's* intended audience as Tucker's dad in *Grange Hill* and its spin-off *Tucker's Luck*. In all of these roles, he used a standard-issue BBC cockney accent ("flippin' 'eck").

• *Gary Cady*. He'd just finished playing a very similar role in the historical comedy *Brass*. This was a compendium of all the "saga"-style dramas set in the industrial North, and which we mentioned in **Where Does This Come From?** Mercifully, perhaps, it seemed to kill off the genre for a while.

• *Terence Alexander*. Presently mid-way through his ten-year stint as the local tycoon Charlie Hungerford in *Bergerac*, which rounded off a career of seemingly doing everything. We'll restrict ourselves to his most obvious roles: *The Forsyte Saga* and *The Pallisers* for costume drama, and a couple of *Avengers* spots.

• *Gawn Grainger*. Another actor you'd see all over the shop, but most recently as Hitler in *Private Schulz* - a comedy based on a true story. You might have spotted him in *Love and Death in Long Island* (but not in the *Hotpants College II* clips). He also wrote for TV.

Oh, and for *very* young readers...

• *Kate O'Mara*. By the time this story was shown, she'd been a star for about fifteen years, and working regularly on television since the otherwise forgettable *Weaver's Green* (which also gave us Susan George - see 5.6, "Fury from the Deep" - and occasional narcolepsy). In the 1970s, after *ingénue* roles in things like *The Avengers* (in an

episode with Roger Delgado!), she hit the big time in *The Brothers*; this was sort-of a British forerunner of *Dallas*, but with lorries. Most of her on-screen smouldering was directed at Paul Merrony, played by a promising youngster named Colin Baker. A similarly unpromising scenario for boardroom / bedroom entanglements was devised for *Triangle* (mentioned in Volume V, and we'll say more in 23.3, "Terror of the Vervoids"), in which she played more or less the same character. (By the way, she had a near-miss with *Doctor Who* in 1970, when she was cast as Petra in 7.4, "Inferno", until another commitment caused her to be replaced by the director's wife at short notice.)

After Kate's first go at conquering time and space whilst ankle deep in Shropshire mud, America beckoned. She did her usual classy bitch type of thing again for a year or so in *Dynasty* as Alexis' sister Caress (this was at its camp peak - Joan Collins escaping from Eastern Europe dressed as a nun, that sort of thing). Once Caress was incarcerated in Caracas, Kate begged JN-T for another shot at being the Rani, and from then on the tabloid interest in her love-life and healthy diet kept her famous even when she was off our screens. More on this later (see 24.1, "Time and the Rani", and "Dimensions in Time" in the Appendix).

Cliffhangers (The Rani reveals her identity by taking off her hat); the Doctor is tied to a gurney and pitched down a mine-shaft, apparently; (the Doctor asks where Stephenson has got to - mercifully, the tree shot was a few minutes earlier, or this would have been the worst cliffhanger of all time).

The Lore

• Due to one of the administrative errors for which they were famous, the BBC had a film-crew going spare for a week, and so producers who thought they could use this bonus were asked to put in bids. Nathan-Turner won, but whilst the film-crew was for free, the accommodation and catering for a location shoot wasn't thrown in. The budget was thus balanced by only having one studio session, so Pip and Jane Baker went along to the shoot and pitched in with rapid rewrites, converting interior scenes to exteriors.

• The Bakers had been writing since the early 1960s, and had done films, television and books.

In the late 1970s, between work on *Space: 1999* and an abortive Season Two *Blake's 7* script, they contacted producer Graham Williams with a view to working on *Doctor Who*. Williams admired their "can-do" approach, but no scripts were finished. A script for a film they had been working on was left in Williams' office, and Nathan-Turner later thought it had potential. He had the film allocation almost worked out, and needed a script with a lot of film in it.

As co-chairs of the Film and TV Committee of the Writers' Guild, the Bakers were well-versed in the practicalities of filming and how it affected scripts. They had not seen much *Doctor Who*, but had worked with Verity Lambert before the series started and therefore felt slightly guilty about their ignorance. On accepting the commission, they watched a few old episodes and produced two basic ideas - a futuristic one and a historical one. The latter had the Rani experimenting with remote-control for her TARDIS and making the Tower of Pisa lean. Saward (author of 19.1, "The Visitation", let's recall) told them that interfering with history was a no-no.

• The Rani had originally been intended as a sidekick for the Master (although with Ainley playing the part as Dick Dastardly, perhaps a sniggering dog would have been more apt). With the Bakers keen to depict an entirely amoral scientist, it became easier to make her an equal. Sarah Badel was approached for the role, but she declined. (Readers of Volume V will doubtless be amazed to find that she'd been in *The Pallisers*.) Once incoming director Sarah Hellings and Nathan-Turner *both* thought of Kate O'Mara (independently but simultaneously), the idea of the Rani as anyone's stooge was abandoned and the part as shown came to life. As we saw in the **Where Does This Come From?** section, the Bakers took the idea of a neurochemist who believes that people are walking test-tubes as their starting-point.

• Hellings was new to the series, and daunted by the script's potential complications. However, she had worked in BBC drama for some years, and before that had done short films for *Blue Peter* and others. Indeed, her 1977 short about the history of Telford and the opening of Blist's Hill is included in the DVD for this story (and is the main reason, frankly, for shelling out good money on it). The Blist's Hill Museum was an ideal choice of location - except, of course, that it was an exact replica of a *late* nineteenth century town, with gas-lighting and advertising hoardings for Victorian wares. A great deal of disguise and redressing was needed, but even so the observant and well-informed viewer can spot a few anachronisms. (Although if you're *that* well-informed you ought to have better things to do with your life... Oh all right, start with the advert for cream teas outside the tea-shop in episode one. Happy now?)

• To begin with, all went well and even ahead of schedule. The sequence of the Master disguised as a scarecrow was a late addition to the script, intended to take advantage of an unused location (and the explanation for this never occurred to anyone, it seems). The horse pulling the cart caused trouble as it was pining for the girl who usually looked after it - she had been sacked the week before and was rehired, at some cost, just for the filming.

• Baker was keen to do his own stunts, and although the fall - had he slipped while dangling from pit-chain - would have been six inches onto a wire mesh, BBC regulations insisted on a Kirby harness for him. During this scene he dislocated a finger, as you may have heard. The other anecdote he retells about this shoot is that the tray of fuller's earth used to besmutcheon his face was, during the lunch break, used by the dog that appears in the earlier scenes. (The same dog caused slight delays in studio, because it kept wandering across the set to see Baker and Bryant.)

Meanwhile, some of the pit donkeys used in the museum wandered around. In the sequence when the Doctor is almost knocked into the river (actually the Severn), one donkey came up behind a girl watching the filming on the opposite bank. The camera crew filmed the donkey tipping her into the river. The Rani's bathhouse was, in fact, a pigsty.

• Then three days of torrential rain blighted the filming. The majority of the Redfern Dell sequences were in the can, but to match them needed another shoot on film. This affected the budget, and Nathan-Turner sent off the paperwork requesting a remount. The BBC said that he could do it, but not in Telford, so the remount was done near Harefield Hospital, at the Queen Elizabeth Country Park. (Baker was left tied to the pole during lunch, although none of the passers-by seemed surprised by his being there.) This happened in between the rehearsals for the studio recording.

• In accordance with the script, a screen depicting JMW Turner's *The Eruption of Souffrier* was built, and the volcano's effect was pre-filmed (for obvious Health and Safety reasons). The Bakers had wanted magma, but this wasn't practicable. The yellow smoke when the rest of this sequence was recorded caused difficulties, and two goes were needed - the cast couldn't see to find, throw or catch the gas-mask.

• Saward was less than happy about the Master coming back. The previous contract for Ainley had been for two stories per annum, but this had expired and the character with it (at the end of "Planet of Fire"). Thus the explanation of his miraculous return was, apparently, left out as a form of protest.

• Amongst his other claims to fame, Gawn Grainger (Stepenson) wrote a biography of Lord Olivier. When this was brought to Nathan-Turner's attention, the producer wondered if Grainger could ask the theatrical giant to make a guest appearance in the show. He may have been joking, but word came back that a small part, entirely on film, might be possible. As it turned out, after the hassles involved in "The Two Doctors", Nathan-Turner had decided not to use film after this year. So only one suitable part remained, and see "Revelation of the Daleks" (22.6) for more on this.

• An odd feature of this era is that Nathan-Turner's closest colleague was Ken Riddington, producer of *Tenko*. Nathan-Turner would turn to Riddington during the Saward hassles of Season Twenty-Three, and the two producers gave each other hints (also note how many of the same directors they used). We mention this here because when the Japanese Women's Prison drama ended, it was Nathan-Turner who nabbed the leftover Convent set and re-used it as the Bathhouse interior.

• As you will shortly discover, this story was made after "The Two Doctors" and brought forward in transmission order late in the day. Jonathan Gibbs hurriedly composed the music while he was preparing to leave the BBC Radiophonic Workshop, after freelance composer John Lewis became too ill to complete his score. This would have been the first score by an "outside" composer since "The Seeds of Doom" (13.6). Lewis, a former colleague of Brian Hodgson (who did 'Special Sound' for the first ten years of the series) died of an AIDS-related condition soon after. Gibbs wasn't told of this, and his main priority was making the soundtrack as unlike "Vengeance on Varos" as possible. Lewis' music,

which is an option on the DVD for the first episode, is much more "Hey-nonny-nonny", like a late 1960s British-made, American-financed horror movie, and fails to drown out enough of the bad Geordie accents.

22.4: "The Two Doctors"

(Serial 6W, Three Episodes. 16th February - 2nd March 1985.)

Which One is This? As the newsletter *Celestial Toyroom* so charmingly put it: "Dago Doctors". Yes, this year they're off to sunny Spain, with the Second Doctor and Jamie and Sontarans and Supreme Commander Servalan off *Blake's 7*, and so much else that a plot would just have got in the way.

But for the British Public, it's the one that was on the week they announced that *Doctor Who* was finishing.

Firsts and Lasts It's the first team-up that hasn't been for an anniversary, the last appearance in the series of Patrick Troughton, the last "beano" to a foreign location (see 20.1, "Arc of Infinity" and 21.5, "Planet of Fire" - we might count 17.2, "City of Death", but that was with a skeleton crew) and - as far as we know at time of writing - the last time the Sontarans pop up. It's also the first time John Nathan-Turner fills in as script editor (see **The Lore** and 23.4, "The Ultimate Foe"). If we count it the way those overseas did, this is the last six-part story. It's also Peter Howell's last score, and Peter Moffatt's last turn to direct.

Six Things to Notice about "The Two Doctors"...

1. As with "Planet of Fire", you're entitled to wonder why they spent so much time and effort going to a foreign location to shoot scenes that look almost homespun. The sequence of the Doctor and Peri fishing, for instance, was done on the last day of filming in Seville, but might almost have been the ever-faithful BBC quarry. Granted, they make a lot of use of one key location, but oddly enough it doesn't look anywhere more exotic and overseas than the opening shots of "Silver Nemesis" (25.3, and shot in Ruislip, Surrey).

2. That said, the urgency with which they try to cram the last episode with Spanish-ness is almost hilarious. Not since the men in stripy jerseys cried 'Beaujolais!' in "City of Death" (17.2) has a tourist

cliché version of a nation been so earnestly presented. So we have a car-chase using a pony and trap, and a really pointless scene with a girl in a flouncy dress lobbing a rose at Dastari (pop to **The Lore** for who she is and why she's there). And over this is so much flamenco guitar, the Sontarans' tight trousers and erect posture suddenly makes a lot more sense. Seriously, you half expect Group Marshal Stike and Chessene O'the Franzine Grig to do a Paso Doble routine on the kitchen table.

3. The Sontaran masks look quite good in still photos. The trouble is, with a big latex mask and no attempt to make it *look* like it belongs on the face of the actor, and the collar floating around the neck rather than connecting the uniform to the face, the overall impression is of someone wearing a Hallowe'en Sontaran mask. Sadly, this is reinforced when the actors try to speak - you can actually see the actors' mouths moving inside the mouths sculpted onto the masks. With gruff, military voices coming from inside what is effectively a latex bucket, some viewers will probably lose the thread of what these characters are saying, and instead wonder what it must have been like wearing that get-up in Spain in summer. Younger, British viewers may also wonder whether they're watching Harry Hill live out his life's ambition of appearing in *Doctor Who*[6].

4. People in this story wax lyrical about the oddest things. Shockeye, an alien foodie, relishes describing how animals - including Jamie - appear likely to taste; Oscar, a poncy actor, eulogises about moths before being asked why he gasses them to death; the Sixth Doctor rhapsodises over the smell of death and, later, the end of the Cosmos; and the Second Doctor delivers a list of his favourite menus and grotesque things done to animals just prior to slaughter. Even Peri manages to deliver a *bon mot* or two.

5. For the fourth time in as many stories, a character comes to the fore from a first draft where s/he was an incidental detail. Like Griffiths, Sil and the Rani before him, Shockeye O'the Quancing Grig is a shining example of a well-thought-out character gaining an extra dimension when an enthusiastic actor takes it on. Holmes kept finding excuses to have him in a scene, and then John Stratton gave the role a theatrical quality almost at odds with the part as scripted. Fortunately, those involved find a means of giving Stratton a whole episode where he and Troughton just throw funny lines at one another

and run off like naughty schoolboys into Seville. Unfortunately, as Shockeye is supposed to be a psychopathic monster, it means that Baker's Doctor has to kill him. The timing of this final chase was therefore rather unfortunate, as it broadcast in a week when the BBC hierarchy wound up saying that the series had become too violent, and when the public were grumbling about this Doctor being a thug.

6. This being Season Twenty-Two, both Jamie and Dastari wear jump-suits. In keeping with the culinary motif running through the story, however, Peri, Chessene and the Sontarans are all dressed in aluminium cooking foil.

The Continuity

The Doctor(s) Both the Second and Sixth Doctors think that Dastari's augmentation of Chessene - resulting in her being a super-genius, but with the base instincts of an Androgum - was a silly thing to do. The Sixth Doctor seems to have picked up oriental medical techniques, here using shiatsu on the comatose Peri and acupuncture on Jamie. Ironically, in view of later events, the Second Doctor tells Jamie that one meal a day is enough [he might just say this on spur-of-the-moment, suspecting that something's afoot in the kitchen]. The Sixth Doctor is, apparently, more appealing to women than Jamie. He doesn't bother to explain how he knows things, simply that he's been around longer than Peri.

Curiously, it seems that the Doctor can "commune" with himself across regenerations. Number Six is alerted to the crisis by a 'mind-slip' / 'time-slip in the subconscious' that links him to his earlier self, whom he believes is in pain and in danger of 'being executed'. [This entire phenomenon is hard to get a grip on, because the tortured "Second Doctor" in this instance is not the genuine article but merely a hologram used to deceive Jamie. It's possible that the Sixth Doctor nonetheless senses the Second Doctor's distress and abduction because they're both in the 1985 time-zone, although this makes the term 'time-slip' even more of a misnomer. As the Second Doctor's TARDIS has been removed from time before whatever-it-is that happens to him, we can rule this out as the cause of the 'mind-slip'. Thus, in the essay we will argue that the whole thing is set up by the Time Lords of the Sixth Doctor's era.]

Six uses - as he puts it - 'telepathy' to track his former self down. This entails placing himself in a trance, and experiencing the world through Two's senses. This communion is said to occur 'on the astral plane' - where time is irrelevant, meaning that Six could have been unconscious for days - but he's fortunately only under for a few minutes. Later, in calculating the coordinates to 1985 Spain, the Sixth Doctor assumes that the Sontarans are only travelling in space. [See last story's essay for more on this.]

Six also claims that he has been feeling out-of-sorts for some time before this, possibly since his regeneration, and worries that he hasn't 'synchronized properly'. [For what it's worth, it's certainly noticeable that he gets along with Peri rather better after this incident, so perhaps mental contact with his previous self brings him (as it were) into "synch".]

• *Ethics*. This week's act of questionable violence: a chase between the wounded Sixth Doctor and Shockeye O'the Quancing Grig ends with the Doctor smothering his pursuer with a handful of cyanide, killing him. [This might not be such an ethical issue in other seasons, but - after the last three stories - it's gotten harder to give the Doctor the benefit of the doubt. That said, Shockeye has proven to be capable of torture (as with his "tenderizing" of Jamie's flesh) and outright murder for petty reasons (as with his slaying of Oscar). He's also armed with a knife, is shouting "Give up, Time Lord! You cannot escape Shockeye O'the Quancing Grig!", has been described as being strong enough to 'break the Doctor and Jamie in half with one hand' and clearly intends on murdering his prey. In such a scenario, the wounded / bleeding Doctor is probably justified in using lethal force against such a foe. As with much of the Sixth Doctor's acts of violence, much of the objection here stems from his final quips to the dead Androgum chef ('Your just desserts...', and later, 'He's been mothballed') rather than his displaying anything approaching regret.]

• *Inventory*. Oddly, the Second Doctor [the one you'd assume would have crowded pockets] is only toting an oil-can [as in 6.5, "The Seeds of Death"] and the TARDIS' so-called 'Recall Disc' [not a disc at all but a black, plastic stick like you'd use to stir cocktails]. Conversely, the Sixth Doctor is carrying a yo-yo, the mirror from "The Twin Dilemma" (21.7), a length of string, a banana, a yellow duster, some acupuncture needles in a carrying-case and a cellophane eyeshade. He hypnotises Jamie with a watch that's different

from the one he uses to tell the time. He's also got, in case of urgent need to find a phone number for a Greek philosopher, a wallet of address-cards [see *Background*]. And he changes into a "summer" version of his waistcoat for the duration of his stay in Seville.

• *Background*. The Doctor apparently attended the inauguration of Space Station Camera, bearing fraternal greetings from Gallifrey, at some point before he 'fell from favour' and became an exile [so this presumably refers to a visit from the First Doctor].

Both Doctors seem familiar with Sontarans and Androgums, and both consider themselves old friends of Dastari. [How many incarnations of the Doctor met Dastari - or whether they even did it in chronological order - is unclear, although Dastari is familiar with Time Lords and presumably the concept of regeneration. See 17.6, "Shada" for a similar situation. The Sixth Doctor obviously doesn't remember Dastari's death even though his earlier self witnesses the event, and many oddities in this story can be resolved if we assume that the Doctor's personal time-line is rewritten slightly when such multi-Doctor events take place. (The Fifth Doctor's comments about being 'whittled away' in 20.7, "The Five Doctors" could be brought into play here.) It's perhaps for this reason that the Sixth Doctor experiences symptoms from his earlier self's transformation into an Androgum - it's all down to "interference" from an aberrant potential time-line opening up and then being closed off. This could also explain why we never witness (for example) an Androgum-inherited Third, Fourth or Fifth Doctor.

[Nevertheless, three other explanations present themselves for Six's memory-lapse. One is that the initial, seemingly unintentional mind-link between the Doctors is perhaps engineered by the Time Lords, whose expertise in messing with people's heads is well-established. We'll explore this notion further in **Is There a Season 6B?** Second, it's possible that owing to an application of the Blinovitch Limitation Effect (as seen in 20.3, "Mawdryn Undead"), the Second Doctor forgets these events. This doesn't account for Jamie's amnesia (again, see the essay), but Holmes' novelisation has them taken out of time and sent on this mission, in a manner like the first draft of 12.4, "Genesis of the Daleks" - and here we refer you back to Theory No. 1.

Was There a Season 6B?

On screen, as the 1960s rolled into the 70s, it seemed so self-evident. The Time Lords finally capture the Doctor in "The War Games" (6.7), then decree that he'll get a new face and be exiled to Earth. The next adventure (7.1, "Spearhead from Space") featured Jon Pertwee flopping out of the TARDIS and the colour era of *Doctor Who* began. So far, so good.

Except that - oh, calamity! - glitches started surfacing with the advent of the three reunion stories (10.1, "The Three Doctors"; 20.7, "The Five Doctors" and 22.4, "The Two Doctors"). To wit, the Second Doctor in "The Five Doctors" claimed to know Zoe's fate and the outcome of his trial - something that should've been impossible, as both events occurred immediately prior to his death / regeneration / renewal (delete according to personal preference) in "The War Games". Then "The Two Doctors" radically ramped up the stakes, as the entire story relied upon an older Second Doctor and Jamie embarking on a mission for the Time Lords - even though there's no point in the Second Doctor's lifetime (again, judging by "The War Games") in which they could've feasibly done so. One could perhaps *try* to overlook that Troughton and Hines had the indecency to age sixteen years between their appearances in "The War Games" (1969) and "The Two Doctors" (1985), but hearing them banter in the latter story about the Time Lords just seemed *odd*, given their existence came as a complete surprise to Jamie in Troughton's final story.

So... latterly, it's been suggested that "The Two Doctors" takes place in some notional gap between "The War Games" and "Spearhead From Space". The idea is that the Time Lords release the condemned Second Doctor from the camera-trick limbo to which he's been consigned (probably the Matrix) and send him off to run a few covert errands for them. He picks up Jamie and Victoria to help him along the way, and has a cobra tattooed on his arm at some point - thus explaining its appearance during Pertwee's shower scene in "Spearhead". As part of this, all sorts of circumlocutions and mental gymnastics have been performed to account for the Chancellor's strangely cagy behaviour in "The Three Doctors". (A quick summary of the argument: he was one of the tribunal hearing the Doctor's appeal in "The War Games" - alongside what may be Chancellor Goth from 14.3, "The Deadly Assassin" - and is in on the scam to use the Second Doctor as a secret agent. Therefore, he's terrified in "The Three Doctors" that

the President's investigations into the Doctor's bio-data will show this up. His objections, even in this catastrophic situation for Gallifrey, amount to hushing up the faked "execution".)

The idea for this extended use of the Second Doctor - called Season 6B - was first floated by Robert Holmes in an interview, at the time when his reputation amongst fans was at its highest (owing partly to his work on 21.6, "The Caves of Androzani"), but even then it was deemed by some to be a mistake. Nonetheless, the mighty Terrance Dicks - as author of both "The Five Doctors" and "The War Games", and story-editor when "The Three Doctors" needed rapid rewrites - in future lent credence to Holmes' theory about a post-arrest Second Doctor doing missions. In more recent years Dicks incorporated the existence of Season 6B into his spin-off novels *Players* and *World Game*. So if you take BBC Books' efforts seriously (and fair enough if you don't), then the idea looks pretty much set in stone. Besides, Dicks and Holmes agreeing on anything is noteworthy, and as counter-intuitive ideas go, you can't get a better pedigree than that.

So advocates of Season 6B have used it as a means of plugging all sorts of little discrepancies. As the theory runs, it was a long period when the Second Doctor "reclaimed" Jamie, reminded him of all the stuff the Time Lords made him forget after "The War Games" (somehow) and then they got Victoria to overcome her fear of time-travel (somehow), went to Planet 14 and got photographed (6.3, "The Invasion") and met some Daleks and again got photographed (4.9, "The Evil of the Daleks") and met an elderly Brigadier, a swarm of furry kangaroos and a lady called Zodin who was (apparently) their travelling companion for a while ("The Five Doctors" and 22.1, "Attack of the Cybermen"). This was all with the full knowledge of the Time Lords, or at least some of them (probably the Celestial Intervention Agency briefly mentioned in "The Deadly Assassin", who are the subject of a lorryload of toss in the spin-off books and elsewhere).

However... the attempt to reconcile Season 6B's convoluted logic with the late 1960s TV stories creates too many extraneous complications to be meekly accepted, and the problems it's intended to fix aren't there anyway. Let's focus on the main justification for Season 6B existing at all: "The Two Doctors", in which the Second Doctor chats happi-

continued on page 59...

ABOUT TIME 1985-1989

[The third option is that Dastari dopes the Second Doctor with Cyrolanamode, which affects memory. That still doesn't account for Jamie, but perhaps he's just traumatised by the sight of the Doctor's faked execution until Six calms him down and hypnotises him.]

The Sixth Doctor can recognise the toll of the Santa Maria bell - well enough to conclude that his other self is in Seville - and the echo of dungeons. He remembers being fond of Jamie. The Sixth Doctor's business-cards include ones for Archimedes, Dante, Aristotle, Brunel [although he doesn't say whether this means Isambard Kingdom Brunel or his similarly-talented father Marc, whom he missed meeting at Lord Ravensworth's bash in the previous story], Columbus, Da Vinci [presumably Leonardo, see 17.2, "City of Death" and many others] and Dastari.

Number Six claims that when he last fished the stretch of water seen here, he landed four magnificent gumblejack in less than ten minutes [see **The Non-Humans**, but bear in mind what's claimed in the novelisation of this story].

The Second Doctor says he has eaten pressed duck at the Tour D'Argent, capercaillies in brandy sauce, pâté de fois gras de Strasbourg en croute and many other rich and sadistically-prepared meals, and that he knows the work of such chefs as Careme, Escoffier and Brillat Savarin. He knows his wine, too. [Something obviously true before 9.1, "Day of the Daleks" but not what we typically think of the Second Doctor as being familiar with. And as part of all this, we assume that Time Lords are immune to gout.]

The Second Doctor has just dropped Victoria off to study Graphology, for some reason.

The Supporting Cast

• *Peri.* She can identify a line from Dr Johnson regarding money, and is none too keen on fishing. She seems to have taken on a role as the Doctor's "beast of burden" in hauling his fishing equipment around [mainly to have an excuse for a good grumble, or maybe she thinks that's how to gain the moral high ground in their increasingly playful arguments]. She remains very worried about him, and when he collapses in the TARDIS, she immediately suggests fetching some celery [21.6, "The Caves of Androzani"] as a restorative. It's Peri who calms Jamie and gets him used to there being more than one Doctor. Her Spanish isn't too hot,

but she's picked up the term 'whopper' from somewhere [surely not from this Doctor, because he'd tell her where the word originated and she'd be too grossed out to use it]. She's been around a fake-English Time Lord long enough to call chips 'chips' and not "fries". All these Spanish back-streets look the same to her.

• *Jamie.* He's *extremely* traumatised by seeing his Doctor "killed", and in the following days aboard the deserted Space Station Camera turns semi-feral, makes a nest in the infrastructure and growls like a beast. Even when Jamie has a blow to the head, giant acupuncture needles in his neck and the Doctor hypnotising him, he remains agitated when asked to remember the sight of his Doctor perishing.

The TARDIS Curiously, the Second Doctor has apparently got the use of the console room as seen between 15.2, "The Invisible Enemy" and 20.6, "The King's Demons". [As the Fourth Doctor moved into this room while claiming he was 'back' (15.2, "The Invisible Enemy"), it's been generally assumed that there were only the two console rooms, and that *this* was the one used up to 14.1, "The Masque of Mandragora". We have also assumed that this was the same throughout the entire series up to that point, and refits (9.5, "The Time Monster"; 10.1, "The Three Doctors") were simply cosmetic. This adventure casts all of that into doubt, especially when you consider Jamie's comments that the Second Doctor's navigation is unusually accurate this time (which true enough, it *is*). Perhaps this console is upgraded - or indeed provided by the Time Lords just for the mission, only to be forgotten when the Doctor is returned to his orthodox time-stream and his memory "modified" (see the accompanying essay for more).

[There *is* an alternative, but it gets fiendishly complicated, and requires a retooling of what's been generally regarded as true. As stated, we know that there are at least two functioning console rooms, and that one seems more wildly remodellable than the other. Thus...

[What we'd suggest is that console room A is the one used from 1.1, "An Unearthly Child" to 6.7, "The War Games". Console room B is pressed into service in "The Two Doctors" when the Time Lords want to have dual-control of the Ship, and again during the Third Doctor's exile up to 9.5, "The Time Monster". It would make sense if the

Was There a Season 6B?

...continued from page 57

ly to Jamie about Time Lords.

Well, as we covered in the last story's essay, let's assume that - with respect to the Doctor's TARDIS - all events of Gallifrey are in sequence, and as far apart for the High Council as they are for the Doctor. Now assume also that this "Gallifreyan Mean Time" (GMT) extends to all TARDISes from the same era (hence the Rani being the same age as the Doctor whenever they meet; 24.1, "Time and the Rani"). Furthermore, assume that the Time Lords of any given year, local to the Capitol, cannot interfere with Gallifrey's past - even if it's just ten minutes ago. (Hence, of course, the First Law of Time and all the others a 'First' law would imply.) With the exception of "reunion" stories, wherein the High Council and a zone outside orthodox time are invoked (including Season Twenty-Three, for that matter), all meetings between the Doctor and his contemporaries have been in sequence. For example, Ainley's Master never popped back to give Sergeant Benton a hard time. (There is a possible exception to this, however: see **The Valeyard, er, How?** under 23.4, "The Ultimate Foe".)

We mention all of this because it's important to recognize that "The Two Doctors" takes place within the Sixth Doctor's period of Gallifrey, not that of the Second Doctor. If you need further proof, consider that the Second Doctor possesses a device in advance of "his" era: the Stattenheim remote control. In "The War Games", it's said that operating a time capsule by remote control will shorten its working life, yet the Rani in "The Mark of the Rani" seemingly has a means of overcoming this limitation. It's hardly a stretch to think that some technological advance has taken place in the intervening centuries.

And if we're going with GMT, "The Two Doctors" so obviously taking place in 1985 would *also* indicate that the Sontarans are messing around with the Third Zone governments in the Sixth Doctor's native Gallifrey era. Why else would *that* Doctor and not (say) the Seventh or the Fourth get a mind-link from his previous self? In fact, further support that we're dealing with Six's era and not that of Two hails from Holmes' novelisation, which hints that the older Second Doctor and Jamie were hauled outside time for their mission. Surely, this nugget straight from Holmes' typewriter is just as admissible as spin-off books by other authors.

So, taking *all* of that into account, we can pro-pose a chronology of events without reliance on Season 6B. Occam's razor at the ready, here we go...

When the Kartz-Reimer experiment scares the (post-"Five Doctors" and pre-"Trial") Time Lords into action, their Lord President - the Doctor - has just regenerated into the patchcoat version and is footloose in the cosmos. To send such a high-ranking Gallifreyan to Space Station Camera to chat with Dastari would make them *look* more worried than they wish to appear. (It's like the difference between allowing a former US president - Jimmy Carter, for instance - to visit somewhere controversial, and George W Bush doing it while he's still in office.) Thus, dispatching the Sixth Doctor to investigate Dastari's actions would be as good as admitting that Chessene's almost cracked the secrets of time travel.

But they *could* check the TARDIS's logs, as they seem to have done in "The War Games" (and the novelisation of 20.1, "Arc of Infinity"), and trace back to a point when the Doctor was - as far as Gallifreyan politics goes - nobody special. From the Second Doctor's perspective, he's being approached from a *possible* future, offered a pardon for something he hasn't done yet and asked to visit his old friend Dastari with a message - all with plausible deniability. ('Officially, I'm here quite unofficially', as he puts it.)

If he failed, then his recruiters would never have done so, and if he succeeded, they wouldn't let anyone know where (and when) he was until after he was reconciled with his people. A win-win situation, it would seem. The only hitch would be if anything happened to the Second Doctor. It would jeopardize his career post-capture - including his involvement in events important enough to warrant intervention by professional agents. To protect the causality of their President, they might've set up a mental link with his younger self, enabling him to serve as his own US Cavalry if needs be. (Frankly, presuming the Time Lords set up an emergency mental link between Six and Two in "The Two Doctors" makes a hell of a lot more sense than thinking it's triggered by Six's previous self being photographed as part of a ruse.) Then when it was over, the Time Lords could just wipe events relating to Dastari and Chessene from the Second Doctor and Jamie's minds.

As for the claim that Season 6B is the *only* means of covering a number of seemingly unshown Second Doctor adventures... let's first

continued on page 61...

Doctor reverted to Room A (rebuilt to try out his control of navigation - Room B, after all, is too prone to being suborned when Gallifrey wants to send him on an errand) from 10.1, "The Three Doctors" to 13.6, "The Seeds of Doom". He uses Room B as a glory-hole, but remembers it in 14.1, "The Masque of Mandragora", and comments on the unreliability of the steering. (As if to confirm all of this, see 13.5, "The Brain of Morbius", in which the TARDIS is steered by remote through brute force, rather than the more elegant hi-jacking of yesteryear in - for instance - 9.2, "The Curse of Peladon".)

[Back to A from 15.2, "Invisible Enemy" to 20.6, "The King's Demons", and then either he refitted Room A... or, well, he didn't. The console room from 20.7, "The Five Doctors" to the classic series' end might be a refitted Room B, but the way Tegan reacts to the new console makes it seem that the Doctor has been rebuilding for a while - part of an overhaul that's been going since Romana arrived, but only really kicked in between "Time-Flight" (19.7) and "Arc of Infinity" (20.1) and which carries on until "Vengeance on Varos" (22.2). So the overall plan we've outlined isn't perfect, but it *might* account for some lingering anomalies, and the business of whether the console can be removed without releasing the power of the TARDIS (1.3, "Edge of Destruction"; 17.5, "The Horns of Nimon") can go away at last.]

The Second Doctor's console has a 'Recall Disc' - a recent addition, as Jamie spots that it's new - that operates via a Stattenheim Remote Control [see last story's notes]. Two can use the Remote Control to summon the TARDIS simply by whistling, and this annoys the Sixth Doctor, because he's always wanted such a gadget. [So wherever Two goes after this story, he doesn't get to keep the Remote Control, nor retains the ability to build one.] Blinovitch-spotters will note that the two TARDISes are, for the Doctors, in separate time-zones by virtue of their being a five-minute walk between them [no, we didn't think you'd buy that]. However, both arrive at Space Station Camera in exactly the same spot.

Six's console room still has that horrid chair facing the viewers, on which Peri places cumbersome fishing apparatus. The Doctor is now using a golf brolly [like the one in the initial press-call in April 1984, if not *the* brolly]. He opens it as he walks into the Ship, which is perhaps why his luck is so bad from then on.

The Time Lords The Second Doctor claims that nobody can travel through time without a 'molecular stabilisation system', and this appears to be the main stumbling block of the Kartz-Reimer project. Several Androgums successfully 'vanished into time', but - for lack of such a stabiliser, evidently - attempts to bring them back failed. Chessene and Dastari accordingly theorized that Time Lords must possess a symbiotic link with their travel machines, which protects them and anyone travelling with them against destabilisation. The villains have therefore kidnapped a Time Lord - the Second Doctor - in the hopes that Dastari can isolate the stabilisation element within his physiology.

The Sixth Doctor subsequently tells Jamie about the Rassilon Imprimature [here we're using the spelling from Holmes' novelisation], a symbiotic print within the physiology of Time Lords. This allegedly enables a Time Lord to safely use and thereby 'prime' a virgin time machine - a process that causes a vital component, the briode nebuliser, to 'absorb' the Time Lord's symbiotic print. Once that's done, allegedly, anyone can use the machine to travel in time.

Later, Six claims that 'None of what he told [Jamie] was strictly true', and was instead a means of fooling the Sontaran Stike, who had snuck up behind him. Nonetheless, Six successfully uses the Kartz-Reimer machine as described, but fools the villains by 'paring' the briode-nebuliser's interface, leaving only a 'thin membrane' of his symbiotic print on it. This causes the machine to work but once more, and it thereafter explodes when Chessene tries to escape in it.

[All right... if we're trying to reconcile all this time-travel gobbledygook, the biggest question is the degree to which Six is lying, as he dumps this vital chunk of information about time-travel as part of a deception. However, much of *Doctor Who* substantiates the notion of a symbiotic link between TARDISes and their operators - the Doctor claiming his Ship is 'alive' and can select destination coordinates according to his desires (11.5, "Planet of the Spiders") is but one example - and the Kartz-Reimer machine *does* work when the Doctor takes a spin in it.

[Ultimately, it would appear that Six *only* fibs about the machine being automatically 'primed' for indefinite use, and that he alternatively knows how to make its function temporary. For better or worse, several of the *Doctor Who* novels have

Was There a Season 6B?

...continued from page 59

acknowledge that the Troughton era contains more credible gaps between stories that people sometimes believe. (Notably, a sizeable one seems to exist between 4.7, "The Macra Terror" and 4.8, "The Faceless Ones".) For that matter, owing to on-screen character development in the Troughton years, it's actually *preferable* to assume that more time elapses than we see in the TV adventures.

Consider this: Victoria "suddenly" goes from blushing at her frumpy dress in "Tomb of the Cybermen" (5.1) and being scandalised by Miss Garrett's shorts in "The Ice Warrors" (5.3) to wearing a teeny weeny mini in the London Underground in "The Web of Fear" (5.5), and later not batting an eyelid at the nude pin-ups on the walls of the Sea-Base in "Fury from the Deep" (5.6, and check the telesnaps if you don't believe us). There's an intermediate stage of her wearing Edwardian clothes, like the cyclist get-up of "The Abominable Snowmen" (5.2) and "The Ice Warriors" and - apparently - the Grecian-line frock that no lady would have worn prior to 1908, but which Victoria apparently wore often enough for the Doctor to recognise it in "Pyramids of Mars" (13.3). It's a bit curious that she does this *after* wearing the mini on Telos, but it's not what you'd call incredible. Also, we're told at the start of "The Two Doctors" that Victoria - presumably during Season Five - has been a student (at Zebedee Univerity, St Cedds or Dellah?). Wherever it is, they must have taught her how to pick locks with hairpins; again see "Fury".

All in all, piffling concerns about the Doctor's hair and tattoos are as nothing to the drastic onscreen change in Victoria's values. If you're still unconvinced, try listening to the "Fury From the Deep" soundtrack, in which she's blubbering - about every five minutes for the last four episodes, or so it seems - about wanting to stay somewhere where she won't get menaced by foam-spurting yeti, foam-spurting Cybermen, foam-spurting seaweed or any other imaginative monsters. How could she *possibly* want to resume her adventuring after this? How could the Doctor, who's spent Season Five looking relieved at talking to adult women, risk her life and his nerves taking her back? If he could actually steer the TARDIS, he'd be far more likely to recruit the secret-agent-style Astrid Ferrier (5.4, "The Enemy of the World") as a sidekick for clandestine missions.

[We've got to say, the contact with his future fellow-countrymen seems to coincide with his acquisition of a second console and a second heart, or at least the start of a process that leads to his body being slightly "rewired". This might cover the grey hair issue and his sudden ability (in 5.7, "The Wheel in Space"), to project his thoughts onto the scanner. See also **When Did He Get A Second Heart?** under 6.1, "The Dominators".)

Of course, we haven't yet covered how the Doctor can remember stuff from his own future in "The Five Doctors", and seems to have been updated by the High Council in "The Three Doctors" - only to apparently have it all erased prior to his exile. The default explanation for reunion stories has usually been that regeneration amnesia covers meetings with future selves, but there's an alternative. Consider that "The Three Doctors" - from the Second Doctor's point of view - happens after "The Two Doctors". And he had a mental chat with his later self on both occasions, don't forget.

If this is the case, then the Second Doctor knew all about one *possible* version of his personal future, which explains his panic and subsequent resignation when the Time Lords come chasing after him at the end of "The War Games". Suddenly, it had ceased to be a possibility and became The Future. (Incidentally, knowledge of his personal future always unsettles the Doctor: see his response to his tombstone in two stories' time (22.6, "Revelation of the Daleks"), his glum acquiescence at the end of 18.7, "Logopolis" and his outright terror when confronted with the truth about the Valeyard in 23.4, "The Ultimate Foe". He's even less cocky than usual in 26.1, "Battlefield".) He therefore recognises Zoe in the Death Zone from his later self's memory, not recent personal contact - a likely scenario if his removal from 'coterminous time' took place while he was still travelling with Victoria. (Again, this is actually cleaner than assuming a clunky block of years happen between "The War Games" and "Spearhead", which were meant to occur back-to-back.)

Ultimately, whichever side of the Season 6B equation you favour, there's a broader aesthetic issue here. The generation who regard Troughton as "their" Doctor have generally found the reunion stories a little gimmicky. His performances (even in "The Two Doctors", where he's the *most* like when he was the star) amount to party-pieces rather than acting - in these stories, he's assuredly "The Second Doctor" (capital S, capital D), rather than

continued on page 63...

upheld the notion of the 'Rassilon Imprimature', so it's a notion that's stuck in fandom's mind as being genuine, even if Six is here shading the truth. We'd be remiss if we didn't revisit this issue in **Things That Don't Make Sense**, however.]

[An interesting tangent, by the way, is to wonder if exposure to TARDIS energy (or if you prefer, journeying with a Time Lord who's in symbiosis with his / her Ship) fundamentally alters those travelling with them. This may be why (just to pick some examples) the first non-Gallifreyan passengers that we see - Ian and Barbara - were knocked unconscious on their first flight (1.1, "An Unearthly Child"), how Jo survived a random transit with the stolen time-controller (9.1, "The Day of the Daleks") and how Ace and the Brigadier withstood Interstitial Time (26.1, "Battlefield"). Indeed, vast chunks of the BBC Wales series require this to be the case. But if that's so, why did Chessene and Dastari come to think that something in Time Lord DNA was the key? But if *human* DNA can contain this vital component as well, then the plot of the McGann TV Movie almost works, but everything else involving time-travel falls apart. And anyway, the Doctor tells Chessene that Peri hasn't got the nuclei, and a lie would be easy to spot at this stage.]

The Sixth Doctor sheds some dark red blood when Shockeye stabs him. [Tom Baker's scheme to give the Doctor blue blood (18.4, "State of Decay") seems to have been abandoned.]

The Non-Humans

• *Sontarans*. In the 1985 time-zone, the Sontarans seem taller than those we've seen before. [In both the past (11.1, "The Time Warrior") and the future (12.3, "The Sontaran Experiment"). More to the point, the Sontarans are reportedly a clone species, but Field Major Stike looks significantly unlike Varl, his lieutenant. There must be more than one strain of Sontaran clones at large, which probably explains why Linx ("The Time Warrior", played by Kevin Lindsay) looks like Styre ("The Sontaran Experiment", and Lindsay again) despite the centuries that separate them, yet neither of them look like the Sontarans here or Stor from 15.6, "The Invasion of Time".] As they are already thinking of altering their genetic make-up, it's possible that they have been bred differently. [In which case, the fact that Varl is the same height and build as Stike is odd but possibly significant. No previous

story has hinted at any "caste" system, and whatever appeared on screen, Sarah mistook Styre for Linx. So the scripts, at least, suggest that all Sontarans actually look alike throughout history. See **Things That Don't Make Sense**.]

The Sontarans are averse to dealing with inferiors, but the concept of adopting Time Lord chromosomal nucleii to facilitate time-travel appeals to them. Sontarans have green blood, as seen when they're blown up by Chessene, or stabbed by Jamie. Coronic acid is especially effective in killing them [or at least in Stike's case, scarring them hideously].

Stike wears girly white shoulder-ribbons to signify his rank [much like the Valeyard in Season Twenty-Two, in fact]. He has a beard and an officer's baton. Sontaran ships revolve in flight [so it's lucky they absorb energy rather than eating anything resembling food] and can be placed 'in clear' (made invisible) to avoid detection.

• *Androgums*. Natives of the Third Zone, and used as servitors by the other races who occupy this area. They're characterized as beings of pure appetite, and use such intelligence as they have to readily gratify themselves. They're divided into a clan system (Karms), are usually designated as "So-and-so O'the such-and-such Grig", and jealously protect this birthright.

Androgums are physically powerful - well beyond human norm - are stocky and tend to have bushy eyebrows (usually orange or pinkish) and warts. To judge by Shockeye, they can consume vast amounts of food in a short time. Their blood is red.

Both Shockeye and Chessene speak English [identified by the Doña Arana as Shockeye's language]. Shockeye can, apparently, read Chinese and Indian cookbooks in Spanish, but the Doctor claims [rightly or wrongly] they can't *speak* Spanish.

• *Chessene O'the Franzine Grig*. Dastari has given her nine 'augmentations', which has raised her intellect to 'mega-genius level' and allows her to assimilate vast amounts of data quickly. She is the mind behind the Kartz-Reimer time experiments, and has worked out that the missing element crucial to time-travel must be within the Time Lords' bodies. She's lost most of her Androgum features, and is human-looking enough to fool the Second Doctor. However, her lineage is not entirely abandoned. She's curious as to how humans taste, becomes bestial when near spilled blood and

Was There a Season 6B?

...continued from page 61

"The New Doctor Who". The people who view the series through the lens of fandom don't really recognize this distinction, and are happy to brazenly use words like "retcon" in public. But - as we have argued at length in these books - the British Public at large see it differently, and *Doctor Who* was made for them.

So for *most* people... the Time Lords caught and punished the Doctor by turning him into Jon Pertwee, who was then made to fend off an invasion of the Home Counties every month or so, and the whole series changed in one fell swoop. The Doctor used to be a magician, but now he's an alien. Hearing Troughton babble about 'Gallifrey' and 'Rassilon' is about as wrong as hearing Harpo Marx talking (see **Did *Doctor Who* Really End In 1969?** under "The War Games"). For fans, it's a generational issue akin to the one about whether Rassilon and Omega had (loud) conversations (see **Did Rassilon Know Omega?** under 14.3, "The Deadly Assassin and 25.1, "Remembrance of the Daleks"). Aesthetically, we can see why many would like to think of the Second Doctor having a more dignified exit than burping and gurning on a big magic telly, but for episode ten of "The War Games" to have anything like the emotional clout it did when we didn't know what would happen next, this needs to be *that* Doctor's death.

refuses to *entirely* betray one of her kind, i.e. Shockeye, even though she forcibly removes some of his DNA to turn the Doctor into an Androgum. She also accedes to Shockeye's request to make camp on Earth, partly to suit her own schemes, but partly to satiate his desire to eat a human.

Chessene has several talents, including a highly-refined ESP and the ability to access the memories of a recently killed human. This occurs without any comment from her associates [and would therefore seem to be a development of natural Androgum skills - see also Morgaine in "Battlefield" and the two-way exchanges of information between the humans and Wirrn, and the Doctor and the Wirrn queen, in "The Ark in Space" (12.2)]. She is also mildly telepathic, able to mentally sense that Peri is constantly thinking about 'the Doctor', but otherwise finding the human brain 'flabby and vague, hard to read'. Notably, Chessene finds Peri's bluff about having friends waiting for her plausible, and is unable to directly read the truth in her mind.

When exposed to an unstabilised time-field, Chessene's augmentations appear to come undone, and she devolves to "pure" Androgum.

• *Gumblejacks*. Described by the Sixth Doctor as 'the finest fish in the galaxy, possibly the universe'. He recommends pan-frying them in their own juices until they're golden brown, and that they taste best when fried quickly. [The novelisation suggests that he was making this all up.] They are one of the things the Doctor would most miss if the Universe came unravelled, along with sunsets and butterflies.

• *The Pandatorean Conger*. Larger than a railway train - or so the Sixth Doctor again claims - and found in the Great Lakes of Pandatorea. [That's the name of an island near Rome used for exiles, so presumably it denotes one of those planets named after an Earth location, such as Navarino (24.3, "Delta and the Bannermen") or Barcelona (X1.13, "The Parting of the Ways").]

History

• *Dating*. It's all, we're led to believe, happening at around the time of broadcast in 1985. With the possible exception of the Doctor and Peri's fishing trip, everything seems to take place in the same time-zone, and the Sontaran ships - not equipped with time-distort [see "The Time Warrior"] - require twelve days to reach Earth from the Third Zone.

Space Station Camera [that's how it's spelled, but everyone pronounces it "Chimaera", which makes more sense really] was once a modest research station in the Third Zone. [It's unclear if this is even a "place" at all, and the ambiguous dialogue makes it just as likely to be a dimension or a kind of League of Non-Aligned Species.] Under the directorship of Professor Joynson Dastari - who was almost present at its inauguration - Station J7 [named that by the computer, and also in the novelisation] has been greatly enlarged. Dastari seems to have been involved in the design of much of the infrastructure and systems, and his voice - if a bit distorted - is used for the computer readouts. It would seem that the nature of the station's research - variously into time-mechanics, pin-galaxies and genetic augmentation - requires the station to be both remote and well-guarded.

It's run by a number of governments but is independent of all of them, and dedicated to pure research [the obvious comparison is with the Think Tank in 17.6, "Shada"]. Dastari authorizes all research conducted at the station.

The Sixth Doctor says that Dastari's people have made some interesting developments on rho mesons as the unstable factor in pin-galaxies, which exist 'within the universe of the atom' for an atto-second (one quintillionth of a second). Dastari has been famous for some time, and worked out his theory of parallel matter many years ago, using pen and ink because he detests computers.

Relations between the Third Zone and the Time Lords are at best described tense. Whilst the Doctor and Dastari are [or at one point were] cordial on a personal level, the Time Lords are particularly concerned that - according to their monitors - the Kartz-Reimer experiment is causing 'ripples' [in time] of up to 0.4 on the Bocca scale. The Second Doctor says that anything higher would threaten the whole fabric of time. In fact, the Kartz-Reimer research is so advanced, Number Six is quite prepared to believe his younger self *was* killed, and that he now only exists as 'temporal tautology', as he was caught in a chronic 'embolism' and was outside the time flow. This would only come to pass if there had been a significant rupture, in which case the collapse of the universe would only take a few centuries. [Fortunately, the Doctor isn't killed at all, so this theory doesn't apply.]

The Sontarans seem able to plausibly blame an attack on Camera as being the Time Lords' work. Dastari knows that the Gallifreyans have 'powers' [or perhaps "weapons"] as yet undreamt-of by Chessene. [See stories such as "Remembrance of the Daleks" (25.1) and "Silver Nemesis" (25.3) for this hint being backed up.]

The Third Zone is sometimes spoken of as including the Time Lords, and sometimes not. Shockeye speaks of 'The Nine Planets'. Apparently they use paper currency, and the twenty Narg note is accepted throughout this system [so don't leave home without it]. Humans have not reached this area of space, although the Doctor seems to say that they will. [Even so, the exact ties between the Third Zone and Earth are a little unclear. Contact between the two seems scant, or else Shockeye would not have to personally go to Earth to cook and eat a human. Balanced against that, Dastari's

office seems filled with what appear to be Earth antiques - especially globes and furniture that seem Georgian - and there's no particularly good explanation for why Chessene and Shockeye seem to speak English, even independently of a TARDIS translation device.]

The Sontaran-Rutan wars continue [as always], and in this phase the Madellon Cluster conflict is going badly for the Sontarans.

The Analysis

Where Does This Come From? Well, there's a sort of debate going on in this season about the use of people as meat. It's stated explicitly here and in "Revelation of the Daleks" (22.6), implicitly in the Cybermen processing humans in "Attack of the Cybermen" (22.1), and with sideswipes like cannibals on Varos and the Rani's lectures on slaughtering animals.

We can't help but notice, though, that the examples of cruel food-preparation cited by Shockeye and the Androgum Doctor are almost all the ones used in both the novel *Do Androids Dream of Electric Sheep?* and its film version(ish), *Blade Runner*. In particular, they're cited as part of the test for empathy, without which one is deemed to be an android. The Sixth Doctor not only berates the Androgums for their lack of what he calls 'emotional capacity', but is chastened by this whole experience, possibly enough make him give up fishing and turn vegetarian. We could extend this to the appearance of Dastari (not a million miles away from Joe Turkel as the geneticist Tyrell in *Blade Runner*) and his pride in his creation, Chessene. This latter strand, at least as written by Holmes, is more akin to Eliza Dolittle from *Pygmalion / My Fair Lady*.

If we're going with Holmes and Saward taking inspiration from 1982's SF blockbusters (not that *Blade Runner* did well in the US, but it made a splash here), then the assault on Camera is a bit familiar. *Star Trek II: The Wrath of Khan* had an old baddie come back and pinning the blame on the Federation for an assault on a scientific research station.

Vegetarianism, though, was suddenly mainstream in the mid-1980s. Not as much so as it became later, with the hype about mad cow disease and the wider knowledge of how meat is processed, but it was certainly no longer faddy. Pop stars, both Indie (obviously Morrissey has to get a mention here) and more commercial (Howard Jones, for instance) and actors (Kate O'Mara cited it as how she kept her looks) weren't treated as freaks. Supermarkets made availability of meat-free products more of a priority. In the overall concern about body-shape, health and lifestyle that dominated much of the 1980s, this was an issue raised far more frequently. Both Robert Holmes and Nicola Bryant were trying to cut out meat, whilst Eric Saward was on a strict diet generally. (And let's not forget the press coverage of "Dr Huge" himself, but that really took off in the eighteen-month gap. *The Sun* had Baker's diet tips.)

Of course, the alternative is to distract attention away from your bulges with loud shirts. We've got to say it, but in the mid-1980s there was a considerable cachet to "bad taste". Things either aesthetically brash or conceptually daring were now challenges. Anthropophagy was a subject hitherto kept for odd low-budget movies. With video making these things available, and connoisseurship of films like *The Texas Chain Saw Massacre* a matter of a weird prestige, it became almost vogueish. The scene at the end of episode two, with Peri being chased by Shockeye, is said by some to look like a famous scene from *Texas Chain Saw Massacre* (those of you with the botched DVD of X2.1, "New Earth" - the Netflix version that, about 32 minutes in, suddenly starts playing *Texas Chain Saw Massacre: The Beginning* - might like to ponder that) but the key thing is that people *could* make that comparison, not whether Peter Moffatt actively shot it that way. (Real buffs preferred Paul Bartel's more stylish *Eating Raoul*, anyway.)

The Twilight Zone had made Damon Knight's story "To Serve Man" a catchphrase (in the US these were in re-runs, but here Channel Four was giving these episodes their first networked transmissions). A sketch hitherto banned from transmission in *Monty Python's Flying Circus* Series Two was shown in the reruns with no comment (see "Revelation of the Daleks" for more). So with Colin Baker presented to the press as the "Bad Taste" Doctor, and the black humour of Holmes' earlier scripts now celebrated by fans, a story like this could hardly be called unexpected. Indeed, Holmes had made notes for such a story when serving as script editor in the mid-1970s. We have to acknowledge how many of the set-pieces here are well-loved Holmes moments from earlier stories. That's not an altogether a bad thing, though, as even "The Talons of Weng-Chiang" ends with a string of set-pieces.

We're also obliged, as employees of Mad Norwegian Press (who published much of *About Time* while operating in the Big Easy), to acknowledge that the *other* other thing for which New Orleans is famous is Voodoo. At least some of the elements in this story would have been more plausibly included into a story set there - we then refer you to "Silver Nemesis" (25.3) and draw a discrete veil over the subject.

Historical note for anyone who wasn't reading lifestyle magazines in 1985: the *nouvelle cuisine* that Oscar mentions (and which should have been *cuisine nouvelle*, but never mind) was a fad for presentation over content. Very 80s. Simply put, celebrity chefs made fortunes by charging vast sums for two asparagus stalks and a rose-petal, so long as it was artistically displayed on an exquisite plate and the sinusoidal curve of the bechamel sauce was mathematically precise. Ironically, this was the same year as Live Aid.

Things That Don't Make Sense Right at the end, Chessene says it's time to kill the 'other' Time Lord ('Six, whom she never finds out is another Doctor). Dastari then panics, claiming that *killing* a Time Lord would ruin them, as the Gallifreyans have powers as yet undreamed-of and so on. So apparently, carving up the Doctor 'cell by cell, chromosome by chromosome' with a circular saw is all right, is it? Especially as Dastari knows that the High Council sent Two to Camera as its (albeit unofficial) emissary.

More worryingly, if the Second Doctor was *not* executed, what - as we've previously discussed - if anything caused a 'mind-slip' with the Sixth Doctor? The way the narrative is presented, the Doctor was weakened by his former self having his photo taken by a mirror, then linked an animation package in Dastari's computer. [This is very silly in terms of the story as broadcast, but we'll at least capitalize on this as possible proof that the Time Lords engineered this whole situation, and thus there is no such thing as Season 6B.]

Oscar the moth-obsessive appears to have just left his nets, lantern and killing-jar in a field and gone to work. [Let's hope he washed his hands thoroughly.] And you don't get Feathered Gothics in Andalucia. While we're on the subject of that open field, it's funny how Shockeye can smell the blood of a Time Lord from over the brow of a hill, but apparently not cyanide almost literally under his nose. This batch of cyanide starts fuming before water is added, and kills when you breathe it in, but *not* if you get it on your hand and then rub a gaping flesh-wound with that hand as the Doctor seems to do. Oscar visibly wears a big sac of blood under his shirt when he's at the restaurant, just in case he needs to entertain the customers with a death-scene.

Arguably, the second-biggest problem of this story is the inconsistency about how exactly Time Lords interact with time machines... we elaborated on this in **The Time Lords** section, but suffice to say it's weird how the "lie" that the Sixth Doctor presents in episode two about how Time Lords control their vessels apparently *is* (give or take) how the Time Lords control their vessels by episode three. For that matter, if Dastari just wants to isolate the prized stabilisation element from the Second Doctor's physiology, why does he need to hack open the Doctor's brain with a saw, as opposed to just taking tissue samples? Worse, if 'priming' the machine were as feasible as Six claims - and as Dastari and Chessene spontaneously seem to know in episode three - then why didn't they save a lot of hassle by just putting a gun to Jamie's head, and forcing Two to "deflower" their machine with his symbiotic print? Under that scenario, the Sontaran assault on Camera, the villains' entire trip to Earth and the intent to dissect the Doctor is a colossal waste of time.

Stike tells Varl to inform High Command that they will return to the battle in the dinky little Kartz-Reimer module, and orders him to set their ship to self-destruct. Whereas the current Sontaran ships are evidently capable of carrying a vast amount of high-tech gubbins - despite being the same configuration as those of Stike and Linx - the Kartz-Reimer buggies differ from TARDISes in being somewhat smaller inside than their phone-booth exteriors. Quite apart from the enforced intimacy this would impose upon Stike and Varl, they're gambling a lot on a machine that has never been properly tested, and which they have only seen other people use. And would the Ninth Sontaran Battlefleet [what a lot of nines in this story] know what it was and refrain from shooting at it on arrival?

As it's their last appearance [unless BBC Wales has a good reason to bring them back, and the Judoon from X3.1, "Smith and Jones" seem like a good reason *not* to] we can finally ask: how can clones, who are literally created equal, have a mil-

itary-style hierarchy? The only way this works is through seniority, and this implies that you get to be Group-Marshal if you are the sole survivor of every battle you are in. So they are either selectively breeding for luck as a genetic trait [and Stike seems to be proof that this hasn't panned out so well] or they have systematically ensured that cowards or egoists have led their campaigns. No wonder the war's been dragging on for aeons.

[All right: a *possible* solution is that they draw lots, and the difference between ranks is purely down to training. That way any Sontaran can be the parent of a future leader, which resolves their interchangeability and lack of any tendency towards self-sacrifice as we might expect from clones. Every Sontaran we have seen has behaved like an individual, despite being raised as a unit of a greater whole. Which raises the question of how they all have such similar names, with so few options for permutations on the basic one-syllable percussive / sibilant theme, but let's not worry about that now.]

The *biggest* Thing That Doesn't Make Sense is that whereas Pennant Roberts could have probably made something of this story, and Peter Moffatt might have done something interesting with "Timelash", their assignments were reversed. Oh, all right... we're getting cheeky, so we'll finish by asking whether it's plausible that Doña Arana has a Chinese recipe book. [Mind, as the late Don seems like a bit of a card, it's vaguely possible.]

Critique (Prosecution) Deep down, some of us had dreaded it would come to this. Back in 1985, there was a certain tier of fandom who'd been sticking with the programme since it went all geeky in 1980, who'd taken to telling people "it'll come right soon", and who'd braved false dawns of quality such as "Enlightenment" (20.5) and "The Caves of Androzani". But almost against their will, this group finally lost patience and stopped even bothering to defend the series, and *this* was this story that extinguished all hope.

It wasn't so much that "The Two Doctors" was made with a tick-box, or that the BBC had announced that they had lost patience too. It's that Robert Holmes betrayed us by writing the most unpleasantly fascistic story imaginable. Attempts to raise the Androgums are doomed because "they're like that" - educating them is a waste of time, and they should only breed with their own kind. Even if he hadn't had both

Doctors saying this (and Troughton even uses words like 'mongrel' for Jamie's attempts at English), the plot valorises this view. The Sontarans' desire to try and steal Time Lord chromosomes is portrayed as a perversion of nature (funny that, since you could say the same about the chromosomes themselves). Chessene cannot help but revert to bloodlust and appetite. Dastari's arguments are actually quite valid, but it's the Second Doctor who opposes him, so we're never going to see Dastari as sympathetic. And the consequences of his beliefs are savage and grotesque, so Dastari is painted as a monster

What *really* hurts is that there are signs of something more dignified and positive underneath this story. The emphasis on empathy, 'emotional capacity' and self-restraint as hallmarks of goodness makes it look as if Holmes was simply unaware that his story was advocating a caste system and a final solution. In print, he tried to remedy some of the script's worst excesses. Unfortunately, we're not reviewing the novelisation, we're looking at the story as broadcast. In this, we find that Oscar's death is a comedy routine gone flat. Shockeye is an out-of-control beast who must be stopped, but his death is botched and topped off with a misjudged quip. With Saward trying to be Holmes, and fandom praising his every move (conveniently forgetting stuff such as 16.5, "The Power of Kroll" and his less-than-sparkling *Blake's 7* scripts), Holmes has started to believe his own hype. He self-consciously writes comic double-acts and black humour. Fine, if they're funny. These aren't.

It's not all his fault, however. The long-form scripts make for *longeurs* even in a set-piece as tried and true as crawling through the interior of a space-station. The pace of these episodes is appalling. Moving the setting to Spain means that all the location footage has to look exotic, regardless of whether it helps the story. Even though doing a shoot in Seville in summer means that the Sontaran costumes get unbearably hot, they go for long takes. And yet it *doesn't* look at all interesting on screen. The location work simply looks like a field somewhere, an old building somewhere, a square somewhere. There's no real sense of the heat, the dust, the flavour of Spain. They could have made this story in Kent.

We might hope for a world where the location filming was the only problem here, but that's not the case. The plotting of episode three in particular seems like it was motivated to get as much goo

and as many explosions in as possible, with no reason for them to be there. The plot-logic is lost amidst the attempts by the different factions to outwit one another, assuming there *was* any plot-logic in the first place.

Even with the logistics of filming abroad requiring almost military planning, the result looks like they were making it up as they went along. The Sontarans are given things to do, but not any reason for them to be there to do them. Besides, they look terrible. The whole subplot of the Second Doctor turning into an Androgum comes out of the blue solely because there's twenty minutes left to fill, and because of this, the whole Oscar and Anita sub-plot is stretched to breaking point. Oscar (yes, the name for an Academy Award, ho ho) is the kind of character that people write when they're doing Robert Holmes-style fan-fic, so it's particularly tragic when Holmes himself walks this route. Essentially, Oscar is a diet version of Henry Gordon Jago (14.6, "The Talons of Weng Chiang"). Fair enough that using him as the lepidopterist when the Doctor needs a bit of info makes the scene a bit more interesting, but then they go and make Oscar own the restaurant too, don't they? And whilst his peroration about moths and Anita's questions about killing them make the (muffled) theme of empathy a bit more clear, the suspicion remains that he's what the author thinks of this mis-conceived Doctor. (Certainly, that seems to be the script editor's take.) We'll have the same aftertaste when it comes to Sabalom Glitz in "The Mysterious Planet" (23.1).

Yet the question remains: how could a story made explicitly "for the fans" kick those same fans in the teeth so often? How could something made with BBC licence-fee payers' money have so little regard for those people paying? The belief that people would sit watching anything that had some sunshine in it in March in Britain is how we landed up with stuff such as 21.5, "Planet of Fire" and 1992's big bummer *Eldorado* (see 4.5, "The Underwater Menace"). Like we said in the previous review, *Doctor Who* might have been wallpaper for most viewers, were it not for the free publicity. That ratings and AI stayed exactly as they were before and after the Suspension announcement, given the massive press attention, speaks volumes.

So what we've got is a story so wrong-headed from start to finish, not even the semi-legendary Robert Holmes of fan lore could have made it work. We have a script that contains things found

ABOUT TIME 1985–1989

in old *Doctor Who* stories, but put together in such a way as to appal anyone who grew up with the series and took moral lessons from it as children. We have an illogical string of badly-executed set-pieces and gimmicks, and some atrocious dialogue. Worse, it does the one thing both Holmes and *Doctor Who* should never do: it is deeply boring. In short, it's typical Season Twenty-Two crap, but whereas we'd no reason to hope for anything better from Eri... sorry, 'Paula Moore' or Pip 'n' Jane, to see this sort of stuff emerge from Holmes' typewriter just seemed like the final straw.

Is there *anything* to be said this story's favour? Patrick Troughton, Frazer Hines, Colin Baker (sometimes), John Stratton, Tony Burrough. All of whom deserved much better.

Critique (Guest Defence by Rob Shearman) It was with an uncharacteristic respect that the production team turned to Robert Holmes. If you're going to bring back the Sontarans, who better than the man who created them in the first place? If you want a story featuring Troughton's Doctor, why not employ someone who actually cut his teeth writing for the man back in the 60s? It all sounds so sensible on paper, but the reality, of course, is that Holmes couldn't be so easily pigeonholed.

For a start, he didn't create the Sontarans - he'd created *a* Sontaran. Looking at Holmes' script editing days, it's clear just how uncomfortable he was with the Generic Alien Monster that had come to symbolise *Doctor Who*, and that he was keen to set the Doctor against a single adversary. In "The Time Warrior", Linx hails from a race of clone warriors, but it's not as if we ever *see* them - instead, we get an articulate foe with intelligence and guile (like Magnus Greel from "Talons of Weng-Chiang", or Solon from "The Brain of Morbius"), but who just happens to have a head like a potato. Asking Holmes to bring Sontarans back as a *race of soldiers* was to misunderstand Holmes' style. Similarly, the reason why Nathan-Turner wanted Troughton brought back was to give an outing to the impish clown that was so popular in "The Three Doctors" and "The Five Doctors", and who fought Jon Pertwee with water pistols on stage at American conventions. Holmes clearly had no interest in this whatsoever - instead, he was drawn to the idea of writing a Doctor of age and experience, and who would provide a real contrast to the more likeable new-

bie still finding his feet. (It's telling that the first time we see the old Doctor, he's hard at work on a mission, being abrasive to all and sundry, whereas "our" Doctor is having a bit of fun larking around with a fishing rod.) Quite rightly, for dramatic reasons, Holmes is expecting audience sympathies to lie with this newer, more light-hearted and more irresponsible Doctor.

And it's this false expectation of what Holmes would bring to these returning characters which is so jarring to fan watchers - and what makes "The Two Doctors" so much more interesting. There was much criticism at the time that Troughton's Doctor was written incorrectly, but this owes to Holmes abandoning the comedic simplification of the character we'd got comfortable with, and put a bit of ambiguity back into it. It's not done through ignorance - indeed, it's done very cleverly, so that the only time we see this Doctor written for comedy (jumping about with the sort of child-like glee we'd been expecting) is when he's been turned into an Androgum and happily watches as truck drivers are clubbed to death before his eyes. To see an object of nostalgia treated this way - to show all those loveable bits of shtick only when he's an alien murderer - is cynical and angry and oh so brilliant. Like much of the story, such as the killing of Oscar in the restaurant (more on this in a moment), it is purposefully jarring, and it's one of the few times when black comedy in *Doctor Who* has been genuinely dangerous.

In the same way, Holmes takes the Sontarans - set up as the main monster of the story - and treats them as comic bits of padding. Fans have ridiculed Peter Moffat's direction as lacklustre, and the introductory scene of the Sontarans shown only in long shot has been used as an example. Whilst it's probably stretching the point to say it's a deliberate joke, there's a comic aptness that these self-important military buffoons are crashing around the story and denied the dignity of a close-up. Instead Holmes focuses upon the Androgums. The Prosecution claims that the eugenics theme in the story is fascistic - well, of course it is. But it's typical of this brave and jarring story that the themes are raised in the first place, and that we're invited to question the standard morality of a *Doctor Who* story. The basic joke of the Androgums, after all, is that if you dressed them with potato heads like the Sontarans, we'd accept their amorality all the more readily. The idea of humanoids upgrading or mutating into other creatures has been a standard staple of Holmes' stories, but whereas in the past it's been easy to reject the Wirrn (12.2, "The Ark in Space") or the Krynoids (13.6, "The Seeds of Death") because of the way they look, here the Androgums have... orange eyebrows. Oh, and a few spots. That's it. So when they look at mankind as cattle, or when they salivate over Scotsmen in kilts, the humour lies in the fact that they look *almost exactly the same* but *haven't the wit to realise it.*

The brave and cruel trick played on us at the story's heart is that all the characters similarly treat the Androgums as if they're *as* exotic and *as* alien as the Wirrn - and we get to see a story acted out with the Generic Monster Race that Holmes found so limiting played out of costume. It'd be a little like watching your standard Dalek story with John Scott Martin and Cy Town without their pepperpot casings - there'd be something much more uncomfortable watching the wholesale destruction that the Doctor visits upon the majority of alien adversaries if (to be frank) the only thing that distinguished them from us was the quality of their eyebrows.

Throughout "The Two Doctors", Holmes takes these standard expectations of *Doctor Who* and turns them back on us as a joke, yet makes the joke just a bit too disturbing to amuse us. In a season which so bravely experimented with black comedy, it's only Robert Holmes - acknowledged by fans everywhere at this point as Elder Statesman extraordinaire - who dares to hold the show's format up to satirical light. A much-loved older Doctor only falls back on his usual quirks when he's literally a monster, and the new Doctor kills Shockeye by a method which would barely occasion the merest shock were the Androgums as alien as they pretend. The main dramatic climax, to all intents and purposes, takes place in a squabble over a restaurant bill. It's what Holmes does best: taking the exotic and giving it the flavour of the banal. It's the same writer who punctured the balloon of the Time Lords by making them all bureaucrats, or who suggested an invasion of the Earth by waxwork dummies.

Ah, yes. The restaurant scene. Your appreciation of "The Two Doctors" probably rests upon whether you consider it the point where *Doctor Who* crashes off the rails into indefensible tastelessness. Robert Holmes had been writing larger than life characters like Oscar for years, but they'd all been untouchable, and their deaths as inconceivable as that of the Doctor. But not only does Oscar die, he does so making jokes about dissatisfied customers usually not leaving tips, and worrying over the safety of his moth collection. In its subtle way, his death is as shocking as Adric's - it savagely breaks the programme's safe conventions, but this time by inviting us to laugh at what should seem tragic. Oscar's last breath sees him trying to soliloquise Hamlet - badly - and there may be no funnier moment in *Doctor Who* than Peri's earnest attempts to chivvy him along and promise they'll all be there to watch his stage-performance on opening night. And it's funny precisely because you're not sure that Peri, or Nicola Bryant for that matter, is in on the gag - you can't be sure whether to laugh or cringe. And that sums up "The Two Doctors" very well, I think.

It's a bold show that plays with its audience's sensibilities so much, leaving you unsure whether it's doing something very clever or whether it's just a bit rubbish. Not until "The Happiness Patrol" (25.2) or "Love and Monsters" (X2.10) do you see *Doctor Who* being quite so daring with its audience's patience. The reputation of "The Two Doctors", then, really wasn't helped by it being the story everyone watched the Saturday after the Suspension was announced. Nor was it what was wanted by a fandom all-but-prepared to canonise Robert Holmes for giving us "The Caves of Androzani": we wanted grim 'n' serious, not this gaudy naughtiness. Really, "The Two Doctors" baffled us - it wasn't the fan treat we'd been promised, but something which felt discordant and not a little sour.

But for all that, I think it's the definitive Holmes story - the *one* time we see him let off the leash and just write for the sheer pleasure of it. It's self-indulgent, yes. It may be Holmes' finest hour - unfortunately, the whole story lasts nearly two and a half. As the Prosecution points out, the pacing is slack, lots of the plotting is irrelevant, and it seems at times to have abandoned all structure. But it's giddily brilliant, perhaps *because* it's so undisciplined. It's the one *Doctor Who* story that has the verve to be a celebration of dialogue over everything else. Dark it may be in concept, but that's offset by the sheer exuberance of a writer just having freewheeling fun. It's clearly not Holmes' best script, but I do think it's his truest, his most personal. And the only one - in its perverse and frustrating way - that ever sees a self-confessed jobbing BBC scriptwriter (who never seemed to understand just how good he was) push towards sequences of pure genius. The death of Oscar is

ABOUT TIME 1985–1989

the most inspired example of it - hilarious, shocking and thoroughly macabre.

The Facts

Written by Robert Holmes. Directed by Peter Moffatt. Ratings: 6.6 million, 6.0 million, 6.9 million. Audience appreciation warbled between 65% for episode one and 62% for episode two, then back up to 65% for episode three.

Working Titles "The Androgum Inheritance", "The Kraglon Inheritance" (although others have been cited, including "The Seventh Augmentment").

Supporting Cast Patrick Troughton (the Doctor), Frazer Hines (Jamie), John Stratton (Shockeye), Jacqueline Pearce (Chessene), Laurence Payne (Dastari), Clinton Greyn (Stike), Tim Raynham (Varl), James Saxon (Oscar), Carmen Gomez (Anita), Aimee Delamain (Doña Arana).

Oh, Isn't That..?

• *Jacqueline Pearce*. In the sixties, she'd played gypsy maidens and doe-eyed vampire victims. In the seventies, she cut off her hair and ruled the galaxy in *Blake's 7*. (For anyone unfamiliar with this series, imagine you're watching "The Caves of Androzani", when suddenly Alexis Carrington sashays across the quarry with a crew-cut, wearing a ballgown and heels. Then imagine four years of this, and that it was all over before *Dynasty* started.) Since then, Pearce has played virtually the same character in various things, often written by up-and-coming kids TV author Russell T Davies.

• *James Saxon*. He appeared in the following year's most pointless film, *Biggles* (the one with helicopters and Canary Wharf - if you bear in mind that Biggles was a WWI plot, the futility of this work begins to dawn on you). Later he was Darcey de Farcey opposite Roland Rat (see 23.1, "The Mysterious Planet", and 21.4, "Resurrection of the Daleks" for how this connects to Rodney Bewes). Most recently, he took over the title role in the remake of *Captain Pugwash* (which uses a big cast to facilitate what Peter Hawkins accomplished, unassisted, in the 60s).

• *Nedjet Salih*. Jose the Waiter will soon get his own eatery in Albert Square. His performance as Ali Osman in *EastEnders* will divide critics on

whether non-speaking roles were a better bet.

Cliffhangers (The computer, in Dastari's voice, claims that Camera's work threatened the Time Lords); an unidentified assailant attacks Peri, which distracts the Doctor from disarming an alarm - and he's gassed as a result; (Anita offers to show the Sixth Doctor to the hacienda); Peri stumbles, and a menacing Shockeye lowers over her intoning, "Here, my pretty one..."; (the Sixth Doctor begins to feel the effect of the Androgum inheritance given to his previous self).

The Lore

• As you'll recall from "The Five Doctors" (20.7), the first draft that Robert Holmes submitted for the Twentieth Birthday story was called "Maladoom" and had Cybermen trying to isolate the First Doctor's DNA to create hybrid "Cyberlords" who could travel freely in time. He evidently left the project because the producer kept throwing in extra ingredients that "had" to be there, but this time around Holmes was on a roll after his "consolation prize" story had shaken everything up ("The Caves of Androzani"). Saward loved him, but Nathan-Turner was still reluctant to have someone from the old days around - at least, behind the camera.

Meanwhile, Patrick Troughton had been sounded out about a return to the series during the making of "The Five Doctors", and the timetabling of his and Frazer Hines' availability was a deciding factor in scheduling this story. Saward and Holmes started making plans, and Nathan-Turner requested that the Sontarans be included. Holmes was reluctant, but was talked around by Saward pointing out how far the aliens had diverged, by their last appearance in "The Invasion of Time" (15.6), from Holmes' introduction of them in "The Time Warrior".

• At the time, Troughton was re-introduced to younger viewers as star of the lavish (by 1985 BBC standards) adaptation of John Masefield's book *The Box of Delights*. In this, he played a Punch and Judy man who turned out to be an immortal time-travelling wizard. He found a whole new way to play this kind of role, and held up well against scene-stealing villains (see 24.4, "Dragonfire").

• This was the peak of U.S. interest in the series. Nathan-Turner had been doing the convention circuit in America, and filming at least one story in the States kept being suggested. New Orleans in particular had beguiled the producer, as he'd been there for Mardi Gras in 1981. In fact, in that same year, Nathan-Turner commissioned Lesley Elizabeth Thomas - an American writer with much soap experience, but based in London - for a breakdown titled "Way Down Yonder", but it simply didn't gel.

By January 1984, the programme-makers felt they had the makings of a New Orleans story. Holmes racked his brain for a justification for this, and toyed with the idea of Jazz-fiend aliens, but finally plumped instead for connoisseurs of exotic food. Anagrammatising "Gourmand", he thought up - or revised from a discarded idea, perhaps - the Androgums, who were the Third Zone's indigenous life-form. They were conceptualized as beings for whom millions of years of evolution and culture were things that had happened to other people, and Holmes' idea was that they served all the other races who had come to this area. (A cut scene from episode one contained a remnant of this notion, with the Doctor telling Peri how the Androgums had millions of years to become accustomed to their lot in life.) It was also decided that the story needed to be longer - like an old-fashioned six-parter (ironically, the format that Holmes had tried to eliminate when he was script editor) - to justify the cost of the overseas excursion.

• Holmes set to making the best of this extraneous strand, and thought up some jokes about the American abuse of English, which he thought would suit this philologically-inclined Doctor. Then the BBC accountants said that visiting New Orleans was a non-starter, so the search began for touristy cities closer to home. Venice had possibilities, but the tourist season would be in full swing during the time-slot when Hines and Troughton were available. Production associate Sue Anstruther suggested Spain, and Gary Downie, this story's production manager, was sent to scout locations. He found a semi-derelict hacienda (two, in fact), a pool for fishing and several good places in Seville out of the way of too many passers-by. Holmes was shown the photos and returned to writing, finding that the character of Shockeye was coming to the fore.

• Baker already knew Troughton socially. Back in the days of "The Curse of Peladon" (9.2), Baker had shared a flat with Patrick's son David. The rehearsals and recording were kept lively with good-natured sniping: in the Las Cadeñas scene,

Baker looked at the table with the dinner and the "unconscious" Second Doctor, and made wise-cracks about the fine old hams side by side. Troughton likewise referred to his co-star as "Miss Piggy". Holmes records that the line about Jamie being hypnotised and "watch(ing) the pretty thing, how it dangles" was milked for all possible innuendoes. The good-natured teasing extended to an elaborate hoax concerning Baker's arachnophobia, with Saward preparing a dummy script and the effects team filling the actor's dressing-room with rubber jokeshop spiders.

• Elizabeth Spriggs (Tabby, one of the murderous middle-aged ladies in 24.2, "Paradise Towers") had been lined up to play Chessene. Jacqueline Pearce was a last-minute replacement, and the wig she wore originally was designed for Spriggs - this was one of the items that was mislaid in transit to Spain.

• The "Fixer" for the location shoot was Mercedes Carnegie, the consular official's wife. She was very obliging, to the point of loaning Carmen Gomez a more in-character dress for Anita. (Mrs Carnegie can be seen wearing the original dress, a flouncy number, when she throws a rose to Dastari in episode three.)

• Gary Downie had found a large hacienda on his original location scouting trip, but the one used in the final shoot was thought more suitable. However, it was being purchased by one of the Hearst family (of kidnap-victim-turned-bank-robber fame and not-at-all-the-basis-for-*Citizen-Kane* fame). Joanna Hearst had chosen Dehera Boyar for its seclusion, which was actually a drawback when it came to filming a low-budget BBC show there. It was a long drive to and from the hotel, and it proved very hard to get logistical support. Spanish customs prohibited the effects crew from importing their own pyrotechnics, so they tried to get something from Madrid - which wasn't possible for reasons of time, so they improvised with locally-sourced gunpowder.

(By the way, the villa has been the site of two return visits. One is a semi-professional "behind-the-scenes" video, presented by Nicola Bryant. The other was an earlier pilgrimage by two fans who went to all the locations and wandered around the road seen in episode three, dressed as Shockeye and the Second Doctor in his semi-Androgum stage. They had a few run-ins with the Hearst security, but found that the locals remembered the BBC crew's visit ten years earlier. It's worth scouting around on the web to find footage from this endeavour - if for no other treason than to see how devoted British fans can get, even though we like to think that only Americans do this sort of thing.)

• The shoot initially went so well, it was decided to do a couple of scenes originally intended as studio recordings. This explains why Varl and Shockeye have that odd conversation on the patio (in which Shockeye is seen chewing raw meat) - in a scene which ordinarily would have been deemed too long to be done in one take, let alone three, in that heat. However, an incident with far-reaching consequences was the costly remounting of a scene with Oscar and Anita. Film shot on location was sent to London for processing, and word came back the negative for one batch had a scratch on it. So they did some frantic rearranging and kept James Saxon and Carmen Gomez to do it again - even though it transpired that the scratch wasn't that bad. At this point, Nathan-Turner decided that film was more trouble than it was worth. The next story in production, "The Mark of the Rani", and the as-yet unwritten season ender (22.6, "Revelation of the Daleks") would be the last stories made with any film (aside from very brief effects shots, such as 24.1, "Time and the Rani").

• Stop us if you've heard these before: during recording, Baker was supposed to sprinkle a little water on Bryant's face when Peri is unconscious in episode three, but he chucked the whole jug at her. Likewise, in a pre-recorded video message for the attendees at WhoCon 21, Bryant made great play of looking up Hines' kilt as he lay supine on the same table. Despite corpsing and caught kilts, the recording went smoothly, and this story - despite the Drama department's decision not to release extra funds for shooting overseas - came in on budget with few real hitches.

• Then, on the Monday following broadcast of episode two, it was announced that the series would not be returning immediately. Regrettably, the way the press handled this news meant the public believed that the show was being axed altogether. What had actually happened was that the cost to the BBC's Drama department in making The Singing Detective and building Albert Square (it's not a real place, you know, it's what used to be Elstree Studios) required a delay in starting work on Season Twenty-Three until the following financial year. Thus the show was continuing, but the transmissions wouldn't resume until September

1986. Once this was clarified, the press - especially The Sun - told everyone they'd "saved" the show.

• However, in the botched handling of the press releases and subsequent furore, it became clear that the BBC weren't that keen to fight for a series they thought was showing its age. To be even slightly fair, many other long-running series were dropped at the same time, and even though the ratings for Crackerjack (oh, go on: "CRA-KERR-JAAAAAKK!!" Feel better?) were healthy, it was dropped too. BBC1's Controller, Michael Grade, no friend of the show (Doctor Who that is, we don't know about Crackerjack - it was probably a bit highbrow for him - and see Volume IV for more on this guy's problems) returned from a skiing holiday and found himself more famous than he'd ever been, but for all the wrong reasons.

But soon, there were mutterings about how Doctor Who had lost its way, was too violent (even though the scripts were cleared by some of the people now griping) and was too "whimsical". We'll be continuing this story as we go, but one detail is worth saying here: Troughton had been doing the rounds of the BBC as part of the build-up to this story, which entailed his popping in on Blue Peter and so forth. It just so happened that he was in the production office when the news broke. He took a stint answering the many calls from concerned fans and the press, and suggested that it was a ploy for the BBC in its latest round of talks about raising the Licence Fee. Nobody is entirely sure he wasn't right. Indeed, ten years earlier, full-page ads had shown an array of 70s monsters and said that the British Public could exterminate the Doctor where these aliens failed - just by not coughing up the cash. (By the way, Bryant was on holiday when the Suspension became public, and when the press rang her up to ask her opinion on "the death of Doctor Who", she thought Baker had died.)

• Later that week, an even worse development: Gareth Jenkins. Using the TARDIS set, the two Sontaran costumes (and the actors who had just filled them), Janet Fielding and a script by Eric Saward, a small boy's dream came true on Jim'll Fix It. For those unaware of this bizarre cultural phenomenon, former DJ and occasional charity-worker Jimmy Savile OBE (now Sir Jimmy, a title which freaks people out) devised and presented a series in which people - often children - wrote in with a wish they wanted made real. And then Savile, well, fixed it. This was surrounded by a ritual involving a badge (actually a medal) and a chair that made tea.

So Jenkins wrote in, and they went all-out to make him the star in a *Doctor Who* sketch. Entitled "Doctor Who in a Fix with Sontarans", it was recorded after Season Twenty-Two had wrapped. Bryant was unavailable to play Peri, hence the unexpected temporary reappearance of Tegan. To get the hastily-learned dialogue right, Baker finally resorted to writing on the console. During the making of this, production manager Corinne Hollingworth (later notorious for dumbing-down *The Bill*) told the studio audience that "this little girl" (pointing to Fielding) had written in. The finished clip is available on this story's DVD (but don't bother, really).

• Although Troughton had shied away from the publicity surrounding the Doctor, his most high-profile role, by the mid-1980s he was resigned to it being a major part of his CV. Indeed, he was now using a hybrid of his own personality and that of his Doctor to make more public appearances than at any time in his career. He was active in fundraising for various charities, which included Baker's favoured Cot Death Foundation, Troughton's own "pet" cause the World Wildlife Fund and the Barnardo's orphanages (for which he went on a sponsored walk with Baker, Bryant, Hines and Fielding shortly before transmission of this story). During that summer, Troughton made his first major UK Convention appearance: at the DWAS event PanoptiCon VI in Brighton.

Although Troughton was still a busy actor, and had a portfolio of films in constant re-run to keep him solvent, ill-health was taking a bit of a toll. He still saw a few close friends, and had regular golf matches with Innes Lloyd (now a very highly-regarded producer of "serious" dramas). As we will see, Troughton's involvement in the backstage story of *Doctor Who* continued until his death in March 1987. While remaining very loyal to Baker, he expressed enthusiasm and curiosity about how Sylvester McCoy would cope with being thrown into the series after such controversy. Troughton was, in fact, wearing his Doctor costume when he died at a convention in America. And there we will leave it.

22.5: "Timelash"

(Serial 6T, Two Episodes. 9th - 16th March 1985.)

Which One is This? 'Pelion on Ossa!' It's the single corniest idea in the programme's history: HG Wells stows away on the TARDIS and writes down everything he sees (invisibility, space warfare, genetic experiments, underground beasts called 'Morlox' and a time machine). However, this isn't what anyone remembers about this adventure: we know this as the one with Paul Darrow playing Richard III, a sock-puppet playing an alien warlord and a blue-faced android WITH-a-sill/ LY-way-of /TAL-king-in/ THE-tune-of/ AN-a-mer/ RI-can-in/ PA-ris. Credibility departs with a scream.

Firsts and Lasts So farewell, then, Pennant Roberts. Appropriately his final story as director is one nobody could have made work anyway (see 21.1, "Warriors of the Deep"; 15.4, "The Sun Makers"), but here he isn't even given any location filming or studio-film to make the VT stuff look like part of something bigger (see 14.4, "The Face of Evil"; 16.2, "The Pirate Planet"; 17.6, "Shada"). This story sees the first major use of a fan's handiwork inside the broadcast story - in this case Gail Bennett's painting of the Third Doctor, based on a publicity photo from 11.2, "Invasion of the Dinosaurs'.

Four Things to Notice about "Timelash"...

1. Like all good *Doctor Who* stories (and "Timelash" is *like* all good stories, without actually being one itself), there are moments when you just know that *no* other programme would show something like this. To be fair, this is usually a good thing, but in this case take a look at the Timelash's interior, Paul Darrow's performance, the unprecedented Morlox and the simply astonishing Bandril Ambassador. "Unforgettable", many fans are tempted to think with a shudder, yet "Timelash" just isn't a story that the general public talk about. This is curious, because it got strong audience appreciation figures, and achieved healthy ratings for what some were branding a "doomed" show. It's also the case that ITV were showing opposite *Doctor Who* a new, home-grown rival, *Robin of Sherwood*, that was less of an immediate success than *The A-Team*. But ask anyone now, and they'll probably claim to have been tuned to the big-haired outlaws rather than Colin

Baker's epic struggle against the Borad[8]. Maybe the trauma of seeing Paul Darrow in a Beatle-wig saying 'most people depart with a scream' caused collective amnesia.

2. *Within* fandom, however, this story's dialogue has been justifiably been held up to ridicule. From the crassest info-dump ever ('What, all five hundred of us?') to lines even experienced actors have difficulty getting out ('He's dangling on the edge of oblivion!' and what sounds like 'Sezom at the felching rock'), at least this story never gets dull. In fact, to while away this story's hour and a half, you can play a little game: some of the scenes were recorded a lot later than the rest, and a couple were squeezed in during the recording of the next story when it became apparent that "Timelash" was under-running. Eric Saward and the cast reworked all of these scenes, so see if *you* can spot where the credited author was kept well away from it.

3. It's 1985, the Year of the Shoulder-Pad. We should expect a fashion-conscious series like this to reflect the styles of the time, but *really*! The rebels-in-jump-suits, the Guardoliers and the Android all have vast sculptures on their epaulettes. (Indeed, the Android looks like he's walked in from the video for David Bowie's "Loving the Alien".) There are snoods! Put it this way: Herbert, from 1885, and the Doctor - that's the *Sixth* Doctor - are the most sensibly-dressed people on this planet.

4. But one way or another, this story isn't even incompetent enough to laugh at properly. The Borad's make-up is quite simply the best of its kind to date, and behind it is Robert Ashby giving a calmly menacing performance that deserves - no, really - to be mentioned alongside Christopher Gable as Sharaz Jek (21.6, "The Caves of Androzani") or William Squire as The Shadow (16.6, "The Armageddon Factor"). The arrival of the burning android in episode one is genuinely shocking and well-executed, and the retroactive set-up for it in episode two doesn't look corny. And in crafting Herbert as being so drastically unlike the real HG Wells as to be ludicrous, the programme-makers inadvertently get right the thing Nathan-Turner's been trying to do, unsuccessfully, since he arrived - make a companion that we like and the Doctor doesn't.

The Continuity

The Doctor He claims to still be President of the High Council of Time Lords [20.7, "The Five Doctors"], which seems to impress the Bandrils. He's pretentious even when talking to himself, comparing the spectacularly ill-timed arrival of a Bendalypse warhead with the Greek story of piling two mountains to make a bigger one. [He declares 'Pelion on Ossa!', even though it's usually Ossa that's put on top of Pelion, by giants trying to capture Olympus. The overall sentiment means "what a lot of effort for no result", not "as if I didn't have enough trouble", or even possibly "crap, we're doomed", as the Doctor seems to think here.]

• *Ethics*. When attempting to stop the oncoming Bandril missile with the TARDIS, the Doctor forcibly removes Peri from the Ship, then tells Herbert - who smuggles himself on board - that they are likely to die in the attempt. [It turns out that the Doctor stops the missile by doing something clever and unexplained, but perhaps he wanted the Karfelons and Bandrils to think he'd committed a noble self-sacrifice, in the interests of re-opening negotiations.] Evidently Megelen's experiments on the Morlox creatures [see *Background*] alarmed his younger self, but he at first treats the Borad as a person who is criminally irresponsible, rather than as a monster. Later, when the Borad captures Peri, the Doctor gains the upper hand by deploying a variety of verbal abuse against him [and in a manner which he would've never used against, say, Sharaz Jek from "The Caves of Androzani"].

The Doctor is well aware that Peri will scream when she sees the Borad, and relies on this to break a stalemate.

• *Inventory*. He has an orthodox screwdriver [fortunately Karfelon technology has not inflicted posidrive screws on the already-beleaguered populace] and a pen-torch, which this time makes a *wheeeee* noise when used. And there's a chain on his person not attached to his watch or keys.

• *Background*. The Third Doctor visited Karfel once before, along with Jo Grant. Both Tekker and the Doctor indicate that someone else was travelling with them at the time. [The extra person's identity is never revealed, but the novel *Speed of Flight* attempts to plug this hole by saying it's Mike Yates].

On that occasion the Doctor 'saved' the planet,

Did They Think We'd Buy Just Any Old Crap?

In **Why Was There So Much Merchandising?** (under 11.4, "The Monster of Peladon") we looked into the ways in which spin-off ephemera made *Doctor Who* different from most other BBC dramas of the 1960s and 1970s. To briefly sum up, the object of the toys and trinkets was to give children a way of keeping faith with the programme during the 167 hours 35 minutes a week it wasn't on screen - and, later, to show allegiance. It's that later phase that needs a bit more investigation now.

One of the side-effects of the increased exposure in the USA was that *Doctor Who* became something that could be treated like a U.S. cult series. That this was not an altogether good idea, as by comparison, the approach stateside was commercial and exclusive. Mainly this meant taking over a hotel for a long weekend and not letting the outside world intrude, but British conventions were not like the American ones, and attempts to shoehorn us into that model didn't go down too well. The outside world was, to begin with, not too different from our own. The venue's staff knew what *Doctor Who* was and assumed - for the first time, at least - that the attendees would mainly be children. But in a disturbing shift, merchandise stalls started to squeeze out fanzine tables.

If you don't know why this matters, you've not read the British fanzines. These were sarcastic, insightful and tailored very specifically to a readership who were almost known by name. As *Doctor Who Monthly* became the in-house organ of the JN-T Personality Cult and toed a party line, so fanzines begged to differ with increasing confidence. Then a semi-professional "rival" to *DWM* emerged: Gary Levy's *DWB* (later re-named as *Dreamwatch*, in case you didn't know) - and this also became predictable in its likes and dislikes, so fanzines started questioning *that* as well too. Imagine if all the newsgroups and websites knew all their readers by name, and met them twice a year. Fanzine reading was an act of collusion, and producing one involved a lot more instinct and thought than just slamming stuff into Dreamweaver and hoping someone would bite. Moreover, a fanzine cost money, and most people making them needed to recoup their outlay (and not a penny more, by law) to be able to afford to eat the following week. You needed to know your audience, or create one. This, in an era of a hundred or so fanzines a month, meant conveying a personality and being unlike all the others.

But the merchandise - or certainly some of the stuff being imported from the US - was embarrassingly gushing. Some of it was slickly-produced, and could have been for any show, just with Peter Davison's face stuck on it. All *Doctor Who* was judged as good (except the black and white stories they hadn't yet shown in America, in which case the fans took the unjustified party line and said that 3.8, "The Gunfighters" was terrible and 3.7, "The Celestial Toymaker" was perfect). So if you wanted a Barry Letts-style TARDIS key, or a pewter sonic screwdriver, or some whimsical badges, these could be had for a bit of money. And if you wanted unbelievably cheesy posters, your luck was *really* in. Being made for an American market, it was a basic assumption that only those who bought them would know what it meant. Whereas newsagents and post-offices in the UK could still sell jigsaws with K9 on them in 1987, the stuff available at conventions was only available there. (Specialist shops would soon emerge, but that's coming later in this story.)

This siege mentality spilled over into the UK, just as the general public started to think of *Doctor Who* as something that *other* people watched. The ratings may still have been buoyant, but for many parents, girlfriends, flatmates and other collateral damage, it was something that was on while they were in the room. (Indeed, with the method of collating ratings changed to account for people recording one show while watching another, many fans weren't actively watching when the episodes were broadcast.)

Once the Suspension crisis made them newsworthy, the media took to covering conventions. Unfortunately, this "coverage" was mainly lazy journos - who often didn't understand one iota about science-fiction - going in search of cut-price Trekkies so they could re-use one of three jokes: "When will you get a girlfriend?", "Why do you buy all this crap?" and "Isn't this a bit excessive for a kiddy show?" They took photos of particularly sad cases in costume - but *only* them, of course. And so people started attending conventions thinking it would all be like that.

In one sense, that actually was the case. American fans did fundraising for Public Television to keep shows they liked - *Doctor Who* included, obviously - on air. With the Suspension requiring a show of force, the potential commercial clout of fandom was one of the strongest arguments for returning stuff like "Timelash" to our screens. Some

continued on page 77...

and gave a brooch with Jo Grant's picture to the rebel Katz's grandfather. Stories of the Doctor's return became somewhat legendary among the Karfel public - until the Borad ordered the stories erased from the history books - and he made enough of an impression to have a mural of him painted under the plasterboard in the Timelash chamber.

During this unseen adventure, the Third Doctor befriended a young scientist named Megelen. However, he reported Megelen to the ruling Council for performing unethical experiments on the Morlox creatures [see **The Non-Humans** for more].

The Doctor recognises the area around Loch Ness [13.1, "Terror of the Zygons" and 4.4, "The Highlanders" were both in that neck of the woods], but he hasn't been to Andromeda for a while. [He specifies this as the 'Constellation of Andromeda', not the galaxy, so 19.1, "Castrovalva" doesn't count.] He doesn't recognise Herbert as anyone special. [So either his namedropping of HG Wells in "Horror of Fang Rock" (15.1) was a bit of a fib, or maybe Herbert is a *different* HG Wells. We think the latter is a better bet, and see **History** for more.]

The Supporting Cast

• *Peri*. Recognises a photo of Jo Grant, and knows that the Daleks [21.4, "Resurrection of the Daleks"] can build Time Corridors. [She might know the latter fact if she was paying attention to the Doctor's stray comment in "The Mark of the Rani", but her identification of Jo makes you think that Peri *did* take a written test on being a companion; see 22.1, "Attack of the Cybermen". Nonetheless, she's unfamiliar with the Daleks' shape when she finally meets some in the next story.] She's worried about her grades, and is using xenobotany as her ace-in-the-hole. [One wonders how her examiners would mark such a project.] All the corridors on Karfel look alike to her.

The TARDIS The chest is back in the console room [see Volume II], and contains a top hat, some boots and a pair of safety-belts. These attach to the console, allowing safe[r] passage through a Time Corridor. [This is obviously a fresh addition to the manifest since the days of regular lurches, as in most of Volume V and Season Twenty-One especially.] Unlike the Rani's vessel, this TARDIS has a fully-functional velocity override [22.3, "The

Mark of the Rani"]. Curiously, the Doctor uses Adric's old star-map [see 19.6, "Earthshock"] for navigation, measuring the distances between stars with his fingers and transferring these relative positions to buttons on one of the console's navigation computers. The Doctor shows no surprise at Vena's spectral appearance in the console room, and works out where she wound up by calculating the distorting effect of the TARDIS on the Kontron Tunnel that she's travelling down. Miraculously this proves correct, as the TARDIS arrives mere feet away from where Vena appeared on Earth.

As mentioned, it's never spelled out how the TARDIS detonated the Bendalypse warhead without sustaining considerable damage.

The Non-Humans

• *The Borad*. As part of his experiments on the Morlox, Megelen accidentally released Mustako-zene 80 - a cellular "solvent" - in the vicinity of one of his specimens. The scent made the Morlox excitable and it attacked Megelen; the Mustako-zene 80 caused a tissue amalgamation that caused Megelen's DNA to fuse with that of the creature. As a result, the Borad - as he is now known - is a half-Karfelon, half-Morlox with a vastly expanded lifespan (of a 'dozen centuries', he claims), amplified intellect, vast strength and a vestige of his still young-looking humanoid face. When the Doctor returns to Karfel centuries later, it doesn't occur to him that Megelen might still be alive. [So Megelen's transformation into the Borad took place after the Doctor's departure, and despite the Council being alerted to his 'unethical' experiments.]

Like the Morlox, the Borad can survive a Bendalypse warhead strike. [This must work like a neutron bomb, see 1.2, "The Daleks", and suggests that the Borad lacks a central nervous system - which makes the next part a little easier to swallow.] The Borad has also cloned himself well enough to transfer his personality and memory. [Even so, we're never sure whether the clone was the one accelerated to death by the Doctor's reflected time-beam, or whether it's the one who comes out of a closet to assault Peri, or even if perhaps *both* of them are clones. Either way, the Borad's whole deception with the face of the Old Man does seem like a level of deception too many, and see **Things That Don't Make Sense**.]

• *Morlox*. [Nobody is sure of the correct plural;

Did They Think We'd Buy Just Any Old Crap?

...continued from page 75

U.S. fan habits flourished here, such as the tendency for longer conventions to have Saturday nights given over to stars doing their party-pieces (instead of just showing old episodes most attendees had not seen, or at least not since transmission - amazingly, this was still possible even in the late 80s). Others, such as slash fiction and filking, never really caught on (not that American academics and Australian scholars twigged this: see **The Semiotic Thickness of What?** under 24.4, "Dragonfire"). But the idea of "fan" as a career-path took hold.

In America, a few groups such as Spirit of Light, Barbara Elder's organisation and the national *Doctor Who* Fan Club of America (publisher of *The Whovian Times*) sprouted as profit-making enterprises. They had exclusive deals with some of the stars and contracts with hotel chains. The BBC's deal with fandom was that if any self-made thing didn't infringe copyright, and didn't make a profit, they would turn a blind eye. British-made semi-pro projects were done initially because it was the only way to make something good enough; making a profit was a compromise between a professional-looking product and the long-term commitment of an amateur. Reeltime, BBV and Big Finish all started in this way.

For a hardcore of fans, spending money on trinkets was not only missing the point, it was a betrayal of what the programme was about. The commodity-fetish of auctions, even for charidee[10], was galling. It was taking the items from the BBC (and thus, effectively, publicly owned by those of us who paid license fees) and concentrating it in private collections. Stalls selling old merchandise were irksome, as the best prices were for the ones that had not been loved enough to get damaged. Worst of all was the assumption that we, as fans, were homogeneous and would buy any old tosh with the logo on.

We've already given the oxygen of publicity to Gary Downie's *Doctor Who Cookbook* (in which John Scott Martin explains how to make "Dalek Bake with Exterminate Topping"- it's fish, basically) and Joy Gammon's *Doctor Who Pattern Book*, advertised with the unforgettable strapline "Knit the TARDIS", but there was more. So was much more...

• **Franklin's Bow-Wows** was an association of fans of Richard Franklin. (If you need reminding, he'd been Captain Mike Yates in the Pertwee stories.) Quite what they did is anyone's guess, and our lawyers have advised us not to speculate. However, at this time he was also playing the Fringe at the Edinburgh Festival with a UNIT-themed farce - *Recall UNIT or The Great Teabag Mystery* - and getting involved in local politics. We're listing him under "merchandise" simply because the badges for the Bow-Wows (the name is to do with the song "Daddy Wouldn't Buy Me a Bow-Wow", as whistled by Sarah Jane at the end of 14.2, "The Hand of Fear" and sung by Yates in a silly costume in the play) were more visible second-hand on stalls than worn by people. At the end of a convention, you could get one free with every purchase. The badge depicted a big bone. Our lawyers have asked us to remove the next comment.

• **Kits and Models.** We've got to mention two in particular. First, Stuart Evans made construction kit Daleks and others. The Dalek models were good enough to be used in "Revelation of the Daleks" (22.6) and his Ice Warriors led to speculation that they would be returning soon (see 23.2, "Mindwarp"). Also, Sue Moore made exquisite plastic models of older monsters, including a very delicate Menoptra and Sensorites more alien than the televised version. Soon, she was making models given as awards to writers who won DWAS and *DWM* polls. By 1987, she was making puppets and prosthetics for the programme, beginning with Eric (the furry thing that nips McCoy's hand) in 24.4, "Dragonfire" and culminating in The Destroyer in 26.1, "Battlefield". (She also worked on the salacious *Spitting Image* style romp *Auf Weidersehen Doc* and the real *Spitting Image*.) But if we're talking about models...

• **Dapol.** In the 70s, Palitoy made Giant Robots (from, errrr, 12.1, "Robot") and a Leela that flattered Louise Jameson. In the States, Bandai made poseable action figures for any show going - except one. So when Welsh doll-makers Dapol, makers of effigies of the Royal Family, moved into *Doctor Who* merchandising, it looked like a guaranteed moneyspinner. Especially as they hardly had to change the moulds. They say they made each one from scratch, but fans have enjoyed

continued on page 79...

the Borad ought to know and calls them "Morloxes", but the Doctor and everyone else dubs them just "Morlox".] They smell like over-ripe fruit, and go wild when exposed to the scent of Mustakozene 80. [They refrain from making 'Boom-Chicka Wah-Wah' noises, mercifully.]

• *Bandrils*. The glimpses we're given via the 3D communicator suggest that they're reptiles. The ambassador who addresses the Karfel Council members looks like a cross between a King Cobra and Prince Philip, and is lit from below in red light. [So they may have a planet orbiting an old sun or have eyes adapted for infra-red - or perhaps they're just developing their holiday snaps.] Like the Karfelons, the Bandrils know of the Doctor and the Time Lords, and they're able to convey messages to the High Council on Gallifrey. Their missiles with Bendalypse warheads are capable of destroying Karfel. For all their skill, the Bandrils face starvation in a recent famine, and it's the negotiations over grain supplies that have led to war with the Borad. [On this point, see **Things That Don't Make Sense.** By the way, we've no way of knowing how big the Bandrils are - they could be fifty metres tall for all we know, and have a dozen arms below the bottom of the viewscreen. To put it another way, we need not assume that they're only the size of someone's hand, even if they *look* like sock-puppets.]

Planet Notes

• *Karfel*. A purple, windswept place, albeit also a heavy exporter of grain to the 'neighbouring' planet Bandril. The ruling Citadel contains - as we're told in a rather blatant info-dump - five hundred Karfelons [although we don't know if that number includes the rebels who occupy the catacombs, and are based at what the novelisation says is called 'the Falchion Rocks' - which is *not* what dirty-minded viewers thought it was named]. Karfel is also home to the Morlox, raven-ous reptilian creatures with elongated necks.

The Citadel's décor is muted, and lacks shiny surfaces and mirrors. [This is apparently in keep-ing with the Borad being unable to stand the sight of himself, although it's arguably overkill since he never ventures out of his command chamber any-way.] Such decoration as there is includes import-ed Bandril plants. The entire complex is moni-tored via CCTV, and the Inner Sanctum where the Council meets has a 3D projector unit for com-muniques from either the Bandrils or the Borad's

public-relations face. There are seven chairs, one of them taller than the others for the Maylin - an appointed administrator - and a diamond-shaped doorway that manifests the Timelash. This is a one-way [albeit two-way if you've got a TARDIS] time-corridor to twelfth century Scotland, used as a punishment for rebels. People fade from view when consigned to this fate, and the Timelash's interior looks like a fridge lined with tinfoil. While lowering himself inside this portal, the Doctor finds a sheer wall of what looks like hexagonal pylons, of various lengths, with striated lights. On some of these are the Kontron crystals used for the time-distortion. [And it's notable that these look a bit like the Crystal of Kronos, from 9.5, "The Time Monster".]

The Borad requires nearly, if not all, of the Citadel's excess energy for his time experiments. Indeed, the Maylin has ceremonial and judicial duties, but is mainly required to switch power through from the generators to the Borad's vault as instructed. Renis, the incumbent Maylin, com-plies with an order to close down the hospital sys-tems, even though his wife is on life-support there [and we're never told if she survives or not].

History

• *Dating*. It's said that the Timelash consigns its victims to Scotland, 1179. The TARDIS deflects Vena's path down the Timelash to 1885, where the Doctor recovers Vena and meets Herbert. At story's end, Herbert drops a name-card that reads 'Herbert George Wells', and so the Doctor and Peri think he's the future author of *The Time Machine* and *Kipps*.

[That's what they *think* anyway, but who pre-cisely is this 'Herbert George Wells'? He's not blond, is rather taller than the famous one, has religious inclinations antithetical to his illustrious namesake, and no trace of a cockney / Kentish accent. He shows no sign of having any knowl-edge of biology, all the ladies in this story find him entirely resistible ("our" HG apparently smelled of honey, according to one of his many, many con-quests, the feminist and novelist Rebecca West) and his eyes are brown rather than blue.

[He lets people call him 'Herbert', rather than the preferred "George" (even George Pal - see **Where Did This Come From?** got that one right), and also seems to be independently wealthy, rather than the son of a below-stairs maid who eked out a living as a student teacher and

Did They Think We'd Buy Just Any Old Crap?

...continued from page 77

themselves trying to prove otherwise. Their first batch coincided with 24.1, "Time and the Rani", and Mel wore a blouse of the kind that nobody had donned since Diana Spencer married into the mob, so that was easy. To some eyes it also seems that Prince Charles is trying to pass as a scarfless Tom Baker.

It gets a bit trickier when you get the improbably svelte Ice Warriors (Fergie?), but by this stage there were other problems. A two-armed Davros did the rounds. The pentagonal TARDIS console raised a few eyebrows, and K9 seemed to come in every colour before they finally issued him in silver. By the way, people openly called the Dapol Sontaran figure "Mr Hankie".

Their Daleks, however, were great fun, especially if you raced them on polished surfaces.

• **Travels Without The TARDIS** by Jean Airey and Laurie Haldeman. One day this will be made into a film, a bit like *Thelma and Louise* but with spray-on water repellent, and two large American ladies standing to attention when *God Save the Queen* is played. Aside from the oft-repeated howler about getting to Leeds Castle (taking a train from King's Cross to Leeds and then a taxi to Maidstone - get a map if you can't see what's wrong), there are many curious notions to be found. Preferring visiting a gravel quarry to going to Blackpool in August, however, is possibly a good call. Full marks for their advocacy of Indian takeaways, by the way.

• **"Doctor Who Is Going To Fix It"** by Bullamakanka. Folk Music Alert! Australian fans invariably apologise for this, but it's infectious (the first few times), affectionate and tongue-in-cheek, and thus scores a lot higher than - for instance - "Doctor ?" by Blood Donor. It's about watching the reruns "half past six on the ABC, just before the news, no ads to interrupt me on an interstellar cruise". The verse is as close as legal to the sig. tune, and the chorus gets better the drunker you are or the less sleep you've had.

There were quite a few bad records based on the show, most from the 1960s, and we ought to mention a few more just to (partially) excuse Ian Levine for thinking that "Doctor In Distress" ever had a hope in hell of charting. After all, Mankind's naff disco version of the theme made it onto *Top of the Pops* in 1978 (vocoder lyrics over the middle-eight: "He is of the Time Lords, Guardians of Time and Space" yadda yadda). The other chart hit is so bizarre we'll discuss it in detail under "Remembrance of the Daleks" (25.1).

But lurking in the back-catalogues of many a Tin Pan Alley hack are lots of ill-judged singles by Roberta Tovey (see the Appendix) and Frazer Hines (see 6.2, "The Mind Robber"). Amazingly, you may have got this far without knowing that "I Want To Spend My Christmas With a Dalek" ever existed. Lucky you. And it's far from being the worst - as anyone who's endured Jon Pertwee's effort "I Am the Doctor" will testify, before breaking into a cold sweat.

• **Make Your Own Adventure With Doctor Who**. The U.S. version was called *Find Your Fate*, which could be a sign that we're more existentialist than the Americans and don't do predestination. It was the Livingstone and Jackson formula, a paperback with multiple-choice endings to each section, so you went back and forth through the text making decisions.

"You" were a ten-year-old boy in this, and the Doctor and Peri needed your help. Six volumes were issued, written by such luminaries as David Martin. You know, the one who'd been Bob Baker's other half in the 70s - amazingly his first effort had his creations K9 (15.2, "The Invisible Enemy"), Drax (16.6, "The Armageddon Factor") and Omega (10.1, "The Three Doctors" and no mention of 20.1, "Arc of Infinity") - but not the Doctor. (That the book was titled *Search for the Doctor* somewhat gave this away.)

However, the balance is restored with his other book (*The Garden of Evil*), in which the human race is relocated to Gallifrey and given an unflattering abbreviated nickname ("Riffs", as in "Refugees"; rather like "Mutts" in 9.4, "The Mutants" or "Trogs" in 15.5, "Underworld"). The "you" in this case is a psychic called "Wings", who isn't remotely like the eponymous *Sky* from that HTV serial. (You know... the one where Bob 'n' Dave tried to prove they could go seven episodes without reusing anything Bob Holmes had suggested to them.)

Also brought out of mothballs was William Emms (3.1, "Galaxy Four"), who recycled "The Imps" (see 4.5, "The Underwater Menace") and showed why the stuff with Professor Zaroff was

continued on page 81...

occasional columnist. It's probably not worth the effort of trying to identify the Doctor and Peri's 'Herbert' - unlike the hoops we jumped through for **Whom Did They Meet at the Roof of the World?** under 1.04, "Marco Polo" - but hopefully we've illustrated that much of what's here differs from the historical record.]

There's no clue of when events on Karfel take place, save that they *don't* occur in 1179, as the Timelash goes there from another era. [There's a discrepancy, though, in that the Third Doctor gave the medallion of Jo Grant to Katz's grandfather, yet the Borad implies that he last encountered the Doctor 'centuries' ago. A few possibilities: the people of Karfel are naturally long-lived, or perhaps the planet has a very rapid orbit of their sun. As neither Jo's photo nor the accompanying lock of hair looks all *that* old, we might assume that the Borad is claiming that he *will* live that long or they have very short years on Karfel.]

The Analysis

Where Does This Come From?   The Ninth Circle, we suspect. But less literally...

American shows of this type almost inevitably include HG Wells, usually as a comical old buffer who talks in what Yanks think is a British accent. And they always assume that, far from just writing up the experiences of his un-named and unreliable friend who claimed to have seen big butterflies at the end of all life (see X1.2, "The End of the World"), Wells *himself* built and operated a Time Machine. And being an Eminent Victorian, he ensured that it was made of wrought iron and quilted leather.

Now, as we've already hit upon in **History**, the biographical details of the Herbert George Wells who wrote the books and the one in "Timelash" are so divergent, it's probably just a matter of mistaken identity. But even if they got it right, the basic idea of Wells' 1895 novella runs very much counter to all the crap that American TV has him saying. For a kick-off, the Time Machine itself is clearly a bicycle.

All right, put a bookmark in at this page, close this book and go away and read *The Time Machine*.

You back already? Right, remember the description of the machine? No, you don't - there isn't one. What you get is mention of a handlebar, a saddle and panniers. As with everyone in 1895, Wells was amused and excited by the freedom

cycling gave the ordinary man and woman (see 5.2, "The Abominable Snowmen"). Allied to that was his enthusiasm for science, socialism and education for the masses. He did a simple thought-experiment on what would happen if the class divisions still dominating education, access to resources and choice of marriage-partner continued into an evolutionary timescale. Thus, the Eloi in *The Time Machine* were tiny, ineffective aristocrats (with a name that's from the Greek for "gods"), and who relied on the lumpenproletariat - now adapted for life in factories - for all their finery. But the Morlocks (the proles) ate the Eloi. This isn't too far from Dickens' *Hard Times*, but with the metaphors taken literally by someone who's read a lot of TH Huxley. (See **What Were Josiah's 'Blasphemous' Theories?** under 26.2, "Ghost Light".)

But, of course, Hollywood in 1960 wasn't about to have any radical ideas polluting the vital bodily essences of its consumers, so George Pal made *The Time Machine* movie as a period-piece, and rendered the Morlocks as simple brutish monsters. As we saw in volumes I and II, the U.S. idea of Victorian Britain as a source for improbable adventure movies kicked off with Disney's *Twenty Thousand Leagues Under the Sea* (and, yes, Nemo hated the British in the book, but they went and cast James Mason, who is unavoidably Welsh). The various undersea / centre of the Earth / moon / North Pole adventure films that various studios churned out right up into the Disco era all have this idea that kids - especially Americans - like seeing Victorian machinery more than they like seeing push-button controls. So Wells' machine, as made by Pal's chums, was trotted out in various disguises (and as itself in *Gremlins*). Even the two Peter Cushing Dalek flicks went in for this, rather than having a futuristic TARDIS (and why not, it was the same Milton Subotsky who made these that had Doug McClure drilling to the North Pole and finding dinosaurs in Atlantis).

Which brings us around to our original point. For all of these reasons, Hollywood has sold us a fictitious character called "HG Wells", usually in a bowler hat. It's the young version of this chap who's (allegedly) presented here, just as Spielberg had inflicted a *Young Sherlock Holmes* on us that same year. Before long, Spielberg and Lucas would provide work for two ex-Doctors (Jon Pertwee and Colin Baker) when they launched *Young Indiana Jones*. Prequelitis hit Hollywood,

Did They Think We'd Buy Just Any Old Crap?

...continued from page 79

more like what they could afford to do in 1967. In Emms' *Mission to Venus*, Captain Burrigan is a more interesting character than this format of book requires, which is a big stumbling block, but alone of all of them he gets the Doctor right. If only his idea about sailing ships in space had been reconsidered *before* "Enlightenment" (20.5)...

The remaining three books were done by Pip and Jane Baker (they were better at this, actually, than writing television), Philip Martin (there was no keeping him away from the show, was there? - he at least seems to have read / played books like this before) and, er, Michael Holt (author of the *Doctor Who Quiz Book* series, copies of which would clutter up remainder bookshops for decades to come). His book (*Crisis in Space*) has a character called Turlough who is almost, but not quite, totally wrong from the TV version. Moreover, it seems to have been written for five-year-olds who might be excited by the Defenstration of Prague and spaghettification by Black Holes. (Ponder, for a second, the fact that this was published and David Banks' proposal - which became the *New Adventures* book *Iceberg* - wasn't.)

Confusingly, two of the later titles were advertised as *The Dominators* (naming no names, but it's set on Tokl, see 22.2, Vengeance on Varos") and *The Space Pirates* (windjammers and self-replicating gold robots suggest that it's "The Imps" / "Voyage to Venus") until someone at the BBC had a word. The British imprint Severn House used illustrations by Gail Bennett (see **The Lore** in "Timelash"), inevitably, but she curiously seems to think Mark Strickson was waist-high to Colin Baker. The U.S. editions were classier, and more readily available in Britain.

While British kids got the single-player gamebooks, RPG purists were catered to by Fantasimulations Associates (FASA) of Chicago who produced a big-boxed *Doctor Who* game and multiple spin-off "game modules" and "sourcebooks". The game was by all accounts unplayable - an alternative system published by Virgin in 1991 was similarly incomprehensible - but the rule books made entertainingly strange reading. (We like the idea, put forward in the Virgin verson, of briefly-fashionable popstrelle Betty Boo being a companion. The video for her "Where Are You, Baby?" looks like "Timelash" with a budget, and it's no more daft than getting Bonnie Langford or Billie Piper. And - gosh, we're excited! - we're get-

ting Kylie for Christmas in X4.0, "Voyage of the Damned", but see also X2.7, "The Idiot's Lantern". She's the first person to get a mention in the series as a real-world "event" and later turn up playing a role, although Ringo Starr came close - see 2.8, "The Chase", 22.6, "Revelation of the Daleks".)

FASA also turned out two "Solo Play Adventure Game" books (won't that make you go blind?) by William H. Keith Jr, who made a living doing such things and is now slightly better known for co-writing a novel with *Babylon 5*'s Londo Mollari.

• **Spirit of Light Posters** came in various degrees of awfulness, from the mildly naff Andrew Skilleter ones that resembled second-string Heavy Metal album covers, to airbrush portraits of the Doctors in the style we associate with Sri Lankan musicals - thence to "The Doctor Lives!" As far as one can tell from looking at it, this depicts the Borad wearing Tom Baker's costume.

Then we had the wildly optimistic "Watch Out America! Who is Here", which showed someone in the Fifth Doctor's clothes striking a stern pose, much like Wolverine or Ice-T. It seemed like the pinnacle of cheese - but we were wrong. The twenty-fifth anniversary ushered in a deeply wrong poster apparently showing seven former Government ministers in bad wigs and with orange skin.

There were some good ones, like the circle-closing one of Tom Baker in the style of Toulouse-Lautrec's *Aristide Briant*. There were big versions of a few over-familiar photos. But then there's the one of the Master (or maybe Derren Nesbitt in a false beard) being pelted with ball-bearings and earrings.

• **Doctor Who: Journey Through Time**. First there were the annuals, which filled stockings at Christmas, featured dreadful stories that bore no resemblance to the series from whence they came, and ended up at the local jumble sale or on the bonfire. World Distributors had been doing these since 1965, though the Suspension killed them off.

Then came the gift books, which repackaged stories and features from earlier annuals. It's beginning to sound a bit dodgier, but it was acceptable in an age when *Doctor Who* fans aspired to own a complete collection of Weetabix cards or Target novelisations. Even the *Doctor Who*

continued on page 83...

and would provide franchise extensions for many characters who - frankly - deserved better. Apparently, Herbert grew up into the annoying little time traveller who provided excuses for parallel-world adventures on *Lois and Clark*.

Meanwhile, in the remains of the British film industry, we're just entering that phase when every film made is set in Edwardian England, includes Judi Dench and Helena Bonham-Carter and is adapted from either EM Forster or something about India - possibly both. Just as the timing of Peter Davison's costume and *Chariots of Fire* was too propitious to be by chance, so Herbert here looks like the kind of male sidekick the Doctor ought to have had in 1985, and the whole thing suddenly looks twice as calculated as it did.

In a wider sense, "Timelash" is a story that really shows how far today's surveillance mentality was viewed (so to speak) whilst it was coming to be accepted. In this adventure, it's a given that cameras and microphones capture everyone's words and actions, and nobody is happy about it. Compare this to the way in which BOSS in "The Green Death" (10.5) monitors 'unauthorised footsteps'. Big chemical compounds doing controversial work have cameras connected to a computer, but the system on Karfel is presented as hysterical science-fiction scaremongering. During the Miners' Strike, which took place in (of all years) 1984, the thing that scared many people wasn't the police wearing riot-gear as a matter of course, nor their being used for political ends, but that they had video-cameras and were taking footage of anyone deemed a potential troublemaker. The same was happening at Greenham Common. Even people who weren't too keen on striking miners and anti-Nuclear protesters thought this was a bit sinister.

Using a one-way time corridor as a penal system is an old idea; Robert Silverberg did it two separate ways. In the early 80s, the most popular version of this was Julian May's *The Saga of the Exiles*, with a whole mini-series-worth of colourful misfits going to Pleistocene Europe and being enslaved by aliens who gave them advanced psychic powers. (Can you see what might happen next?) As with so many bestsellers of this period, this fashionable "science-fiction-for-people-who-don't-like-science-fiction" title is a one-line pitch someone could have told you about, without your having to bother reading the stuff (see 19.3, "Kinda").

More overtly (and we have to say it somewhere), Paul Darrow has pilfered his entire Maylin Tekker schtick from Sir Laurence Olivier's *Richard III* (see 6.6, "The Space Pirates" and of course 1.6, "The Aztecs"). Admittedly, there were some vague hints of this even on paper, but at least Darrow's alterations allow for a few hints of character in such a linear role. We could make some crack about the use of a benign 'public relations' face for a hideous alien government, and how anyone would have to be mad to rip off 4.7, "The Macra Terror", but it's beneath us.

Things That Don't Make Sense Fundamentally, the Timelash is a daft idea. You send rebels back in time to an inhabitable planet, on which each new arrival would be greeted by the previous anti-government forces. After a few years, you've created a community united in their hatred of you, and they've probably got enough technological nous to overcome the locals and turn them into an army. After a few centuries, it's entirely possible that their descendants will come and beat up your ancestors.

Indeed, were it not for the fact that the banished Karfelons appear to have all wound up splashing down in Loch Ness - and arguably drowning on arrival - we could surmise that a big Karfelon rebel population lives in Inverness, established since 1179 at the latest. If so, and leaving aside the possibility of three women mysteriously appearing a bit earlier circa 1050 AD and telling Macbeth a thing or two, the biggest Thing That Doesn't Make Sense about "Timelash" is that the "rebels in Inverness" scenario was totally ignored, even though it's far more interesting than anything that made it onto the screen. Besides, what if the Karfel exiles established themselves as the Scots royal line? This makes all British history, especially since 1603, very weird. Never mind Queen Victoria being a werewolf, why have we not heard more about this?

Back on Karfel, the government has a problem with rebels, yet the Guardoliers leave acid-spitting plants lying about in the municipal flower-beds. And as Peri proves, this acid can harm the Guardoliers despite the bee-keeper veils on their helmets. [Surely, the whole point of having the veils is to protect the Guardoliers from *some* sort of attack? Unless, that is, the actors playing them requested anonymity.] Speaking of plants, we're told that Bandril is a world that's stricken with

Did They Think We'd Buy Just Any Old Crap?

...continued from page 81

Special of 1985, the heaviest of these compendia, was basically aimed at this market but...

It was reprinted. In America. In 1986. With horrid new cover art (British readers got a publicity photo of Colin) and a slipcase decorated with *exactly the same cover art*. It was no longer a book aimed at Weetabix fetishists, but at the people who were willing to stump up $1,500 for Al Hirschfeld caricatures of the Doctors. And inside were reprints of the incoherent stories and unrecognisable art that had blighted British Christmases twenty years ago. On the plus side - and anyone who's forked out for the recent wafer-thin new series annuals will sympathise - you got a big book for your money.

• **The Key to Time. (Yes, the actual one!)** At an auction at PanoptiCon in 1987, the prop for the complete Key was the prize lot. Never mind that there were so many components already on the market, and that the complete Key was never seen on screen (except the one that exploded), this was the proverbial It. Bidding was brisk, and a price of several hundred quid for this lump of perspex seemed possible.

Then from the back of the auditorium came a clear, loud voice. *One... Thousand... Pounds!* A gasp went up, and those who recognised the voice knew that it was no joke. Andrew Beech had the money and the will to do it. As co-ordinator of the Doctor Who Appreciation Society (DWAS) he was a name, and even to this day is the press' go-to guy for opinions. Earlier that week, he had publicly slated Sylvester McCoy's debut. The cheque was paid and Beech vanished as swiftly as he had come.

Another Key to Time showed up later. Beech, a lawyer, made enough money eventually to quit and just be a fan full-time. In the early days of 2007, he was hoaxed by Channel Four's *The Friday Night Project* (with guest host David Tennant) when Big Finish owner Jason Haigh-Ellery secretly made off with Beech's Key to Time, and it was offered at a fake auction while Beech was present. Despite moments like this - or perhaps because of them - Beech is less of a figure of fun now than he is a role-model, someone who has his priorities sorted out and is a lot more comfortable with life than he seemed back then.

• *The Key to Time* (not the actual one). Home computers were now affordable and widespread,

especially in the homes of pasty young men who were now felt to be *Doctor Who*'s default audience (see **LOAD: "What Did the Computer People Think?"** under 21.6, "The Caves of Androzani" - and indeed much of Volume V). The BBC had their own branded machine, marketed by Acorn, which possessed of a mighty 32K RAM and was ubiquitous in schools and on Sunday afternoons in *Micro Live*.

This was called "synergy" and *Doctor Who* had its part to play, with BBC Software issuing two games that - unhelpfully - were only available as BBC / Acorn-friendly software. Perhaps realising this was a mistake, the BBC subcontracted the third game - *Doctor Who and the Mines of Terror* - to Micro Power for release in several formats. It was launched to coincide with *Doctor Who*'s triumphal return to our screens in autumn 1986, and promoted in popular gaming magazines by full-page colour adverts showing a close-up of a human brain and very little else. This was, perhaps, a tactical error.

Undeterred, the BBC licensed *Dalek Attack* in 1992, then returned to the fray themselves with *Destiny of the Doctors* in 1997. This was meant to cash in on another triumphal return of *Doctor Who* in its new multi-million dollar Americanised format, but actually surfaced to appalling reviews, dreadful sales and legal action. Since then - and despite the obvious potential if they got it right - the BBC has been reluctant to exploit *Doctor Who* in software form. (The sad fact is that the Master hosted this game, and Anthony Ainley is better here than he was in most of his TV appearances in the role. Nevertheless, when discussing his adversary in various incarnations, his comment on Tom Baker is, 'Don't make me laugh'. At this point, fans invariably shout at the screen: "No, *don't* make him laugh!")

While the BBC flailed, the home computer boom put the technology into the hands of people with enough ingenuity, enthusiasm and programming skills to write their own games, and it's not surprising that there was a boom of unofficial and parody games based on TV series. Text-based "adventure games" were easy to write and easier to mock up on commercially available software packages. The Doctor's most memorable appearance in the 8-bit world is as a character in Runesoft's *Spoof* in 1984. The same year, Lumpsoft issued a parody of the series as *The Key to Time*, fol-

continued on page 85...

famine and therefore importing grain from Karfel - a planet that's rendered on screen as a barren and probably uninhabitable.

The Citadel looks like the product of a technologically advanced race, yet they apparently can't power the local hospital's life-support equipment and the Borad's time experiments at the same time. And what exactly *are* these 'time experiments'? All we see are the Timelash and his time-acceleration ray - the latter of which he only uses when punishing people for plotting against him. Or, apparently, when he just feels like aging them just for a lark. [We tried and failed to think of a reason - other than pure sadism, perhaps - why the rebel Aram is hauled before the Borad early on to get zapped, as opposed to just casting her down the Timelash with the rest of her cohorts.]

Alleged "time experiments" aside, the other big scientific undertaking that we learn about - in what looks like a flagrant exercise in stretching episode two out to 45 minutes or so - is the Borad's clone. He uses this because he worries that the people will destroy him if they discover his true form, even though he on occasion reveals himself to his foes before vanquishing them. But otherwise, he uses his Ventriloquist's doll. So the point is... do the Borad and his clone have a power-sharing arrangement? Because if not, two (awkward) possibilities present themselves: either the Borad in the chair was the clone, which suggests that the genuine article is directing both him and the Old Man from inside another, even-more-secret secret HQ, *or* the one that grabs Peri was the clone and left growing in a vat in case of emergencies - and was instantly updated on recent events via some sort of telepathic feed. The latter is more plausible in plot terms, but either scenario raises the question of how you accurately clone a Karfel-Morlox hybrid that was created by a freak accident. Plus, if the Borad has cloning technology, his scheme to breed with a Peri-Morlox hybrid (which biologically is just as likely to go wrong as right) seems misguided when he could just make an army of Mini-Borads. [The novelisation tells us what this could have been like. Maybe even Saward knew there were limits...]

The Borad must prize loyalty among all else, because he kills Maylin Renis for ignoring Mykros' vague talk of treason, yet overlooks Tekker's gross incompetence for letting Vena steal the all-important amulet and falling down the Timelash with it. Fine, that sounds plausible, but it's later amazing - after much of episode one is spent retrieving the amulet from Earth - to watch Tekker brazenly strut about the Timelash chamber (now packed with even more rebels than before) with the recovered item as if nothing had happened, and he doesn't even chain the amulet around his neck this time. [To lose one irreplaceable amulet down a non-stop time corridor to twelfth century Scotland might be considered an oversight, but to wilfully risk it happening a second time...]

While we're discussing Tekker: he clearly wants to hold Peri's life to ransom, yet he seems utterly unconcerned if she sticks her face into an acid-squirting plant while the Doctor is in the room. As a means of forcing the Doctor to do his bidding, letting Peri get scarred worse than The Abominable Dr Phibes out of sheer laziness seems an odd way of going about it. Then Tekker finally decides to rebel against the Borad, but he foolishly threatens the dictator while standing directly in front of the super-aging ray that he's seen the Borad kill someone with an hour earlier. Anyone care to guess how Tekker's term as Maylin comes to an end?

Back to the Borad, who seems to treat Peri's arrival as a marvellous opportunity to create a mate for himself, which makes one wonder if Karfel women are such dogs that he hasn't tried to create a female Morlox hybrid well before now. When the rebels prevail in the council chamber against four Guardoliers and one Android, the Doctor urges everyone to leave because the Borad will soon 'flood the area with troops'. True, so why - if the Timelash is so important - didn't the Borad just do that in the first place? It's not like the rebels were in danger of going anywhere, so committing more resources to the assault seems like common sense.

We should expect anachronisms in a story about time-shenanigans, but nothing as grotesque as someone from Victorian England saying 'Holy mackerel!' [It was popularised in the 1930s radio series *Amos 'n' Andy*, and was the title of a Lodge chief. There's some debate about the origins of the phrase, and it might date back to the early 19th century - either way, Herbert would be very unlikely to use it.] But then, even setting aside the evidence which suggests that young Herbert *isn't* HG Wells [and here we refer you back to **History**], let's just consider his response to having unaccompanied ladies materialising in his room. There are books of etiquette for all circumstances

Did They Think We'd Buy Just Any Old Crap?

...continued from page 83

lowed up with an *Avengers*-spoof in 1985. The highpoint of this mini-genre of TV parodies was a merciless pisstake called *Robin of Sherlock*; even in the world of computer-gaming the Doctor was being outclassed by the other side.

The Oric 48K computer had a few borderline-legal crossovers in its games (it was named after Orac, the annoying computer in *Blake's 7*, so what did you expect?), *Brian Bloodaxe* had a cameo appearance by a Dalek (fortunately nobody bought it, so Terry Nation's rottweiler-like lawyers didn't sue), and another game was in fact called *Attack of the Cybermen* - but these alien menaces were seen off by the hero, Percy the Robot.

• **The Doctor Who Stained Glass Window.** Produced by the Doctor Who Fan Club of America in 1985 for $125 as an attractive collectible item that would appreciate in value over time. A recent *Doctor Who* merchandise guide ventured the opinion that a near mint example today would now be worth... $125.

• **Video Nasties.** By the mid-1980s video hardware had become comparatively inexpensive and was soon embraced by fans looking to make their own homebrewed *Doctor Who* stories. Some took this more seriously than others - particularly in America where companions were invariably played by chunkier performers than their TV equivalent (see, for instance, Jonathan Blum's "Time Rift"; inadvertently hilarious on so many levels) - but those with professional ambitions saw the potential in non-fiction videos. Enter Keith Barnfather's Reeltime Pictures, whose interview series *Myth Makers* ran for almost twenty years and made presenter Nicholas Briggs a fan celebrity long before he was hired as BBC Wales' renta-monster-voice. *Myth Makers* got increasingly ambitious, adding elaborate effects and fictional components. Why not, some fans whispered, actually make some proper *Doctor Who* stories for the direct-to-video market...? Well, because it was illegal, but let's not worry about that right now.

Reeltime got round it by acquiring the rights to use Sergeant Benton "from television's *Doctor Who*" as the star of his own story, the vaguely supernatural thriller *Wartime* (1988). Aside from demonstrating why John Levene never became a leading man, it's now memorable for the behind-the-scenes incident in which Briggs and future TV series composer Mark Ayres were almost shot by anti-terrorist police who'd mistaken the production for an IRA cell. (See also **What Are the Dodgiest Accents in the Series?** under 4.1, "The Smugglers"). *Wartime* was reasonably successful and Reeltime began plotting a follow-up, *Downtime*, with a script by proper telly writer Marc Platt, direction by Christopher Barry (see 1.2, "The Daleks" and nine others) and starring Nicholas Courtney, Elisabeth Sladen, Deborah Watling and indeed anyone else available and willing to recreate their TV roles. The rights to the Yeti weren't a problem, curiously (see 6.1, "The Dominators" for why this is interesting), but they played second fiddle to 'Chillies' (zonked-out students) as the Great Intelligence's pawns in his fiendish scheme to conquer Hampshire. This didn't appear until 1995, by which time *Doctor Who* was long off the air and unofficial semi-pro video spinoffs were everywhere, feeding a demand for fans who liked their spinoffery to have proper telly actors, no matter how much they might have let themselves go in the interim.

(And this cannot be overstated: the people who bought these things did so for the stars, not the plots. A video with a cast of twenty was sneered at within earshot of one of the authors because "there's nobody in it" - meaning no washed-up hams who'd been monsters in televised stories. And the actors, who were mainly recruited at conventions over drinks, were often pathetically glad of the work but justified it by giving promising youngsters a leg-up.)

First off the mark was Southampton-based Bill Baggs, erstwhile producer of the *Audio Visuals* series of amateur audio stories (Briggs had his finger in that particular pie as well). Baggs moved on to the BBC Film Club, where he assembled Colin Baker, Nicola Bryant and Michael Wisher (who dedicated his twilight years to appearing in this sort of thing) for a short film called "Summoned by Shadows". Baker and Bryant played mysterious time travellers called "The Stranger" and "Miss Brown". You can see where this is going. In 1991 Baggs released "Summoned by Shadows" via his own company, BBV ("Bill and Ben Video", which says a lot if you're British), and it was a big hit with a fandom starved of a TV series.

More *Stranger* videos followed, some based on old AV scripts, but gradually evolving away from *Doctor Who*. In 1993, Briggs reappeared with a

continued on page 87...

in 1885, and the first rule of hospitality is to make a guest feel welcome. If she's an angel, as he suspects, he ought to ask if she requires refreshment after such a long journey, or indeed enquire as to her needs rather than make such rash assumptions. He doesn't offer her so much as a cup of tea and a bath oliver. And he's at a picturesque loch near Inverness - and the main railway - out of season, so there's going to be a lot of curious villagers scrutinising his activities. This isn't how a well-brought-up person treats a guest of any kind, spectral or not. What about the local gossip? [Mind you, he has a lady's mirror in his drawer, so he must have entertained at least one local girl quite regularly.] And why, prior to Vena's arrival, did the glass move on Herbert's Ouija board?

So someone hands Peri a piece of paper bearing the message [in English, unless the TARDIS translation system has undergone an upgrade]: 'Sezom at the Falchion Rocks'. [Stop giggling.] This is never properly explained, although it's suggested that the note hails comes from one of the rebel spies, and we might assume that they hear about the Doctor and Peri's arrival and hope that the travellers can help against the Borad. Okay, but why didn't the same spy a) write a message the Doctor and Peri stood a chance of understanding, and b) alert the rebels that the travellers might be paying them a visit, thus eliminating the possibility that Sezom would want to torture or kill the supposed interlopers? And why does Katz think that Peri's identification of Jo Grant - a character from a story that used to be in the school History curriculum - is proof of bona fides, when even Tekker knows about her?

And how did Sezom, stuck out in the Fel... err, in his base, know that Tekker had replaced Renis as now Maylin?

If shiny surfaces and mirrors are now verboten, then why did someone cover the mirror in the Council chamber with a naff painting of Pertwee, and cover *that* with a piece of chip-board painted beige? Why not just remove the mirror, and the painting? [It's possible that this was concealed as part of an underground movement against the Borad's oppression, but it's questionable how this act of discretion could be carried out in the ruling Council chamber.] And if the painting was done after the Doctor left Karfel, why is he here confident that the mirror is still behind the chip-board, and that the painting will bust if he hurls a chair against it, but that the mirror will remain intact?

For that matter, why does one of the Androids recoil at the sight of itself in the Doctor's hand-held mirror? Perhaps this is meant to symbolize the Borad's own fear of mirrors, but it's a rather silly vulnerability for such an advanced machine to have. And notice how the Doctor decently grapples with one of the Androids, even though you'd think the machine would be super-strong like Lt Data on the *Enterprise*, or the robot Frankenstein Monster at the Festival of Ghana in 1996 [2.8, "The Chase", as if you could forget].

Not impossible, but certainly unlikely: Bandril is cited as Karfel's 'neighbouring planet', yet it's in another solar system. It might be the nearest *inhabitable* planet or somesuch, but then we've still got the small matter of how a missile sent across star-systems arrives in under a day. [Yes, all right, warp-drive on a missile isn't impossible, but it makes the TARDIS stopping it by standing in its way far too complicated even for a convoluted mess like this story. Of course, the Bandrils seem to be launching the missile from a spaceship, but that ship doesn't look much bigger than the missile, so perhaps it's effectively the same as a missile with a warp-drive for its first stage.] Moreover, this being *Doctor Who*, terms like 'intergalactic' are bandied about (which would make the missile's arrival in such a short time even more strange). Oh, and the Timelash space-time portal strangely still looks "open" - albeit less illuminated - after the rebels destroy its control unit. [Are we to presume it's some sort of interface?]

A big one: the Bandrils are starving, so obliterating their only source of wheat in a fit of pique seems a bit rash. Even if the Bendalypse warhead doesn't irradiate the grain, it would presumably kill all the farmers who cultivate it and put it into sacks. Fine, perhaps they use robots for that, but even then a bomb isn't likely to help matters. So really, refusing to abort the missile on a technicality (the Borad's body is not available for inspections) is daft and petty. If nothing else, Mykros' ability to make such anti-Borad statements without fear of retaliation should be as good a sign as any. Besides, if the Bandrils have been as badly misled as everyone else, then showing them the Old Man's body would do.

The Doctor tells Herbert that should anything happen to him while confronting the Borad, Herbert should find Peri because she 'might' find a way of getting him home from Karfel - an alien planet in the future. [Sorry, we *are* talking about

Did They Think We'd Buy Just Any Old Crap?

...continued from page 85

one-off story, "The Airzone Solution?" that reunited all the living Doctors (except Tom) in totally different roles and cannily cashed in on the mass-disappointment when "The Dark Dimension" failed to happen (see A1, "Dimensions in Time"). BBV then began to include proper *Doctor Who* characters with two new series, Mark Gatiss's *P.R.O.B.E.* (featuring Caroline John as a pipe-smoking Liz Shaw) - now routinely revived as "camp classics" by *League of Gentlemen* fans - and Briggs' *Auton* trilogy (with shop-dummies invading various parts of the UK that all look remarkably similar to Southampton).

Also contributing to the boom were the publishers of *DreamWatch* magazine (formerly *DWB*), whose "Shakedown: Return of the Sontarans" could boast a script by Terrance Dicks, stars of *Doctor Who* and *Blake's 7*, and the rights to the Sontarans - though not to their BBC-owned likenesses, hence their redesign as yellow cane toads. Sophie Aldred now seemed to be popping up in these as frequently as Michael Wisher and got to play the *New Adventures* version of Ace (ssshh - don't tell the lawyers) in Reeltime's *Mindgame* series, also largely by Dicks (and more Sontarans, the estate of Robert Holmes being particularly amenable to this sort of thing).

Eventually these releases petered out as audio production and direct-to-video documentaries proved to be a lot more cost-effective (ie people bought them). Later videos tend to play down any hint of a *Who* connection (BBV's *Cyberon* is almost embarrassed by its Not-the-Cybermen-Honestly monsters) or were out-and-out spoofs like "Do You Have a License to Save This Planet?" or "The Few Doctors" (in which the Sixth Doctor memorably defeats a Vervoid by eating it). BBV might have made a go of their unofficial *Professor and Ace* audio stories, begun in 1998, if the BBC's lawyers hadn't noticed and Big Finish (a rival outfit but employing many of the same people as Baggs, including Nicholas Briggs again) were awarded the official audio rights. It was hardly the best-kept secret in the world that Big Finish ultimately hoped to get permission to make proper licensed direct-to-video *Who*, but the advent of the BBC Wales series put paid to that ambition.

BBV had one last crack at Not Quite *Doctor Who* videos in 2002, when they joined forces with some, er, legitimate businessmen from America to make a film that would appeal equally to *Doctor Who* fans and the US porn market by combining Zygons with full frontal female nudity (mainly that of BBV stalwart Jo Castleton). The Zygons are shapeshifters, so would never appear in their blobby, BBC-copyright and expensive form, thus saving even more money from the costume budget. Sadly the project was shelved after most of the filming was complete and no one has seen it, although - at time of writing - it's again being rumoured as an upcoming release. Writer Jonathan Blum is occasionally spotted online defending his script against the misconception that it was anything other than a tender, mature and emotional drama that just happened to be about Zygon-humping.

And now - *stop press news* - you have the chance to find out for yourselves. As this book was being typeset, it was announced that a heavily revised edit of this has made it to DVD and is (so to speak) coming very soon. Not soon enough for us to comment on its merits, but just in time to avoid us getting into trouble for repeating the rumours and accusing the distributors of all sorts. *Zygon* has the tagline 'When being me is not enough' (We were hoping for "Organic Crystallography means never having to say you're sorry".) By the time you read this, we'll all doubtless know a great deal more than we ever wanted to about the Skarasen's lactic emissions, and will never be able to watch Broton manipulate the controls of his spaceship and keep a straight face (13.1, "Terror of the Zygons"). If you've not seen this bit, we're very sorry if talk of *Zygon* affects your response when you *do* finally get to watch this terrific little story, especially when Sarah looks at a sausage-like homing-device that vibrates and moves across the table.

• **Royal Doulton Plates**. See, British companies of good reputation could do tacky too. Just to complete the fun, the company who hired them to make these was called "Bona-Plus" (see 10.2, "Carnival of Monsters" for notes on Palare).

• **Clothes Make the Fan.** As we'll see when we get to "Time and the Rani" (24.1), there's a lazy journalist cliché about fans who (as TV's Eric Roberts would say) "drezz for the occasion". But before organised fandom, there was Dalekmania. Think back to 1964/5, when young fans had a choice of two different toy Dalek suits - or would

continued on page 89...

the same 'Peri', right?] And why would Herbert carry around a card with just his name on it and nothing else? [Perhaps he's so dim, it might be in case he forgets who he is.]

Critique Based on the anecdotal and audience-research evidence, this was the Colin Baker story that non-fans enjoyed the most. No continuity references surface that aren't explained (at length, and to stories never shown anyway), and this adventure was playful in ways the series hadn't been for a while. And these days, we can't help but notice how having a Big Name from History as a one-story companion is the recipe for pseudo-historicals, BBC Wales style. (Although if we're evoking the new series, Herbert looks more like a Mickey prototype than anything else.) So we have every reason to buck the trend, and say that "Timelash" is an enjoyable romp and not the disaster everyone thought at the time.

... but we're not going to. This isn't a flawed gem, but rather a terrible story with good parts almost smuggled in. It's not that Tekker is a desperately interesting part that Paul Darrow hams up, but that it's a dire role that he *almost* salvages by grandstanding. It's not that the horrid sets and lousy costumes bury a neat premise, but that it's a grindingly dull story only memorable for being made as a school panto with belated New Romantic 80s fashion errors.

Most damningly, this is the story where Eric Saward's padding - the "TARDIS bitch scenes" and the frantic bulking-out of the second episode - provide the only tangible entertainment. Yes, Saward's interjections actually *improve* a story, which just shows you bad things have become. Those trying to redeem this period sometimes claim that the Doctor-Peri sniping makes Season Twenty-Two seem like '*Frasier* in Space'. "Timelash" is the closest we get to this, but even then you wish for Eddie the dog to come along and relieve the tedium of the Karfel scenes.

In all fairness, so much here is *nearly* right that the badness really screams at you by comparison. Most of the cast are committed and pitch-perfect. As director, Pennant Roberts has picked up the pace and spared us some longer-drawn-out, political infighting dialogue scenes (which is why the padding was needed). The slapstick, for once, comes off. There's only so much even an expensive post-production can do with a horrendous set like the Timelash interior, but this whole sequence

was the last to be made (until the rewrites and the 'then I'll be unreasonable - get out!' sequence) and there are a lot of visual flourishes. No, with obvious caveats like Paul Darrow, the Bandril Ambassador and the Timelash itself, the problems begin long before the studio recording, and no director could have saved this.

Quite simply, a storyline like this - not to mention the dialogue - belongs in the World Distributors *Doctor Who Annual*, with jobbing artists[9] making the most of two publicity photos and a wonky translation of the text to illustrate it. That the general public seemed to go along with this story just shows how far expectations of the series had slid, not least since the BBC have made public their wish to be shot of the show.

The Facts

Written by Glen McCoy. Directed by Pennant Roberts. Ratings: 6.7 million, 7.4 million. Audience appreciation was a solid 66% and 64% (so you see what we mean about lowered expectations).

Supporting Cast Paul Darrow (Tekker), David Chandler (Herbert), Robert Ashby (Borad), Jeananne Crowley (Vena), Eric Deacon (Mykros), Neil Hallett (Renis), David Ashton (Kendron), Peter Robert Scott (Brunner), Dicken Ashworth (Sezon), Tracy Louise Ward (Katz), Steven Mackintosh (Gazak), Denis Carey (Old Man), Dean Hollingsworth (Android), Martin Gower (Bandril Ambassador).

Oh, Isn't That..?

• *Paul Darrow*. He was, of course, Avon in *Blake's 7*. Earlier, he was Captain Hawkins in 7.2, "Doctor Who and the Silurians". He's done other things, probably.

• *Eric Deacon*. With his twin brother, he'd just made Peter Greenaway's *A Zed and Two Noughts*. This is as unlike "Timelash" - and yet, oddly, as much like *Doctor Who* as we generally understand it - as you can get. The Deacons will be back in *Drowning By Numbers* (which sounds like a Bond-movie credit, but is so marvellously wrong that we won't correct it).

• *Jeananne Crowley*. She'd just escaped from *Tenko* (early episodes of which were directed by Pen Roberts, which also explains why Louise Jameson had a career after *Doctor Who*). She'd

Did They Think We'd Buy Just Any Old Crap?

...continued from page 87

have done, if Scorpion Automotives versions hadn't gone up in flames in a factory fire that we wouldn't dare to call "suspicious".

The distinction to be made is that these were seen and sold as *toys*. Most items of practical clothing connected to the series seemed designed with one of three purposes in mind: a) to brand the wearer as a *Doctor Who* viewer, i.e. consumer, b) to make them look like a pillock, or c) both. Basic items like hats, slippers, gloves, jackets and (of course) T-shirts are easy to manufacture and stamp with the *Doctor Who* logo. These proliferated in the mid-1980s, but some manufacturers applied ingenuity to come up with some genuinely idiotic items of costume. Step forward anyone wearing a "Resurrection"-style Dalek hat, complete with bulbous and increasingly - as the elastic gave out - detumescent eye-stalk. (At least one person connected with the *About Time* series owned one of these, though even he admits he never actually wore it out of doors.)

Ponder the question, though: is owning one of these novelty items any sadder than wearing a *Doctor Who* kimono, which is less embarrassing to the untrained eye but somehow much more pointless? Or what about the *Doctor Who* designer T-shirt - a fad in bold and breathlessly cool fashion statements that boomed in 1989, about five years after Frankie Said It Was All Over and just as the TV series keeled over and died?

There also was a report of a special *Doctor Who* shirt with matching tie. If this had been released in the early 1970s they might have got away with it, but this was 1985.

What's rarely noted about convention fancy dress is the effort that must have gone into getting the costumes right(ish). Authentic(ish) *Doctor Who* costumes have never caught on, though Dapol attempted to crack the market with Seventh Doctor and Mel costumes - timed to launch exactly three months after Bonnie Langford's departure had been screened. For months afterwards, *DWM* carried an advert with an uncomfortable duo posing in matching question mark tanktops, a look of quiet desperation in their eyes. The sad fact is that in an era when the Doctor started wearing a uniform for easier branding purposes, he stopped dressing in anything that a normal person might want to wear.

• **The TARDIS Inside Out.** John Nathan-Turner tells all! Sort of. Actually, it's forty pages of stuff for £7.50. (This is 1985, so a four-hundred page novel by someone who could write would have cost about that much, as would a family meal in a decent restaurant.) Whilst the illustrations are often quite good (reprints of Andrew Skilleter's better efforts, portrait photos of the cast and a whole page with a drawing of some celery), the text is at best perfunctory. Apparently Sarah Sultan and Jane Fielding were in the series (a similar gremlin has recently rendered Billie Piper unable to spell "Eccleston").

A couple of years later, JN-T struck again with *The Companions*, in which all the detail about Mel's background and that fateful encounter with the Master got page after page (and completely contradicted what we saw on screen), whereas "Vicki travelled with the First Doctor" is as far as the rest of it goes for her. Nice photos, though.

Later on, when he was allowed to tell rather more, the Nathan-Turner Memoirs in *DWM* filled out issue after issue, usually amusingly.

done *Reilly - Ace of Spies*, now mainly remembered for inflicting Sam Neill on the world.

• *Dicken Ashworth*. Here appears fresh from a stint in *Brookside*, a Liverpool-based soap we'll be hearing a lot about in later stories.

• *Tracy-Louise Ward*. She wasn't famous yet, but would be in *CATS Eyes*. On paper that sounds a bit like *Charlie's Angels*, but you simply cannot imagine how unlike it this programme could be.

• *Denis Carey*. As you probably know, he was the eponymous Keeper of Traken (18.6, "The Keeper of Traken", dummy!) and Chronotis in 17.6, "Shada".

• *Stephen Mackintosh*. Well, he's been in lots of things. Yes, amazing, isn't it; someone who stands out as underwhelming even amid the opening minutes of "Timelash" became a star. There's barely a week when he isn't in a well-regarded drama, most recently *The Amazing Mrs Pritchard*.

Cliffhangers (The Doctor tells Peri not to go wandering off, and she snippily replies, "Yes, Sir!"); an Android herds the Doctor toward the Timelash; (a Morlox menaces Peri, who's chained to the wall - not bad for an artificially imposed cliffhanger).

ABOUT TIME 1985-1989

The Lore

• Glen McCoy was a former ambulance driver who'd written a few episodes of medical soap *Angels* (see Volume V) and was author of *Jobs in the Ambulance Service and Hospitals* (Kogan Page books, 1981). He submitted a story to Saward on spec, which was a bit like the finished version but said out loud what's been deliberately not-said since 1963... that the Daleks were straight out of HG Wells. With the usual legal wrangles over scripts with Daleks in, Saward declined but didn't entirely reject McCoy as a writer.

• One of the script's singular virtues was that it looked easy to make entirely in the studio, with a small cast and fewer sets than usual. In other words, it could be done on the cheap. There were a few differences between McCoy's next version and the final product, mainly concerning the Gurdels (later Bandrils) and their attempts to send diplomats to resolve the crisis. (This sequence was perhaps too much like the end of 18.1, "The Leisure Hive". 'You mentioned... Foamasi?'). McCoy's revised draft was submitted soon after 21.7, "The Twin Dilemma" had aired, and was very much in the same vein. It needed softening, as Peri and the Doctor were supposed to get on better by the time of "Timelash". Once Saward had resolved a few wrinkles, saved Sezom from a gory death and cleared up Tekker's death (if you can call it "cleared up"... see **Things That Don't Make Sense**), he found that the finished scripts were a bit asymmetric. Episode one was an epic, episode two almost an afterthought. Rather than lose a potentially good cliffhanger, Saward reworked the bulk of the dialogue himself.

• Nathan-Turner had approached Paul Darrow about appearing on *Doctor Who* during a convention - Darrow had been typecast since *Blake's 7*, and suggested playing Tekker as Richard III. In the *Blake's* episode "The City on the Edge of the World" (famous as the story where Vila gets the girl) Darrow had worked with Baker (who was playing Bayban the Butcher / Barbarian / Berserker) and as such almost been relegated to a supporting role in his own show. With recordings just before Christmas and a chance at some pay-back, Darrow embraced the new role.

• In comes Pennant Roberts, by now almost the patron saint of lost causes (see 21.1, "Warriors of the Deep"; 17.6, "Shada"). As always, he took a small part and made it female (in this case Aram,

as small a part as you can get in this story). He shaved a bit off the budget by making the Bandril a puppet and getting Martin Gower - who'd been Tyheer early on in the story - to do the voice.

• So they got it all into the can, edited it and found that episode one was *still* too long, and episode two was *still* too short. But the cliffhanger was still deemed sacrosanct, despite Roberts' plan to move it a few minutes earlier (probably in favour of Guardoliers busting in on Sezom's party). A few trims were made, and some brief scenes were re-written in longer form, to be recorded at the end of the next story (22.6, "Revelation of the Daleks"). The music was by Elizabeth Parker, soon to have a big hit with the soundtrack to *The Living Planet*, one of David Attenborough's blockbusters. She'd done some of the sounds in "The Stones of Blood" (15.3), but this is her only official *Doctor Who* moment. Almost the whole of her score was included in the thirtieth anniversary CD put out by the BBC Radiophonic Workshop (and is probably the best thing about this story).

• Fast-forward to the time of broadcast. People are beginning to wonder whether the series is actually worth saving, especially with the advent of a half-decent British-made fantasy for the family on Saturday teatimes on ITV. Finally, they've cracked it (see 13.1, "Terror of the Zygons" and accompanying essay for how long it's taken). The day before episode two aired, Baker became a father again. The next year or so will see him take on all sorts of odd jobs.

• Meanwhile, the first of a string of rumours and plans about a feature film based on the series appeared in the press. It will get a bit confusing from now on, but this is the one by a company called Coast to Coast, whose make-up division would shortly become famous for realising Max Headroom. Over most of the rest of this book, we will be tracking the three main attempts to make a *Doctor Who* movie, culminating in the Paul McGann debacle.

22.6: "Revelation of the Daleks"

(Serial 6Z, Two Episodes. 23rd - 30th March 1985.)

Which One is This?   It's Colin's turn to taunt Davros and shout 'Aim for the eye-piece!'; this time it's in a futuristic funeral parlour with posthumous hospital radio.

Firsts and Lasts   It's the last time they do location filming on film, and the final story in the experimental / accursed (depending on your point-of-view) 45-minute format. For the first time we *see* a Glass Dalek (although it was mentioned by David Whitaker way back in 1964, *Doctor Who in an Exciting Adventure with the Daleks*) and - lo! - the buggers can levitate now. (Mind, it takes a lot of goodwill and faith to see this - especially when Davros apparently amputates William Gaunt's *other* leg.) Unfortunately, this long-desired advancement of Dalek technology won't stop cruddy stand-up comedians making the same "stairs" joke for the next twenty years (see X1.6, "Dalek" for the last time this is possible and 25.1, "Remembrance of the Daleks" for the Doctor abruptly realising this error). The Daleks that can do this are a new design with a new colour-scheme (white with gold bits) a subtly different voice. One of the Dalek props is being retired, after having seen action against William Hartnell, and the rest of the grey ones are pensioned off after this.

And goodbye to Peter Howell's arrangement of the theme-tune, still thought of by many as "the new version" as late as 2004. The title sequence, however, will linger for another year.

Four Things to Notice about "Revelation of the Daleks"...

1. Eric Saward's Big Idea for this year had been the Greek Chorus commenting on the story, and Graeme Harper's serendipitous "trademark" had been the asides to camera in "The Caves of Androzani" (21.6). So it seems like an obvious idea that Saward and Harper would combine forces and make a story where everyone sees everyone else on CCTV and has dramatically-motivated eye-contact with the viewers, but it raised eyebrows (so to speak) in 1985. Not least, because the first half of the story has interjections from an omniscient observer - a DJ who plays mid-twentieth century rock and dresses accordingly, played by Alexei Sayle (see **Oh, Isn't That..?**).

2. But this didn't grab as much notice as the *other* major Saward theory of this era - namely, that the worlds the Doctor visits are more interesting for what happens away from the main plot. In this instance, it means that the majority of the story happens while the Doctor is en route to the action, or while he's locked up and can't do much beyond ask questions. Some may say that this is how the series should have developed, but it's significant that the following year sees the introduction of a narrative device by which the Inquisitor can say "I'm bored with this, let's get back to the plot". Indeed, the next story to develop the background and leave the Doctor out almost entirely (X2.10, "Love and Monsters") is discussed even as late as 2006 as being an "experiment" and an "embarrassment". But at least "Love and Monsters" had the monster in the forefront, whereas *here* the big shock is how everyone seems to accept Dalek patrols as routine in a morgue.

3. And yet another of Saward's pet theories gets a road test, as Davros and the noble assassin Orcini are carefully underwritten to demonstrate how killers and psychopaths can be done with restraint. We'll explore why this is the case in **The Lore**. For now, just notice how once Orcini and Davros actually meet, the only way to avoid it seeming like snooker commentators competing to see who can be more hushed and silky-voiced is for Davros' rotating head to abruptly reveal that it's got a body after all, and for him to start ranting away like billy-oh.

4. But the *main* thing everyone remembers from this story is the bonkers set design. Coming at the end of the year, the budgets for "Revelation" had to be stretched out, so a lot of this is borrowed from other sources. As a result, it all looks like a real place rather than the unnatural uniformity of most other planets visited in this period of the series. (Maddening, isn't it? The first time this year we've had actors who are more watchable than the sets, the sets themselves repay close examination.) Anyone who doesn't already know can have fun working out which series provided which bits (Davros' lair is the one you'll not get in a million years without help).

The Continuity

The Doctor Now sticking to his vegetarian diet [22.4, "The Two Doctors"], and making Peri go along with him, but he doesn't seem to have lost any weight as a result. The sight of his own tombstone unsettles the Doctor more than he thought possible. [Someone who has risked death on a weekly basis since records began, and who lectures others on the transience of all things, suddenly finds his gut reaction to his own mortality is worse than the death itself. He's less stoic than he thought.]

Incidentally, he's suddenly started claiming to be nine-hundred years old. [He was seven hundred and fifty-six while knocking around with Romana in the late 1970s, and the only significant gap for him to have aged such duration is between "Time-Flight" (19.7) and "Arc of Infinity" (20.1) - hence the theory that a long-lived Nyssa and the Fifth Doctor travelled for about fifty years with no incidents worth televising. (See **The Obvious Question: How Old is He?** under 16.5, "The Power of Kroll" and **Who Narrates This Series?** under 23.1, "The Mysterious Planet".)]

• *Ethics*. This time around [as opposed to 12.4, "Genesis of the Daleks"], the Doctor has no worries about causing the prevention of a new species - in this case Daleks bred from human tissue - and he seems prepared to allow Orcini to kill Davros and / or Davros' business partner Kara professionally and dispassionately. Indeed, the Doctor's only moral anguish comes when Orcini wants to personally detonate the bomb rather than allow the Doctor enough time to rig up a timing mechanism. Yet with Orcini's over-riding concerns about redeeming his lost honour, the Doctor is willing to assist this suicide and help the disgraced Knight clear his name posthumously.

• *Inventory*. Peri breaks the Doctor's pocketwatch while scrambling over a wall, and he doubts he can get another one quite like it. [In subsequent stories a half-hunter with various unlikely functions is shown - by Season Twenty-Five, this has become almost a surrogate sonic screwdriver. We'll list each one as it comes along. Stay tuned.]

• *Background*. The Doctor knew and respected Professor Arthur Stengos, as both a friend and 'one of the finest agronomists in the galaxy', and is puzzled by this great man's apparent decision to be interred in Tranquil Repose. Despite this friendship, the Doctor doesn't recognise Stengos' daughter Natasha. Somehow, the Doctor has been able to 'hear' disturbing rumours about the situation on Necros. [This is left ambiguous, just as it's unclear how precisely the Doctor learned of Stengos' "passing".]

The Doctor sees taking on a Knight of the Order of Oberon as self-evidently dumb, and it's implied that he knows where their regimental HQ is. [For all the talk of the Order being a secretive and select order, Orcini seems to think the Doctor would be able to return his medals to the group, which suggests that Orcini knows the Doctor by reputation and that his name would open doors.]

The Supporting Cast

• *Peri*. She's no fan of nut-roast - at least, not the way the Doctor makes it - and mutters to herself that she's longing for a burger [again, see "The Two Doctors"]. She's clearly homesick, despite her frequent denials, and finds an approximately American-accented DJ as too intriguing to pass up. The Doctor trusts Peri to get to the TARDIS unaided and contact the President's incoming spaceship via the Ship's comms [so there's been at least one unseen adventure where she learned how to operate this]. She seems well-versed in deflecting the advances of creepy older men.

The Supporting Cast (Evil)

• *Davros*. Not to give too much away, but he's crafted a public identity for himself as 'the Great Healer'. Since arriving at Tranquil Repose funeral home [after his escape in 22.4, "Resurrection of the Daleks"], Davros has established himself as the benefactor of the starving masses, and the compassionate innovator who has made death a lifestyle choice. The day-to-day running of the establishment interests him as much as the Big Picture, it seems, as he monitors the DJ's broadcasts, the CCTV and the business deals with Kara (a local industrial tycoon). When soft-soaping his associates, Davros soft-pedals the ranting and is witty, quiet and almost mellifluous. But during his many soliloquies, he abruptly reverts to his old ways.

As 'the Great Healer', Davros appears as a disembodied head in a cylindrical glass tank, able to revolve and scrutinise every readout and monitor. Of course, this is a [mechanical, biological or otherwise] ruse: he is as he always was, but with two new features. He can now hover - with his

What Would the *Other* Season 23 Have Been Like?

Season Twenty-Two ended with the Doctor threatening to take Peri to 'B....' (and a freeze-frame). The word they recorded him saying was 'Blackpool', and this was done with the next story - "The Nightmare Fair" - already budgeted. Written by former producer Graham Williams, a version of this adventure later emerged as a Target paperback in 1989. From Williams' comments, this is another story like "The Two Doctors" (22.4), where John Nathan-Turner had made a list of old villains, setting and style (ideally something fashionable, or at least like a recent movie) and sent an experienced writer to deliver a pretext for these.

Actually, Blackpool makes a lot of sense as a location. Not only is it a town with a long association with the *Doctor Who* Exhibition (opened in 1974), but it's the UK's equivalent of Coney Island. Not an *exact* equivalent, mind you, but still well-known, fondly-regarded and in keeping with the Sixth Doctor's gaudy persona. Indeed, after opening the newly-refurbished Exhibition, Colin Baker was on hand to endorse the "Space Invader" roller-coaster ride - it would have been odd for even a BBC producer to resist cross-promotion like that. Thus, Nathan-Turner managed to sweet-talk the proprietors of several local attractions, and got some nifty deals on the back of the free publicity they'd get. Out of season, Blackpool is one of the convention capitals of the country, so facilities for a BBC crew would not be a problem. All that was needed was a story worth doing there.

So, insert an old villain and a recent film: the idea was supposedly a variation on *Tron* (only just out on video then) with the Celestial Toymaker (see 3.7, "The Celestial Toymaker"). As the novelisation cover makes clear, the idea was that Michael Gough would return as the Toymaker - but BBC regulations at the time made an actor playing two guest-roles in one series in under three years impossible, or so Nathan-Turner later claimed. And Gough had Chancellor Hedin in "Arc of Infinity" (20.1), which might've posed a problem.

One rumour doing the rounds (and never entirely dismissed by the BBC, although under the circumstances, fans had other things to ask about at the time) was that Rik Mayall was being considered for the role. This was when Mayall was at the height of his popularity, between *The Young Ones* (op cit) and *The New Statesman*, and just before his barnstorming rendition of Roald Dahl's "George's Marvellous Medicine" on *Jackanory*. It's certainly true that once the idea took hold, it became hard for anyone to imagine the Toymaker being played

any other way. (This is, we must repeat, a fan rumour, but it's from the same source that got Bonnie Langford's casting and the shortened seasons right.)

A feature worth noting is that at the time, the Toymaker's mystique was at its peak. Some of the lost stories needed redoing (or so the production team were persuaded, see 22.1, "Attack of the Cybermen"), and "The Celestial Toymaker" was held to be the next unavailable classic. Everyone involved (or near enough) was keen to be credited for this "masterpiece", but then disaster struck: the final episode was found. The BBC took delivery of "The Final Test" - the grand finale to this story - and many deemed it rubbish. Everyone involved (or near enough) started trying to offload responsibility onto others, ideally people who'd died since. Williams saw it and knew at once that it wouldn't even have been broadcastable in 1985 - so the Toymaker as a concept needed a rethink.

So *could* this have worked? If done on film with the increasing use of stunts since Season Twenty-One, not to mention at least one cliffhanger involving a roller coaster, there's potential. If (as is reported) it was conceptualized as a two-part story in the new 45-minute format, on VT, it would need a lot more than hi-octane thrills and manic energy, plus a strategic timing of such set-pieces as were available. Williams went on just about every ride available (on Saward's instructions: research, really it was) and saw ways to make it visually interesting.

But once again, with hindsight of the *real* Season Twenty-Three, one can see all sorts of problems with it being made on VT, not to mention possibly directed by one of the less flamboyant regulars like Peter Moffatt or a *Who*-virgin like Nicholas Mallett. Matthew Robinson was offered a contract to direct this story, but hesitated. He was just coming to the end of his stint setting up *EastEnders*' visual style, and he might've applied the fluid camerawork he developed for the soap to locations in Blackpool, rendering this already extraordinary setting alien and alluring. His salary, though, was another matter. On the strength of the previous two years and what we finally got in 1986, it's also possible that this could've been the calling-card for a fresh director.

Another advantage, however, is that Williams' novel shows signs that he "got" the Sixth Doctor and Peri, and provides many opportunities for a

continued on page 95...

"buggy" able to negotiate stairs - and he can fire static electricity from his fingertips. [Yes, just like the Emperor in *Return of the Jedi*. We assume that it's static - it would be very weird if the creator of the Daleks used any other kind.]

Notably, Davros has developed a means of converting humans into Daleks, and has been using some of those interred in Tranquil Repose for this purpose. However, despite his success at crafting a new Dalek force, Davros spreads news of Arthur Stengos' "death" as a means of luring the Doctor to the facility. [It is almost as if Davros needs the Doctor's appalled admiration as much as he craves power itself.]

The TARDIS   Seems to have acquired a new lamp [see **The Lore**] and has some kind of radio that can contact nearby spaceships. Peri can apparently use this [so it can't be part of the guidance systems (see 10.1, "The Three Doctors") or telepathic circuits (18.7, "Logopolis", 9.5, "The Time Monster").]

The Non-Humans

• *Daleks (Davros' new and improved ones)*. They have nice straight backs and an extra slat around the "collar". Their arms only have two telescopic sections, not three, and their voices are slightly higher in pitch. Davros has finally made the breakthrough he was planning, and can now convert humans into Dalek mutants, rather than having to start from scratch with cytoplasm and growing each one in a lab. [This development is something that will carry into the new series, see X1.12, "Bad Wolf" and more pertinently X3.5, "Evolution of the Daleks". There, however, each time is more or less presented as if it's the first time.]

The humans Davros selects have to be intelligent and either legally dead or willing volunteers. Judging by Arthur Stengos - who undergoes the transformation before his daughter mercy-kills him - Davros conditions his subjects with mind-altering chemicals, and adapts their DNA so that internal organs grow from the head. They are loyal to Davros alone, and have been told what the Doctor looks like.

Davros' Daleks are cream, with gold appurtenances. Yet they are outgunned by...

• *Daleks (the old-fashioned ones)*. Presently based on Skaro, and loyal to the Supreme Dalek. They only know what the Doctor previously looked

like, and don't recognize his current incarnation. We never see if they can levitate, but they're now using spaceships unlike any we've seen them use before [possibly a commandeered civilian ship?].

Curiously, instead of instead of just wiping out Davros' new genetic "perverts" and eliminating him for good, the grey Daleks take him off to face a trial. [This seems downright bizarre, but when we get to the TV Movie's pre-credit sequence it will - comparatively speaking - be as sensible as Barbara Wright's shoes. It would appear that the Daleks' legal system has become so refined that even Time Lords are allowed to give evidence and are granted diplomatic immunity for the duration. Thus, in the TV Movie, the Master's remains are taken to Gallifrey by The One They Call Doc-Torr - who is, we later gather, what Mummy Daleks tell their mutant embryos about to make them behave. See 25.1, "Remembrance of the Daleks", plus 27.0, "The TV Movie" and X2.4, "The Girl in the Fireplace".] As we now know, one possible future for the Daleks has the Cult of Skaro set up to brainstorm off-the-wall ideas for avoiding defeat (X2.13, "Doomsday") so at some stage the division of Dalek forces between "pure" and "impure" becomes negotiable: this might be invoked to settle the age-old question of how genetically-engineered blobs can have a hierarchy. The flipside of this is that the debate on how "Daleky" a Dalek is has never been entirely about genetics, as 4.9, "The Evil of the Daleks" and X3.5, "Evolution of the Daleks" demonstrate.

[NB. It was hard enough filling in the gaps between the state-of-play at the end of this story and the start of the next Dalek adventure, without BBC Wales messing it about further. For the purposes of this book we will assume that the Dalek history here is entirely separate from that we hear about in X1.13, "The Parting of the Ways" and X3.4, "Daleks in Manhattan", but will suggest possible links for those who want it all to be one big story. Suffice it to say, Davros is wheeled off to Skaro on the orders of the Dalek Supreme at the end of this story, and we only ever hear of one of these antagonists again.]

Planet Notes

• *Necros*. Appropriately named, for a planet of the dead. From space it looks like Earth, and it's shown to have woods, lakes and hills, albeit coated with snow. The trees look like oaks [which, if we take seriously the comment in "The Android

What Would the *Other* Season 23 Have Been Like?

...continued from page 93

director to put his or her own stamp on it. In the era of *Labyrinth, Willow* and *Time Bandits*, animatronic dwarves would've been exactly what *Doctor Who* needed to be doing (we're not sure about the morally-ambiguous intelligent cloud, though). With the story's emphasis on video technology, though, the risk was always that we'd get someone playing with the toys and making unholy messes like the disco dream-sequence from "Mawdryn Undead" (20.3).

Fiona Cumming is said to have been pencilled-in for Wally K Daly's "The Ultimate Evil". This too was novelised, and we can't help noticing how it's sort of a mish-mash of "The Caves of Androzani" (21.6) and what eventually became "Mindwarp" (23.2). The basic story entailed a malignant little arms-peddler - the 'Dwarf Mordant' - messing with people's heads to make two neighbouring pacifist species go to war. However it's hard to see how anyone could have made Mordant significantly different from Sil, who would've returned either way, as we'll see. (And "The Nightmare Fair" had evil dwarves too. Warwick Davies, Kenny Baker and David Rappaport would have been quids in...) This was intended as a two-parter in the 45-minute slot, and the novelisation yields about six places to have put the cliffhanger. Again, the book goes into details that wouldn't have made the screen, including some nasty business with Peri and broken glass. (It's also worth mentioning that naming "nice" aliens 'Tranquelians' and 'Amelierons' is crass even by Terry Nation standards.)

Meanwhile, Ron Jones would doubtless have been first in the frame for the next story, "Mission to Magnus". This was also novelised by its scriptwriter, Philip Martin, and - as indicated - featured Sil. As we know from "Mindwarp", the possibilities of the digital technology, and Martin's keen interest in making his alien worlds work, needed a more pragmatic director. Jones showed his true colours in casting people who could plausibly have lived in places like the titular worlds seen in 21.3, "Frontios" and 22.2, "Vengeance on Varos"; this admittedly came a bit unstuck in "Mindwarp", but even there the "stunt-casting" made up for it.

Who would have played the Time Lord named Anzor in "Mission" is an open question, especially as we suspect this idea would have been dropped fairly early on. From the novelisation, we have a pretty good idea of what Martin was up to, although once again it's suspiciously "high-con-

cept". The person who bullied the Doctor at school pops up (the aforementioned Anzor), as do the Ice Warriors, an impending environmental catastrophe and a matriarchal society. (*Why* is the latter always lurking in any list on unmade stories? See **What Else Wasn't Made?** under 17.6, "Shada".)

This is clearly too many elements, even for Eric Saward. Given that the story scheduled to follow this was to include the Master and the Rani, the Anzor subplot looks like the sacrificial victim (especially as he disappears partway through the book). Again, we have to consider the timing, and the then-imminent release of "The Seeds of Death" (6.5) on BBC video. Commissioning an Ice Warrior story was plausible for the first time since *Star Wars* had made Ice Lords look like wannabes. Mind you, with the trouble they could've had with that story, we have to accept that the commissions at this early stage entailed an element of "belt and braces". As early as July 1985, the Trial idea and the order to limit Season Twenty-Three to fourteen episodes was being discussed. We have only a sketchy idea of how early the fourteen-episode "cap" was given to the production team, but if it *was* March - along with the alleged "cancellation" - then any two of the stories just outlined and the next (the six-part Robert Holmes Auton / Master / Rani / Singapore chop suey) would take us up to the end of the year. This is the only other story ever mentioned in any detail, but we have tantalising details of others (and will explore them in a moment).

Holmes' story is generally referred to by his working title "Yellow Fever (And How to Cure It)". With Singapore the most likely site of un-wiped telerecordings of black and white stories (see **What Were The BBC *Thinking*?** under 3.1, "Galaxy Four"), Nathan-Turner was able to take a working holiday and scout out locations. He and Downie took some home movies, to which they later subjected Holmes and Saward. Had this story gotten made, we could inevitably have expected a scene in the Raffles Hotel. Whether - as is sometimes reported - the Brigadier would've appeared is open to question, but the Master and the Rani were definitely meant to be included. Holmes appears to have been unhappy with his brief, and asked for a deferment on developing the story. It never got beyond a sketchy outline; all the speculation we've read over the years is fun, but there's not much else to go on. Singapore exports rubber,

continued on page 97...

Invasion" (13.4), would mean that this isn't Earth's galaxy (see **Dating**)]. Native life is limited to speelsnapes, voltrox and the weed-plant. The latter is like a purple lily, and used in the funeral decorations.

The planet's main place of interest is Tranquil Repose, a necropolis within a circular wall. This complex has many concrete slopes and under-passes, but is predominantly vast pyramids. The Garden of Remembrance, lined with tombstones, is on the path into the main reception area. Whilst the bulk of the facility's work is preparation of the deceased, most of the area is given over to those near death and in cryonic suspension. In order to preserve each subject's mental function and mem-ories [cf 24.4, "Dragonfire", where total suspen-sion destroys memory traces], the clients awaiting cures for their complaints are fed an update on galactic affairs and a selection of Oldies, as pre-sented by the in-house DJ. The occupants of the vaults are legally dead, and thus they have bequeathed their worldly goods even if they are cured and awakened.

Outside the perimeter wall, the entire area is monitored on CCTV. The escaped [or released] products of some of the Great Healer's experi-ments are allowed to roam free or lurk in the water. [So this is a "Lake of Mutations", in a "Dead Planet"... did the Doctor not get *déjà vu*?] The Daleks have already taken up much of the day to day patrolling of the complex, and also check peo-ple's passes. Many of the ancillary staff are interns, usually medical students. All wear powder-blue uniforms, like scrubs used in surgery, with cotton gloves, felt caps and make-up. The main com-plex's walls are blood-red marble, inset with mon-itor screens that have the company logo as a screensaver.

History

• *Dating.* No date is given, but it's obviously after Davros escaped imprisonment in "Resurrection of the Daleks". [The DJ is terribly excited that Peri is from the United States of America, on Earth. So either this story is set in the comparatively near future, or the Earth authorities have re-formed the old nations and re-introduced regional accents. Or maybe Earth is now so remote and forgotten, foreigners think they *still* have a USA - the way present-day Americans think that Britain has steam-trains and outside toi-lets. The DJ's great-grandfather visited Earth and

picked up some recordings of American DJs - we assume these are from the twentieth century, between the invention of sound recording and America's downfall (see **Whatever Happened to the USA?** under 4.6, "The Moonbase").

[Another wild card, though: our best-guess for the Davros Era - meaning the block of four Davros stories from "Destiny of the Daleks" (17.1) to "Remembrance of the Daleks" - puts this story suspiciously close to the fiftieth century, which is when time experiments seem to have taken off again (X1.9, "The Empty Child" and "The Girl in the Fireplace", plus their source 14.6, "The Talons of Weng-Chiang"). More on this when we get to "Remembrance of the Daleks". We might also, after all that wrangling about when "The Ice Warriors" (5.3) is set, surmise that the 'Artificial Foods' which Leader Clent whitters on about includes Kara's version of Soylent Green.]

In this era, the professional killer Orcini belongs to an organization called 'the Knights of Oberon'. [The name is usually associated with the King of Fairies as featured in Shakespeare's *A Midsummer Night's Dream*. If we forget the Victorian frilliness and recall what people of Shakespeare's time thought, Faerie was a wild and dangerous 'parallel world' inhabited by capricious forces (see 26.1 "Battlefield"). So the implication is that Orcini and his brethren are ninjas. However, fan lore and several mentions in Virgin *New Adventures* and BBC novels have made the equally logical leap that 'Oberon' denotes one of the moons of Uranus - named after the Shakespeare character - which could be the Knights' base. In which case, Orcini was trained on the third satel-lite of a planet nineteen times further from the Sun than Earth, orbiting at almost right-angles to the plane of the ecliptic. So, very close to the moon Sycorax (X2.0, "The Christmas Invasion") and handy for mining Taranium (3.4, "The Daleks' Master Plan").]

The Galaxy has a President, whose wife has recently died. Davros is sort-of famous, although even a professional hit-man like Orcini has trou-ble putting a name to the face. [Not for the first or last time, the analogy with Nazi war-criminals like Martin Bormann is unavoidable.

[Note that they don't say that it's *our* galaxy. A lot of this story makes more sense if one assumes that a recent development in space-drives has facilitated inter-galactic travel, and that a big and largely empty galaxy has been colonised.

What Would the *Other* Season 23 Have Been Like?

...continued from page 95

so at least one possible Auton-related storyline (and any number of funny ones unsuitable for family viewing) opened up, and a big revelation about the Master's improbable escape in 21.5, "Planet of Fire" has been mooted.

Pause to consider all of this, and you see a trend emerging, don't you? Three of the four potential stories all fit the template of "The Two Doctors" and "Time-Flight". A lot of the planning was connected with what BBC Enterprises had scheduled for video release, and what audio versions of wiped stories could be sold. The exception ("The Ultimate Evil") seems overly-familiar too, and is written by Wally K Daly - an experienced comedy writer for radio, but not, on the strength of his novelisation, a natural *Doctor Who* author. But the big hit from the last year had been Philip Martin, a TV writer from a totally different discipline, so you can see why they were tempted to try that strategy again. That would account for Michael Feeney Callan - an Irish writer who had worked on *Shoestring*, *The Professionals* and some less routine thrillers for RTÉ television - submitting something called "The Children of January". His website fails to mention this, but proudly cites his work on *Perry Como's Christmas* (the 1994 one, Como's swansong). Could a writer who'd not seen much of the series do the trick? Well, so long as he didn't muddle it up with *Fortycoats*[12], it could've worked.

Looking at the other proposals... Peter Grimwade's 'pure' historical, "The League of the Tancreds", was also being considered favourably. It seemed to be too lavish, but got as far as a scene-breakdown. Christopher H Bidmead was trying to get "In the Hollows of Time" to work within the format, and it's been suggested that his idea was about assassinating old companions. That's probably untrue, and although the idea *may* have been in one or more of the other scripts, it most likely derives from a fan-hoax script of this period, titled "The Death of Yesterday". It's perhaps relevant that Michael Craze - whom Nathan-Turner had wanted to use in a totally different role - was sounded out as making a final appearance as Ben (Anneke Wills was in an Ashram in India, probably), but Bidmead himself doesn't recall much about this. Fan lore contends that the fifth slot was a shoo-in between "The Children of January" and something by Bill Pritchard; unfortunately no one knows anything about the latter.

However, many hangovers from previous seasons were not completely abandoned, and we can't rule these out as possible. After all, "Vengeance on Varos" took years and rewrites to reach the screen, so perhaps Peter Ling's "Hex" and some of Barbara Clegg's ideas (the one about Quetzecoatl and Christopher Marlowe perhaps) were still on the blocks (see Volume V). Other leftovers included Ingrid Pitt and Tony Rudlin's "The Macros", Ian Marter's "Volvok", Andrew Smith's "The First Sontarans", Robin Squire's "Ghost Planet" and an outline by Chris Boucher (who by now was busy setting up the new BBC2 series *Star Cops*). Paula Woolsey had another partly-scripted story still on file (possibly in an attempt to prove she was real), while fan-turned-pro Gary Hopkins was commissioned for an episode of a nuclear thriller titled "Meltdown" and Jonathan Wolfman's possible entry for the season is as elusive as Bill Pritchard's.

So, if one of *these* was in the fifth slot, anyone who recalls what was actually made will probably ask themselves, "What about Pip and Jane Baker?" An astute question, because was no way they were *not* going to come to the party. Their story was called "Gallifray" (sic), was a definite season finale, and was commissioned soon after the Suspension was announced. All signs are that this would have concerned the last days of the Doctor's homeworld, but whether it was the Daleks or the Master that destroyed it is another matter for conjecture. (Apparently, the Bakers never got around to writing any of it. We note, though, that when hurriedly asked for a story to end the broadcast Season Twenty-Three with, they had the Master lead a coup and the Valeyard attempt to assassinate the hierarchy.) This is considerably bolder as a story than anything we've seen so far in this putative season, or indeed in the whole of this book. The effect of the programme's brush with mortality seems to have made everyone ask what was previously unthinkable - namely, how to end the series. It also meant that the long-term plan to make this Doctor mellow over time had to be sped up. But as you inevitably know, the Suspension meant that the whole of this proposed season was put on ice, although the authors were asked to submit new (or revised) ideas. For whatever reason, the Trial format was judged a more sensible idea because it shook things up. Daring, therefore sensible.

It wasn't as daring, though, as the ideas for the

continued on page 99...

Certainly, the grey Daleks' ability to turn up unannounced, right on the heels of an expected visit by the Galactic President, is a tiny bit more plausible in a frontier setting.]

Necros borders a part of the galaxy [all right, *a* galaxy] that's been recently colonised, and is now undergoing massive famines. Names like "Arthur" and "George" have apparently come back into vogue. One of the people stored in Tranquil Repose has Beck's Disease, which has been curable for forty years [so Tranquil Repose must have been open long before then].

Notably, the purple flower *herbabaculum vitae* (AKA "staff of life") grows on Necros and is similar in food value to soybean plants on Earth. The Doctor advises cultivating this flower as a protein source to alleviate the widespread famine. [In fact, the alternative name "staff of life" - here mentioned by the Doctor - might've come about in a future time when the plant's value was known; even so, see **Things That Don't Make Sense**.]

Orcini explains the concept of a sword to his squire, implying that the weapon has fallen into obscurity.

The Analysis

Where Does This Come From? It's routine to trot out all the similarities with Saward's holiday reading - Evelyn Waugh's *The Loved One* - and all the references to his holiday destination, Rhodes. We'll do that in a moment, because there's a lot else we need to say.

In 1983, smug film critic Michael Medved came to these shores to sneer at old films he'd already ridiculed in his book *The Golden Turkey Awards*. Channel 4 showed a season of these flicks on Saturday night, prefaced with Medved's observations and snide remarks, and the films themselves had superimposed captions pointing out "Here comes a good bit". British viewers largely resisted this attempt to create a "cult" for movies like *Eegah!* - partly because commentator Clive James had already covered most of the good ones, and partly because the "funny" moments had hours of tedious ineptitude between them, but mainly it was because we resented being *told* that something was funny. In those days, we preferred to discover these things for ourselves, and cherish some works for their hopeless optimism. (And anyway, how can any list of "Worst Movies of All Time" that fails to include Norman Wisdom, Cliff

Richard or Hugh Grant be taken seriously?)

We have to admit, though, that the plot of "Revelation of the Daleks" is pretty near to being a sequence of *hommage* moments to Medved's choices. Davros has his head in a glass case for most of the story - there's no reason why this should be, except that it looks like the signature shot from *They Saved Hitler's Brain*. The tussle with the Mutant was changed to account for the snow, but it's not hard to see resemblances to the gorilla-with-spacesuit lumbering out of the woods in *Robot Monster*. The basic premise is - ahem - "grave-robbers from Outer Space", as in *Plan 9*. More significantly, the series' overall tone, with so many of the specimens coming from the late 1950s, was of kitsch nostalgia, and the theme was a rough take on "Wipeout" by the Surfaris. So when a DJ narrates and links separate storylines as they unfold - just like Wolfman Jack did in *American Graffiti* - we shouldn't be too surprised. (See our comments on 24.3, "Delta and the Bannermen" for more on the re-imagining of the 1950s that went on in 80s Britain.)

One thing we've got to say right now: this is the story in which Saward gets his way and turns the Daleks into second-rate Cybermen. He insisted in interviews at the time and afterward that the Daleks were no longer frightening, represented an out-of-date kind of horror, couldn't do long speeches and were therefore dramatically redundant. We'll leave anyone who's come to this series as a result of seeing the BBC Wales version to answer that charge, because the point is that the new model army Davros has recruited from the dead are "converts" to the cause, just as Cybermen were to theirs. Dramatically, this is a Cyberman story with Davros as guest-villain. (The logical way to follow through on this is to have Cybermen with a mad creator in a wheelchair, but that would be silly.)

In devising this story, Saward was told by Nathan-Turner that he needed to include a tombstone depicting the Sixth Doctor. The original script was called "The End of the Line", so we might surmise that the mellowing of this Doctor and his initial abrasiveness - planned from the outset by the producer and the star - were somehow connected with this. It's certainly true that the Doctor we see in Season Twenty-Three is more chummy with Peri and an altogether wiser person. With this in mind, the choice of a funeral parlour as a setting seems incumbent on the script

What Would the *Other* Season 23 Have Been Like?

...continued from page 97

last two stories in that format. Before we leave this topic, we have to look briefly at what the Trial might have alternatively been like.

The diptych of two-part stories to introduce Mel were David Halliwell's "Attack from the Mind" and Jack Trevor Story's "Second Coming". When these didn't work they were replaced by Christopher H Bidmead's four-part "The Last Adventure" (latterly "Pinacotheca"). This didn't have the Master in it and wasn't about computer fraud at all, despite what you might have read. Rather, it was about a museum of pictures / recordings / frozen chronosynclastic interstitial engrams - a bit like the one in "All Our Yesterdays", the penultimate episode of *Star Trek* - and String Theory. Also being considered for one of these slots was PJ Hammond's "Paradise Five" (AKA "End of Term"), which would have given the Valeyard a villainous companion of his own.

These two stories cropped up in the dying days of this production team, with the producer and the script editor reputedly championing the two rival stories over the other (Nathan-Turner preferred the Bidmead, Saward wanted "Paradise Five"). The ultimate replacement - "Terror of the Vervoids" - may well have been the result of a half-hearted compromise between the two. Hammond, creator of *Sapphire & Steel*, is an interesting choice. News that he was contributing to *Torchwood* raised more speculation concerning this *Angel*-style spin-off than almost anything else. (And amongst the *Torchwood* Series 1 episodes, Hammond's story certainly had the most coherently thought-out plot.)

Jack Trevor Story's contribution has acquired a mythology all its own. As writer-in-residence at Milton Keynes, Story had become re-invigorated after many years chasing money. He had launched his own small press, and had taken on many quick commercial jobs to fund it - usually anything that presented him with a challenge. Story is a writer who attracts indulgent friends and unlikely anecdotes, even after his death. So when his proposal for a Season Twenty-Three story was rejected, the myth grew up that it was "too shocking" for the BBC. Eric Saward's account is that it was half a page of notes about a man in an empty gasometer playing a saxophone. Story's unauthorised biography seems to back him up on that, claiming that gasometers and saxophones figured prominently into his childhood nightmares from pre-war

Cambridgeshire. Another clue is that David Halliwell (author of such plays as *Little Malcolm and his War against the Eunuchs*, more recently revived with Ewan McGregor in the title role) says he was asked to give Story a starting point from the end of "Attack from the Mind". They liaised closely enough for Story to lend Halliwell a biography of Ernest Hemingway, which was never returned. It involved a planet called Penelope, inhabited by beautiful Penelopeans and ugly, rat-like Freds (yes, really) and the novel twist that the Freds were the good guys. (No, really, it could have been good. Just because it's been done a dozen times since 3.1, "Galaxy Four" and never particularly well doesn't make it automatically a bad idea.)

The Penelopeans were in fact psychically gifted and were manipulating the Freds. Halliwell's story ends with the start of a genocide (one which has not yet happened but will if the Doctor is released, so he is to be executed preemptively), so the precise lead-in to Story's script is unclear. However, looking closely at the elements we know about and Story's track-record in TV drama, we can't rule out the possibility that we were in for something involving time, memory, Hemingway, childhood fears and old songs. (Something very similar was on our screens when the real Season Twenty-Three was broadcast. Imagine Saward being given the script for *The Singing Detective* and telling everyone: "It's just a kid up a tree and a scarecrow waving at him." In fact, come to think of it, hasn't Steven Moffat carved himself a niche doing stories like this lately?)

(Incidentally, the apparently curious turn of events with Saward working with people like Halliwell and Story makes more sense when you factor in David Rose, producer of *Gangsters* and so much more, moving to Channel Four and setting up their feature film unit. Writers he had championed were finding it harder to make purely televisual projects. Philip Martin - who had acted in the first production of *Little Malcolm* - was telling anyone who'd listen that *Doctor Who* was the only place left for non-naturalistic drama on television.)

One thing we do know is that the grand finale of "Trial" that Saward wrote involved a vast circular building, because that's why Chris Clough scouted out the Potteries (see 23.4, "The Ultimate Foe"). So soon after *Brazil* had ended inside something similar, we can speculate that this is the image Saward retained from Story's script, however long it was,

continued on page 101...

editor, and his choice of paperback for a trip to Rhodes far more premeditated than is usually assumed.

For those who've not read it, Waugh's novel is a tale of how British expats fit in (or failed to fit in) to Hollywood. The general tackiness of that city is represented by two funeral homes - one for pets (where the protagonist has wound up working) and a more pretentious affair called Whispering Glades. The latter is described in the kind of bemused tone that Waugh's friend Jessica Mitford (who seems to have drawn it all to his attention) would do rather better in *The American Way of Death*. It's run by an unseen magnate called "The Dreamer", and he's revered by junior embalmer Aimee Thanatogenos (whose first name denotes her religious upbringing - as in Aimee Semple McPherson - but the surname means "death-maker"). She is, in turn, worshipped from afar by Mr Joyboy, her boss.

OK, it's not *that* much like "Revelation of the Daleks", is it? Well, Joyboy is plump and wears a pince-nez, and all the girls want him - but he is dominated by his mother and desires Aimee, who wants Dennis the dog-burier. Or at least, she does until she witnesses his frivolity toward religion and how generally "European" he is. (This was written in 1947, so you can work out what Waugh is getting at.)

So when you get down to specifics, *The Loved One* isn't much cop as a source. A couple of scenes about the routine workings of Tranquil Repose are pretty close, but the tone is different. Still, funerals are going to be increasingly important in the series, though, so it's worth dwelling on this. A show like *Doctor Who* is one in which lots of characters die, and those bodies have to go somewhere. Zombies of one kind or another have been around in the series since the Cybermen arrived, and the Hinchcliffe / Holmes phase of the show made it almost standard.

However, the use of death as a form of punctuation - removing surplus characters the second they have no plot function - is something Saward did a lot (e.g. 21.4, "Resurrection of the Daleks" and 22.1, "Attack of the Cybermen", even though Saward didn't write that one at all, honest). Usually, said characters were evaporated by magic rays, or crumbled to dust that blew away in a wind that somehow arrived at precisely the right time but - again - Holmes changed this by making the discovery and utility of dead bodies significant

for the drama. With the whole of this year's stories seemingly worrying at the idea of people as meat this looks like an obvious conclusion. Back in the 70s, *Monty Python* had run into censorship for a sketch about eating dead relatives as a cheap and tasty alternative to funerals (a version of it made it on to the record *Another Monty Python Album*), but by now *Dotcor Who* could do it for the kids.

1980s audiences, however, were more used to seeing things done to bodies, and indeed in the majority of horror films, the utility of corpses was key to the plot. So cannibalism was "in" in 1985 (see 22.4, "The Two Doctors"), but funerals have a dual purpose. For the participants, they're the means of what in Oprah-speak is called "closure". But for the practitioners - the people who make a living out of other people's raw emotion - it's a branch of showbiz. That multiple perspective - the play of appearances and sincerity - makes for grim ironies, as many fantasy shows had hitherto discovered. (See, for example, the last "proper" episode of *The Avengers*, "Bizarre", and its apparent precursor "The Terribly Happy Embalmers" - an episode of the hapless *Adam Adamant Lives!*) Even in a squeaky-clean era like Season Twenty-Two, a story about tidying up corpses is possible, and indeed by "Delta and the Bannermen" (24.3), a body being 'ionised' into just a pair of smouldering blue suede shoes is strictly for laughs.

Additionally, the script to "Revelation of the Daleks" is littered with throwaway references, most of which should be obvious ('a box of delights'... 'an offer I cannot refuse'...), but some may need a bit of glossing. The concern with famine relief and Orcini's donating his fee to charity are apparently oblique references to Band Aid and other efforts to do something about the Sub-Saharan famine. (**The Lore** will discuss another bizarre sidelight on this surge in high-profile munificence.)

When on holiday, Saward encountered a lot of useful historical details. There was a monastery called Tsambika (say it three times quickly if you can't see why this matters), and ruins belonging to the Knights Hospitaller - they ran Rhodes for a couple of centuries, and were fearsome and Vatican-approved mercenaries. One of their later leaders was - lo and behold - a Grand Master Orsini, but with Saward's interest in mercenaries, this may be superficial. It was during rehearsals that Graeme Harper and William Gaunt seem to have hit on Don Quixote as a model for the char-

What Would the *Other* Season 23 Have Been Like?

...continued from page 99

and found a way to justify it. (There is, of course, a simpler explanation, as we will discuss when we get to that story.)

In a wider sense, what would the season we didn't get have been like to watch? We know that Colin Baker and Nathan-Turner had discussed a story arc for the Sixth Doctor in which we discover why he was such a git to begin with. We also know that the starting-point for what became 22.6, "Revelation of the Daleks" was a scene with the Doctor seeing his own grave. If we compare his existential rant in 21.7, "The Twin Dilemma" and his sullen acceptance of an eternity stuck in limbo in 22.2, "Vengeance on Varos", we might have a clue. Broadly, it's starting to look as if the pointlessness of his "crusade" and the fact that once he'd started he was committed to it for centuries to come might have been getting to him. Thus, Season Twenty-Three would have been where he found a solution. Some dark and terrible secret may have emerged. Baker often makes the comparison with Mr Darcy from *Pride and Prejudice*. Jane Austen's romantic hero is someone who is protecting someone else from scandal, and can only cope by keeping people at arm's length. "The Two Doctors" reveals a momentary willingness to face the possibility that the Time Lords are corrupt. Destroying Gallifrey may have been something he knew in advance that this incarnation would do.

Consider also that Nathan-Turner was by now planning to move on. His term as producer was now as long as that of Barry Letts, and once this milestone was reached he could have been wondering what else he could do. Eric Saward was re-contracted after "Revelation", so he would have had longer-term plans. He was contacting more experienced television writers, such as David Halliwell and Jack Trevor Story, who were new to the series. As we have seen, old *Who* hands were given the nod for the projected Season Twenty-Three and the televised one alike. Yet the real shape of things to come was 22.5, "Timelash", with a writer new to television.

Another big question is whether the experiment of using 45-minute episodes to get away from simply telling the story would have continued. When "The Trial of a Time Lord" reached us it had the Valeyard and the Inquisitor saying, in effect, "skip this bit", a complete about-face from Saward's previous policy of going off at tangents and exploring the world around the Doctor. This was after the BBC had cut the amount of screen-time per episode and halved the amount per year. Had this decision been taken before the scripts were commissioned, then it's likely that Saward would have found other ways to cut to the chase.

---

acter. Certainly the presence of an earthy sidekick, Bostock, must have made this an inescapable conclusion. Orcini may not seem literally quixotic ('the Knight of the Sad Countenance' is a wannabe, Alonzo Quesana, trying to live up to fictitious standards in a world he thinks has declined), but his comments about the spiritual aspects of swords and 'like the old days' (not necessarily in his own lifetime, though) are in keeping.

Moreover, the whole of this season has seen the Doctor being judged against rumours of his former abilities and reputation. In Book II of *Don Quixote*, Cervantes has his fictional hero-*manque* running into the bootleg presses running off unauthorised sequels to Cervantes's Book I (itself supposedly a translation of an older book), and encountering avid fans of Book I who know more about Quixote's adventures than he does himself. In the mid-1980s, there was a sudden spike in interest about the book when people started using terms like "postmodern" and "magic realism" in polite conversation - some of them accurately. Even people who had never got beyond the bit about the windmills in ch 8 (out of 52 in Book I) could talk authoritatively about it. Saward will discover postmodernism in the following year (see, in particular, 23.4, "The Ultimate Foe").

The Knights of Rhodes, though, were inescapable for a while in the mid 80s, with a sudden rediscovery of 1941's *The Maltese Falcon* after the success of the superficially similar *Raiders of the Lost Ark*, and the publication of books like our old chum *The Holy Blood and the Holy Grail* (see 5.2, "The Abominable Snowmen"). This sort of thing will become a bigger part of *Doctor Who*'s diet after Andrew Cartmel takes over as script editor (see "Remembrance of the Daleks").

Things That Don't Make Sense Astonishingly, nobody in the widespread galaxy seems to have noticed that the source of the miracle foodstuff is the same planet where all the dead people get sent. Besides, how much protein *can* they get out of one stiff? Surely not enough for a famine-relief programme. Unless the *entire* dead of the rest of the galaxy are sent to Necros (and the cost of this, to say nothing of the environmental effect on all those other planets with all that biomass gone, would be huge - never mind that Tranquil Repose is said to have only a 'few thousand stiffs'), it simply can't be done. Also, we're told that Tranquil Repose is a costly and exclusive service, and it's not like the facility has the staff to handle a whole galaxy's ex-plebs anyway.

One more point: nice as the Doctor's "Why don't you cultivate the purple weed-plant for protein?" solution is, are we to assume that agronomy in this period is so crap that *nobody* has thought about cultivating the plant as a famine-remedy before now? Especially as the plant 'grows almost anywhere' and - to rub salt in the wound - Professor Stengos was reportedly 'one of the finest agronomists in the galaxy'. Didn't his old chum the Doctor ever suggest this solution in all these off-screen meetings they supposedly had? And although the plant is decently pretty, isn't decorating elaborate funeral services with something widely referred to as 'the weed plant' just a bit gauche?

Just how public *is* Davros' guise as the 'Great Healer'? It seems like a well-known identity, but if even Bostock recognises Davros as a wanted war-criminal on sight, how come the President of the Galaxy has no idea? Never mind that Davros previously busted out of a top-security space-prison, so he'd be pretty famous just for *that*, without all that "creating-the-most-vicious-race-of-monsters-ever" business.

But the *big* shock about Davros is that his "disembodied head" is just a ventriloquist's dummy placed in a glass tank in case of assassins. All right, but how did he operate it, and how did he read all these dials arrayed around the dummy head? And did Saward honestly think we'd forgotten that the Borad did exactly the same trick in the previous story? [We'll leave aside how Davros is so well-informed about the Order of Oberon, and file it with all the other Things He Didn't Oughta Know, like the Time Lords.] How is the dummy-Davros able to send a static charge through a glass case anyway? And given the chance to create a new identity, he makes his Public Relations face identical to his old, well-known, galaxy's-most-wanted

one, rather than Max Headroom, Denis Carey or Graham Leaman.

Natasha and her associate Grigory find that her father's corpse has been replaced with a stuffed dummy. Seriously, have they replaced *every* purloined body with one, and if so, why bother? Do the Daleks make them out of old clothes and straw? Maybe they have a production-line, like in 4.3, "The Power of the Daleks", but making scarecrows. [With Davros looking the way he does, complete with pushchair, many British fans have made the obvious joke here; Nyder saying 'Penny for the Guy' as they sneak into the Thal Dome. We just like the idea of Daleks with woolly hats and scarves, drinking Bovril and saying "Oooh" when fireworks go off. See **When Did Susan Go To School?** under "Remembrance of the Daleks" for the obligatory historical footnote.]

Amid all his scheming, why does Davros allow the distraction of Natasha and Grigory sneaking into Tranqil Repose? Why not just stake out the tomb of Natasha's father, and avoid wasting time with searches? How, for that matter, do Natasha and Grigory "track" Stengos' body - or rather, the dummy serving as his body? They can't be sniffing out DNA because the dummy doesn't have any, but why would the dummy have a tracing device on it?

This brings us to the biggest problem with the story: perhaps we're missing the point of Davros' megalomania, but isn't it stupidly risky of him to lure the Doctor to Necros just as his plans are reaching some fruition? It's as if he's put out an advertisement saying, "Any passing Time Lords who wish to prevent Davros' latest goofy plan, ring 0800STRANGELOVE". Besides, if the whole object of the exercise was to have the Doctor say something like: "Blimey, Davros, you've finally done it! I'm scared!", why risk keeping Orcini alive during the final confrontation, when the two of them are almost guaranteed to team up against their mutual foe?

Botany student Peri says that the weed-plant is 'the only plant' that grows in the wilderness. She says this whilst standing in front of a bloody great oak tree.

Critique One of the advantages of doing a 1980s Dalek story was that any actor who was approached actually knew what a Dalek was. Regardless of what else was going on with *Doctor Who*, the chance to appear with Daleks made actors who wanted to do it for their kids a bit more inclined to say "yes". As a result, a script as grim and self-consciously "sick" as this nets a cast who probably would've turned up their noses at an identical story featuring - say - the Trods or the Voord. And it's the cast and what Graeme Harper did with them that make this story function at all, let alone shine as it does.

In our comments on the last two stories, we've noted what a difference swapping the directors could have made. Imagine Pennant Roberts or - heaven forbid - Peter Moffatt having been given this script. Worse, imagine it without Clive Swift (as the mortician Jobel), Alexei Sayle (the DJ), William Gaunt (Orcini) or Eleanor Bron (Kara). Suddenly, it's a lot more ordinary. Without them, all that bold dialogue and conceptual daring becomes a little boy trying to shock. Just as "Resurrection" had bad fake policemen simply because *Doctor Who* had done this before and got into trouble (8.1, "Terror of the Autons") for it, Saward builds a whole scene around the bit that Philip Hinchcliffe cut from "The Ark in Space" (12.2) - 'Kill me, Vira' becomes 'Kill me, Natasha'.

We fully expect someone from BBC Wales to come and beat us up with a *Torchwood* prop for saying this, but doing televised *Doctor Who* for adults only is about as pointless as making an X-Certificate weather forecast. A crucial point of the series is to show that the priorities that grown-ups fret over aren't the Big Picture at all. Love and death happen, but sex and violence is almost beside the point. "Revelation of the Daleks" (and what an absurd, pretentious title), has a sense of wonder about the *presentation* of things, but not in the things presented. The mystery of what's going on is pretty redundant as soon as Davros and a Dalek appear (assuming you missed the title of the story), but what kind of world this is occurring in still keeps smaller viewers interested. This is almost an accidental side-effect, when it should have been the object of the exercise.

One thing we *don't* have to imagine is a script like this without the Doctor or the Daleks. It's almost that already. Because Eric Saward has "issues", and is hell-bent on doing it all his way, this story gets as close as you can imagine to alienating the children who are still the ostensible core audience. Yet the inclusion of the Doctor, Peri and the Daleks helps frame all this radical and iconoclastic material in a format that is familiar and reassuring, ensuring that it gets to where it's supposed to go. Moreover, it gives the script a chance

to be as clever as Saward thinks it is. Made outside *Doctor Who*, this would have been too inconsequential to function as drama, and too costly to do as a sitcom (even if the comedy department would never have commissioned a sitcom in space). In the year of *Edge of Darkness*, this was never going to be made any other way.

However much Saward may have resented the Sixth Doctor, he writes quite well for the character - certainly better than he did for Davison. Six is basically a dumb person's idea of a clever person, or (to be fair to Saward) a parody of overeducated speech. Baker's delivery smoothes over a few odd bum notes, so instead of a Doctor who doesn't understand the word 'guy', we have one who's alarmed that someone as famous as Arthur Stengos isn't - to judge by Peri - a household name in 1980s America. This is a Doctor who's using the banter with Peri to distract himself from a sense of foreboding - not someone who counts the hours before another chance to snipe at her, as we've seen so far this year.

Before leaving the script, we have to say something: we've sometimes been harsh on his work, but Eric Saward is a decent thriller writer and should have worked on *The Sweeney* or *Taggart*. It's clear from this story that he has a complex about stepping into the same job as Robert Holmes and Douglas Adams, and that he wants to write at least one script that bears comparison with their work for *Doctor Who*. Since the interviews for *Doctor Who: The Unfolding Text*, Saward has realised that problem-solving can be a creative move as well as mere crisis-management. All his frustrations in trying to write for the Daleks two years ago have become the subject-matter, and this should have been the point where he truly found his own voice as a writer. Instead, with "Slipback" and this story's uneasy similarity to "The Two Doctors" (22.4), he comes across as a wannabe. Saward is torn between writing for quirky characters and writing action, and where this story resolves these tensions he produces his best work. Like X3.4, "The Daleks in Manhattan", a story more like this than people are willing to admit, he manages to make the Daleks a conceptual threat without a single extermination in the first forty-five minutes, then unleashes them in the next episode.

But the script is the sponge-cake at the base of a trifle. On top is a look that is like the routine 1985 *Doctor Who* sets, marble-effect and inset monitor screens, but is all done proficiently, and yet is *also* like several other types of set. Not just TV sets (although the bulk of the interiors were pilfered from other shows) but films, stage-plays and pop videos. It is stylistically promiscuous, in a way that helps Harper's plan to make this story look like channel-zapping between several other programmes.

Into this come actors from a wide range of disciplines: a stand-up comic, a stage-actor, the star of a 60s adventure-show, someone from a costume-drama, some new to television... nobody looks any more or less like they belong in this world. It's a world where performance matters, after all. Funerals are public shows, and everyone in this story is to some extent hiding behind a front and playing up to the ubiquitous cameras. We'll see this done more overtly in stories like "The Happiness Patrol" (25.2) and "The Greatest Show in the Galaxy" (25.4), but here it's part of the fabric of as routine a *Doctor Who* format as you can get. It would be nice to think of the last five stories as leading up to this, but we have the uncomfortable feeling that it's the result of a director whose instincts are sharper than the scriptwriter.

Unfortunately, if a director just gets good actors, colourful characters, crazy sets and electronic tricks, this doesn't make the final result worth watching on its own. What we have here is something rare and strange, a story where the faults of the production and the faults of the script cancel each other out, and their strengths reinforce one another. This rarely happens all at the same time - look at 23.2, "Mindwarp" for what *could* have happened. There, we have lots to look at, lots to listen to and enjoy, a big mystery that reassures the casual viewer that it's *supposed* to be confusing for now - but, overall, there's a feeling that it's a lot of good moments, not a story or a world-view. Some might excuse both of these stories by saying that we're not so much interested in linear plot as in a visual environment, which would (almost) hold water if the whole of this two-episode romp was consistent.

Yet the fact remains that once the Doctor arrives at Tranquil Repose, all such effects are curtailed in order to tell a bog-standard Daleks and Davros yarn. The DJ loses all his mystique, Davros reverts to being his usual ranting self and the visual narrative becomes very orthodox. Watched in one go this is tolerable, as the mysteries and atmosphere of the first act retain the viewer's goodwill through all the latter half's running around corridors and big explosion. Seen over two Saturdays or, worse, in four very uneven episodes, the gulf between intention and execution widens.

The 45-minute format is the culprit. Whilst we don't waste any time with people talking about "...them" until the first Dalek appears at 22 minutes in, we don't see Orcini early enough (for those watching it overseas) and everything conspires to keep the Doctor's arrival as the big turning-point, when in fact the crisis has already begun. It's episode one that earns this story its reputation for daring, atmosphere, wit and panache. Episode two is very much a dull thud of Season Twenty-Two-ness returning after a flirtation with quality.

The Facts

Written by Eric Saward. Directed by Graeme Harper. Ratings: 7.4 million, 7.7 million. Audience appreciation was 67%, then 65%.

Working Titles "End of the Road".

Supporting Cast Terry Molloy (Davros), William Gaunt (Orcini), Eleanor Bron (Kara), Clive Swift (Jobel), Alexei Sayle (DJ), John Ogwen (Bostock), Jenny Tomasin (Tasambeker), Hugh Walters (Vogel), Stephen Flynn (Grigory), Bridget Lynch-Blosse (Natasha), Trevor Cooper (Takis), Colin Spaull (Lilt), Alec Linstead (Head of Stengos), Ken Barker (Mutant), Roy Skelton, Royce Mills (Dalek Voices).

Oh, Isn't That..?

• *Alexei Sayle*. He began as a stand-up, with a persona that affected to be "just out of prison" (hence the shaven head and 60s suit several sizes too small). As one of many alumni of the Comic Strip - a club that became a TV anthology series - and the "other" regular cast member of *The Young Ones*, he was well known as a shouty leftie scouser but had other strings to his bow. He'd had a hit record (*Ullo John, Got A New Motor?*), a radio series and several written pieces (he soon got a regular column in *The Sunday Mirror*), including an affectionate piece for *Foundation* entitled "Why I Should Be The New Doctor Who: The Case for a Marxist in the TARDIS". (Track it down if you can: it's worth a look for capturing the viewpoint of those who'd grown up with the series, and later felt betrayed by Nathan-Turner.) You've probably seen Sayle's cameo in *Indiana Jones and the Last Crusade* (in which he's a Sultan) without knowing it was him. By that time his series, *Stuff*, had secured him a place as a National Treasure.He is now mainly active as a novelist and short-story writer, and might well wind up being remembered for this rather than for anything he did on screen.

• *William Gaunt.* The sardonic English one in ITC's spooky action show *The Champions*, but by 1985 he was the harassed father Arthur Crabtree in *No Place Like Home.* This was an almost self-consciously retro sitcom about an empty-nester whose adult kids all moved back in, and those kids included Martin Clunes (Lon in 20.2, "Snakedance") and Dee Sadler (Flowerchild in "The Greatest Show in the Galaxy").

• *Eleanor Bron.* Icon or what? She'd been the queen of the 1960s satire "boom", doing elegant skits with (usually) John Bird and John Fortune. She'd been Paul McCartney's love-interest in *Help!* (although off-screen "is not the right Beatle he") and avoided being upstaged by Leo McKern. She played Patsy's mum in *Absolutely Fabulous* and... well, look, in any other story she'd have been the biggest star in the cast, but here and opposite John Cleese (17.2, "City of Death"), she's kept from dominating proceedings.

• *Trevor Cooper.* It seemed he was barely off our screens in the late 80s. He was a lecturer at Lowlands University in *A Very Peculiar Practice* (the cast of which would mainly be familiar to anyone reading this, not least David Troughton, Peter Davison and Graham Crowden from 17.5, "The Horns of Nimon"), was cast by Graeme Harper in *Star Cops* as the token "bloke" in a Moonbase full of ethnic stereotypes and was drowned by Juliet Stephenson in Peter Greenaway's film *Drowning By Numbers* (see last story). Then the next year...

• *Hugh Walters.* At that time, he played a camp tailor in daytime soap *Gems* (written by Tony Slattery - see the Appendix). He'd been in the one-off *Callan* revival, "Wet Job". You probably already know, however, that he'd been Shakespeare in "The Chase" (2.8) and Runcible in "The Deadly Assassin" (14.3).

• *Jenny Tomasin.* Of course, she was Ruby in *Upstairs, Downstairs.* She also did a stint in *Emmerdale Farm* (as it was then) and a few other rural dramas of that period.

• *Clive Swift.* He'd been in *The Barsetshire Chronicles* (yet another Anthony Trollope adaptation, this time about Victorian clergy), but is now doomed to be remembered as Richard Bucket (that's pronounced "Bouquet") in *Keeping Up Appearances*, a sitcom about pretension from the pen of Roy Clarke. (Clarke also did *Open All Hours* and *Last of the Summer Wine* - cited all through these books, so we won't list them all.) Curiously, *Keeping Up Appearances* has made Swift moderately well-known in India, where an adaptation of the sitcom has been a massive hit and spawned interest in the original. Swift was also, in fact, in David Lean's *A Passage to India.*

Cliffhangers (Natasha and Grigory hide from a Dalek patrol); a vast marble tombstone, bearing an unflattering likeness of the Doctor, falls onto the camera; (Peri uses the PA to contact the Doctor, who tells her she's in great danger); the lead-in to the (unmade) next story, the Doctor suggests he and Peri enjoy a holiday in 'B...'

The Lore

• Originally, the official colour of mourning on Necros was white (not blue), but with the unexpected snow-cover it's as well they changed it. The snow, in January 1985, caused a rapid rethink of many of the scenes, including the first sight of a flying Dalek attacking Orcini and Bostock. On the plus side, the lighting crew determined that there was about half an hour's extra filming time as a result. (In January, in Britain, this was a definite plus. The available hours are essentially 9am to 3pm.) Many of the exteriors were shot at the IBM complex near Southampton, which had various security restrictions on where they could film.

• As we mentioned in "The Mark of the Rani" (22.3), Lord Olivier had let it be known that he would do a small part in the series if it was on film. As the decision had been made that this would be the last story to do any location filming (see "The Two Doctors"), the only suitable role was the Mutant that tangles with the Doctor and Peri. The octogenarian screen legend declined, and Ken Barker, who was also the underwater hand in the opening minutes of the story, took the part.

• The filming was hastily rescheduled to get the close-ups first, then all the rolling around in snow later, when they could have a break for hot baths and so on. The big wall was actually Goodwood race course. The scene where Orcini and Bostock encounter a Dalek was to have entailed a stunt-Dalek (an empty prop) flung from a catapult to make it "levitate". However, the snow prevented the effects crew from reaching the original location (Butser Hill; see 23.1, "The Mysterious Planet"), and so it was relocated to the same disused airstrip where the entrance to Tranquil Repose was filmed. Thus they had an empty Dalek hanging around, so the shot of Peri not-quite seeing one running behind her was improvised, using wire to pull it along. (And this shot became the trailer for the story when first broadcast.) When mounting the materialisation - carefully placing the TARDIS prop in front of where all the footprints in the snow were - they found they'd left the lamp in London.

• As we discussed, Saward's misgivings about Baker's casting were compounded by the actor stating that there was no other way he could've played Bayban in the *Blake's* 7 episode "The City on the Edge of The World". (To be fair to Baker, underplaying while opposite Paul Darrow was never going to work.) In scripting Davros and Orcini, it would seem, Saward was attempting to prove Baker wrong. Saward claimed later to have conceived Orcini as the kind of character that Christopher Lee would have played, and his doubts about the casting decisions were to grow over the next year.

• It had always been intended that Saward would have another crack at writing for the Daleks, after he wrote what he *thought* was a perfunctory story for Season Twenty's finale. (This was, of course, later moved to the middle of the next year - see 21.4, "Resurrection of the Daleks" and comments around 20.6, "The King's Demons".) In order to avoid self-commissioning and concomitant hassles from Pip and Jane Baker - co-chairs of the Writers' Guild at that time - Saward timed his holiday to come between the end of his contract and the start of a new one. Thus, writing a script whilst on holiday and then taking over the script-editorship effective immediately after his stand-in (Nathan-Turner) had commissioned it wasn't breaking any rules. However, the one-page outline was accepted in March, whilst Saward was still in his post. (It's a bit complicated, but Jonathan Powell, then Head of Drama and a figure we'll be coming across a lot in these anecdotes, insisted that Saward was to do it while off contract, much to Nathan-Turner's annoyance.)

• Budgetary concerns forced designer Alan Spalding to ignore Saward's suggestions for the appearance of Tranquil Repose. The script wanted a blank white and chrome area, with hi-tech fittings (so not even slightly like 12.2, "The Ark in Space", then). Spalding picked up on the Egyptian hints, but took what he could get from other series. The catacombs were mainly from Civil War drama *By The Sword Divided* (hence the Norman arches for the doors, although they look pleasingly Dalek-shaped). Davros's lair - with the Hindu, Catholic and Russian Orthodox trappings - was recycled from various sources, but the bulk of it was from Culture Club's three-minute spot on *The Kenny Everett Television Show*. (Bear in mind that programmes deemed to be Light Entertainment - a different department altogether - always got bigger budgets than drama per minute of screen-time.)

Inside this set, the booth for Davros was constructed without reference to how big Terry Molloy was. He had a swivel-chair and handrails inside there, but no room for his legs. The idea that Davros' head would be in a tank of liquid was vetoed - probably for the same reasons that Sil was kept high and dry (22.2, "Vengeance on Varos"), i.e. fear of children trying to copy it. The Main Hall's central arch was pilfered from *The Little and Large Show*. (Anyone not in Britain at the time should just accept that this series was worse than it sounds: like being trapped in a lift with a drunk who thinks he's funny, but with a stooge who's like the Earthling from 18.2, "Meglos" only less charismatic.)

• Similarly, Pat Godfrey, with £5,000 to spend on all the costumes, opted to take Orcini's clothes from stock and add a few details, ignoring the script's recommendations. The majority of the uniforms at Tranquil Repose were dental nurse scrubs. The Dalek props were a mixed bag: the Imperial ones were all new, made following the original templates but constructed from fibreglass and with small modifications. By contrast, the Grey Daleks were a motley assortment of parts from stories dating back to the 1960s, with one complete shell (made for 3.4, "The Daleks' Master Plan" and later painted gold for 9.1, "The Day of the Daleks"), and tops and bottoms mixed with more recent components ('recent' meaning 1975). To offset the cost of making the new ones, a plan was hatched to lease them to BBC Enterprises for promotional work, but nothing came of this. The new ones were later painted grey and became the "Rebel" Daleks in "Remembrance of the Daleks".

• Alexei Sayle was slightly concerned that the Dalek operators seemed to shun everyone else. Meanwhile, Nathan-Turner was concerned that Sayle's performance was muted in the rehearsals, and they contemplated replacing him. They had no lack of options, as Harper had made a wish list for this part that would take up the whole of this page. The one everyone knows is Ringo Starr. More curiously, it seems that David Bowie, Rowan Atkinson, Roger Daltrey and Jasper Carrott were considered. As it turns out, the shy Sayle was saving his energy for the take, and was closer to his delivery as MC of the Comedy Store. (Nicola Bryant reports that off camera, Sayle is pretty much the DJ as Peri sees him.)

• The bulk of the music used is cover-versions of the originals, flanged by Roger Limb. Two actual proper recording were OK'ed by the copyright-owners, A Whiter Shade of Pale by Procul Harem and Fire by the Jimi Hendrix Experience. (The latter isn't sanctioned for DVD or video releases, but is used in broadcasts; a similar legal hassle afflicts 7.1, "Spearhead from Space" episode two.)

• Because Baker and Bryant were in panto in Southampton during Christmas, the location was handy for them. However, it meant that they missed the first recording block in the studio - less of a problem in this story than it would normally have been. One snag was that in addition to all their scenes for this story, the remount for the newly extended TARDIS scene for 22.5, "Timelash" was recorded in the second block. The panto, Cinderella, also starred Anthony Ainley, Mary Tamm and Jacqueline Pearce; it was directed by Fiona Cumming, and produced by Nathan-Turner. In the end it lost an estimated £30,000.

• Jane Judge, the departing production secretary, was by now Saward's main contact with the day-to-day running of the series. Indeed, she was with him on the holiday to Rhodes (where they stepped onto the tarmac at the airport and heard Levine's big hit of that year. Hi-Energy). Gary Downie would later make a big deal out of this relationship, saying that it gave Saward a distorted view of conversations he shouldn't have known about. Saward counters that Downie's belief that he was being groomed to take over the series deluded him into prima-donna-like behaviour. (See, for instance, "The Greatest Show in the Galaxy") Curiously, the code to detonate Kara's 'great big bomb' is E.N.A.J.

• Colin Baker got himself nicked for speeding shortly after this story was shown. He conducted his own defence, but wound up with a ban. This affected his charity work a bit, but not unduly. (With hindsight, though, it makes the next year's worth of episodes a bit more silly than they already are.)

• On the strength of just two stories (this one and 21.6, "The Caves of Androzani"), Graeme Harper was considered enough of a "star" director to be mentioned in connection with the alleged thirtieth anniversary special, "The Dark Dimension" (see the Appendix and weep). We cited him as one of the recognised stylists (see **Which Are the "Auteur" Directors?** under 18.5, "Warriors' Gate") and evidently Russell T Davies agreed. Harper got to do the two Cybermen two-parters for Series Two (X2.5, "Rise of the Cybermen" / X2.6, "The Age of Steel"; X2.12, "Army of Ghosts" / X2.13, "Doomsday"). In the first two of these, Colin Spaull - who'd played Lilt in "Revelation" - was Lumic's associate Mr Crane. Harper was back in Series Three, and is now the only director to have supervised two regenerations in different stories (Yes, one of them was the Master, unexpectedly returning an episode ahead of the leaked "surprise", but other than Barry Letts' double regeneration at the end of 9.5, "Planet of the Spiders", this is unique.)

• As we've seen, Colin Baker and Nicola Bryant weren't left idle despite having an extra-long break between Seasons Twenty-Two and Twenty-Three. Baker had recorded "Doctor Who in a Fix with Sontarans" (see 22.4, "The Two Doctors") shortly before news of the hiatus broke. By calling the BBC every day for the subsequent year, he was able to ensure he was still paid under the terms of his contract as the Doctor, while pursuing other work. As it turned out, this other work included more Doctor Who for the BBC, on the radio. Publicity around the cancellation had caught the interest of light entertainment producer Jonathan James-Moore - then preparing a children's summer magazine show called Pirate Radio Four - and he contacted Nathan-Turner to see if this could include a one-hour Doctor Who serial.

It was agreed that Saward would write the script and Baker and Bryant would star in it. Initially titled "The Doomsday Project" (but changed to avoid confusion with a BBC schools' initiative planned to coincide with the 900th anniversary of the Domesday Book), "Slipback" would see the Doctor and Peri trapped on a spaceship with ravening monsters, obsequious servo-drones, thick policemen, a villain capable of psychosomatically cultivating plague spores on his own body, plus various other elements seemingly pinched from Robert Sheckley via Douglas Adams. The plot revolved around a megalomaniac computer with a split personality accidentally travelling back in time and creating the universe... again. (See also 20.4, "Terminus", which Saward script-edited.)

Doctor Who had come to radio before - in 1976, when Tom Baker and Elisabeth Sladen recorded the school's series *Exploration Earth* episode ("The Time Machine") as a mini-*Who* drama. (Other near-misses are cited at the end of this book.) Saward wrote "Slipback" very quickly, and the story was recorded in early June. Valentine Dyall (the Black Guardian in 16.6, "The Armageddon Factor"; 20.3, "Mawdryn Undead" et seq.) also appeared in this; it was his last acting role, as he died two weeks later. The cast also included Ron Pember, Jane Carr, Nick Revell and various other people who ought to have been in the TV series but weren't. Saward was still enthusiastic about the series even at this stage - something to bear in mind as the story of Season Twenty-Three unfolds.

Saward padded "Slipback" with extensive humorous digressions for the Target novelisation, which hit the shelves in 1986 around the same time as his *Starburst* interview. Featuring one of the ugliest covers in the range - by Paul Mark Tams, and we'll learn more of his crimes in just a bit - it was reputedly one of Target's poorest sellers. "Slipback" became a perennial BBC Audio Collection release (usually paired with the bowdlerised soundtrack of 12.4, "Genesis of the Daleks") and kick-started the BBC's on-off flirtation with the idea of putting *Doctor Who* on radio for the nation (see the Appendix). In the case of "Slipback", "the nation" meant England as it was broadcast in VHF / FM, then largely unavailable in Scotland, Wales or Northern Ireland. Two 10-minute episodes of *Slipback* were broadcast at unscheduled moments in the three 3-hour editions of *Pirate Radio Four* on Thursday mornings over the end of July / start of August 1985. As we'll see, this was just about the only airplay *Doctor Who* received in 1985...

• We've put it off long enough. As you'll know from volumes IV and V, Ian Levine has a life outside *Doctor Who* as a record producer and DJ on the Northern Soul circuit. So when another well-placed fan, Paul Mark Tams, came to him with a protest song about the Suspension Crisis, Levine ensured that it got made. If you've heard Levine's work, even just the theme from "K9 And Company" or the early, unsuccessful Take That singles before *Could It Be Magic?*, you can perhaps imagine the sort of thing - mind, whatever you imagine is a lot better than the result.

In the style of *Do They Know It's Christmas?* and *We Are The World* (and any number of lousier ones after that), they herded a lot of people into a studio, gave them the lyrics, told some to do some lines and others to do others, and pointed a camera at them while they did it. Except that, where the two singles we previously named had people the average person might have identified (such as David Bowie, Billy Joel and Bob Dylan to pick but a few), "Who Cares" (and a name like that was asking for trouble) had Colin Baker, Nicola Bryant, Anthony Ainley, Nicholas Courtney, Faith Brown (Flast in 22.1, "Attack of the Cybermen"), Sally Thomsett (from *The Railway Children* and *Man About the House*), Rick Buckler (formerly of The Jam), Justin Hayward (of The Moody Blues), Bobby Lee (AKA Bobby Gee of Buck's Fizz), Phyllis Nelson (a one-hit wonder, but "Move Closer" is as good a one-hit wonder as any) and Matt Bianco[11].

So they weren't *total* unknowns, despite what the press claimed, but they were hardly Wham! or Culture Club. Everyone managed not to look too embarrassed, as they sang a potted synopsis of 1.1, "An Unearthly Child" and yelled: 'Eight-teen. Months. Is. Too-long. To-wait. Bring back the Doctor, don't hesitate.' The first verse is odd but commercial... and then they wheel on the *Who* cast. Ponder Baker singing, or Courtney almost pulling off the Rex Harrison *sprechgesang*. Most people give up when Ainley goes 'heh-heh-heh'.

However, this was all for charidee - in this case Levine and Tams picked cancer research. This looked like a flimsy pretext, but it helped. The record got to 130 in the UK charts, despite the BBC not giving it airplay. (This wasn't censorship, nor indeed an aesthetic judgement. The problem was that it's hard to figure out the lyrics, and they have guidelines about that.) The music press - at their most sarcastic in that era - had great fun with the project and its cast of not-quite big names. The video, directed by Keith Barnfather, was more imaginative than the song and better than most of this kind of record's promotion.

• Then Levine addressed fans at a convention, DWASocial V. Some eye-witnesses call it "The Nuremberg Rally", others tried to suppress giggles as Levine - fresh from a photo-call where he kicked in his TV - railed against Radio One (the main pop channel) and various news and entertainment programmes that had ignored his record, plus the BBC in general. He was mainly angry about reports that the next season would only have twenty twenty-five minute episodes, a rumour the production office said was "ludicrous" and "scaremongering". Levine then turned his ire against Nathan-Turner...

... who did a panel immediately afterwards. Even those who had doubts about him, and Baker, found themselves won over by the tactful, witty and direct approach of producer and star that afternoon. For better or worse, Nathan-Turner was still a BBC staff-member, and was in rather urgent need of a fresh project. Such a public humiliation as his series being lambasted by the Corporation's hierarchy (not to mention getting trounced in the ratings) didn't help his career prospects, but he understandably couldn't appear on a panel and slag off the BBC1 bosses. Levine's request for a repeat season was one he thought a fan letter-writing campaign could fruitfully follow, but the suggestion of co-production with America would not work. (In fact, since 20.7, "The Five Doctors", the series was technically a co-production between BBC Drama and BBC Enterprises, the semi-autonomous merchandising wing of the Corporation.)

• After the Suspension was announced, the production team began revising plans for the next season, not least with regard to the number and length of episodes. (We've given over this story's essay to the various options.) Nathan-Turner took advantage of this break to claim all the accumulated leave he'd been able to take, owing to one crisis after another, since his break in late 1982.

23.1: "The Trial of a Time Lord: The Mysterious Planet"

(Serial 7A, Four Episodes. 6th - 27th September 1986.)

Which One is This? The Doctor is put on trial for his life, and the prosecution shows an escapade involving mud-huts, robots and a lot of running about in corridors. Well-spoken Celtic warriors inhabit future-London, but cockney wide-boys have claimed every other planet, apparently. Peri gets engaged several times, and the Earth moves.

Firsts and Lasts Format-wise, it's the first of the 14-episode seasons that will define the show from here to its conclusion, and it's the debut of Dominic Glynn's rendition of the theme tune. (To be fair, this sounds better on a stereo - but not much - than through TV speakers.) It's the first of three appearances by the supposedly loveable rogue Sabalom Glitz, and although his sidekick Dibber doesn't appear again, this was Glen Murphy's first major TV role (see Oh, Isn't That...?).

Most significantly, this adventure begins with the first episode since the Suspension, and a lot was riding on it. The aforementioned 14-episode format is here engineered to make the whole year's run one long story about the Doctor fighting for his life. (If you couldn't guess that from the "Trial of a Time Lord" title, see if you can spot the sub-text in the Valeyard's opening lines.) Thus it is also the story that introduces the prosecuting Valeyard, the adjudicating Inquisitor and the Trial Room set (along with the model-shots to establish this). Mike Tucker here starts his stint as Special Effects dude, and having a fan around to do this sort of thing makes a noticeable difference.

Four Things to Notice about "The Mysterious Planet"...

1. Finally, after a few faltering attempts (18.2, "Meglos"; 21.4, "Resurrection of the Daleks"), *Doctor Who* enters the age of motion-control cameras. That being the case, there's a big show-offy opening sequence of a beam of light pulling the TARDIS into a vast space station, with lots of cam-

Season 23 Cast/Crew

- Colin Baker (the Doctor)
- Nicola Bryant (Peri, 23.1 and 23.2)
- Bonnie Langford (Melanie, 23.3 and 23.4)
- Michael Jayston (the Valeyard)
- Lynda Bellingham (the Inquisitor)

- John Nathan-Turner (Producer)
- Eric Saward (Script Editor, 23.1, 23.2 and 23.4 "Part Thirteen" only*)

* As we'll see, no script editor is credited for 23.3 and 23.4, "Part Fourteen".

era-swoops around the place - and, it would seem, blowing the whole year's effects budget on the first forty seconds. Yet as impressive as this was at the time - especially compared to most of the previous decade's efforts - it only made the remaining 354 minutes of this season look more shoddy than ever. In particular, notice the contrast when the Doctor emerges from the spectacularly hijacked TARDIS and enters the nasty-looking Trial Room set, with its mood-destroying lighting.

2. In fact, with everything lit so flatly, it's hard to get any sense of scale. So even when, at last, we get a corridor set big enough for the Doctor to speedily run around in, it looks cramped. And when we see a ginormous robot towering over people already established as fairly tall, the proportions are misrepresented - and the depth-of-field so compromised - that the effect is lost. So while you're watching this, observe carefully the relative heights of Drathro, the Doctor and the tribe-queen Katryca, and try to imagine what her death *should* have looked like. Similarly, the Trial Room is actually quite vast, but looks like the cardboard-box *Doctor Who* theatre they showed you how to make on *Blue Peter* (see the DVD of 14.6, "The Talons of Weng Chiang").

3. So the Tribe of the Free are post-Apocalyptic warriors combining trashed technology with Celtic folk-art. It could have looked horrible, like a Toyah Willcox video[13], or it could have looked frightfully nice and hand-knitted. It was certainly intended to look sort of like *Mad Max* and its sequels, with a dominant matriarch like Auntie Entity. Indeed, short of actually getting Tina

Who Narrates This Programme?

Obviously, someone does. Although *Doctor Who* is shown to us without - a few exceptions aside - any voice-over telling us that this is anyone's story in particular, the series' presentation as a work of television suggests a continuous, coherent point of view. There's music from somewhere. There's a definite decision to cut from one camera-angle to another, sometimes for obvious reasons of narrative tension (both "The Mysterious Planet" and 8.2, "The Mind of Evil" construct cliffhangers around someone apparently shooting the Doctor, but in reality pointing at someone else). There are points when that week's episode stops. Yet this clearly isn't CCTV footage - it's not a news feed, and this is obviously a story being told to us. So what's the provenance of this story? How reliable is it? Is there any bias, or omissions for more than narrative pace?

The question becomes more complicated the closer you look. Yes, it's a BBC production, but it isn't like most of them. Soaps do not have especially commissioned scores (well, ours don't). Big dramas either have a voice-over narrator, or a central character whose adventures and crises we follow. We had that to begin with, but she left with Ian in 2.8, "The Chase". (The 2005 series had one too, and she *did* narrate whole episodes - see X1.8, "Father's Day"; X2.12, "Army of Ghosts" / X2.13, "Doomsday".) Legitimate drama productions tend not to have cliffhangers at all, unless they're Dickens adaptations, and we'll come back to them in a moment. But as we've seen before - and will again - the orthodox narrative practices of even bog-standard mimetic television break down every so often, and we see things that are either hallucinations or flashback memories, presented to us on the same level as things all the characters can see and photograph. (See, if you haven't already, Is "Realism" Enough? under 19.3, "Kinda".) Only very rarely do soaps do the sorts of things we see in episode three of "Ghost Light" (26.3), when Ace's sense of oppression causes her (and us) to hear fire engines and see flashing blue police-car lights.

So on the one hand, we have a highly symbolic use of narrative, but in a context of media SF that relies on and demands the absolute assumption that the spaceships and monsters aren't representing emotional states, but are really there shooting at the characters. Earlier in the same story, we skip eighteen hours. In the majority of television dramas, we'd be told this with a shot of a clock. Or the sun rising. Or something.

And if you're not watching this as *EastEnders* with ray-guns or a freaky form of costume-drama, but have come to it from the background of "Cult" TV - and are therefore thinking of it as somehow belonging with other such shows - the question is more complicated yet. Habitually, such people think of series as being set in self-contained "Universes", and each such show has its own ground rules and house style. That style is part of the signature of any given show, and includes things like the way they go from scene to scene.

Which brings us, strangely enough, to "The Gunfighters" (3.8): far from being a freakish aberration, "The Ballad of the Last Chance Saloon" was only an extreme logical conclusion of the tendency of the preceding stories to use music representative of the world in which the episode was set. Space adventures had brassy discords and *musique concrete*, and historicals had roughly right music (a possible exception being 3.5, "The Massacre" with sort-of spy movie music, but that was itself a comment on what they thought this story was about). The house style of mid-1980s *Doctor Who* is noticeably more coherent than that of its mid-60s version or that of the present day, which is why nearly every cliffhanger of Season Twenty-Three ends with a crash zoom on the Doctor's face. Yet the series' original point was that, in the cult-TV fan's terminology, the TARDIS travelled between "universes". One week it was in one kind of story, with *that* story's style of delivery, the next we would be in another type of narrative entirely. Nobody would think it odd when Marco Polo did voice-over for seven episodes, and then the next week we pop to *Flash Gordon* in (very) slow motion. Nobody in 1964 had any problem with that, because *Doctor Who* was sort-of an anthology series. It was only when people applied the rules of Cult TV to it, long after the fact, that this looked strange.

It's an odd thing, but the fans only pondered this when they came to write original novels. Why did - for example - first-person narratives, the oldest and most durable form of prose, seem wildly experimental when used on occasion in a *Doctor Who* book format? Statistically and aesthetically, such narratives should have been the norm, as they are in all other fiction. In fact, why did the use of a third-person narrator who told the story in character strike anyone as odd? And why did books deviating from this apparently "natural"

continued on page 113...

Turner to play Katryca, what more could they have done? Well, Eartha Kitt was in Britain a lot that year, plugging her rancid dance album, so Nathan-Turner asked her - and got no reply. Plan B was, um, Joan Sims (see 19.6, "Earthshock" for *deja vu* and **Oh, Isn't That..?**, should you need telling who Joan Sims was.)

4. If "The Caves of Androzani" (21.6) was Robert Holmes redeeming ideas from earlier stories that hadn't quite fulfilled their potential, this story might almost be an effort to take the best bits from previous Holmes hits and do them as badly as possible. Observe in particular how Glitz and Dibber recycle dialogue from Garron and Unstoffe in "The Ribos Operation" (16.1).

The Continuity

The Doctor He was deposed as Lord President of Gallifrey because he neglected his post [20.7, "The Five Doctors"], and the Inquisitor claims this was done legally. [As he later claims to be 'President Elect' we have two options: either he was re-appointed by a new High Council, somehow, or the deposition took place later in Gallifreyan Mean Time than the later stories. More on this to follow.] During the course of this affair, the Doctor believes that defending himself is a better move than accepting a court-appointed defender. [For the particular charges against the Doctor and more on this, see **The Time Lords**.]

In court, the Doctor is contemptuous of basically everyone present, but most particularly the Valeyard. He indulges in self-congratulatory comments when watching the replay of his adventure on Ravalox, and many schoolboy puns about the word 'Valeyard'. When riled, he makes grandiloquent speeches with big gestures. He's particularly pleased about his "stratagem" for using his umbrella to deflect a volley of stones, even though this fails and results in his being bashed unconscious.

The Doctor is still writing theses, and briefly considers staying on Ravalox for a year to research one entitled *Ancient Life on Ravalox*. He stops short of revealing his pen-name. He's still claiming to be 'only 900 years old' [as with 22.6, "Revelation of the Daleks"]. The thought of leaving the mystery of Ravalox unsolved seems anathema to him [and he emphasises that he personally has to solve it]. While imploring the robot Drathro to let the humans under his control live, the Doctor argues

with him about the purpose of organic life, claiming that even *he* hasn't figured it out yet.

He seems familiar with the characteristics of Black Light, and proves somewhat adept in manipulating machinery that regulates it, but says this isn't his field of expertise [cf 24.1, "Time and the Rani" and 11.1, "The Time Warrior"].

• *Ethics.* The Doctor seems to prefer someone in authority asking for help before intervening, but it's mostly his own curiosity that keeps dragging him into various conflicts. [His actions here reflect the programme's usual stance on potential being more important than mere survival (i.e., he knows that Marb Station is viable in itself, but its people must shed their fear of venturing onto the surface if their society is to change). Yet when trying to persuade Drathro of the superiority of humans over machines per se, he doesn't play this "adaptability" card.]

• *Inventory.* On the conveyer belt tonight: a slightly different golf umbrella, a slightly different waistcoat, a black cat-badge, a teddy-bear, a bag of sweets, a big torch, an oil-can and a carnival cat-mask

• *Background.* At some stage, he's read the [edited] Time Lord files on Ravalox. [It's hard to gauge when this might have happened, although the Doctor's contact with the Matrix in 15.6, "The Invasion of Time" is a possible suspect.] As an apparent side-effect of his being pulled out of time for the Trial, the Doctor doesn't recall what he was doing prior to his abduction, nor remember Peri's location. [Both are explained in the next story.]

The Doctor has read *Moby Dick* and *The Water Babies*.

The Supporting Cast

• *Peri.* Her hair has grown a bit since we last saw her, and [judge for yourselves if this is a good thing] she's started dressing in very colourful clothes, rather like the Doctor. She's enjoying this whole time-travel lark now, and finds Ravalox strangely familiar. However, she freaks out upon discovering that the planet is actually the doomed planet Earth, two million years into her future. This upsets Peri to the point that not even the Doctor's peroration on transience can soothe her. [And after all, she's just seen him freak out about his own mortality: "Revelation of the Daleks".]

When the Tribe of the Free takes Peri captive, the prospect of forced marriage doesn't disconcert her as much as the notion of polyandry.

Who Narrates This Programme?

...continued from page 111

style of telling the story - the one Terrance Dicks taught us - have to *explain* how we came to be holding this text in our hands? After all, we'd never asked where the TV stories came from. But in books, you can do a lot with the omissions and lies inherent in a single narrator, and one of the key problems of adapting Dickens (to take only the most adapted of all "classic" authors) is that when you do it on screen, Dickens himself isn't there. His persona - in print and when he read from the books in front of audiences (see X1.3, "The Unquiet Dead") - affects how we interpret the stories. (For this reason, we've seen it seriously argued by otherwise sensible folk that this makes *The Muppets' Christmas Carol* the only faithful Dickens adaptation, since Dickens - looking very like Gonzo - is present throughout and addressing us.)

Along those lines, the recent version of *Bleak House* (the one with Gillian Anderson and Burn Gorman) has all sorts of flashy editing to stop you seeing any one character as central, but their version of the plot makes Esther seem superhumanly virtuous and sympathetic. If you've read the book, you'll know that alternate chapters are told by her, and the others are told by Dickens in the third-person casting doubt on Esther's version. Once you pull at that strand, the "real" story emerges. The only time *Doctor Who* attempted this was in X2.10, "Love and Monsters", and Cult TV fans somehow think this is a kind of "experiment".

The question we started to ask, then, is one that might not strike many of this book's readers as worth asking. But in the context in which *Doctor Who* was created, it was the key question. How do we get to see and hear these events, and who is deciding what we don't see and hear?

During the course of the evidence in the Trial, the Valeyard seems to answer this question. The TARDIS has a psychic 'collection field' that allows it to collate the subjective impressions of those in range - not just the Doctor - and relay them to the Matrix. But even this doesn't answer anything. Apart from raising the prospect that stories in the Trial narrative itself probably aren't reliably told (see the essay for the next story), it opens up far bigger questions.

For direct comparison, let's take an example each from the authors this season. "The Ribos Operation" (16.1) has the Doctor's strand of the story running in a zone outside time, then in the TARDIS and then on Ribos. Meanwhile, Garron and

Unstoffe are flogging a planet to the Graf Vynda K. Except... what does "meanwhile" mean? Is the TARDIS able to pick up Garron's mental traces from *before* it materialised? If so, why wait until what we experience as episode three before revealing that he's running a hookey planet scam? In "Vengeance on Varos" (22.2), we have the main plot and a counterpoint, the latter being a couple who have no direct causal connection to events. Nothing wrong with that, but why pick *this* couple? In "The Mark of the Rani" (22.3), it's left until the cliffhanger's reprise that we see George Stephenson dash to the Doctor's aid. And with *three* TARDISes around in that adventure, why are so many plot details left unresolved? Ultimately, being told that the TARDIS is collecting mental data only sketches in where the raw material comes from, not who chooses it. (And this still doesn't address the awkward questions offered by 7.4, "Inferno", or 9.1, "Day of the Daleks", in which there's no TARDIS present to collect anything not entirely from the Doctor's point-of-view.)

If you start thinking like this, it blows things wide apart. Where did the incidental music come from? Why do some scenes in black and white stories carry on after the TARDIS has left? Can we legitimately assume that *all* written data, unless specifically left impenetrable, appeared to the Doctor and his chums as English? That last point seems like a detail, but it's especially pertinent. We've assumed a "translation convention" on occasion, but always for the benefit of the characters in the story, not specifically for us at home.

Which brings us to the main point: if this all *really* happened, why are we being told about it? Who is telling us about aliens and time travel, when we're constantly warned in the stories that Earth isn't ready for this knowledge? The existence of 158 televised stories before the 1989 cut-off point, another forty-one (or forty-two, if you include the McGann film) to date and a vast corpus of spin-offs and unauthorised material about the Doctor's exploits could be a softening-up exercise, preparing us for contact. Alternatively, the existence of a well-known show might be a means by which the Government could plausibly cover-up the presence of *real* aliens and time-travellers. If anyone actually sees an Ice Warrior on Hampstead Heath, the official denial would be "they were filming *Doctor Who*", rather than anything about Martians going "looking for badgers" (see 6.5, "The Seeds of

continued on page 115...

ABOUT TIME 1985–1989

• *The Inquisitor*. The judicial overseer of the Doctor's Trial looks like a [Gallifreyan] woman of indeterminate age, and who seems to hide a mix of confusion and contempt behind a professional mask. She wears a white robe, with a red diagonal sash, and a white skullcap [similar to the collars of senior Time Lords] with lace "wings". Her status is unclear, but she's obviously of enough rank to administrate a court composed (according to the Doctor) of 'distinguished' Time Lords. Somewhat oddly, she seems not to know the Doctor even by reputation [see **History** for what this *might* mean about the court's temporal relation to Gallifrey].

She knows little of the Doctor's past, and has to consult notes to see that he's previously been tried for a similar offence [6.7, "The War Games", and again, see **The Time Lords**]. The Valeyard offers that the Inquisitor can privately view information withheld from the Court. [Yet we're annoyingly never told if she does. If so, and as this information pertains to secrets being lifted from the Matrix, then the Inquisitor is a lot more complicit in the High Council's cover-up than is often thought - see the next story for more on this.]

The Supporting Cast (Evil)

• *The Valeyard*. As mentioned, he's the appointed prosecutor in the Doctor's Trial. He seems to know the Doctor's past and *modus operandi* in some detail [for reasons revealed - as if you didn't know - in 23.4, "The Ultimate Foe"]. He attempts to play the authority figure, allowing the Doctor's flippancy to work against him.

The Doctor says - and the Valeyard confirms - the term 'Valeyard' means 'learned court prosecutor'. [And at no point on screen does it mean, as is often claimed, "doctor of law". This "fact" was invented by malicious fans, who persuaded a *Doctor Who Magazine* reviewer to mention it in print - shout us drinks at the Fitzroy Tavern and we'll name names.] The Valeyard is clearly antagonistic to the Doctor, but speaks appropriately according to his post, and uses archaisms in his indictment. He also plays to the gallery, seizing on every occasion where the Doctor's own words do the prosecution's job for him.

As proof of the Doctor's misdeeds, the Valeyard proposes to show two 'separate epistopic interfaces of the spectrum' - meaning he's going to screen events from the Doctor's visit to Ravalox and one other escapade [see 23.2, "Mindwarp"].

The Supporting Cast (Evil-ish)

• *Sabalom Glitz*. Criminal who claims he's the product of a broken home, and has seen 'dozens' of prison psychiatrists. Glitz and his apprentice Dibber visit Ravalox to retrieve scientific secrets as held by the L3 robot Drathro, and Glitz is ruthless enough to contemplate gassing the several hundred humans underground to death to achieve this. [This clashes considerably with the "loveable rogue" persona Glitz later sports; see "The Ultimate Foe".] Glitz's prize is destroyed when Drathro overheats and perishes, but as a consolation, Glitz and Dibber decide to plunder the lucrative Silictote from Drathro's Black Light aerial.

Glitz claims to have the death penalty on him in 'six galaxies' [probably true, as there's no point in his making such an idle boast to Katryca, who's got no idea what a 'galaxy' is].

The TARDIS In accordance with the 'latest surveillance methods' - and without the Doctor's knowledge - the TARDIS was 'bugged' on a previous occasion. [We presume this happened the last time the Ship was in dock, 20.1, "Arc of Infinity", although it's worth reiterating that Time Lord technicians are only mentioned as working on the console in the novelisation, and aren't seen on screen. Still, if the bug *was* installed in "Arc", then it's quite possible that Maxil did it - which might explain a great deal.] Owing to this, the evidence presented at the Doctor's Trial has been harvested from the TARDIS' 'collection field' [evidently an extension of its telepathic circuits], which contains visuals and audio on anyone within range of the Ship.

[Incidentally, we never see where on Ravalox the TARDIS has been parked. It must be within walking distance of what's now Marble Arch tube station, so unless the Thames has run dry, we'll assume it's somewhere in the West End. Although given the Ship's perverse sense of humour, it might as well have been Buckingham Palace.]

The Time Lords To examine the peculiarities of their system... authorities at the Doctor's Trial include the Inquisitor, the Valeyard, some assorted guards and one Gallifreyan [in Patrex robes, judging by 14.3, "The Deadly Assassin"] whom the Inquisitor seems to indicate would have served as council for the Doctor's defence. Also in attendance are about twelve Time Lords in full regalia - they're seated behind the Inquisitor, and

Who Narrates This Programme?

...continued from page 113

Death" and the essay with 25.2, "The Happiness Patrol"). Either way, someone with knowledge of *real* extraterrestrial activities would have to be behind the broadcasting of this series.

Who might this be? An obvious candidate is the Doctor himself. He might be retrospectively telling us all about his exploits, possibly as a thought-experiment. The one instance where we know the Doctor is narrating and "weaving" the mental impulses into a "story" is the repeat showing of "The Evil of the Daleks" (4.9) following "The Wheel in Space" (5.7). He begins with a teaser "trailer" of Kennedy being exterminated, and then, with a bit of spoken commentary (like a BBC announcer), he allows it to run on exactly the same way we saw it thirteen months earlier - music, cliffhangers, logical flaws and all. So what BBC1 showed in the summer of 1967 is in every respect like the Doctor's attempt to tell his memories like a story.

This raises some interesting problems. If this is the case, how do we know he's not slightly exaggerating, or putting a rather slanted account forward? Why does he sometimes "imagine" stock music (sometimes Dudley Simpson, sometimes the BBC Radiophonic Workshop and so on) and really ghastly lapses of judgement in some cases? Might it not all be an attempt by one of the most evil and corrupt beings in the universe to "spin" the events of his life to us as a series of benign interventions? Why should we believe that it's just bad luck that wars start wherever he lands? (The astute amongst you will recognise this as a variation on the theory that Jessica Fletcher was, in fact, America's most prolific serial-killer - but that she got Angela Lansbury to play her in *Murder, She Wrote* so that no jury would convict her.)

If you've been reading these essays in sequence, you'll remember how the TARDIS Scanner provides a bit of evidence. Sometimes it shows what is objectively outside, like a TV screen. But sometimes it shows drawings, diagrams or photos (examples would include 19.4, "The Visitation"; 1.3, "Edge of Destruction"; "The Wheel in Space" and 10.4, "Planet of the Daleks"). Occasionally, like showing Zoe the video of "Evil" or "The Keeper of Traken" (18.6), it converts memories into narrative. Similar non-mimetic sequences happen in instances like the climax of "The Massacre" (3.5), the linking scenes of "Marco Polo" (1.4) and the end of "The Chase" (2.8). We also have the big screen (we suspect it's the Matrix, but it's

not explicitly stated as such) in "The War Games" (6.7). The Time Lords, who seem capable in other stories of watching live coverage of history happening, not only rely in the Doctor's psychic affidavit but show drawings instead of footage.

So maybe it's not the Doctor doing it, but rather the Time Lords. This was tenable back when there *were* Time Lords, just about. Although the High Council tended not to come out of these stories too well, it's possible that these tales were selected to reflect badly on the *ancien regime* after a more Doctor-friendly generation had come to power.

That said, if the programme we've been watching was propaganda intended for Gallifrey, how did BBC television get hold of it? And why is there a whole new batch of adventures set after the Time Lords' destruction? (The other question here - How can the Matrix contain knowledge of what happens after it ceases to exist? - is trivial. It's the Matrix, it knows bleedin' *everything*. The whole point of the APC net, as originally explained in 14.3, "The Deadly Assassin", was to calculate the future of the one planet where laws of physics and protocol prevented actual first-hand investigation: Gallifrey itself.) Surely knowing about the Time War would wreck history, and maybe that's exactly what happened - a small clique of Time Lords saw it all coming, and ensured that at least one small planet knew that things had once been different.

Another possibility is that someone from outside the Matrix is tapping it. We know that this is possible, as the entire plot of Season Twenty-Three is about these bootleg videos. What makes less sense is that the whole scam was done expressly so that Cold War-era British schoolkids could get a cheap thrill every Saturday. (Seen in this light, the High Council's decision to wipe out all life on this planet seems entirely proportionate and reasonable.) Here, X2.0, "The Christmas Invasion" is worthy of note: if the Doctor was trying to send out a warning to other species not to bother coming to Earth, "accidentally" leaking Time Lord records of how many times invaders have come unstuck is a cheap, low-maintenance way of doing it. That being the case, what if the *Doctor Who* we watch is a series of dramatised reconstructions?

The obvious comparison on that score is Sherlock Holmes. In the 1930s, Monsignor Ronald Knox (see 19.7, "Time-Flight") posited the most

continued on page 117...

it's their mental energy that draws the Doctor and his TARDIS 'out of time'. [Thus, although they're constantly referred to as 'members of the court', they seem to serve the double-function of jurists and effectively court bailiffs, bringing the Accused to face the inquiry. Although it's a little debatable, we'll henceforth refer to them as 'the Jury'.]

The Valeyard charges the Doctor with 'conduct unbecoming a Time Lord', and 'transgressing the First Law'. [Meaning the First Law of Time, whatever that might be at present. Essentially the Doctor is put on Trial for meddling in the affairs of other races, although the hypocrisy of these charges later gets all the more confusing - again, see "Mindwarp".]

The proceeding against the Doctor is opened as an 'impartial inquiry', although by the end of this adventure the Valeyard wants it to become a full-blown Trial and impose the death penalty against him. [Note that we repeatedly use the term 'Trial' instead of 'inquiry' for simplicity's sake, even though it's technically the former for this adventure. Also, determining just *when* this affair moves into the Trial phase is difficult, as we'll discuss over the next two adventures.]

The Doctor indicates that the Lord President of Gallifrey cannot be put on Trial. [At least, not while that President is in office. Mind, this adds a whole new spin to Borusa's meglomania in "The Five Doctors".]

• *The Courtroom...* is located in a vast, rusty, hexagonal space-station. The numerals "5" and "6" appear on the station's exterior [judge for yourselves - as with much of *Doctor Who* - if this is a translation device for the viewer's benefit], and seem to indicate there are at least six courtrooms. The TARDIS appears to be pulled into Courtroom No. 5.

Each "courtroom" has a hemispherical silo, which opens in six segments to pull in the accused [and witnesses, as in "The Ultimate Foe"] via a psionic tractor beam. Within the station, the Trial room is dominated by a screen that displays recordings from the Gallifreyan Matrix. This is behind the jury, who are seated in three rows on swivel chairs. Outside the Trial Room is an ante-chamber with steps, stained-glass windows and decor very like that of Gallifrey in "The Five Doctors".

Planet Notes

• *Ravalox*. According to [the official, it would seem] records on Gallifrey, Ravalox is located within the Stelion Galaxy [another name for the Milky Way?], and has the same mass, angle of tilt and period of rotation as Earth. This is apparently owing to the fact that Ravalox *is* Earth, but situated 'a couple of light-years' away from Earth's location [for reasons explained in "The Ultimate Foe", but see also **Things That Don't Make Sense**].

• *Salostophus*. Found in Andromeda, and apparently the birth-place of Glitz and his apprentice Dibber [see **History** for more].

History

• *Dating*. The Doctor dates his visit to Ravalox as being 'two million years' after Peri's era. Five centuries previous, Earth and its entire 'constellation' [!, see **Things That Don't Make Sense**] were apparently shunted two light-years across space.

This transition triggered a solar fireball that nearly destroyed the planet. [It's enticing and aesthetically pleasing to link this to the 'solar flares' incident circa 6,000, as described in another key work by Robert Holmes - "The Ark in Space" (12.2) - but this doesn't at all fit what's said on screen.] Life on the surface apparently perished, but an L3 robot named Drathro (a.k.a. 'The Immortal') set up an underground biome habitat for three cryogenically-preserved 'Sleepers' from Andromeda [the 'constellation', not the galaxy, it appears]. Drathro calls this facility Marb Station, and it's located near the remains of the Marble Arch tube stop; the dwellers within call their world UK Habitat. Drathro's habitat contains five hundred humans, who serve as 'work units' and are culled when in access. The Sleepers died anyway when a relief ship from home failed to arrive.

Earth's surface has become habitable in the intervening centuries, and the Tribe of the Free - containing many humans saved from Drathro's culls - now lives there and has declared Drathro's Magnum Mark 7 light converter a totem of their god Haldron. The device converts ultra-violet rays into Black Light, a more powerful energy source [see 11.1, "The Time Warrior"]. Being made of rare metals such as Silictote - described as the 'hardest known material in the galaxy' - the aerial has attracted off-world visitors, each with a different excuse for taking it away. The Black Light system becomes unstable upon the destruction of its light converter, which threatens to trigger a Black Light explosion. The Doctor claims that such an explosion has never occurred, but that some have

Who Narrates This Programme?

...continued from page 115

popular theory amongst fans - namely that everything Doctor Watson told us was true, but, as they say on *Dragnet*, "the names have been changed to protect the innocent". Indeed, some small details like distances and dates were deliberately fudged, but in such a way as to be easily checked against maps and newspapers. Another comparison is with Thomas Hardy's "Wessex" novels, where place-names are inverted or shifted to create a fictional world replete with closely-observed real details, but organised to fit Hardy's moral vision (see **Does Plot Matter?** under 6.4, "The Krotons"). So it could well be that someone is feeding the Matrix recordings of the Doctor's exploits to someone at the BBC, who is then hiring writers, directors and designers to remake these stories.

Certainly, this would explain the curious casting decisions and odd plot developments. After all, nobody just making this stuff up and trying to simply entertain would abruptly recast the protagonist as someone utterly different (nine times, apparently by sticking a pin in *Spotlight* at random at odd intervals). No sane producer would decide not to show the major events on Planet 14 (6.3, "The Invasion") or skip the Great Time War (X1.2, "The End of the World et seq) in favour of a bunch of people running around Cardiff and having dinner (X1.11, "Boom Town"). It would account for otherwise quite unbelievable conversations that explain apparent anomalies. We've noted the strange discussions that people seem to have rather than running around screaming or giving orders (e.g. 19.6, "Earthshock", where the Captain's horror at seeing her ship infested with aliens is used as a pretext to clear up a continuity query, rather than for - as would really happen - Beryl Reid to start swearing. Well, assuming that a space-

captain would be in any way like Beryl Reid.) It also explains why when someone outside the BBC gets a chance to do it, the whole thing looks and sounds ludicrous.

Giving the BBC the rights to do this makes sense, provided this is the case. The BBC has the Public Service remit written into their charter, so anything that broadcasters are obliged to do - whether or not there's a big or hard-to-reach audience for it - is their job. Everyone knows they're a bit short of money, so *Doctor Who* aliens look unconvincing on occasion; that way the real aliens only have to put on rubber masks to pass unnoticed amongst us. (By the same token, really nasty aliens who wanted to soften us up for conquest would make slick-looking pap where all aliens are nice and technology always provides solutions. Not that we're saying Gene Roddenberry had sinister ulterior motives...)

The trouble is, of course, that the identity of the narrator(s) of this series is something that could only be revealed in the very last episode. Until the story is finally over, all regenerations used up and the Universe comes to an end, we have no-one to take a curtain-call. In 1990 it *looked* over, and because the story had halted with the Doctor's relationship with his own people apparently up for grabs, it *felt* finished. Now, obviously, things are different. It can be argued that the 2005 series is a totally new timeline, and not in any way connected with the previous programme of the same name. 2006's offerings made this ambiguous, bringing elements from the past but rewriting the chronology. But a possible way out is that everything from "Rose" (X1.1) onward is narrated by someone other than the narrator of everything up to "Survival" (26.4), and so inconsistencies are as inevitable as a different look and a sudden explosion in the number of Welsh supporting actors.

---

speculated it will create a chain reaction that consume all matter in the galaxy. Alternatively, some believe it will cause dimensional transference, and threaten the stability of the entire universe. [And now you really *must* proceed to **Things That Don't Make Sense**.]

Queen Katryca leads the Tribe, and a gender imbalance allows women to can multiple husbands. The Free's legends state that their ancestors used to travel the stars, and that the gods punished them for this by sending the 'Great Fire'. Because of this, star-travel is 'forbidden by the

gods' on pain of death. [Yet Katryca wants Peri to join the Tribe, so it's apparently only a lethal offence if you're male.] The Free have developed a form of agriculture, despite the evident lack of mammals or birds, and the surface rain is not toxic. Both Katryca and the Doctor - who look middle-aged at best - are deemed 'old' [which suggests that human longevity has been curtailed, understandable in such conditions].

Drathro has a limited learning capacity, but is chiefly trained in installation and maintenance - not repair - and thus has a dilemma when its

ABOUT TIME 1985-1989

Black Light system starts to fail. To compensate, Drathro routinely recruits the two most promising young people from Marb - here seen as the youths Humker and Tandrill - to research the problem [as we'll see, this is very similar to another Holmes story, 6.4, "The Krotons"]. Also at Drathro's disposal is a box-like L1 service robot, which proves vulnerable to gunfire.

Drathro maintains water rationing in Marb Station, despite knowing that the surface has rainfall. The Marb Station dweller Balazar has been designated the 'reader' of 'The Books of Knowledge' (meaning the only three books to have survived the planetary catastrophe): *Moby Dick*, *The Water Babies* by Charles Kingsley and *UK Habitats of the Canadian Goose* by H.M. Stationary Office.

Glitz's homeworld of Salostophus has a well-developed penal system, and is the hub of a well-established commercial network. The 'grotzit' is the common currency there, and hard-wearing metals such as Silictote and Machenite are worth a lot of these. Glitz suggests that there's a big market there for technical secrets, and says that the "discoveries" he hopes to procure from Ravalox include anti-gravity power, dimensional transference and 'travelling faster than light'. [There's every reason to think that he makes up this list on the fly, however, because the 'faster than light' reference sounds spurious whichever dating you favour for "Dragonfire" (24.4) - a story that seems to occur in Glitz's home era.]

Women on Salostophus can also have as many as six husbands at a time.

The Analysis

Where Does This Come From? Let's start with the Trial format. The premise of the Doctor being put on trial seems to have been developed very early on, possibly within a fortnight of the Suspension being announced. John Nathan-Turner claims to have always had the model of *A Christmas Carol* in mind and commissioned fresh stories to fit. This is something we'll look at under **The Lore** for each story, and we'll consider the "surprise" twist of the Valeyard's identity under "The Ultimate Foe". Yet we can't help but notice that Cliff Richard was facing a trial on stage, in the musical *Time*, in which his accusers were called "Time Lords". It co-starred Dilys Watling (sister of...) and a projected image of Lord Olivier (see "Revelation

of the Daleks") that was recycled in the dismal flick *Sky Captain and the World of Tomorrow*. This gained the play a lot of publicity at the time (as did Ken Russell directing the video for the song "She's So Beautiful") and we bet Gary Downie knew at least half the dancers. So if Nathan-Turner went to the Amazon Basin and stuck his fingers in his ears and went "la-la-la", it's *just* about possible he could have not known about it.

Another trial was occupying the minds of many people in Britain at the time. Former MI6 operative Peter Wright had written a memoir called *Spycatcher*, and the Government wanted to stop it being published. As it turned out, Chapman Pincher - a long-established writer on such matters - had written about almost all of it in another, widely-available book (*Their Trade is Treachery*, available in most second-hand shops) and nobody had batted an eyelid. Still, it was the principle that mattered. So Wright went to Australia - where he bought a silly hat that he wore in court when he was hauled back to London - and millions of pounds of taxpayers' money was spent on trying to silence this self-important little man. The trial in Australia was in the news as this story was being written, but the main one in the UK took years. By the time it all ended, you could - strangely enough - buy *Spycatcher* in Moscow, Beijing or Washington, but not Britain. This whole situation came on top of a number of other attempts by the Government to silence the citizens, including the BBC's investigations into a borderline-illegal spy satellite, and a plethora of lawsuits filed by the Crown. The *Spycatcher* trial resulted in all Wright's piddling secrets[14] being put into the public domain by way of the headlines, and is thus emblematic of that whole litigious mindset of 1980s British politics. Count the times the Valeyard uses the usual excuse of 'not in the public interest' when denying access to information.

More obviously, there's a large slab of *Mad Max* in this story. It would've been surprising if nobody had thought to try this, and there's going to be a lot more post-punk trappings in later stories (see particularly 25.2, "The Happiness Patrol"; 25.4, "The Greatest Show in the Galaxy", and 26.4, "Survival"). We could point out that everyone was doing this sort of thing in the mid-80s (and if you're up to it, check out flicks like *Spacehunter: Adventures in the Forbidden Zone* as a typical specimen - and not for a cheap laugh about Molly

Ringwald's lack of work since), but there's more. The Celtic thing was getting fashionable at the time, particularly when combined with synthesisers and hair-gel. HTV's *Robin of Sherwood* made a big deal about it. The BBC had done a big documentary series about the Celts with music from nearly the same source (launching Enya's career, but never mind). So when everyone started having Oirish broaches and strapwork tattoos - almost as a "uniform" for anyone not in the mainstream - Britain had its own equivalent to Native American trappings. Australia adds punk and Aborigine to car-chases and gets *Mad Max*, America goes all techno-retro and has the Burning Man festival, and in Britain - especially prior to the Criminal Justice Act 1994 - Goths, Crusties and Punks raise families in fields, go to raves and oppose US nuclear missiles being plonked in our ancient common land.

Post-apocalypse cliché-lovers will doubtless have recognized the parody of Walter M Miller's *A Canticle for Leibowitz* in Balazar's library. The same people may be thinking of *Dune* when the water-theft is met with Sharia justice (of sorts), but this is closer to the sort of thinking associated with near-future space-travel and architecture. (Marb Station is a sort of Arcology, the type of self-sustaining city-system proposed by Paolo Soleri in the 1960s.) That said, the music seems to think that David Lynch's film of *Dune* was worth plundering. Using tube stations as air-raid shelters is nothing new (see 5.5, "The Web of Fear"), and we'd had five years of grim jokes at the expense of the patronising and stupid advice the Government's *Protect and Survive* leaflet offered. You have to remember, in the mid-1980s we were convinced that the Americans were planning a nuclear war any day.

As we mentioned in discussing "Attack of the Cybermen" (22.1), the mid-80s were the golden age of British TV's obsession with cockney con-men. The previous Christmas had seen *Minder* go head-to-head with *Only Fools and Horses*, and so it's hard to imagine a Season Twenty-Three without characters such as Glitz and Dibber. Indeed, the main surprise is how unpleasant and callous they are on first appearance, even compared to other such characters in Holmes' work (again, the obvious comparison is Garron and Unstoffe in "The Ribos Operation"). Other well-worn Holmes plot details are the post-solar-flare London wilderness (12.3, "The Sontaran Experiment", credited to Bob Baker and Dave Martin but virtually dictated by Holmes as script editor), the robotic Minotaur selecting the two brightest humanoids ("The Krotons") and a regimented society believing something that was true centuries ago (both "The Krotons" again and "The Ark in Space").

Drathro's logic resembles that of "Cutie" in the Asimov story "Reason" (adapted for *Out of the Unknown*, hence the White Robots in 6.2, "The Mind Robber"). Oh, and when Drathro's right-hand man Merdeen shows the Doctor into the 'Castle', the music quotes the old music-hall song "Oh, Mr Porter".

But in the wider scheme of things, this story - and indeed this season - has something about it that is never explicitly stated. In the previous two autumns, the BBC had shown a series called *The Tripods* - a family SF adventure series shown at teatime. The first year's-worth stretched an already sedate book (yes, it was a literary adaptation, that's how Michael Grade was prevented from stopping it) into weeks of travelogue in future Europe, treading grapes and stealing loaves[15]. Then year two saw the groundbreaking special effects go beyond the use of the Paintbox computer to matte in hundred-foot-high walking tanks, whenever the charms of Wales-pretending-to-be-Tuscany palled. Today it looks horribly mid-80s, like the titles for *Going for Gold*. (Or any daytime quiz, for that matter. Nonetheless, the combination of Australian finance and mittel-European accents makes this analogy irresistible - *Going For Gold* had people from across Europe taking part in a quick-fire quiz in English. To make it more fair, the host was an Irishman who'd clearly been the subject of an exclusion order around the Blarney Stone, so even the British contestants had difficulty understanding the questions.)

What they ultimately achieved with Series Two was astonishing, but not enough people watched it for the cost to be justified, so the BBC cast around for any other family science-fiction show that could be shown in Autumn 1986 in 13 or so twenty-five minute episodes. You guessed it... for accounting purposes, it seems, *Doctor Who* Seasons Twenty-Three to Twenty-Six are actually *The Tripods* Series Three to Six, and the emphasis on Paintbox effects and big explosions will be more obvious as the McCoy era progresses. And in many ways, "The Mysterious Planet" - set in a future like Britain's past, and with humans enslaved by a giant who lives inside a secret citadel - is the ideal way to ease hardcore *Tripods* fans (if such people existed) into watching its replacement series. (It's sometimes stated that the first episode of *Tripods*, directed by Christopher Barry - see 1.2, "The Daleks"; 8.5, "The Daemons" and many others - played up to this by having the first speaking role given to John Scott Martin, the famous non-speaking Dalek operator and expendable Security Guard. In fact, someone else has a line before he does.)

Things That Don't Make Sense   Are you sitting comfortably? Then we'll begin...

Overarching Problem No. 1 [and sorry to jump ahead to revelations in "The Ultimate Foe", but it seems fair as "Trial" is designed as a 14-part epic, and it's easier to discuss the issue here]: we later learn that the Doctor has been put on Trial to cover up the High Council's culpability in the Ravalox affair, and that they cut a deal with the Valeyard to this end. But if that's the case, then it's incredibly stupid to show the entire Ravalox affair to the attending court, as it's the key to the very scandal the High Council wishes to keep secret. Surely, the Doctor's history is rife with better examples of his meddling with time (such as 14.4, "The Face of Evil" or 9.3, "The Sea Devils" to pick just a couple) than this one? Or for pity's sake, if the TARDIS really *has* been bugged since "Arc of Infinity", then the Doctor's involvement in 21.3, "Frontios" - in an era where the Time Lords are expressly forbidden to go - must be on file.

Overarching Problem No. 1A: in addition to the Valeyard's presentation later blowing the lid off the High Council's conspiracy, the Ravalox adventure actually shows the Doctor acting courageously and morally, and potentially saving the entire universe. Bear in mind that Glitz and Dibber blow up Drathro's light-converter - and thereby threaten a universe-wrecking explosion - totally independent of the Doctor's actions. Also, despite the Valeyard crowing that 'lives were lost', on screen there's only three deaths worth mentioning: Katryca and her associate Broken Tooth (who pretty much doom themselves by challenging Drathro), and the enforcer Grell, who's killed by Merdeen to protect the Doctor. So that's arguably *one* death, versus the Doctor saving the hundreds in Marb Station if not - again - all of creation.

Overarching Problem No. 2: the footage from Ravalox has Glitz telling Dibber about the (- bleeped out word -), a source of unimaginable secrets that he suspects the Time Lords have sent the Doctor to investigate. Why on Earth [or Ravalox] didn't the Valeyard just excise this pointless scene entirely, instead of bleeping out the word and glaringly citing the equivalent of Executive Privilege? Worse, for benefit of anyone who can't deduce the word by just *reading* his lips, Glitz goes on to describe the source as 'the biggest net of information in the Universe'. How can *anyone* in the Trial room not be thinking, "Hrmmmmm... that sounds a little like the Matrix..."?

Overarching Problem No. 3: Ravalox is Earth moved 'two light-years' or so away. So... that's less than half the distance to Alpha Centauri, then. Yet the Doctor failed to spot that his favourite planet is absent from its location of the last five billion years, and that another one exactly like it is just a spitting distance away (in cosmic terms), and that it coincidentally was hit by a solar fireball at exactly the same time that Earth's solar system went missing. And he lectures Balazar on trusting experience over something you read somewhere...

[Moreover, we have to presume they really mean "Earth and its solar system" were moved, not 'Earth and its constellation', because moving *that* many stars would draw even more attention to the anomaly.]

Overarching Problem No. 4: the Doctor says that a Black Light explosion has never occurred, and that some theorize it could destroy the universe. Okay, but Drathro's system isn't presented as unique, so how can such an explosion *not* have occurred? [If you think such futuristic technology could be foolproof, think again - blowups happen. Remember Three Mile Island and Chernobyl?] And if the technology is *that* dangerous, why haven't the Time Lords moved to suppress it? Never mind concerns about body-swapping in the next adventure, this allegedly threatens the whole of creation, and should be cause for more worry.

Relatively smaller concerns now: we're asked to accept that Marble Arch station has somehow been kept as it was in the 1980s for two million years, and *then* adapted into a survival chamber. If water is so precious in Marb Station, why do the overseers leave jars of the stuff in the open and hide behind sliding doors, rather than - say - just guarding it? [Are they trying to make their quota for stonings this week?] Merdeen covers his headset while speaking conspiratorially with Balazar - to prevent Drathro overhearing - yet later takes no such precautions while talking freely about letting the Doctor escape. At the Tribe of the Free, Glitz tells Dibber to holster his weaponry because he might get a back full of spears - then Glitz is subsequently foolish enough to pull a pistol on Katryca while there's a whole gaggle of men behind him.

In the Trial Room, the Doctor ends this adventure by saying that his presence on Ravalox was 'specifically requested' - by whom, exactly? [He certainly seems to be acting solo when the adventure opens.] Based upon the Doctor's instructions to Peri, the best way to help contain a Black Light explosion is to randomly hit keys on an English-labeled keyboard. [Although it's more entertaining to think that this has no effect, and he's just providing her with a distraction during a crisis moment.] Grell hardly seems sneaky while "stealthily" sauntering along beside Merdeen. Later, Merdeen and Peri seem intent on infiltrating Drathro's abode by - oddly - walking into a giant fan, and this strange endeavour is only interrupted when the fan *behind* them switches on.

The Tribe of the Free have an imbalance of women to men, and have had for generations. How is this possible? Unless being male is somehow toxic, or they do some kind of dangerous hunting for the non-existent wildlife, this imbalance is unlikely to last as long as three generations, but it's said as a matter of long-established tribal policy. Conversely the lads in Marb Station seem to be reproducing without female assistance (which would explain a lot about Humker and Tandrill), but if there's a population of exactly 500 and we only get to see a sample of 20, all boys, either they have some kind of men-only rule for Guards (unlikely in a small population artificially preserved) or the women are kept in purdah for breeding (unlikely, if the population is to be kept to a precise number). Are they eating the womenfolk or something? [We wouldn't put it past Holmes to have suggested this in an early draft, but then Peri's free passage through the tunnels becomes a bit odder still.]

Any ornithologist would know, upon hearing the titles of Balazar's books, that it's not 'Canadian' but "Canada Goose". And the geese's 'UK Habitat' is, basically, everywhere in the UK except Scotland [with over-hunting and migration, there are more breeding pairs in Britain than Canada or the US, their original native land].

Finally, how can Drathro - advanced robot that he is - not be programmed to know what "hubris" means? Do they not *have* hubris in Andromeda?

Critique Imagine for a moment how this adventure looked back in 1986, as the first out of the gate after the Suspension crisis. The first episode looked promising, especially on a big screen in a roomful of expectant fans (see **The Lore**), but overall, with a *lot* riding on this story to perform well... it's a mess. Only episode one actually *sounds* like vintage Robert Holmes, and the rest seems suspiciously like someone (Holmes himself, or Saward, or both) trying to match that. Even as a Holmes pastiche, it tellingly lacks the trade-marked Holmes set-pieces, and everything in this story is like a set-up for something to come - but which never seems to arrive. Even the visually impressive L1 Robot bursting through the walls seems like an incident along the way.

All of which, admittedly, is to damn with faint praise. There's nothing disastrous here, and no performances really stand out as bad (Tom Chadbon comes close as Merdeen, but he's just subdued amid some over-enthusiastic newcomers, as opposed to being dull), no effects fail (except that the zapping in the food pipe is a bit perfunctory). It doesn't go off the rails, but it merely chugs along. And as we've indicated, "just chugging along" just isn't an option for a story as important as this. This is effectively the relaunch of the entire series, so everything needs to be cranked up to eleven but isn't.

You might think that we're picking holes *now* with benefit of hindsight, but in truth many of the problems here should've been spotted in pre-production. You've got the most impressive giant robot since, um, the Giant Robot (12.1, "Robot"), but nobody seems to have asked themselves what made K1 such a workable character. Partly it was Michael Kilgarriff's theatrical reading of the role, but it was also because we saw him towering over Sarah, Benton, the Doctor and various short actors. Then he went out on location and kicked UNIT's butt (and then he hilariously grew even bigger, but never mind that). The point is that for Drathro to *really* work, he should've left the "Castle" and smashed up Katryca's wigwams - and if the premise of the story didn't allow that, or it just wasn't feasible as an effect, then the premise should have been changed to keep the casual viewer interested.

While they were making changes in the conceptual stage, the Tribe of the Free should have been scary headhunters, not fugitives from a Jethro Tull gig. The stakes were high for this Tribe, so they should have sounded desperate - and it's not like the story as made rules this out. The two sets of humans are both living in marginal circumstances, and only iron discipline should be preventing starvation or a massacre. Holmes commissioned "The Face of Evil", so he knew it could have worked that way. And the Tribe is really symptomatic of a bigger problem - that while all the material in this story has the potential to make something strong, memorable and entertaining, it just doesn't happen. So why not?

Well... at this point, we have to acknowledge that the Trial format did nobody any favours. As episodes one to four of a long story, "The Mysterious Planet" seems designed as an extended set-up, not a story in and of itself. All right, sometimes it does, but on other occasions it seems like an autonomous story that's punctuated by irrelevant stuff about some courtroom - usually just as it looks like getting interesting at last. Just look at the cliffhangers. One is the Valeyard telling us what we already know from the story's title: that the Doctor should be put on trial. The next is the Doctor thinking his last hour's come, when we know that he survives long enough to get hauled before the Time Lords and watch this episode on a big screen. The third is one of the lamest clichés imaginable - someone's firing a weapon at someone else, but we can't see the intended target, so we think it's the hero. And then the final episode concludes with the Doctor admitting it's all been pretty unsubstantial until now. By the way, all of this is accompanied with momentum-killing interruptions from the Valeyard and the Inquisitor, mainly to settle dull continuity points.

We can lay the blame for this at Jonathan Powell's door if we so desire, especially as he sent out contradictory instructions about the level of humour and seriousness (which he thought were mutually-exclusive) that caused Saward and Holmes to amend things continually until rehearsals. But really, a more basic flaw is the worrying sense that none of the programme-makers seem to know what they're doing any more. Is this a story or *part* of a story? Is this farce, satire, drama or just a lot of (very pretty) explosions and effects? Who, if anyone, watches *Doctor Who* these days? Everyone involved seems to have had different answers for those questions - and nobody in charge was giving answers.

And therein lies the *real* problem here: the show just can't afford such creative ambiguity with its future on the line. Looking at the ratings

slump since "Attack of the Cybermen", if ever there was an argument *against* playing it safe, this was it. Trying to get out of the jam by largely carrying on as before - albeit smoothing out a few of Season Twenty-Two's rough spots - was just idiotic, but we can't pin the blame on *just* Nathan-Turner or *just* Saward or anyone else. Whether you're mostly positive or negative about the decisions made with *Doctor Who* in the last few years - and despite the creative renaissance to come in the McCoy era - at *this* juncture in time, the whole production team should have been fired and a complete break with the past made.

The Facts

Written by Robert Holmes. Directed by Nicholas Mallett. Ratings: 4.9 million, 4.9 million, 3.9 million, 3.7 million. Audience appreciation was remarkably decent, ranging between 69% for episode two and 72% for episodes one and four. (It's probably worth mentioning that from now on, even though the ratings are calculated without regard for home taping, the portion of the public who are watching are doing so by choice - meaning that the AI figures will reflect this somewhat. That split of the public into fans and the majority is no longer a matter of whether one is a paid-up, card-carrying "fan", but simply whether the three other channels are showing anything the sample viewers would rather watch. Bear this in mind when the series goes head-to-head with the most watched and loved show in British TV history from 1987 on.)

Working Titles "The Robots of Ravalox", "Wasteland".

Supporting Cast Joan Sims (Katryca), Tony Selby (Glitz), Roger Brierley (Drathro), Tom Chadbon (Merdeen), Glen Murphy (Dibber), Adam Blackwood (Balazar), David Rodigan (Broken Tooth), Timothy Walker (Grell), Billy McColl (Humker), Sian Tudor Owen (Tandrell).

Oh, Isn't That..?

• *Michael Jayston.* Somehow, he'd avoided being upstaged by Tom Baker's portrayal of Rasputin in *Nicholas and Alexandra.* He'd also been in the famously low-rent spy hokum *Quiller* and was Alec Guinness' foil in *Tinker, Tailor, Soldier, Spy.* After this season he gets kinda-sorta honorary

Doctor status - again (oops! Spoiler) - in the *Press Gang* episode "UneXpected", wherein he plays the actor who played "Colonel X" on Saturday teatimes in the seventies. (The fake archive clips, in fact, make you wish they'd shown this instead of Season Eleven.)

• *Lynda Bellingham.* For older viewers, she'd been the loveable fat nurse in ATV's *General Hospital* (as unlike the US show of the same name as you can get). For younger viewers, she'd been the "Oxo" Mum, heroine of a series of sardonic ads in the 80s (replacing an earlier couple, Philip and Katie, who were like Ian and Barbara but with a hostess trolley instead of a Food Machine). After this, she was the replacement for Carol Drinkwater on *All Creatures Great and Small*, a series with too many connections to *Doctor Who* to list again (see Volume V). And look... she's also acting alongside Peter Davison in *At Home with the Braithwaites.*

• *Tony Selby.* He'd been in *Up the Junction*, a groundbreaking TV play from the 1960s, and then was Sam in *Ace of Wands* - the nearest Thames got to a rival to *Who* (see also 26.1, "Battlefield" for what we'll charitably call a *homage*). In the 1970s, he'd been in hit sitcom *Get Some In*, about 1950s National Service.

• *Joan Sims.* One of the few *Carry On* regulars to change the type of character she routinely played. In the early ones, she was the slightly frustrated girlfriend, usually of Sid James. Later, she became Sid's nagging wife, and he thought she'd failed realise he was chasing Barbara Windsor. She did a nice line in cockney women trying to sound posh - which is odd as she didn't sound cockney in real life.

• *David Rodigan.* A familiar voice to Londoners, as he did the reggae specialist shows on Capital Radio.

• *Glen Murphy.* He's a few months away from stardom, when the one-off play *London's Burning* became a series. Sunday nights started to have regular spectacular stunt sequences as part of bigger fires - not to mention more perilous rescues that interrupted Blue Watch's complicated love-lives.

• *Adam Blackwood.* Would become one of the Drones who made life perilous for Bertie in Granada's *Jeeves and Wooster*, back when Hugh Laurie was English. His character, Barmy Fotheringhay-Phipps (that's "Fotheringhay" pronounced "Fungi", unlike the real place), was later played by Martin Clunes (20.2, "Snakedance").

Blackwood has been various foppish types, and was the voice for James Bond on the *The World Is Not Enough* computer game, but now arranges corporate events.

Cliffhangers The Valeyard demands that the inquiry becomes a Trial, and that a guilty verdict should result in a termination of the Doctor's life; the Doctor's party finds themselves squeezed between the advancing L1 robot and the gun-totting Tribe of the Free, and the Doctor thinks this could be 'the end'; Merdeen raises his crossbow, announces that he's hunting the Doctor, and fires. And the lead-in to the next adventure: the Valeyard (here we go again) says the most damning evidence is still to come, and that when he's finished, the Court will demand the Doctor's life.

The Lore

• So... after the decision to rest the series for a year was taken, the production team hunkered down and rethought the forthcoming season. In March 1985 the first version of Season Twenty-Three (see **What Would the *Other* Season 23 Have Been Like?** under the last story, if you somehow missed it) was well-advanced, with scripts for "The Nightmare Fair" already sent out. Nabil Shaban claims that he was paid for "Mission to Magnus" without seeing a script. It was soon clear that the episodes would revert to being 25-minutes each (a decision that irked Saward in particular). How many per annum was still unclear, although Ian Levine claimed, in the so-called "Nuremberg Rally" at DWASocial V, that it was to be cut to twenty episodes a series. By the summer it had emerged that in fact there were to be fourteen episodes. (The BBC had sent a fax to the US distributors, Lionheart, but had misdialled and sent it to American fan Ron Katz. Allegedly. Then he told Levine, who told the tabloids.)

Saward was credited with Plan B, the Trial format, with Nathan-Turner suggesting the model of *A Christmas Carol.* Although the eventual season wound up being the work of old hands such as Robert Holmes, there was a concerted attempt to get other experienced television writers to try doing a *Who.* Holmes was asked to submit a four-part introduction and the two-part climax, with other writers slotting in their ideas between them (see the previous essay for far more on this).

It was decided very early on that the Prosecuting Council was to be an evil version of the Doctor from some time in his future, but that the judge was to be sympathetic and competent, to avoid accusations that the series was becoming "satirical" again. The plan of '*Doctor Who* on Trial' was announced to Michael Grade, who used the line in press briefings. Bizarrely, and despite the sharp ratings dive in Season Twenty-Two, the series' public profile was as high now as it had ever been. With merchandising proliferating (Nathan-Turner's book *The TARDIS Inside Out* was published on the same day as his partner's *The Doctor Who Cookbook*), Baker's Cot Death charity work (Baker, Saward, Nathan-Turner and Ian Ogilvy, of *Return of the Saint* fame, did a parachute jump in July) and the growing uncertainty about the future of a series only recently described as an "Institution" making headlines, *Doctor Who* was inescapable that summer. Notably, "Slipback" got about as much press coverage as the series' twenty-fifth anniversary would receive two years later.

• Fast-forward to January 1986, and everything is different. The first batch of scripts are in, but Jonathan Powell doesn't like them. Saward is dismayed. You've probably heard about Saward's fall from grace, and the precise sequence of events leading up to his departure and tell-all interview in *Starburst* magazine (there's more on this article, unavoidably, under **The Lore** in 23.3, "Terror of the Vervoids") is a complex matter, and everyone involved has said their piece.

Most agree that Saward's withdrawal from the show's day-to-day operations had begun before this snub, but that Powell's treatment of Holmes - a writer Saward now revered - was crucial. Saward claims that the increasingly odd casting decisions were a contributory factor; Gary Downie counterclaims that Saward was hearing garbled versions of confidential discussions via Nathan-Turner's secretary, whom Saward was dating. Certainly, Saward was working from home much more, so many decisions were taken while he was absent. It's also true that when writing the scripts with more humour - to please Grade, who had specifically asked for this - they wound up with a story that Powell dismissed as "lightweight". Holmes was in no mood for this malarkey, as he was ill. He was in close collusion with Saward over the final two-part story - then still called "Time Inc" - and it was becoming obvious that Saward would have to take over completely.

• Meanwhile, the rumour was going around that Bonnie Langford was to become Nicola

Bryant's replacement. Nathan-Turner flatly denied this to Ian Levine, but when the publicity photos of Baker and Langford were released in January, much of the public at large, fandom in general and Saward began to wonder if the producer had lost his mind. (This strategy might sound more sensible twenty years on, after Billie Piper's stonkingly successful use of a spot of time-travel to overcome typecasting as a former child-star, but it's important to remember the pop culture landscape in 1986. We'll pick this up under "Terror of the Vervoids".) The fact remains that this and the Powell memo in rapid succession seem to have finished Saward's appetite for the series.

• By April, when studio recording had begun, Saward made plain his intention to quit, and Powell - curiously, perhaps - advised Nathan-Turner to do whatever was needed to keep his script editor on the team. The producer cannily negotiated that Saward should complete Holmes' final script and *then* leave. (This one will run and run, and the rest of this year's **Lore** entries will try to clarify the sequence for you.)

• One element that Powell found pointless was Glitz and Dibber. Ignoring this, Nathan-Turner found this element was one that appealed to actors. Although the dialogue - especially Dibber's mockney slang - was toned down, the casting of the major roles proved very easy on the strength of the script. Tony Selby even came off a diet to bulk up for the role of Glitz. (He tells many anecdotes about the location filming and catering - one involving a lobster, another about how he, Baker and Joan Sims had a pudding-eating contest.)

• That opening effects-shot cost £8000, about a tenth of the budget per episode in 1986. The model was six feet across, and the sequence was made at Elstree's Peerless Studio. Originally, the sequence was to have been of a storm-lashed Sargasso of wrecked spaceships, with the Trial ship revealed slowly to be a cathedral-like, eerie vessel several times larger than the rest. This idea is continued in the later scripts, and Dominic Glynn's decision to use a church-organ sound and chimes in his score. After a career in local government, Glynn had recently turned pro and sent in demo tapes. To scotch a well-worn myth, nothing Glynn has recorded for the series was done in his or anyone's bedroom. He did, however, require the use of his girlfriend's spare room to get the theme done in time. Nathan-Turner suggested that the best "shop-window" for an up-and-coming composer was the theme-tune, and Glynn took five weeks to make the version we hear (which was released as a single, as the Peter Howell version had been in 1980).

• When Frankie Goes to Hollywood - *the* hype sensation of 1984 - finally made a second album, the second single from it was called "Warriors of the Wasteland". Thus, for their appearance on *Top of the Pops*, they wanted to borrow the costumes from this story, which had been hanging in the BBC studio awaiting return to the warehouse. In fact, some reports say they tried them on and were reprimanded by BBC bigwigs. This is almost the last time that classic *Doctor Who* was considered hip, and also the last thing the band did that made the headlines.

• When the new season made its debut, it was consciously placed in the context of the 1970s Saturday night line-up of yore. Since Day One, *Doctor Who* had followed a puppet show. (Seriously, for the Saturday teatimes of the 60s and 70s to lack puppets was almost unheard of. The first and oddest was *Telegoons* - but there's a whole book to be written explaining *that*.) Where we had had Basil Brush or Lamb Chop, we now had Roland Rat preceding the new episodes. Two years earlier, Roland Rat had been the saviour of the ailing TVAM (ITV's first Breakfast TV franchise, amazingly made to look safe and dull by the BBC's "spoiler"). Poaching the puppet rodent and his chums to BBC looked like a certain ratings-winner. Then *Doctor Who*, then Noel Edmunds and his tremendously popular *Late Late Breakfast Show* in the old *Generation Game* slot, then *Juliet Bravo* in place of *Dixon of Dock Green*, then *Dynasty*, news and football. What could possibly go wrong?

Well, two things. One was that *Roland Rat - The Series* was painful even for small children, the other was that by this stage ITV were still milking *The A-Team*. Still, expectations were high, especially for the thousand or so of us who packed into Imperial College London to watch episode one on a giant screen as part of PanoptiCon VI. A thousand party-poppers went off... for a trailer for *The Late Late Breakfast Show*. Oops!

23.2: "The Trial of a Time Lord: Mindwarp"

(Serial 7B, Four Episodes. 4th - 25th October 1986.)

Which One is This? Sil meets Brian Blessed on Planet Disco. Peri dies (but later gets better, apparently).

Firsts and Lasts Nicola Bryant leaves, shortly after she stops playing Peri. Nabil Shaban makes a farewell as Sil. (Yes, it's only the second of two appearances for him, but he *still* dominates this phase of the series.) We've also got the first real barnstorming use of the new improved digital paintbox, in case you failed to spot it...

Four Things to Notice about "Mindwarp"...

1. The TARDIS here lands in a lurid setting: a pink sea under a green sky with purple rocks on the shore. Just to make sure we get the point, they make sure we have a good long look at it - something that even the Inquisitor and the Doctor say is a bit gratuitous. So then they fast-forward to... the Doctor and Peri explaining the plot while walking on purple rocks near a pink sea, under a green sky, with a big ringed planet nearby. And then in episode two, a reason surfaces for Peri to be lashed to the purple rocks under the green sky, with pink waves crashing. Proud of their new toy, aren't they?

2. Another way in which colour is used is in making the "interlopers" (the Doctor, Peri, the raving warlord Yrcanos and the calculated brain-surgeon Crozier) the only Caucasian humanoids in the story. These days it would pass almost without notice, except when they overdo it and cause anachronisms (X2.7, "The Idiot's Lantern" and - unforgiveably - X3.2, "The Shakespeare Code"). But at the time it looked excitingly futuristic, even if some casting decisions seemed questionable. To blur the ethnicity further, they have everyone dressed as an amalgam of Inca and Bollywood (dayglo saris and hijabs, thick knitted ponchos) except Brian Blessed, who's dressed as a samurai, but with thick eyeliner.

3. Just about every two years, the producer of *Doctor Who* - whoever it happens to be - decides that they've never done a werewolf story. So every couple of years, you get an adventure that has mentions of lycanthropy, is shot like a werewolf story, or just has men turning hairy. (Examples include 7.4, "Inferno"; 13.1, "Terror of the Zygons"; 15.1, "Horror of Fang Rock", and several others.) So here, we have Yrcanos' associate Dorf turned into a dog-man - and once again, everyone forgot about it. Two years later, the same producer decided that it was about time *Doctor*

Who did a werewolf story in 25.4,"The Greatest Show in the Galaxy". (We might at least excuse Russell T Davies on this score - see X2.2, "Tooth and Claw" - because eighteen years really *is* an awful long time for people to forget about this sort of thing.)

4. Just as Terry Nation Dalek stories have an episode's worth of people talking about "them" before the cliffhanger reveals (*dun dun daaah*) a Dalek, so anyone with any foreknowledge will see the first episode (or "The Trial of a Time Lord Part Five" as it's called here) as playing for time until Brian Blessed and Nabil Shaban turn up. Although Baker is on screen more than he was in "Revelation of the Daleks" (22.6), he's even further from centre-stage, and scripted as acting out of character for much of the time. Indeed, he's having so much fun as comic relief in his own series, and letting Nicola Bryant take over the Doctor's usual plot-function, that the return to the Trial and business as usual for Baker is disappointing.

The Continuity

The Doctor   Still has an annoying habit of going 'hmmmmm' as if agreeing with something Peri's saying, even when he's absorbed in something technological. He puts his hand up in court - as if he's still in school - and is pertly smug for most of the courtroom presentation, and later seems to use this to cover anxiety. His relief when being told that Peri didn't die in an ambush is palpable, but upon later discovering that she has been killed - by order of the High Council - his bluster is replaced by cold fury.

• *Ethics.* [This is a bit tricky in a story where the Doctor is acting strange as part of a ruse, and we're lead to believe that the Valeyard has been editing the narrative shown on the big-screen. Therefore, we'll confine our comments to the stuff we're certain happened as shown.]

As with "Revelation of the Daleks", he's started investigating - based on rumours and unsubstantiated reports - things he thinks need sorting out. [We'll see a lot more of this in seasons Twenty-Five and Twenty-Six, but we should note that it's already becoming routine behaviour for him.] Thus, the Doctor has decided to investigate the death of the Thordon warlord by taking Peri to Thoros Beta, knowing that she would never have agreed to such an excursion if she'd realised that Sil and his people were present. [In this *one*

regard, the Valeyard actually has a point - the Doctor of late has been almost brazenly dragging Peri into potential danger. It's not like she's Ace, and can bash Daleks with a magic baseball bat.]

He's not particularly upset about his role in killing the augmented Raak creature. [Although, to be fair, the creature attacked first and the Doctor says his handgun discharged accidentally.]

• *Background.* Shortly before the start of this story, he met a dying Thordon warlord who indicated that parties on Thoros Beta were providing the warlord's forces with futuristic weapons. His intervention on Thoros Beta is therefore dictated by a need to stop an advanced civilization from unduly influencing a lesser one. [It chimes with the oath we heard in 14.2, "The Hand of Fear". So not exactly 'conduct unbecoming of a Time Lord', then.] The Doctor claims to have some knowledge of transfer technology, and seems adept at helping to repair Crozier's wrecked machinery.

The Supporting Cast

• *Peri.* She's fit, healthy, well aware that the Doctor dislikes anyone stating the obvious, displays suitable compassion for the chained-up Dorf and theorises about the effect of Thoros Alpha on the tides of Beta. [So she *was* listening to the Doctor's lecture in 21.6, "The Caves of Androzani".] As is traditional in a companion's last story, Peri expresses both homesickness and a slight contempt for home, plus a concern for someone other than the Doctor. In this case she displays warmth for King Yrcanos, whose warrior ways amuse her once she stops being scared of him. [By now, being involuntarily engaged to a middle-aged loon must seem familiar - not that we see Peri discovering Yrcanos' intent - and she gets on with saving a planet as if it's her job.]

Even when Peri finds that the Doctor has duped her into visiting Sil's homeworld, she doesn't give him the verbal roasting she would have done even three stories before. Peri's final fate, as shown here: the scientist Crozier erases her as a mental being, then transfers the mind of the Mentor named Kiv into her body. Moments later, Yrcanos - unknowingly acting as the High Council's assassin, bursts into Crozier's lab and apparently kills Kiv-Peri, Crozier and Sil. [Spoilers be damned: "The Ultimate Foe" (23.4) explains that Peri's death was part of the Valeyard's faked evidence, and that she became Yrcanos' Queen. We'll pick this up two stories hence.]

How Warped Was the Doctor's Mind?

Episodes five to eight of "The Trial of a Time Lord" are a bit of a mess. Not in terms of watchability (in fact, they're the only bit that you can sit through in non-fan company without setting off a smoke-detector with your blushes), but the internal logic is a touch awry. Whereas the rest of "Trial" (barring Part Fourteen) is too obvious to be any fun, this story - when considered as part of the whole umbrella-season-arc-tosh - is puzzling because parts of it actually make *too much* sense.

If that sounds like an odd complaint, it's because we're repeatedly told that the evidence is inaccurate. Suffering from amnesia, the Doctor is trying to piece together what happened based on the Valeyard's presentation. We're led to understand that the Doctor in the Thoros Beta story is a) acting out of character because of Crozier's scrambling his brains at the end of episode one, b) acting out of character as part of a cunning plan to ingratiate himself to the Mentors and then thwart their aims and c) acting out of character because this version of events is a fake, a farrago, a travesty, a farce and so on. There is also option d) all of the above. Basically, it's a story in which the evidence is allegedly tweaked to make the Doctor act strangely, when he's already got plenty of justifiable reasons for acting strangely.

Furthermore, we later have the Master's word (for what it's worth) that the ending is baloney and Peri survived. And we have the Doctor's assurance that Part 5 is substantially correct. Soooooo...

In rehearsal, Colin Baker reportedly asked author Philip Martin how much of what he was doing "really" occurred (to adjust his performance for the benefit of confused viewers), and was told to ask Eric Saward. But the script editor apparently didn't know either. Baker's performance only really alters in three scenes - one is when the Doctor alerts the guards in Part 6, but this seems to be confusion owing to Crozier's brain-blast, as he regains his wits if not Yrcanos' trust. Later when giving Sil advice on investments, he seems his old self again - not enjoying marsh-minnows and giving (erroneous?) forewarning of a war on the galactic rim. If his advice had altered history significantly, this might be another charge for the prosecution, but it's apparently ignored as if part of the Doctor's ruse. Similarly, blowing the whistle on Peri and taking her to the rocks is of a piece with the revolt he starts in Part 8, but the interrogation itself is another matter.

It could be argued that this is the *only* fake before the end. Consider how the "real" interrogation might have gone, with the Doctor using the lack of surveillance to brief Peri on how to get Yrcanos and Tuza to unite and overthrow the Mentors. She appears to achieve this anyway, by accident as much as design. If this interrogation *is* false, it would have made sense for the consequences of it to be altered and the Doctor's intervention to have seemingly caused a pointless massacre. Instead, the Time Lords (apparently) see fit to intervene themselves because the"'villainous" Doctor hasn't made enough of a mark on the situation to affect Crozier's work. So why would the Valeyard change one small aspect of the Doctor's behaviour - one which made no material difference to the outcome - only to have the Time Lords erasing it all anyway?

Assuming Peri *didn't* die, and therefore wasn't separated from Yrcanos and wasn't injured in the battle, then the whole of Part 8 has to go. The Doctor instigating a near-bloodless coup - thus preventing the alteration to evolution threatened by Crozier's work, and avoiding Yrcanos getting his hands on weapons of mass destruction - would be a good day's work but hardly incriminating. Aside from the overtly silly bits with the old Mentor (which the Inquisitor could have asked to skip) and Peri's "ooh!-bit-of-politics" outburst - both of which seem like the Valeyard's pride in his work outweighing their relevance - much of it is noticeably different from the story's first episode.

The point at which the Time Lords take the Doctor is particularly cruel, and their use of Yrcanos as a "hit-man" is unlike anything we've seen them do. Yet the "summoning" of the TARDIS is explicitly stated to be by the mental effort of the Jury, so they *should* know if this part of the story is untrue - as would the Inquisitor. (Notice that the Inquisitor seems to get a paragraph of the Valeyard's closing speech about why Peri had to die. Living up to her title, she's been asking questions throughout and has obviously no idea what was going to happen - so why is she suddenly so well-informed? If, as we are told, the intervention is part of an outcome that didn't even take place, how could she know so much about it?) We could speculate that the distortion used to make Yrcanos "pause" before attacking the lab would have needed High Council sanction and thus - as they are in cahoots with the Valeyard - could be faked. But this *still* leaves us with the question underlying the entire Trial storyline - why did the prosecution choose to show the Ravalox business, and thus expose the whole Trial as a fraud?

The Supporting Cast (Evil)

• *Sil*. [Last seen in 22.2, "Vengeance on Varos".] He knows that the Doctor is a Time Lord and - upon thinking that the Doctor has become the Mentors' ally - uses the Doctor's knowledge of the future to help decide upon applications for funding. In his native clime, Sil's colour is more green than brown, and his neck-frills are more abundant. He's far more subservient to Kiv than his previously demonstrated arrogance would have suggested. Nevertheless, he goes against Lord Kiv's wishes and indulges in speculation, hiring the zonked Doctor to tell him of financially-sensitive near-future events. In this scene, which is to be approached with caution, it seems that Sil knows a lot more about Time Lords than he did before.

• *The Valeyard*. Has his sycophantic side, and makes a point of calling the Inquisitor 'sagacity' [cf 15.4, "The Sun Makers"]. He claims not to need anything as 'crude' as shock tactics in prosecuting the Doctor, but uses them nonetheless. At one stage, the Inquisitor deems his presentation 'highly prejudicial'. [That said, check out *her* actions under **Things That Don't Make Sense**.]

The TARDIS Briefly loses [for whatever reason] the "Officers and Cars" sign from the right-hand door when it materializes. The Ship arrives on Thoros Beta on the shore, but is later hijacked by the Time Lords' mental power [as witnessed last episode] and used to transport the Doctor down a time corridor to face the Court.

The Time Lords By order of the High Council, Yrcanos and Tuza are caught in a time-bubble until conditions are right for their final attack on Crozier's laboratory. The Doctor counters that the High Council has no right to authorize someone's death.

The Non-Humans

• *Mentors*. We see three representatives of the species: Kiv, Sil and an older Mentor who objects to people shouting. Sil seems to be the runt of the litter.

The Mentors are cold-blooded and appear to have slow pulses. They're born in 'mires' [which seem to be both places and clans], and as a species seem to remorselessly exploit those around them, but only in sure-fire deals like slavery and arms trading. They have at least one god, called 'Morgo'.

Sil is the servile second-in-command to Kiv - the Mentors' unchallenged, ruthless, and canny leader. Kiv is a hybrid, and so his skull isn't designed to accommodate the growth of his brain - meaning he's only a few days away from a fatal brain compression. Alphan bodies cannot support Kiv's brain. Crozier transplants Kiv's brain into the body of a brown-coloured, similar hybrid found adrift off the 'islands of Brac' - the hybrid's skull is slightly larger, and this buys Kiv some time. The hybrid hails from Kiv's home mire, and thus has the same facial features. [That both Kiv and the hybrid look like the actor playing them - Christopher Ryan - would often be deemed a glitch or a conceit, but it's plausible as we don't learn much about Mentor physiology.] The hybrid has retained his primeval stinger, and his tail - unlike Kiv's or Sil's - contains enough venom to kill.

A curious phenomenon is that some of the hybrid's brain cells escape death by laser-isation, and the hybrid's memories start to influence Kiv's mind. [This would suggest that the Mentors' memories are encoded in their cells - again, not impossible for their species.] When transferred to Peri's body, Kiv finds finds warm blood and smooth skin very much preferable to his normal form [but this is part of the faked evidence, and therefore highly suspect].

We never see any Mentors who aren't called 'he', so it's unclear if they even have females. [Sil's reaction to humanoid females - and his labelling of Peri as 'disgustingly ugly' - makes it seem that he distrusts and is repelled by them.]

It's hard to tell if Kiv's relative stillness compared to Sil's agitation at all times is a characterpoint or a species trait. The majority of Mentors seem to be calm in proportion to their seniority, and physically larger too (Sil only needs a lightweight cradle, and can easily be carried in his bearer's arms in an emergency).

• *The Krontep*. [Note that the term "Krontep" is both used to describe Yrcanos' tribe and their place of origin. However, Yrcanos' people seem to inhabit the same planet as their rivals, the Tomkomp Empire, and their world is *probably* called "Thordon". The alternative is that they're located on two different planets, in which case we have to wonder how such barbarians can fly spaceships.]

From what we can gather, the world of Krontep is located a reachable distance from Thoros Beta, and is in a state of perpetual war. Yrcanos practices a religion akin to Hinduism, but with the twist that upon death each Krontep gets reincarnated in a more noble warrior, eventually being born as a King. After a King's death, his spirit takes up residence in the Field of Verduna, 'the home of the gods', where the dead kings fight for eternity. [This winds up a bit Viking-ish, and akin to Valhalla.] The alternative seems to be the Plague-halls of Morgdana. [Kiv also cites this locale as a hell-equivalent.] Warrior Queens are expected to fight alongside their King. Yrcanos cites himself as King of the Krontep and Lord of the Vingten.

The warriors consume something called 'flay-fish' - dried into strips, this serves as emergency rations to 'fuel the fighting spirit', but can promote irrational behaviour. Incidental details about their mythology include mention of the 'seven-legged charger of Koraljam'. [This and Dorf being called the King's 'equerry' suggests that they have horses, of some kind.] Yrcanos swears by the 'Great Jeweled Sword of Krontep', and makes reference to the 'sewers of Skulnesh' [possibly a location on Thordon, or another planet].

• *Possicarians*. An ambassador with a crimson face and ferocious-looking teeth represents Possicar in business negotiations with Kiv. He [at least, we *think* it's a he] is apparently bipedal [although we can't see the feet under his flowing robe], has big hands and stands only just over a metre tall. We can't understand the squeaky language he speaks, but Kiv can. The ambassador's head is bulbous, beneath his hood, and his entire nose and mouth are in one big snout. [If you think this sounds like a Teripleptil (19.4, "The Visitation"), you're not wrong - see **The Lore**.]

Planet Notes

• *Thoros Alpha*. It's a ringed planet, inhabited by humanoids who appear to be of South Asian origin. The Mentors and their servile humanoids on Thoros Beta [assuming these humanoids are themselves native to Beta] have subjugated many Alphans as slaves. One of the Alphan rebels on Beta formerly worked as a spice trader.

• *Thoros Beta*. The twin of Thoros Alpha. It has pink seas, lilac rocks and a turquoise sky. Originally aquatic, the native Mentors are now carried around in litters. Tides on Thoros Beta are artificially amplified to maximise their use as a power-source. [The script indicates tidal power itself, but the energy unit's design looks like it's more likely to be deuterium extraction and some

kind of cold fusion.] References are made [figuratively or otherwise] to the seas of 'Loss', 'Turmoil', 'Despair and Longing' and 'Sorrows'.

Contrary to Sil's comments the last time we met him, Thoros Beta's gravity doesn't seem to be much lower than that of Varos.

• *Wilson One*. Has a Spondilex crop [you'll need to know this one day].

History

• *Dating*. The Valeyard clearly establishes that the Thoros Beta adventure begins in the 'twenty-fourth century, last quarter, fourth year, seventh month, third day' - so that's 3rd of July, 2379, then. [And owing to Sil's presence, this helps to specify the dating for "Vengeance on Varos".]

After 'a decade of hard work', the surgeon Crozier - a blonde man who looks like he's in his 30s, and who's in Kiv's employ - has perfected a serum that can nullify tissue rejection. Thus, he can put any brain into any body. By story's end, he develops a means of transferring just the contents of someone's mind to another subject [but see **Things That Don't Make Sense**].

Crozier's experiments have yielded several corollaries: implants of his invention can block slaves from forming rebellious thoughts, and it would appear that the Mentors can also revive corpses. [Not only does Crozier transfer Kiv's brain into a hybrid that's apparently been dead for a while, but the rebels claim they can't leave the bodies of their opponents intact, otherwise the Mentors will use brain surgery to create creatures like the wolf-man Dorf.]

Crozier's work also leads to augmentations on the Raak - a toothy sea creature that's upgraded to work machinery - but the Raak becomes unstable and dies while attacking the Doctor and Peri. Later, Kiv's guards here perform an experiment that apparently uses circuitry to age rebels to death. [As shown, this comes precariously close to being a Thing That Doesn't Make Sense at the climax of episode three, but it's workable. It would appear that the head guard Frax and his men ambush a rebel weapons store and affix the rebel guards with circuits that make them decrepit. They then allow one to escape, luring Yrcanos' party into a trap.] Crozier also keeps a living brain on his desk as a side project, or maybe just as a paperweight, and *seems* to be studying the healing rate of its ganglions.

The Mentors have influenced events on the planet Thordon - a world inhabited by what the

Doctor calls 'a bunch of skullcrackers' - by supplying the Krontep warriors with multi-setting CD Phasers capable of stunning opponents or liquefying rock. This has lead to the defeat of the 'massed hordes' of the Tonkomp Empire, and the Mentor leader Kiv now wants Crozier to mentally pacify the Krontep King, Yrcanos, to facilitate contract negotiations. Kiv wants to establish business dealings that cover scientific advancements - major discoveries would be leased from the Thordonians for thirty years, at a royalty rate of 40%.

Sil has access to all the universe's stocks and commodities via a 'Warp Vault' relay. The Doctor says [unless he's bluffing] that a great many wars will occur around the rim-worlds in the near-future, and that a salvage operation working from the planet Tokl could harvest a large amount of battle-cruiser debris. [Presumably this refers to the business around *Invasion of the Ormazoids*, Martin's *Make Your Own Adventure* book, in which Tokl is described as looking almost exactly like Thoros Beta.] Sil thus extends credit to Search Con Corp., a group of space-rangers who retrieve wrecked spaceships. [This entire scene seems to confirm that the 'space-time craft' Sil mentioned on Varos are just ships with warp-drives: if they had time-travel in any serious sense, this project would not be viable, and Sil would not be so pleased to have the Doctor around helping.]

The Doctor labels the Court's proceedings as the biggest 'travesty of a trial' since the 'so-called Witches of Enderheid'.

The Analysis

Where Does This Come From? It's the 1980s, and everyone's obsessed with money. Well, that was the cliché. In fact, everyone was obsessed with how obsessed everyone was with money. Whilst the Government was privatising anything they thought they could get people to buy, and a lot of publicity was given to the traders in the City of London (not the physical city, but the financial district), it was a boom time for parodies of conspicuous consumption, moral treatises on the pursuit of wealth as a corrupting influence and those who got rich quick indulging in almost self-parodic ostentatious affluence. By 1986, even Oliver Stone had noticed and made *Wall Street*, a film almost exactly like a 1930s Warner Bros flick but with Martin Sheen doing what Pat O'Brien's character would have done in a Jimmy Cagney movie. Some people failed to spot that this was a diatribe, and idiots who thought Gordon Gekko was a role model started dressing like him. Michael Grade, for instance, adopted the look and the combative style. Del-Boy Trotter, in *Only Fools and Horses*, did so to comic effect just after Grade left the Corporation. People remembered Gekko's "Greed is good" speech, but forgot what happened to him at the end of the film. Admit it, so have you.

But even in the 1970s, this equation of moral degradation with parasitic wealth was fairly well-worn. Philip Martin's series *Gangsters* had taken the tropes of Blaxploitation movies, Fritz Lang films and those Warner Bros movies previously mentioned and thrown them into grotty Brum, with a cynical examination of people exploiting racial tensions. Like Sil, his crime-lords worship wealth and adopt near-comedic power-relationships. (The lackey Kuldip goes from sinister to slapstick, and his mangled English is - like Sil's - a running gag. But mainly he's the hapless foil of the "respectable" Mr Rafiq.)

Even in *Doctor Who* terms, this was old news (see "The Sun Makers"). What had changed was that this was no longer a ridiculous exaggeration or a rhetorical stance - but was now mainstream, even Government policy. "There is no such thing as society", said Mrs Thatcher, and society, for a few years, believed her. As we saw in the last story and "Attack of the Cybermen" (22.1), the new folk-heroes were dodgy entrepreneurs, so this year's crop of comic baddies are more monstrous to us now than any Dalek. Sil endorses slavery, and Glitz plans genocide in the course of retrieving some prized documents, but we're supposed to love them and laugh at their foibles.

When this story was broadcast, the media were obsessed with the impact of technology on finance - especially the so-called "Big Bang", when the Trading floor and all those hand-jiving berks in stripey blazers were replaced with coke-addled prats with red braces at computer terminals. The stuff with Sil and his 'warp-fold relay' is clearly akin to what the press said it would be like. (And the backstory for Mel in Nathan-Turner's book *The Companions* - not to mention the rumoured Bidmead tale for the original Season Twenty-Three - supposedly connected with this. We note that one version had the Master creating something very like what happened a year later - see 24.2, "Paradise Towers").

The scene of the released slaves with the malfunctioning implants running around causing a distraction is familiar. With this being an underground base, with a multi-ethnic crew of baddies and someone yelling and karate-chopping, it's obviously meant to look like *Enter the Dragon*.

Things That Don't Make Sense To go straight for the jugular, and examine the greatest problem here: the Court can't seem to decide what offence the Doctor has actually committed. Allegedly he's charged with meddling / 'interfering in the development of alien life forms', but the ending [as much as we might appreciate its drama] relies upon the Court deciding that Crozier's totally independent discovery of mind-transfer threatens the whole course of evolution, and is therefore the greatest threat of all. Consider that the Time Lords then remove the Doctor from Thoros Beta at a crucial juncture - so basically, they deliberately stop him halting Crozier's work, then add any consequences owing to his absence to *his* charge-sheet. Are they outraged, then, that he intervened on Thoros Beta, or that he didn't intervene enough? After all, the Valeyard proclaims that the Doctor 'abandoned Peri', even though the Jury *themselves* were responsible.

Moreover, after Peri's second apparent death, the Inquisitor suddenly knows a lot more about the proceedings than at any stage before, drops all pretence of impartiality and lectures the Doctor - almost as if she's reading a speech written for the Valeyard, in fact. Worse, judging by the Valeyard's comments during the last story, the imagined outcome of Crozier's surgery has to be pure speculation - once the TARDIS has been removed from time, how can it collect the mental impulses of people around where it had been? Besides, we later learn that the climax in Crozier's lab was bogus, yet the Inquisitor and the Court claim to have time-freezed and manipulated Yrcanos in this entirely false sequence of events. Is *everyone* in on the High Council's conspiracy? It's almost looking that way [and see the accompanying **How Warped Was the Doctor's Mind?** for more].

Crozier in the space of a day goes from surgically swapping brains around to transferring only the *contents* of someone's mind, when surely the two skills are entirely different disciplines. [Again, we probably have to rule this as part of the faked evidence, meaning it simply never happened. If Crozier *did* spontaneously develop this skill, then it's possibly the inadvertent result of the Doctor's

tinkering with his equipment, but there's not a shred of evidence for this. And if Crozier never honed such a process, meaning it's the Valeyard's invention, then the Court's intervention to quash the innovation is even more of a farce.] Besides, if the ability to transfer minds into new bodies is such an evolutionary no-no, why were so many beings that the Fourth Doctor encountered able to do this unimpeded? [Our count includes three possessions, another three godlike beings using human bodies, memory transfer - Noah's 'I'm Dune' from 12.2, "The Ark in Space" - and a threatened brain-swap. Then there's Salyavin, who arguably doesn't count because the Time Lords *did* intervene.] If the mere ability to do this must be stopped, shouldn't the Empire of Traken - given the Master's abuse of the Source in "The Keeper of Traken" - have been the subject of a surgical strike on the orders of the High Council?

Quite why *does* Crozier have a pulsating brain in his in-tray? With all those nice china teacups [apparently pilfered from British Rail], you'd think he'd at least have a cake-tin handy, but the brain just sits on his desk, throbbing a bit, without even any clingfilm to stop it drying out. For that matter, you'd think that Crozier's brain-transference lab would be kept sterile, yet he's seen sipping tea, and Sil eats Marshminnows during Kiv's all-important brain surgery. Wouldn't removing Peri's windchime-sized earrings have been a good idea too?

The Doctor and Peri seem to leave the TARDIS door ajar while it's in the ocean, yet it's apparently unaffected even when the tide comes and goes. Frax thinks that the mutated Dorf will finish off the escaping Doctor and Peri, which is rather optimistic considering Dorf is actually rather friendly and - more to the point - chained to the wall. Frax's competence is further called into question, though, when he lets Peri escape after she gives him a good kicking. Crozier's laboratory is of the utmost importance to Kiv, yet nobody bothers to lock the door or post a guard so the Doctor and Peri just stroll in toward the end of episode one. [And it's possibly a glitch that Yrcanos declines to kill one of his oppressors - Sil - after busting free at the start of episode two, but perhaps his honour demands only killing rivals in battle.] Oh, and the Doctor keeps expecting the Court to recognize Earth terms such as 'barmy' - a curious reversal of his irritation when Peri uses words like 'guy' ["Revelation of the Daleks"] or 'set them up' ["The Two Doctors"].

ABOUT TIME 1985-1989

One Thing That *Does* Make Sense: an urban myth, still being relayed as fact by the BBC's own website, claims that the third Mentor is watching *The A-Team* on his monitor. Aside from the fact that the recordings were on weekdays in May and June - so it would have to have been a recorded episode rather than one on air - it just isn't true. Yet people choose to believe it rather than look for themselves.

Critique   More like it! If the problems of "The Mysterious Planet" were mainly because nobody was in charge behind the scenes, the main problem here (if we're trying to get this out of the way) is that the Doctor is not the cohesive force this story needs. However, not only is that part of the story's point, it allows Peri to finally step into the breach as a pro-active, self-motivated character rather than a victim. She's been the object (in *many* meanings of the word) of other people's interest and ambition for so long, it's as much a relief to see her taking control of a situation as it was when Jo Grant told the Master that hypnosis didn't work on her no mo' (10.3, "Frontier in Space"). This should've been cause for celebration - a major turning point like Mickey Smith deciding not to be the Tin Dog (X2.3, "School Reunion") - but unfortunately it comes out of nowhere. It just *looks* like Philip Martin wrote for a generic companion - even though we know he probably didn't, because he'd written for Peri before and should've known her frailty, so perhaps this was a result of Saward's rewrites.

We're obsessing on this because it's crucial to why this story isn't perfect. Everything around it, in some regard, is exactly as it should be - and indeed as *Doctor Who* should've been five years earlier. All the technical wizardry seems belatedly in line with the public's expectations for the series: technicolour skies, robotic voices, a few "how did they do that?" moments, funny characters, really *alien* aliens and a lateral-thinking element to cover the lack of budget. For too long the target audience's visual acuity and the look of every other similar series has marched steadily on without *Doctor Who* - now they can do this sort of thing properly, but apparently at the expense of what kept people watching the series *in spite* of technical deficiencies. Simply put, nobody's been thinking about character, plot or dialogue.

Almost nobody, that is. We've seen what Philip Martin can achieve with minimal gimmickry

when it comes to making a world out of throwaway lines. Here he does it again, but with the digital tomfoolery on top. What stops King Yrcanos from being Brian Blessed doing his usual schtick is the idea that he's from a planet where they're *all* like that. It's the same trick that made Sil work on Varos, and now we see a planet where he's nothing special (apparently) and the novelty alien becomes a character. Unfortunately, not enough of Martin's script made it to the screen.

So it's left to the actors to bring this world to life, and most of them succeed. The rebels that Tuza leads are so wet, it's amazing they don't smell of fish too (and note that Martin denies all knowledge of this subplot). Nevertheless, you have a feeling that this planet was there *before* the Doctor arrived, and that the ones mentioned - but which go unseen - are almost as real. Every character seems to know what they're doing there (again, except those amateur rebels), both as people with lives and as characters in a *Doctor Who* narrative. Watch Baker's face as Frax hands him the gun and says 'cover me': the look says "will they never learn?" Even without the added layer of complication about what really happened, this double-vision - with everyone acting like they know they're in *Doctor Who* - makes this worth re-watching. Everyone is motivated by a need to stay in character: Yrcanos wants to die heroically, and he knows rebels will appear because that's what happens in this sort of enterprise. This is what makes the Doctor's abandonment of the role of hero so disruptive.

Yet this occurs because we're given an on-screen critique of the Colin Baker Doctor, with the Valeyard plausibly suggesting that this one isn't up to the standard we expect of the character. Of course it's not true, but if you read the tabloids and didn't actually watch Season Twenty-Two, you might buy it. Whether this was part of the overall plan to mellow this Doctor is beside the point - the fact is that no other Doctor (even early Hartnell) could viably be traduced or misrepresented that way. It's an opportunity too good to miss, and allows the real Sixth Doctor to pass judgement on his critics. For once, the premise of the Trial works, and the Doctor is allowed to defend not just the actor playing him, but the entire premise of the series.

This would all be pointlessly clever if the surrounding story was no good. In fact, even without the flashy effects, stunt-casting and self-conscious metatext, this is a classic *Doctor Who* set-up: an experiment into mind-transference and a consideration of where personality ends and biology begins. Although it's kept fairly low in the mix, this is an interesting idea in itself and allows the stakes to be raised in the final episode.

So they can have their cake and eat it too. Peri dies, and doesn't. Nicola Bryant, fresh from rewriting the character she's been playing for two years, gets to play a different one inside the same body. Even so, the story's ending is a misfire - not because of the "it didn't happen" Liberace moment in Part 14, but because the cliffhanger is moved to yet another crash-zoom on the Doctor's face rather than ending with the white-out as Yrcanos fires randomly.

In short, this story marks the point where the Sixth Doctor era should have begun - with Bryant making Peri likeable, Baker making the Doctor unpredictable, Ron Jones giving us a lot to look at and Philip Martin braining up the scripts (even if Saward screws it all up again). It's taken a while, but here *Doctor Who* looks like it belongs on Saturday nights again. One week is all it will take to remove this, but don't think about that for now. Anyway, when the payoff finally arrives in December, the story will turn out never to have happened at all.

But just *look* at it. Good sets, amazing locations (even without the colour), visual panache and funny characters who do things for good reasons (as well as because it's what that kind of character does). If there's "false" material in this, maybe the Valeyard should have written more stories. This is, quite frankly, the only Sixth Doctor story you can still watch these days without making major allowances, and the only one you can show small children (even if you have to reassure them Peri's all right).

The Facts

Written by Philip Martin. Directed by Ron Jones. Ratings: 4.8 million, 4.6 million, 5.1 million, 5.0 million.

Working Titles "Planet of Sil"

Supporting Cast Brian Blessed (King Yrcanos), Nabil Shaban (Sil), Christopher Ryan (Kiv), Patrick Ryecart (Crozier), Alibe Parsons (Matrona Kani), Thomas Branch (The Lukoser, AKA Dorf), Trevor Laird (Frax), Gordon Warnecke (Tuza).

Oh, Isn't That..?

• *Brian Blessed*. At this stage, he was just on the cusp of being the actor Brian Blessed, and being the character Brian Blessed always plays. He'd been in *Z Cars* for ages, then was Augustus in *I, Claudius*. In *Space: 1999*, he'd played the leader of a race called... "Mentors" (see 17.2, "City of Death" for who played his daughter). However, after playing King Vultan in *Flash Gordon* and Richard IV in *The Black Adder*, he was seemingly always playing shouty, bearded psychos. With his chat-show appearances, mountaineering (he's "done" Everest), autobiography and appearance in Kenneth Branagh's film of *Henry V* he'd become more famous for being Brian Blessed than for anything else. (Let's face it, who *else* could be instantly recognisable behind a CGI blob, talking gibberish, in *The Phantom Menace*?) In 1983, the press had been convinced that he would follow Peter Davison as the Doctor, and these days advertisers use Blessed and Tom Baker almost interchangeably for voice-overs.

• *Alibe Parsons*. She was in *Gangsters*, playing Sarah Gant, the Madame-turned-CIA agent. As Crozier's assistant, Parsons is enough like the earlier character - similar eye make-up included - to make some critics wonder if the part was written for her. She was also in *Space: Twenty Quid*, as a character called 'Alibe'. Clever, huh?

• *Gordon Warnecke*. He was quite good in *My Beautiful Launderette*, but never really managed to capitalise on it. He also was in several episodes of *Boon*, a series that was very popular but nobody knows why.

• *Patrick Ryecart*. Later the straight man (in *so* many ways) in *The High Life*, the sitcom that gave the world Alan Cumming.

• *Christopher Ryan*. Hitherto best known as "Mike, the Cool Person" in *The Young Ones,* Ryan had been doing stage-work before and smaller TV parts after. You do a kooky drama where the hero hallucinates Trotsky, you call Chris Ryan and give him a goatee. This story was his first major TV role after getting to Number One in the charts with the charidee version of *Living Doll* (with the other Young Ones and Cliff Richard).

• *Trevor Laird* is now Martha's dad in TV's *Doctor Who*. (We make the distinction on the grounds that "Mindwarp" and X3.1, "Smith and Jones" barely seem to be from the same planet, let alone the same series.)

Cliffhangers   Crozier subjects the Doctor to a brutal mind-probe; Yrcanos readies to shoot the Doctor for betraying him; the Mentors' troops gun down Peri, Yrcarnos, Tuza and Dorf. And the lead-in to the next adventure: Peri is dead, and the furious Doctor declares that the Trial is rigged.

The Lore

• With Sil such a hit with younger viewers, a rematch was inevitable. As we have seen, "Mission to Magnus" was commissioned very promptly, and even when this was scratched, the Mentors and Thoros Beta were on the "wish-list" for the "Trial" storyline. Another idea included very early was that Peri should die as part of some experiment - Nicola Bryant had wanted to play an "evil" double of her character, and the mind-swap idea seems to have been a means to that end (possibly replacing the idea of an Auton replica in the unused Holmes "Yellow Fever" story).

• When studio rehearsals began, on 24th of May, news broke that Robert Holmes had died. Eric Saward was especially upset. This ended Saward's formal connection with the series, but his involvement was to have included the final two-part story of the year (and we'll tell that story when we come to it). Colin Baker, puzzled at which bits of his performance were supposed to be "really" happening and which were faked evidence, was asked to consult Saward on it, but got no help.

Likewise, Martin found that some of the parts he thought were "true" were being over-acted as though fake, and much of what was broadcast came as a surprise to him. Martin had been told to include more humour, then had to fight for it as Saward trimmed the jokes. Then, when the resulting episodes under-ran, Saward introduced less amusing gags - such as the whole spiel about the Mentor who hates Yrcarnos' shouting - and entire subplots, such as the business of Tuza's rebel faction. Martin was also perplexed at being asked to write material to tie up with later stories, even though nobody was sure which of many possible third stories was to be used.

• This story's production coincided with the first serious attempt to sell *Doctor Who* in France. French television executive Alain Carrazé had long been a fan of the series and - after attempts to get the rights for *The Prisoner* and the revived *Twilight Zone* fell through - convinced channel

TF1 to buy the first two Tom Baker seasons for inclusion in the magazine programme *Temps X*. Appropriately for this era, it was presented by two people in jumpsuits: Igor and Grichka Bogdanoff. A 16-minute promotional feature was made covering the making of "Mindwarp", including with Nathan-Turner and Baker. These were shown, oddly captioned, at PanoptiCon VII. Publishers Garanciere translated eight Target novelisations to tie in with the launch of the series, with photos of the Brothers Bogdanoff plastered all over the attractively cartoony cover art. Clearly, a big push was underway.

Then TF1 was privatised, Carrazé was given the push and *Temps X* cancelled. *Doctor Who* was now under the purview of a form children's presenter named Dorothé, and buried at 7am on Sundays. Specially filmed introductory material was omitted - though American fans who remember Howard Da Silva's intrusive recaps of the late 1970s might not see the problem here - and the series began with "Genesis of the Daleks", then worked backwards towards "Robot". No one watched (understandably) and *Doctor Who* wasn't seen again in France for almost twenty years, when Christopher Eccleston's series (dubbed remarkably accurately, *tournevis sonique* and all) was flogged to a cable company. They put it on between *The West Wing* and soft porn, where it tanked (but then, French mainstream TV doesn't usually touch anything thought to be American these days). On the plus side, Eccleston went down well in Russia.

• With only a few minutes left in which to record one last scene, Blessed dried and replaced the word "Mentors" with something we can't repeat. Being Brian Blessed, he was not given the usual roasting from Nathan-Turner that would have followed, but instead a calm, diplomatic reminder of the word.

• Given the programme's long association with confectionery, it should come as no surprise that Trebor-Bassett were interested in jelly 'marshminnows'. A trial batch was used in this story, replacing the dyed peaches from "Vengeance on Varos". Martin and Nathan-Turner were in favour of the idea. As part of his abasement after the botched handling of the Suspension, Michael Grade was often involved in launching drives to promote the series in the US. This coincided with the Food and Drug Administration's reversal of the ban on Jelly Babies, so Grade trotted out the old joke about male ones having a bit more. (Bassetts eventually lost patience with Nathan-Turner, however: see 25.2, "The Happiness Patrol".)

• Grade's comments came as part of the launch of a tour. The travelling *Doctor Who* Exhibition was sent on its way in Washington DC by Grade and Peter Davison just before this story began recording, and allowed interested fans to view a mock-up of the TARDIS console room, some of the monsters and even Bessie. Later, Janet Fielding took Davison's place. (Reports coming to us about this make it seem like a weird road-movie. Try recasting *Paris, Texas* or Fellini's *La Strada* with Colin, Nicola and Janet. Or *The Adventures of Pricilla, Queen of the Desert*, if you can avoid imagining a new use for Dalek ping-pong balls. Strange days...)

• Those big round doors were actually just one prop over and over again, and it was a loaner. Bryant was peeved that the cost of hiring the door was more than her fee. The Possicar Delegate was another example of recycling, this time of the Terileptil mask from "The Visitation", but coloured pink this time. Inside the costume was Deep Roy, formerly Mr Sin in 14.6, "The Talons of Weng-Chiang", later the entire Oompa-Loompa nation in the 2005 film of *Charlie and the Chocolate Factory*. If you're the sort of person who watches old British fantasy shows, you'll be able to add to this list, no bother.

• This was an unusual production in that the location work was done after the studio material. After a long search for a suitable coastal location, one was found about a mile from where Nathan-Turner lived in Brighton. The downside was that this was a nudist beach, and also (coincidentally, of course) popular with dog-walkers. New production secretary Kate Esteal was being assessed by a prim BBC personnel lady, whose embarrassment amused the crew. Unedited location footage shows that miscalculations about when high tide was caused problems.

• The location material was amended in post production by the new HARRY computerised paintbox system, and we'll be seeing a lot more of this later on. The BBC had been using two of these for the weather forecasts, but hadn't allowed the technology to be exploited for silly things like *Doctor Who* until now. The music was the one score by Richard Hartley for the series. Although Malcolm Clarke had been scheduled to do it, Hartley - who had arranged the music for *The Rocky Horror Picture Show* (see 24.4, "Dragonfire")

and *Shock Treatment* - was apparently given the job well in advance.

• Martin's novelisation was delayed for two years after its scheduled publication date, leaving a gap in Target's wholly arbitrary numbering system. By the time Book No. 139 appeared, even the editors were getting confused. In fairness Martin was busy with episodes of *Star Cops* and a *Make Your Own Adventure With Doctor Who* book (see **Did They Think We'd Buy Just Any Old Crap?** under 22.5, "Timelash"). Despite rumours that he'd be writing a third Sil story for Season Twenty-Four, his subsequent *Doctor Who* work consisted of a novelisation of "Mission to Magnus" and 2004's "The Creed of the Kromon", a frankly underwhelming Big Finish audio starring Paul McGann. "Kromon" is notable for regurgitating themes from Martin's two televised stories and introducing a six-foot tall psychotic religious grasshopper as the Doctor's new companion.

• All right, we have to mention it: the novelisation claims that Peri is alive and well and living in California, where she is married to Yrcanos and managing his successful Pro-Wrestling career. Voroomnik!

23.3: "The Trial of a Time Lord: Terror of the Vervoids"

(Serial 7C Part 1, Four Episodes. 1st - 22nd November 1986.)

Which One is This?   Bonnie Langford and the Killer Tulips.

Firsts and Lasts   In case you missed it... Bonnie Langford. It's true, it's all true!

More importantly, the workhorse director of this final spurt of the series, Chris Clough, begins here. For three years running, he'll do six episodes (out of fourteen) per annum. The BBC Radio-phonic Workshop - in the shape of Malcolm Clarke - contributes their last music score to the series. Clarke had done their first one without an "outside" composer (9.3, "The Sea Devils") as well as many others, but this one isn't particularly memorable. Adric's old star-chart makes a farewell visit, seen on the wall of the corridor outside the cabins. And it's technically the last story Colin Baker made (on TV, at least).

Most important of all, due to BBC Health and Safety regulations (see 25.4, "The Greatest Show in the Galaxy"), this is the very last sighting of that quintessential *Doctor Who* feature (at least as far as crap comedians and TV critics are concerned): the Wobbly Set. Watch Colin take the axe from the wall at the end of episode two, and prepare to sob.

Four Things to Notice about "Terror of the Vervoids"...

1. We all know that Bonnie Langford is a true pro, a tireless trouper and showbiz royalty. The trouble is, her time on *Doctor Who* entailed a slight credibility-gap. If you lived in Britain in the 80s, she wasn't so much a household name as a punch-line - every cliché about stage-school brats, or any gag you wanted to make about obnoxious child stars, had her name at the end. For us, she was like Shirley Temple and all the Kids from *Fame* in one tiny, flame-haired package. Observe how Pip 'n' Jane have written for her *perceived* character, rather than create a character and have someone play it who's in past played loathsome children. Proof of Langford's professionalism comes in the first cliffhanger where, to mix into the theme-tune "sting", she's asked to scream in the key of F.

2. As you might expect from a Pip 'n' Jane script, there's some ripe dialogue. 'Don't prevari-cate, Professor' is borderline witty, but much of the rest is clunkingly cumbersome. 'Why can't you use plain language?' asks the Commodore, before continuing, with *Airplane!*-style urgency, 'Whoever's been dumped in there has been pul-verised into fragments and sent floating in space - and in my book, that's murder!' Compounding this is the fact that much of the Doctor's presenta-tion has apparently been tampered with, but there's no discernible difference between the "faked' dialogue and how people in Pip 'n' Jane scripts *always* talk.

3. Incredibly, the appearance of the main mon-sters seems not to have struck anyone as rude until transmission. Seen "in the flesh" (as it were), they look like tulips on top of piles of maple-leaves. From different camera-angles, however, they alternate between looking like female geni-talia and male genitalia. Occasionally, for variety, they look like a baboon's bum. And when steam exudes from small pipes at the, um, business end, and the dying Vervoids make low moaning noises and occasional squeaks, you wonder if *anyone* in the BBC hierarchy was paying attention. (Yet clearly someone *was* concerned enough to prevent the fanzine *DWB* publishing photos of the

Vervoids in advance of transmission - resulting in an issue punctuated with blank spaces where the pictures would have gone.)

4. In Andrew Rose's last two outings as costume designer, menswear had been tracksuit and shoul-derpad themed (13.2, "Planet of Evil" and 21.6, "The Caves of Androzani"). It makes sense to con-tinue in this vein for a story made in 1986, but in a story set in 2986 - one that discusses aerobics, actually includes the line "if you've finished with my tracksuit..." and has treadmills in the gym - it's starting to look like an obsession. And however gynaecological the Vervoids' heads may have seemed to some, their bodies below the neck are even less well-thought-out. Basically, they're tracksuits too, with leaves stuck on them. So when the Vervoids die, and the leaves go brown and fall off, you can see the drawstrings of the trousers and the black fabric underneath. Some claim you can even see the word 'Adidas' in white on the legs. There, you now have motivation to stick it out until the last episode. (Oh, and they've got rubber-soled plimsolls on their feet.)

The Continuity

The Doctor He's now decided that his best course of defence is to show that his behaviour will change. He therefore consults the Matrix files, and elects to show an escapade from his future - one in which he intervenes to stop the Vervoids from slaughtering everyone aboard the Hyperion III in 2986. As shown in court, the evidence features the Doctor's future companion, Melanie, saying that he usually goes charging into danger regard-less of the risk. [You'd think the Doctor would have cut that line from his submission, so it's probably down to the Valeyard's editing - even if it's generally true.]

The Doctor has taken to performing *Vesti la Gubbia*. In future, he'll wear a waistcoat with satin diagonal stripes of bright colour, and a different cat-badge. His cravat will change, too, being a yel-low one with white stars [and yet he'll have ditched this outfit by 24.1, "Time and the Rani"]. He's able to discretely procure a leaf from Hallett's pocket even with a small group of people around him. On the whole he'd rather be in Pyro Shika. [This planet is described more in the Bakers' *Make Your Own Adventure* book. Its residents, the Shikari, taught him the trick he used to avoid being hit by a box in 22.3, "The Mark of the Rani", apparently. Never mind that "Shikari" is the name of a real tribe in Africa.]

• *Ethics.* [Let's assume that the alleged genocide happened the way we see it, because the Doctor doesn't refute the event.] The Doctor "solves" the Vervoid menace by accelerating their lifespans unto death. His perspective is that the Vervoids are acting in accordance with their nature, and view humans as hostile because animals - one way or another - subsist on plant-life. Effectively, he seems to regard the idea of co-existence between Vervoids and humans as being impossible. [There's none of the consideration for the Vervoids' point-of-view, as with the Silurians and Sea Devils in the Pertwee years. That the Vervoids seem to have some reasoning ability is almost irrelevant, as the Doctor apparently believes they'll never learn to behave better - this is a little out of keeping with his usual methodology, but not much.] Notably, he doesn't justify his actions to the Court by arguing that Vervoids were an artificially-created life-form, or that even their creator (Professor Lasky) concurred with the need to destroy them [see 12.1, "Robot" for a comparable example].

• *Inventory.* He's got a bunch of fake flowers up his sleeve, and a boxy gadget for picking locks. [Remember, they wrote out the sonic screwdriver because it made things "too easy".] His new watch needs winding more frequently.

• *Background.* At some time in this incarnation, he encountered Commodore "Tonker" Travers when he was just a captain - an incident that Travers claims involved 'a web of mayhem and intrigue'. The Doctor evidently saved Travers' ship on that occasion, although it's implied [possibly owing to the Valeyard's edits] that he might have endangered it in the first place.

The Doctor also knows Hallett - the secret agent that everyone seems to recognise from Stella Stora - and claims he admired him. [Proceed to **Things That Don't Make Sense.**] He also seems to have visited Mogar at some point.

• *Foreground.* He's been travelling with Mel long enough to vouch for her without reservation, but he's still getting used to her exercise regime, and has yet to ask her if she's enjoying this life of adventure. Weirdly, he's become concerned that his ears are growing longer. [This appears to be a spectacularly lame joke about a donkey, and suggests he thinks that Mel is about six years old.]

The Supporting Cast

• *Melanie.* [Various guides and publications identify her last name as "Bush" - probably true, but this is never said on screen. In fact we might conclude from the ritual introduction that her surname is "knownasmel".] It's said that she hails from Pease Pottage, and the circumstances concerning how she met the Doctor are never revealed. [Nathan-Turner's book *The Companions* fills in some of the blanks, though, and Gary Russell's novel *Business Unusual* offers itself up as the first time - from Mel's perspective - that she meets the Doctor.] The Doctor hints that she's been with him for a while already, when they discuss her life so far as a companion in episode one.

Mel already knows her way around the TARDIS console, and is confident that she can use the Hyperion's communications rig. She's credited as having total recall, and is usually able to identify the Doctor's literary allusions, although she teases him for his 'antediluvian' vocabulary. She isn't much into agronomy. She is, however [and not without justification], on a mission to get his weight down. More curiously, she's obsessive about exercising - even though she's petite to the point of being skinny. [So she's hoping to build muscle, then, and note her similar interest in swimming in 24.2, "Paradise Towers". Or more plausibly, and in keeping with concerns of the time, she's borderline anorexic and connects control of her weight with self-esteem. It seems like a stretch but this was also how Peri was originally conceived according to some sources] Despite [or perhaps because of] this apparent dysmorphia, she screams at things she considers ugly. Or when anyone gets into any trouble. Or when she hasn't had a line of dialogue lately.

The Supporting Cast (Evil)

• *The Valeyard.* Curiously, he's allowed the Doctor to pursue his argument that the Matrix has been interfered with. [We've moved from "if" or "is it possible?" remarkably quickly.] Moreover, rather than letting the Doctor's outbursts incriminate the defendant, the Valeyard seems to be downplaying their significance. He even allows the Doctor to demonstrate his cleverness by showing how he identified one of the Mogarians as an impersonator. [To many observers, this has been taken to indicate that the Valeyard actively *wants* to be found out, apparently so he can gloat about his cleverness in outwitting the Court, the High Council and the Doctor. Watch his reaction when the Master blows his cover next episode - it's not shame or anger but surprise, almost relief.]

The TARDIS Now registers the text of SOS messages on the panel that controls the scanner. The Doctor works out on an 80s exercise bike that's taken up residence in the console room, and there's evidently a supply of carrot-juice on board.

The Time Lords Article Seven of Gallifreyan law relates to the outlawing of genocide, and the Valeyard claims there are no exceptions given for this crime.

The Non-Humans

• *Vervoids.* They're essentially humanoid plants that walk, talk, hunt and think. The Vervoids are slightly taller than the average human, and "hatch" from three metre-high seed-pods upon exposure to high-intensity light. Their "hands" have six digits and seem more like stamens; in the centre of this is a toxic dart that must be "placed" rather than fired over any distance. As another means of attack, Vervoids can exude a poisonous "marsh-gas" that's a methane derivative. The Vervoids are covered in palmate [i.e. maple-like] leaves, which they shed [almost like deliberate calling-cards], and they appear to have ivy growing on their surfaces. Vervoid chloroplasts function like those of normal plants, and trap sunlight.

From the neck up, the Vervoids are utterly unlike humans. They have vertical slats at the centre of the bulbous, pink "head", from which small fronds emerge. A horizontal fold bisects this; the hemispheres are pale pink above the fold, but redder below. The surrounding leaf-structures are like a Savoy cabbage, only inside two layers of petals. These form a high collar that is yellow, and in two shades.

• *Mogarians.* Bipedal, basically humanoid creatures from the airless world of Mogar, which means that oxygen - even in water form - is toxic to them. Accordingly, they are encased entirely in protective suits - these are golden in colour, and apparently all identical save for the differing colours of their translation devices. The Mogarians' helmets are brassy-looking - rather like 1930s microphone casings - and contain breathing apparatus and some kind of eye protection. The one unmasked Mogarian that we see appears to have mouthpiece - or possibly a natural filter - and golden skin. [It's possible that their skin changes colour upon contact with air, but it's easier to assume that this is their natural hue.]

Untranslated Mogarian speech sounds like a recording played backwards. They largely seem to be polite - save when one of them upends a stewardess' tray [presumably owing to Hallett's death by poisoned tea], and when they hijack the *Hyperion III* to steal back their planet's ore from Earth's authorities. They've bribed the *Hyperion III* security office, Rudge, to help with this plan.

Planet Notes

• *Mogar.* Seen from space, Mogar looks brick-red. It's located in the Perseus Arm of the Milky Way, and rich in minerals including vionesium - a substance similar to magnesium, and which accelerates the Vervoid life-cycle when exposed to oxygen (by giving off bright light and CO_2.)

History

• *Dating.* The Doctor supplies the date as 16th of April, 2986, and crewman Edwardes' readouts confirm this. Three years previous, the older traveller Mr Kimber encountered the investigator named Hallett when the latter investigated 'shortages in the grainery on Stella Stora'. [Quite why a special investigator was called in regarding such a matter is a puzzle, like basically everything else related to Hallett. And why didn't they just buy a cat like any other farmer would in these circumstances?]

Class One Security vessels conduct runs between Earth and Mogar. *Hyperion III* Flight 113 is here seen transporting a 'top-priority consignment' of Mogar metals to Earth. Life-support equipment is heard on board [and sounds like that used for the Tharils in 18.5, "Warriors' Gate"]. Aerobics seem to be back "in" [although having a gym aboard a space vessel travelling for any duration seems sensible enough].

Earth has apparently forged a relationship to mine Mogar, but some Mogarians are upset about this, claiming that the humans have gone from a limited concession to wholesale strip-mining. [Given that something similar is happening in the other thirtieth century story, 9.4, "The Mutants", we can surmise that Earth's government is really hell-bent on making itself unpopular. It seems a heck of a coincidence, by the way, that both stories have space-liners called 'Hyperion'. It might have been a nice touch if Cotton had been on his final voyage home from Solos when the Vervoids

How "Good" is the Doctor?

Over the years we've got used to assuming that the Doctor triumphs through virtue, and that therefore he embodies the values to which the programme-makers would want us to aspire. We had all taken as read the summaries of his heroic status in various introductions to the show, be it Terrance Dicks' often-quoted "mission statement" from *The Making of Doctor Who* (to which we'll return) to Harlan Ellison's typically excitable peroration from the Pinnacle editions of the Target novelisations.

Ellison's is especially interesting, as it allows us to examine a generational shift in perceptions of the Doctor. For Ellison, the Doctor's gifts are intelligence and curiosity, and his willingness to put these at the service of others in trouble are what make him a hero that one can imitate. Concepts such as regeneration and a time machine are minor plot details. For people who came to the series later (i.e. after Tom Baker), the Doctor is an alien with superpowers, and must therefore be rendered morally ambiguous to make the stories interesting. In part, this is a function of the way the last phase of the series borrowed from mid-1980s comics, and how the authors of the spin-off books all fell over themselves to prove that it wasn't in any way infantile to be interested in *Doctor Who*.

This assumption that nobody would "buy" a straightforward hero is typically 1980s. We had no end of flawed, vulnerable protagonists in that era, from Indiana Jones down, and in comics the whole adolescent obsession with turning Batman into "The Bat-Man" and then "The Dark Knight" contaminated all forms of popular culture. Once Andrew Cartmel got his hands on *Doctor Who*, it seemed, the Doctor became questionable by the standards of the time of broadcast. This looked, to many, both "mature" and unprecedented.

Of course, in actuality it was neither, because the Doctor's motivation had been questioned throughout the run of the series. Often, this was an opportunity to show how far his view of things - the Big Picture, if you will - alienated him from his friends. Sometimes, it was because he was keeping something from us and his companions. In incidents like the Laurence Scarman's death (13.3, "Pyramids of Mars") or tricking Jamie into rescuing Victoria (4.9, "The Evil of the Daleks"), it turned out he was right, but that didn't make him any more pleasant to know at that time. But go back further, and the matter becomes more interesting.

We have to remember that the Doctor was originally there to get Ian and Barbara into trouble, and that he was as much a plot-contrivance as a character. In the first three stories, he allowed his own selfish interests and impatience with slower minds to place everyone in danger. Barbara and Ian get ample opportunity to lecture him. Perhaps because they were schoolteachers, or perhaps because Ian was formerly Sir Lancelot (the sanitised TV one, not Mallory's Ill-Made Knight) as far as viewers were concerned, we assume that they're right and that therefore the Doctor is wrong. He admits as much at the end of "The Edge of Destruction" (1.3). Is that the case, though? Look again at "An Unearthly Child" (1.1), and you find his intelligence is at odds with his instincts. He does questionable things when he *thinks*, but he's as heroic as we ever see him when he *reacts*.

In later stories his thoughts and deeds are in synch, but not always what we would think of as "good". In "The Macra Terror" (4.7), the Doctor seems to be committing genocide. Obviously the Macra are treating the humans in a way that should be stopped, but to be fair, they *were* on this planet first. (Of course, we can't see what really happens to the Macra, but we assume they all died as a result of the Doctor's actions. It's significant that out of all the also-ran, Vauxhall Conference-level Troughton monsters they could have brought back, X3.3, "Gridlock" inflicted shopping mall-sized Macra on the viewing public, with a whole new backstory to exonerate the Doctor for wiping out an intelligent species - by suggesting that they were a galaxy-wide "scourge" and not native at all. So those fans peeved with Ian Stuart Black for making a story where the Doctor wipes out a life-form are now irate at Russell Tiberius for ignoring Black's "classic" script. No pleasing some people.)

Was the Doctor correcting a sin or committing one? The logic of the 1967 story is that the Macra surrendered their right to live when they overstepped some line. They enslaved the humans, robbing them of free will, and this is the traditional *Doctor Who* definition of "a fate worse than death". But is this enough to cost the Macra *all* rights? When defending the Vervoids' actions to Mel, the Doctor says that they are simply following instinct. If this is an excuse, then Daleks should be just left to get on with dominating the cosmos. (Note that in X1.6, "Dalek", the Doctor realises that the prisoner he's spent the whole story trying to kill is in pain because of a conflict between genet-

continued on page 141...

ABOUT TIME 1985-1989

over-ran the ship he was on, but this story is quite silly enough without Rick James in it.]

Professor Lasky specializes in thrematology ('the science of breeding and propagating animals and plants under domestication'). With her two assistants - Bruchner and Doland - she created the Vervoids in the course of their work on Mogar. [Why they needed to conduct such advanced agronomy work on an airless planet is never clear, unless it was to avoid Earth jurisdiction. That doesn't seem right, though, as Lasky's party is here en route to Earth without much fear of sanctions.] Doland - if not Lasky and Bruchner also - believes the Vervoids have potential as a ready-made labour force, and will be far more affordable in the running of factories and farms than robots. The team also seems responsible for the creation of silver Demeter seeds - so-named by Bruchner [but see **Things That Don't Make Sense**] - which can increase potential yields three-fold, and grow in desert sand.

A mishap in the course of the Vervoid research caused a spec of pollen to penetrate a minute scratch on the thumb of Doland's lab assistant, Ruth Baxter, and she's consequently been turned into a half-Vervoid creature. [If this is a function of Vervoid biology, then the Doctor is right - they're a formidable threat to humanity in more ways than one. Maybe Lasky was breeding them as weapons.]

Bruchner has training as an astronaut, as it was an obligatory requirement for someone on Lasky's team to do so. Anyone receiving a Mayday signal is required to respond. Equipment aboard the *Hyperion III* includes a laser-lance, capable of burning through doors.

The Mogarians are seen playing *Space Invaders*, or a 3D projection of a similar 2-D game.

The Analysis

Where Does This Come From? This story is a fusion of two of the oddest programmes the BBC made in the 1980s[16] - one a serious drama intended for adults, the other...not. One was a children's crime series, *Captain Zep: Space Detective*, the gimmick of which was that only the three regular actors were real - the rest were drawings onto which they were CSO'd. Zep was now senior lecturer in Super Space Detecting, and so addressed a class full of students (stage-school kids in lurid jump-suits and hair-gel) with recordings of his

best cases. The bit in "Terror of the Vervoids" where the Doctor robs us of five minutes of our lives by explaining how he knew Hallett wasn't a Mogarian is like a *Captain Zep* episode, only condensed from twenty-five minutes. And save that the hand-drawn alien criminals over which the rostrum camera roamed were marginally less crap than the aliens in this story.

However, the *real* freakshow of early 80s BBC drama was *Triangle*. Twice a week, in the slot used for Davison-era *Doctor Who* (6.55pm, after *Nationwide*) they told a tale of passion, chicanery, wheeler-dealing and intrigue on the high seas. Well, the North Sea, anyway. Yes, it's a soap set on a ferry. And Pip 'n' Jane wrote for it. Kate O'Mara's smouldering half-smile may have been an attempt to avoid becoming seasick, as they actually recorded this whole show on the ferry between Harwich, Gothenburg and Rotterdam (that's the eponymous "triangle") during winter. The North Sea's grim enough in summer even without storms and violent lurches, and attempting to do a glossy-looking shoulderpads-opera with BBC resources was doomed anyway (see our comments on *Howard's Way* under 22.1, "Attack of the Cybermen", then watch the second series of *A Bit of Fry and Laurie*).

Triangle was a kitsch classic. Words cannot express how contrived the plots got over the three years that our license fees paid for this to be made. Seriously, it ran for three years, and how many different plots do you think running a ferry can generate? Well, there's the "I was in charge of security for twenty years and they're throwing me on the scrap-heap" chestnut. Nigel Stock (he's Professor Hayter in 19.7, "Time-Flight") had that one. There's the "will-they-won't-they" sexual chemistry thing too; in this case Michael Craig (appearing in "Vervoids" as the Commodore) and Kate O'Mara got it until she left at the end of Season Two, deciding that watching wooden mock-geordies turn into non-wooden trees was a better move (see "Mark of the Rani"). Sadly, she was right.

The point is that all of the subplots simmering away in "Vervoids" episode one are there to develop at different speeds (like in a soap), and not naturally likely to come to a head together (as in a detective story). Indeed, the main villains haven't been born when the first death (the sizzled Edwardes) occurs, so classic detection plotting has been junked pretty comprehensively. But this

How "Good" is the Doctor?

...continued from page 139

ically-engineered bloodlust and an accidental transfusion of Rose's attitudes. As we saw in "Robot" (12.1) the capacity to imagine the pain of others seems to be some kind of litmus test, a theme we've seen in garbled form when discussing the morality of Androgums in 22.4, "The Two Doctors". See **Does the Universe Have an Ethical Standard?** under "Robot").

As we've seen in earlier essays, the series' basic morality allows us to speculate on what criteria the Doctor may be using. He mustn't wreck history, if at all possible (**Can You Rewrite History, Even One Line?** under 1.6, "The Aztecs"); he should resist anything that makes life more predictably conformist, as part of an overall policy of resisting Entropy (**What Do the Guardians Do?** under 16.1, "The Ribos Operation")[17]; and he shouldn't inflict unnecessary suffering. Within those limits he has some leeway, and often the most characteristic moments are when he goes the extra mile and makes one person's life better when it strictly speaking isn't necessary. More often, the only time this makes his behaviour any different from what we'd expect of a routine TV hero is when two or more of those criteria are in conflict. We can cite any number of examples, but let's stick with the big ones: not preventing the Daleks' creation when ordered (12.4, "Genesis of the Daleks"), not rescuing Adric (19.6, "Earthshock") and turning down the offer of Enlightenment (20.5, "Enlightenment").

The last one brings us to a complicating factor. For obvious reasons of not ending the series, the Doctor has to remain fallible and engaging, so he has often refused godlike powers. Whilst the usual reason for this is the classic Greek-inspired Enlightenment European traditional plea of self-knowledge - of not being "good" enough to be trusted with such ability or responsibility - the Doctor has on occasion said that nobody else should have such power either. Under his comic turn as what would happen if (so to speak) Rasputin became all-powerful (16.6, "The Armageddon Factor") is a serious point. Without total knowledge, including self-knowledge, the Key to Time is simply too powerful to exist in the hands of any being - even the Guardians. His characteristic refusal of responsibility, in the sense of duty, used to be an endearingly child-like trait, but now we have the spectre of responsibility in the sense of guilt. The Doctor has been forced to make

decisions that - in his own eyes - prove that he isn't up to his own standards. Even before the mysterious events of the Time War (X1.2, "The End of the World" et seq.), he's always acted as if carrying the burden of culpability for something terrible, something that happened because he was inadequate to the task. This is, again, a classic storytelling convention, and in keeping with that whole Romantic / Enlightenment tradition to which the series was heir. (See **Did Sergeant Pepper Know the Doctor?** under 5.1, "The Tomb of the Cybermen".)

From this we come to another development at half-time. Whilst the series' first two years were a concerted move to bring the Doctor from being a slightly unpleasant character to being a hero, Season Ten saw a shift to having the Doctor trade vast knowledge for wisdom. Under Barry Letts, the Doctor became someone still very much on a learning curve. Letts introduced a strand of Buddhist thought into the longer-term storytelling, and attempted - in 11.5, "Planet of the Spiders" - to have regeneration accompany a spiritual upgrade. (We note that the word "regeneration" was hitherto one used by priests for their programmes of evangelical work.) So individual stories have been allowed to show the Doctor as less "good" at the start than he was at the end. However, with an overall trend now well-established that the Doctor is the hero, this became increasingly untenable. "Snakedance" (20.2) is the nearest they came to pulling it off, and it seems to rely on the Doctor forgetting things he's told other people in the past. Seen with hindsight, even the "shock" twist in "The Curse of Peladon" (9.2) requires the Doctor to begin the story as a bigot.

This seems to be how the production team for the new series are thinking, as each new Doctor seems to have to learn it almost from scratch. If regeneration is a chance to start again and invent a personality, it's also a chance to learn from whatever killed the last one. Fall from a Radio-telescope and you get vertigo (19.1, "Castrovalva"), but if what led you there was a need to show off (look how often the Doctor's self-doubt in 18.7, "Logopolis" is expressed as hubris), you spend your next life having quiet words with authority-figures (see, for instance, "Enlightenment"). Noble self-sacrifice leads to a new life as a monstrous egoist (21.6, "The Caves of Androzani"). Guilt over the Time War and an inability to wipe out the

continued on page 143...

adventure is nonetheless swaddled in the trappings of Agatha Christie, so we'd better look into why this was deemed a good idea. In 1986, you could barely switch on at prime-time without adaptations of old detective novels. Present-day cops like *Bergerac* were still selling well overseas, but that was mainly the location filming in Jersey. (American readers please note: we mean the *real* Jersey, an island almost in France and thus outside UK tax law. Where the cream and potatoes come from, and the knitted tops.) What US and Australian TV wanted was lavish-looking country-house murders with well-spoken thesps and vintage cars. The BBC's *Miss Marple* Christie adaptations were a case in point.

Oh yes, talking of Australian co-productions, we can't avoid David Maloney's post-*Blake's 7* project: an adaptation of John Wyndham's *Day of the Triffids*, shown after *Top of the Pops* in September 1981. It had killer plants with stings, so we have to mention them here (although they are as unlike Vervoids - the name comes from "vervain", if you hadn't guessed - as you can get). The TV series had Maurice Colbourne in it briefly but memorably, and obviously made a huge impact on the makers of *28 Days Later*... Bits are point-for-point identical, except that the character that Christopher Eccleston played in the film is done by the fat bloke from *2 Point 4 Children*.

The Mogarians are obviously intended to be analogous to the "Trail of Tears" of Native Americans, who were moved from their lands because of mineral claims. (Or the Australian Aborigines, who were a more "fashionable" subject for Western angst in the late 80s.) Their appearance is suspiciously like the Japanese film *The Mysterians*. And anyone buying consumer electrical goods would have known the names "Commodore" and "Lasky" back then - just anyone who's seen the Davison years should know why the stewardess is named "Janet".

Things That Don't Make Sense Brew some tea before starting this bit, because we could be here a while...

On the face of it, the entire notion of the Doctor presenting an adventure from his personal future is completely bonkers. Surely, this would automatically suggest that the Trial will end in an acquittal and he's going to be set free? Unless we're meant to take this as merely a potential future, but it's never named or even intimated as such. So even going by Time Lord logic, shouldn't the Court find it a *little* strange that the prosecutor keeps asking for the death penalty, but they're watching a video of the accused intervening in 2986, and after he's met a new companion?

And with such high stakes, it's certifiably insane for the Doctor to select *this* adventure to prove he's a good egg, given that it ends with him utterly annihilating his enemy. He's obviously familiar with Article Seven, so the thought of getting smacked in the face with a charge of genocide never occurred to him? Never mind that he's an idiot for here presenting his defence in the style of a Poirot novel - as the TARDIS' collection field should have harvested that everything that occurred on board the *Hyperion III*, there's no need to be coy about the murderer's identity and such.

Moreover, Gallifreyan law has some incredible loop-holes if it allows someone accused of meddling in time to review his future activities as recorded in the Matrix - even if he's barred from seeing the Trial's outcome, this could provide him with some potent foreknowledge, and rather seems like giving a shotgun to an accused serial killer [more on this in the next adventure]. For that matter, the Doctor doesn't *need* to look to the future, because - even setting aside controversial adventures such as "The Invasion of Time" (15.6) - his past is surely littered with commendable works. Of particular note, there's "Terminus" (20.4) - in which he both saved the entire universe and with a zero body count to boot - and the service he performed for Gallifrey in dealing with Omega not once but twice (10.1, "The Three Doctors"; 20.1, "Arc of Infinity"). We could go on, but suffice to say that the Vervoid escapade seems penny-ante by comparison.

Oh, and the basis of the Doctor's defence ("I improve in future") really is crap - if it's not immediately obvious as to why, we refer you to the *Monty Python* sketch where Eric Idle is accused of murdering several people and claims, "I'm very sorry and I won't do it again." We also need to inquire when, precisely, the Valeyard edited the Doctor's footage - even for someone of his talents, he'd almost need to be altering the film as the Doctor *is watching it* to make it back to the Courtroom in time. We might also question why the Valeyard bothers to amend little statements here-and-there in the evidence, but shockingly fails to strip out the on-hand authority figure -

How "Good" is the Doctor?

...continued from page 141

Daleks seems inevitably to lead to a quietly ruthless Tenth Doctor ('no second chances' and so on) who's tempted by the Krillitanes' offer of remoulding the "great work of time" until Sarah Jane starts talking like the older Doctors (X2.3, "School Reunion"; X1.13, "The Parting of the Ways"; X2.0 "The Christmas Invasion"). Well, at least he *talks* tough, even if he never really gets nasty.

Which brings us to a final point. The Doctor might say the right things, but given a chance he sometimes fails to do them himself. He becomes suddenly squeamish about performing surgery on the Krynoid-stricken Winlett (13.6, "The Seeds of Doom"), is freaked out by his own tombstone (22.6, "Revelation of the Daleks") and indulges his own curiosity (so many examples, let's pick 26.2, "Ghost Light") when wisdom says, "Leave!" However, in most cases he knows when he's being self-indulgent, and knows that really he can't trust himself. However, his willingness to get involved in the lives of ordinary people, and to try to help them - which is usually a virtue in this kind of series - is a potential source of damage. He knows that, too, but can't help himself. The correct thing to do is remain in Olympian detachment from the petty lives of lesser beings, but his own code says that this makes him the pettiest and least of all beings: someone who could have helped but didn't. Given a straight choice between being "good" as defined by the Time Lords, and doing the "right" thing as humans (and especially those who write family-orientated TV dramas) define it, he usually thinks he ought to do the former but reacts by doing the latter. By his own apparent standards, it's not "good" because it's mere instinct - like Daleks killing someone or salmon spawning - but the effect is the same.

If copyright permitted, we'd reprint the end of Terrance's piece, but you should all know it by heart anyway. The point is that the Doctor conforms to our ethical and moral expectations for reasons of his own, but not so often as to be boring or end the series.

Commodore Travers - explicitly asking for the Doctor's help.

[There's a possible solution if we buy the theory that the Valeyard is also the Keeper of the Matrix throughout 24.4, "The Ultimate Foe", and is using multi-temporal pretzel logic to be in two places at once. This might also explain how someone who apparently didn't know that he was going to need an imaginary world has one readily to hand when the Master unexpectedly intervenes. But it opens up so many new problems that we'll just mention that it exists and walk away, quietly.]

And if we're talking about the Trial... when precisely did this *become* a Trial? The Court began its session as an 'inquiry' in "The Mysterious Planet", yet for awhile now everyone's been treating it as though the Doctor's life is on the line, even though the Inquisitor never actually ruled that matters had gone beyond the fact-finding stage. One presumes that the charge of genocide would put the Doctor in genuine peril, but this only comes along at the end of Part 12. In which case, the proceedings against the Doctor are a "Trial" only for the duration of one cliffhanger and a few minutes into Part 13, meaning that the seasonal title "The Inquiry of a Time Lord" or even "The Probing of a Time Lord" would be more accurate than the one everyone's been tricked into using for more than two decades.

For a story patterned after Agatha Christie, there are an *awful* lot of unanswered questions here. Eventually, the Doctor blames Lasky's assistant Doland for crewman Edwardes' electrocution, Investigator Hallett's poisoning, the failed attempt on Mel's life and the deaths of the hijacking Mogarians. Well, okay, except that... Doland had no reason to commit the first two crimes. If he's hoping to exploit the Vervoids for profit, then leaving an alleged 'booby trap' that kills Edwardes and makes the Vervoids emerge from their pods is just about the most counter-productive thing he can do. It's likewise never said why he might deem Hallett as a threat [although there's an off-chance that he just pissed himself upon realizing Hallett was an Investigator, and brashly decided to poison the man - as if that wouldn't arouse suspicion from Earth authorities, goodness no].

Even then, it's never established how Doland recognized Hallett in his admittedly incompetent Mogarian disguise, which he must have done *before* the Translator gaffe, nor indeed where and when he slipped the drugs into the correct teacup without Janet or anyone else spotting it. [A close examination of the scene, however, seems to reveal Janet herself dropping something into

Hallett's tea before he dies - so is *she* working for Doland, even though it's never said? That might explain how Doland so easily slips away from her company to eliminate the Mogarians.] Also bear in mind that Doland later confesses to gassing Mel - but that he thereafter had any number of ways to bump her off "accidentally" and never did - and he somehow failed to hear the Vervoids plotting to kill everyone while stuffing Mel into the laundry.

And what's with Investigator Hallett, Inept Man of Mystery? The Doctor says he 'admired' this 'maverick' of a secret agent, so it's astonishing to think that Hallett made known his occupation and real name while investigating matters on Stella Stora - which here lets Mr Kimber recognise him - and that he isn't smart enough to "switch on" his translator while disguised as a Mogarian. [The Saint, he isn't.] Hallett couldn't be more conspicuous while sniffing around the hydroponics lab dressed as a Mogarian Power Ranger, and he's careless enough to leave the door open and the lights on while stealing Lasky's Demeter seeds. And how on Earth did Travers and company fall for Hallett's limp "I'm faking my death" scenario? Did they foolishly assume, "Well, the pulveriser gate is open, so *someone* must have fallen inside..."?

Besides, why the hell does Hallett's Mayday to the TARDIS claim that a 'traitor' must be identified? What traitor, precisely? Is he using dramatic license in referring to Doland? Because otherwise, with Hallett / Grenville / Enzu [as Mogarian III is styled in *Radio Times*] busily making a complete red herring of himself, the only possible way this relates to the story is if he's asking the Doctor to unmask him. And if he *knows* the Doctor already, then it's bewildering why he doesn't have a quiet word with him, rather than being needlessly cryptic and leaving silly clues like Demeter seeds about the place.

So the Doctor's description of Hallett as a 'maverick' secret agent is starting to look like a euphemism, and we never actually find out who employed the man, nor why he was aboard the *Hyperion III* anyway. [One scenario - based on Travers' blocked inquiry with the authorities - is that a government on Earth learned that someone on Lasky's team was forging illicit deals with the consortium that Doland mentions. That would maybe, perhaps, just about explain the still-exaggerated 'traitor' reference. But not the decision to become a murder suspect by faking his own death

and thus alerting his quarry that security will be tightened up. Undercover work requires allowing those being investigated to relax, not making them more suspicious of everyone.] And under any circumstance, there's the immense coincidence that the TARDIS just happened to materialise in the Perseus arm of the Milky Way in April 2986 - because you need to be in deep space in the thirtieth century to do an aerobics work-out with Mel, obviously - which allowed any passing secret agent to know that the Doctor was on call.

[Stop for a rest. Have some Kendal Mint Cake, like they do when climbing Everest.]

We can't avoid saying it: nearly everyone in this story seems afflicted by Stupid Gas at *some* point. Mel wonders how the Doctor will obtain a gas mask to enter the Isolation Ward, when - as we discover seconds later - there are gas masks hanging off-camera but directly in her line of sight. The Commodore wants an explanation as to why two if not three people have been murdered, and Mel's incredibly serious yet dense reply is: 'You've got a killer on board.' Upon being menaced by a Vervoid, the doomed guard outside the Isolation Room wastes precious seconds fiddling with the communicator in his right hand - as opposed to (say) firing the pistol he's got in his left. Rudge is a security officer who's foolish enough to let two of his captives - the Doctor and the Commodore - whisper and potentially conspire in front of him, and he then falls asleep to boot. [The Hyperion's owners deciding to hand him a pink slip suddenly makes a lot more sense.] And when the as-yet-unexposed Doland is interrupted while telling Mel, 'We don't want you breaking your neck, at least not until...', what is he *trying* to say? "Not until you've filled out some insurance forms naming me as beneficiary"? "Not until you've autographed my copy of *TARDIS Inside Out*"? Or, as we'll see, perhaps, "Not until I've changed my tracksuit" is in keeping.

The Mogarians are so vulnerable to oxygen that they perish if you sprinkle water on them, yet they're seen drinking tea through straws. And doesn't the ease with which Doland murders them - by simply splashing a glass of water in their direction - strike you as a bit of a design flaw with their all-covering environmental suits? One carelessly overturned drink at dinner in the ship's lounge, and they're goners. Mind, consider the context of their deaths - the Mogarians have just captured the ship, and ordered that everyone stay off the bridge lest the hostages die. But when Doland enters bearing drinks, their response isn't something like, "Fool, you've signed the death warrant of your comrades!", but a ridiculously pedestrian, 'We did not order refreshment.'

How, we may ask, do plants speak? There *are* ways they can exude gas, but these all require them to do things we don't see them do, like take in water or have roots. And if they've got lungs, what are all those leaves for? [Photosynthesis just needs chlorophyll, so they don't need leaves as long as a lot of their surface is exposed - presumably the maple-leaves are the optimum shape for the chloroplasts to take in carbon-dioxide and give out oxygen.] If it's marsh-gas they exude to speak, shouldn't talking be a symptom of their impending decay, rather than a handy plot-exposition device? And why should plants that need light spend so much time lurking in gloomy ventilation-shafts?

More intriguingly, how is *any* life-form, animal or vegetable, capable of figuring out how to turn on the shower less than an hour after being born? We can just about accept newly-hatched killer plants that speak English, but innate instinctive plumbing ability? [Later, one Vervoid tells the others 'forget your previous orders', as though they have had a conference and briefings with flipcharts.] And anyway, the Vervoid that searches Janet's cabin is doubly curious - failing to find anyone or anything, it evidently decides to spray the place with deadly marsh-gas for the heck of it. That poses a threat to Mel, who's hiding in the loo, but why did it bother? And here's the *big* issue with the Vervoids: if you were genetically engineering a race of beings for use as slave labour, would you really think including lethal stings and deadly marsh-gas as part of the specs was a nifty idea?

As for Brucher's attempt to destroy the *Hyperion III*... imagine you're a spaceship pilot. There are any number of ways to destroy the ship instead of slowly aiming it at a handy Black Hole. [You could overload the engines and make it go "bang", or switch them off and let everyone die of natural causes centuries before anyone finds the ship. Space is pretty big, and they're off their scheduled course already, so this would be as melodramatic and self-pitying a death as the spaghettification by a singularity he has in mind. Then there's all sorts of stuff you could do with the hull, especially if you try flying a dirty great liner like it was the three-person vessels he's trained to pilot. Pulling a

handbrake turn would snap the ship nicely.] Lucky he unexpectedly embarks on the Black Hole gambit, though, because Rudge's plan to help the Mogarians hijack the ship seems to depend on this happening.

Moreover, note how Brucher just waltzes onto the flight deck with a pistol and seizes control, making the Commodore's subsequent claim that the ship is 'designed to be hijack proof' more than a little ironic. And ultimately, if it wasn't the Doctor, then who *did* sabotage the ship's communications unit? [Doland eventually seems guilty of everything up to and including the killing of Richard III's nephews, but this probably owes to Rudge as part of the hijack scheme.] Why is Lasky in such a hurry to get to Earth anyway? They evidently want to smuggle the Vervoids through customs before the pods burst, then they want to get the goods off the ship as soon as possible for other reasons. But Ruth Baxter is in quarantine, as Lasky must know because it was she that declared it, so a quick flit through the usual channels is impossible. [Moreover, the quarantine is because of an alien infection, so allowing passengers and a stewardess on board is really silly.] A small but amusing detail - with so much neurotic continuity-referencing going on, we have to assume that the duplication of the name 'Hyperion' from 9.4, "The Mutants" was premeditated. See, this story *could* have been worse.

Sorry to nit-pick about the special effects, but the "Black Hole" seen here looks blatantly squarish and rather like a stained glass window in parts. [Even after X2.8, "The Impossible Planet", the most scientifically accurate depiction of these events in *Doctor Who* is still 10.1,"The Three Doctors". And have you *seen* that?] 'Demeter' does not mean "Food of the Gods" as Lasky claims, but is the name of a harvest goddess. [The Greek for "Food of the Gods" is, as you all know, "Theobromide" - as in the cocoa bean. The Mogarian-who-isn't even uses the word 'bromide' in the same scene, and note that chocolate is, of course, a religious beverage - see 1.6, "The Aztecs".] And where did the budget for extras go in this story? Because we keep hearing about other passengers, but for the most part we only *see* These Our Players and the token old man Mr Kimber, meaning the ship's lounge is conspicuously sparse most of the time. [British viewers were amused by the similarity of Arthur Hewlett's performance to the semi-legendary "J.R. Hartley" from the *Yellow Pages* ad of the late 80s: if you know this, try listening to Janet's suggestion that he might like some light reading with a straight face. If not, imagine him reading a book in the shower, as she seems to be suggesting.]

Last, and perhaps most entertaining [well, as entertaining as *anything* gets in this story], keep track of Lasky's movements and clothing changes in the first three episodes. When she's not dithering about her research, she splits her time between exercising in the gym (where she wears sweats) and reading in the ship's lounge (where she sports a casual mauve outfit). Fine, except nobody gave any thought to her relation between the two locations and the rest of the adventure. The result is that in the space of a few hours, Lasky seems to undertake two if not *three* separate workout routines - diligently showering and changing after each one, then reading a few pages of *Murder on the Orient Express* before heading back to the gym. We can't rationalize this away with Matrix-editing, so perhaps they're very obsessive about aerobics in this era. At the very least, that might explain why Doland tells Lasky, 'I know how much you object to your *work* schedule being interrupted' while she's pedaling on a bike in the gym.

Oh, all right, just one other thing: did *nobody* involved in designing or shooting the Vervoid husks see *This Is Spinal Tap*?

Critique Poor, poor Bonnie... We'll never give her less than full marks for effort, dedication and tenacity, but the material she's given here doesn't make the most of what she does best, and forces her to do things that simply go against her talents. At the time we all joked that casting her was a masterstroke, as no *Doctor Who* girl ever had a career afterwards. As regards television this was almost true, but (like Deborah Watling before her) Bonnie's former career as a child-star tainted how the script-writers thought she ought to behave.

Which is to say: this is a gut-wrenching case of the wrong writers being chosen for the job at hand. Pip and Jane Baker were never going to be the natural authors for a modern, hi-tech career-woman of the 80s, and their idea of "Youth Culture" was the *Just So* Stories. Sadly, this team wrote nine of the twenty episodes featuring Mel. Now, the Bonnie Langford of today - the charming, self-deprecating star of *Sweet Charity* and *Dancing on Ice*, who sent herself up on *The Catherine Tate Show* - could have pulled off the

lines she's given here. But with - as even *she* said - more thought going into her costume than her character, she didn't have a prayer.

All of that said, don't think we're trying to demean Bonnie's contribution, because she's just about the best thing here. However clever it might look on the page, the Bakers' dialogue can never be made to sound like what real people would say. This is true of all *Doctor Who* (and possibly all drama), but there's a line between heightened expression with no mumbling or swearing, and OEDema - the painful swelling of the lexicon. Any one of these characters may have spoken like that once or twice a day, but *all* of them, *all* the time, is highly improbable. Colin Baker has figured out that it's best to do this slightly bigger than normal - as if trying to distract those around the Doctor from what he's really thinking - but he's playing a bloke who dresses like PT Barnum on Benzedrine. Michael Craig (as Travers) gives it a schoolmaster-ly drawl, as if relishing chances to tell people off creatively, because it's his only release from the tedium of space-liner captaincy. It *sometimes* works, but when he has to become "Tonker of the Yard" and solve Hallett's alleged murder in the pulveriser, it goes painfully wrong. Furthermore, Professor Lasky (who's obviously what they originally wanted the Rani to be like), Bruchner and Doland are the dullest debating society ever to try to kill one another.

In its defence, we might say that the script is intended as a small child's idea of how grown-ups and scientists talk. Although hardcore fans who'd tried to bring the series back through sheer willpower might've wondered why they bothered upon seeing this, the fact is that - in one small detail - Michael Grade had a point. *Doctor Who* had traditionally relied on a new audience of kids coming along every few years, not on a diehard group of a few thousand. So if children weren't bothering to watch, why make it? And some of the most self-consciously child-friendly material of the last few years was Pip 'n' Jane's "The Mark of the Rani" (22.3), even if it was done badly.

But now the pendulum has swung too far in the opposite direction, by which we mean that some of the most successful *Doctor Who* models entailed doing material for *families*, and which by consequence caught the imagination of children. By here making a story that, arguably, *only* a child of seven could find interesting, the story-makers are alienating everyone else. Compare "Vervoids" to even a bad Pertwee story, and you'll see what we mean. In "Planet of the Daleks" (10.4), there are scenes that make the average kid go "uh?" then ask a grown-up. Liquid ice, a silly idea (except that NASA recently claim to have found some on Europa, one of Jupiter's moons) is explained as an 'allotrope', so you get down a big dictionary when you go back to school on Monday, and look it up. It's a real word. Hot air ballooning, explained perfunctorily by the Doctor, really does work the way he says. There are plants that squirt their spores in jungles on Earth. *Doctor Who* has made the real world more exciting. But Pip 'n' Jane, who seem to be writing from a folk-memory of Pertwee scripts most of the time, never quite get the difference between exposition and demonstration right. The payoff to this story should have been in the same league - clever to anyone who knows a bit of plant biology, and the first time that smaller viewers learned that leaves go brown in autumn for a reason. Yet it's none of those things, and if we're comparing any story unfavourably with "Planet of the Daleks", then things have gone *badly* wrong and there's a more cogent comparison...

A lot of people noted the coincidence of the musical version of *Little Shop of Horrors* hitting the big screen here at almost the same time as this adventure. Why did a low-budget undertaking quicky become a Broadway hit, then a megabucks musical film? Because the story worked on a variety of levels, that's why. The Frank Oz film changed the ending, but if we go back to the source(s) we can see why "Terror of the Vervoids" didn't hit home. The man-eating plant in *Little Shop*, Audrey II, tempts a put-upon human into doing its killing. It stays put in the florist's shop, plotting and growing. It's all very *Faust*, with slapstick and blood (actually, so's Marlowe's version).

But we also said in "The Seeds of Doom" (13.6) that having the Krynoid talking was a mistake - and in *that* kind of story, it was (even if the dialogue was written by someone who could do it *well* for humans). It's theoretically possible to have the Vervoids as weapons (yes, possibly landmines) and move the emphasis to the people tempted by their potential. In a story about confinement - they're on a spaceship, for Heaven's sake - and ambitious scientists conspiring against each other, a Vervoid leader who stayed in the Hydroponics bay and sent "sproutings" to kill or blackmail Lasky into doing its bidding would have been dramatically and logistically more plausible. It would have also given Honor Blackman a decent part.

Yet the Vervoids we see, even if they looked better from the neck down (or less amusing from there up), are rubbish monsters because they're a silly idea. They didn't scare children, either.

Meanwhile, Malcolm Clarke's music - another familiar bone of contention - suffers from the same flaw as everyone else we've discussed. He's doing what he does best, just a bit too vigorously. The only person showing any restraint is the set designer, Dinah Walker. With the director's idea of a luxury liner instead of the space-faring banana boat that the script suggested, the story almost makes sense. Any other director would probably have gone all-out for *Alien*, and the already tenuous plot logic and character developments would have *really* come unstuck. Clough also keeps his directorial flourishes to a minimum - when they come they're welcome, but it's obvious he's finding his feet in this series, after an (as yet unseen) rather spectacular debut on location in very trying circumstances.

But the *big* fault with this story - as with the two before it and some in the previous year - is that it has all the elements for success, but each of these is in the abstract, not connected to the rest. It's like a cake with wonderful ingredients and an ingenious recipe, but someone's forgotten to switch on the oven. Is this just the fault of the Trial format? Is it the lack of a full-time script editor? Has the producer taken his eye off the ball? Or is it that nobody involved can agree on what *Doctor Who* is really for any more?

The Facts

Written by Pip and Jane Baker. Directed by Chris Clough. Ratings: 5.2 million, 4.6 million, 5.3 million, 5.2 million.

Working Titles "The Ultimate Foe" (see **The Lore**).

Supporting Cast Honor Blackman (Professor Lasky), Michael Craig (Commodore), Denys Hawthorne (Rudge), Tony Scoggo (Hallett), Malcolm Tierney (Doland), David Allister (Bruchner), Yolande Palfrey (Janet), Arthur Hewlett (Kimber), Simon Slater (Edwardes), Barbara Ward (Ruth Baxter).

Oh, Isn't That..?

• *Michael Craig*. He was in *Triangle*, playing almost exactly the same character. He's got a long list of other, nearly identical characters up his sleeve since the 1960s.

• *Tony Scoggo*. He came with director Chris Clough from a stint in *Brookside*. As did...

• *Malcolm Tierney*. Recently played Charlie Gimlet in *Lovejoy* (see 25.4, "The Greatest Show in the Galaxy") and was in *House of Cards*.

• *Denys Hawthorne*. He was in ITV's long-running women's prison drama *Within These Walls*. (Typecast? Never!)

• *Yolande Palfrey*. She was in *Pennies from Heaven* (the Bob Hoskins TV play, not the Steve Martin movie version) and *Dragonslayer* - Disney's attempt to do something like *Hawk the Slayer,* but with the annoying little bloke from *Ally McBeal* as the hero.

• *Honor Blackman*. Obviously, she was Dr Cathy Gale in *The Avengers*, and later starred in *The Upper Hand* - a British rendering of *Who's The Boss?* She was Hera in *Jason and the Argonauts*, in one of the few parts not to be upstaged by a Harryhausen model sequence. These days, she's mainly famous just for being Honor Blackman.

• *Bonnie Langford*. Well... she's been in showbiz since she could eat solids. She was in children's variety show *Junior Showtime*, played a pushy starlet in *Bugsy Malone*, was on stage in *Gypsy* as the obnoxious Baby June (wherein she became the subject of one of Sir Noel Coward's last *bon mots*, but we won't repeat it) and then did a long and career-defining stint as Violet Elizabeth Bott in *Just William*. Faced with a lifetime of people repeating the catchphrase *I'll thqueam and thqueam and thqueam until I'm thick* at her, she took to being a song-and-dance girl, and co-starred with Wayne Sleep in the successful TV variety series *The Hot Shoe Show*. This was another victim of Michael Grade's axe, so she returned to theatre and played Peter Pan. We'll pick this up in **The Lore**.

Cliffhangers Crewman Edwardes flirts with Mel but is then electrocuted - sparks create the prohibited white light, and the mysterious giant pods start twitching as Mel screams in the key of F; the half-plant Ruth Baxter (a particularly excited vein pulsing down the middle of her face) wakes up and stares at the Doctor while Mel again screams; the desperate Bruchner steers the *Hyperion III* into the Black Hole of Tartarus (or more accurately, we

get a close-up of the Doctor as he explains Bruchner's intent). The lead-in to the next story: the Doctor is accused of contravening Article Seven of Gallifreyan law, i.e. wilful genocide.

The Lore

• The complications of this adventure's production make more sense when you recall that "Vervoids" and "The Ultimate Foe" were made as one story. For a start, the whole location shoot for the Matrix sequence was completed *before* any work was done on the four episodes we're treating as a story now. So after a frantic start and a baffling initiation, Bonnie Langford had a month to get used to the series before making her introduction story.

(Indeed, one of the snags when differentiating this year's stories is that the title "The Ultimate Foe" was originally applied to *all* six episodes, and this bit of it in particular, and has now been reallocated to the final two episodes. The commonly used title, "Terror of the Vervoids", was never used by the production team but was invented for the novelisation published in 1987. The story also appears to have been referred to as "The Vervoids", but it seems that no one was paying too much attention to story titles by this point.)

• This production was the end of the 14-part "Trial" series, and was always intended to be done entirely in studio. With the Bakers known to be fast and reliable writers, the missing third four-part story was given to them. (As you will recall, there were many other candidates considered over the previous year, but with Saward now only nominally involved, the negotiations had ground to a halt.) As it turned out, they also had to patch together the final episode too. Apparently, Nathan-Turner met the Bakers by accident at a lift in Television Centre and greeted them like lost relatives, so it seems their selection to do this story was a *fait accompli*. Whether this is after the Saward Split is unclear (but think about it: a producer who shuns Robert Holmes and literally embraces Pip 'n' Jane might further incline the script editor to think it was time to jump ship.)

• Bonnie Langford had the same agent as Colin Baker, so negotiations were conducted fairly casually. Mel had been thought up in the Summer of 1985, but it seems that the character may have been created with Langford in mind. She had mentioned to Faith Brown that doing *Doctor Who* might be fun (this would be after Faith appeared in 22.1, "Attack of the Cybermen", and possibly after the recording of *Doctor in Distress*). The casting happened some time before Christmas, and was formally announced with a photo-shoot at the Aldwich Theatre (where Langford was starring in *Peter Pan*) in January. However, word was out before Christmas amongst the hardcore fans, and when Saward asked if it was true, Nathan-Turner flatly denied it. Saward had written an audition piece for the character, so at least one other person must have been up for the role (this piece became the core of his un-used final episode for the season). With hindsight, Saward claims that Langford's screen-test was a lot better than he'd imagined.

• Detailed background notes were prepared for Mel - but as always, the more complicated a background they create for someone, the less it turns up on screen. (Compare the pages of stuff on Able Seaman Ben Jackson and his difficult relationship with his father to the Ben we get in 3.10, "The War Machines" and after, and then look at the description for Polly - *she's a secretary and a bit posh*. She didn't even get a surname.) In Nathan-Turner's book *The Companions*, there's no end of stuff about Mel living in Pease Pottage, being a computer programmer, meeting the Doctor when he tried to prevent the Master's plan to bankrupt the world by fiddling the Stock Exchange computers, and general notes on how beguiling and fascinating this woman is.

• Chris Clough, as we have noted, had directed several episodes of *Brookside*, Channel 4's Liverpool-set soap. However, it was his subsequent work on *EastEnders* that had got him noticed by Nathan-Turner. His earliest directing work had been in Granada's current-affairs series *World in Action*. After his baptism of fire on "The Ultimate Foe", this was almost light relief, but he found the prospect of planning a whole space-opera slightly daunting. He decided to make the *Hyperion III* cabins and corridors small, to look like a luxury liner with all the space given over to cargo, and to avoid the cliché of *Doctor Who* spaceships being vast and spacious.

One of Clough's touches was to decorate the cabins (actually the same set redressed each time) with framed front-pages of *The Eagle* showing Dan Dare (see **What Kind of Future Did We Expect?** under 2.3, "The Rescue"). He also had Professor Lasky reading Agatha Christie's *Murder on the Orient Express*, just in case nobody at home spotted the similarities.

• During the recording of this story, the BBC's press office got wind of another potential problem: Saward had done an interview for the magazine *Starburst*, and it wasn't what you'd call helpful. In fact, it was downright bitchy - mainly about Nathan-Turner's style, priorities and methods; the "miscasting" of the main roles and several smaller ones; and anything else that irked him. The press got hold of this, and the BBC asked the producer some very searching questions (mainly "How could you spend five years working with this berk and not know he felt like this?"). Jonathan Powell had a word, saying that legal action would make Saward look more plausible, so it was best not to bother. (Remember, the Drama Department heads had suggested letting Saward go after the break during which the latter wrote 22.6, "Revelation of the Daleks", and it was Nathan-Turner who stood up to Powell and said that Saward should have been on the BBC contract throughout. Saward's position in this phase had been a legal grey area, and only the producer's loyalty to his deputy had prevented the Corporation from offloading another hotshot youngster they were fast-tracking onto *Doctor Who* and giving the script editor's job to a newcomer. This is, of course, exactly what happened before and after Saward's stint, with Antony Root and Andrew Cartmel more or less presented as done deals, but it seems that Nathan-Turner put his own job on the line to keep Saward on the team. You can see how even people who thought Saward's comments had a grain of truth decided to support the producer on this matter.)

Saward's beef, in brief, was that the producer was obsessing about the minutiae and not paying enough attention to the overall direction of the series, and that he didn't care about the scripts. He was furious at the "light entertainment" tendency of the series, the stunt-casting and the ill-thought-out characters. He resented the amount of attention being given to American fan conventions instead of the British public, or the needs of the day-to-day production of such a complex series. His comments struck a chord - especially with the increasingly belligerent *DWB*, the semi-professional fanzine run by Gary Levy, and its excitable readers. Levy, now "Gary Leigh", had enjoyed a close association with the production office, but shortly before the start of the new season this had gone badly wrong. Unhelpfully, all the people Saward cites who'd back him up on this are now deceased.

• Despite everything happening backstage, the actual making of this story proved fairly relaxed. Both Honor Blackman and Michael Craig giggled a lot in rehearsals, and the idea of a Vervoid called "Pepe" (actually dancer Peppi Borza) caused a few chuckles. Borza had a bad time with the smoke device used for the marsh-gas scene. The wrap party for the season included a comedy drag act by Malcolm Tierney and David Allister (who'd been the strangled Mr Stimson in 18.1, "The Leisure Hive") as the BBC cleaning ladies.

• At around this time, Colin Baker recorded inserts for the second edition of *Roland Rat: the Series* in the "future" costume; these were shown before episode two of 23.1, "The Mysterious Planet". His two cat-badges for this season were made by Maggie Howard and based on Baker's own cats, Eric and Weeble. The tradition of adding a black cat to the inner lining of his coat for each completed story seems to have stopped with the Suspension.

• The first episode was broadcast in the weekend that marked the fiftieth anniversary of BBC television, and so came ahead of a special retrospective show that included clips of old *Doctor Who* stories - just not the ones they'd hoped to show. A combination of clearances, picture-quality and the non-existence of many episodes made the archivists realise what we'd been telling them for ages: the wiping of VT and junking of film copies of episodes was a short-sighted move. (See **What Was the BBC *Thinking*?** under 3.1, "Galaxy Four".)

This marks the beginning of the Corporation's more conciliatory approach towards amateur investigators. Fan Paul Vanezis had independently asked Cyprus Television what they had, and gained copies of several lost Hartnell episodes during the Suspension - he's now a consultant to the BBC Archives. The *Radio Times* for that week - as well as making heartbreaking reading for anyone watching BBC's output these days - had a feature on Mel in the children's section, *John Craven's Back Pages*. A compilation repeat of "The Chase" (2.8) was under consideration for broadcast during the week, but this failed to materialise. (It was at around this time that the Saturday line-up changed abruptly. *The Late Late Breakfast Show* was pulled after a member of the public died in a stunt, and was replaced with a variety of popular re-runs. *Hi-de-Hi* was rescheduled - see 24.3, "Delta and the Bannermen" - and *Doctor Who*

ceased to be part of a coherent line-up.)

• Now, remember that "Terror of the Vervoids" was made *after* the two episodes we're treating as the final story of this season. August, when the story was recorded in studio, leads into the transmission of the first episode of the year (and Baker and Bellingham doing early-evening chat show *Wogan*). Late October sees the second press-launch. By this time, it's coming up to Christmas, and Nathan-Turner's doing another panto with Colin, Hugh Lloyd (he's Goronwy in 24.3, "Delta and the Bannermen") and Wendy Richard from *EastEnders* (or Miss Brahms from *Are You Being Served?* if you're American). Bonnie's back doing *Peter Pan*. So at the press-relaunch they sat the assembled journos down, in a darkened room, with Bonnie and Nathan-Turner and all. As the footage of Mel skipping commenced, Langford wanted the floor to swallow her.

• Then in November, Powell wants another word. In accepting Nathan-Turner's resignation, he lumbers the producer with one more task: tell Colin Baker he's fired. As it turns out, the fan-moles have had an inkling of this, so Nathan-Turner decided to tell his star straight out rather than have him hear it from the press. The deal was that he not to go public with it until after transmission of the final episode.

• At the end of November, just before rehearsals of *Cinderella* begin, Powell strikes again. It turns out that the various parties asked to take over the series think Nathan-Turner is too tough an act to follow (or that being producer on a series that's seemingly doomed would be the kiss of death), so his resignation is un-accepted. With no script editor, no scripts, no Doctor and no time before work has to start on the next series, we hear what is to be a familiar catch-phrase: "I've been persuaded to stay."

It was hoped that Baker would be similarly persuaded to come back and do a regeneration story. You should be able to work out his reply; if not, go directly to 24.1, "Time and the Rani".

23.4: "The Trial of a Time Lord: The Ultimate Foe"

(Serial 7C Part 2, Two Episodes. 29th November - 6th December 1986.)

Which One is This? The Valeyard's an evil future incarnation of the Doctor who did a deal with the High Council to cover up the pirating of the Matrix, so both sides of the Doctor fight for possession of his soul inside a nightmarish version of Victorian London. Who didn't see *that* coming?

Firsts and Lasts The end of the Trial, and so the final appearance of the Inquisitor and the Valeyard. In fact, it's the final use of the Time Lords' high-collared costumes, the Gallifreyan Matrix and any sort of Key of Rassilon.

Dominic Glynn's theme gets its final airing. (At the time we thought "No, they can't do any worse" - see the notes on 27.0, "The TV Movie" for how wrong we were). Episode one (or Trial 'Part Thirteen', if you prefer) is the last involvement either Robert Holmes or Eric Saward had with the series. Indeed, the final episode - like the Vervoid story - has no credited script editor.

It's also, bizarrely, the first and only time a thirty-minute episode has been aired (see 26.3, "The Curse of Fenric" for a near-miss on that score). It turns out that this is the only time three actors (Baker, Jayston and Geoffrey Hughes as Popplewick, the Valeyard in disguise) have played the Doctor when neither of the "others" were returning former stars of the series, and some people think that there's a fourth (James Bree as the Keeper of the Matrix, assuming he's the Valeyard right from the start). Bree in fact makes his last of three appearances (having previously been the Security Chief in 6.7, "The War Games" and Decider Nefred in 18.3, "Full Circle"). It's also our final glimpse of the Master's TARDIS, disguised for the occasion as a statue of Queen Victoria.

Most significantly, on the day the final episode aired, it was announced that Colin Baker had been sacked. This declaration rendered the climax of the story a lot more exciting than it otherwise would have been, or - indeed - is now.

Two Things to Notice about "The Ultimate Foe"...

1. Notoriously this story is regarded as a mess, but with effectively four writers (Holmes, Saward, Pip 'n' Jane) and no script editor, it surprisingly coheres a lot better than the rest of this season. However, so many inconsistencies and logical flaws can be found, it's almost too easy to pick it apart. The chief problem is that the scenes inside the hallucination-space of the Matrix have causal logic and rationales when they shouldn't, and actually make more sense than the stuff happening in the real world of the courtroom. (The Bakers later attempted to explain some of the goofs in the novelisation to this adventure, - but they only corrected the errors most people hadn't spotted, and "fixed" these so ineptly that they probably shouldn't have bothered.) Still, even when you've read **The Lore**, and seen how much of a crisis the last episode created, you may wonder why a few moments couldn't have been spared to rewrite a couple of the Valeyard's lines. You know the ones we mean.

2. So far in this season, the Matrix has been the repository of the Doctor's adventures. Thus, it's perhaps telling when Glitz attempts to steal a prized Matrix master tape that contains 'phases three, four, five and six', and the officious Popplewick says: 'The primitive phases one and two have been relegated to the archives.' In case you missed this subtext, the object Popplewick hands Glitz is a 2" videotape case - as was used in the BBC Archives.

Meanwhile, the source of all this material is a circular building full of petty-minded Victorian pen-pushers, called 'The Fantasy Factory'. You don't think Eric Saward was perhaps a bit fed up with working at Television Centre, do you?

The Continuity

The Doctor Seems horrified [understandably] to learn that the Valeyard is apparently his evil future self. He can already spot flaws in the Valeyard's Matrix-generated illusion of Mel, and second-guess his future self's plans. He allows himself to be sidetracked by the [hallucinated, it would seem] steam-engines within the Matrix, but isn't snared in the Valeyard's various booby-traps. The Doctor indicates to Mel that he and the Valeyard have the same handwriting. [This suggests that the Doctor's handwriting is constant throughout his lives - see 2.3, "The Rescue"; 18.6, "The Keeper of Traken"; 26.1, "Battlefield".]

As a 'defence mechanism', the Doctor's mind instinctively shuts itself off as protection against a visual and audio assaults of sufficient magnitude. [This is probably an instinct inherent to all Time Lords, and was previously witnessed in 11.4, "The Monster of Peladon". As in that story, the "sensory overload" seen here looks and sounds like a bad early 90s night-club.]

When all's said and done, charges against the Doctor are dropped and he declines the Inquisitor's recommendation that he stand for the

ABOUT TIME 1985-1989

Presidency again - advising that she stand instead. The final line we hear spoken by this incarnation: 'carrot juice, carrot juice, carrot juice.' [This is said when Mel suggests that they return to their exercise and diet regimens, but it consequently means that Colin Baker's last televised line is even more ludicrous than William Hartnell's ('keep warm').]

Curiously, upon learning that Peri didn't die - but was instead made a Queen by King Yrcanos [as you probably knew that from the 23.2 "Mindwarp" entry] - the Doctor never shows an inclination to visit and ask if perhaps she doesn't want to be married to a hissing, shouting Samurai-helmeted alien warlord. [He might consider their relationship closed - as with his reluctance to visit Sarah Jane after 14.2, "The Hand of Fear"; see also X2.3, "School Reunion" - but his decision still leaves Peri stranded. One follow-up to this occurs in the novel *Bad Therapy*, and see **The Lore** for another.]

• *Ethics.* Err... well, he *says* a lot of fine-sounding things about sacrificing himself for the good of all, lest the rule of law become compromised and anarchy spread - but this is when he knows he's being set up, and is for the Valeyard's benefit. More genuinely, he expresses anger about the High Council's corruption, and how ten million years of absolute power has made his people more contemptible than Daleks, Cybermen and other would-be monsters. Yet the Doctor never says that there shouldn't *be* a High Council, and never gets much opportunity to comment on the apparent mass-lynchings that break out on his home planet.

Notably, he displays no qualms about leaving the Valeyard - his future self - behind to perish as the villain's machinery implodes.

• *Background.* Surprisingly late, there's a sign that the Doctor has read the Bible. People he cites as notorious liars: Ananias [mentioned in the *Acts of the Apostles* as someone who lies to both God and Peter about the proceeds from a land-sale, and drops dead as a result] and Baron Münchhausen [1720-1797, and someone who told outrageous tall tales].

Once again, the Sixth Doctor cites his age - claiming he's already lived 'over nine hundred years'.

The Supporting Cast

• *Melanie.* Appears as a witness that the Master procures, even though she hails from the Doctor's future. The story ends with the Doctor and Mel leaving in the TARDIS - even though he chronologically hasn't "met" her yet. [In the novelisation, the Bakers try to salvage continuity by adding a coda in which a Trial-style beam of light propels the TARDIS to Oxyveguramosa, where a second TARDIS is parked. Mel walks out, and from the other Ship steps the Sixth Doctor - now a few pounds lighter - to ask where she's been.

[Here we should add that the books and audios have routinely assumed that the Sixth Doctor spends many years - decades even - travelling on his own or with various companions (Evelyn Smythe in the audios, Grant Markham in the books, etc) between the end of his Trial and his fated "first" meeting with Mel in the BBC book *Business Unusual*. Expect this gap to become further pillaged for storytelling in future.]

Mel knows her Dickens, and calls the Doctor 'Doc' to his face, but says 'disinterested' when she means "uninterested". She's somehow able to identify the advanced contraption in the Valeyard's cupboard as a 'megabyte modum' [see **Things That Don't Make Sense**, as if you couldn't guess], and can't tell when the Doctor's hamming it up for public consumption.

It turns out that Mel doesn't recognize the Master. [This caused great amusement to everyone who read Mel's character notes in Nathan-Turner's *The Companions* (1986), which claim otherwise. Eleven years later, *Business Unusual* would jump through some considerable hoops to reconcile the two accounts.] By her own admission, Mel states she's 'about as truthful, honest and about as boring as they come'. [No, we're not saying anything.]

• *Glitz.* Was apparently working for the Master while trying to nick the Matrix files that were lost on Ravalox [23.1, "The Mysterious Planet"]. Glitz doesn't seem perplexed by the notion of time travel, and seems familiar with the Master's TARDIS. [Depending on which position you favour, this will simplify or vastly complicate the dating of 24.4, "Dragonfire".]

Glitz seems to have softened from his former stance as a ruthless killer, and proves immune [possibly owing to his sheer greed] to the Master's hypnotism. He seems scared of ghosts, and prays to the 'cosmic protector of grafters and dissemblers' for deliverance. Glitz keeps swapping sides during the dream-battle in the Matrix - grudgingly helping the Doctor, sometimes serving the

The Valeyard - errr... How?

In the brief explanation the Master offers, we gather that the Valeyard is not *all* of the Thirteenth Doctor, but just his bad half. Actually, he might not even be Number Thirteen - what we're told is the curious formulation 'somewhere between your twelfth and final incarnation'[18]. This was a compromise, intended by Nathan-Turner to prevent future producers from being contractually obliged (in whatever fashion) to have to cast Michael Jayston. So the plan was that the Valeyard was (if you will) "Doctor 12A", from a future that was contingent.

Of course, this raises all sorts of problems. It's entirely within precedent for a potential future Doctor to meet his present-day self in a zone set outside time by the Time Lords (see **Why Do Time Lords Always Meet in Sequence?** under 22.3, "The Mark of the Rani"). It's plausible that a future Doctor could set in motion the chain of events that led his younger self to become the version he eventually became: i.e., the Trial might be what created the Valeyard. (Well, maybe. We're not given much to go on here.) But what makes all of this odd is the Master's intervention and the precise role of the High Council. On the face of it, the Master seems to vouchsafe the Valeyard's existence in the Doctor's future as a pre-ordained fact. If the Master has met the Valeyard out in the Universe, then we can scrub Gallifreyan Mean Time and say goodbye to the idea of 12A - this is the one and only Twelfth Doctor.

But on closer examination, this doesn't appear to be what is happening. The Master talks about the Valeyard as a challenge, a rival, but mainly a distraction from his long-term aim of killing "his" Doctor. The Valeyard is dismissive of the Master, as though he's faced far bigger threats. The relationship between the Master and the Valeyard is therefore different to the one between the Doctor and the Master. The Master is curious about the Valeyard, which could indicate that he only knows this version of the Doctor by reputation. (And when the Master says, 'You pretend not to know me, do you?', he might just be indicating that the Valeyard should have the Doctor's memories of him.) The Master's taunting of the Court and Mel is largely theorising; the Master thinks he still has a chance if the Doctor wins, but if the Valeyard comes into existence, it could be trouble for him. (We note that this is in Part 13, written by Holmes and Saward. Their version of Part 14 goes further and has the Master refuse to kill the Doctor even when the High Council try to bribe him - in an echo of 20.7, "The Five Doctors", only without the pesky business of saving the Doctor's life - with a free pardon for everything.)

The obvious question we need to ask is *which* High Council ordered this inquest in the first place. If we're going with GMT, then the whole scam with Ravalox must have happened 'centuries' before in the Sixth Doctor's timeframe, *if* it's his own High Council that did it. But - and it's a *big* but - the make-up of that High Council has undergone a few changes just lately. The longest-serving member would have been Chancellor Flavia, and she only got a seat in "The Five Doctors". It's likewise doubtful she would have been involved in deposing the Doctor, as she recommended him for the Presidency in the first place. (Then again, unless Gallifreyan law allows for the indefinite absence of the President, her hands might've been tied in this regard.)

Suppose for the moment that it's the High Council of the Valeyard's time. That's superficially more appealing, but also raises problems. The Doctor recognises the members of the Court (or "Jurors", if you prefer), and identifies their names on Mr Popplewick's list. The Valeyard is intent on bumping off the Court, to effect (all together now) 'the catharsis of spurious morality'. We have to assume that this is the Valeyard's back-up plan when the Master wrecks his original plot to get that Court to convict the Doctor and hand over all remaining lives to him. (How exactly he'd profit from eliminating the Court is another matter.)

So after twenty years of thinking *very* hard about this story, the only logic some people have found to the Valeyard's actions is that he is... trying to prevent his own creation. At least, that *seems* the logical corollary of the Valeyard trying to eliminate his previous self, which would effectively send his timeline up its own arse, but c'mon... not even the Valeyard is *that* stupid. Except that we've possibly been a bit misled about his precise relationship with the Doctor (which we'll get to in a moment) and he seems to have even less time for this particular High Council and Jury than the Doctor did. If he could change the circumstances of his coming into being without removing himself from the timeline, it would be in character for him to do so whilst causing as much collateral damage as possible. If there's a way of making

continued on page 155...

Master and often just prioritising his own needs. Eventually, he gains an increased respect for the Doctor's wiles and experience.

Glitz shows absolutely no respect for the law, and is more impressed by the Trial Room's expensive furnishings than the Inquisitor. He routinely wears a Mark 7 Postidion Life preserver, a sort of Kevlar underwear. He's last seen paralysed by a booby trap in the Master's TARDIS, but the Doctor pleads for leniency on Glitz's behalf. [And the Time Lords must consent, as Glitz is seen at liberty in "Dragonfire."]

The Supporting Cast (Evil)

• *The Master*. Whilst the Doctor blundered into the Ravalox affair and the High Council's dirty dealings, the Master seems to have been piecing the story together over time - with the evident intent of exposing the Council's corruption and triggering a crisis. [This would explain why the Master sent a small-time trasseno like Glitz to Ravalox instead of just going himself, as Glitz could better operate under the High Council's radar and be sacrificed if caught.] The Master has access to the Matrix, but his movements within seem limited by the Valeyard's corrupting and more secure influence. He does, however, have the ability to bring Mel and Glitz - the former hailing from the Doctor's future - through space-time to serve as witnesses. [This is slightly odd, as the Doctor was snatched out of time by the Court's 'mental energies', although it's *just* possible that the Master could tap the Court's minds without their even knowing it.]

The Master intervenes in the Trial, it would seem, because he finds the notion of the Valeyard - a being possessed of the Doctor's talents, but with none of his self-limiting morality - a far more dangerous an opponent than the Doctor himself. Also, a victory on the Valeyard's part would deprive the Master the pleasure of destroying the Doctor himself. [At least, that's what he *says*. But more significantly, if we assume that the only thing that prevents the Valeyard's timeline from being the Doctor's inevitable future is the intervention of another Time Lord, the Master seems to be instrumental in rewriting the entire future of his people. So, ironically, it seems that the Master's greatest single victory is one that requires him to save the Doctor. This isn't entirely unexpected: all through his lives, the Master's main motive has been to earn the Doctor's respect and fear. Note

his own worst nightmare in 8.2, "The Mind of Evil": namely, the Doctor towering over him, laughing. Note his endless prevarication over killing the Doctor, wanting always to see his rival cower (hence his reluctance to fire missiles at the Doctor's ship in 10.3, "Frontier in Space", to cite just one instance). Look at how the High Council persuade him to rescue the Doctors from the Death Zone (20.7, "The Five Doctors"), the whole malarkey with framing him for shooting the President (14.3, "The Deadly Assassin") and the otherwise inexplicable behaviour of both in X3.13, "Last of the Time Lords".]

The Master here exposes the High Council's cover-up with regards to moving Earth across space ["The Mysterious Planet"], thereby proves the government to be corrupt and causes a regime change [see the accompanying essay for speculation on *which* High Council this topples]. This throws the Time Lords into disarray, and the Master believes himself well situated as the only one who can impose leadership and order. [He cannot, of course, become President until the Valeyard has been cleansed from the Matrix, but he can demonstrate the permeability of the Matrix and prove that things have to change pretty drastically. The Master has previously demonstrated almost unfettered access to the Time Lords' files - see "Colony in Space" (8.4), "The Sea Devils" (9.3), etc - and hacked into the APC net with no bother (14.3, "The Deadly Assassin"). So apart from the data contained therein (which would only be of use if he was getting a sneak preview of Gallifrey's future from his point of view), it must be the symbolic role the Matrix plays as the sign of Presidency - and communion with the most sacred traditions of his people - that matters.]

In fact the master tape has been swapped for a 'Limbo Atrophier' that seems to act like a slow-time trap, and restrains the Master and Glitz against the walls of the Master's console room. [The term 'Limbo Atrophier' comes from the novelisation by Pip 'n' Jane, which makes sense of the slurred words on screen. As usual, we never learn how the Master escapes, but he's next seen in 26.4, "Survival."]

The Master can somehow, and from a distance, make his voice heard in Glitz's mind.

• *The Valeyard*. He's the Doctor's possible future - notoriously described by the Master as being 'an amalgamation of the darker sides of your nature, somewhere between your twelfth and final incar-

The Valeyard - errr... How?

...continued from page 153

himself come into being earlier - say as the Seventh Doctor - then some of what we see here might possibly make some kind of sense. (Either way, if we assume that we're dealing with a Twelfth Doctor-age High Council, the Time Lords of that era are boned: either the Valeyard bumps them off, or the Doctor wins and thus closes off the timeline so they never exist.) This has been plausibly argued, so we've mentioned it here, but there's a simpler mechanism which we'll suggest shortly.

If the Valeyard isn't trying to prevent his own creation, perhaps he's trying to here facilitate it with the Trial, meaning that the High Council have agreed to make Doctors Seven to Thirteen turn out like the Valeyard, and Doctor 12A is hell-bent on eliminating the McCoy, McGann, Eccleston, Tennant and Chegwin[19] versions to guarantee his ascendancy.

This makes a cognitive sense, save that you'd expect the Valeyard to remember the events of his creation, as he's already lived through them once, yet he's defeated anyway. (This can easily be resolved if we assume that the Master's intervention is "unscripted", and we note that the Valeyard looks surprised by this turn of events. Everything from then on is improvised by both variants of the Doctor.) But it doesn't match the egotism that is the character's main trait. Once again, the wording makes a more complicated possibility seem likely. The High Council - and the Indemnity waiver that Popplewick makes the Doctor sign - hands over all the Doctor's remaining lives to the Valeyard. So we return to the idea in 20.3, "Mawdryn Undead" that the power of regeneration is almost like currency, and therefore transferable. The Valeyard is 12A and wants to assure there is a Doctor 20.

This almost makes sense. If the High Council had the ability to offer the Master a complete new regeneration cycle ("The Five Doctors") then they could offer it to the Valeyard, with his previous self as a donor. (The Trial is, after all, occurring outside time, which might aid the Valeyard in maintaining his causality.) Look again at the wording;'between your twelfth and final incarnation'. So the Valeyard probably came into existence during a regeneration, which offers a slightly Star Trek possibility. We've seen how regeneration can create "avatars" like Cho-Je (11.5, "Planet of the Spiders") and the Watcher (18.7, "Logopolis"). We've had Romana apparently using this facility to road-test her next body (17.1, "Destiny of the Daleks"). Maybe the dis-

tillation of all the Doctor's evil tendencies was a side-effect of distilling his goodness. Perhaps there's an anti-Valeyard, all sweetness and light and totally ineffectual.

If you've read all these books, or seen all previous stories, one obvious candidate springs readily to mind. If the boosted regeneration over-rides the Blinovich Limitation Effect, the anti-Valeyard could meet the earlier Doctors with no adverse consequences. (See **What is The Blinovich Limitation Effect?** under "Mawdryn Undead", then go to 18.4, "State of Decay"; 9.5, "The Time Monster" and above all "Planet of the Spiders".) Yes... K'Anpo Rinpoche, like the Valeyard, rejects the hypocrisy of Time Lord society and has also kept an eye on the Doctor's development. Were it not for this inconvenient Gallifrey Mean Time (GMT) theory, this would be so obvious as to be accepted without question. But if an iconoclast like the Valeyard is following the rules, they must be laws of physics, not mere legal restrictions. The Trial must be at the earliest possible juncture where the Valeyard can affect his own past, and even then only because they're outside time. Otherwise, he would also go back into the Doctor's childhood and tell him stories. (That said, we note that K'Anpo uses some form of astral projection instead of a TARDIS, so may be free of these restrictions.) Ah, but if we are arguing, as we have, that each Doctor is a different consciousness, then this must surely go double for refinements of the Doctor. The main difference between the behaviour of the Valeyard and K'Anpo is that the former acts and talks like an element of the Doctor's persona trying to get a separate life, whereas the latter already has a distinctly individuated self (but, as a Buddhist, is trying to get rid of it).

But GMT affects the interpretation of this story in another way. If the High Council is from the future, as seen from the Doctor's perspective, and the Jury and the Inquisitor are from the present, on which Gallifrey did the Master cause a riot? The logic is such that the Master has been supplying a feed from the Trial room to Gallifrey and stirring up dissent against a High Council that doesn't yet exist. He (briefly) overthrows the High Council of his own time, and blows the whole Ravalox scam wide open - entering the possibility that it will now never have happened. So on the plus side, Earth's future is safe and we can happily work out a timeline that merely has it fall into the Sun some

continued on page 157...

155

nation.' [See, of course, **The Valeyard, errr...
How?** It appears that the Master's intervention is a
surprise to the Valeyard, which has been taken to
suggest that this is the point at which his memory
of how the Trial went - back when he was a fat
idealist with no dress sense - diverges from his
own experience as Doctor Number 12 1/2. It is
certainly true that from here on, he's less reliant on
a pre-arranged trap than on hasty exploitation of
back-up facilities that he's hidden inside the
Matrix.]

The Valeyard shares his earlier self's penchant
for Victoriana, Shakespeare, the French Revolution and elaborate disguises. He says he wants to
kill the Doctor so he can 'operate as a complete
entity' and 'obtain his freedom' - something he can
only accomplish by eliminating the Doctor's 'mis-
placed morality and constant crusading'. Perhaps
for this reason, he touts his intended destruction
of the Court as the 'catharsis of spurious morality'.
[That phrase, so often ridiculed, suggests that the
Master, the Doctor and the Valeyard agree on one
thing at least, just differing on what should
replace the present arrangement and how change
is to be effected.] As part of his deal with the High
Council, the Valeyard was promised the remainder of the Doctor's regenerations [see the essay
regarding this major concern].

The Valeyard has established 'The Fantasy
Factory' as his stronghold within the Matrix, and
has adopted the identity of its proprietor, 'J.J.
Chambers'. The Fantasy Factor has big carnival-
float lighting [rather appropriate, considering the
Doctor wanted to go to Blackpool - see 22.6,
"Revelation of the Daleks"], and it amuses the
Valeyard to go undercover as the various Messrs
Popplewick. [We note, though, that the plan -
such as it is - requires him on site to micro-man-
age the traps rather than leave them running.
More evidence, it might be said, for the theory
that he's operating Plan B by the seat of his pants
rather than relying on the memory of his previous
self.] Eventually the Doctor unmasks the Valeyard,
and Popplewick's face peels away as if it's one of
the Master's old disguises [see, just for a start, 8.1,
"Terror of the Autons"]. Within the Matrix, the
Valeyard can also throw explosive quills, teleport
from place to place and shrug off energy bolts
fired from the Master's Tissue Compression
Eliminator.

After the Doctor thwarts his plan to assassinate
the Court with a particle disseminator - a device

capable of destroying even sub-atomic particles
such as quarks and gravitons - the Valeyard is
briefly seen "dying" under an energy barrage from
the device. Later, the Valeyard appears to have
escaped and taken on the persona [or at least the
hat and frock] of the Keeper of the Matrix. The
Inquisitor walks straight past "the Keeper" without noticing that he bears the Valeyard's face.
[Unless the Keeper is just wearing a rubber
Valeyard mask as a gag. Again, this has been
argued to be proof that the Keeper was *always* the
Valeyard, which might suggest that everything
after "Mindwarp" was a bad dream (see **Who's
Narrating This Series?** under 23.1, "The
Mysterious Planet"). Alternatively, it could just be
the case that the Valeyard murders the Keeper off
screen in the finale, when the Keeper unexpectedly leaves the Courtroom for no good reason.]

The TARDIS(es) The Master's console room has
its usual black décor [21.5, "Planet of Fire"] and
appears to dematerialise as if on a pre-set timer
["Planet of Fire" again], but now has a couple of
odd features. It has disco lighting effects that can
overload the Doctor's senses and send him into a
stupor. [Whether the Doctor subsequently obeying the Master's verbal commands owes to this or
a follow-up dose of the Master's hypnotism isn't
clear.] It also seems that the Master can make
broadcasts from the Matrix - with an electronical-
ly-produced backdrop of blue chevrons - from a
small studio to the right of the console. The base
of the console contains a slot for loading "car-
tridges" such as the alleged Matrix master file, but
in this case triggers the concealed Limbo
Atrophier.

The corridor outside the Master's console room
appears to have a secondary viewing screen. [The
Master and Glitz are seen chatting in front of this
device, although it's a curious place to put one.]
Like the Second Doctor, the Master has a chest
lying around the console room; unlike him, he
keeps jewellery in it. [By the way, we might
assume that the Doctor's Ship is capable of finding
the time-space co-ordinates to reunite Mel with
the Doctor's future self.]

The Time Lords The Gallifreyan Matrix is
described as a 'micro-universe', and can be physically entered through several 'doors' - the seventh
of which is conveniently located outside the
Courtroom. Persons who do so can participate in

The Valeyard - errr... How?

...continued from page 155

ten million years hence and then get blown up in a nova in 5 Billion AD (3.6, "The Ark"; X1.2, "The End of the World"). On the minus side, we have to account for the Master and Glitz running a scam in their past, but as we now know, memories of aberrant timelines remain with time travellers (X1.8, "Father's Day"). We can therefore assume that the deposition of President-Elect Doctor didn't take place and the apparent anomalies of seasons Twenty-Five and Twenty-Six with regard to the Doctor's activities is cleared up nicely. He's President, so whatever he does is sanctioned by the High Council (either as part of a deal he cut when restoring order after the Master's coup, or as a blank cheque they've agreed just to keep him out of their hair). As no subsequent story ever acknowledges the existence of Season Twenty-Three, and the books and Big Finish audios (in the main) have President Flavia handing over to Romana, we can be forgiven for making out none of it is real. Except Mel.

the hallucinations therein. 'The Key of Rassilon' opens these doors, and purportedly never leaves the person of a Matrix-overseer named 'the Keeper'. [*Another* Key of Rassilon? One was used to create the Demat Gun in 15.6, "The Invasion of Time", but this one serves an entirely different function - unless it's the same Key but with its former power discharged. The Keeper seems to perform functions hitherto reserved for Coordinator Engin (14.3, "The Deadly Assassin"), and fandom has sometimes speculated that it's a revision of the same post.]

The Keeper's tunic is very like the Prydonian Chapter's ceremonial drag, and he admits to lending out the Key to 'qualified experts' who must perform maintenance on the Matrix - such as to replace a transductor - once a millennium or so. Yet the Master has a copy of the Key, and the Valeyard has access to the Matrix through unknown means. The Seventh Door is stained-glass, but one enters the Matrix by means of a beam of light [similar to the one that guides the TARDIS to the space-station, and here propels Glitz and Mel in their coffin-like travel units].

Curiously, the Matrix master file - a document cache so powerful, the Master believes it will give him the leverage needed to become Caesar of Gallifrey - is contained within the Matrix itself. [This is a notion so gonzo as to be brilliant, except that it looks like an accident of the frenzied script revisions. Either way, we might presume this is a "Greatest Hits" anthology of Time Lord secrets that's been packaged for convenient bootlegging, even if that in itself raises more questions than we've got time to answer. But even if someone - the Sleepers, the Valeyard, etc - bothered to do this, how can a copy of the master file have been *physically* removed from the unreality of the Matrix and hidden on Earth in Drathro's time? Oh, well, assume that it's feasible. The Master certainly seems to believe it's possible for him to take the heart of the Matrix out of the Matrix and into his TARDIS.]

The Time Lords' legal system continues to be downright peculiar. Here the Court hears testimony from Mel, a character-witness for the accused even though she technically hasn't met him yet. The Inquisitor finds the revelation that the Prosecuting Council and the Accused as the same person as 'irrelevant' to the proceeding at hand. [Unless she's making a limp attempt to continue covering for the High Council - not impossible, given hints that she's overlooking or actively aiding their deception in "The Mysterious Planet" and 23.2, "Mindwarp".]

The Doctor refers to the Time Lords attending his Trial as the 'Ultimate Court of Appeal, the Supreme Guardians of Gallifreyan law'. Glitz says the "jury box" in the Courtroom is made from real Machenite ["The Mysterious Planet"].

History The Doctor claims that his people have been running things [or rather, ensconced as the Lords of Time] for 'ten million years'. [This tallies with Andred's throwaway comment in "The Invasion of Time" that Rassilon has been dead 'millions of years', although it may or may not be relevant that the Doctor supplies the 'ten million years' comment while the Court is outside time.]

Here it's revealed that the High Council - in order to keep the Sleepers from Andromeda from obtaining secrets taken from the Matrix - authorised use of the Magnetron to pull Earth 'and its constellation' away from its native position. This caused the fireball that nearly destroyed the planet. [See "The Mysterious Planet" for more, and once again it's said that "Earth and its constellation" were towed out of place, when the writers probably mean just "Earth and its solar system".]

When knowledge of the Ravalox affair becomes public, 'insurrectionists' run amok on Gallifrey and depose the High Council. [See **Things That Don't Make Sense,** but it seems a given that a new, hopefully less-corrupt regime will take charge. We'll return to this in the **The Valeyard, errr... How?** essay, and more importantly under 25.1, "Remembrance of the Daleks".]

The Doctor claims that the Council kept secret its relocation of Earth for 'several centuries'. [It's unclear whether this means 'centuries' of time on Gallifreyan or in the non-Gallifrey universe, but it's probably the latter - meaning the duration of time Earth was believed to have been Ravalox. Here we should note that some of the books seem to favour the idea that the next Time Lord administration undid the relocation of Earth and nullified its effect on history, which explains how Earth is recognizeably Earth in all future adventures (including 3.6, "The Ark", and X1.2, "The End of the World", if you like). Nothing on screen substantiates this, however, and we'll elaborate on another possibility in the essay.]

The Analysis

Where Does This Come From? The Sixth Doctor getting his dignity compromised by hallucinatory pranks wasn't entirely unprecedented. The comic strip in *Doctor Who Magazine* had been doing this sort of thing for ages. In particular, the storyline running from "Voyager" to "Once Upon a Time Lord..." in 1984 and 1985 had the Doctor trapped in increasingly unreal environments (and generic parodies up to and including a page from the *Rupert Bear Annual* - which explains the Doctor's trousers if nothing else). His foe was an elderly, garrulous, unstable ex-Time Lord called Astrolabus, who was trying to prolong his life with stolen documents.

Sound familiar? Steve Parkhouse's script - and John Ridgway's art - took the Doctor into trippy and sinister worlds with sparkling wordplay (and when you think that "normal" in this strip was a wisecracking penguin, you can see how odd it got). We are, of course, loathe to suggest that any-one involved in Season Twenty-Three was actively ripping off the *DWM* strips - just as we would hesitate to suggest that X2.12, "Army of Ghosts"

or X1.13, "The Parting of the Ways" had any uncredited inspiration from the *DWM* comic "The Flood". (But if you're curious about the similarities, check out the "ghost" Cybermen infiltrating London in the first part of each, and compare both redesigns of the Cybermen. The Doctor defeats them by ingesting the Space-Time Vortex, but refrains - unlike Rose - from tagging his handle across time and space.)

In a wider sense, this story is in line with overall comic-book thinking. Evil future incarnations of the hero were by now as routine a nuisance as surrendering your superpowers to marry a mortal girl (Paul Cornell, we're looking at you), alternate universes where gorillas wore clothes and robbed libraries and Jimmy Olsen playing checkers underwater with a mad computer. (You wouldn't believe how often these happened over the years.) In the mid-1980s, DC Comics were attempting to retcon the mutually-exclusive backstories of their characters with the twelve-issue all-time-geekiest crossover, *Crisis on Infinite Earths*. In so doing they reset all the chronologies of all the titles, but more significantly made a big splash in the outside world. Evil future incarnations of superheroes were now in the public domain, with all the press coverage of this comic-book "event" singling out silly inconsistencies. Soon, as we will see, self-consciously "hip" comic fans would no longer be quiet about their obsession, and one of them will step into Saward's shoes with the next story. This development will surprise no-one who read Volume V, nor should the similarity between 22.4, "The Two Doctors" and those smug team ups between - say - Aquaman and the "Golden Age" Aquaman.

Since the last time we wandered around in the dreamscape of the Matrix (ten years previous in "The Deadly Assassin" in 1976), this sort of thing has gone from being strange and experimental to being almost humdrum. Films such as *An American Werewolf in London* and, more cogently, the *Nightmare on Elm Street* franchise have, as part of their narrative style, a radical instability about what's objectively happening and what the protagonist is experiencing in his or her sleep. The entire premise of the original *A Nightmare on Elm Street* was that when asleep, the victims were inside Freddy Kruger's world and his laws applied. These became increasingly ludicrous, a game for the audience rather than genuinely unsettling. The second film in the series almost killed the franchise, with what the hardcore horror buffs thought was a cop-out ending. It showed that Freddy - the child-molester killed by the parents of his victims, and who kept coming back to seek revenge - would lose his power upon a display of unconditional love. In fact, whilst this sort-of acknowledges the debt all such films owe to Ray Bradbury, and *Something Wicked This Way Comes* (note that this aspect of the book was skipped in the film version, and then see 25.4, "The Greatest Show in the Galaxy"), this is in keeping with a big trend in 80s fantasy films and TV.

When people realised - thanks to the release of *The Empire Strikes Back* - that the *Star Wars* story was somehow more powerful than all the other spaceships-and-princesses flicks, the press and TV were full of psychoanalysts pontificating about it. This confirmed what anyone interested in serious fantasy had been saying for a decade or more: that it helped to have a working knowledge of Carl Gustav Jung's writings. Certainly, the interviews Christopher Bailey (he wrote 19.3, "Kinda" and 20.2, "Snakedance", remember) gave in *Doctor Who: The Unfolding Text* made clear that at least one TV writer was thinking in those terms. (See **Could It Be Magic?** under 25.4, "The Greatest Show in the Galaxy".) So suddenly, the media were filled with "Archetypal" figures like Tricksters, Wise Old Men and (cue dramatic chord) the Shadow.

This isn't the place to summarize all of Jung's work, but in essence the idea was that old stories - and new ones that hit the right notes - had recurrent characters who reflected the process of becoming an adult. Basically, they were core components of a complete person. The Hero (or in German, *Der Held*, which sounds less embarrassing) undergoes transformations, the biggest of which is acknowledging and coming to terms with the unpleasant aspects of his own nature. Those aspects are usually manifested as another character who is like a photographic negative of Der Held, a figure called the Shadow. By accepting the Shadow's existence and influence, Held-boy becomes the Wise Old Man. (It works for women too, of course, but most heroic tales are about boys: Jung has the process of integrating the feminine aspect as part of Held's "individuation", and vice versa for female heroes to become the Great Mother.)

So for anyone up on this mentality, the big surprise in *Star Wars* wouldn't have been Darth Vader saying, "Luke... I am your father", but rather "Luke... I am Han Solo's father". Or in the case of "The Ultimate Foe", with the Valeyard turning out to be just some bloke who hated the Doctor getting all the attention. Jung was in vogue all over the place. The Police's last single, "Wrapped Around Your Finger", aside from containing some of the oddest words to appear in a pop single ever, is just part of Sting's attempt to enlighten the readers of *Smash Hits*. After *Dune*, he shut up about Jung, oddly. The last series of *Robin of Sherwood* (just ending when this season began) had Locksley (the new, blond Robin) turn out to be Guy of Gisbourne's half-brother.

Also on ITV shortly before was the Granada version of *Sherlock Holmes*. With the Centenary coming up, all things Sherlockean were being revisited. Jeremy Brett (who would shortly be touted as the ideal next Doctor) had made the part his own (at some cost to himself) and the adaptation of "The Final Problem" looked sensational. (It included Action by Havoc... or at least Alan Chuntz, who got Champagne bought for him by Brett. Incidentally, hardliners objected to the padding of the episode with a subplot pilfered from 17.2, "City of Death": Moriarty had six copies of the Mona Lisa, so he could sell the stolen painting seven times over.) So the prospect of the Doctor and a new arch-nemesis tussling over an abyss (see **The Lore**) was as good a season finale as any.

This is the start of that era of script-gurus who offer advice on how to make things "mythic" (ie sell as well as *Star Wars*) and so we have to take into account the baleful influence of Joseph Campbell's *Hero with a Thousand Faces*. All arch-nemeses have to be fought to the death as part of a quest, the end of which is to redeem or educate one's own clan or nation. (See 27.0, "The TV Movie" for John Leekley's attempt to do this.) We could argue from this that Season Fifteen is "mythic", as it follows a fight against Death Incarnate (15.3, "Image of the Fendahl") with a trip to the "Belly of the Whale", i.e. the Underworld (15.5, um, "Underworld") and a reconciliation with a lost father and uniting his home tribe (15.6, "The Invasion of Time"). But then we'd wind up defending "The Armageddon Factor" (16.6) on Jungian grounds. You see how daft this stuff gets?

Shortly after "Revelation of the Daleks", Channel 4 showed a 75-minute TV film that tied in with the style of *Brazil* and *Blade Runner*. It ended with a computer-generated talkshow host called Max Headroom presenting 80s pop videos. Soon after, he got a show on Channel 4, presenting pop videos. Now look at the Master's appearance on the Matrix screen - it's either a *homage* or a *rip-off*. (But he's in good company either way. In the 1987 Election, SDP leader Dr David Owen tried to appeal to the Youth vote with a similar technique. Oddly, it failed to make the correct impression.) We will hear more about *Max Headroom* and Coast to Coast as we go on.

Mr Popplewick's speeches about order and bureaucracy are oddly like Dickens' narrative introducing the Circumlocution Office in *Little Dorrit*. In this, Dickens is satirising the governmental oversight committees that delayed clearing funds and resources for his friend Charles Babbage (rendered here as the character Daniel Doyce) to build the Difference Engine. And this is odd, as Dickens attributes exaggerated thoughts to the Office which suggest that civil service policy exists to ensure that all innovation is stillborn - whereas Popplewick says it out loud, as though it's what such clerks genuinely believe.

We've mentioned the *Spycatcher* trial under "The Mysterious Planet", but a far bigger legal ruckus was breaking in the USA at almost the exact moment that the Doctor was denouncing the Time Lords as "decadent, degenerate and rotten to the core". The Tower Commission was uncovering the Iran-Contra Affair - a massive scandal within Ronald Reagan's presidency, which had been selling arms to the fundamentalist Iranian regime and funnelling the proceeds to South American terrorists. Robert Holmes had certainly referenced American dirty politics before in stories such as "Genesis of the Daleks" (12.4), "The Brain of Morbius" (13.5) and "The Deadly Assassin". However, any possible rumours aside, news about Iran-Contra didn't become public until early November 1986. (At least, not in the US. The British press had a sense that something was in the air for over a year beforehand, and had never forgiven the US for overthrowing a democratically elected government. Nobody had been able to find the smoking gun, but this didn't prevent circumspectly-written pieces appearing here, nor ex-members of the deposed Sandinista regime speaking at rallies in London. Proof that American intervention in Nicaragua was illegal as well as immoral was treated in Europe as "I told you so".) So it's doubtful that it was a direct influence, but it still resonated that this story revolved

around the Time Lords putting their President on trial as the capstone of a huge cover-up.

That said, it's just as likely that the *real* reference here is to Watergate, and the subsequent mini-genre of paranoid political thrillers made by Hollywood in its wake. The business of the TARDIS' 'collection range' and the editing of the Matrix's evidence could be seen as allusions to the infamous White House tapes made by - and then used to topple - Richard Nixon. The Master, then, is here cast as a Deep Throat figure - passing on evidence that will crack the conspiracy (although with considerably less skulking around in dimly lit car parks). But before we get too smug about all this transatlantic corruption, we should remember that both Watergate and Iran-Contra unfolded in the glare of TV cameras. The Doctor's trial takes place *in camera*, and the Inquisitor takes a dim view of the idea that they might have unauthorised viewers. It's a very *British* conspiracy.

Things That Don't Make Sense By now we've covered most of the issues / entanglements related to the Vervoid adventure hailing from the Doctor's future, yet the point remains... the Doctor here departs the station after having seen *two* versions of the *Hyperion III* incident - one on the Matrix screen, and one while preparing his defence. So perhaps the Time Lords tinker with his memory - like they do when he meets his future selves, apparently - although this might suggest that his first act would be to pop back to Thoros Beta and rescue Peri, thus altering the timelines even further. Or, worse yet, he might remember the Vervoid incident and - when the occasion finally arrives - act precisely the way he remembers seeing himself act. The legal and moral implications of *that* would keep Gallifreyan lawyers on the gravy-train for several lifetimes.

The Inquisitor demands that the Doctor produce witnesses to substantiate his version of events, and the Doctor declares that any such witnesses he might procure are scattered all over the Universe and throughout time. Both of them seem to have forgotten that they hail from a race that's perfected space-time travel, and you'd think the Trial of an ex-president for genocide would warrant TARDISes being dispatched to pick up a witness or two.

In the Matrix, the Doctor becomes so eager to confront the Valeyard that he signs a parchment that surrenders his future lives, claiming it hardly matters because the Valeyard can try to kill him at any time. But if the document is so legally binding, why is the latter fannying about taunting his younger, cleverer self and dressing up as Popplewick? Why not just kill him and get this stupid [not to mention mentally draining - for the Valeyard and probably the viewer too] hallucination over with? Along the same lines, the Valeyard could have operated his Particle Disseminator at any time, so why not just use the damn thing if he wants to slaughter the Court? Why instead tell the Doctor, "*Disseminate* the news...", and with such a dramatic flair that his rival immediately deduces the purpose of the Valeyard's fiendish contraption? Does the Valeyard *want* to be defeated?

Indeed, we've done a whole essay on the Valeyard's wonky logic, but it's still worth highlighting that we're never given a reason why he wants to particle-disseminate the Court *at all*. What does he stand to gain from this? If he's forged an illicit deal with the High Council [of either the present or the future - see the essay], then offing a number of 'distinguished' Time Lords sounds like a very good way of make them renege on the deal. [Perhaps the Valeyard is preparing to cover his tracks should the Doctor be found guilty, or perhaps murdering of the Court in front of the Doctor's face is just a massive rebuke to his benevolent self. Well... maybe.] And either way, if he wants to kill the Court, why bother with such a fancy, advanced weapon? Why not just sabotage the space-station's life-support? Or if the Valeyard is safe in the Matrix, then he could just blow up the station with no ill-effects, problem solved.

Reality within the Matrix seems to bend to the Valeyard / Popplewick's will, except in instances where the plot requires that it doesn't. Specifically, if Popplewick is the Valeyard and goes to shoot Glitz, then how can Glitz's previous removal of the bullet without Popplewick seeing him have any effect? As far as Popplewick, the creator of this universe, is concerned, there's a ball of lead in the pistol that will kill Glitz despite his body-armour. And why use a bullet when you can turn this Victorian theme-park into Toon Town at will, and send Glitz, the Doctor or everyone involved falling through the floor into a pit of shark-infested custard? [At least none of them turned into a tree.] How can the Doctor bind the Valeyard with wire even temporarily, as the Valeyard should be able to banish it with a thought?

Right, we've got a physical door into the dreamscape of the Matrix. We'll accept that through gritted teeth. And bootleg copies aside, this door - named the Seventh Door - has only one key. So either this is a rather inconvenient system (seven doors, but only one key) or there *are* six other keys, and the Keeper is guilty of gross understatement when he says there's no security risk. And the Master can steer a TARDIS inside this imaginary world. Well, maybe he can once he's *inside*, but from outside a non-existent place in a courtroom outside time, this must have been a challenge. Either that or he shoved a statue of Queen Victoria through a small doorway that isn't supposed to be opened at all, and nobody noticed.

A well-worn irritation: how can Mel look into the Valeyard's closet and recognise his steam-driven disco lighting rig as a 'megabyte modem'? Well, apparently it's not a modem at all, but a 'modum'; presumably it grinds and filters coffee as well. Even so, how is one little megabyte going to convey live coverage of the collective unconscious of dead Time Lords? Come to that, what does it have to do with conveying a particle disseminator's products in a collective hallucination to a courtroom full of real people?

Mel runs into the Courtroom, and tells everyone to switch off the big telly. They can't, so she says that they have to evacuate the Trial Room. Fine, except who legs it first? The guards, who leave the elderly Jurors to amble slowly away or - as it turns out - crouch down and somehow not get their particles disseminated seconds later. Talk about a lack of discipline and respect. But it turns out that you can survive the disseminator's dinky triangles by simply ducking - even though the triangles' contact with even air particles alone should release intense heat and radiation. We might suppose that the Valeyard *imagined* the disseminator within the Matrix out of sheer force of will, but then his slowness to use it becomes even *more* silly, and it's rather haphazard to imagine something that fails to have a "real" effect in the "real" universe.

And how, precisely, do the 'insurrectionists' on Gallifrey find out about the High Council's culpability in the Ravalox affair? [It's reasonable to assume that the Master broadcast events and revelations within the Courtroom, but this is never said, and the uprising seems to occur in record time.] Also note how the Court relaxes at the end, and the Inquisitor seems to saunter off for a cup of tea, even though anarchy is still presumably raging on the Gallifreyan homeworld. 'Repair the

Matrix, Keeper; requisition anything you need', she says, as if the downfall of the Time Lord government happens on a weekly basis. And anyway, why was the Inquisitor so eager to recommend that the Doctor stand for President again, considering he *still* appears to be guilty of genocide for wiping out the Vervoids, and the Court has just witnessed that his future self is a murderous loony who tried to slaughter them wholesale?

'Gallifrey doesn't have any Crown Jewels', claims the Doctor. So what are the Sash of Rassilon, the Seal of the High Council, the Rod of Rassilon, the Coronet of Rassilon, the Matrix Coronet, the Ring of Rassilon, the Great Key (of Rassilon)...? [Basically, if you're going to do a story that rips off "The Deadly Assassin", at least remember what the story was about.] And as we see in "The Invasion of Time", there can't be a new High Council without a President to make the appointments legally, and there can't be a new President without a High Council, and in particular a Chancellor, to ratify the President's nomination. So this story ends with Gallifrey still in a state of chaos and the one person who could fix it sauntering off with Mel, whittering about carrot-juice and being allowed to go off and have genocidal adventures with Vervoids.

Critique If you'd managed to take a video copy of these two episodes back in time to the day the Suspension Crisis began, and shown it to people *then*, they'd have stared at it in disbelief. OK, mainly at seeing Colin's bubble-perm and Bonnie Langford as Peri's replacement, but they'd also have gaped at the slickness, the pace and the daring of the whole production. This is frantic stuff compared to the sluggish tempo of Season Twenty-Two, and it looks like it was made *years* later, not a handful of months. Sure, those 1985 viewers wouldn't have understood the story - but neither did most of the 1986 ones, and therein lies the main concern here.

Because it's not just the occasional line of dialogue that's confusing. Yes, many lines are quite quotably ludicrous, but that's not really unexpected after the scripting of late. But what the viewer needs, at the end of a fourteen-episode build-up, is some point to this endeavour. Why was the Valeyard doing all this? What exactly was the reason for the Master's intervention, and how did it topple the High Council? Why present evidence that makes it clear that the High Council was cov-

ering something up, if the intent was to silence the Doctor about it all? We've theorized some explanations, but we shouldn't *have* to fill in such very important blanks. If the three previous stories didn't really seem to be headed anywhere, then it was vital that *this* story make it all worthwhile, yet they don't really pull it off.

Worryingly, it would again seem - as with all of this year's output - that there's no one person in control. To something this "high concept", you need a neurotic control-freak in charge - someone who micro-manages everything and ruthlessly removes all obstacles or ambiguities. Nathan-Turner was so keen to be everyone's friend, he could never be the relentless monster this type of project requires. Saward was asleep at the wheel until he jumped ship (yes, that's a mixed metaphor, but it reflects the confusion surrounding this situation). So it was left to new boy Chris Clough to unify the production, and try to get a workable story from last-minute writers *after* the locations have been scouted.

And as we've hinted, the creative confusion is all the more annoying because we have a production that's reliably worth looking at. Out of context, the Matrix sequences are visually arresting, and the location material gives the lie to the usual maxim about film inevitably being more atmospheric. There are certainly moments - such as the Gallifreyan guard leading a tumbrel through cobbled streets at night, then abruptly vanishing when Mel says it's an illusion - where you know no other series could do this at all, let alone as well. The clever editing - rather than elaborate digital effects - makes this dream-like, but they've accidentally got the right location for this sort of thing.

Yet it would've taken an act of faith for someone to tune in for such a visually arresting production, but *then* they'd have to get around all that tiresome piddling about in court, Bonn... sorry, Melanie Knownasmel... emoting all over the shop, and the pretty awful dialogue (not just in the final episode, but in the bits allegedly written by the master-craftsman Holmes). This is frustrating if you're just watching "The Ultimate Foe" to see how it all ends, but especially with the hindsight of what's to come in the McCoy era, it feels enormously irritating because so many of the people involved should've known better.

So... we've now reached the culmination of the 1985 and 1986 seasons, in which the viewership slumped to the point that this professional-looking, but altogether sterile, show struggled to get five million viewers for the climax of a long-running story. Things can only improve.

The Facts

Written by Robert Holmes and an uncredited Eric Saward (episode one), Pip and Jane Baker and an uncredited John Nathan-Turner (episode two). Directed by Chris Clough. Ratings: 4.4 million, 5.6 million. Audience appreciation was 69% for both instalments.

Working Titles   "Time Inc"

Supporting Cast   Anthony Ainley (The Master), Tony Selby (Glitz), Geoffrey Hughes (Popplewick), James Bree (Keeper of the Matrix).

Oh, Isn't That..?
• *Geoffrey Hughes*. He was, of course, the voice of "Paul McCartney" in *Yellow Submarine*. More to the point, he'd just finished a long stretch as Eddie Yates, the whimsical binman in *Coronation Street*. (This is set in a fictionalised Manchester, so they always have a character from Liverpool to be the butt of the jokes.) After this, he was the embarrassingly common brother-in-law of Hyacinth Bucket (you know how it's pronounced now) in *Keeping Up Appearances* (see "Revelation of the Daleks").

Cliffhangers   Within the Matrix, several flailing hands pull the Doctor down into soft, bubbling quicksand; the Keeper of the Matrix turns to the camera and is revealed as... the quietly cackling Valeyard.

The Lore

• So, this was made in June 1986, *before* work on the story with the Vervoids. Indeed, until fairly late on, the third section of the evidence was unwritten. However, with the decision to use the same crew on all of the last six episodes, it made sense to go ahead with the finale - set in the Trial Room and a few locations, and later make the third section entirely in studio. This decision was informed by the earlier choice to avoid doing a six-part story (i.e. a two-parter bolted on to a four-parter) but instead write them separately, with Robert Holmes coming back to tie up the whole

season's plot with "Time Inc". However, with three or four different possible four-parters being considered, the writing of the final section had been messed about. Meanwhile, Holmes had Hepatitis C, and was increasingly unable to work. Saward had been taking what Holmes had done and patching it together.

What we see as 'Part Thirteen' is almost all Holmes up to the Doctor walking into the "waiting room" that turns out to be a beach, even if the material from the entry to the Matrix was probably rewritten. Saward had thought of using a studio set, and once the Bakers had been hired to do a kind of "Agatha Christie In Space" the option of using the *Hyperion III* set again was considered. Saward had an elaborate plan for a final episode, in keeping with what he and Holmes had discussed, and ending with a cliffhanger (we'll go into details later). Nathan-Turner was against the idea, as it would give the BBC an excuse to end the series. Saward brooded on this.

• It was agreed by all parties that Sabalom Glitz should return. Tony Selby even turned down other work to keep himself available. Other than this, the only other parts were a Dickensian clerk named Mr Popplewick (scripted as a thin, Uriah Heap sort of character - see 24.1, "Time and the Rani") and the Keeper of the Matrix. Casting Popplewick was difficult, whilst they kept within the original brief, but James Bree seemed an obvious choice for the Keeper. He was reportedly a little annoyed when the revised script needed him less.

• Yes, about that revised script... Saward quit during the writing of the final episode and forbade the use of anything he had contributed in whatever they finally broadcast. This was after actors had been cast, the locations had been scouted and props made or bought for the last two episodes. Jane Baker received a desperate phone call from Nathan-Turner explaining that they would have to write a new ending using these locations, characters and props, and a taxi arrived bearing the script for Part Thirteen for them to follow. They had ten days to do it.

For a document that was shredded, the unused Part Fourteen is remarkably well-distributed. Significant changes are: the Master refuses the High Council's offer of a pardon if he kills the Doctor; a fake Mel almost leads the Doctor into a circular corridor that is a time-loop intended to trap him for eternity; the Valeyard is old and frail and fears death; the Valeyard's TARDIS is materi-

ABOUT TIME 1985–1989

alised over a 'Time Vent' inside the Matrix, which if left open for longer that seventy-two seconds will rip the Universe asunder; the Doctor and the Valeyard grapple over the rupture and fall in, like Holmes and Moriarty.

The original version had a lot of recycled material (some of it written by Saward as Mel's audition piece, even though Nathan-Turner had as good as cast the part already). Thus Clough had looked at various round buildings before opting for the Gladstone Pottery Museum near Stoke on Trent. This was another of those industrial heritage showcases (see 22.3, "The Mark of the Rani" and "The Mysterious Planet"), and was in use during the day. The Bakers wrote around this and the beach location used for the cliffhanger. Clough showed the Bakers all his photos of the chosen locations, and asked if they could use the Trial Room as much as possible. The Queen Victoria statue was commissioned for the earlier draft, and made from fibreglass. It was later offered free to a good home by the DWAS. (The shed-TARDIS on the beach was a real shed, already there and occupied for several years, and it was paintboxed out of the picture when not needed.)

• Not only did the Bakers deliver the goods on time, they wrote an episode that was 38 minutes long. The cast tried to speed it up, but a lot of comic scenes were trimmed (Selby pretended to be upset that it was all his lines that went). Even with as much whittled away as possible, the running time couldn't be brought down below 30 minutes without making an already complex plot baffling (we'll see this situation a lot more when Andrew Cartmel takes over Saward's chair). Jonathan Powell agreed that this episode needed to be longer, and sanctioned the only half-hour episode in the programme's history.

• As many of you will know, this was far from the end of the Sixth Doctor. Although Colin Baker's television reign was cut short, he's come into his own on the Big Finish audio plays. These have been commercially available since 1999, and despite the higher profile of those featuring Paul McGann (which have been broadcast on the digital radio network BBC7), it's Baker who has won most praise. Before this, various fan-produced videos had used him as "The Stranger" (accompanied by "Miss Brown", played by Nicola Bryant).

• Baker also has the unique distinction of being (so far) the only Doctor to write a comic strip for his character. The Age of Chaos in fact gives most of the best material to his companion, Frobisher, and tells the story (which we'd all wondered about) of the Doctor's quest to find out what happened to Peri and Yrcanos - and shows him meeting their granddaughter. For those who didn't follow the DWM strips (which are arguably the best Sixth Doctor adventures of all), Frobisher was a Whifferdill, a shape-shifting alien who had been working as a private eye when, like the TARDIS, he stuck in one shape - that of a penguin. As voiced by Robert Jezek (see 26.1, "Battlefield"), he's been given the best lines in some of the audios, too. However, it's in John Ridgway's illustrations - especially for Steve Parkhouse's crazed, unsettling stories - that we see what this Doctor could have been like, and almost nobody who followed these comics month-by-month can forget the sheer frustration of watching the ponderous TV equivalent.

• After the last episode of "Trial" (which - like all preceding it this year, and for a year to come - had "story so far" introductions by the BBC Continuity Announcers), the floodgates opened. The Daytime TV discussion series Open Air - usually given over to bland discussions of where Selina Scott got her hair done - was the scene of a furious exchange between members of the Merseyside Local Group (then led by Chris Chibnall, now the main writer for Torchwood and so himself guilty of a shockingly lame and pointless season ending) and the spectacularly-trousered Pip and Jane Baker. The host, Patti Caldwell, was out of her depth (she'd only seen Part 14) and it got into an unedifying mess. Very funny to watch, though.

• Incidentally, this business of "Trial" being one long story confused a lot of people, especially when "Dragonfire" came along and needed a publicity boost. Suddenly, to make that one the 150th Doctor Who adventure, "Trial" was counted as four stories.

24.1: "Time and the Rani"

(Serial 7D, Four Episodes. 7th - 28th September 1987.)

Which One is This?   The BBC camera crew referred to it as "The Two Bonnies". We can't say fairer than that, as a lot of it really is Kate O'Mara pretending to be Mel.

Firsts and Lasts   With the exception of the Hartnell clip from 20.7, "The Five Doctors" or the recap at the start of 19.1, "Castrovalva", this is the first time they went ahead with a pre-credit sequence. In this, we get Sylvester McCoy's first appearance as the Doctor, and the first use of the new titles and theme-tune arrangement that characterize his three seasons.

It is our sad duty to tell you that this is Keff McCulloch's first attempt at a score; although he gets better as he goes along, his soundtracks tend to be - how shall we put this? - rather excitable. This also is the first story shown in the 7.35pm slot (i.e. opposite *Coronation Street*), the televisual doldrums hitherto reserved for dire imported sitcoms and strange cheap shows (see 24.3, "Delta and the Bannermen" for a real doozy). So, as we move forward, the *big* surprise is that there's a Season Twenty-Six at all...

It's also the final outing for Pip and Jane Baker, and for Kate O'Mara as the Rani[20].

Four Things to Notice about "Time and the Rani"...

1. Err, yes, that pre-credit sequence. The TARDIS is sent hurtling around as zap-bolts knock it about like a billiard-ball, the Sixth Doctor and Mel are on the floor (which is *filthy* by the way - don't they have any mops?), then the Ship lands with a big rainbow, falling out of the (pink) sky into a quarry. Then in comes the Rani, looking dead butch with a big gun, and drawling 'Leave the girl - it's the man I want!' Just as you're thinking this can't get any sillier, Keff McCulloch's mighty Emulator parps up some power-chords, and a thing in furry boots turns over someone wearing Colin Baker's clothes and a Harpo wig. With a squeal of synthetic guitars and a squall of digital inlay, this person's slightly blurred face is revealed to be that of children's entertainer

Season 24 Cast/Crew

- • Sylvester McCoy (the Doctor)
- • Bonnie Langford (Melanie)
- • Sophie Aldred (Ace, 24.4 only)

- • John Nathan-Turner (Producer)
- • Andrew Cartmel (Script Editor)

Sylvester McCoy. Did they do this for a gag? See **The Lore**, but in all truthfulness...

2. Keff starts off overblown and gets louder. For the maximum effect, go straight to the first cliffhanger and note the disparity between what we're hearing (imagine the Day of Judgement, as Afrika Bambaata might have scored it) and what we're seeing (Bonnie Langford doing pirouettes inside a giant paperweight). We should also note the silly use of the theme tune inside the incidental music, but we'd fill every story McCulloch scores with comments on this. (For a really lurid example, check out "Delta and the Bannermen" and his late-sixties *Perils of Penelope Pitstop* riffola version, which accompanies a shot of an empty field with the Doctor and Ray arriving on a scooter.)

3. The featured aliens of this story - the Lakertyans - are impounded in the 'Centre of Leisure'. Unlike Leisure Centres in 80s Britain, there are no tracksuited kids tagging their handles outside, and no people with bad hairdos attempting aerobics or pensioners playing bowls, but a fountain with a disco-ball above it and a catwalk about ten feet off the ground are present. (You'll see that catwalk a lot from now on.) To make these Lotos-Eaters sympathetic, the story kills off a young female (who runs in a very distinctive fashion like the Lakertyans all do - those who can muster a run, anyway). Later in episode four, *another* young female is killed to demonstrate the explosives the Tetraps attach to the socks of the indigenous population. Two things to observe about this: one is how little fuss anyone else makes, the other is that the only on-screen violence to leave remains (a skeleton with a tail and a head-crest, used both times) is against young women. This is very unpleasant, and especially disquieting in such an otherwise lightweight story.

4. On the whole, the exterior set-dressing is

quite impressive. The entrance to the Rani's castle is as good as anything we've seen (certainly streets better than Omega's pad in 10.1, "The Three Doctors"), and the mesh between built objects and special effects is almost faultless. The Centre's even got a moat with a set of stepping-stones, a level of thought we've been praying for over the last few years. However, there's one scene where Mel and the rebel Ikona hide in a concrete drainage tube. Nothing wrong with that, as there's a long and honourable tradition of sewers and ventilation shafts in the series, but someone's decided that a concrete tube doesn't look alien enough. So they've hung a bit of tinsel on it.

The Continuity

The Doctor Appears to have regenerated after hitting his head on the console during the Rani's hijack of the TARDIS. Yes, really. [It's bizarre that the exact cause of this "fatality" this isn't actually said on screen, although the novelization by Pip 'n' Jane specifies that the Doctor hits 'the plinth of the console' head-first. Moreover - and laugh if you must - page nine of this book specifies: 'Regeneration had been triggered by the tumultuous buffeting.'

[Understandably, fandom-at-large has deemed this a daft way for one of the Doctors to go, and it's long been held that the Sixth Doctor was dying already from an unseen and far more glorious adventure - and that he just *happened* to regenerate after the TARDIS got snared in the Rani's time beam. It took some time, but a "final" adventure for the Sixth Doctor finally saw print in 2005 as *Spiral Scratch* by Gary Russell, who also gave us Mel's proper debut (in *Business Unusual*) and the Foamasi-Wirrn team-up story to end all Foamasi-Wirrn team-up stories (in *Placebo Effect*).]

The Doctor refers to his new form as his 'seventh persona' [see **Who Are All These Men in Wigs?** under 13.5, "The Brain of Morbius"]. Upon first regaining consciousness, this new Doctor starts to plan his day before recognising the Rani and gabbling at her at top speed. He's significantly shorter than before, and a lot slimmer than when we last saw him. [To be fair, he might've shed a few kilos well before the regeneration.] His hair is now dark and wavy, his eyebrows thicker and downcast. Somehow, he's acquired a lilting Scots accent to go with his new body, and his speech has an odd cadence. At this stage, he routinely mangles proverbs [see also 18.1, "The Leisure Hive" et seq]. He says he's concerned about a 'temporal flicker' in Sector 13, has thoughts of popping over to Centaur 7, and then perhaps wants a quick holiday. [So those who think that the Doctor's "To Do" list of planets to save begins with Ace's arrival in "Dragonfire" (24.4) should note the distinction he makes there.]

After several false starts in selecting a new outfit, he finally chooses to dress like a prewar Oxbridge don on a golfing holiday - with a panama hat, soft collared shirt, paisley tie, sleeveless pullover, cream cotton jacket, brown check trousers and golfing shoes (but without the studs). The pullover [annoyingly to some] has question-marks knitted into the pattern. He has a bandanna in his left pocket that matches his hat-band, and a yellow duster in his right. This time - but not afterwards - he wears his braces over his jumper, and has a red woollen tartan scarf. [The overall effect is to look like someone who would wear tweeds and a waistcoat to work - as indeed McCoy does in "The TV Movie".]

This Doctor seems to appreciate all forms of Earth's culture - from Princeton physicists to Elvis, from Louis Pasteur to Mrs Malaprop. He can, apparently, detect Mel's pulse with his own thumb [humans can't do this]. Likewise, she can detect his double pulse. He's concerned not to pollute [see **History**]. His regeneration took place next to the exercise bike and toolkit in the console room [suggesting a continuation of Mel's fitness regime; see 23.3, "Terror of the Vervoids"]. Like his former incarnation, he apparently hates carrot juice.

When the Rani's Big Red Brain gestalt comes up with a wrong answer to a sum as part of its equations, the Doctor can't help himself from correcting this out loud - even though it helps to facilitate the Rani's dreaded plan. [If *you* were not only smarter than a Big Red Brain, but a Big Red Brain that was connected to the mind of Albert Einstein, you'd show off a bit too. That said, this sort of carelessness will later become unthinkable for this incarnation.]

The Doctor gives no sign that returning the fifteen or so geniuses that the Rani snatched from their native times [and places, as one of them seems to be an Argolin; see "The Leisure Hive"] will pose a problem. [So he must be confident that the TARDIS won't go astray. This is, in fact, a central characteristic of the Seventh Doctor's era - on

What's All This Stuff About Anoraks?

During the course of these books, one stray comment has probably caused more confusion amongst overseas readers than any other. It appears that outside the UK, the assumption that a specific type of *Doctor Who* fan wears a specific type of overcoat - and the use of this as a pejorative term - has no cultural context. Apparently, no other countries save Australia have trainspotters either. What curious nations you all inhabit.

We'll start at the logical place to begin, 1980. This is the year when a line was drawn in the sand, and either you watched *Doctor Who* or you didn't. Up to that date everyone sort-of watched it now and then, but from "The Leisure Hive" (18.1) on, the show increasingly adopts a tone of being for a smaller section of the Licence-fee paying British Public than the series had been for hitherto. (See Volume V for the reams of debate about this. And of course, blaming any one story or season or incident for a long-term trend like the one we're discussing is a crude simplification, but we need agreed landmarks before we get into the hazy areas.) Meanwhile, ITV found that the series wasn't invulnerable, and put on *Buck Rogers in the 25th Century* - finally tempting away a significant percentage of the supposed core *Who* audience of teenage boys.

Then in 1983, we have Longleat: the BBC puts on a small event, but underestimates the amount of public interest by a factor of ten. Some fans don't like the direction of the show under Nathan-Turner, but - and this is what's important - already it's becoming clear that *most* of the attendees (including the JN-T dissenters) like the *idea* of the series. With the sales of *Doctor Who Monthly* holding stable, it was obvious that the whoever-it-was-that-was-watching was a sizeable body of people, somewhere else. At least, that's what most people seemed to think. The fact that this book is written by people who bought *DWM*, but thought of themselves as members of the public (and indeed thought *like* those people who believed the "real fans" were elsewhere), should give you a clue as to what was really happening.

Those "real fans", though, what were they like? Well, everyone knew that they went to conventions, and dressed as their favourite characters. Because that's what Trekkies do, and *Doctor Who* fans are supposed to be just like Trekkies, aren't they? Well, except that - according to the stereotypes - Trekkies are fat middle-aged women with hair dyed the colour of Ribena, and *Doctor Who* fans (no suitable name existed for them then,

except the American thing "Whovian", which nobody here uses) are all geeky boys. Or slightly creepy older men with no kids. Just like trainspotters.

(Seriously? You *don't* have trainspotters where you come from? OK, let's start again. On a small island where trains were invented and running since the 1840s, you've got a large but finite number of engines in service. Each engine has a name and serial number. They run on specific lines in particular services - originally for a small number of private companies, but then after 1948, for British Rail. So if you knew which engines were running on which lines - and had a timetable, a notebook and a packed lunch - you could, in theory, log the number of every locomotive in service in the UK before you died. Except that some trains were retired from service, some replaced at short notice due to damage and some were more noteworthy than others. In the age of steam, this made sense to everyone, even if they couldn't see themselves doing it in winter.

(Once diesel trains came in, the obsessiveness of it all seemed to outweigh the appeal. It's that completist gene - something we've all got, but most people try to hide. It's the camaraderie of fellow enthusiasts going through it too, something only you and they really understand, combined with fierce competitiveness, an urge to trump your rivals. When Irvine Welsh wrote a book about a close-knit band of drug-addicts, the metaphor he picked for that intensity of obsession was *Trainspotting*, and every reader "got" it. Except that his characters were vaguely romantic figures, and "everyone knows" that trainspotters dress in anoraks and have no social skills. American readers should by now be aware that your "railfans" aren't really in the same league as these spods. Back to the story.)

The BBC went and wrote a *Who* fan into *EastEnders*. A series made by ex-*Who* personnel (by and large) bit the hand that fed it with its portrayal of a fat, shambolic creep with a long scarf (because we all wore those in public, of course) and an anorak festooned with badges. Conveniently, just as it suited Michael Grade to have an aunt-sally of his most organised and intractable critics, BBC1 had one to order. (In fairness, it should be pointed out that said character was the creation of long-time *Doctor Who* fan and *EastEnders* script editor Colin Brake. But screw fair-

continued on page 169...

ABOUT TIME 1985-1989

screen he appears to have near-absolute control of his Ship, and from now on random landings (the start of "Delta and the Bannermen" being a possible exception) will fall by the wayside.]

• *Ethics.* When the Rani attributes her opinions on the Lakertyans - that they're lethargic, and failed to reach their full potential - to the Doctor himself, he's mildly concerned and says, 'The more I know me, the less I like me'. However, he's later silent when Ikona tips away the antidote to the deadly insects in the Centre of Leisure [so he probably agrees that the Lykertians *should* get off their scaly butts a bit more]. Although he's predictably abusive to the Rani - and initially decides to smash whatever it is she's built on principle, without asking what it is or what she's doing - his real venom is saved for the *collaborateur* Beyus.

As yet, the new Doctor's code regarding the deaths of other beings seems ambiguous. He says he feels sorry for the Rani when he thinks she's died in one of her own traps, but also remarks there's not a spark of decency in her. He's initially disheartened to discover the 'sad' skeleton of a Lakertian, but gives it a friendly little wave before moving away. He shoves a menacing Tetrap onto one of the Rani's deadly tripwires, but it's uncertain if this occurs as an act of cold calculation, spontaneous opportunity or simple forgetfulness - and he at least takes off his hat when the creature perishes. Later, the Doctor shows no hesitation in telling the Rani that the Lakertyans are attacking, even though he must know this will make her trigger the explosive bangles and kill Beyus (who admittedly volunteered to sacrifice himself).

• *Inventory.* At last, he's got a real Swiss Army knife - and a wristwatch *as well as* the pocketwatch as before, on a chain from his lapel. The umbrella that accompanies him here is smaller than the previous golf umbrella [23.1, "The Mysterious Planet"] and has a shoulder-strap.

• *Background.* The Doctor specifies that his age, and that of the Rani, is '953'. [See **Why Do Time Lords Always Meet in Sequence?** for what this implies about encounters away from Gallifrey. The Sixth Doctor kept claiming he was 'nine hundred' (22.6, "Revelation of the Daleks") or 'over nine hundred' years old ("Terror of the Vervoids"), which further implies the long, unbroadcast post-Trial period for him that the book and audio-makers seem happy to mine.] Apparently, the Doctor specialised in Thermodynamics at University [this is news to anyone who's seen 18.7, "Logopolis" -

then again, it's not said that he *excelled* in the topic], and the Rani therefore kidnaps him when her faulty machinery requires such an expert. It's established that the Doctor and the Rani went to university together, where he bitched about the morality of her work.

The Doctor seems a bit casual when talking to Einstein (but the latter seems unfamiliar with the TARDIS interior). At some stage, he [the Doctor that is; we can't speak for Einstein] has learned to play the spoons. He spins Mel around on his shoulders [possibly a trick he picked up from his time with the Mountain Mauler of Montana (2.4, "The Romans")]. The Rani says there's no evidence that he's visited Lakertya before now, and the post-regenerative Doctor doesn't disagree.

When one of the various genii in the Rani's Big Red Brain gestalt says, 'It is a fundamental postulate that all motion is relative,' the Doctor replies, 'You wouldn't say that if you met my uncle'. [This could easily be a joke and nothing more, and it'd certainly be suspect if he'd been conscious while saying it. However, this is the Doctor's mind talking, so we might have to take it seriously (see 9.5, "The Time Monster" for more of the Doctor's uncensored thoughts).]

Even in his post-regeneration, amnesia-induced state, the Doctor doesn't think it at all odd that "Mel" should know about the conductive substances phb and pes. It takes him ages [or more specifically two episodes] to recognize that "Mel" is actually the Rani in disguise [so maybe he doesn't know Mel as well as we think].

The Supporting Cast

• *Melanie.* She admires scientist / novelist CP Snow, and has read all his books. [This is improbable as there's a lot of them - besides, they're dreadful. There was a BBC adaptation of Snow's *Strangers and Brothers* books, but not even *we* watched that. Suffice to say, there wasn't much call for a TV tie-in edition. We can find any sign of tie-in reprints before 1999 - but hey kids! *The Two Cultures* came out in America in May 2007! - so his books would have to be from a library or jumble-sale.] Mel also says she 'of course' knows about regeneration [suggesting she took the same companion quiz as Peri - see 22.5, "Timelash" among others]. Somewhat unexpectedly, she can hurl the Doctor around as she's though trained in all-in wrestling. [She never demonstrates this talent again, however, and it might've come in handy

What's All This Stuff About Anoraks?

...continued from page 167

ness: this is the author of *Escape Velocity*, and thus deserves all the contempt we can muster.)

The *Eastenders* character didn't last long, but the stigma associated with still watching a series deemed long past its best grew more intolerable. Caring about a television series that wasn't a soap was "sad". Sad people wear anoraks, talk in croaky voices like Mr Bean or John Major and need to Get A Life. Of course, "A Life" means liking the same things as everyone else, and only caring about making more money. Otherwise, no matter how you dressed, you were an anorak-wearing spod.

It wasn't flattering, but to a certain extent this caricature covered up what was really happening within fandom. You might expect that the "sad-case" label was something we all tried to avoid. It has to be said, some *did* rebel against it and - predictably, perhaps - most of these expressed their individuality in the same ways as each other. Fandom had - proportionately, when compared to the rest of the demographic - more than its share of tragic Goths (black nail-varnish, Sisters of Mercy T-shirts, smelly leather greatcoats and so on), Casuals (designer sportswear, pastel shaded jumpers, conspicuous consumption trappings) and amusing moustaches, but the *real* statistical anomaly was how gay it all was.

Perhaps spending so much time in an environment where people already knew the most embarrassing thing about you made it easier to make the *second*-most awkward admission of your life. Perhaps some people found that a hero who never quite belonged, and had other priorities than getting the girl and looking cool, helped them though difficult school years. Or perhaps it was the fact that the Nathan-Turner years were the most overtly homosexual mainstream TV ever transmitted at that point (see **What Are the Gayest Things in *Doctor Who*?** under - where else? - 25.2, "The Happiness Patrol"). Whatever the reason (and entire theses have been written on this topic), a significant percentage of fandom in the UK - and a very high proportion of the high-profile fans and future spin-off creators - were gay or bi. If you weren't, you either accepted those who were, or grumbled darkly in the bar at conventions and missed out on all the good parties. Because let's face it: in a building full of people who profess to be fans of a series about tolerance and different perspectives, being homophobic would get you about as far as expressing racist

opinions, even if you were amongst the slim majority of straight fans. Besides, if you were into *Doctor Who* in the 1980s, you were already in an oppressed minority and sometimes had to admit to a Camp sensibility (see **Is *Doctor Who* Camp?** under 6.5, "The Seeds of Death") to disavow taking it at all seriously.

But, amazingly with hindsight, the trainspotter cliché allowed fandom to keep this from the public view. Michael Grade made jokes about how the *Doctor Who* fans probably didn't have girlfriends and we laughed along - because the joke was on him, really. After the series ended, and the programme became "ours" in ways it could never have been before, the public slowly got used to the idea that being obsessive about something was better than sheeplike conformity. And as football reclaimed its family heritage after twenty years of hooliganism and bad press, nerdy obsessiveness became chic. In dance music circles, "Anorak" became a term of affection for people who knew all the white-label trivia (and the garments themselves were reclaimed, first by Britpop stars Jarvis Cocker and Noel Gallagher, then as "urban" wear by UK rappers). In 1992, the BBC's *Late Show* crew (pretenders to the crown of *Late Night Line-Up*, see Volume II) launched reruns with a spoof documentary (entitled *Resistance is Useless*), narrated by an anorak with the East Midlands accent associated with the truly sad (see 25.4, "The Greatest Show in the Galaxy"). It was, apparently, Nathan-Turner's idea. But the laugh was on him too, because as his career sputtered out, the anoraks were taking over the asylum.

And just to show you how things change, there came a point in early 1999 when we stormed the mainstream. It was easy for anyone who'd been in 80s fan circles (ooer!) to spot how series like *The League of Gentlemen* were the work of People Like Us. *Spaced* (the stoner / anorak crossover sitcom that spawned *Shaun of the Dead*) and *This Morning with Richard Not Judy* (Stewart Lee and Richard Herring's odd show) had overt references, yes, but more importantly they had an overall sensibility of cult-TV dues having been paid.

Most striking, of course, was *Queer as Folk*, the original Channel 4 version, which had the first realistic portrayal of a fan ever in Vince Tyler (what is it with all these Tylers?[21]). He watched gay porn for sake of the plot, but preferred Hinchcliffe stories when he'd been stood up (again). At least three of

continued on page 171...

when matronly cannibals jump her in the next adventure.] Mel claims that her speciality is computers, not physics, and she's now able to use the Doctor's key to get people into the TARDIS.

[Incidentally, Mel here wears what would have been the height of fashion for Spring 1982, but was terminally naff by 1987. Does this clue suggest when she *really* met the Doctor? Her chronic fashion-sense is equally retro in the next story, and nothing she had on before gives any hint that she's from the era of Terence Trent Darby and Debbie Gibson. Perhaps this is why she thought in the last story that a 'modum' should be big enough to need its own cupboard. Then again, the Doctor is disappointed that she didn't know about Strange Matter, theorised in 1984 (she doesn't get a chance to say "that's after my time", though), and ultimately most guidebooks and much of fandom regards Mel as being contemporary with her broadcast stories.]

The Supporting Cast (Evil)

• *The Rani*. She now has a nose-stud [as befits a Rani] and has done her hair. She drew the TARDIS off-course with a large, conical device that looks like a gun - something the Doctor calls a 'Navigational Guidance System Distorter'. [This is an amazingly powerful gadget - apparently able to pluck a Gallifreyan space-time vehicle out of the Vortex, yet it's not even the size of a cricket bat.]

Here the Rani's arsenal includes lethal insects, which are hidden in a revolving globe in the Lakertyans' Centre of Leisure, and used to punish any acts of insurrection. She's also booby-trapped the area around her base with tripwires - stepping on one traps victims in an energy sphere, which dashes itself against the nearby terrain and turns those within into skeletons. The Rani can also generate a non-speaking hologram of Mel.

In a curious development, the Rani needs the Doctor's help with the aspects of her plan to do with time travel and Thermodynamics [we've suggested several connections between the two fields throughout these books], as even Einstein can't give her cerebral stamp-collection his 'unique understanding of the properties of time'. [See **Things That Don't Make Sense**.] At University, the two trainee Time Lords argued over ethics, despite specialising in different fields. [Some of the books make the assumption that each fresh intake at the Academy is numerically pretty small: the Doctor is maybe only one of a dozen or so

Prydonians of his generation. The mother-lode for info on this, 14.3, "The Deadly Assassin" is ambiguous, as Runcible knows the Doctor and Borusa remembers him - both seemingly familiar with his shady past, like he was one of about a hundred students - but Engin and Spandrell act as though he was one of thousands and have to look up his records. The most simple explanation is the most worrying: all these renegades were at school together simply because there was something about the Class of 92 that made them all go bad. (See 9.3, "The Sea Devils"; 16.6, "The Armageddon Factor" and the essay on the abortive Season Twenty-Three.) It certainly appears that something may have been seeking a recruit amongst the kids selected for the Academy that year, if the Doctor's account in X3.12, "The Sound of Drums" is to be believed.]

The TARDIS(es) The Doctor says the Rani took an 'incredible risk' by maneuvering her TARDIS close enough to take detailed footage of a supernova. [This suggests that there's a limit to how close even Gallifreyan vessels can get to such an event. See X2.13, "Doomsday".]

The Doctor says he needs to sechedule his TARDIS' bi-centennial refit. The Ship has a new wardrobe area - like the "costume room" from 21.7, "The Twin Dilemma", and even containing some of the same clothes. However, it's so dark as to be almost an abstract space [like the zone with the old fridge in it in 16.3, "The Stones of Blood"]. The room includes a chest [with the same stuff as in 22.5, "Timelash"] plus a hideous Hawaiian shirt [in-jokes, dontcha love 'em?] and a full-length Victorian mirror. For some reason, there's also a Napoleonic tunic and hat in the new Doctor's size - as well as a schoolteacher's mortar-board and gown, a Prussian Shako and several of the previous Doctors' outfits.

The Doctor fetches a radiation wave meter [different from the similar device seen in "Ghost Light" (26.2)] from the TARDIS tool room, which is mentioned but not seen. The Rani's vessel has materialised some way away from the Tetrap base. [Don't ask why, please.] Like much of the base's design - which is founded on square-based pyramidal shapes - her Ship has the outward appearance of a metal and glass pyramid, with mirrors on each of the base vertices. [With the Lakertyan sky like it is, and the TARDIS exterior reflecting it, the Ship is - you've guessed it - a

What's All This Stuff About Anoraks?

...continued from page 169

the mishaps that befell Vince are known to have happened, sort of, to prominent fans. Russell T Davies (oh, you *did* know he wrote it, didn't you?) had previously written a Virgin *New Adventure* and several fannish children's TV shows - *Century Falls* is "Image of the Fendahl" (15.3) with money spent on it - and made no secret of his inclinations. He was a fan, out and proud. Listen to him and Phil Collinson on the DVD commentaries if you don't believe us. You'll see few if any overt references to old stories, but the thinking behind the new ones is shaped by this, as we'll explore in a later essay. (See **The Semiotic Thickness of What?** under 24.4, "Dragonfire".)

Unlike the Trekkies / Trekkers (incidentally which *is* the preferred term these days? - whatever it is, we'll use the other one to annoy them), *Doctor Who* fans in the UK didn't think of the series as in any way "Cult". It was as mainstream as it got until 1980, and the foundation of fandom came at a time when activities associated with Punk and New Wave seemed more useful to us. Sarcastic fanzines and meeting in pubs was how we began, so when some bright spark had the idea of running conventions along the lines of *Trek* cons, we were already slightly uneasy about looking like the kinds of people who wear costumes and buy action figures. We weren't yet that different from the general public. Once this division set in, some of us bought into the Convention lifestyle wholesale, and started doing other things American fans did, but they got laughed at even by other anoraks. To reiterate; British *Doctor Who* fans love *Coronation Street* far more than they like *Stargate SG-1*, and were in those days more prepared to stay in for *House of Elliot* than *The X-Files* although *Top of the Pops* and *Later with Jools Holland* were more vital than either. It was a very blokey world, characterised by piss-taking, quite unlike the suspiciously gushing American scene. Even with a new series being shown and the majority of the nation on our side, we are wary of being too enthusiastic. We've been let down by this show before, and mocked for our love of it.

Moreover, there is a sense in which enthusiasts of anything are wary of allowing the outside world to see their affection for something so insubstantial, especially when the object of that love is risible. Rock music theorist Greil Marcus commented on how people like him, who'd built their lives around a form of entertainment, were mildly traumatised when *The Rutles* confronted them with the silliness of even the most hallowed and iconic band, the Beatles. Old *Doctor Who* looked creaky and odd in the 80s and 90s, even to fans, so what chance was there of explaining the appeal, let alone the fact that the original object of fan activity was left behind like trainer-wheels years ago. We'll pick this up in the essay with "Dragonfire", too, but it's significant that when Davies wrote an entire episode of his revamped *Who* about a version of fandom (X2.10, "Love and Monsters"), those of us who were "there" in the 80s for the fun loved it and those who used it for their own ends hated it. It's also worth noting how unlike a real Local Group that LINDA was: predominantly female, and not so inclined to berate one another's tastes in music.

So the years when we couldn't say the word 'Dalek' in public without people laughing and pointing at us have - for some - left deep scars. Davies has justifiably been ruthless in omitting from "his" series anything that would send us back to the them-and-us mentality of Nathan-Turner-era disasters. Sure, he's brought back elements from the classic show, but he's explained them in detail, as though for the first time, and not just put them on screen in the vague hope that people will realise why they're there. (21.1, "Warriors of the Deep" for example, expects us to go "Wow! Silurians!" and just looks silly if you don't. Well, sillier.) We have a word for this condition - "Anoraknophobia". Davies simply won't risk doing the things many might say *Doctor Who* ought to be doing, in case it goes wrong like it did in the early 80s. (See also **What Happened at Longleat?** under 20.6, "The King's Demons" and **Did *Doctor Who Magazine* Change Everything?** under 18.2, "Meglos".)

whole bunch of pink triangles. They really aren't being very subtle with the subtext this time, are they? And we're still a year away from 25.2, "The Happiness Patrol".]

Inside, there's a big room with what looks like rock walls, with two passages branching out from it. The room contains a vertical laser that the Rani uses to mill the surface of a slice of phb. At the end, this room appears to be the ideal place for the Tetrap named Urak to suspend his former mistress from the ceiling in handcuffs and chains.

The Non-Humans

• *Tetraps*. They're large and shaggy, with matted fur and leathery wings. And yep! They look rather like giant bats, but with four eyes - one in the front, one on either side and one at the back. Even with this extra vision, however, they still need to turn their heads at times.

The Tetraps also have snubby, pig-like snouts and large fangs. They appear to sleep while hanging upside down from the ceiling, and drink a sort of blood serum that Beyus slops into their trough. They've got big flappy ears, elephantine feet and tufts of white hair, from which a bony ridge descends to the mouth. [The overall effect is like a composite of all four of the *Banana Splits*.] They have forked tongues, pot bellies, and tongues that contain some means of paralyzing humans and Time Lords stiff as a board. For whatever reason, glitter frightens them. They're armed with web guns that render people unconscious.

Urak, the obsequious Tetrap leader, claims that their home planet is called "Tetrapriapus". [Well, that's what it *sounds* like, although that might suggest that they've got other things in fours besides eyes. Once again, the Bakers' prose-style has many distractions, and we had to wait for the novelisation to work out what was being said, although the smut version of the word had taken control by the time it published. It's *actually* spelled "Tetrapyriarbus", which sounds like a gum infection.]

• *Lakertyans*. As the name would imply [but only if, like Pip 'n' Jane, you read dictionaries over breakfast], they're lizard-like with green skin and scales. They have a strange way of running - arms behind them, almost like basilisks. Their skeletons reveal vestigial tails and a bony crest on the skull. But they wear circlets on their heads, so we can't say if the bony surface on their scalps is skull or hat. Either way, a single strand of hair - which gets bushier with age and extends down their backs - extends from this. [Think of a dayglo wild boar if that helps.]

The Lakertyans all wear bright colours, usually yellow and orange. [Combined with their lime-green faces and the pink sky, this makes the exterior sequences look like an ad for Opel Fruits.] The Rani says that the benevolent climate on Lakertya induced lethargy, and that the people consequently failed to reach their full potential. [She might be making this up, but it's perhaps notable that the only Lakertyan structure we see is the Centre of Leisure, and the majority of the Lakertyans seem relaxed and blasé about the threat from the Tetraps. However, Ikona seems to indicate that the Centre provides for the pleasure seekers' needs, which amazingly - and despite the barren terrain - suggests they're advanced enough to effortlessly produce food.] The Lakertyans use 'fireworks' or glittery stuff in their carnivals.

The Lakertyan leader, Beyus, advocates co-operating for the duration - especially because the Rani has enough deadly insects at her disposal to wipe out his people - whilst young rebel Ikona favours resistance. Similar to Sil's regarding Peri as revolting in 23.2, "Mindwarp", Ikona thinks the Tetraps are 'almost as hideous' as Mel. [One has to wonder about his point of reference for this claim, however.]

Planet Notes

• *Lakertya*. The parts of the planet seen here look like a slate-quarry, with a bit of lichen but no other vegetation [see **The Lore**]. Lakertya has a pink sky, a few wet areas (one of them being a sizeable pond) and some tall cliffs. The Centre of Leisure is presented as a gaming and relaxtion room with beige walls and a little pond. To enter, cross a small moat on stepping-stones, then ceremonially kiss your hand and place it on a rock at the doorway.

The Rani has constructed a fortress for the Tetraps and her own laboratory, and Ikona comments that constructing this 'cost the lives of many Lakertyans'. [So the people really *are* lethargic, if Beyus' word alone has quelled them from rebelling against the Rani's lethal slave-labour.] The fortress has a protruding spar on either side of the gateway, each with a dragon-like head on the end (and this motif is picked up in the chamber with the Rani's Big Red Brain). There's a balcony overlooking the door, and a chute for launching the Rani's rocket on its fixed trajectory over that. The Tetraps have a basement to sleep in, with suitably gothic bars and a chute for warm blood, but in the main level there's a basic theme of square-based pyramids, some inverted.

History

• *Dating*. Absolutely no clue. [Although the Rani mentions 'returning' Earth to the Cretaceous Age, so - for what it's worth - the story probably can't take place before that.]

The Rani's fiendish scheme this time around:

kidnap geniuses such as Einstein, Hypatia, Pasteur and others, plug them into a gestalt creature [which we've taken to calling the "Big Red Brain"], and get them to develop a formula for a lightweight substitute for Strange Matter. [The implication is that the 'genius' potential in these people is more useful than knowledge itself, which would *almost* make sense of the Master's plan to harness the geniuses of the Industrial Revolution in 22.3, "The Mark of the Rani". It also might explain why people from the past seem sufficient to the task at hand, and why the Rani doesn't stick to nabbing beings from more advanced eras. Still, it's amusing to think that for all her effort here, something similar was almost achieved in X2.3, "School Reunion" with thirty fourth-formers and a bag of chips.] Strange Matter is an incredibly dense substance (a lump the size of the Big Red Brain would have the same weight as a planet) that only explodes in reaction with itself. The bit of the formula for the faux-Strange Matter that we can hear: '87K to the power of 19B, correlated with 52 to the power of 6.4 equals 39B'.

The synthetic Strange Matter is then loaded onto a rocket and fired at an asteroid of Strange Matter near Lakertia. The resultant explosion would have created Helium-II, as well as released a burst of gamma rays equivalent to a supernova. The Helium-II would fuse with the upper atmosphere of Lakertia to form a shell of Chronons - discrete particles of time - and the gamma rays' hothouse effect [Uh? Up until now, this has *almost* made sense...] would make the Big Red Brain go into chain reaction and fill the gap between the planet and the shell. This would create a Time Manipulator - a cerebral mass capable of dominating and controlling time anywhere in the Cosmos. With such a device, the Rani hopes to bring 'order' to creation. Among other things, the Rani wants to use the Manipulator to return Earth to the Cretacous Age, as she feels the 'potential' of the dinosaurs was never fully realised. [The Rani expressed interest in dinosaurs in "The Mark of the Rani", but it's almost as if she doesn't know about the Silurians, the Sea Devils and all that. See 7.2, "Doctor Who and the Silurians" for why this is interesting.]

The Doctor says a Princetown physicist discovered Strange Matter in 1984. Both phb and pes [or 'ps', as the Doctor alternatively calls it] are heat-conducting materials suitable for the Rani's machinery. The Doctor favours using phb because it's bio-degradable, and suggests it can be fermented from sugar and starch. Pes is a petroleum-based plastic, slightly amber and almost opaque, and isn't as good for the environment.

A 'micro-termistor' is such an irreplaceable part of the Rani's equipment, the Doctor can bring her entire operation to a halt by stealing it.

The Analysis

Where Does This Come From? In amongst all the science - enough of which is accurate for us to discuss in a mo - there's a lot of fairy-tale thinking. As we said when Luke Ward turned into a tree, the Bakers have a way of hitting on these ideas without really making them sing. Here, we have a lot of Hans Anderson-like concepts. The story about the Rani making the Doctor forget the real Mel - not to mention her being a witch-queen who keeps talking animals as slaves - is enough like "The Snow Queen" to make it frustrating that Mel resolves the issue with two episodes to go. The business of the hologram of Mel in exchange for the missing component is similarly witchy. The trip-wires aren't just grenades, they're glass balls (all right, force-fields) that bounce you off mountains until you explode. It's Glinda the Good Fairy gone wrong (and don't think that's the last we'll hear of *The Wizard of Oz* this year).

How did the Bakers come up with so many ideas in such a short time? Well, it helped that they'd written a "Make Your Own Adventure" book (*Race Against Time*) with the Rani building a Time Destabiliser to re-write Earth's history. The more affordable bits of "Time and the Rani" seem to have been recycled from this work (but these days, they could do CGI Cryogenates firing shards of ice and melting when exposed to ethylene glycol), as do bits of "Terror of the Vervoids" - which was also written in a hurry. (Seriously, the book is great fun, and shows that the Bakers "got" *Doctor Who* as it had been made in the Hartnell and Pertwee years. You'll never leave home without a handy guide to Morse Code once you've played it. It's just a shame they wrote such unsayable lines, and that television required linear plots.)

As might be expected of a writing team whose male half is named after someone from *Great Expectations*, there's another Dickensian hint. "Urak" is named after and very loosely based on the scheming Uriah Heap from *David Copperfield* (see our comments on Mr Popplewick and the Circumlocution Office in 23.4, "The Ultimate Foe". With this in mind, it's odd that the Gordon

Riots weren't mentioned in "The Mark of the Rani" - maybe not even the Bakers could finish *Barnaby Rudge*.)

Right, let's talk Quarks. Not the dodgy robots with schoolboys inside (6.1, "The Dominators") but very tiny particle-oids. You only really *need* to know just a few details, but they won't make much sense without the bigger picture. There are six "flavours" of quark, and six types of lepton (those are particles with no mass - like electrons - that can move at lightspeed and don't get affected by the Strong Force). Protons and neutrons are made of combinations of the two most common quarks, Up and Down. Similarly, most leptons that stick around for more than a fraction of a second are electrons or electron-neutrinos. If the rest went away one day, maybe the Universe wouldn't notice. (X3.0, "The Runaway Bride" suggests that something like that has already happened during a pretty hefty redraft of the Laws of Physics - see also X3.2, "The Shakespeare Code" and 10.1, "The Three Doctors".)

Now, so long as the total charge of any combination of quarks is either 0, +1 or -1, we're in business. The thing is, quarks have fractional charges, of 2/3, 1/3, -1/3 and -2/3 (at this level we're dealing with antiquarks too). So two Ups (+2/3 each) and a Down (-1/3) make a proton, two Downs and an Up make a neutron. Then in the 1950s, they found a much heavier particle and called it Strange, because it should have decayed faster than it did. (It didn't because it's a quark, so the Strong Force can't touch it, but it took a while to figure that out.) Just with these three you get eight baryons (the heavier particles that the Strong force can pull, like protons), and throw in quark-antiquark pairs and you've got half a dozen mesons. Strange quarks, which also have -1/3 charge, can mix with Ups and Downs - and if you've got one of each, it's a Lambda particle. (All together now, "One Up, one Down, one... Strange Matter".) You don't get many of them to a pound. Think about all those pop-science examples of how many elephants weigh as much as a spoonful of neutron star, and you've got some idea. (If you don't know, the other quarks are named Charm, Top and Bottom. Flavour can change with a Weak force interaction, but don't let's get started on that, or we'll get into something they call "Colour" that isn't. Worse, we'll land-up using terms like "anti-green gluons", and it'll start sounding like Terry Nation explaining how Daleks can turn invisible.)

The mid-1980s saw a rash of popular books about the wonders and oddness of Quantum Physics, and newspaper articles about the quest for the Grand Unified Theory. It meant that a lot of people started pontificating at parties about particle-wave duality, even though they couldn't figure out Young's Modulus of a plastic ruler when they'd done science at school. (It also meant that a lot of people saw a cat go into a box in X2.11, "Fear Her" and thought it was a clever joke about Erwin Schrödinger - as opposed to the second *Sapphire and Steel* knock-off of the year.)

And if you didn't know, or hadn't worked it out, "Loyhargil" is an anagram of "Holy Grail".

Things That Don't Make Sense   The Rani is a Time Lord with enough advanced know-how to build a Big Red Brain gestalt that exploits various genii, and to construct machinery that can pump out a Strange Matter substitute within moments of being fed a chemical formula. Yet against all odds, she's apparently unable to equip her rocket with a targeting system or navigational device, meaning it's ridiculously stuck on a 'fixed trajectory' and she's screwed when lift-off is delayed a bit. [The near-miss is stupid for another reason, as we'll explain.]

But then, we *might* take issue with the Rani's entire plan. She's using various geniuses from history to power her Big Red Brain, but as the point of the exercise is to eventually alter time and the course of evolution on planets such as Earth, then these people paradoxically won't have been born if she succeeds. [That said, perhaps the Time Manipulator is *so* powerful that it overrides such concerns. This might alleviate the hitch that if the Rani "brings order" to creation as she wants, it might eventually generate an awful lot of immensely powerful beings who resent being told what to do by a silly woman with shoulder-pads.] And ultimately, considering they've been abducted from their homeworlds by a harpy with a nose-stud, forcibly compelled to meld minds and possibly man-handled by giant bats, the kidnapped geniuses are an awfully passive bunch when seen in the TARDIS console room.

[We've got to say that she may have made a really big mistake in collecting Einstein. Her fiendish scheme relies on calculations connected with quantum theory. Not only was Einstein's mental arithmetic notoriously wonky - he was a brilliant theoretician, but don't let him do your tax returns - he spent the last thirty years of his career trying to find a way to avoid having to use this "voodoo" science. "God doesn't play dice with the Universe", he said, and whilst Relativity seems strange enough to most people, it's still counted as a Classical theory, almost impossible to reconcile to quantum mechanics. Steven Hawking's whole body of work is about trying to arrange a shotun wedding between quantum and relativistic physics. Anyway, everyone except the director of this story knows that Einstein refused to wear socks.]

To judge from what we're told, an asteroid composed of Strange Matter would be so dense and massive, Lakertya would orbit *it* rather than vice versa. And assuming that such an asteroid could remain in existence for longer than the duration of the new title sequence (which is doubtful), it would probably implode into a small black hole. If it somehow didn't, then it would almost undoubtedly have enough mass to pull any passing rocket toward it - along with the odd star - so the "delayed lift-off" that supposedly prevents the rocket from hitting the asteroid is immaterial anyway. Also please note that the Rani's desperate to launch her rocket at the time of a solstice, even though there's no relation between one and the orbit of an asteroid. While we're focused on science matters, fibre-optic cables - of the type that the Doctor uses to disarm the lethal Lakertyan bangles - don't conduct electricity.

[We could, if Dr Science had his way, continue in this vein for several pages. Trying to get the science right creates too many hostages to fortune, unless you really know what you're doing. The Bakers have got the "patter" right, but made crass errors with the basics that any schoolkid would know. So just one more, because it highlights the rod the Bakers made for their own back...]

The Doctor claims that the big mistake "he" (or rather the Rani) made in constructing the laboratory equipment was that he 'broke the Second Law of Thermodynamics'. The solecism aside - because it'd be like breaking the Law of Gravity - this ironically happens in a story that mentions the works of CP Snow. He said in his "Two Cultures" lectures, later his most famous book, that nobody could consider themselves truly cultured unless they knew some science as well as Latin and Beethoven, and - lo and behold - the example he gave was the Second Law of Thermodynamics. And as we saw in volumes IV and V, the Second Law was the one bit of science

Victorians and 70s arty types all knew about already. So getting this wrong would be dumb under any circumstance, but to do so in an adventure where you've claimed that Mel has voluntarily read Snow's entire catalog is just idiotic.

If the Rani at all expects that she's going to impersonate Mel, why leave the real one on the TARDIS floor so she can recover, wander free and potentially confuse the Doctor? Why not just kill the meddlesome redhead, or have the Tetraps dangle her paralyzed upside down in their lair? And unless we're to presume that an unseen adventure took place between this and "The Mark of the Rani", how does the Rani know Mel's characteristics (or even her name) to imitate her from the get-go? Because as far as we're shown or told, they've never met. Mel certainly doesn't know who the Rani is. Worse, Sarn bumps into Mel while fleeing the Rani's fortress, but the Rani - who's watching the escape on her monitor - later hasn't realized that Mel is out wandering free.

For that matter, before the Rani's equipment broke down and she decided to coerce the Doctor's help, how was she planning to give the Big Red Brain an understanding of time mechanics? She might've been planning to add her own mind to the Brain after all, but she certainly bitches enough about *not* doing this. And how, exactly, does the Rani activate the scanner of the Doctor's TARDIS and "see" through Urak's eyes? [This might be feasible if the Tetraps had demonstrated *any* level of telepathic ability, but they don't. It could be down to the Rani's technology, then, but we never see her fiddling with the console, and she seems to achieve this weird effect at the flip of a switch.]

The Rani "locks" the Doctor in her laboratory, but this uselessly only seems to affect one door, as Mel can waltz in easily enough from the outside. Then in episode four, the Rani decides that she might still need the Lakertyans as a labour force, and has the Tetraps fit them with deadly bangles. All right, except her entire timetable relies upon this 'solstice' thing - which is now imminent - and it's very hard to see what the Lakertyans can possibly do for her in that time. Basically she's got little to gain, other than providing the Doctor and his allies with a ready-made source of explosives. Besides, if she's confident that the indolent Lakertyans can't remove the bangles, why didn't she distribute these sooner, rather than faffing about with the deadly insects? And in neutralizing the bangles, the Doctor asks Mel for advice - even though she's supposedly a software expert, not an electrician. [Thus prompting fan jokes where the Doctor is continually asking "Mel, you're the computer expert - what's the capital of Nebraska?" and so forth.]

'Look out! They kill!' someone seems to shout about the Rani's deadly insects a split-second before anyone has actually dropped dead from them. Also notice how the panic gets going when the insects have done nothing but flit out of the globe, when you'd think the pleasure-seekers would first respond, "Oooo... pretty lights." And do the few insects that get out of the globe perish after biting someone, or do they fly away to the Lakertian countryside to breed? In which case, given the right conditions, Ikona's noble sentiments about his people finding their own way might've doomed them to extinction.

If only for the excuses Pip 'n' Jane would have contrived, Mel should have asked: "Why have you got a Scottish accent?" Do lots of planets have a Scotland?

Critique There comes a moment, in episode four, when the Doctor mentions Elvis. A lot of people had stopped watching by this stage, but those of us who stayed thought maybe things were about to improve. There's now a Doctor we can believe in, under the children's TV goofing about. He's someone who could *almost* pass unnoticed in England in 1987, and here seen in a world that looks like a quarry (of course), but *not* any quarry we've ever seen before, and with what looks at first sight like a very expensive castle built there. Sure, a lot of the worst features of this story are hangovers from the Saward / Colin Baker days, but there are also a lot of the innovations of that time, applied almost casually.

Watched with the sound down, this is more visually impressive than anything from the last five years. Moreso even than "Mindwarp" (23.2), this looks like a product of its time, and how *Doctor Who* should have been looking since Nyssa left. At least twice we have a clever edit between the threat of impending violence and a bang at the start of the next scene. All the digital jiggery-pokery is fine, and none of it fails to come off, which is a plus. (The interior of the Rani's TARDIS threatens to be a Mrs Farrell Moment - see 8.1, "Terror of the Autons" - but just gets away with it.) But it's what the people *inside* this box of tricks get up to that matters. That we can concentrate on this is

another plus - there's no wobbly sets or bad CSO to distract us, so we can turn our full and undivided attention to the script and the acting...

Oh well. It's not as if the writing credit for Pip and Jane Baker raised anyone's hopes unduly. And, to be fair, they've learned from their mistakes. Ikona gains some character from his not liking Mel to begin with, and his learning to trust *some* aliens is the nearest we get to an emotional core for the story. He gets to say a lot of what the audience is thinking, just as the Rani's impatience with this goofy little Doctor must have elicited a few cries of "here, here" at home. They must have realised, after the scenes with crewman Edwardes ("Terror of the Vervoids"), that viewers wouldn't buy Mel flirting. This time around, the Rani is contemptuous of everyone, is obviously lying when she claims to be dispassionate, and now has goons who talk back. She's also avoided landmines in favour of tripwires - a much more sensible precaution, and recognizes that (this being *Doctor Who*) a lot of people will be running from something and not looking where they're treading. And, hey, nobody turns into a tree.

So if we disregard the Rani's bonkers plan, and the apparent decision to have some of the most unspeakable lines of exposition ever at the climax, the story is simple enough to follow. What we miss in the rushed ending is that - in the space of four episodes - the Doctor has gone from confused clown to devious manipulator, and the story ends with him making the Rani do exactly what he wants. That's how it's going to be from now on. If anyone withstood the embarrassing first episode, they would have realised that things were only going to improve.

McCoy figures out how to play this role in front of us. We may not spot it, with all eyes on Kate O'Mara, but the gulf between those painful early scenes and how the Doctor persuades Beyus to make a stand is huge. He's not quite right yet, so bringing back a much bigger star as the focal point was a shrewd move. Not content with playing Mel more entertainingly than Bonnie, O'Mara fills the Doctor-shaped hole in this story for the first three episodes.

But then the Doctor mentions Elvis. Apart from priming us for "Delta and the Bannermen", it also prepares us for a series where Mel isn't needed. She's supposed to be our link to present-day Britain, but even back in 1987 she didn't seem like anyone the viewers would know (or would want to, if we're honest). The Doctor is now more of an identification-figure than the companion, and that's fundamentally wrong. Fortunately it will all change utterly in the stories to come, but this adventure may have helped to ensure that only a handful of us recognize that, even today.

Because fanboy thinking means that you *must* have a regeneration sequence, and a whole story about how the Doctor goes a bit mental before settling down. The public at large aren't married to this idea, and would have accepted a new Doctor who started off as he meant to continue, but for the sake of a few letters to *DWM*, we have to sit through this stuff. Mercifully, this is the end of that whole trend. When old things from the series return in Seasons Twenty-Five and Twenty-Six, they'll either be killed off completely or rethought from scratch. But before that, we have to first sit through the most excruciating single *Doctor Who* episode ever (yes, it's even worse than Episode Three of 4.5, "The Underwater Menace", episode three of 15.5, "Underworld" and episode two of 20.4, "Terminus" - all of which have *something* to commend them), and then three more that are just a bit silly but look pretty good with the sound down. Even then, the resemblance to that annoying kiddy series *Emu's Pink Windmill Show* is worryingly close.

The Facts

Written by Pip and Jane Baker. Directed by Andrew Morgan. Ratings: 5.1 million, 4.2 million, 4.3 million, 4.9 million.

Working Titles "Strange Matter"

Supporting Cast Kate O'Mara (the Rani), Donald Pickering (Beyus), Mark Greenstreet (Ikona), Wanda Ventham (Faroon), Karen Clegg (Sarn), Richard Gauntlett (Urak); Peter Tuddenham, Jacki Webb (Special Voices).

Oh, Isn't That..?
• *Donald Pickering.* You might remember him as Captain Blade in "The Faceless Ones" (4.8) or even as the corrupt prosecutor in "The Keys of Marinus" (1.6), but he's done other stuff, honest. Usually set in World War II.
• *Wanda Ventham.* She's of *UFO* notoriety, but was also the doomed Thea Ransome in "Image of the Fendahl" (15.3) and was the airport Commandant's secretary in - crikey! - "The

Faceless Ones". As well as appearing in every second episode of *The Saint* - or so it seemed - she was the *ingénue* in Amicus Films' 1968 classic *The Blood Beast Terror*, which starred Peter Cushing and had Kevin Stoney (3.4, "The Daleks' Master Plan"; 6.3, "The Invasion") in it too. We could explain what happens to her character, but you wouldn't believe it. She was Nick Courtney's love-interest in *Watch the Birdies*, in 1967.
• *Mark Greenstreet.* Probably wasn't in "The Faceless Ones" (but for all we know, he may have been a toddler wandering around Gatwick Airport when they were filming). He played both the leads in *Brat Farrar* and was in the wondrously ludicrous *Trainer* (which everyone here thinks was by Jilly Cooper but was actually the work of Gawn Grainger, TV's George Stephenson from "The Mark of the Rani"). He had one of the more fruitful auditions to become the TV Movie Doctor (see 27.0, "The One With The Pertwee Logo").

Cliffhangers Mel steps in one of the Rani's booby traps - which has previously been seen to turn people into skeletons - and screams as she's tossed through the air in a giant sphere; the Doctor hides in the slumbering Tetraps' lair, but they wake up hungry; the Doctor is added to the Rani's collection of genii, and the Big Red Brain becomes active.

The Lore

• Understandably, Colin Baker flatly refused to come back for one last story after his sacking. This was just too much to ask, although he said he had no regrets about his three years in the role. (His comment in his final appearance as the Doctor - in the *Tomorrow's World* quiz - was that he wished he had a TARDIS to go back and do it all again.) Pip and Jane Baker accordingly found themselves halfway through a story that was supposed to build up to a regeneration, and had to rewrite it to *start* with one. If you've been reading **The Lore** sections in order, you'll understand that the Bakers were - as far as scripts for a first story were concerned - the only game in town. Nathan-Turner believed that he could rely on them to deliver the goods without supervision. (Andrew Cartmel's memoir of this era, predictably, gives a different version: *Script Doctor* is an entertaining read but not always for the right reasons. We will be returning frequently to this very partisan account.)

• Stepping into the script editor's seat was - as we've just mentioned - newcomer Andrew Cartmel, a former IT consultant who had caused a stir with a script about phone sex. He had been involved in the Drama Unit's scriptwriting workshop. In fact, a lot of his "finds" as scriptwriters were from the same source. He had big ambitions for the series (in the job interview, he expressed a desire to bring down the Government with it), and saw it moving in the same direction that comics had been veering in the last five years. Indeed, his reading recommendations for series writers were IPC's *2000 AD* (the source of *Judge Dredd* and several others in similar vein), particularly Alan Moore and Ian Gibson's *The Ballad of Halo Jones*, and also Moore's *Swamp Thing* and *Watchmen*. One character from the latter - Dr Manhattan - was Cartmel's idea of what the Doctor was like.

• Nathan-Turner had other ideas, and told the press he was looking for a "true eccentric" as his new lead. This time around, with the recent unpleasantness in everyone's minds, the BBC insisted on auditions, screen-tests and rigorous interviews. One early front-runner was writer and performer Ken Campbell, whose adaptation of the *Illuminatus* trilogy ran for nine hours. He had a "roadshow" of unlikely performers, putting on shows that combined slapstick, satire and symposium. Star players like David Rappaport of *Time Bandits* fame and Sylveste (sic) McCoy of *Vision On* and *Tiswas* fame found work in other shows. Campbell's former leading lady Janet Fielding was less lucky, and after three years playing Tegan (see Volume V) and a few stage performances, more or less quit acting, later becoming an agent.

However, Fielding was asked in to play Mel and "Ms X" against the various auditioning Doctors. One of these was Chris Jury, then out of work as the series he'd been in - *Lovejoy* - had ended after one year. (Fortunately for Jury, it was revived a year after the plug was pulled on *Doctor Who* and became a big hit. He additionally wound up in a guest-starring role as Deadbeat in 25.4, "The Greatest Show in the Galaxy".) Andrew Sachs, still haunted by having played Manuel in *Fawlty Towers*, and then playing Father Brown on radio, also threw his hat into the ring. Campbell was very close to what Cartmel had in mind, but was too scary for the BBC bosses (but not as scary as Nabil Shaban was for Granada heads, which is how Campbell landed up playing *Erasmus*

Microman in a series created for Shaban).

• Clive Doig, once a vision-mixer at Lime Grove in the Hartnell days, and now a successful Children's TV producer, had worked with McCoy on three series. In *Vision On*, McCoy had played epeP, the person who lived in a mirror-world and did everything backwards (because they ran the film in reverse), to the accompaniment of Haydn's Clock Symphony. In *Eureka*, he was various characters in comic versions of the invention of various things. (As such, his photo appears in the same *Radio Times* with the painted cover for 20.7, "The Five Doctors" - and he's even wearing a straw hat!) In *Jigsaw*, McCoy and Rappaport had been the "O-Men" - lousy superheroes who turn up whenever six words with two "O"s are used. And so, Doig suggested McCoy - now trading as "Sylvester" - as the new Doctor. But could a man famous for banging six-inch nails into his nose be a Time Lord?

Well, he'd done *other* things as well. He was a member of the Royal Shakespeare Company, and straight roles had been written for him (the version of *The Pied Piper* performed in schools across Britain was created on his behalf). He'd been in a major feature film (the version of *Dracula* with Lord Olivier and Donald Pleasence), and a significant TV drama demythologising Scott of the Antarctic. He'd also done six months in *The Pirates of Penzance* - opposite Bonnie Langford, as it happens. Basically, and as we hope you're gathering, all that stuff with ferrets down his trousers was a side-line. He'd also been a presenter on *Tiswas* - ATV's chaotic Saturday morning series - in the late 70s. Edited video compilations make this series look rather ordinary, partly because it was so influential, but mainly because they omit the sense that it was all going to go wrong at any moment. (And usually it did, just not on camera. Imagine a kid's show that went from custard-pie fights to a clip of Sid Vicious murdering first "My Way", then his audience, from *The Great Rock and Roll Swindle*.)

By 1987, McCoy was at a crossroads. By day he was playing the comic stooge in *Knightmare*, a grim kids Sword 'n' Sorcery-themed gameshow, and by night he was the jester Feste in the RSC's *Twelfth Night*. Apparently, the night Nathan-Turner went to see McCoy perform in this is the same night Cubby Broccoli went to see the star, Timothy Dalton. (Imagine if they'd got their notes muddled up: Dalton as the Doctor we could cope with, but McCoy as James Bond?) One role McCoy had played at the Young Vic in 1986 is worth a mention, partly because it's been erased from the records for some reason, but mainly because it's a good indication of why McCoy should have been thought a worthy applicant. The Oxford Theatre Company's production of *The Caucasian Chalk Circle* had him as Azdach. The character is a mercurial dispenser of justice, champion of the underdog and instinctive maverick. McCoy ran amongst the audience playing the spoons in the encore, but in the play itself he was meditative and explosive by turns.

• It's obligatory at this stage to say that McCoy was born Percy Kent-Smith, grew up in Dunoon, went straight from school into a monastery, left it in the early 1970s, went to work in the City but got sidetracked by Ken Campbell's Roadshow and took the lead (and the character's name) in their play *Sylveste McCoy: The Human Bomb.* (Remember that William Hartnell's early films included *I'm an Explosive!*) We ought to say that it was actor Brian Murphy - later star of *George and Mildred* and now doing time on *Last of the Summer Wine* - who was on the box office and recognised him coming back several times. Murphy is said to have told Campbell, "We're playing at being nutters, but this guy's the real McCoy". It should be noted that it was Gary Downie - whose network of friends in the stage-dancing world would have mentioned if there were any tales of McCoy being difficult to work with - who suggested that someone who did so much slapstick could probably do stunts and all the running around that the part of the Doctor required. Consider it done.

• Kate O'Mara sent Nathan-Turner a postcard from the set of *Dynasty* saying how much she'd rather be in mud. She'd been playing Caress (Alexis' sister) for about a year and felt like a return to Britain and more theatre, but also a spot of telly here and there. The producer had accepted his fate to produce another year of *Doctor Who*, but had decided to become more pro-active whilst withdrawing from actively engaging his critics as before.

• Director Andrew Morgan had hitherto made HTV's near future Arthurian tale *Knights of God*, with a cast mainly made up of people that *About Time* readers would recognise (including Patrick Troughton, Gareth Thomas, etc). Morgan was recognised in the industry as a safe pair of hands, having been the unsung hero of many 70s BBC drama productions. His main decision - told as a

joke by Cartmel but a serious point - was that an alien planet shouldn't have recognisable trees. So the script's forests became yet-another-quarry.

• Keff McCulloch was engaged to one of the backing singers from Nathan-Turner's pantos: Tracey Wilson. She was the niece of Dolore Whiteman (who played Aunt Vanessa in 18.7, "Logopolis") and was chums with the producer thereafter. McCulloch had a varied background, including Pickettywitch, arranging albums for Rose Marie (she's one of those artistes who remains popular, despite nobody you know ever having heard of her), and a bit of work with David Bowie. At this stage, he was having to hire an Emulator for £90 a day.

• Cartmel wrote the audition piece for the new Doctor, with a slight nod to Alan Moore, and included a Thatcher-like villain and a speech about the Doctor's life being fragmented. (This would be recycled as Mel's farewell scene in "Dragonfire".) Morgan directed the screen-tests in mid-February.

• It appears that, what with Oliver Elms having been hired to make a swish computer-generated title sequence, the Bakers decided that the Doctor's face had to appear on screen *before* this was premiered. Hence the pre-credit sequence. Or maybe not: one version holds that they shot it as a gag-reel, but Nathan-Turner said "Brilliant! Let's use it!" Whatever the case, and for better or worse (mainly worse), it's the most quoted scene of the story. In the broadcast episode four title sequence, they experimented with the Doctor's face only partially appearing, but this freaked some kids out.

• The idiotic decision to put *Doctor Who* head-to-head with *Coronation Street* was Michael Grade's. Who'da thunk it? He calculated that nobody in Britain liked both series (see the accompanying essay for why this was wrong). The 7.35 slot had hitherto been the preserve of anything that went well after *Wogan* - the celebrity chat-show on three nights a week - and was 25 minutes long (like *Head of the Class* or *We've Got It Maid*). Meanwhile, after a serious shooting incident in the town of Hungerford, ITV had yanked *The A-Team* from the screens. Saturday Nights would, from now until the late 90s, belong to Cilla Black (see "The Faceless Ones"). Who knows what *Doctor Who's* ratings would have been against this?

• It wasn't just *The A-Team* that caught the backlash from the Hungerford incident - violent scenes in all children's and family programming came under scrutiny from people with too much time on their hands. A BBC *Panorama* documentary screened in February 1988 pointed the finger primarily at *Captain Power and the Soldiers of the Future* (even though the series hadn't actually been seen in the UK), but also at *Doctor Who*. Clips from this story were shown to illustrate its extreme and unsettling content. And they showed... Donald Pickering standing around looking stoic, and the Rani climbing over some rocks.

• We have to mention it: Andrew Beech, who had pulled the DWAS out of a financial pickle and bought a few items of memorabilia, was quoted in the press as not being too keen on the first episode. That the press deemed this newsworthy is the most significant fact. From now on, all coverage that isn't about the one or more of the *Doctor Who* feature film projects on the blocks is about how even fans hate the current series, and how the ratings are plummetting. It's odd that a show the tabloids insist nobody watches any more is worth that many column-inches, especially as "nobody" in TV terms is still three times the sales of even the bestselling tabloid. Anyway, Beech's credibility within fandom took a knock that same week (see **Why Did They Think We'd Buy Just Any Old Crap?** under 22.5, "Timelash").

24.2: "Paradise Towers"

(Serial 7E, Four Episodes. 5th - 26th October 1987.)

Which One is This?   Richard Briers plays Hitler (and loses).

Firsts and Lasts   This is the first story commissioned by script editor Andrew Cartmel (though it was John Nathan-Turner who opened discussions with writer Stephen Wyatt), so in many ways it's the real start of Season Twenty-Four and the McCoy era. It's also the first one for ages not to refer to any previous story.

Four Things to Notice about "Paradise Towers"...

1. This story has been reclaimed by a section of fandom, who've pronounced it almost a pilot episode for *The League of Gentlemen*. And, yes, it's easy to see traces of Tabby and Tilda (two "kindly" women who are closet cannibals) and the

Chief Caretaker in characters like *Gent's* Tubbs and Edward. So imagine how people reacted when *League* writer / performer Mark Gatiss wrote "The Idiot's Lantern" (X2.7) and included a disembodied being attempting corporeality and groaning 'Hungreeeee'. Anyone unsure what we're on about will just have to accept that the idea of an enclosed community of monomaniacal grotesques had more potential as a sitcom than as a *Doctor Who* four-parter. (And then you should look up *League* online, if only to see photos of Christopher Eccleston's appearance on the series, because he's dressed as we all thought the Doctor should look.)

2. And, like that story, this one got a lot of publicity for the stunt-casting. Richard Briers, the king of the middlebrow, claimed later that he took the part of the Chief Caretaker specifically to give himself an excuse to "act badly". It's actually hard to tell, though, as he gives almost the same performance he gave in *Ever Decreasing Circles*, and has given in everything he's done since. (Even Briers' "possessed" performance in episode four resembles his turn as a mafia boss in a dream sequence from the final episode of this sitcom.)

But in amongst so many, um, "rich" performances in this adventure, Briers hardly stands out from the other sitcom fugitives playing the older occupants. Simultaneously, the younger ones all seem to be straight out of stage-school, well-enunciated future-slang and all. The final result, tragically, is that the different species fighting spacewars in 1970s *Doctor Who* had more in common than the different cliques living in this one building.

3. The disparate elements of this world are each sorta-kinda plausible on their own terms, but it needs to be set at a remove from our own. This could've been achieved with music that says "we're following our own rules", like - just for example - *The League of Gentlemen's* gothic mambo soundtrack. Or even "The Mutants" (9.4) would have done. But Keff McCulloch gives us the sort of music 1987 viewers would have heard all day - especially if they were put on hold whilst phoning a big corporation, or were watching the selections from Oracle or Ceefax that took up hours of daytime TV back then. Most absurd is the "regional sports round-up" style theme for the Robot Cleaners. Amazingly, McCulloch's score was a last-minute replacement for another by someone else, and which was deemed far worse (see **The Lore**).

4. The infomercial about Paradise Towers turns out to be recorded on a CD. This is 1987, and nobody's got around to inventing CD ROMs yet, let alone DVDs. At last, a *Doctor Who*-predicted future that happened!

The Continuity

The Doctor This Doctor is a lot less stand-offish than his previous incarnation, and engages the people he meets with a willingness to listen, and an apparent desire to talk to them in their own terms. To an enquiring mind, he says, even rubbish is instructive. He sketches things that interest him. He also bemoans Mel for her lacking a "spirit of adventure".

[Here we must consider the degree to which this adventure is unplanned. On the surface, it appears as though the Doctor has innocently suggested he and Mel visit the luxuriant Paradise Towers, and she's agreed to appease her swimming fetish. However, we'll later see - in most of Seasons Twenty-Five and Twenty-Six, in fact - how this incarnation takes very deliberate trips to deal with evil-doers, and often doesn't inform his companion of such missions. Arguably, the trip to Paradise Towers could be the new Doctor flexing his muscles and "warming up" in his crusading, and he only starts going after bigger fish such as the Daleks (25.1, "Remembrance of the Daleks") once Mel is gone and he's got Ace at his side. Many of the *New Adventures* writers make a big deal of the fact that the Seventh Doctor knows he is destined to do Big Things, but the on-screen evidence, as we will see, is sparse and ambiguous.

[Still convinced that the adventure in the Towers is entirely unexpected? Then consider how the Doctor early on "wracks his brains" to remember details about the Great Architect, but later "spontaneously" knows all sorts of stuff about the Architect turning Miracle City into a slaughterhouse. That said, he does seem to be able to metally look up facts somehow, as we've seen in stories as diverse as 2.5, "The Web Planet"; 14.2, "The Hand of Fear" and X1.5, "World War Three". We'll see a lot of this in the next two years, notably his patchy and sporadic insight into the Cheetah People in 26.4, "Survival". But let's ask ourselves how the Doctor knows that Paradise Towers won some awards, yet allegedly *doesn't* know that it's fallen into such blight. Does he remember every single magazine article he's read? The difference between his personal experience and things he

just knows about is remarkably variable over the twenty-six years he spends telling us to find things out for ourselves. Mind you, if he *is* still President, he has the Matrix as his own personal internal Google.]

The Doctor is made an honourary Red and Blue Kang, and given a scarf with both colours to represent this.

• *Ethics.* When it appears that the Blue Kangs have won their contest against the Red Kangs, the Doctor doesn't say that the games are irrelevant, nor that the impending death of everyone in the building makes their lifestyle pointless. Instead, he just calmly suggests that they shelve their differences for the time being. Ultimately, the Doctor seems to end the unsustainable and grotesque lifestyles of three sections of community in Paradise Towers, although this is something of a side-effect of his dealing with Kroagnon and insuring everyone's survival. [Earlier Doctors would have jumped in with both feet and said, "This is wrong, you should live like___".]

• *Inventory.* His wristwatch is for telling the time, but his pocket watch for something else. [We don't know what, just yet.] He's no longer using his previous self's colourful brolly, but he keeps mislaying his new one, which is black with a curved wooden handle. He's also changed to the paisley scarf he'll favour from now on, and his pockets contain a hardback notebook and a pencil.

The Supporting Cast

• *Melanie.* Her devotion to swimming almost borders on the obsessive, as she remains eager to swim and laze in the Paradise Towers pool even after she's: been captured by big-haired, crossbow wielding amazons; separated from the Doctor; almost plunged to her death in an elevator; terrified near-witless by whatever's lurking in the basement; and nearly eaten by a pair of "sweet" middle-aged ladies.

For reasons best known to herself, Mel is wearing a polka-dot tail-coat over her swimsuit. Her manners remain immaculate, but in this case - considering the duplicitousness of some of the Towers residents - that's something of a liability. Mel is unimpressed by the "hero" Pex's physical prowess, but wants to believe in him. Nonetheless, she seems to deem his lying about his nobility as worse than people tying her up with shawls, prodding her with toasting forks and wanting to eat her. [In fact, Mel's moral rigidity, freakish memory and obsessive behaviour have led some to suspect that she's mildly autistic. Autism was recently rather fashionable in fiction, so maybe soon she'll be found to have synaesthesia, this year's must-have disability.]

The Kangs finally accept Mel as one of their number, but don't give her a scarf.

The TARDIS The Doctor evidently had to jettison the Ship's bathroom because it was leaking. [This isn't the calamity that American readers might be imagining, because 'bathroom' here just means a room with a bath in it. We're less prissy about talking about toilets, despite the egregious anachronism in X1.10, "The Doctor Dances". (They establish that the man fooling around with the butcher has an outside khasi, then show a metal bathtub hanging on the wall, *then* have Nancy use a phrase nobody here had heard in 1941: 'Can I use your bathroom?') We might also wonder if the discarded 'bathroom' was the one seen in 15.6, "The Invasion of Time", because that much water getting into the works really *could* have been nasty.]

The new hatstand is a horrid 80s chrome thing, and the Doctor here just puts his hat on the Time Rotor.

The Non-Humans

• *The Golmeries.* A species of flesh-eating octopi who reside on the planet Griophus, and have rather a nice swimming pool for their exclusive use.

Planet Notes

• *The Unnamed Planet That's Home to Paradise Towers.* [It's identified in an early script as "Griphos", and in an earlier version still as "Kroagnon", although that's hard to credit.] The sky seems blue-ish, and the gravity seems Earth-like but could be slightly lower. [This would be helpful if the Towers are as high as they seem.] Atmospheric pressure must be about right, with all those cans of fizzy pop and kettles being boiled. [And that's about it... sorry we can't be more helpful.]

History

• *Dating.* The Doctor talks about the Towers winning awards 'way back in the twenty-first century'. [He says this, however, while he and Mel are in the TARDIS and en route from who-knows-

when, so it's potentially a bit misleading if you're thinking that the story occurs well after that time. If we're looking for further evidence, the robotic Cleaners' design might provide a clue, as they're hardly any more advanced than the Servo Robot from circa the 2030s in "The Wheel in Space" (5.7) and not up to the standard of (say) the Mechanoids, circa 2200, in "The Chase" (2.8).

[Another sideways glance provides another hint, when it turns out Kroagnon has built lots of famous things on other planets but that the informercial has to tell the viewers what these were. So we can surmise that lots of planets have been colonised, but they don't have much to do with each other. This could put us in the same sort of period as "Nightmare of Eden" (17.4) - which occurs in the early part of the twenty-second century - as does, we might conjecture, the comic-opera uniforms of the authority-figures in both stories.

[However... we *also* know that the able-bodied men of this society went off to fight a war. The apparent age of the Kangs suggests that everyone arrived at the Towers - and the men went off to fight this conflict - no more than a dozen or at most 15 years before, at what the Kangs now call "Time Start". We know about one major conflict in this era, but it's a touch later than we're used to seeing for "Paradise Towers" in guidebooks (except for *The Terrestrial Index*). "The Dalek Invasion of Earth" (2.2) has humanity's home-world conquered in 2157, so if other planets near-by are attacked at the same time or thereabouts, we've got a good reason for why the women and children were left in safety on a remote planet, and the possible big leaps in robot design after-wards. Either way, you'd think the Towers residents would know more about whoever they were at war with, including pejorative nick-names. Yet there's not a sausage. Very odd.]

Prior to this time, Kroagnon - AKA "the Great Architect" - won awards for Golden Dream Park, the Bridge of Perpetual Motion and his 'master-piece': Miracle City. He initially refused to leave the latter and was finally forced out, but those who moved in were killed by various booby traps [or so it seems], because Kroagnon couldn't abide the 'mobile litter' (i.e. people) making changes after he'd got everything how he wanted it.

No wrongdoing could be proved, and space is a big place, so Kroagnon got more work. He similarly wanted to stop anyone using Paradise

Towers, but it appears that just before anyone's arrival, the Kangs' parents rose up and imprisoned him in the basement [unsurprisingly, see **Things That Don't Make Sense** on this point]. Kroagnon's fate was lost to history, but his body was apparently destroyed, and his mind kept alive in a mechanical apparatus. Since then, he's been perfecting a method of electroscopy that will facilitate mind-transference, and he finally uses this to take over the Chief Caretaker's body. [Kroagnon's choice of placing himself into a fat old man is curious, as he's been given any number of more promising specimens beforehand. However, he says that the other bodies 'weren't right', and (tellingly) that 'they couldn't understand', which might suggest the process is as much psychological as physical, and he needed to make the Chief *so* servile that his mind became receptive as a host for Kroagnon's brainwaves or whatever.]

Paradise Towers itself is a massive tower block that's 304 floors high, and each floor has its own "streets". Potassium Street is the only one named on screen [which might suggest that they're named after metallic elements, allowing for a vast expansion of the periodic table in future], and there are concourses such as Fountain of Happiness Square. The top floor is given over to a swimming pool - which is booby trapped with a yellow crab-like robot - but entrance to the Basement is forbidden on pain of death. There are express lifts between floors, and service lifts for the Caretakers. Megabotic Mark 7Z Cleaners equipped with 'bi-carbal scraping blades' are supposed to cleanse the building, but the Chief Caretaker has usurped these to murder people, out of a strange desire to feed his 'pet' (actually the bodiless Kroagnon) in the basement. At least some Towers apartments have XY3 standard issue waste disposal units.

Establishing shots show several similar towers in close proximity to the Towers. [The story plays out as if Paradise Towers is just a single structure, so quite what these other buildings are for is a mystery.] Phones in the Towers contain coinage bearing Kroagnon's name, and a 'Fizzade' machine dispenses (according to the Doctor) 'refreshing' cans of soda-pop.

Persons living in the Towers include the officious Caretakers, who live their lives by a Rule Book (yet simultaneously don't seem to know its contents very well, enabling the Doctor to trick them and escape). Regulation ZZZ overrides all other rules and regulations, and it's implied that the Caretakers must always obey the Chief Caretaker unless an imposter has usurped him. The Chief can authorize a 327-Appendix-3, Sub-Section 9 death, and this is deemed exceedingly nasty. It's implied he can also mete out death to his Deputy Caretaker, although this would involve more paperwork. The Rule Book allows condemned persons a Last Request. Regulation 13, Appendix 2 Final Conversation details an interrogation procedure, but this entails nothing more than the Chief shining a bright light in the Doctor's face and asking, 'Are you the Great Architect?' The Caretakers know all the numbers of all the regulations, and use complex designations as names. They salute the Great Architect by placing their hands, palm down, under their noses like a moustache.

The actual Towers residents (AKA "Rezzies") are older women who harmlessly knit tablecloths and have tea - that is, when the more predatory of them aren't luring hapless individuals into their apartment to become dinner. They have plans of the Towers and seem to be able to get hold of jewellery and knitting facilities without difficulty.

Also in the building are groups of young women - the Kangs - who've organized themselves in groups according to colour. There's Red Kangs, Blue Kangs and Yellow Kangs, the latter of whom are exterminated by the Cleaners. The Kangs play non-lethal games that involve out-maneuvering one-another and entering their rivals' 'Brain Quarters' [headquarters]. They like to spray graffiti [in English], and address themselves with names such as 'Fire Escape', 'Bin Liner' and 'Air Duct'. [Cumulatively, this is all a bit odd. The Kangs know how to spell and write their wall-scrawls, which suggests they were taught to read at some point. Yet they don't demonstrate any comprehension of their real names, as if (say) 'Fire Escape' is the only name the Red Kang leader has ever known.] The Kangs have pyramid-like arrangements of junk to conduct funeral rites around, sometimes designate their affiliation with bracelets, and tend to salute each other with 'build high for happiness' (the slogan from the Infomercial). They use complex salutes, such as the 'How-You-Do' and the 'Build High' version of "one potato, two potatoes". They seem to have had no difficulty getting colour-coordinated outfits in their size, despite puberty happening after they were abandoned. Like denizens of dystopias throughout 80s *Who*, they can get hold of hair-care products and weapons more easily than food.

[See 21.3, "Frontios"; 23.1 "The Mysterious Planet"; 25.2, "The Happiness Patrol" and of course 22.2, "Vengeance on Varos".] Their highest compliment is 'Brave and Bold as a Kang should be'.

The last resident of note is Pex, a physically fit, slightly dim lad who dodged the draft and smuggled himself into Paradise Towers, and now parades around as its self-appointed guardian. Yet he's generally cowardly, and the Kangs regard him as a 'scaredy cat', although he redeems himself by giving his life to blow up Kroagnon.

The Analysis

Where Does This Come From? It's common practice to say that writer Stephen Wyatt told Cartmel that this stemmed from J.G. Ballard's book *High Rise*, so everyone's gone off and found the bits that resemble "Paradise Towers" and accepted that was that. However, few people ask *why* Ballard, of all people, was suddenly thought a suitable "source". It's not immediately apparent why a series that had just featured Kate O'Mara whittering about Helium-II and killer bees would abruptly embrace the author of "The Assassination of John F Kennedy Seen As A Downhill Bicycle Race" as a mentor.

Well, let's recall that Ballard was suddenly respectable, after *Empire of the Sun* had been nominated for the Booker Prize (and by this time was being filmed by Spielberg), and his previous association with SF was quietly forgotten by the Sunday papers. He was now the nation's premier satirist of the suburban (after a close-fought battle with Victoria Wood: Ballard won by two falls to a submission). He was the bard of officialese, and as the nation slowly came around to his way of thinking, he was finally taken as seriously as he'd always wanted. (This process was accelerated by the public hilarity at the Government's "lightning response" to a radiation leak from Windscale power-station - renaming it "Sellafield" and opening a Visitor Centre.)

However, Ballard would always claim that his books were only mild exaggerations of things he'd observed about the thin veneer of calm over bourgeois England. And *High Rise* so closely resembles mainstream thought from the mid-seventies, it's debatable whether he should have been paid for it at all. In many ways, it's almost a soap-opera setting of the theories of historian / literary critic Lewis Mumford. Ballard's friend Brian Aldiss had been telling anyone who'd listen that Mumford was worth reading since the mid-60s. By 1987, people were very used to some of his ideas, even if they didn't know his name.

Architecture was tremendously fashionable and contentious in late 80s Britain. In colour-supplements, news programmes, even "Yoof" TV (that mysteriously fashionable trend of the late 80s, beloved of every TV executive but not the intended audience), you would find interviews with Sir Richard Rogers and reappraisals of Ove Arup and Le Corbusier. These were names to drop in conversations, back then. Angular, stylish, conceptually-challenging buildings made good television, and directors loved editing shots of the Lloyds Building (with its famous "inside-out" design) to electro music. Let us not forget that it was in items about Mies van der Rohe and his big glass towers that most people first encountered the term "Postmodernism". After all, when you think of "Modernism" as a movement, you might have a vague notion of James Joyce's influence, or Picasso, but a big rectangular concrete building says it so much more clearly.

And when you have people rebelling against this with "quotations" from earlier styles and playing about with the way a building does its job, you can see instantly what people mean when they talk about (nostalgic phrases, these) "discontinuous signifiers" and "incredulity towards metanarratives". Showing people film of a building with mock-Georgian eaves, Egyptian pillars and big glass walls showing the plumbing off - accompanied with similarly "sampled" music - makes it all make some kind of sense. The consensus was that old-fashioned Modernism (especially as most people encountered it), with its 60s high-rises and concrete office blocks, was a blind alley and we were well shot of it. Postmodernism is young, playful, sexy and you sound clever talking about it. And that was what Yoof TV was all about. Hence, a bizarre 1987 memory for anyone who saw it, a feature on Robert Venturi on *The Tube*.[22]

The low-cost public housing solution of the post-war years - concrete estates - were a massive improvement on the slums and bombed-out streets they replaced, but they created isolation, anomie and concentrations of deprivation. The facilities didn't work, and shopkeepers moved away. It didn't help that one of the most high-profile building programmes of the early 70s was tainted by a major corruption scandal, as John Poulson's "City in the Sky" in Newcastle went over-budget and those involved were tried and (in many cases) jailed. In another estate, the Broadwater Farm estate in Tottenham, North London, there were riots (this was rare enough to make headlines, about two years before this story was shown). It has recently been back in the news as a spectacular example of a transformation - indeed, the tide is turning back towards Modernism and buildings for public use, rather than show-offy monuments like Canary Wharf (X2.12, "Army of Ghosts") and the Swiss Re "Gherkin" (X2.0, "The Christmas Invasion"). But in 1987, it was a cliché that 60s concrete blocks actually *caused* bad behaviour.

... which is what Mumford had been saying since the 40s, actually. He didn't specifically mean 60s concrete estates, but he drew links between environment and attitude. It was part of a much wider concern with the uses to which we put our abilities, and how those uses then start to condition us. (He's got more in common with those gonzo cyberneticians we mentioned under 4.2, "The Tenth Planet" than with the usual anti-concrete lobby, whose main champions were Prince Charles, Sir John Betjeman and Hitler.)

The main problem these people (barring Hitler, obviously) had was that monumental buildings imposed a top-down system onto people, rather than emerging from the bottom up. Mid-century thinking had been all about big systems, from Freud to Stalin to BF Skinner (the leader of the Behaviourists, of whom we've spoken a lot in earlier volumes). These were now called "metanarratives" (or in foreign, *grands recits*) and we weren't supposed to like them now. First they got the trains running on time, next thing you know it was big gas chambers and Cultural Revolutions. So Great Architects who resent real people inhabiting their nice, clever buildings were a common figure of fun. (*Monty Python* had done it, and it led into a sketch about Freemasons. After all, Freemasonry had a lot of stuff in it about architecture, so a lot of people watching "Paradise Towers" made that connection too, but it's not really relevant. Many of this kind of guidebook will state it as fact, but Hyacinth Bucket is much more of a "source", as we'll see.)

Wyatt had hitherto made a bit of a splash with his TV play *Claws*, which was ostensibly about a cat-show but was *really* about rivalry between middle-aged women. Can you see where we're going with this? The whole subplot about the "Rezzies" is in keeping with much mid-80s comedy, especially to do with Northern women of a certain age. Victoria Wood made an art-form of it, but the real strides in making this mainstream came from Roy Clarke (op cit) and Alan Bennett. His world-view is crueller than is often supposed, and his current status as "National Treasure" has obscured how much suppressed anguish underlies the comic characters in his work. The then-recent film *A Private Function* is a tale of an attempt to secretly slaughter a pig during the immediate post-war rationing, but is really a sort of Yorkshire *Macbeth* about a passive-aggressive wife manipulating her weak husband. Where this connects with "Paradise Towers" is in the ostensible authority figures' attempts to constrain, and the manner in which apparently ordinary housewives subvert or ignore this. Every Sunday night since the Dawn of Creation, it seems, the same battle had been going on in *Last of the Summer Wine*. "Paradise Towers", *Claws* and *The League of Gentlemen* all spring from the same soil.

The feral kids (all right, the Kangs as seen aren't *kids*, but that's the idea), with their garbled language and oral history backed up with wall-paintings, come mainly from *Mad Max: Beyond Thunderdome*. However, that was at least partly inspired by Russell Hoban's gibberish-epic *Riddley Walker* (written in the garbled, half-remembered English that the post-holocaust clans speak). The Kang's "How You Do" ritual owes a lot to the dance moves to *Prince Charming* by Adam and the Ants. If you want, you could find references to Hansel and Gretel in Tabby and Tilda, and of course Freddy Kruger in the way the Kangs' parents killed someone in the basement and he came back as a ghost (see 23.4, "The Ultimate Foe"). And if we're thinking of British versions of teen anarchy, the two to mention are *Lord of the Flies* (which has itself hints of cannibalism, borrowed from Circe's island in *The Odyssey*) and the 1962 novel *A Clockwork Orange*, with its verbally inventive narrative derived from Russian. In the film version, as you probably know, the location work was mainly done on those award-winning estates around Chelsea when they were new and exciting - not the way they were routinely shown in the 80s, after rain and poverty had made them more like Soviet housing.

Wyatt's main concern in this and his later story (25.4, "The Greatest Show in the Galaxy") was the betrayal of optimism and the way idealists "sell out". Architecture had previously been for the people, whether the people liked it or not. Now it was for big corporations and moguls to stamp their egos on the landscape, like dogs spraying on street corners. Kroagnon is bad not because he's killing people per se, but because he's making people live by his rules and imposing his will so firmly that humans become an obstacle. Nobody looking around London, Birmingham or especially Manchester could entirely disagree.

A small piece of social history: Esther Rantzen's TV series *That's Life* was an uneasy but massively popular combination of social crusades, consumer advice, personal tragedies and vegetables that looked like genitalia (see 23.3, "Terror of the Vervoids", as if you weren't thinking it). As well as providing work for Adrian Mills after his performance as Aris in "Kinda" (19.3), it gave the world the noun "Jobsworth" - meaning a minor official who prevents people from doing simple things, on the grounds that it's against regulations and "more than my job's worth, mate". Rantzen instigated an award of "Jobsworth of the Week" and presented the winner with a satin-covered peaked cap - which may or may not have been the one worn by Ken Dodd in 24.3, "Delta and the Bannermen".

At the further end of this, a lot of people were citing - often without having read it - Hannah Arendt's essay on the way Nazi atrocities were allowed because they were so ordinary and routine. "The Banality of Evil" became something of a buzz-term, with people observing that the train timetables for extermination camps were the same ones used for public holidays. Hitler and Stalin became emblems not of pure evil (well, that too), but of bourgeois taste and conservative opinions allowed free reign. Blandness in art and lifestyle was the true harbinger of atrocities (or at least so people said when asked why they weren't happy to join the rest of the country in watching *Little and Large* and buying Dire Straits records).

But the *real* influence here, and one we'll be considering a lot, is Cartmel's favoured reading: comic books. Essentially, there are elements of *2000 AD* all through this story. The anal-retentive Caretakers - with their reeling off numbers with oblique-slashes - aren't just a form of bureaucratic silliness, they're entropy incarnate. (The best example, though, is in the *DWM* strip "Polly the Glot", in which nerdish aliens have a 'Grey Alert' on their spaceship.) The Chief Caretaker is fearful

of the Great Architect's return because Paradise Towers is almost the way the Chief wants it, meaning run by blind obedience to the rule-book. (Now that we've had a conscious and acknowledged reference to the vigorously-average character Max Normal - X3.3, "Gridlock", although most right-minded people were thinking "it's Mr Benn!" - *2000 AD / Doctor Who* crossovers are back in vogue.) If the resemblance to *Judge Dredd* wasn't clear enough, we have Pex as a comedy Rambo character who's 'sworn to put the world of Paradise Towers to rights'. All that's missing is the Umpty Candy (and we get that in 25.2, "The Happiness Patrol"). If we're generalizing, then control freaks and long fingernails are to Cartmel what possessions and flatulence were to Robert Holmes, or mercury and loonies called 'Bennett' were to David Whitaker.

Things That Don't Make Sense Everyone seems to notice the big age imbalance in this story - primarily that the Kangs are clearly women in their 20s when they're probably intended as teenagers - but the problem runs deeper than that. Some of the Caretakers look suspiciously *young*, and no explanation is provided why they weren't shipped off with every other male their age to fight for their country. Perhaps they were assigned to Paradise Towers by some sort of Selective Service Act, but this makes the entire premise of Pex and the Kangs even less watertight than it seems.

But the *real* curiosity is the relationship between Pex and the Kangs. Assuming he's about five years older than they are [but again, the casting of the Kangs runs counter to the script's notion of them as early teens], then at some point in the last five years, he must've been the only adult or even near-adult male interacting with them. Leaving aside the issue of whether Kroagnon or the Chief put bromide in the water, it's hard to see how a bunch of nine-year-old girls (however tuff) would have ignored a fourteen-year-old boy's offers of help and guidance. Compared to their stage of life, he would've been far stronger, taller and more experienced. So in this *Lord of the Flies* set-up, he could've built a power-base from this even if he was the fat kid with glasses and asthma. And depending on when the Kang warfare started, he would've been one Kang group's equivalent of a tactical nuke.

More worrying is the point many critics have raised, that the Kangs' parents were a bit daft in apprehending this psycho architect and locking him in a cellar with a device that's capable of transferring minds. It's not *quite* as silly as Horus' design for a prison for Sutekh [13.3, "Pyramids of Mars", which this story obviously has somewhere in its DNA along with 13.5, "The Brain of Morbius"], but it's still a bit of a problem, especially if this is set before 23.2, "Mindwarp", when such activities scare the willies out of the Time Lords. [And we'll revisit this "as prisons go, that's idiotic" notion two stories hence in "Dragonfire".]

As much fun as Tilda and Tabby's efforts to placate Mel might seem, they're also a bit pointless. After all, she first arrives at their apartment with her hands bound, so they could've just overpowered her from the start. Early on, Mel's claim to the Kangs that she doesn't 'have a colour' strains credibility, given she's wearing *that* blue outfit, and has *that* red hair. And after she swims in the pool, why isn't she shivering for the rest of the story? Because she's got no opportunity to change out of her bathing suit. Given the Towers are in such disrepair, Tilda and Tabby seem especially lucky to have their Pex-dashed door fixed by the time Mel returns in episode two. Then in episode three, the Chief Caretaker bribes Maddy with the promise that she can have their quarters; she accepts, apparently unconcerned that the former occupants have met a grisly end down the waste disposal chute. And how did the bulky Cleaner get its arm up the chute to grab them anyway?

In preparation for the final struggle, the Deputy Caretaker remembers that Corridor 75 on Floor 245 contains a secret emergency supply of explosives for dealing with 'pests'. All right, but what sort of 'pests' require explosives? They've got rats the size of elephants on this world, apparently. Besides, the entire scheme to position Kroagnon in front of an exploding door seems needlessly over-complicated - once he's been lured out of his headquarters and is slowly shambling around the Towers, it'd be far simpler to just have the Kangs' best sniper pick him off with a crossbow bolt, explosive-laden or otherwise.

At risk of seeming trivial, why is Bin Liner not more prominent in the final scene? An urban myth has arisen that she vanishes altogether, and there was speculation that, like Steven in 2.8, "The Chase", she was hiding in the TARDIS to be revealed as a surprise new companion a few stories later. [By our count there are three Sontarans, a Cyberman and a 1920s police constable rattling around in there somewhere as well - see 15.6,

"The Invasion of Time"; 19.6, "Earthshock" and 19.5, "Black Orchid". Never mind fan-fiction, this is an RPG waiting to happen.]

And why does Pex have a mushroom tattooed on his neck?

Critique   Here's a good rule of thumb when reviewing the first few stories of a new Doctor. The first story is everyone running around like headless chickens trying to get it made, and the second story is usually something left over from the previous incumbent and just slightly redressed. The third adventure is usually an attempt to go in a direction that wasn't available before, and the fourth story is sort-of how things are going to be from now on.

But interestingly enough, within this framework "Paradise Towers" is an exception. However much of a stretch it might be to imagine "Doctor Who and the Silurians" (7.2) with Patrick Troughton, it's nothing compared to what's needed to conceive of Colin Baker in the Towers. Despite Wyatt having been approached before Cartmel was appointed script editor, this is often seen as unmistakably the kind of story that the last three seasons always did. It so obviously belongs to the phase of the series where its closest BBC drama stablemate is *Casualty*, with hindsight it looks almost routine. Thus, we forget how much this story makes for a startling change from "Time and the Rani" and Season Twenty-Three. Looked at as the middle of a loose trilogy - between "The Mysterious Planet" (23.1) and "The Happiness Patrol" (25.2) - its virtues seem more apparent.

In many ways, this is a rerun of the Ravalox incident, with girl gangs instead of Celtic warriors, little old ladies instead of skinny boys, and Caretakers and robot cleaners instead of Marb Station guards and the L3 robot. The pull back from the Doctor on a monitor to the revealed villain in his lair is almost identical. (Although, as one of these malefactors is a huge robot, and the other is Richard Briers dressed as a competitor in the SS Ice Dance finals, it's forgivable if you didn't make that connection.) It's all so simple when it's pointed out, so why does nobody immediately think this? Well, it's because Nicholas Mallett has seen where he went wrong since he directed "The Mysterious Planet", that's why. He's turned down the lights, made the camera a participant in the action and above all used the script as a springboard, not a straitjacket.

That script, however, has a *big* flaw. Whilst it

has better dialogue, more witty wordplay and characters with motives (however odd some of them are), it's pulling in two directions at once. Part of this script wants to be a sitcom about life in a dystopian high-rise, and to explore characters and situations arising from this premise. The other half wants to be a traditional four-part narrative about zombies and a gathering crisis. This schism between a linear plot-driven drama and a character-led sketch-show is typically 1980s: writers Andrew Marshall and David Renwick managed it with nuclear-war gagfest *Whoops! Apocalypse* (the film version of which shows how emphasising the plot over the characters would have doomed the TV series), then two series of *Hot Metal*. So as a six-week comedy-drama with no real need to provide a definite conclusion - much less a happy ending - "Paradise Towers" could have worked. But the only way the BBC would pay for anything like that would have been to make it as *Doctor Who*. So this story was given four episodes opposite *Coronation Street*, and they have to include the Doctor and thus make everything all fall into place too quickly.

But it does mean they've also included Mel. She's the one doing all the exploring here, trying to find the pool and running into Pex and the predatory Rezzies. Unfortunately, Pex is sadly miscast. Howard Cooke was the only applicant who could handle the humour without playing it for laughs, but he isn't the meat-head Stallone / Schwarzenegger figure that the script needs. As with the very similar Nord in "The Greatest Show in the Galaxy", he has to completely lack self-awareness and try to inhabit a function in this society, even though he's woefully inadequate to this task. Cooke comes across as too clever to do this.

Mind, no discussion of erroneous casting can proceed without mentioning Richard Briers. If he'd played the part as written, he'd have been perfect. The Chief Caretaker is almost exactly the kind of character Briers had developed over the years, especially in *Ever Decreasing Circles*. He's content with the Towers as they are, save for a few odd Kangs messing the place up, but the Great Architect threatens to take it from him and change things. That's this character's motivation, and it's the kind of cheery anal-retentive petty official we all know, taken to extremes. The whole point is that he's not so much a monster, but instead exemplifies anyone who's reluctant to rock the

boat when things are going wrong.

But against all this, Briers opted to play the Chief as almost as bad a figure as the Great Architect, which not only robs us of the horror of the last cliffhanger (why should we care if one fascist steals the body of another?) but makes him a less credible leader for the other, more Trainspotterish caretakers. A similar problem affects the Red Kang leader. It's obvious that none of these actors has ever been anywhere near a council estate, but the *real* problem is why the Red Kangs treat Fire Escape as their head when it's obvious that Bin Liner is the alpha female. On paper, Julie Brennan has been given the prime role, but Annabel Yuresha grabs the subordinate part and steals all the scenes.

Watching this in the context of British television, that's what *really* strikes us as odd. On screen, the scenes with Richard Briers and Judy Cornwell (as the resident Maddy) look like padding. (A similar problem afflicts the movie *Street Fighter*, which this story resembles in many peculiar ways.[23] We're supposed to be watching Raul Julia and Jean-Claude Van Damme, but everyone in the UK is waiting for Simon Callow and Kylie Minogue, and thinks this silly kick-boxing stuff is there to fill time.) Briers has taken the decision to over-act, and the other sitcom stalwarts follow his lead. The result is that the hungry newcomers are almost in a different programme to the grown-ups. In many ways, this is what a story like this needs - a sense of worlds colliding and antithetical tribes coming together.

But what it *also* needs is two more episodes to do this properly, but nobody would have put up with six weeks of this story even in the twenty-six-episode-a-year days. In short, this story should have been done in Season Twenty, before griping about housing was fashionable, before the Suspension made people forget that *Doctor Who* was intended to do this sort of thing, and before Janet Fielding left. Mel's lines are actually good, and what Langford does when allowed space is good, but the two don't quite match. When it's just her and the similar mis-match of Pex's character and Howard Cooke's version of the role, you really *want* one of the crap robots to bear down on them - if only so the painful music will drown out their dialogue.

Thelonius Monk said that writing about music was like dancing about architecture. As the Kangs do the latter, let's ponder just how bad David

Snell's rejected score could possibly have been for McCulloch's attempt to be deemed an improvement. About the only thing you can say in McCulloch's defence - apart from this being a rush-job - is that it doesn't sound like any other *Doctor Who* story so far broadcast (except, of course, "Time and the Rani"). It's not just that the score is intrusive and repetitive, but that so much of it is simply wrong for the visuals. You could argue that the music is so clearly of its time that it spoils the effect of making a TV play in a style we became more used to in the 90s (with a constantly-moving camera and lots of high angles), but it all seemed terribly wrong in 1987. Some of McCulloch's music in other stories make a virtue of finally sounding like the same year as the rest (the next one, "Delta and the Bannermen" plays with the anachronisms by juxtaposing pastiche Shadows against stuff very like what Prince was doing in his prime, a couple of years either side of 1987). This story suffers from sounding like everything else on telly that night. More damagingly, it seems almost to overdo the "look at that!" stuff to the point where it's like someone saying "Wow!" in a sarcastic tone of voice. Turn off the sound, and "Paradise Towers" looks very 90s. With the music it's October 1987 - not a good time for music in any case.

But even if the mix isn't quite right, the ingredients are finally all there. If you watched "Paradise Towers" during the aftermath of a hurricane and stock-market collapse in late 1987, it was clear that the series had turned a corner. Now, almost two decades on, it looks like a bold experiment. It seems more like *Doctor Who* than the entire previous year, partially because of the sudden absence of all the references to old *Doctor Who* stories. Significantly, Cartmel's stable of writers all stopped watching around 1980 and are attempting to recapture their collective memory of what the series was *like*, not what the guidebooks say happened in old stories.

The Facts

Written by Stephen Wyatt. Directed by Nicholas Mallett. Ratings: 4.5 million, 5.2 million, 5.0 million, 5.0 million.

Working Titles "Paradise Tower"

Supporting Cas Richard Briers (Chief Caretaker), Clive Merrison (Deputy Chief), Howard Cooke (Pex), Julie Brennon (Fire Escape), Annabel Yuresha (Bin Liner), Brenda Bruce (Tilda), Elizabeth Spriggs (Tabby), Judy Cornwell (Maddy), Catherine Cusack (Blue Kang Leader), Joseph Young (Young Caretaker).

Oh, Isn't That..?

• *Richard Briers*. He was familiar to TV viewers from two different types of programme. In sitcoms, he had been the unctuous middle-class drop-out Tom Good in the hugely-popular and endlessly-repeated quasi-utopian *The Good Life* (called *Good Neighbors* in North America, and by 1987 widely-perceived as the last word in BBC Twee). More recently, he was the unctuous middle-class anal-retentive Martin Brice in *Ever Decreasing Circles* (the fourth series of which began the day before "Paradise Towers" episode four was broadcast). For those who were kids in the seventies, he was the narrator of jittery cartoon series *Roobarb and Custard*, plus other more sedate animations. He's concentrated on stage work more recently (specialising in Alan Aykbourne) and "mad old man" parts in series such as *Monarch of the Glen*. (He also did a lot of advert voice-overs, but not as many as people think: half of them at least were Terry Molloy doing his Briers impersonation.)

• *Brenda Bruce*. She'd been in *Connie* and was Bertie Wooster's nice Aunt Dahlia in *Jeeves and Wooster*. She was also a devious Madame in the fondly remembered Colin Watson adaptations televised as *Murder Most English*.

• *Judy Cornwell*. Yet another regular from *Keeping Up Appearances*, where she played Hyacinth Bucket's sister. More amusingly, she appeared in Anthony Newley's 1969 egotrip *Can Hieronymous Merkin Ever Forget Mercy Humppe and Find True Happiness?* as a character called "Filigree Fondle".

• *Clive Merrison*. Since his last *Who* jaunt (with ill-advised accent) as Jim Callum in 5.1, "The Tomb of the Cybermen", he's been busy. Notable TV appearances include the Shakespearian magician Hathaway in the BBC's 1992 adaptation of *Archer's Goon*. He's been the most industrious of all the radio Sherlock Holmes, and scored a hit on stage, screen *and* radio as the headmaster in *The History Boys*.

• *Elizabeth Spriggs*. She'd specialised in playing eccentric and / or severe old women at least as far back as *Fox* and *Shine on Harvey Moon*, and more recently in *Martin Chuzzlewit* (as Mrs Gamp) and

Taking over the Asylum. (The latter was a show about a hospital radio station with a difference - and guess what the difference was. A promising youngster called David Tennant was in it, and stole scenes from Ken Stott and Spike Milligan.) "Paradise Towers" coincided with her starring role in the BBC children's series *Simon and the Witch* (hint: she wasn't Simon). She co-starred with Cilla Black and David Warner in a bizarre obscure drug-themed comedy film *Work is a Four-Letter Word* circa 1966. Later she was the Fat Lady in *Harry Potter and the Philosopher's Stone*, and she was Bertie Wooster's nasty Aunt Agatha in *Jeeves and Wooster*.

Cliffhangers The Caretakers hail the Doctor as the Great Architect returned, and the Chief Caretaker then declares that they should kill him; the *real* reason Tabby and Tilda have been plying Mel with cake is revealed, as they net her in a crochetwork shawl and approach her with toasting forks; in the basement, the Great Architect possesses the Chief Caretaker while a robotic Cleaner tries to strangle the Doctor.

The Lore

• Stephen Wyatt came to television via the BBC script unit and sending spec scripts to BBC producers. In 1985 he'd written *Claws*, which was intended as a pilot for a comedy-drama series about schisms in a cat breeders' club, but was ultimately made as a one-off play for BBC1. This had garnered a lot of interest in the industry, and thus Wyatt discussed ideas for *Doctor Who* with Nathan-Turner before Cartmel's arrival. The new script editor wasn't impressed with the story Nathan -Turner had asked Wyatt to develop, and "Paradise Towers" emerged from further discussions. *Claws* was eventually broadcast on Sunday, 4th of October, 1987, the day before "Paradise Towers" episode one.

This was also the week a hurricane hit southern Britain, whilst a devastating slump in share prices (caused by the so-called "Big Bang" we mentioned earlier in this volume) was unchecked as dealers were unable to get in to work. The long-term consequences of this concatenation of events will play out over the remainder of this book, and look at the abrupt dip in the ratings for the first episode.

• Wyatt's script specified that the Chief Caretaker would be an elderly man in a shabby

version of a South American dictator's costume. The decision to give him a Hitler-moustache was made in production. Wyatt was reputedly unhappy that the Caretakers included a number of young, healthy extras, as he'd imagined them as decrepit old men. Wyatt later regretted killing off Tilda and Tabby so early on (and Brenda Bruce and Elizabeth Spriggs were keen to return in a later story) and proposed a sequel about the Kangs escaping from a boarding school to search for their brothers. Cartmel expanded on the Cleaners - only a minor element in the original storyline - as the requisite "monster" for the serial. Director Nicholas Mallett pulled out of a German-made mini-series by Pip and Jane Baker to work on *Doctor Who* again (so many possible comments we could make...). A recurring problem was that the costumes and sets were too clean, and needed to be dirtied up for recording.

• Edward Hardwicke was originally cast as the Deputy Chief Caretaker but found himself committed to another project; he was then a familiar face on British television from playing Watson in Granada's *The Return of Sherlock Holmes*. Philip Jackson and The Who's Roger Daltrey had also been invited to try for the role. (What *is* it with directors and Roger Daltrey? Graeme Harper wanted him as Sharaz Jek in 21.6, "The Caves of Androzani" and the DJ in 22.6, "Revelation of the Daleks", and for all we know Daltrey was the other person who auditioned to play Mel.) Richard Briers was equally unlikely casting for a part that had also been offered to sinister and heavyweight performers such as Ian Richardson, Ronald Lacey and T.P. McKenna (see "The Greatest Show in the Galaxy").

• Julie Brennon (Fire Escape) was then the wife of Mark Strickson (see 20.3, "Mawdryn Undead" et seq.), and Nathan-Turner had wanted Mrs Turlough to be in the series for ages. Catherine Cusack, as the Blue Kang Leader, was a member of the Cusack acting dynasty. (Remember Cyril Cusack from our list of people Verity Lambert approached before getting Bill Hartnell to be the Doctor?) She hadn't acted before (so an Equity card was hastily arranged), and she became famous as Carmel, the psycho babysitter in *Coronation Street*. Joe Young (as the Young Caretaker) also came to *Doctor Who* through family connections, as his parents were friends of Nathan-Turner. Young later cropped up in various BBV audio dramas, including as Guy de Carnac in a spinoff from David McIntee's *New Adventure* book *Sanctuary*.

• The only location work was for the swimming pool scenes, taped at Elmswell House in Chalfont St Giles in May 1987. This was owned by an Arab sheik, and had been left empty for months. The indoor pool wasn't heated, and both Bonnie Langford and her stunt double Ellie Bertram - who was Mel in the sequences where the pool cleaner attacks her - were kept warm between takes by hair-dryers. The BBC technicians later announced that they'd found a shower that worked, which would have made her day go better had she known. Though the pool scenes were restricted to the final two episodes, a good proportion of the cast and extras were needed for the OB taping.

• During the production of this story, McCoy and Langford appeared in costume outside BBC Television Centre for publicity shots of children from Tadnell Middle School, Portsmouth, cleaning the TARDIS police box prop. It was part of an annual car-wash for charidee involving schools nationwide.

• The Paradise Towers prospectus was comprised of stock footage from heavyweight Australian art-critic Robert Hughes' groundbreaking documentary series *The Shock of the New*. Mallett had arranged this specially with the series' distributors, then found there was less useful material than he'd hoped, and the chosen shots had to be doctored with video effects.

• David Snell was initially commissioned to score the serial. No one is entirely sure why it wasn't used, and by all accounts his work for episode one was effectively dramatic and atmospheric. The official account is that the complete score was monotonous, repetitive and "too intrusive" - so they hired Keff McCulloch instead. Go figure. Snell was understandably upset, but has since acquired a successful career as a conductor of film music. McCulloch's replacement score for episode one was written in three days. (And here we refrain from further comment.)

• "Paradise Towers" was caught up in the backlash against media violence following the Hungerford killings of August 1987. The scenes of Mel being threatened by everyday kitchen items - though cleared for broadcast - drew a couple of complaints. In the sensitive climate, this led to close-up shots being deleted from the version offered for sale abroad. (Because, of course, German and Australian viewers would be upset by any reference to Hungerford... hang on, run that by us again...) The order for this came directly from Michael Grade, in what must've been one of his last acts as Managing Director of Television at the BBC (see "Dragonfire" for where we go from here).

• In her recently-published autobiography, Elizabeth Spriggs (Tabby) confesses to not remembering much about the recording, but mentions it anyway for fear of fan reprisals. Her main anecdote is of complaining that her costume made her look like a tea-cosy, and Dickie Briers saying something like, "You think *you've* got problems?"

24.3: "Delta and the Bannermen"

(Serial 7F, Three Episodes. 2nd - 16th November 1987.)

Which One is This? The tabloids and the production team called it "Hi-De-Who": Mel goes by time-travelling charabanc to a 1950s Holiday Camp. Not much of a holiday, but very camp. The Doctor dances and Mel meets a Llanelli child[21].

Firsts and Lasts It's the first three-parter since 1964 (see 2.1, "Planet of Giants"), and also the first one to be *scripted* as one (unless you count 22.4, "The Two Doctors", and nobody does). It's also the first story to be entirely made in Wales (almost; see **The Lore**). It's the very last appearance of those helmets they've been using since 19.6, "Earthshock". For the first time since "The Dalek Invasion of Earth" (2.2), the companion gets to wear blue jeans. And speaking of fashion, from now on the Seventh Doctor's umbrella handle will have a red plastic question-mark on it. (For goodness' sake!)

Three Things to Notice about "Delta and the Bannermen"...

1. Introducing Ray, the Sam Briggs of the 80s (see 4.8, "The Faceless Ones"). In the first run of children's TV spin-off series *Totally Doctor Who*, they had a feature called "Companion Academy", wherein ten-year-olds have to do a lot of things a TARDIS crewmember would be expected to do, and the one who comes last each week is eliminated. (*DWM* editor Clayton Hickman served on this as a sort of cuddly Simon Cowell.) Weirdly,

with benefit of hindsight, Season Twenty-Four looks a lot like that. Everyone knew Bonnie was going as soon as she could, so suddenly we have these pert young girls popping up to aid the Doctor.

First there was Sarn (who was bumped off as soon as it was obvious that Mel was staying) in the season-opener, then Bin Liner in the world of Paradise Towers, then Ray in this story and finally Ace in "Dragonfire" (24.4). Readers of Virgin's *New Adventures* might want to take a moment and ponder what these could've been like with Ray as the companion. (Hmmm... a "mature" version of *Doctor Who* with an odd-looking Welsh bint as the sympathy character. Maybe not such a good idea.) And those of you who need subtitles to figure out what she's saying might want to imagine two years of Sara Griffiths and Sylvester McCoy. Instead of already-dated early 80s teenspeak, we would have had the catch-phrase 'He was i-i-ionised!'

2. Oh look, it's Keff McCulloch with a *really* anachronistic pony-tail, and his chums Tracey and Jodie, accompanying Billy onto stage for the dance in episode one. At least once in the last couple of stories, music has been featured that the Doctor and company could have heard in addition to the viewer, but now this comes right to the fore. This happened before when Gerry Davis was story editor (3.8, "The Gunfighters" to 4.9, "The Evil of the Daleks"), and in Seasons Thirteen and Fourteen. (The last time the series' principal composer made a guest cameo, in fact, was 14.6, "The Talons of Weng-Chiang".) But here, this story's use of music from the period - or covers thereof at least - includes appropriate radio theme-tunes and singing Redcoats... sorry, Yellowcoats.

The "fictional" music score is also in period, and the two sources of music cross over, especially towards the end of episode two. Anecdotally, people watching this on first transmission looked at each other when a particular radio theme - *The Devil's Galop* - was briefly quoted, and said: "They wouldn't dare." (See **Where Does This Come From?** for what that tune meant to two different generations.) Seconds later, when it came back in full force, everyone watching had to decide if *Doctor Who's* creative drought was finally over, or had become terminal.

3. If it helps you make up your mind, watch the scene of the Tollmaster's death. Normally we keep comments on the guest-stars for **Oh, Isn't That..?**, but seeing Don Henderson as a Spaghetti-Western

desperado arrive in a spaceship and shoot Ken Dodd was simultaneously bizarre, funny and (for many people watching) a sign that the right people were making the series at last. In trying to conceive of an equivalent for American readers, the best we can come up with is Peter Falk as The Man With No Name shooting a Borscht-Belt stand-up who's dressed as Ziggy Stardust. This is, however, an inadequate measure of how odd it looked to us in 1987.

The Continuity

The Doctor Evidently has a price on his head, one that the bounty hunter Keillor thinks he can claim. [It's never specified that the reward is offered for *this* Doctor, however, so the bounty could've been posted at pretty much any time in his past or future.] While staring down the barrel of Keillor's gun, the Doctor doesn't beg for his own life, but does ask Keillor to let the similarly threatened Ray go free. Once Gavrok disposes of Keillor by remote [but see **Things That Don't Make Sense**], the Doctor comments that Keillor's death is: 'A poignant reminder that violence always rebounds on itself.' [This might well be viewed as this Doctor's new motto.]

• *Ethics*. Whilst advocating or employing fairly inoffensive methods to ward off the Bannermen, he isn't entirely heartbroken when Delta shoots one and Gavrok (the Bannermen leader) blows himself up. He's concerned about Billy's abrupt decision to ingest alien goo and turn himself into a Chimeron-human hybrid, but does nothing to stop him going through with it.

• *Background*. The bounty hunter Keillor recognises him [and not just by reputation, so he's possibly seen a photo], but Gavrok doesn't. The Doctor seems familiar with Chimerons, Bannermen and Navarinos. He's also apparently seen at least one episode of *Rawhide* [hence his shout of 'Head 'em up! Move 'em out!' in episode three]. He can handle a Vincent motorcycle with sidecar [a different proposition to all the motorbikes he rode in his third life] and seems to have taken jive lessons. He knows his honeys, and seems a big enough cheese in wherever these aliens all come from to offer Gavrok some hope for leniency, offering to testify on Gavrok's behalf if he lets his prisoners go. [As Gavrok could face trial on a charge of attempted genocide, it's suspect how much this could help, because even the

What are the Oddest Romances in the Programme's History?

In "Delta and the Bannermen", the Doctor tells Billy, 'Love has never been known for its logic'. Certainly in *Doctor Who*, the absence of any kind of plausible motivation for why people get together is matched only by the odd relationships you see in real life. Abrupt cast-changes, writers who've not seen the programme before and producers who aren't sure what they can show in a family series have all caused baffling romances, often right out of left field and a total shock to the actors playing the roles. What follows, then, is just a handful of egregious instances from the classic series.

• **Billy and Delta.** We're tempted to echo the Doctor's comment in "Rose" (X1.1). Billy and Delta are doomed because: 'It'll never work! He's gay and she's an alien.'[27] Billy doesn't just fail to respond to Ray's charms, he's completely oblivious to girls. It has been noted that young men with mildly slicked-back hair tend to be confused about these things in *Doctor Who* (as part of an overall semiology of hairstyles in the series that should have its own essay, but we ran over the word-count for Volume V), but that really oily barnets are a sign of lost innocence. The trouble is, when and how did Billy change?

Because the story focuses on his ingestion of the green goo *after* he's already smitten by Delta, we never spot that this wide-eyed yokel has fallen for an alien he hasn't actually spoken to yet. She's politely tolerant of him sitting at her table, which he does because it's the only free seat. He can't think of anything to say, and he seems more interested in her immaculate overalls than anything else. She smiles. It could be a polite, embarrassed acknowledgement of his presence, but it looks somehow... predatory. We don't know what happens next, but he dedicates a song to her and she stomps off, coldly determined. Then Billy turns up at her door, which means that he's fraternising with a guest (a sacking offence), out after hours (a sacking offence) and finds out that a single mother has got onto the premises (which he doesn't report, a sacking offence). And he's obtained flowers (from somewhere).

Think about it. Flowers... for a Queen Bee. Seen in this light, with Delta desperate for a drone to impregnate her and continue the species, the use of scent may be significant. Let us not forget, Billy doesn't run screaming from the Chimeron baby, and automatically accepts that there's a single mum in a holiday camp in 1959. In fact, he accepts a *lot* that even the average twenty-first century motor mechanic would find hard to swallow (as the BBC Wales series has proved, at length). For a lad from 50s Wales (not that he sounds local), it would be strange enough that middle-aged people were wearing Teddy-Boy clothes. So let's stop beating around the bush and name the obvious explanation for his suddenly amorous behaviour: Delta is giving off mind-altering pheromones. *That* is why fools fall in love.

There's all sorts of unpleasant possibilities concomitant on this. Some species of insects eat the males after insemination. Others fuse with them, using the genitals as a reservoir of DNA but biting off the head to stop the bloke resisting. If human-Billy was a suitable match *before* taking in the green goo, then the Chimerons must be able to mate with anything. Perhaps Delta is upset, then, because the goo will change him too much to be edible. Still, there's a half-dozen Bannermen left on the ship if she or the Princess get peckish or randy.

• **Jo and Cliff (10.5, "The Green Death").** Traditionally, boy meets girl, they have a fun time together (unless it's a TV adventure show, in which case they have a fun, exciting and *life-threatening* time together), fall in love, kiss, get engaged and then have a big party. The iconoclastic Welsh genius Professor Cliff Jones would never be that bourgeois or predictable, however. Despite his winning chat-up lines ('You clumsy young goat, you've contaminated my spores!') and Jo's coquettish ripostes ('The ambient temperature suits me just fine, thank you'), this is not a straightforward romance. Cliff doesn't kiss his girlfriend until after the engagement party is well under way. He also told everyone about the honeymoon up the Amazon before proposing to Jo, and in fact made the travel arrangements before he met her. Meanwhile, she's besotted with him without knowing what he looked like, and risked losing her job and being court-martialled in order to run off and be with him.

Surely, this was true love, as neither the lithe young lady who tied herself in knots during dinner-parties, nor the sensible Earth-Mother Nancy appears to have turned Cliff's head beforehand. Everyone knew their relationship was meant to be - even Jo's uncle in New York, who somehow arranges in record time that Wholeweal is going to

continued on page 195...

Doctor can't wriggle out of that. Oh, wait, he did, last year.]

The Doctor hasn't seen many examples of cross-species breeding working out well, and warns Billy that his mating with the Chimeron could lead to all sorts of mutations.

The Supporting Cast

• *Melanie*. Claims to have never won anything before. She knows all the words of "Rock Around the Clock", and not just the chorus like everyone else on the bus. Judging by the hurried decision to join the Navarino 50s tour, Mel can pack a suitcase in record time. [And this item of luggage is, apparently, a TARDIS-like reticule - containing far more clothes than seems feasible.] Mel has the same dress-size as Delta [as we discover when Delta needs a change of clothes; as Ray would say, "there's handy, isn't it?"], and by a similar quirk of fate has packed a white frock with green polka-dots.

In this, her second-to-last televised story, Mel finally wears something vaguely like the viewers might have worn or seen other people wearing. She looks like she means business when she trains a gun on a surviving Bannermen.

The TARDIS Not so powerful that it can avoid being pulled to the Toll-Port [see **History**], but it enables the Navarino time-bus to survive a plunge to Earth when the Doctor reroutes the 'vortex drive' to create 'an anti-gravity spiral'. [Not only is this something of a pre-cursor to the gravity-can-celling field the TARDIS generates in X2.9, "The Satan Pit", it's interesting for several reasons. One is that the Doctor can only do this by operating console switches on either side of the navigations controls, which doesn't seem a terribly efficient design. (He taps one switch with his foot, like Jerry Lee Lewis, and the other with his umbrella.) Also, he must do this because the Nostalgia Trips bus hits a low-orbital satellite. This means the bus was in normal spacetime, and the time-travel element is over before they arrive in Earth orbit, so the collision affects their transponder.]

The Doctor keeps a spare Quarb crystal in his Ship, and says it's the only such crystal 'this side of Sophtel Nebula'. When *this* crystal is also broken, the Doctor accelerates growth of a new one in the TARDIS' 'thermal booster' and generates a new crystal in 24 hours.

The Non-Humans

• *Chimerons*. They're are a bit of a puzzle, frankly. Gavrok's forces appear to devastate their homeworld, but mention is also made of a 'brood planet' where the Queens mature. Delta looks human [either owing to the fact that she's a Queen, or maybe *just* because she's female], but the male Chimerons seen here are green-skinned humanoids with blobby, undefined mouths. [With the apiary motif running through this story, we may be best thinking of these as "drones".] They're wearing what looks like helmets, but could be bony extrusions.

The Chimeron offspring seen here hatches from a spherical egg. [These look worryingly like Sontaran spaceships.] The child is also green-skinned to begin with, bearing a huge bulbous head and a comparatively tiny body, like the Mekon from *Dan Dare*, appropriately. Within hours the child is still green but starts to look like a human baby, and seems generally covered with a hexagonal pattern of ridges. [Provided you can detach yourself from the sight of a real-life baby in a sort of "alien" coverall, it's never clear whether this *is* a form of clothing or skin. Delta seems able to remove hers, but Billy gets one when he trans-forms, so maybe there's a tiny jump-suit dispenser in her handbag.]

The green goo [apparently akin to the "royal jelly" that bees make] that Delta feeds this "Princess" from a syringe helps the child boost her energy for the rapid-fire changes that she here undergoes. In quick succession, the "larva" becomes rapidly taller, more nordic-looking and better able to protect herself. In the first stage of change, the sprog can double her weight in an hour. Then in "The Singing Time", she visibly grows taller in seconds, and emits a vocal chord that shatters windows and repels the Bannermen. Delta never demonstrates a comparable ability [suggesting it fades with maturity]. Chimeron Queens have augmented hearing via scaly / shiny protrusions behind the orthodox ears, and these apparently enable Goronwy's bees to loosely com-municate with Delta.

[We should say that the name "Chimeron" sug-gests hybridity. Under "The Two Doctors", we mentioned the word 'chimaera', and this has been a thread running through a number of stories late-ly. This could explain how Delta accepts the human Billy as the possible progenitor of a new generation, against all apparent logic. It's also curi-

What are the Oddest Romances in the Programme's History?

...continued from page 193

need UN Schedule One status and funding. Blimey, even the TARDIS seems to have known that it was time to look out that special gemstone for the occasion. And the Doctor's reaction? He tries to sabotage the relationship - and when that fails, he seeks solace in physical violence and cross-dressing (a classic "cry for help"), then picks up a bottle of booze and drives away really fast. Next thing we know, he's got himself a flashy new car (11.2, "Invasion of the Dinosaurs"). Textbook stuff, and a sure sign that he feels like he's been dumped. And to look at another angle from the same story...

• **Stevens and BOSS (10.5, "The Green Death").** Global Kemicals (as we will call them, because the *real* "Global Chemicals" made such a fuss that the novelisation for this story had to rename it "Panorama Chemicals") is a caring employer. It has facilities for torture and bondage, with chains hanging from the ceiling (unless it's an extreme crèche - maybe the brainwashed Ralph Fell plummeted to his death from the mother of all Naughty Steps). All the senior staff seem to have the keys to the Executive Dungeon, so they're obviously fairly open-minded (as far as zombie wage-slaves of a megalomaniac computer can be). So the Managing Director's complex domestic arrangements go almost un-noticed. Well, we say "domestic" but Stevens never actually goes home. His burly minder, Hinks, is permitted to smoke his suspiciously fat hand-rolled ciggies in the office. Neither seems to leave, except when Hinks is sent to fetch a maggot-egg. It has all the comforts of home, including a hi-fi unit that doubles as brainwashing equipment. And you thought the Googleplex was laid back.

Stevens may be indulging in rough trade activities with Hinks, but the love of his life is his BOSS. In a first for children's television, "The Green Death" provides us with an openly gay mad computer. ("Tim" from *The Tomorrow People* was not all that mad, really, just lacking in any aesthetic judgement.) BOSS has pet-names for Stevens ('My little ubermensch'), mis-quotes Oscar Wilde and speaks of his bonding with Stevens' brain as a wedding. Even his dying words are a paraphrase of the Wicked Witch of the West. And BOSS' wails and sobs at the end aren't anything to do with being destroyed, it's because he's been jilted at the altar.

• **The Brigadier and Doris (11.5, "Planet of the Spiders", 26.1, "Battlefield").** This one's peculiar, because the Doris we finally see in "Battlefield" is nothing like the Doris we hear about when the psychic "Professor" Clegg does his stuff in "Spiders". When we hear about Doris' past with the Brigadier on this occasion, it's described as a good old-fashioned 50s-style dirty weekend - they booked into a hotel in Brighton (presumably as "Mr & Mrs Smith", which is so traditional that the Doctor has a knowing look when he suggests using the name "Dr John Smith" in 7.1, "Spearhead from Space"). However, the Doris Lethbridge-Stewart who meets the Seventh Doctor is just too nice to give watches to soldiers, or to have ever been that kind of girl. In fact, she's not really the kind of lady to have the name 'Doris'. Nobody old enough to be called that would have that accent or those habits *and* the name. The 1974 model is clearly a 1950s good-time girl, and it doesn't appear that the older version ever was.

Then there's the Doctor's reaction. In his third life, he enjoys the Brigadier's embarrassment and observes that Clegg has uncovered a naughty secret. Yet why did the Brig hand over the watch at all if there was any risk of this coming out? And why be embarrassed in the presence of someone already on first-name terms with him, and who takes him to tacky working-men's clubs to watch exotic dancers? Later, in the middle of a gunfight against supernaturally-assisted knights in armour and daemonic beings, he mentions Doris and the Seventh Doctor is amused that 'She finally caught you'. Well, was the Brig avoiding her for decades? And if that's the case... he was the head of a top-secret security agency, so how hard can staying out of her way really be?

• **Leela and Andred (15.6, "The Invasion of Time).** Of the many things that make people watching this story go "Uh?", this entirely spurious romance is one of the biggest. It comes right out of the blue. Prior to this, Leela has enjoyed more chemistry with even K9 - including episode one, in which the tin dog points a gun at her.

Then again, maybe that's what first attracts her to Andred, who's one in a long line of Security Guards that she's antagonised. It was only in the previous story that it was "amusingly" out of character for her to be smitten by the space-pilot Orfe, but it's not as if she was unaware of boys. Contrary

continued on page 197...

ous that the baby-food syringes contain green goo, something that's well-established in *Doctor Who* lore as a means of fusing human DNA to other types - see 12.2, "The Ark in Space"; 10.5, "The Green Death"; 7.4, "Inferno" and now X3.4, "Daleks in Manhattan".]

• *Bannermen*. Even though they're named in the title, there's not much to say about them. They're humanoid warriors who have protective eyewear and stick out their tongues while emiting a sort of strangled "victory cry". For reasons known only to them, they here come perilously close to wiping out the Chimerons. [A clue might lie in their apparent over-reaction to Goronwy's bees. If the Chimeron drones pose such a threat to the Bannermen - despite their being obviously outgunned - it must be because of something in their bodies. Many humans have extreme anaphylactic reactions to bee-stings, so it's not impossible. It's also notable that the song of the young Queen scares the Bannermen off but doesn't seem to affect anyone else. With the emphasis in this story on biology, there's material here for endless speculation.]

The Bannermen leader, Gavrok, blows a hunting horn to rally his troops for battle. He's also got a taste for raw meat, and oddly likes to eat it on a stairwell while at least six of his men guard two tied-up, unarmed civilian prisoners. Gavrok spits out his meat to show contempt for justice, and it has to be said that for all his bullying, he doesn't keep a very disciplined army. In fact, they're a bit of a rabble.

• *Navarinos*. Ordinarily, they look like mauve root-vegetables with eyes; their arms, head and legs being lumpy and asymmetric. But they can use a Transformation Arch to feign human form, and this equips them with lurid but just-about authentic clothing. [This is apparently removable, as Murray changes into pyjamas for the night.] Navarinos have a very high metabolic rate, unsuitable for sustained bopping. [And see **History** for more on them.]

Planet Notes

• *Gthaal*. Has glass-eaters. [This is bad news, apparently.]

History

• *Dating*. It's summer 1959... but not as we know it, although hula-hoops are in vogue. [Yes, it's warm and sunny as everyone remembers, but

US space technology isn't quite where it should be. The US government agent Jerome P. Weismuller and his partner Hawk have been sent to find a very crude downed US satellite (more of a space-bleeper, really) that was launched from Cape Canaveral. They've been equipped with a lamentably shoddy tracking apparatus, and you'd expect US agents of that period to have something with transistors in - for portability and reliability - but they've got a big box of valves and a wire aerial instead. Then again, it's possible that they're actually low-level Walter Mitty-ish fantasists who've been posted to Wales to keep them out of harm's way, which is implied in their general demeanour and a sequence deleted from the broadcast episodes.]

The satellite's purpose isn't explained, although it's possibly a surveillance probe. [This would explain why it's not headline news, and why our hapless Yanks mistake the Bannerman spaceship for the satellite - if it's so secret that even US government agents haven't been provided with photos, then it must be for something politically-sensitive and dodgy. That said, this is *Doctor Who*, where American space-tech is routinely streets behind that of Britain - see 7.3, "The Ambassadors of Death" and 13.4, "The Android Invasion" - and the American electronics industry is in the stone-age compared to Tobias Vaughn's advances (see 6.3, "The Invasion"; 26.3, "The Curse of Fenric" and **Whatever Happened to the USA?** under 4.6, "The Moonbase"). A slower development of US technology could also account for why Hawk says the satellite's launch is 'history in the making' - as if it's the first-such US endeavour - when in real-life, the US put up *Explorer I* more than a year earlier in January 1958.]

The summer of 1932 was hot and abundant in cherry blossom. Over the years, the beekeeper Goronwy says he's seem a number of odd phenomena, including lights in the sky. [It's very tempting to cross-reference this with stories such as "The Unquiet Dead" (X1.3) and "Boom Town" (X1.11), but that way madness lies. Mind you, we'll revisit this notion if we see Hugh Lloyd in a jar of formaldehyde in a *Torchwood* episode. Incidentally, some have taken the fact that Goronwy has a casual attitude around the Doctor, and his unflinching attitude despite all these weird events, to speculate that he's also an alien, if not a Time Lord, himself. There's really no evidence for this on screen, though, and - frankly -

What are the Oddest Romances in the Programme's History?

...continued from page 195

to what's sometimes said, there *are* other women among the Sevateem, but Leela is definitely the Alpha Female. Note how she knows exactly what Adam Colby's thinking (15.3, "Image of the Fendahl").

It's odd, though, that she's got *that* far past puberty in a tribe of savages without littering a dozen or so kids. Andred, on the other hand, is from a planet of monks. Even though writers Graham Williams and Anthony Read introduce a female Time Lord in "The Invasion of Time", the simple fact is that they're dating across species (Leela and Andred, not Williams and Read). Andred might have become more xenophobic than ever after facing an invasion from *two* lots of aliens, but the first alien to be allowed into the Capitol since history started is the one he winds up dating. It's a strange first date, though: running around the TARDIS getting shot, and watching every law in the book being broken. He's clearly bewildered, so her abrupt decision to stay on Gallifrey and break yet *another* law must leave him so nonplussed that he accepts the situation. The Doctor more or less orders him to marry her, within hours of their first meeting. In a story so much like a Marx Brothers film, anything like a proper romance would have been as irritating as the cute couples in those.

Since then, the spin-off books and CDs have detailed how Leela and Andred's mating had big exciting consequences, and has forever changed the way things are done on Gallifrey. Fortunately, then, both the books and *Doctor Who* on telly have blown up the dreary planet.

• **K1 and Sarah (12.1, "Robot").** When they first met, his eyes lit up. She was the first person to worry about him. He came into her life when the man she'd been running with had forgotten her - he just wasn't the same any more. Others told her not to see this new love. They told her he was bad, but she knew he was sad; he's no rebel, no no no, just mixing with a mean crowd.

So she did what any girl would do: went home to meet his folks. Pa Kettlewell thought he was long gone, running with that gang had bought him nothing but an early end. Or that's what he told her. It was a lie: Kettlewell was preying on the boy's sweet nature and making him do bad stuff. Then Kettlewell was shot in a heist gone wrong, and the boy took his new sweetheart hostage. He

told her of his dream - to live someplace where there were no guns, no bad guys, no-one to keep them apart and they could live off the fat of the land and keep rabbits.

But someone tipped off the heat, and the place was surrounded. He swore they'd never take him alive, and as soon as he was sure she was safe he went on a killing spree. He was betrayed - not shot, but poisoned. Her ex and some sailor he'd picked up got him from behind ("look - bunny-rabbits!"), then drove off.

(And what makes it really sad is that, as we find out a lot later, this is the nearest Sarah got to a relationship before or after meeting the Doctor. No wonder she put so much emotional investment in a tin dog with a similar name - see X2.3, "School Reunion".)

• **Susan and David (2.2, "The Dalek Invasion of Earth").** Another cross-species romance? Well, if she *is* the Doctor's granddaughter, it's weirder with hindsight than it looked at the time. It's a peculiar courtship by any standards, starting with the fish-slapping dance. (Besides, cooking a fish you've caught in the river Ouse soon after a plague and after you've seen aliens going for a dip in the Thames, sounds risky to us.) He tempts her with promises of sheep-farming. Oddly, David accepts that Susan's from another planet, and it never occurs to him to ask what it's like where she comes from. As her only relative is the Doctor, he may have had occasion to think twice. But look at how he treats the paterfamilias: downright obsequiously. The Doctor's idea of match-making is to lock the TARDIS doors and deliver a long speech before stranding Susan on what's left of the South Bank.

• **Joseph C and Gilbert M (25.2, "The Happiness Patrol").** They're such a sweet couple, but the sad thing is how long both parties were stuck in damaging co-dependent relationships. Of course in Gilbert's case that was a hard habit to break, and the griping about his ill-treatment is one of his main pleasures in life. The only time we see this pair together - before they elope - is when they find the Kandy Man's remains, and it's obvious from that conversation that Joseph knows next to nothing about Gilbert. So how long do these two have? Especially as Gilbert is griping about Joseph within seconds. If Joseph - who has

continued on page 199...

it's a stupid idea.]

As for the native time of the Chimerons, Bannermen and Navarinos, all we know is that... errr, well, it's in the future, possibly the *far* future, and certainly at a point when the Bannermen and even a Navarino holiday tour have time technology at their disposal. In this era, the Navarinos love 1950s American culture [this might explain a lot about the DJ in 22.6, "Revelation of the Daleks"], and have '1950s nights' back on their homeworld. The time-active Nostalgia Trips have obviously been operating for a while, despite their apparently being disaster-prone, and the Navarinos are only one of the species using their services. The Doctor says Nostalgia Trips is the 'most notorious travelling firm in the Five Galaxies'. At some point, he and Mel have heard an amusing anecdote about a Nostalgia Trips jaunt getting stuck on the Planet of the Glass Eaters.

The departure point of *this* Nostalgia Trips tour [licence plate No. VWW 361, a bit of an anachronism] is Toll-Port G715, which exists as a grotty way-station in space and time. [Exactly who gave them the authority to regulate such traffic isn't said, although it's sometimes been speculated that the Port owners have some sort of lease or permit agreement with the Time Lords.] We only see the Port in semi-darkness [so either night lasts a long time there, or it's very far from a sun]. It's looked after by a garishly-dressed Tollmaster, who's enthusiastic because the Doctor has won a prize for being the joint's ten billionth [and they use the American billion] customer. Even the Tollmaster knows about rock 'n' roll. [So the Doctor's comments about Elvis in 24.1, "Time and the Rani" and the DJ in "Revelation of the Daleks" would indicate that Earth has become renowned for this. It certainly might explain why the peak time for invasions of Southern England occurs between Merseybeat and the New Romantics.]

Delta says she wants to take her case against the Bannermen to 'Judgment' [and she says this as if it's a place, rather than a concept], whereupon 'they' will send an expeditionary force to rout the Bannermen for their slaughter of the Chimmerons. The Doctor alludes to Gavrok potentially being put on trial, and says Delta has sworn a statement detailing the near-genocide of the Chimerons. [All told, it's pretty clear that a formidable justice system is operating in the Bannermen's home time, and that it could scuttle the Bannermen's goals if everyone lives long enough to make the proper entreaties. And if 'Judgment' is a place of, err, judgment, that it's possibly where Delta and Billy haul the surviving Bannermen off to at story's end.]

Murray's Nostalgia Trips bus is equipped with a Hellstrom Two (AKA 'Hellstrom Fireball') engine, capable of Warp 5 in a good tailwind. However, his vessel requires a Quarb crystal [see **The TARDIS**] to function. Murray tries, and fails, to speed up growth of the Doctor's Quarb crystal with 'mind power'. [The evident joke here is that Murray's too dim to mentally generate growth, but this suggests that certain beings *can* make the crystals grow faster using their mind.]

The Bannermen's ordnance destroys the Nostaliga Trips bus, almost to the point of disinegration. [We should perhaps assume that the bus' eradication owes to the Fireball engine detonating - because if Bannermen weaponry were *that* powerful, then the pair who later spy Delta and the child through their binoculars are wasting their time trying to get a closer shot.] Gavrok has a detector that registers the TARDIS as advanced tech. His weaponry includes a 'sophisticated' sonic cone - a small device that he can place atop the TARDIS, and which projects an explosive energy field around the Ship. The Doctor speculates that it's possible to tunnel under this cone, but the problem is solved when a stunned Gavrok falls against the field and is killed, thereby draining its energy. [A pity the Doctor didn't realize this, because the heroes could've just chucked lumber or somesuch against the field until it deactivated.]

Gavrok offers a reward for the Chimeron Queen in 'units' (one million, to be precise). The Doctor says the White Flag is the accepted signal for truce throughout the civilized universe, and unless it's part of his posturing, he expects Gavrok to honour it.

The Analysis

Where Does This Come From? Let's get this out of the way now: *The Devil's Galop* (by "Charles Williams", who was born Isaac Koserbreit) was the theme for BBC radio's stirring post-war adventure serial *Dick Barton, Special Agent*. "Post-war" is the key term here, because it kept the nation enthralled during the privations of the late 1940s, but was replaced in 1950 by *The Archers* - as unthrilling a serial as you can imagine. (Despite this

What are the Oddest Romances in the Programme's History?

...continued from page 197

after all put up with Helen A for some years - can accept that Gilbert needs to vent, then they look likely to have a happy retirement on Terra Omega (so long as the authorities from Gilbert's home-world of Vasilip don't turn up and ask awkward questions). One imagines the two of them doing a cookery series on daytime TV.

- **Troilus and Cressida (3.3, "The Myth Makers).** We did a whole essay about this (**Marrying Troilus: What *Is* She Thinking?**), but we nonetheless wonder how exactly Vicki, who's from the twenty-fifth century, would adapt to life on the run in the Mediterranean some thirty-eight centuries earlier. What would she tell her kids? (We assume she'd have some, although - puerile joke for American readers, this - she has a ready supply of Trojans.) And what would she and hubby chat about? Venderman's Law? We're talking about Vicki here - the girl who didn't spot that Koquillian sounded just like Bennett, only shouting; the girl who gives any passing alien or robot a cute name. Assuming she wasn't slaughtered, and that Troilus survived his bout with Achilles, she'd've been along for the ride as far as Latium, and had a pet-name for the Sea-Serpent that ate Laocoon ('Hisso'), Cerberus ('Mr Woofy'), Three-bodied Geryon ('Big-shirty'), Cacus the fire-breathing giant ('Flame-grilled Whopper') and Venus ('Auntie V').

- **The Doctor and Cameca (1.6, "The Aztecs").** Men are such bastards, a Time Lord doubly so.

it's still going, and is required listening for anyone wishing to understand rural Britain.)

So, kids who grew up with Dick, Jock and Snowy saving the nation from spies - often by being tied to bombs every fifteen minutes - later used the series' theme and urgent narrative style for parodies. Thus another generation only knew *The Devil's Galop* from *Monty Python's Flying Circus*, and as aural shorthand for pipe-smoking heroes in desperate races against time. Southern Television, in a firmly retro phase in the late 70s, tried a TV version to match their remakes of *The Famous Five* and *Dan Dare* (see 21.4, "Resurrection of the Daleks"), but it bombed. (Alec McCrindle, who played Snowy in the original, was a rebel general in *Star Wars: A New Hope* and got to say "May the Force be with you", but even this failed to publicise the TV show.) Incidentally, "Galop" is spelled with one "l" (as it is a musical term, not an equestrian one), so forget what you might have seen in *DWM*.

When the BBC had its 60th birthday bash in 1982, it issued a record of old themes. Apart from reminding many people of an age of certainties - when reassuringly brisk music announced regular fixtures in the schedules - *On The Air* was a gold-mine for samplers. Moreover, the themes used in "Delta and the Bannermen" are all Keff McCulloch's best attempts at reproducing the selections from the 1950s section. "Puffying Billy", which American readers might know from *Captain Kangaroo*, was used for *Children's Hour*; "In the Party Mood", heard when Weismuller and Hawk arrive, is from the 9.00am show *Housewives' Choice*; and the lunchtime selection "Music While You Work" was a wartime measure retained until 1967. (For more on the music selection, see **Things That Don't Make Sense.**)

But the warm cozy glow of 1950s nostalgia was beginning to pall in the late 80s. Although the charts were full of Golden Oldies, usually recycled as part of advertising campaigns for jeans or Baby-Boomer American films, Britain was mildly sceptical of this trend. At the back of everyone's mind was how much this fondly-remembered period was built on hypocrisy and repression, how grim the real fifties were, and how the American model failed to match circumstances here. *Our* 1950s were the era of Gilbert Harding (8.5, "The Daemons"), Muffin the Mule (X2.7, "The Idiot's Lantern") and race-riots. There weren't *many* of the latter - and ironically the racists were all keen on rock 'n' roll, a black form of music co-opted by rednecks - but it happened.

Many of the bright young talents of the first flower of British rock were being promoted in clubs run by hoods, and this was now being talked about. The last hope for the 1980s British film industry was a big-budget spectacular about how the two versions of 1950s Britain - the squalid Soho scene and the lurid mythical version - met up in the summer of 1958. *Absolute Beginners* was based on one of Colin McInnes' novels of Soho life, but made into a gaudy fantasy with an all-star cast (although nobody can remember who played the lead). The film is remembered now as one of the big bombs of 1986, but you can see in it the first serious attempt to make a point about the US version of the 50s (all Fonzie and milkshakes) and our collective memory of snobbery with violence. Look at the contemporary rash of films set in that era: *Dance with a Stranger*, which was about the last woman to be hanged in the UK; *Scandal*, which was about the Profumo affair (see "Remembrance of the Daleks"); and *Prick Up Your Ears*, which was about the playwright Joe Orton (see 4.5, "The Underwater Menace"). Yet American films of the time made this period seem much more innocent. To the US, this is the age of *Dirty Dancing*, *Hairspray*, and the one that mysteriously went straight to video here: *Shag!*.[25] It was no surprise to some that George Lucas went from *American Graffiti* to *Star Wars* - because 1950s America, to us, looks like science fiction.

So what we had were bad cover-versions of the hits from the US, and our own forms of music. We could explain some of this but really, you have to find it all out for yourselves. Meanwhile, *Doctor Who* had inherited the slot previously reserved for a bizarre series called *The Golden Oldie Picture Show*. This took old hits and tried to do clips for them as if they'd had MTV in 1957. Tragically, for a while this was the only work Graeme Harper could get. Also in that slot, in re-run, was *Hi-De-Hi!* - a sitcom about a holiday camp in 1959. It was set (perhaps) in Wales, but with a couple of prominent Welsh cast-members. Seriously. It had been, and would be for a couple more years, one of the biggest hits of the time. Like much of *Doctor Who* at this point, it dealt with the disjunction between being cheerful for the public and loathing your job. Leslie Dwyer (the showman Vorg in 10.2, "Carnival of Monsters") played a Punch and Judy man who hated children (and we'll pick up this thread in later stories). Inevitably, any story set in a holiday camp in Wales in 1959 is going to be riding that show's (yellow) coat-tails.

One other factor, before we leave the 50s to fester, is that we're in Season Twenty-Four. There's an anniversary coming up, so they need a trial run for any story set in 1963 that they might be planning. Except, of course, that they weren't as organised as that. (see **Did Cartmel Have Any Plan At All?** under 25.3, "Silver Nemesis"). The scripts were written by someone who was a film-buff (hence the Bannermen, a nod towards Akira

Kurosawa, as we'll see in **The Lore**), but more to the point someone who'd grown up with *Doctor Who* and knew what worked and what clichés to avoid. This is a trend worth noting, as it will define this period.

One other obvious "source" ought to be considered. This story entails what's effectively a virgin birth, and a fugitive mother forced to take shelter in an insalubrious place. There's a tyrant who slaughters a lot of innocent people to try to kill this child, and two dumb agents from the West are told to follow a satellite. Just as this looks contrived, at *exactly* the place in the story where shepherds ought to appear, a bee-keeper shelters the child and provides gifts. That leaves Billy and his Vincent motorcycle as Joseph and the donkey.

Things That Don't Make Sense   Almost all of Billy's odd romantic behaviour can be explained by a very nasty theory - which is covered in this story's essay - but on the face of it, just so we're clear, a member of staff meeting a single mother after-hours in a 50s holiday camp would be a sacking offence for at least three reasons. Billy doesn't even react to the sudden appearance of a green baby (something that seasoned time-traveller Mel screams at), and seems able to get flowers from somewhere despite the late hour.

Then, Mel goes to sleep after she's all screamed out, even though she knows that the mysterious roomie who swore her to secrecy is a fugitive from genocidal time-travelling aliens who are probably on their way. Well, we say, "swore to secrecy" - actually, the first chance she gets, Mel blabs to the Doctor *in public* about this [it's amazing Keillor didn't make that call there and then] but she only mentions about Delta, *not* the baby. She's got a very curious set of priorities, has our Mel. So Delta and Billy vanish, not leaving a note in case of emergencies.

The Navarinos know enough about the 50s to correctly execute the dances, yet they have clothes nobody over twenty would be seen dead wearing. The Teddy-Boys, rockabilly thugs with pseudo-Edwardian clothes, were about as popular as Qaeda at holiday camps. Despite this, the camp-master Burton maintains enough professionalism to not react as if he's just seen a horde of fifty-year-old Hell's Angels in lamé. And if we're addressing historical details, another oddity is the radio music. Even allowing that pirate stations could play this stuff as far from the North Sea as Barry

Island, the BBC themes seem to indicate that the holiday-camp residents have lunch ("Music While You Work") before breakfast ("Housewives' Choice"). Indeed, the 5.00pm Children's Hour usually began three hours after we hear the theme from one of its main programmes (*Larry the Lamb*: seriously, don't ask), yet we hear no chart hits under two years old. Indeed, if it's the summer of 1959, you'd expect to to hear bloody "Volare" everywhere. There's also no Everly Brothers, no Russ Conway, and nothing by Pearl Carr and Teddie Johnson - in short, none of the year's biggest sellers.

So, imagine for a moment that you're Delta. Your people have been butchered almost wholesale, and you're pursued by thugs who want to deal you the same - but then you reach the safety of a holiday tour. Some discretion might go a long way at this point, but instead of just saying "yes" when Murray asks if she's a late-arriving Navarino, Delta replies 'I'm a Chimeron' for benefit of anyone who wishes to hunt down and slaughter her. But then, Murray later proclaims to any human in earshot that he's an alien, and the Doctor confirms this at equal volume.

And what *was* Keillor, the bounty hunter, doing on the holiday tour anyway? Is he just coincidentally part of the tour, even though a nostalgic 50s fest to Disneyland hardly seems like the type of vacation a relentless murderer would take [maybe future film buffs took out a contract on Annette Funicello after *How To Stuff A Wild Bikini*?]. Or is he *so* incredibly up-to-date on the Chimeron-Bannermen conflict that he guesses the last Chimeron Queen will seclude herself amongst the Navarinos? Eventually this unsavoury character meets his maker when Gavrok sends a high-impulse beam down Keillor's transmission track and disintegrates him... actually, that bit *does* make sense, insofar as Gavrok understandably wants to avoid paying the bounty of 'one million units'. However, Gavrok later curses himself because Keillor's death leaves him without a beacon to track Delta's location with. Was there really *such* a rush to vapourize Keillor, then? Do they have such an advanced form of PayPal that Gavrok needed to eliminate him right this very second rather than transfer the cash?

In fact, Gavrok is *so* ruthless that he shoots the Tollmaster in the back just because he feels like it, making it later seem incredibly out-of-character when he spares Weismuller and Hawk's lives for no good reason - especially as he has to detail two

Bannermen to guard them. Even when the Bannermen are recalled, Weismuller and Hawk are just shackled with a throat collar as opposed to being more simply shot in the back of the head - never mind that the collar is hardly the sort of thing that could stop them just up and walking away.

As the story opens - and in typical *Doctor Who* fashion - one of the Chimeron drones drops dead after taking what appears to be a bullet to his bicep. (All right, it *might've* gone through his chest, but it's still amusing to watch.) American and British relations are at an *amazing* point in this period as Weismuller can go to a countryside police box and ask to be connected to the White House ('Priority Call, Code 11'), as if the rural police make such high-security phone connections all the time, and can reach 'the President's right-hand man' in seconds. And why is a police box out in rural Wales anyway? Owing to editing issues, the Doctor sometimes wears glasses while driving Billy's motorcycle, and sometimes doesn't.

It's actually in keeping with the story's mood that Gavrok's spaceship has a map of Earth with the border between England and Wales clearly marked. However, might they not have followed through and marked "Wales" as "Cymru"? More curious is the later map shows the as-yet unbuilt M4 motorway.

Gavrok sends up a flare that apparently signals his troops in the field to "observe the vehicle passing by your position, wherever that is, and fire a tracer at it". So it's lucky that no other vehicles ever pass close by a holiday camp, isn't it?

And over on the right of the screen as Ray storms off from the dance: what the *hell* is Richard Davies doing?

Critique   This is the story that separates even those who saw the whole of 1980s *Doctor Who* as a criminal waste. In one corner, we have a group who see it as the last straw, a story that is "silly". This is a crime, apparently. The opposing view, more common now than at the time, is that "Delta" is part of Season Twenty-Four's effort to shake off the baleful influence of Ian Levine and the army of anorak-clad zombies... control has now been wrested from people who measure a story's worth by how many other stories it references, not whether anyone outside fandom can watch without feeling confused or ill. So the argument seems to go that "Delta and the Bannermen" is either bad because it doesn't take itself seriously, or magnificent because it doesn't take The Fans seriously. Yet to be honest, it's not quite either.

Of all people, it's Keff McCulloch who had the most interesting insight into Season Twenty-Four as a whole, and this story in particular. He observed that the writers were all convinced that they were making *film noir* thrillers, whilst the directors all seemed to think they were working on goofy comedy. Here - and in one scene in particular - you can gauge which side McCulloch is on. The Nostalgia Tours bus and all within are blown up (in one of the big explosions that the location crews have begun to make a speciality), and Gavrok shoves a gun in Mel's face. It's a grim moment. For a few seconds the music stops, Bonnie Langford acts her socks off and Don Henderson is genuinely menacing. Everything is tense... and then the *Dick Barton* theme returns, and an assortment of strange-looking people in vintage vehicles are seen tooling up the coast road, scaring a few seagulls.

There we have it. The stunts are almost back up to the standard of the "Action by Havoc" era, the Paintbox work to turn yet another use of *that* quarry into something rich and strange is better and less show-offy than "Mindwarp" (23.2), and the spaceship landing scenes are the kind of thing we wish they could have done in the 70s. Yet everyone thinks of this as a throwaway story - as a "romp".

Not that this makes anyone's commitment any less necessary. If anything, the use of experienced comedy actors spares us the embarrassing mugging and goofing that happens when so-called "straight" actors decide they want to play *Doctor Who* for laughs. Nobody is actually giving a comic performance here (except McCulloch, actually). Yet whereas watching "Paradise Towers" (24.2) with the sound down makes it a darker, more stylish production, it isn't possible to do Kurosawa in Butlins. Even with no music and no dialogue, this is obviously intended to be entertainment. Not - as Saward would claim - light entertainment (although the use of music is more prominent and subtle than recently), but this story is there to keep as wide an audience as possible happy, amused, excited and curious. Of course, most of the potential audience was all off watching ITV when "Delta" was first broadcast, but never mind.

Under everyone's noses, *Doctor Who* has detached from its past. Cartmel has recruited writers who all loved the show in their youth and

stopped watching when Peter Davison came along, meaning they're writing from a folk-memory of what and who the series is for. The Doctor is back to being a curious traveller who intervenes to help, not a-Time-Lord-from-the-planet-Gallifrey-in-the-constellation-Kasterborous. This is the second story in a row not to have any mention of anything from the programme's past, nor hints of Something We Haven't Been Told. The people making it are properly interested in and fixated upon what the series *can* do, not what it's done.

And under all our noses, the regulars have figured out their characters. McCoy's still a bit incomprehensible, but he's getting better at doing regret and simmering anger. Langford is finally showing signs of The Right Stuff (ironically, she's arguably the only companion to be redeemed by having a script written for Generic Girl Sidekick). Sara Griffiths had potential as Ray despite a very limited role, Henderson's idea that Gavrok had an even nastier twin brother should have been followed up, and Goronwy deserves a spin-off series far more than Sarah, K9 or Captain Jack.

The Facts

Written by Malcolm Kohll. Directed by Chris Clough. Ratings: 5.3 million, 5.1 million, 5.4 million.

Working Titles "Flight of the Chimeron". (This and "Delta and the Bannermen" seem to have been batted back and forth as potential titles throughout the production.)

Supporting Cast Don Henderson (Gavrok), Belinda Mayne (Delta), David Kinder (Billy), Stubby Kaye (Weismuller), Morgan Deare (Hawk), Ken Dodd (Tollmaster), Richard Davies (Burton), Sara Griffiths (Ray), Johnny Dennis (Murray), Brian Hibbard (Keillor), Hugh Lloyd (Goronwy).

Oh, Isn't That..?

• *Ken Dodd.* We are legally obliged to say at this juncture: "By Jove, Missus!" Comedian Ken Dodd had briefly been the most famous person from Liverpool in the early 1960s, and combined Music Hall's last embers with television technique. At best, he was an encyclopaedia of jokes and a master of word-play, and used to hold the record for continuous gag-cracking (three or four days). He used props - his "tickling stick", his mussed-up hair and his goofy teeth, which he had insured in case they went straight - and branched out into children's TV with the Diddymen, originally puppets with regional accents and then children in costumes. What made this odder still was that - with his hair combed and his teeth covered - he was a crooner and launched a parallel career as a housewives' favourite, having a string of hits including a Number One in 1965 with "Tears". By the time this story was broadcast, he was about to become famous for something else (see **The Lore**).

• *Don Henderson*. Suddenly, he was all over television. He'd been playing cops for a while, and one in particular. From *The XYY Man* onwards (see 22.2, "Vengeance on Varos"), he'd played Detective Inspector George Bulman - a character who got odder as he developed, eventually getting his own show (the imaginatively named *Bulman*). It was being used by Granada as their Saturday night filmed show, opposite *Bergerac* et al. Henderson was now guesting on other series, and he lent his support to any project that looked fun. (There's a fifteen-minute student film adaptation of William Gibson's story "The Gernsback Continuum", renamed *Tomorrow Calling*, that was filmed in Blackpool and had Toyah Willcox in it too. Hearing Henderson growl "Just listen! Really bad media can exorcise your semiotic ghosts!" in it is an experience.) When "Delta" was broadcast, he was also appearing as a villain in TVS's near-future Arthurian epic *Knights of God* (which had been made two years before, but was shown concurrent with Season Twenty-Four) and almost everywhere else. His brief moment in *Star Wars* - as the general who warns that the rebels might still destroy the Death Star - is now greeted with chuckles by anyone who thinks he'll revert to type and pull out a chip butty and a bottle of stout as soon as Grand Moff Tarkin leaves the room.

• *Richard Davies*. He was one of those faces that kept popping up in ITC shows in the 60s, although obviously not as often as Derren Nesbitt or Edwin Richfield. Then in 1969, he got the role as the teacher Pricey in London Weekend's school sitcom *Please, Sir,* and has played Welsh jobsworths since. He was also in *Oh No, It's Selwyn Froggitt*, but even if we told you it was ITV's answer to *Some Mothers Do Have 'Em*, you'd be none the wiser.

• *Stubby Kaye*. As the king of Broadway, he played all the roles that Nathan Lane would be the first choice for now. In movies, you'll have seen him in *Guys and Dolls* (he sang "Sit Down, You're Rocking the Boat", but we hope you knew that), *Cat Ballou* and as the murder victim Marvin Acme in *Who Framed Roger Rabbit?*, where he played pat-a-cake with Jessica. At around the time this story is supposedly set he was in *Cool It, Carol!*, which is almost the kind of film "Delta" is parodying. And anyway, when he was in London he drank at the Fitzroy Tavern, so he's an honorary Fan[26].

• *Hugh Lloyd*. Can still be seen playing every third character in repeats of *Hancock's Half Hour* from the 1950s. He acquired his own sitcom, *Hugh and I*, in the following decade. Around the time he played Goronwy, Lloyd had been in *Victoria Wood - As Seen on TV*.

• *That Bloke From The Flying Pickets*. The alien bounty-hunter with the Brummie accent, Keillor, is played by Brian Hibbert. He was in a radical fringe theatre that, for budgetary reasons, had music done by a collective of *a capella* singers with the topical name "The Flying Pickets". It was entertaining enough when they did arrangements of old Motown songs, but their version of Yazoo's "Only You" got the 1983 Christmas Number One. For three weeks, The Flying Pickets were everywhere you looked. And, as they dressed like all the people you try to avoid talking to at the Fitzroy Tavern, it was inevitable one of them would make it onto *Doctor Who*.

Cliffhangers While Mel screams at a newborn baby, the Doctor and Ray face certain death in a laundry-cupboard from a menacing bounty hunter; the Doctor comes close to liberating Gavrok's prisoners, but hears the Bannermen cock their pistols, and thinks he might've overplayed his hand.

The Lore

• "Delta and the Bannermen" and "Dragonfire" were produced as a single six-part serial with the same production personnel, with the two stories split between one recording entirely on location as Outside Broadcast, with a mobile facility and different equipment, and one recording entirely in studio. As you'll recall, something similar had been tried with the last six episodes of Season Twenty-Three, and Nathan-Turner craftily juggled the budgets to get four stories with the budget allocation for three. Get used to this, because it's going to be this way from now until the end of the series. (The sharing out of resources between two different serials had previously been tried a decade earlier on 12.2, "The Ark in Space" and 12.3, "The Sontaran Experiment" but OB drama work was now more commonplace than it had been in the mid-1970s.) Two studio scenes in the TARDIS were recorded (and a third was made, but cut from the finished broadcast) as part of "Dragonfire" a month after OB work in Wales wrapped.

• Knowing their two stories were intended to be broken up this way, writers Malcolm Kohll and Ian Briggs discussed ideas in advance. They decided that Kohll would write the "serious" three-parter, while Briggs would tackle the "funny" one. No one else involved in the production seems to have got this, which might explain the occasional uncertainties of tone in both stories. Like many of the writers from this point onwards, Kohll was known to Cartmel from workshops at the BBC script unit.

• Nathan-Turner suggested South Wales to Kohll as a potential location, but the writer seized upon this because he knew the Barry Island area (his brother lived there), and because it would get *Doctor Who* away from quarries. It seems no one is prepared to own up as to who suggested the holiday camp setting, but Kohll had holidayed at Barry Island, and we suspect he may have been the guilty party. His scripts originally contained much more background and motivation for the Bannermen - they had invaded the Chimeron planet after polluting their own to the point where it became uninhabitable. The Bannermen themselves were inspired by Kurosawa's film *Kagemusha* and this prompted the title "Delta and the Bannermen" as a play on the post-punk band Echo and the Bunnymen (itself named as a parody of 1950s-style rock 'n' roll handles, although the eponymous "Echo" was a drum-machine).

• Hawk and Weismuller were added after Kohll was told the story needed more humour. At this point, the setting was 1957 and it was intended that the American satellite was the first such body launched into space - predating Sputnik - but was hushed up when it crashed. The date was shifted to 1959 to allow for a greater variety of music, but the dialogue referring to the launch as 'history in the making' was confusingly retained in the final broadcast. In the event, most of the period rock 'n'

roll used in the serial were cover versions performed by Keff McCulloch. Nathan-Turner hoped the score could be released commercially.

• Stubby Kaye was in the UK a lot anyway, but at this stage was making *Who Framed Roger Rabbit?* (like most technically-demanding big movies in those days, it was made in Britain). Once Kaye had been cast, Morgan Deare abandoned plans to play Hawk as a New Yorker and played it as a Southerner.

• As previously mentioned, it was clear from an early stage that Bonnie Langford would be leaving *Doctor Who* at the end of the season. Both Ray in Kohll's script and Ace in "Dragonfire" were potential replacements. However, the production team decided that "Delta and the Bannermen" was the wrong story for the end of the season, and that Ray herself wouldn't strike a sufficient contrast with Mel. Chris Clough cast Ray and Ace from the same pool of auditioning actresses, eventually narrowing the choice for the former down to Georgia Slow, Lynn Gardner (who was also still under consideration for Ace) and Sara Griffiths.

One auditionee for Ray, Sophie Aldred, was - unlike all the others - an experienced motorcyclist, and put 'has own leathers' on her application form. These three words had far-reaching consequences, but oddly enough she was passed over in favour of girls who had to be shown how to ride bikes. Gardner was cast as Ray, but broke her arm while practising riding a scooter in a BBC car park two weeks before production began. The role was recast with Griffiths. Gardner - who was still paid for the serial - ended up with a small voice-only role in "Dragonfire" as a consolation.

• Ken Dodd was required for only one night's work, on Tuesday, 7th of July, with the Tollport actually being a former RAF base that had been converted into an industrial estate. The hangar we see was, in fact, filled with containers of toilet rolls. Dodd's casting garnered a lot of pre-publicity in the press, and a short feature for the childrens' magazine show *But First This...* was taped during the day's rehearsals. The casting was met with fan disquiet that would have a knock-on effect when the season was finally broadcast, but it was rare good publicity for Dodd, as he spent the rest of the decade embroiled in accusations of tax evasion (of which he was eventually cleared). Indeed, before he was arrested, Doddy told the press that the Tollmaster was "a cross between David Bowie and Nigel Lawson" (the Chancellor of the Exchequer), because he had to "dress up in satin and take people's money away".

Dodd was actually the third choice for a role, which had clearly been marked for a high profile celebrity cameo. First was Christopher Biggins, whom we hope readers will remember as Nero in *I, Claudius*, and many of you reading this will think of him as the conman Banto Zame from Big Finish's "The One Doctor". At the time, he was co-presenter of garish LWT light entertainment show *Surprise, Surprise*, but the majority of the viewing public regarded him as Adam Painting from *Rentaghost* (see 1.8, "The Reign of Terror"; 6.7, "The War Games" and 21.1, "Warriors of the Deep" for more on this show) and presenter of ITV kid's quiz *On Safari*. Biggins, who was obviously a major star - at least in his own mind - wanted a bigger role, preferably as a villain (but it's hard to imagine him as Gavrok).

Second choice was Bob Monkhouse, a comedian and comic actor then familiar as the host of game shows such as *Family Fortunes* and *Bob's Full House*; however, the recording date clashed with scheduled surgery. (Monkhouse was a brilliant choice - as a friend of Dennis Spooner and a major silent movie archivist, he was someone known to have a keen interest in *Doctor Who*'s early years. He'd also been the ostensible star of *Carry On Sergeant*, so had worked with William Hartnell, and as his later appearances in semi-serious roles - such as in *Jonathan Creek* - showed he could do straight drama.)

The Tollmaster was actually Dodd's first dramatic role for the screen (some sources list a Ken Dodd as "Second Ninja" in 1980s action flick *The Ninja Mission*, but somehow we doubt this is the same person) and his last before appearing as Yorick in Kenneth Branagh's bladder-weakening film of *Hamlet* almost a decade later.

• The principle location for the serial was the 1960s Majestic Holiday Camp on Barry Island, as other suitable venues in the region were fully booked for the peak holiday period. The camp was undergoing renovations at the time, and the production was recorded at the still-unmodernised Yellow Camp. The production base was a nearby hotel rather than Butlins itself - perhaps fortunately, as the team soon discovered that the abandoned Yellow Camp was infested with rats. The interiors of the Bannermen spacecraft and the Nostalgia Tours Bus were constructed in the camp corridors. The bus proper was bought by the BBC, and later reused in "The Greatest Show in the Galaxy" (25.4). For the shot of it crashing outside Shangri-La, it was dropped a short distance from a crane; nearby flowerbeds had to be removed and replaced after the shot was complete. The crane was a last-minute replacement for a larger one that had proved too heavy to cross the causeway to the island, causing further delays.

• Burton's dog is Pepsi, who as you may know from *A Day With A Television Producer* (see 18.1, "The Leisure Hive"), was Nathan-Turner's pet. She'd been staying with the producer's parents, but recent ill-health meant they had to return the pooch. We'll see Pepsi again, shortly before she died, in Season Twenty-Six.

• Four performers appeared as the Chimeron Princess in various stages of development: six-month-old Jessica McGough, four-year-old Amy Osborn, nine-year-old Laura Collins and twelve-year-old Carley Joseph. The "monster" form of the baby was played by two elaborate props built by Susan Moore and Stephen Mansfield, and McGough was also doubled by a doll because she cried too much.

• Don Henderson threw himself into the role of Gavrok, suggesting details like the Bannermen war cry and purple tongues, and his chewing raw meat in the scene where the Doctor confronts him. He also proposed a sequel. Henderson's frustration at being unable to deliver the line about "advanced technology emissions" correctly is the highlight of a compilation of outtakes and skits that circulated among the cast and, later, at conventions. McCoy, Langford and Hugh Lloyd also recorded special linking material for a trailer compiling material from the first three stories of the season - which was shown at the press launch and in truncated form on BBC1 - in the lead up to the autumn season.

• Deleted material included all the dialogue for Navarino tourists Adlon (Leslie Meadows) and Bollit (Anita Graham), who are nonetheless credited both on screen and in the *Radio Times*. Adlon is the ageing Ted we have dealt with, but Bollit is the bottle blonde in a black dress with tartan accoutrements. Their principle contribution to the story was a scene where Billy shows off his Vincent, cut from episode one.

• Kohll found the experience of writing for *Doctor Who* exhausting, and declined the opportunity to write another serial. He novelised the story for publication in 1989, though a typo on the spine reduced Gavrok's hordes to a single Bannerman. Meanwhile, the version sold for broadcast in West Germany was retitled *Delta und die Bannermänner,* which sounds charming. (Yes, they'd succeeded in flogging this show to the German-speaking world via Radio-Television Luxemburg. This will have far-reaching repercussions, as we will see in "Silver Nemesis" and "The Curse of Fenric". Interestingly, they had retained the same actor across regenerations in dubbing the series, so Sylvester McCoy was made to speak like Tom Baker. The German version of "Remembrance of the Daleks" has Ace watching *Doctor Who*, and 26.1, "Battlefield" permits Bambera to shout "Scheiße".)

24.4: "Dragonfire"

(Serial 7G, Three Episodes. 23rd November - 7th December 1987.)

Which One is This? Film Theory 101, on ice.

Firsts and Lasts Mel decides rather abruptly to leave, taking Glitz with her, and the Doctor decides to let his new friend Ace come along for a ride. (Why, you may ask? See 26.3, "The Curse of Fenric" episode four.) This is the last time the BBC see fit to have their hard-working continuity announcers give plot summaries before each week's instalment. It's also the start of a trend for visual quotes from *Indiana Jones*, but in this story it's just one film *homage* among dozens. And after years of making condoms into monsters (as in 10.5, "The Green Death"), we finally have an inflatable sex-toy as part of the story's signature Special Effects sequence (see **The Lore**).

And a round of applause, please, at what's arguably the last instance of a companion tripping over their own feet for no good reason. Watch in episode two as Mel takes a sudden spill and knocks herself out on some metal stairs. With the ice motif in this story, you almost want a slow-motion replay and marks for Artistic Impression and Technical Merit.

Three Things to Notice about "Dragonfire"...

1. Film-buffs will have lots of fun trying to spot all the cinematic allusions. Indeed, the script has so many, it looks like a commentary on the promiscuous borrowing done by *Doctor Who* writers. If this seems accidental, consider that almost all the characters have the names of prominent film theorists (Bazin, Kracauer, McLuhan,

Pudovkin, Belazs; the novelisation gives us an Eisenstein and the original scripts included a Sarris). If this *still* seems like a coincidence, consider the question the unusually bright Security Guard asks the Doctor. If you don't recognise it, see the essay with this story.

2. And yet, with all this graduate-level malarkey, the scene where waitress-Ace hands in her notice - by dumping a milkshake on her boss' head - is straight out of children's television. It's noteworthy, because this strangely schizoid production repeatedly goes from maturity to stupidity and back - sometimes within the same scene. The script does the same curious dance, with deft wordplay in some scenes and idiotic faff right after it. As further evidence of this, compare the two cliffhangers. The one has the Doctor deducing the whole story from clues we've seen but not comprehended until now; the other shows him deciding it's time to do some pointless slapstick. Quite why he opts to hang from his umbrella over a precipice is never made clear (see **The Lore**), except that someone decided it was time for a literal cliffhanger.

3. OK, so *Raiders of the Lost Ark* had a scene where Ronald Lacey's character, the Gestapo man Todt, melts quickly and comically. Done by Industrial Light and Magic, this shot cost as much as William Hartnell's whole time as the Doctor. It also had an A rating - the equivalent to today's PG - at the cinema. So it's interesting to consider that in "melting" the villain Kane, *Doctor Who* - that cheap, tacky kids' show - does the same shot only better, more gorily and on the budget of Harrison Ford's pedicures. If the public had been watching in larger numbers, this would've caused a storm of protest.

The Continuity

The Doctor In searching for the Dragon *and* in accepting Ace aboard his Ship, the Doctor says he wants 'a quick adventure, then back in time for tea.' He seems very excited at the prospect of exploring areas of the Iceworld outpost that're labelled the 'Lake of Oblivion' and the 'Death of Eternal Darkness'.

• *Ethics.* He stops Glitz from shooting the Dragon dead, and throws Glitz's gun away too - a fact that makes the Dragon trust him. He finds the idea of running away from responsibilities, even big ones, anathema. [This is ironic, as the Doctor traditionally legs it as soon as anything like responsibility is offered to him, but this is about to change, big-style.] He pities Belazs - who sold her liberty to Kane years ago - but can't help her.

The Doctor's questions to the Abnormally Well-Read Security Guard indicate a growing interest in theology [cf. "The Curse of Fenric" and his discussion with the Reverend Wainwright about Nietzsche], although he knows a lot about Existentialism. He believes that just taking what you want is wrong. [Again, words like "pot" and "kettle" spring to mind, especially when we remember the contents of the TARDIS' auxiliary power control room in 15.6, "The Invasion of Time".]

• *Inventory.* He's reading a 1950s Penguin edition of Shaw's play *The Doctor's Dilemma* [See 2.8, "The Chase" for comments on the line 'stimulate the phagocytes', and note that this is the first of a string of 'Doctor'-titled books to be found nestling in his pockets alongside the scripts.] Although it's not used, there's an abacus briefly visible in another pocket, that will be brought to the fore later.

• *Background.* He's been monitoring signals from Iceworld 'for some time'. [This is his alleged reason for going there, and it's an angle that's become more interesting with hindsight. It seems pretty safe to conclude that the "signals" he mentions are actually Ace's time-trail, so he's investigating Fenric's bait. All the business with the dragon and the treasure-map is probably just a means of stirring up whatever he's there to find. Note in particular the almost questioning look he gives Ace in the café, just after she puts two drinks on the table and Glitz starts talking philanthropy. Naturally, all of this makes events in this story seem a lot less innocent - and see "The Curse of Fenric" for why. Then again, if this is the 'temporal flicker' he said he'd detected in Sector Thirteen at the beginning of "Time and the Rani" (24.1), then the last two stories and whatever happened in between may only have been this new Doctor flexing his muscles after an unexpected regeneration.]

The name of the planet Proamon nags at him, bit he says he can't recall where he's heard it recently. He can recognise a Stradivarius and an authentic Old Master.

The Supporting Cast

• *Melanie.* Seems to have loosened up since her trip to the fifties, and can see through the Doctor's attempts to be casual about the visit to Svartos [although she's left believing that he's there to investigate the dragon and its treasure]. However, it's more of a struggle for her to tell if Glitz is lying, and she's rash enough to declare 'If you kill him, you kill us too!' to the authorities before realising that Glitz genuinely owes them money.

In her dealings with Ace, Mel at first seems to adopt a maternal attitude, then joins in the fun of blowing things up. Her throwing arm is better than Ace's. Interesting side-note: Mel's got an earring - the clasp type worn by students - half-way up her left ear.

Mel spontaneously ends her travels with the Doctor by declaring that "It's time to go", and she exits the TARDIS to take up travel with Glitz [we presume as "just good friends", otherwise... ewww] in the *Nosferatu II*. She says she's got 'much more crazy things' to do before returning home. [Really, this is the most spurious companion departure since Leela decided to stay with Andred on Gallifrey ("The Invasion of Time"). The novel *Head Games* suggests that the Doctor used his hypnotism to subliminally put Mel off the Ship, believing that she wasn't up to the great struggles that lay ahead of him. Even if you're the type of fan who ignores the books wholeheartedly, this makes far more sense than what we're shown on screen. Unless that blow to the head did her more harm than we thought...]

• *Ace.* She's sixteen, but sometimes tries to pass herself off as eighteen, and hails from Perivale. She gets terribly upset when Mel inquires about her parents, claiming she 'doesn't have and doesn't want' a Mum and Dad. Ace's real name is "Dorothy", and believes this signifies her parents weren't genuine, because her true Mum and Dad would never saddle her with such a naff name. [See **Where Does This Come From?** for more on "Dorothy". At the risk of jumping ahead, the TV show never much addresses Ace's anger toward her parents, although the implication is that she's from a broken home. The novels reunite Ace with her mother after an awful lot of angst, and the Big Finish audio "The Rapture" both says her father is dead and reveals that she's got a half-brother named Liam. Yeah, right.]

Here we discover that Ace is quite interested in homemade explosives[28]. She did A-Level Chemistry [but doesn't seem to have sat her exams], and her sloven room on Iceworld includes a small shelf of retorts and test-tubes. She keeps handy a supply of deodorant cans filled with her explosive of choice: Nitro-9.

ABOUT TIME 1985-1989

She has a habit of giving people peculiar soubriquets - Mel is 'Doughnut', Glitz is 'Birdbath', and the Doctor is 'the Professor'. She's also given to proclaiming terminology such as 'Ace!', 'Brill!' and 'Wicked!' [Fandom has almost universally assumed that Ace is contemporary with the broadcast of "Dragonfire" in 1987, yet outdated phrases like this make you wonder if she's actually stepped foot on Earth since 1982. See "Ghost Light" (26.2), though, for what's probably the definitive evidence on her year of origin.]

Ace says she was attempting to extract Nitroglycerin from Gelignite when something about her endeavour generated a time-storm that ferried her to Iceworld. [On the face of it, this is almost - but not quite - as daft a means of time-travel as the 144 static-charged mirrors used by Waterfield in 4.9, "The Evil of the Daleks". Fortunately, "The Curse of Fenric" offers a rather better explanation. Then again, it was a chemist, the Rani, who figured out how to run a TARDIS by remote control - see 22.3, "The Mark of the Rani".] On a separate occasion, she was suspended after blowing up the art room [she elaborates on this in "Battlefield" (26.1)]. After her suspension, she worked as a waitress in a fast-food café.

She somehow seems to have packed her bags before the trip [unless some of the contents of her room travelled with her], as she has a nylon rucksack, cycle-shorts, a puffa-jacket festooned with badges and a T-shirt from Top Shop. The badges indicate she's got an interest in old TV, especially *Blue Peter* and Gerry Anderson puppet shows. Items in her backpack include a flask of coffee, a rolled-up metal ladder [seen again in "The Curse of Fenric"] and her Nitro-9 explosives. The latter are described as 'like ordinary Nitroglycerin, but with more wallop', and seem capable of sticking to ice. [In later stories, they'll just be deposited on the ground in front of whatever needs demolishing.] Two Nitro-9 cans can bring down a door-high ice wall.

The Supporting Cast (Well Dodgy)

• *Glitz*. He owes 100 crowns [see **History**] to Kane, as he sold him a space-freighter full of rotting frozen fruit. Glitz also sold his crew for 17 crowns each (or 102 crowns total), but lost it in a rigged card game. He more than once seems to think that action and adventure are "too dangerous for girls". [More likely meaning that he would get too distracted - the novelisation and the *New Adventures* suggest he got it on with Ace at least once.]

The flight cabin of Glitz's spaceship, the *Nosferatu*, contains a pair of fuzzy dice, a Stradivarius and a painting by an Old Master [i.e. Dutch of Flemish, from the seventeenth century, give or take a couple of decades]. Somewhere on the ship, he also has 600 kilos of commercial explosive.

The TARDIS The hatstand has been painted white, and the scanner can evidently supply star-maps that are contemporary for the era of arrival.

The Non-Humans

• *Kane*. As a native of the planet Proamon, Kane's body temperature is considerably below zero. It's low enough that he can "freeze-burn" people to death by touching their heads with his hands, but he regularly warms to -10 Celsius, whereupon he must lie in a chamber in his 'restricted zone' and bring his body temp down to -193 Celsius. [He seems to do this rather often - three times in three episodes, in fact - so perhaps all this "hand-freezing my enemies to death" really takes a toll on a person.] He can easily plunge his hand into liquid nitrogen, which is at -200 Celsius. Temperatures above zero Celsius greatly sap his strength, and exposure to concentrated sunlight melts / vapourizes him in seconds. Kane's people are likely extremely long-lived, as he's been exiled from home for 3,000 years, yet in no capacity acts decrepit.

• *The Bio-Mechanoid Dragon*. [It's unclear if the one seen here was crafted especially to keep Kane restrained, or if it's part of an entire species.] A tall, purple, pickle-headed bio-humanoid that the Doctor describes as a 'semi-organic vertibrate with a highly developed cerebral cortex'. It seems adapted to the cold, and augmented with electronics. The top-heavy design appears to be either reptilian or insectoid, and entails a vast head atop a humanoid body, with spines along the back. The Dragon can fire lethal laser beams - which the Doctor estimates are 'in excess' of 1500 Celsius - from its eyes [although it can see through these as well, apparently]. Within its cranium lies the jewelled 'Dragonfire' power-crystal. This is revealed when the bio-mechanoid's entire head segments into four, with the face tipping forward and the rest opening like a musical box.

Although charged with keeping the Dragonfire

The Semiotic Thickness of *What?*

If you think about it, nothing that's lasted as long, changed as often and been such a part of British pop-culture as *Doctor Who* could have escaped the attention of academics. But what's amazing - when you consider the ways that shoals of papers follow the same subjects around, like pods of dolphins - is that so few of any note have been published. Compared to how Donna Haraway's flimsy piece about the links between Deleuze and Guattari's writing on the "Body Without Organs" and the dated concept of the Cyborg (which she seems to have picked up from a Frank Zappa record) spawned an entire industry - Google it if you don't believe us - it's remarkable. Compared to the volume of stuff about *Nationwide* (which went off-air in 1983), it's downright bizarre. And what's really odd is how much of what exists was done by Australians.

In 1983, John Fiske (most of the Australian academics are named "John") made some observations on "The Creature From the Pit" (17.3) that only someone who's never seen any other British television could make. His basic point, however, is that programmes like this are popular because they don't make the viewer ask awkward questions about their lives. This was commonplace amongst theorists in the 1970s, and has its origins in Pre-War German scholarship. The starting-point for anything interesting about mass culture is the Marxist literary critic / philosopher Walter Benjamin, and the text of his to begin with (which many students never get beyond, because this one essay is so useful) is "The Work of Art in the Era of Mass Reproduction". Benjamin's worry is that individuality is an illusion catered for and fostered by business making so much stuff for people to pick and choose from. His version is a bit more complicated than that, but this is a short essay and we've got a lot of ground to cover. (Unlike most of the people we'll be citing, Benjamin writes for a general readership, so check out *Illuminations* one day.)

Benjamin was writing in the context of the group we now call The Frankfurt School - a centre for neo-Marxist social theory - and another member of this, Theodor Adorno, disagreed with him and got the last word by not dying. (Benjamin's death is the type of thing they wrote operas about, but that's another story.) Adorno and his followers said that anyone who liked something popular was a stooge of the state. We are all stupid cattle-like consumers, being lied to and loving it. (Again, this is a very crude summary of half a century's work.) Only people who've been to University - and even then only the ones who've read Marx (and of course, Adorno) - can be free of this conditioning. Everyone else needs to be forced to see the Truth.

So this was the mainstream view when John Fiske wrote his 1983 paper "*Doctor Who*: ideology and the reading of a popular narrative text". For Fiske, the fact that mining and Free Trade in "The Creature From the Pit" are seen as "natural", and Lady Adrasta's efforts in to stop this are associated with "evil" and "strangeness", is all part of the BBC's conspiracy to make us accept Capitalism without question. He notes that Romana's name comes with imperialist associations of Law and Justice, and that she's dressed as a vestal vIrgIn. He observes that only the comedy proles lack the "aristocratic" speech. He *doesn't* note that Romana dressed as a schoolgirl the previous week (in 17.2, "The City of Death"), in a story about a mad capitalist alien that amounted to a Frankfurt School critique of Commodity Fetishism. Nor did he mention that Tom Baker learned to talk posh to lose a Scouse accent. He ignores the semiology of Adrasta and the Hunstman, which derives in part from Disney's *Snow White*, and in part from fetish culture. He misses the significance of the BBC's strained relationships with the Conservative Party *and* the Unions *and* that the Corporation - as he suggests - is not run by the Government. Being an Australian, and mainly watching American TV, it doesn't occur to him that the link between communications and commerce in the UK might be different. He's so in thrall to the Frankfurt School, he can't see how something can be publicly funded and not state-run. What Fiske needed was the Big Picture - and in the same year, we got it.

Well, sort of. Wind back to 1977, and the British Film Institute suddenly notice that there's never been a book where outside observers watch an entire TV series happen, from the initial idea to the viewers' reactions. So Edward Buscombe (BFI's publications editor) and Manuel Alvorado (from the Society for Education in Film and Television) - neither of them Australian, by the way - go to Thames and ask if they can sit in the back and watch. Thames lets them in on the making of a *noir*-ish comedy-drama, *Hazell*. The resulting book is a real eye-opener on how too many cooks can spoil a broth, but one of the main players - and someone who comes out of the book very well - is

continued on page 211...

out of the wrong hands (i.e. Kane or his henchbeings), the Dragon accepts the Doctor as being worthy of knowing about its greatest possession. From this and other characteristics, it seems to have a reasoning intelligence but no verbal abilities. It first communicates with the Doctor, in fact, by copying his hat-raising gesture. The creature seems generally benevolent and able to distinguish between right- and wrong-doers, as when it aids the little girl Stella.

If the Dragon is killed and beheaded, the Dragonfire emits a final burst of residual energy that slays those attempting to procure it.

Planet Notes

• *Svartos*. Has a permanent dark side, on which the space-trading outpost of Iceworld is located. [The planet seems to be made entirely of ice, with a breathable atmosphere and tolerable gravity. It's generally implied that it's in captured rotation around its star, although in truth it might as likely to be a moon of another world. More on this in **Things That Don't Make Sense**.]

Svartos seems to have been hollowed out into caverns, tunnels and caves, but the bulk of the population seem to inhabit or visit Iceworld's frozen food outlet. This has catering facilities, and is arguably at room temperature. The complex has a public-address system, and a two-leveled control complex where Kane keeps his cryogenically-suspended soldiers, and his lackeys control and monitor all activities on Svartos.

• *Proamon*. Kane's homeworld, an icy planet orbiting a Red Giant. The sun went supernova a thousand years after Kane was exiled, to the apparent surprise of the space-faring people who lived there. [A nasty thought: if Proamon is orbiting a star on which a device to blow up stars was tested... we're not saying it *was* necessarily the same solar system as Skaro (as we'll see in 25.1, "Remembrance of the Daleks"), but Kane's curious punishment might make a *bit* more sense if it was part and parcel of the Daleks' very odd legal system (see also 22.6, "Revelation of the Daleks" and 27.0, "The TV Movie"). This is only remotely feasible if you prefer a future dating for "Dragonfire" - and see **History** for that can of worms - because if we're operating in the present day, then the star blew up around 15 BC, and it's got nothing to do with the Hand of Omega or even the Doomsday Device (8.4, "Colony in Space") then. Further debate gets murky because we've no idea which

galaxy we're in, even though Glitz's presence suggests Andromeda, and because the Kaleds in 12.4, "Genesis of the Daleks" don't believe there are other planets capable of supporting life (so presumably they've looked in their own backyard).]

History

• *Dating*. Quite contentious, and no date is given on screen. [Right, let's run through the possibilities here. Glitz first appeared in "The Mysterious Planet" (23.1), and the Doctor dated that story to circa 2,000,000. This could well be Glitz's native era, so Occam's Razor would seem to suggest - allowing that the Time Lords sent Glitz home after "The Ultimate Foe" (23.4) - that "Dragonfire" occurs shortly afterward.

[Alternatively, it's been noted that Glitz might've been moved through time by the Master, who assigned him to hunt around Ravalox for the Matrix files ("The Mysterious Planet" again). If so, pinpointing Glitz's time becomes a lot more awkward. Either way, "Dragonfire" *still* might occur at some point in the future, as Ace is carried to Iceworld by a 'time-storm'. Using conventional English, the obvious implication is that she's been carried away from her native time. Fine, you could argue that Ace is a teenager from Perivale, 1987, and doesn't know the proper terminology, but the Doctor uses the exact same wordage in 26.3, "The Curse of Fenric". Nor does it seem likely that Fenric would conjure a 'time-storm' for the sake of pushing Ace forward just a few weeks or months, as he could've just spared that temporal energy and had her wait until the Doctor showed up. (Unless you start to call upon the sort of physics they use in *Star Trek*, but now we're getting entirely theoretical.)

[The fly in the ointment is that at the end of "Dragonfire", Glitz offers Ace a lift back to Perivale. He surely doesn't mean to take her back to Ravalox, given the primitive conditions there, yet the story's entire dynamic would be a lot different if the Iceworld / *Nosferatu II* were capable of time-travel. (Just for example, Kane could've foregone that whole suicide thing and instead flown straight back to Proamon three thousand years earlier, then done something nasty to his people before the sun went pop.) Along similar lines, it's bewildering that Mel seems to have no problem disembarking the TARDIS in the future without the time-technology required to return to her native era. Hopefully she's been made aware that

The Semiotic Thickness of *What?*

...continued from page 209

Thames' head of filmed drama, Verity Lambert.

It all makes sense now, doesn't it? The logical next thing to do is combine the practicalities of making a TV show with theoretical perspectives and interviews with key players. So Alvorado and another Australian, John Tulloch, get on the phone. Tulloch was editor of the journal where Fiske's paper was published. Soon Tulloch and Alvorado are interviewing Lambert about her first big project. (See **Where Does *All* Of This Come From?** under 1.1, "An Unearthly Child" if you seriously don't know what that is. Clue: this book is about it.) Then they ask Barry Letts, Terrance Dicks, Douglas Adams, Graham Williams and the current production team. However, the team in question is in flux at that time, as Christopher H Bidmead is giving up the script editor's seat to Eric Saward, but on the plus side this allows them to watch a story being made. Their luck's in, because that story is "Kinda" (19.3), a story that *needs* foreign eggheads to ask the writer and director what the hell is supposed to be happening.

A bit more context. Tulloch's later work shows a certain impatience with the pat assumptions of Adorno and his posse, but this is 1983 and Media Studies is still a subset of Film Theory. In the late 70s, the magazine *Screen* had featured many articles taking the Russian Formalist approach to cinema, and dissecting plots and montages according to a form of symbolic logic. Vladimir Propp's *The Morphology of the Folk-Tale* and AJ Griemas' diagrams were the common currency of this approach. If you couldn't do it with hieroglyphcs, it wasn't worth doing. (The example in *The Unfolding Text* of 6.4, "The Krotons" is pretty entry-level, but still causes nosebleeds for the uninitiated. See 26.3, "The Curse of Fenric".) There was a backlash brewing, as we'll see in a moment.

Meanwhile, US universities had noticed that SF was being read, so they got people to teach courses in reading it. Unfortunately, the people they got weren't always the people who should have taught this sort of thing. A few of the resulting textbooks are like listening to people who've never seen cricket played try to explain googlies to people who've never *heard* of the sport. Some of these were fruitful, but the ones that got into print were - with the exception of those by Samuel R Delany and his followers - appallingly schematic and obsessed with "definitions". Many of these were in the wake of Tsvetan Todorov's work on

Fantasy and the Uncanny, and Darko Suvin's crud about "Cognitive Estrangement".

Alas, there was no backlash. Tulloch and Alvorado tried to resolve all of this theoretical mess into a coherent book by stepping back from Film Theory and discussing *Doctor Who* as though it were a stage drama, a spectator sport and a critique of SF. And, being the early 80s, they used the word "Semiotics" an awful lot.

Almost a quarter-century on, we may need to explain what "Semiotics" means (start with the last paragraph of this essay), but back then real people used it in real conversations. Not, however, Ian Levine. That's right... Tulloch and Alvorado asked fans what they thought about the recent changes to the series - but the fans were the ones like Jeremy Bentham, the Liverpool Local Group of DWAS (the people who tore into Pip 'n' Jane on *Open Air*; see 23.4, "The Ultimate Foe") and Levine. Tulloch recycled these interviews to "represent" British fan opinion in the late 90s, but that's later. The book was advertised in *DWM*, and sold a lot of copies, some of which were read cover-to-cover. (Soon, fandom would start sending emissaries into the Ivory Towers, as we'll see...)

The immediate impact of *Doctor Who: The Unfolding Text* was that Eric Saward started to think that Robert Holmes was The Man. A slower impact was that the fanzines started digesting bits of the theory and applying them to stories not covered. Tulloch and Alvorado asked some interesting questions, but if they'd watched a few more stories than the ones in the BBC2 repeat season and borrowed a couple from friends, they would have come to different conclusions. It's significant that they never once mention "The Daleks" (1.2), even when they give a whole chapter to the superficially similar "Kinda". There are some hilarious moments, like when they show "Kinda" to Asian Buddhist students at the University of New South Wales, seemingly unaware that these kids had barely seen any television before.

However, by showing the process of making the series as part of a dialogue between viewers' interpretations, institutional requirements and technical capabilities, this formed a welcome opening out of the debate from knee-jerk Frankfurt School contempt. "Cultural Capital" was the new buzz-term. People who might be economically marginalised could use information or a social position of influence the way people use money or status.

continued on page 213...

the Trial Earth is effectively a wasteland, unless going to Ravalox and getting forcibly married to six hairy men is one of the 'crazy things' she wants to do. *Head Games*' allegations that the Doctor gave Mel a mental whammy and put her off the Ship seem all the more feasible, but even so...

[We *might* have to accept that "Dragonfire" is more or less contemporary with broadcast in 1987 - if only to make sense of the ending, which is rather important in that it swaps one series lead for another. The big hurdle there is that - talk of a 'time-storm' aside - you've got to assume that no-one else seen on Iceworld is human. All right, this doesn't require *much* more of a leap of faith than "The Daleks" (1.2), and the signs in English might (as is often the case) be a translation device. But once you factor in that Ace works in an Earth-style malt shop, the idea that these people *aren't* humanity's descendents starts to get extremely dubious. So it's entirely possible that "Dragonfire" is set in 1987, but very, very far from anywhere the programme has ventured before, but it's hardly what you'd call a flawless theory.

[One final note: if we *are* wedded to the idea that Iceworld is in the far future, we could assume that Glitz - who's never, as far as we know, told that Ace has been bumped through time - simply believes she travelled to Iceworld by spacecraft like everyone else, and that her home is within reach of the Nosferatu's engines. It *is* Glitz we're talking about, so he might just think that 'Perivale' is another colony planet. Either way, the Doctor mentions that Glitz could take Ace home by 'the direct route', but he could just be speaking figuratively, comparing it to the TARDIS' winding route through space-time. As we will see, Ace occasionally gives out signals that she's from 1982 or 1983 rather than 1987.

Three thousand years ago, the 'notorious' Kane-Xana gang carried out systematic violence and extortion that was deemed 'unequalled' in its brutality. Xana - clearly Kane's mate, as he here has an ice efficgy sculpted in her honour - killed herself in the final siege on the gang's headquarters. For the 'sheer evil' of his crimes, Kane was exiled from Proamon to the dark side of Svartos. One thousand years after his exile, Proamon was destroyed when its Red Giant sun went supernova and became a neutron star.

Many alien races travel to Iceworld, including at least one Argolin [18.1, "The Leisure Hive", and note that Argolins are "in" this season - see 24.1,

"Time and the Rani"] and a furry baby lizard [called Eric]. Iceworld is capable of flight, as driven by a 'starflight photon drive', but requires the Dragonfire to power it.

Through the centuries, travellers claim to have seen the terrifying Dragon that lurks in the lower passages of Iceworld, and it's legendary for guarding a treasure. Features in the lower levels include the 'Singing Trees' (ice crystals that resonate with the air currents) and the 'Ice Gardens' (an outdated star chart at the Dragon's disposal), and also - according to Glitz's map - the 'Lake of Oblivion' and the 'Death of Eternal Darkness'. The Planetary Archives from Proamon run off the Dragon's 'optical' energy, and Kane's history is found in Segment 931203.

In preparing for his revenge, Kane has assembled a band of soldiers that he keeps in cryo-freeze - this process freezes the neural pathways and causes complete memory loss, save in cases of overwhelming hatred or anger. One of these "zombies" withstands two of Ace's Nitro-9 explosions. [So the condition arguably enhances one's endurance.]

The Iceworld freezer section has phoenix eggs labelled as being free range. The Crab Nebula Pasties are on special offer. Glitz has an Asteroid Express card, but the local currency is the crown - a coin that bears Kane's profile. The value of a crown isn't clear [it's agreed that seventeen crowns isn't much money, but Glitz cannot repay Kane a sum of 102 crowns]. A photon refrigeration unit looks as though it's priced at 24.95. Grotzits are, apparently, also accepted. Kane freeze-brands the palm of those in his employ with "the mark of the Sovereign", meaning the face of such a coin.

Kane and the Doctor make mention of 'the Twelve Galaxies'. [The novelisation claims that Iceworld is somewhere in 'the Ninth Galaxy'. See **How Many Significant Galaxies Are There?** under 2.5, "The Web Planet", and give Briggs a pat on the back for getting it right.] Kane's lackeys sport guns that look very much like plastic. [But who knows? In this era, perhaps guns *are* made of plastic.] The Doctor seems to imply that Perivale is 'an idyllic place', but hastily revises his opinion when Mel reminds him that Ace comes from the twentieth century.

The Semiotic Thickness of *What?*

...continued from page 211

Look at the way people who know Latin or opera have a position as "refined" and "elite", regardless of how much they earn or what job they do. (And we'll return to this in a bit, but observe how even the most geeky *Doctor Who* fan tends to know about capital-C "Cultural" things far more than Trekkers generally know about anything outside the Federation's prescribed list of "Classics".) It came at around the time that Dutch theorist Ien Ang made a bolder statement about how people who like *Dallas* weren't all "fooled" by it, and how in fact it empowered women. She'd read Adorno, but she liked *Dallas* anyway. Then came Queer readings of *Dynasty*, that showed how little fun Camp can be when academics get their hands on it (see **Is *Doctor Who* Camp?** under 6.5, "The Seeds of Death"). And then came film studies professor Constance Penley's forays into the strange netherworld of the Trekkies...

...which is where the Shatner hit the fans. By making the undercurrents of slash fiction[30], Filk singing and scratch video seem like the whole of US media fan activity, Penley unleashed a torrent of confessional papers. American scholar Henry Jenkins made a stand against the cliché of Trekkies with no social lives, buying any old crud with the logos and sucking in junk TV like piglets. His approach was a form of self-conscious ethnography, studying his own kind like an anthropologist, but deeply critical of the way outsiders equate "viewing" with "consumption". Jenkins' book *Textual Poachers* is very much of its time (the early-1990s), when "Cult" TV was big business but seen by TV bosses as a male preserve. By showing what women "did" with such apparently technical, militarist, "male" shows, Penley and Jenkins created a new orthodoxy. Adorno was out, and French scholar Michel de Certeau was emphatically in (because you still need to drop an imposing European name to make it "safe" to like this stuff). Audiences can be "active", collecting a form of worth through what they know and how they produce new ways to re-write (or at least interpret differently) the shows we watch. And of course, as everyone knows, these conventions that people go to are almost entirely run and attended by women. Err... Go back and read **What's All This Stuff About Anoraks?** under 24.1, "Time and the Rani", if you can't see why applying all this to the UK is monumentally dumb.

What UK fan-academics eventually found was that the work on Football and Rave Culture was closer to our own experience. Novelist Nick Hornby's anguish at Arsenal's appalling run of failure - but his dogged determination to stay with "his" team - was echoed by anyone who'd sat through "The Trial of a Time Lord". Ethnographer Sarah Thornton's notion of "Subcultural Capital" seemed to explain how the things that might make someone seem geeky earned that person kudos within a very small frame of reference. This formed a challenge to the assertions of sociologist Pierre Bourdieu, who found a way to detach status from income with the original "Cultural Capital" idea.

The other thing was that - even in the mid-90s - the general public knew about *Doctor Who*, and so the boundaries of fandom were more porous here than in the States. That said, we were fairly close knit. That had a big impact, as we sort of patrolled one another's tastes and memories. Education psychologists - and there's a large number of schoolteachers in UK fandom - will recognise this as a nationwide version of Vygotsky's "Zone of Proximal Development". It basically stated that a community has a bigger collective memory than any one member, but that memory is distributed so that individuals can access it better than individuals not in such a network. Thus, fans of a particular football team will be better-equipped to know stats about any other team than anyone who just doesn't like football.

Similarly, members of the general public who claim to prefer *Star Trek* to *Doctor Who* will nonetheless have less good recall of individual *Trek* episodes than even *Who* fans who claim to hate *Trek*. (A fair amount of us seem to feel that way, actually. Ask us about something like *The West Wing* or *Butterflies* though...) Similarly, the process of assimilating new information or attitudes is faster in a group of like-minded individuals than done alone or in a crowd of "others". There was a funnel effect. So, far from being powerless parasites, British fandom was a mechanism for educating and training people in how to be a Fan, and this was transferable expertise for the wider world and in particular Higher Education. People could join this "Invisible College" almost by accident, by knowing a fan socially, and become sucked in to Our Way of Thinking without actually seeing that many old episodes. A handful joined via *The New Adventures*. Some just shared houses

continued on page 215...

The Analysis

Where Does This Come From? As we've hinted, the names of the characters are mainly taken from film theorists, and the conscientious viewer who looks them all up could get a Media Studies A-Level without even trying. Some of them were also practitioners. Vsevolod Pudovkin directed *The Mother*, a masterpiece of silent Soviet film (which ends with ice melting, calamitously) and had some interesting ideas about how to act for film. Siegfried Kracauer wrote *From Caligari to Hitler*, the best book on the psychology of German pre-war cinema. Andre Bazin co-founded *Cahiers du Cinema* - it was the magazine that made cinema theory happen (which is why so much of the terminology is French), but he's the only significant contributor not to have made famous movies as well. Marshall McLuhan was mentioned quite enough in Volume II, thank you.

Bela Belazs was another theorist, with whom Bazin had a sort-of debate about editing over the course of decades. Ace's boss is named Anderson (after Lindsay, the director / New Cinema theorist) on screen, but gets rechristened Eisenstein (after Sergei, the director / Marxist Cinema theorist) in the book. Kane was originally called "Hess" (but this was deemed a bit too Nazi) and officially was renamed in honour of *Citizen Kane* (as the original poster says, "It's Terrific!"), hence a lot of the other names being critics who've said how good it was. (One who disagreed - Pauline Kael - was originally mentioned in the PA dialogue.)

However, "The Mark of Kane" sounds a bit familiar, Biblically speaking. And if we're talking about Space Opera crime-bosses, we need only look as far as *Buck Rogers* for a slightly better fit. Kane's death is only the most flagrant visual "quote" in the story, and was far from being the most obvious steal from *Raiders of the Lost Ark* that Cartmel would sanction. The Red Sun business, with all the caves of ice with hi-tech plot-explaining hologram technology and a nice lady telling us about escaped criminals, is right out of *Superman II*.

Although the overall feel of the story is intended to echo *The Maltese Falcon*, there's more than a bit of *Treasure of the Sierra Madre* about how people fall out over treasure. The name *Nosferatu* is clever, as not only was it a silent vampire film, but it had been remade towards the end of the Werner Herzog / Klaus Kinski dysfunctional co-depend-

ent set-up. Moreover, it's enough like "Nostromo" to suggest *Alien* without actually copying it. Except that, of course, they *did* copy it (and its sequel) with the Dragon design and mention of the "ANT hunt". And, of course, Stella is like Newt (the little girl from *Aliens*) only more likeable, even putting Teddy to sleep in a cryo-pod. Stella being rescued by the monster is a tip of the hat to Boris Karloff and James Whale (*Frankenstein*).

We could go on like this for ages. Outside cinema, though, is something more prosaic. Iceworld is manifestly Iceland - a chain of low-budget freezer-centres, selling some of the most disgusting processed comestibles on the planet (but really cheap and in bulk, so don't knock it). The description of the Kane-Xana gang is very like the Baader-Meinhof organisation, who thought of themselves as revolutionaries but who never got much further than bank-jobs, clumsy murders and kidnappings.

Most importantly, though, this is the first *Doctor Who* story for some time to seriously consider the everyday lives of the majority of the target audience. The 1980s were mainly a period of high unemployment, but many teenagers had menial jobs just to earn cash, and some came to believe that without one you might as well not exist. With high unemployment comes an attitude among bosses that anything the staff are asked to do is acceptable, because the alternative is being replaced by someone who'd be glad to do it. (Funny how writers who were leaving school just then remember this - see X3.4, "The Daleks in Manhattan" for an example.) In 1987, McDonalds had almost ceased to be a novelty in Britain. Other junk-food chains saw the employment practices imported with the style of meal as the way forward. The nation's teens learned to mouth horrid platitudes and catch-phrases through gritted teeth, and all dreamed of escape. The entire Rave culture of the late 80s was paid for by fast-food wage-slavery. (We'll pick this up under 25.2, "The Happiness Patrol", but bear in mind that Ben Aaronovitch was an enthusiastic participant in this scene.)

Ace's entire look is one associated with House music, then almost emerging in the mainstream after a few years underground. Like all American fads associated with Da Ghetto, it's mainly middle-class white kids and ageing hipsters who get into it most deeply. Ace is from Perivale, a suburb in

The Semiotic Thickness of *What?*

...continued from page 213

with fans. The point is, more people know the phrase "reverse the polarity of the neutron flow" than actually saw "The Sea Devils" (9.3), and they had access to this vast mutual-aid affiliate. (Need we add that being a fan here meant something almost unrecognisable to anyone expecting us to be like Penley and Jenkins said American Treksters were? Apparently, we can't say this often enough.)

Fiske, of course, chimed in that this may well be true, but in the wider scheme of things it still made us powerless consumers. Not so, said everyone else, because with *Doctor Who* off the air, we own it now. It's fans who write the books and audio dramas, fans who find the missing episodes in vaults, and fans who get to patrol what the public think of it as a social phenomenon. Inevitably, Jenkins and Tulloch teamed up. Tulloch did some original research about Australian *Doctor Who* fans, and regurgitated all the interviews with Ian Levine from 1982. Jenkins re-thought some of his original assumptions about Trekkers and Trekkies (of course there's a difference: Trekkers are more fun to annoy). Obviously, the Jenkins material was of far more use to British *Who* fans (even if it assumed that anyone who didn't write slash was an anomaly, whereas 95% of us only heard of this silly habit through books such as his), but it began a worrying trend. Nobody was talking about the programme any more.

At least, not in book form. One of the side-effects of *The Unfolding Text* was that a generation of fans got curious and looked up all the long words. In the medium term, the most obvious sign of this was *In Vision*, a partwork analysis of every story from 12.1, "Robot" on. (It succeeded an earlier, less rigorous chronicle called "Adventures in Time and Space".) This raised the bar for even the most dryly factual behind-the-scenes analysis, but also tried to be more incisive than *DWM*'s meticulous Archive features. Others followed suit, usually to disagree with *In Vision*'s commentary.

The fanzines of the 1990s were amazing for many reasons, but one of these was the "arms race" that went on. Fan A would-be sat in a university library, nonchalantly reading Mikhail Bakhtin's *Problems of Dostoievski's Poetics*, when suddenly s/he would see the handy spotter's guide to the Menippean Satires in Chapter 4 and think, "So *that's* why I prefer Season Six to *Who Framed Roger Rabbit?!*"[31] Fan B would be hiding a copy of semi-pro fanzine *The Frame* under a copy of *Barely Legal*

and become incensed at the completely wrong-headed use of Andre Bazin's theory of the Associative Montage in an article about Douglas Camfield, and would hastily fire off a 5000 word rebuttal. (Or just harangue the author at the Fitzroy Tavern for hours on end.) Fan C would decide to launch a new fanzine and invite A and B to write for it, so both pieces would appear, separated by a photoshopped picture of a boy-band with one of the heads almost flawlessly replaced by that of Jon Pertwee.

In his continuing criticism of Fiske, Tulloch uses similar material - well, not the Pertwee photo, but Bakhtin and Ang - in his 1990 book *Television Drama: Agency Audience and Myth*. But when he mentions *Doctor Who* at all, it's Fiske's essay and his own book he discusses, not the programme. This is another difficulty with the way academics handle this kind of subject. If someone else has written about a TV series, the writing about it is the subject for all subsequent published work. It takes a brave soul like Jenkins to raise his or her head above the parapet and say "this is worth looking at", so the more freakish the phenomenon (and you don't get more freaky than slash fiction about *The Professionals* or *Top Gear*), the more likely it is to get into print, and be lightly retouched and submitted elsewhere to bulk up one's publication-list. Small wonder that fans A, B and C drift away from academia and write reviews for dumbed-down laddish TV magazines to pay off student loans. Some - like Matt Hills and Tim Robins - stuck it out and became lecturers, but their work is largely preaching to the converted.

After all, a lot of fans would have wound up in academia anyway - it's part of what we're like. As you'll recall from the essay with 2.6, "The Crusade", British fans wound up as bibliophiles, and wanted to know everything. Most of us would have been like this anyway, but we had an emotional core and a "narrative" linking otherwise disparate material. Many of us used our *Who*-learning as a framework in which to place any new theories or information we gathered, and happened to manifest this as an ability to do well in studies of pretty arcane stuff; others found ourselves "cursed" with this series and its lore and tried to understand ourselves better using the insights of sociology, psychology and literary theory. (We would humbly suggest that this marks out what Hills thinks is a distinction between "fan-scholars" and "scholar-

continued on page 217...

West London (home of Janet Street Porter, op cit), but she acts like she's from Hackney or Brixton. The dead giveaways are her dated slang ('Ace', 'Wicked', 'Brill', the last tainted by its use in *Little and Large*), and the fact that all this trendy badge-wearing includes two *Blue Peter* badges and one for "Fanderson" - the Gerry Anderson fan club. She is, however, an amalgam of real street-kids that Briggs knew, and so in his hands the character is less contrived than usual. She is also, if you hadn't guessed, yet another film *homage* - this time to the 1939 MGM version of *The Wizard of Oz*. Her name would have been 'Dorothy Gale'[29].

We've cited some of the most obvious film quotations, but what's really new is that the audience is not only expected to pick up on these, but to appreciate the way they've been pummelled together into a story. Mid-80s culture did this a lot - sampling here, alluding there and plonking in *homages* whether they needed to or not. It was how American television had started to do things, with shows like *Moonlighting* and films like *Gremlins*. We needn't labour the point that this is how 70s BBC shows like *Gangsters* and *The Goodies* had worked, except to say that those were treated as innovative exceptions in their day, whilst the constant stream of pastiche and parody was now treated as almost compulsory.

Things That Don't Make Sense Just like two stories earlier [24.2, "Paradise Towers"], there seems to be a massive and totally unbelievable backstory at work here. How on Earth did Kane come to be exiled in the elaborate spaceship that is Iceworld, the power-source of which resides inside the Dragon? Fair enough that Kane's people might not be into the death penalty and would opt to exile him instead, but did they *really* need to devote so much time and resources to building the means by which he could escape and exact vengeance upon them? [And it's no less illogical to say that Kane had Iceworld built after his arrival, because if he had the means of crafting such a vessel, he surely could've had its power-source installed too.]

So basically, the only safeguard to Kane's prison is that he never gets around to murdering his jailor - something his lackeys readily accomplish once he orders them to do so. Of course, it's only in *this* story that Kane deduces that the rumoured 'treasure' that the Dragon protects and his power-source are one and the same - even though he's

had three thousand years to obsess upon the subject. It would also appear that none of the myriad of space-travellers who've visited Iceworld throughout the centuries have casually mentioned that Proamon's sun went nova a couple of millennia back, so Kane is astonishingly in the dark about that as well. But then, the total obliteration of Kane's space-faring people seems rather suspect, as their star would've exhibited warning signs of going supernova for several million years beforehand. [Unless some of Kane's people *did* survive and were told to steer well clear of Svartos.] It's also remarkable that Kane suffers so much from the temperature rising above zero Celcius, yet fails to get horrible hand-burns while killing people. [As Kane's victims have an internal body-temperature of 37° Celcius, "hand-freezing" them should've practically felt like he was touching a volcano.]

If Iceworld *has* got a permanent dark side, then it must orbit another planet and have captured rotation. Like our Moon, captured rotation is a result of an imbalance in a satellite's mass, so the side that's physically lighter would become the dark side, if you see what we mean. The problem being: Svartos' dark side is the side with a bloody great city-sized spaceship, so unless the ship is generating anti-gravity [and consider that everyone's walking about more normally than you would on an ice moon, which would be have barely any attraction for anything smaller than an elephant], the orbit would be made wonky. And it's going to become wonkier still once the ship takes off.

Ace informs Mel that she's 'never told anyone' that her name is Dorothy, as if nobody at home - not her school teachers, not her classmates, not her parents' friends in Perivale - were ever aware of this. This is a bit dubious, you must admit, as the sort of secret that you only tell *one* person in your lifetime. In episode three, why does Glitz go searching for Ace in her room, when he told her and Mel to stay put in the ice caves? [The novelisation says he's there to search for her Nitro-9, but this isn't what happens on screen.] And how does the little girl get into Kane's Restricted Zone - did he not bother to lock the door behind him? He would surely have felt a warm breeze, and everyone else a cold draft. (But then, the Restricted Zone's status as a high-security area is already open to debate, considering Belazs can apparently spy on Kane through an open doorway.)

The Semiotic Thickness of *What?*

...continued from page 215

fans", us-in-academia and them-writing-about-us.) The audience for Hills' exemplary book probably knew most of the content already (except the chapter about Elvis impersonators), whereas the fanzines - like the series itself in the early days - served the function of what Antonio Gramsci called "Organic Intellectuals", bridging the gap between the campus and the work-place. (We offer *this* as a thesis subject for anyone reading who wants to try.) And compared to the early years of Tulloch and Alvorado, we ask very different questions as fans than "not-we" academics might. We're better-briefed in the wider context of British television and popular culture. You need a *Who* fan on your quiz team, especially in the rock-music and movie trivia rounds.

Once a fan got to make the series in Wales, Fiske's Adorno-flavoured interpretation became more relevant. There's still a trend towards fan-wank, but it's only to do with things Joe Public might know about, like Daleks, Cybermen or BBC Wales' own new monsters. Think how often the Slitheen are name-checked in Series Two. So far, they're reluctant to have too many overt acknowledgements of the "old" past, unless you count the Macra in "Gridlock" (X3.3) and the Isop Galaxy references. (Funnily enough, a Spider-robot ran into the camera *just* like the Zarbi in 2.5, "The Web Planet" within minutes of the Face of Boe making his debut in X1.2, "The End of the World".) Fans once again look like an excluded minority, but so many are in such a lot of interesting positions in wider society, BBC Wales is finding it hard to police the PR distribution.

Even when Manchester University Press launched a new book on the back of the new series, it was about what we're now supposed to call the "classic" series. The submission date for all completed papers was December 2004, three months before "Rose" (X1.1). *Time and Relative Dissertations in Space* is the first textbook since Tulloch and Alvorado to talk about the series rather than its fans, and should be coming out around the time this volume sees the light of day. Many of the contributors' names will be familiar to Mad Norwegian's core readership. Twenty-four years since *The Unfolding Text*, Media Theory has developed out of all recognition from the Structuralist consensus of those days. However, the main strength of *Doctor Who* for academic study now is as a core-sample through twenty-six years of rapid change. It is, for many people, about the only black and white BBC archive material available.

Right, so back to "Dragonfire" and That Security Guard's question to the Doctor. ('Tell me... what do you think about the assertion that the semiotic thickness of a performed text varies according to the redundancy of auxiliary performance codes?') On page 243 of *The Unfolding Text*, stage theorist Kier Elam's work is cited as a way to evaluate the way we might interpret "City of Death". In a nutshell, if we've got people in loud ties and fedoras holding the Doctor at gunpoint, we think "30s gangsters". Whereas with a well-dressed man with a posh voice and a lot of ornaments giving them orders, we think "Bond villain". A man in a raincoat talking like Mickey Spillane is supposed to reinforce the former, but he's obviously English and nobody's taking him seriously. But the Doctor and Romana, dressed like students, aren't taking the Bond villain seriously either, which makes the hoodlums behave more hoodlumly. Then Dudley Simpson adds *Pink Panther* music over shots of Catherine Schell. And so on. We've got many systems of signs and references at work, but each trips the other up and acts as a commentary on the limits of systems like those. (The study of how signs form systems is called "Semiology" and the number of semiological systems at work at once is "semiotic thickness".) And sixteen million people tuned in to "City of Death", so it's not some elitist game. Like we said at the start, it's amazing more people aren't writing about this stuff. But you can also see how anyone in a film-theory class might read this and want to have a go himself, hence "Dragonfire" and "The Curse of Fenric".

The emergency services team on Iceworld are so inept they think the best way of clearing a door-high ice blockade is for two of their members to push in it with their bare hands. [If they keep at it long enough, they might melt it with body-heat, perhaps, eventually.] And while we've ridiculed the "Doctor dangling" cliffhanger enough, the scenario becomes even stranger in long-shot, where it looks like there's an iron railing beneath him as part of a catwalk. So there *must* be a safe route down to it, in which case all the scaling the ice-wall business has just become doubly pointless.

An aesthetic concern... the caverns of Iceworld are allegedly frigid, and even Kane's headquarters is probably at most zero Celsius. Yet you can't ever see anyone's breath, nobody seems to shiver, and Ace and Mel loaf around inside a glacier in shorts and T-shirts. They even take their jackets off to chat over the coffee. And note how the Doctor, with spikes on his shoes, is slipping around on the ice when nobody else is.

Critique   Chris Clough has many virtues as a director. He made some savvy casting decisions, and found ways to make locations work that really shouldn't have come off. He also tackled the logistics of night-shoots and scenes where the general public might have intervened diligently, but it's in the studio that his faults are more apparent.

We're mentioning this here rather than in stories where it's a big let-down, because in those cases there were mitigating circumstances. "Dragonfire" has fewer reasons to look so stagey than, say, "The Happiness Patrol" and should by rights look more cinematic than "Terror of the Vervoids" (23.3). So in a story where nearly every character is named after a film theorist or director, it looks a bit perverse to almost draw attention to the limits of cheap television drama. The scenes in episode one that really stand out as exposing the drawbacks of three-camera gallery direction are Ace's tipping a milkshake on someone (to be fair, that's a scene that could hardly have worked if John Ford or Orson Welles had made it) and the first cliffhanger. No, not the cliffhanging *itself*, daft as this was, but the lead up to it. Cutting to the Doctor from the Dragon approaching Ace and Mel only puts the emphasis on the wrong part of the narrative.

This script was admittedly written as a comedy, so the peril for the Doctor was a good time to do a bit of Harold Lloyd, but the point is that he's thus unable to rescue the girls and explain what's going on to them (and us). We're labouring this point to illustrate (again) how unlike usual Clough-directed stories this is: even a confused mess like 25.3, "Silver Nemesis" or "The Ultimate Foe" makes a kind of sense when we're watching, because director and cast have figured out what the viewers want to know and how to deliver this information clearly.

A drawback of the producer's cunning plan to make two three-part stories for the price of a six-parter is that Clough seems inclined to polarise his two back-to-back stories. It's slanted so that one is

all location and the other is all studio, but *also* so that one is all comedy and the other is all action, or one is character-led and the other is plot-driven. It's not quite as linear as that, but this is a definite tendency. A script like "Dragonfire" has an inherent leaning towards playing it for laughs, and yet because we're coming to it straight after 24.3, "Delta and the Bannermen", Clough opts to follow the old maxim about farce being tragedy speeded up. All the performances are solidly motivated characters, and such gags as there are come from the situations, not the performances. On the whole, this is a good call.

Where this falls apart is when the plot requires characters to abruptly change their views. Within minutes, Glitz goes from vowing vengeance on Kane for blowing up the *Nosferatu* and causing thousands of casualties to passively observing Kane's apparent victory and then cheerily welcoming new customers (should more than two remain alive) to Iceworld / *Nosferatu II*. Kracauer goes from obsequious Kane-man to treacherous assassin in moments. Mel flips in the last scene from boring engineer to wild and crazy party girl. One-dimensional characters can do this with ease, but after putting that *bit* more effort into it, each actor is painted into a corner with regard to plausible motivation. This schism is largely down to the script.

As a plot, "Dragonfire" is clever enough, but where it *really* scores is in dialogue. Someone from an ice planet would use metaphors like 'the past is an empty sled'. Under the dated teen-speak and odd nicknames, Ace is already defined as a character by her analogies: 'd'you wanna argue with a deodorant that registers nine on the Richter scale?' Unfortunately, as will happen a lot, Aldred will say this when walking away from a microphone ("The Happiness Patrol" suffers from this in particular). Still, speech-patterns come out of the character's point-of-view, rather than being imposed on that character almost at random, as was happening too frequently before. Go back to "Attack of the Cybermen" (22.1) or even just "Time and the Rani" (24.1) and you'll see what we mean. This allows characters who are doing bad things enough self-awareness to know that other people (and us viewers) might conceive of them as villains. Rather than deliver long speeches explaining their motives, they express their positions in throwaway remarks, in connections they make that others wouldn't, in misapplied intelligence...

and, in a word, "wit". We understand more about Kane in three brief episodes than we do about the Rani in three hours of screen-time.

While script-editing the early Nathan-Turner stories, Christopher H Bidmead claimed that the art of a good *Doctor Who* story was to create an odd but logically self-consistent world, then throw the Doctor at it and see what happens. But in actuality, Cartmel seems to have taken this idea as his starting point, and run with it far more than Bidmead. It's unlikely that Bidmead would have commissioned anything as (how can we say this?) "courageous" as "The Happiness Patrol", "The Greatest Show in the Galaxy" (25.4) or "Ghost Light". In fact, Cartmel's villains seem to be the very control-freaks Bidmead wanted us to admire.

Meanwhile, the Doctor of "Dragonfire" wins through a mix of experience, deductive reasoning and treating people fairly in good faith - all traits we recognise from earlier Doctors. It's almost as if the series is no longer afraid of comparisons with its former glories, even while it's still recognisably Nathan-Turner's show. The guest casting sees to that, but there's no grounds for complaint on this score. Bonnie's still around, but having Ace around makes Mel (belatedly and frustratingly) snap into place as a character. And for all of Briggs' complaints about this, Glitz being put into the story in place of a generic bad-boy treasure-hunter saves a lot of time on motivation and forming all-iegancies. Tony Selby is happy to be there, and one of the odd things about "Dragonfire" is that whilst the novelisation reveals that Glitz doesn't actually get the best lines, on screen it's his dialogue we recall fondly.

The Facts

Written by Ian Briggs. Directed by Chris Clough. Ratings: 5.5 million, 5.0 million, 4.7 million.

Working Titles "Absolute Zero", "Pyramid in Space", "The Pyramid's Treasure".

Supporting Cast Tony Selby (Glitz), Edward Peel (Kane), Patricia Quinn (Belazs), Tony Osoba (Kracauer), Leslie Meadows (the Creature), Stuart Organ (Bazin), Sean Blowers (Zed), Nigel Miles-Thomas (Pudovkin), Miranda Borman (Stella), Shirin Taylor (Customer), Daphne Oxenford (Archivist).

Oh, Isn't That..?

• *Daphne Oxenford.* For the post-war generation of British under-fives, she was the nice lady who asked, "Are you sitting comfortably? Then we'll begin". (Yes, just like X2.7, "The Idiot's Lantern".) This was the ritual start of a story on *Listen With Mother* on the Home Service (later Radio 4). So for anyone in Britain, she's the voice of childhood (at least until Nerys Hughes from 19.3, "Kinda" took over in 1982, and the BBC began moving it around the schedules as a pretext for dropping it). Oxenford was also in the first cast of *Coronation Street* and was later a semi-regular in *All Creatures Great and Small*. She's now approaching her late eighties, and Big Finish recently coaxed her out of semi-retirement to guest-star in the *Sapphire and Steel* audio "Cruel Immortality".

• *Edward Peel.* Shorn of his trademark moustache, and without the Yorkshire accent he'd used then, it may have taken some viewers a while to realise that he was the bloke from *Juliet Bravo*. In a series about a female chief of police - and who was single (as was her replacement, a couple of years later) - it was obvious that they'd try some "will-they-won't-they" stuff. Peel later went on to *Emmerdale Farm*, although he got out before the *New Adventures* crowd took over and made it aspire to kitsch status.

• *Tony Osoba.* He'd been in smash-hit prison sitcom *Porridge,* where his native Glaswegian accent had been used for comic effect. (In 70s Britain, we were used to seeing black actors, and used to people who talk like Billy Connolly, but not both at once.) He'd also been Lan in 17.1, "Destiny of the Daleks".

• *Patricia Quinn.* She's got four noteworthy roles to her name. In 1985, she'd been Sylvia Daisy Pouncer in the BBC's borderline-awful, occasionally bewitching adaptation of *The Box of Delights*. (That everyone reacts to her as if they've read *The Midnight Folk* - to which this is a sequel and in which Sylvia was prime villain - is part of the series' odd charm.) But ten years earlier she'd made a film you may have heard about: *The Rocky Horror Picture Show*, which is as good a pension plan as any. She was Biba-clad vamp Magenta. Between these she was - as most people try to forget - the witch-cum-plot-dispenser in camp classic *Hawk the Slayer* (see "The Mark of the Rani"). Her character is called "Meena", but you have to read the novelisation to know that, and be prepared to admit to having done so. More commendably, she was also the title character's sister -

and Patrick Stewart's mistress - in *I, Claudius*.

• *Stuart Organ*. He did long stints in *Grange Hill* and *Coronation Street*. Round these parts, that's like getting your face onto the stamps.

• *Sean Blowers*. Here playing the bit part as Zed - the crewman killed by Kane at the start of episode one - but soon to be a familiar face on British TV as one of the regulars in *London's Burning*.

Cliffhangers Mel screams as she and Ace finally confront the Dragon beneath Iceworld, even as the Doctor - for reasons best known to himself - dangles over the precipice hanging from his umbrella; the Dragon reveals the location of its treasure - the jewelled 'Dragonfire' - to the Doctor's party, but Kane is eavesdropping and declares it shall be his.

The Lore

• Like many writers new to *Doctor Who* in this period, Briggs came direct from the BBC script unit, had little previous writing experience and initially suggested several ideas that Cartmel felt were too reliant on both general SF and *Who*-specific clichés. As previously noted, Briggs felt that he would write the comedy serial of the season and his storyline (titled "Absolute Zero") reflected this. In this the villain was a 14-year-old business genius, with an oleaginous henchman named Mr Spewey.

• Briggs' scripts were very long, with episode two reputedly running to almost twice its intended duration. This problem with script overruns would become a recurring problem for the series' final two years. Among the material deleted before production was a long subplot involving Ace's toy dog Wayne, which is stuffed with Nitro-9 and used to blow up the zombified mercenaries. A lot of material with the little girl (initially unnamed in the scripts, but credited as 'Stella' on screen), including an encounter with Kane, was also dropped. Among the many film references, the bar was intended as an *homage* to the *Star Wars* Cantina (itself a series of quotes from classic Westerns), but as it was realised on a BBC budget with BBC lighting, this isn't immediately apparent on screen. In the original scripts the character that the Doctor and Mel meet here is a roguish space pirate named Razorback (Swordfish in some drafts) inspired by Han Solo. Nathan-Turner sug-

gested re-using Glitz in this role instead. This, of course, led to Briggs having to insert lots of dialogue with "grotzit" in, which he hated.

• So who actually created Ace? One of Andrew Cartmel's jobs upon arriving at the production office in January 1987 was to collaborate with Nathan-Turner on creating a new companion to replace Mel. 'Alf' (also an early stage-name for Yazoo singer Alison Moyet, which would've been clever five years earlier) was to be a teenage girl from 1980s London. She's described in strikingly similar terms to Ace, except that she ends up working as a checkout girl in a distant galaxy, and gets intentionally sacked by emptying a drink into her till. She was also much inspired by Sigourney Weaver's character in *Aliens*, released the previous autumn, but this shouldn't come as much of a surprise. Briggs was specifically instructed not to include Alf in his scripts, but he still drew on her heavily when developing Ace. With hindsight, Ray didn't stand a chance of becoming an ongoing character. Briggs also drew on aspects of three different girls of his acquaintance, including one who had actually blown up an art room at her school. Nevertheless, the writer later had to sign a waiver handing all rights to the character over to the BBC. (Characters who unexpectedly became companions were generally the property of the first script's author, hence Haisman and Lincoln getting a five pound cheque whenever the Brigadier turns up, whereas companions devised by the producer and script editor and farmed out to a writer to introduce are BBC copyright. Ace was in a grey area between Alf and Briggs' composite teen. The DVD of 26.4, "Survival" makes the agreement seem more casual than the extant paperwork suggests.)

• Sophie Aldred was one of more than 100 actresses to audition for Ace and Ray, and - as previously stated - was considered a likelier prospect for the latter role as she could ride a motorbike. By 26th of May, 1987, the casting had been narrowed down to Aldred, Lynn Gardner (who played the announcer in this story, see "Delta and the Bannermen") and Cassie Stuart. Three weeks later, Aldred was offered the three episodes with an option on a further year. She was appearing in *Fiddler on the Roof* in Manchester at the time, and delivered a heartier-than-usual rendition of the line "Mazeltov, Rabbi!" on the evening she got the news. (One of the other cast members was John Scott Martin, who was on hand when she took the phone-call backstage and welcomed her to the "family".) By his own account, Andrew Cartmel spent the next two and a half years infatuated with her. At McCoy's suggestion, Cartmel rewrote Briggs' scripts to end with Mel's departure rather than Ace's, incorporating elements of the audition piece he had written for McCoy. Briggs was reputedly unhappy with this scene.

• Ace's look was inspired partly by the picture of a girl in a badge-covered bomber jacket that had appeared in *The Face* (the "Troupette" look favoured by Salt 'n' Pepa, although they eschewed shocking pink tights). Aldred and costume designer Richard Croft went shopping on the Kings Road for the right look. A pair of yellow and black striped tights caught her eye, but proved unsuitable for recording as they made the cameras strobe. Aldred's visibly unshaved armpits distressed the cameraman for aesthetic rather than technical reasons. (Cartmel thought Aldred's posture quite sexy, but was out-voted.)

• Some of Ace's badges were bought specially, but others were from Aldred's own collection, including the two *Blue Peter* badges. You really have to earn these, they are not given out lightly - an illicit trade in them on Ebay in 2005 led otherwise sober commentators to call for the death penalty for this specific offence - and the production team had to clear Aldred's credentials with the indomitable Biddy Baxter before allowing them on screen. (If you're still unclear about how much value is attached to these badges, consider how Ray Cusick had to plead with them to give him one for designing the Daleks.)

Aldred's life-long ambition was to become a *Blue Peter* presenter. She never managed this, but soon after getting the "Dragonfire" gig she was hired as the presenter of a new BBC pre-school series, *Corners*. Production began less than a week after "Dragonfire" wrapped. (We note that soon afterwards *Blue Peter* hired Katy Hills, who was sort of a downmarket Sophie.) As "Dragonfire" was Aldred's television debut, she needed to be given directions to Television Centre, and was "adopted" by Langford. One piece of advice, about how microphones can hear *everything*, seems to be the reason there's so much less salacious gossip about Aldred than, say, Katy Manning.

• Ronald Lacey, who had turned down the role of the Chief Caretaker two stories earlier, was also offered the part of Kane. Lacey had played the flesh-seared Nazi named Todt in *Raiders of the Lost Ark*, and may have declined out of fear of being typecast in "melty face" roles. (The effect was mainly done with wax, although the body slumping to the floor was the aforementioned sex-toy deflating). David Jason and John Alderton were also considered. Briggs hoped to write a prequel story about Kane's background at one point. In rehearsals, Edward Peel and Patricia Quinn took it upon themselves to corpse McCoy - when their best efforts failed, they both seem to have begun to enjoy a job they'd taken on as just work a lot more.

• Briggs was unhappy with the realisation of the Dragon, which was designed by Andy McVean. Chris Clough tried to shoot the costume in shadow as far as possible, and to avoid showing its legs. For his novelisation, Briggs reverted to his original description and vetoed the inclusion of the TV design from Alister Pearson's cover. *Doctor Who Magazine* commissioned an illustration of Briggs's version from artist SMS, and to be frank it looked barely distinguishable from McVean's. And, speaking of the novelisation...

• What exactly is supposed to be happening at the end of episode one? As *broadcast*, the Doctor is seen to climb over a railing to dangle pointlessly over a precipice from the end of his umbrella. As *scripted*, the Doctor is following a map and attempting to clamber down to a ledge that proves rather more distant than he supposed. Sadly, this doesn't come across at all on screen, where the ice face is shown to be a sheer drop and the resolution in episode two - showing the Doctor and Glitz reaching the lower level safely - is simply nonsensical. Briggs was asked about this at various events after the story was broadcast and his response was invariably, "Read the novelisation". Some felt that this was more than a little patronising, and also impractical since the novelisation was delayed until March 1989. It didn't help that one of these events was a DWAS convention where Briggs and a pair of co-conspirators had drunkenly stormed the stage to hold an impromptu panel before being ordered off by Andrew Beech.

• Recording on "Dragonfire" concluded in mid-August 1987, less than a month before Season Twenty-Four began transmission. Sylvester McCoy's debut was met with almost unanimous disapproval from the press, and even those critics who praised his performance tended to concentrate on his voluble eccentricity at the expense of other qualities. At this point, there was little goodwill towards *Doctor Who*. For fans, the stakes were raised on 12th of September when the *Daily Mail* published a lengthy article by DWAS co-ordinator Andrew Beech that attacked McCoy, Nathan-Turner and the BBC's decision to retain Nathan-Tuner as producer following the 1985 cancellation (see "Time and the Rani" and the essay with 22.5, "Timelash"). The article - and the failure of "Time and the Rani" to make the hoped-for break-through against *Coronation Street* - polarised fandom into those who felt that the series desperately needed a change at the top, and those who felt that a critical response was both disloyal and would hand the BBC an excuse to cancel the series for good. (In fact, the series had been renewed for Season Twenty-Five in late August.)

In this hostile atmosphere, McCoy, Nathan-Turner and Langford appeared on the daytime phone-in series *Open Air* on 29th of September. Some fans who phoned in to voice complaints found themselves being cut off, and the strongest criticism of the series came from schoolchildren in studio. Soon after - and in a move that would be unthinkable today - the BBC dedicated an edition of the BBC2 television review *Did You See...?* to airing fan complaints against *Doctor Who*. This was broadcast on 22nd of November, the day before "Dragonfire" episode one went out, and featured contributions from fans Ian Levine (see most of the previous volume and this one) and Jeremy Bentham, academic Manuel Alvorado (see the accompanying essay) and fan-posing-as-academic Peter Anghelides. Soon afterwards, the notoriously militant fanzine *DWB* launched a campaign named "Operation Who", whose object was to get Nathan-Turner sacked and replaced. This alienated many fans, even those who might've agreed with the sentiment

Nathan-Turner considered suing *DWB* but was dissuaded by his boss, Jonathan Powell, who felt that this would be counterproductive. The producer had agreed to continue with the series for another year in August, unable to resist the prospect of handling the twenty-fifth anniversary season. At the start of 1988, it was reported that the next series would be Nathan-Turner's last and a hunt for a new producer was underway. "Operation Who" appeared to have succeeded in its aims, but the arguments between fan factions continued in the letters pages of *DWM*, *DWB* and numerous fanzines for months to come. As you have probably guessed, there has never been a

time (before or since) when the atmosphere in *Doctor Who* fandom has been more rancorous. It was all terribly funny.

• The general public (remember them?) were canvassed for their views on the series for an annual Audience Research report. McCoy's performance rated a poor 46% - the same proportion that wanted the series to continue - and Langford's a dismal 34%. (Objective statisticians, however, might wonder if questions such as 'Do you wish Mel had been eaten by the dragon?' didn't have a bias somewhere.) Sophie Aldred was more popular than either by a considerable margin.

• Meanwhile, the BBC needed a new Controller of BBC1. They discovered this when they turned on the TV one morning in October and saw news reports of Michael Grade arriving for work as Chief Executive of Channel 4. This was just the most visible of a series of seismic upheavals in the BBC hierarchy, coming at the end of a near decade-long struggle between the Corporation and a hostile government. Margaret Thatcher's ultimate aim of privatising the BBC had been decisively thwarted a year earlier, but in the process government pressure had squeezed out Director-General Alasdair Milne. Grade had put himself up for the vacancy, unsuccessfully. The new D-G was Michael Checkland, who was felt by many to be a compromise and a place-holder. The *real* power at the BBC now was the Deputy imposed on Checkland, one John Birt. There was room for only one powerful ex-LWT light entertainment yuppie whizzkid at the Beeb, and for many Grade's defection had only seemed like a matter of time.

Yes, *of course* this is relevant! Birt's ascendancy at the BBC would have a long-term effect on *Doctor Who's* prospects after the cancellation in 1989. More immediately, it removed from the scene an individual that many *Doctor Who* fans regarded as the villain of the piece, but his replacement as Controller of BBC1 was hardly more sympathetic to the series. This was the head of Drama, the aforementioned Jonathan Powell, who had previously produced classics like *Tinker Tailor Soldier Spy* and overseen a golden age of BBC serials. His five-and-a-half year stint as Controller is less fondly remembered by industry professionals. Most insider accounts suggest that Powell was even less-enamoured of *Doctor Who* than Grade had been; both Nathan-Turner and Cartmel would later intimate that their encounters with him were (to put it tactfully) unhelpful. And *he* was now in charge of the programme's future.

• "Dragonfire" was promoted as the 150th *Doctor Who* story in *Radio Times*, which also noted that the first episode was broadcast on the series' twenty-fourth anniversary. The numbering of the story was an extraordinary volte-face from Nathan-Turner, who'd spent a year saying that Season Twenty-Three was one long story. Additional publicity for *Doctor Who* came on the evening of 23rd of November 1987, as the BBC evening news covered an incident in Chicago the previous night when a repeat of 15.1, "Horror of Fang Rock" had been briefly interrupted by a TV hacker dressed as Max Headroom. You'd think this would have been etched onto the collective memory of fandom, but apparently not. (If you're so inclined, the footage from this is available on YouTube, but it's really not worth your time or trouble.)

• After leaving *Doctor Who*, Bonnie Langford failed to continue with the serious acting career she had hoped for (though this was hardly unusual for a *Who* Girl), but continued to appear in stage musicals, in light entertainment and as the butt of a thousand unfair jokes (including a long-running advert claiming to show her parents, with the cruel tagline "If only they'd worn a condom"). But then, she morphed into a National Treasure. After the surprise success of *Strictly Come Dancing* - which spawned America's *Dancing With the Stars* and a host of unauthorised knock-offs - everyone was just as surprised that ITV's "me-too" project was a hit. But by having ice dance - something Britain won Olympic medals for in 1984 - and *celebrities we'd actually heard of*, they did it. Unfortunately, all the people who would have put money on an all-*Who* final - Bonnie vs. John Barrowman - were thwarted by her getting injured and his being unexpectedly voted out in the semis. Jokes did the rounds about Jeb Bush supervising the count, that's how rigged it looked. But it did the trick for Bonnie - nobody thinks of her as Violet Elizabeth any more, they think of her as middle-aged gay icon Bonnie Langford.

25.1: "Remembrance of the Daleks"

(Serial 7H, Four Episodes. 5th - 26th October 1988.)

Which One is This?   *Doctor Who* plays at being kids playing *Doctor Who*: a spaceship lands in the school playground, and Ace hides behind the sofa on a Saturday evening in 1963.

Firsts and Lasts   It's the last appearance of Davros, and of series stalwart Michael Sheard (sob), who here marks his sixth appearance in the show since 1966 (3.6, "The Ark"). It's also the last time that an obvious pseudonym disguises an actor's presence (in this case, episode three credits one 'Roy Tromelly' as playing the Emperor Dalek, fooling no one).

For a generation of *Doctor Who* fans, the key moment is the first cliffhanger, in which a Dalek "chases" the Doctor up stairs. It's not the first time we've seen floating Daleks (that was in 22.6, "Revelation of the Daleks"), but this *is* the first time it's been done as something other than an odd-looking process-shot. And while a Dalek Emperor had appeared before (4.9, "The Evil of the Daleks"), this one is right out of the 60s *TV Century 21* strip (albeit the wrong colour and sans eye-stalk), as is much else on display here.

A couple of new Dalek-related features here will become so warmly regarded, they'll get recycled into the new series. Levitation (on the command 'Elevate') has become standard, but there's also the Daleks' Head-Up Display, which makes it look as if they're hunting their foes as part of a video game; the "skeletal effect" that characterizes someone dying from a Dalek energy bolt; and the very notion of a young female serving as a Dalek controller - all of which reappear in "Bad Wolf" (X1.12).

As "Battlefield" (26.1) didn't do it after all, episode one will stand as the last episode with a pre-credit sequence until 2005, when suddenly almost every story has them. This was the first story broadcast in Nicam Stereo, not that many people could get it then. And McCoy gets to yell "Aim for the eyepiece!" - the last time anyone will do so on TV for 17 years.

Season 25 Cast/Crew

- Sylvester McCoy (the Doctor)
- Sophie Aldred (Ace)

- John Nathan-Turner (Producer)
- Andrew Cartmel (Script Editor)

Four Things to Notice about "Remembrance of the Daleks"...

1. Look, kids, it's 1963! There's nothing on telly, the money's all weird, the jukebox plays hits from the 50s and people drive Commer vans with sliding doors. They've even found the right shape of milk-bottles for one scene, and looked out specific newspapers. Such a shame that every location they visit has 80s buildings in shot, spray-painted graffiti and the odd anachronistic bus. And those newspapers and the calendars are a problem - even allowing that you have to pause the video to them clearly - because they appear to indicate that it's November, when it manifestly isn't (see **When Did Susan Go To School?**).

2. Here writer Ben Aaronovitch - how shall we say this? - works through some "issues". The neo-Nazi Ratcliffe was originally named after a member of the Thatcher government, Professor Rachel Jensen's original surname was "Israel", and there's a cut scene where Sergeant Mike Smith suggests that he wouldn't fancy Ace so much if he learned she was foreign. But to be fair to Aaronovitch, for the most part this is seamlessly worked into the plot's main thrust about Daleks and notions of "purity". He's also made a conscious decision to have positive rolemodels, including strong women. Hence we have Ace going ninja on three Daleks and firing a bazooka at another, Rachel getting all the sarcastic one-liners and Allison... um...

3. Season Twenty-Five's policy of including a token black person in every adventure is obviously intended to be terribly "right-on". After all, racism is an Issue in this story, up to and including the 'No Coloureds' sign in the boarding house run by Mike's mum[32]. (But if this is intended as a clue that Mike himself might be a bit fascist, his working for a man with a black star badge - and

When Did Susan Go to School?

As you will know, the very first episode of *Doctor Who* begins with a mysterious schoolgirl walking home, followed by curious teachers. The school's terribly modern, and has no uniform but an official tie, and the pupils are vaguely hip and given to doing Kenneth Williams impressions. It's the early sixties, but when exactly?

It's become tradition (largely owing to sentiment) to think that "An Unearthly Child" (1.1) occurs in the week of 23rd of November, 1963 - the same as the first episode's broadcast that Saturday night - but if we look at the actual on-screen evidence, then we're no nearer to an answer. On the blackboard in Ian's lab is biology homework set on a Tuesday for completion by Thursday, but It's also there In flashback from "the other day" when Susan finds the chemistry lesson too simple. It's after dark when school ends, which suggests that it's probably the second half-term of the Christmas Term or the Spring Term. All right, but Spring Term 1963 would have been during the worst winter in memory, with snow staying on the ground until April. So it has to be after the clocks go back, which is half-term, and the homework on the board wouldn't have been set until the work assigned for half-term was marked and returned.

First week in November at the earliest, then. Which, if we take seriously Susan's comment to Barbara in "An Unearthly Child" that 'The last five months have been the happiest of my life', it suggests that she was enrolled at the end of summer term, and spent three months at liberty in London at the height of the Mersey boom. Now suppose that "Remembrance of the Daleks" (25.1) occurs a month later. (Most people surmise this from the conversation in the funeral parlour, assuming the 'old geezer with white hair' was - as was presumably intended - the First Doctor). Rev. Parkinson confirms that four or five weeks have elapsed since the arrangements were made for the Hand's interment.

So if Susan's abrupt departure from the school *did* happen in November 1963, i.e. on the day of transmission or thereabouts (not the Saturday itself), the funeral and the Dalek-on-Dalek action would occur just before the Christmas holiday. If so, the school should have been amateurishly decorated, and after-school activities such as rehearsals for carol concerts and a panto would have taken up much of the Head's time. Anyone living near a school will know how close Christmas is from the sound of badly-played recorders in the street at 3:30pm. This state of affairs didn't begin in August - as it seems to now - but certainly any later than the third week of October (half-term, the week when the clocks go forward), and the place would have kids wheeling dummies about demanding "Penny for the Guy"[34]. There might conceivably have been some Hallowe'en stuff *if* it was the very end of October.

Other discrepancies need to be taken into account. In "Remembrance", Coal Hill School has a uniform. We know from 2.5, "The Web Planet" that there's an official school tie (used as a belt). Maybe - and this runs against what we are told in books but never on screen - Susan is a Sixth-Former and Coal Hill's Sixth Form are allowed to wear their own clothes. Well, this book's author knows from bitter experience how hard it is to do A-Level History and Physics at the same time, as schools timetable the lessons on the assumption that nobody will do both. Nope, she's Fifth-Form, doing O-Levels, and yet her class are exempted from the Uniform regulations. (Although these can't be *too* strictly enforced, since - as we've mentioned - one of the kids at the start of "Remembrance" episode one is wearing Levi 501 jeans.)

It seems Susan's entire class are also doing History and Science. The jukebox in Harry's Café has a couple of hits from April 1963 (along with rather older stuff, much of it from 1959, oddly enough - see 24.3, "Delta and the Bannermen"), but nothing from after the sudden shift in the nation's tastes that took place in that summer. Even the sound-collage from the pre-credit sequence has nothing later than July in it. (If you're as sad as us, you will have scanned the newspaper headlines for clues: Mike's *Daily Mirror* is from May. But some cafés even today have out-of-date papers lying around so people can do crosswords while waiting for their meals.)

The clincher here is the one that every school-child spotted in 1988, when the story was first shown: if it's 5.15pm and time for "Do-" (and we'll address what the announcer on telly was about to say in a bit), why is it broad daylight outside? Any later than mid-October and it should be pitch black and the streetlights (even the anachronistic ones we see in the streets on location) would be on. Mrs. Smith would have banked up the fire, drawing it with a nice big newspaper so we could read the headlines and date this story better. Indeed, at 5.15 on a Saturday, she'd have the radio or telly on already so she could do the Pools, and

continued on page 227...

who was locked up in World War II for sympathizing with the Nazis - is a bit of a giveaway too.)

So we get John, who here runs the café when Harry's away, and who talks about how his ancestors were stolen from Africa. In *this* context it's quite clever, but later on, when the only person of colour on Terra Alpha (25.2, "The Happiness Patrol") is only one who can play blues harmonica, and when the only African-American dude on Segonax (25.4, "The Greatest Show in the Galaxy") is the embarrassing Rappin' Ringmaster, and when Jazz is used against Nazis and Cybermen (25.3, "Silver Nemesis", and it ain't Ronnie Scott or Andy Sheppard they invite), it cumulatively looks a bit off. Well-intentioned though it may be, the effect is that Season Twenty-Five accidentally reinforces some stereotypes, and today looks unbelievably patronising. Still, compared with what was to come, it's just about acceptable if you don't watch this whole season in one go. (Actually, there's another, albeit non-speaking, black character. He's one of Ratcliffe's gang. We'd like you to ponder that for a moment.)

4. Here we see the curiously-wrought invective of Ace: when not giving people odd nicknames, she indulges in G-rated swearing. Even in 1963, girls would use worse words than 'toerag'. Any real 1980s teenager - upon discovering that she's been flirting with a Dalek stooge - would have yelled at Mike with the same volume that Ace does, but would also have used more immoderate language. We may choose to think of this as a translation anomaly, or as a side-effect of the BBC dramatising these events from Time Lord files (see **Who Narrates This Programme?** under 23.1, "The Mysterious Planet"), but it jars more than real swearing would have.

The Continuity

The Doctor   Somehow, he's able to calibrate the radio frequencies of a Dalek transmat with his umbrella and hankie. He sometimes takes sugar in his tea, and seems to enjoy wiggling his ears while sitting in thought [or letting people know he's listening, which is at least polite]. He can make objects appear from the air, by old-fashioned conjuring [cf 19.3, "Kinda"; 8.3, "Colony in Space" and of course 7.3, "The Ambassadors of Death"]. By now, he's so prone to sneezing while hiding from an enemy [see also 24.3, "Delta and the Bannermen"], it's starting to look as if he's got a

dust allergy. [Ace has the same problem in "Silver Nemesis".]

The Doctor can fiddle with a Dalek transmat device, and thereby destroy an incoming Dalek by making both halves of the creature materialize in the same location - causing their mutual annihilation. He says that such rewiring is easy, 'when you have nine-hundred years' experience'. [Compare with 24.1, "Time and the Rani", in which his total age is 953.] He also knows how to "short out" a Dalek pilot by touching a few wires together, and to rewire a Dalek shuttlecraft's communications system so it relays signals to a TV in the school cellar. He can also rig a device that interferes with the Daleks' control systems [similar to a device he rigged on Spiridon, "Planet of the Daleks" (10.4)]. He's now making a habit of getting his umbrella stuck in closing doors [see also 24.2, "Paradise Towers"].

The Doctor thinks begonias are lovely. He appears to sign a military inventory form with a question mark [and see *Inventory*].

• *Ethics.* To say the least, they're becoming rather complicated. As opposed to a myriad of instances where the Doctor just stumbles into trouble completely at random, here he goes out of his way to pre-programme the Hand of Omega to fly into Skaro's sun and turn it into a supernova. He then leaves the device where the Daleks can find and use it, allowing them (or specifically Davros) to "press the button" that dooms Skaro to obliteration. [Many commentators have questioned why, if the Doctor wanted Skaro destroyed, he didn't simply use the Hand and do it himself. We'll never know the answer for sure, but a clue might reside in his comment in "Delta and the Bannermen" that 'violence always rebounds on itself'. Arguably, the idea is that using the device himself is a line he doesn't wish to cross, but it's another matter entirely if evil-doers blow themselves up in a mad quest for unimaginable power. Sun Tzu, in *The Art of War*, suggests that one should always offer your opponents a dignified way out and, if they refuse it, show no mercy. The Doctor has always followed this line, punishing people as much for ignoring pleas for mercy as for whatever they did up to that point. If they bring about their own destruction after he warned them, his conscience troubles him far less. The line between shooting a villain and handing them a gun to let *them* do it might seem thin, but it's a line nonetheless.] The Doctor technically offers

When Did Susan Go to School?

...continued from page 225

we'd know from the scores when it was. Or at least, know from some sad-case who knew what the scores were.

Therefore, many have concluded that the First Doctor's depositing the Hand actually happens about a month before "Remembrance" episode one, and the two visits to Coal Hill School happen afterwards in very close succession. This seems to have been the reason Ace found a book on the French Revolution in the lab (although it's a completely different book from the one Susan took home with her in "An Unearthly Child", never mind that it's presumably still on board the Ship somewhere). But if that's true, why did Susan seem so much odder to Ian and Barbara than a series of scorch-marks in the playground, shattered windows everywhere and an entire neighbourhood kept awake by Dalek space-shuttles coming and going? (Even if they immediately forgot, as the story suggests, the pupils all yawning must have seemed a bit suspicious even for 1963 - see **What Are The Most Mod Stories?** under 2.7, "The Space Museum".)

And why did Susan's transistor radio not pick up the transmat signals from the cellar? Even if we invoke the difference between AM and FM, the power of the signal would have swamped John Smith and the Common Men (whose hit, we must assume, is being played on a pirate station out at sea - see 4.7, "The Macra Terror" and 5.7, "Fury from the Deep"). And of course, the police would all be using FM frequencies, if they had patrol cars there. The majority in London did, even though police boxes were in use until 1969.

And if Susan's been gone less than a week, and the Daleks recruited Ratcliffe and his 'Association' a while back (as they'd have to, to get Mike into place unless they were phenomenally lucky), then she was in extreme danger - as someone associated with the person who hid the Hand - when she went to Totter's Lane to meet her grandfather. And the Dalek stationed there failed to act on there being a TARDIS present, and a couple of people with alien physiologies right on its doorstep? ... It's looking like we have to start again.

We know that there *isn't* a police box in Totter's Lane in "Remembrance", but the Doctor knows that Harry's wife will have twins (suggesting he was in the neighbourhood some time later - chronologically speaking - on what was to him an earlier visit). We also know that the Chameleon Circuit used to work and that, given accurate data, the TARDIS can go anywhere the Doctor chooses. So it's worth asking: did the Doctor leave Susan at school while he did something else?

Well, he *didn't* attend Parents' Evening. Ian and Barbara would have met him before, had Susan been at school throughout the Autumn Term. If she was provided with somewhere safe to go at night, or a supply of money if she was spending the time out of school at swinging hot-spots in the capital, the Doctor could gallivant off to Quinnius or a spot of night-fishing on Venus. (Contrary to what you might think, we simply have *no* data on how well the Doctor could steer the Ship before the schoolteachers wandered in. The assumption throughout Season One - aside from Susan's suggestion that the Doctor is simply forgetful - is that with the correct starting co-ordinates and no mechanical faults, navigation is easy. Again we have to wonder if the wayward steering, stuck Chameleon Circuit and other faults all happening just as the first human passengers arrive is coincidental, but if we follow that train of thought we'll get into that whole Rassilon Imprimatur business again - see 22.4, "The Two Doctors". Just listen to Susan and the Doctor reminiscing about previous journeys, and draw your own conclusions.)

But would the overly-protective Doctor leave Susan alone for such a period, let alone knowingly send his granddaughter to a school whose head is in the power of a Dalek faction? He claims to not even know who the Daleks *are* four episodes later. So he may have detected alien instrumentation (and a nearby transmat) and removed the TARDIS to avoid his own cover being blown - the first episode could be interpreted as a pre-arranged rendezvous. So when the Doctor tells Rev. Parkinson that he was 'called away unexpectedly', this could be something else entirely - and nothing to do with Ian and Barbara (which was later, after he returned to pick up Susan).

Depending on how you play the cards, then, "Remembrance" could actually *predate* "An Unearthly Child" by anything up to four months, although that requires disregarding the calendars that say 'November'. (There's one in Harry's café, and one in Ratcliff's office, but you have to look fairly hard to see them.) This would explain why it's still light so late in the day. The decision to drop the uniforms worn in the Dalek romp might have come into effect during half-term. The events and

continued on page 229...

Davros the chance to back down and surrender the Hand of Omega, but he also goads the villain an awful lot, and thus practically guarantees that Davros will order the device's activation. Afterward, the Doctor says that Davros 'tricked himself' and that he 'has pity' for him.

The Doctor tells the last Black Dalek how much its forces and ambitions have suffered total defeat, and this - coupled with the Doctor's mentioning how very much alone the creature is - persuades it to self-destruct. [In a cut shot from the start of this scene, the Doctor tells Gilmore that dealing with this straggler is his responsibility because 'I started this'. It's understandable that the Doctor can't allow a demented Black Dalek to roam around killing people, but one could also argue that - as much as anything else - he's putting the creature out of its suffering. See X3.5, "Evolution of the Daleks" for a comparable example.]

• *Inventory*. He carries a calling-card made from what looks like gold-embossed plastic, and which bears some Old High Gallifreyan scribble [see 20.7, "The Five Doctors"] and a symbol that looks suspiciously like a question mark. The Dalek Controller and the Black Dalek immediately recognize this card as the Doctor's handywork.

He's still got that abacus [24.4, "Dragonfire"], and a copy of Richard Gordon's *Doctor in the House* [it's a first edition, and long after the films with Dirk Bogarde and Leslie Phillips]. He's also got a clothes-brush that in future will get a lot of use whenever Ace blows things up, and a box brownie camera. [This might be something the Doctor borrows, or one of the items he takes from the TARDIS in a cut scene, but in the transmitted version he seems to have had it on his person throughout. Either way, it would've been old compared to when this story is set.] He's got cash on hand, and a bag of pre-decimal coins for Ace. [Originally, he paid for his tea in the "sugar" scene with 1991 coins. We'll revisit this "coinage anachronism" in "Battlefield", also by Aaronovitch.] By the end of this story, he has more government-issue pens than at the start.

• *Background*. Here the Doctor proclaims himself as 'President-elect of the High Council of Time Lords, keeper of the legacy of Rassilon, defender of the laws of time, protector of Gallifrey'. [And note that whereas the Doctor was put on trial for interference / meddling in time in Season Twenty-Three, he here facilitates the Dalek homeworld's destruction without any apparent fear of retribu-

tion from his own people. Clearly, something has happened off screen between the Doctor and the Time Lords, and it's hard to imagine he could take such momentous action against Skaro without the High Council's sanction. So at some point recently - perhaps even prior to his meeting Ace - the Doctor has been in touch with the Powers-That-Be, and the new regime is more prepared to give him a free hand.]

In explaining the Hand of Omega to Ace, the Doctor mutters, '... and didn't we have trouble with the prototype'. When Ace wonders what the Doctor means by 'we', and he revises his words to say, '*they*' and seems to furrow his brow in discomfort. [There are two ways of looking at this. This could simply be a Time Lord talking to a human, meaning he's using 'we' as when the authors of this book tell the American readers about who invented computers ("The Curse of Fenric") or Americans tell us who got to the Moon. However, the obvious implication - and what the production-team was hinting at - is that the Doctor hails from a much earlier point in Gallifreyan history, and could be (along with Rassilon and Omega) one of the founders of Gallifreyan society. The infamous cut scene in which the Doctor replies to Davros' taunt, and says he's *more* than just a Time Lord, might substantiate this view - although it could equally mean that he's just not like the majority of the "dormice" on Gallifrey. He's just said he's President. The eventual answer to this question - revisited in "Silver Nemesis" - is never answered on screen, so we'll have to refer you to the spin-off material. See **Did Cartmel Have *Any* Plan At All?** under "Silver Nemesis"]

New information is presented about what the Doctor was doing prior to the first televised adventure. [1.1, "An Unearthly Child". We're told that 'an old geezer with white hair' left the Hand of Omega at the funeral home - this is probably the First Doctor. See the essay for more.] It appears that the First Doctor left the Hand of Omega behind for the Daleks to find, yet here the Seventh Doctor doesn't recognize the Headmaster of Coal Hill School, and he has to figure out the building's layout. The groundplan of 76 Totter's Lane is familiar to him, however, and he knows in advance that Harry's wife will give birth to twins. The Reverend Parkinson indicates that the Doctor made preparations for the Hand's gravesite 'a month' ago, and the funeral director acts as if the

When Did Susan Go to School?

...continued from page 227

all the military kerfuffle in Totter's Lane would require the gates to be repainted, and they do look a lot shabbier in their first appearance than the last. (This could also explain why the spelling of 'Foreman' changes on the gates in Totter's Lane.)

We're never given the full title for the BBC's touted new family science-fiction serial ("Do-"), so it could be just about *anything*. Given that no-one ever, in twenty-six seasons, says, "It's just like something off *Doctor Who*", we can rule out the existence of such a series within *Doctor Who* itself, so maybe Saturday teatimes in September 1963 saw a short-lived series called *Dolphins From The Fifth Dimension* or *Dogs On Mars*. (The spin-off books have picked up on the idea of *Professor X*, the alleged attempt to sell the franchise overseas rather than flog the actual episodes. In particular, there's a tradition that the fictitious avatar *Colonel X* - as seen in the *Press Gang* episode "UneXpected" and mentioned a lot elsewhere in this volume - is what the BBC shows on Saturday teatimes in the fictive universe of *Doctor Who*. Professor X himself became an honorary colonel when exiled to twentieth century Earth in the early 1970s episodes.)

We know that there was an ITV series called *Emerald Soup*, which was on opposite the first broadcast episode of *Doctor Who* and vanished shortly afterwards, so TV executives at the time must all have been trying to make a fantasy adventure for kids of all ages. Anyways, that the announcer says we're about to watch 'another instalment' of 'Do-' suggests the series has been going over a fortnight, so it can't simultaneously be *Doctor Who* and be November. (As you'll know from the notes in Volume I, "An Unearthly Child" was shown on 23rd of November in amongst the fallout from Kennedy's assassination, and was repeated the following week before "The Cave of Skulls" - meaning "another instalment" would not have appeared any earlier than 7th of December. And if that were so, even if people didn't put up their decorations until Christmas Eve, you'd've had *some* indication of impending festivity - not least with Phil Spector's album selling better here than in the States.) In fact, with the time given by the announcer as '5.15' and everyone apparently going to lunch something like three hours later, this is perhaps a later addition to the story. Either we disregard this or the sun set around eight PM - which is right for the very start of September in London.

Dating "Remembrance" to September has the immediate advantage that nobody would know about Kennedy's impending assassination, nor yet that Harold Wilson would be Labour leader in a month and start talking about decimalization. The Government was in flux that month mainly because Harold Macmillan had resigned, ostensibly for health reasons. Lord Home had to renounce his peerage to stand for Tory leadership (despite rumblings from a faction loyal to Rab Butler, a former chancellor removed by Macmillan for what seems to have been a personality clash). Then there's the business of Lord Boothby's former affair with Macmillan's wife, which had been known to many In the press all summer. 'Chunky' Gilmore alludes to this general shakiness, rather than anything specifically to do with the Test-Ban Treaty or Profumo (almost a dead issue by August, although it's Christine Keeler who was the subject of that *Mirror* headline, asked to surrender her passport after it turned out that Profumo had lied to the House of Commons), and certainly not to the murder of the President of the United States. So we're looking at early autumn.

We can finally try to pull all of this together. The Doctor arrives in June, enrols Susan in Coal Hill School and visits the funeral parlour with regards to the Hand of Omega. At around the same time - or maybe even before this - he finds a blind vicar and makes the burial arrangements. Perhaps this is where he decides that tagging along with Susan is not his cup of tea - we know that at some point he develops a loathing for Cliff Richard movies (X2.7, "The Idiot's Lantern"). Someone or something requires his immediate attention elsewhere, so he asks Susan if she wants to stay put (perhaps in digs - she's certainly untroubled by money worries, not even knowing about pre-decimal currency, so maybe she's pretending to be a trust-fund kid) or come with him. She chooses the former and has a smashing time in Swinging London.

July: term ends, and the Imperial Daleks occupy the abandoned school. Rebel Daleks set a trap at the designated rendezvous at Totter's Lane. (What other reason do they have for placing a Dalek in a junkyard miles from anywhere? The only connection between the school and the yard is the Doctor and Susan.) Term starts, the school caretaker abruptly vanishes (did he look in the cellar?) and a Third-Form blonde girl - the Dalek Controller

continued on page 231...

"burial" arrangements were made at roughly the same time. [And again, see **When Did Susan Go to School?**]

Upon meeting Rachel Jensen, the Doctor says that he's "sure he has heard" of her before. [Either he's just ingratiating himself to her, or she's more distinguished than she might appear.]

The Supporting Cast

• *Ace*. She regards the Doctor's plan to give the Daleks the Hand - and his overall deviousness - as 'brilliant', and displays no reservations about the risks involved. [It's hard to imagine Mel giving the Doctor such a blank check, so Ace's arrival in the TARDIS might well explain why - six incarnations after he planted the Hand - this Doctor feels the need to follow through on his masterplan. For that matter, it's also hard to imagine Bonnie leaping through windows, charging down stairs and slugging Daleks with an energized baseball bat.]

Two of Ace's Nitro-9 charges can destroy a Renegade Dalek at close range, and she and the Doctor are already playing a game in which he strenuously warns her to leave her homemade explosives behind, but obviously knows that she's carrying some [see also "Silver Nemesis" and more]. The ten-second fuses on her Nitro-9 canisters seem prone to going off early. When the Doctor tries to pull the brainwashed Headmaster out of harm's way, Ace sounds incredulous that he'd try to save someone who just tried to facilitate his death.

She seems to place a great value on listening to her tunes - which sound like mid-seventies, mid-Atlantic rawk noodlings - and which she listens to on a boom box that the Doctor made for her. [The Doctor replaces the boom box in "Silver Nemesis" after a Dalek blows this one up, but see **Things That Don't Make Sense**.]

Ace doesn't understand the basics of pre-decimal currency, and she's starting to show a tendency to fancy boys who anyone watching knows will be dead by the end of the story [see also "The Curse of Fenric"]. Like all suburban 80s British kids, she's delighted to be given a baseball bat. [We didn't like having American missiles on our soil, but we loved their pop culture - or we certainly did then.] Unlike most students her age, Ace almost immediately figures out how to fire a hand-held rocket-launcher [our schools didn't get that rough until at least 1994]. She's wearing a skirt now.

The Supporting Cast (Evil)

• *Davros*. As the Doctor puts it, Davros has now 'cast off the last vestiges of [his humanoid] form' - meaning he's got very little body left. Instead, he looks heavily wired into the giant sphere of an Emperor Dalek, which sits atop a reconfigured Dalek skirt. The sphere has one hexagonal gold plate [possibly a sensor array], but has no gun or plunger. Davros' familiarity with the Time Lords - and their abilities and policies regarding time travel - seems greater than ever. He ends his *Doctor Who* tenure by departing in an escape craft. [Again, the spinoffery wouldn't let it lie - see *both* the novel *War of the Daleks* and the Big Finish audio "Terror Firma" for where matters go for Davros from here. Oh, and Big Finish has also given Davros a whole backstory in the *I, Davros* mini-series.]

The Time Lords

• *The Hand of Omega*. Pretentious name for Omega's stellar manipulator [see **History**], which has the ability to 'customise stars'. The Hand is a coffin-shaped device with a misty, bright energy within, and which is 'alive, in a manner of speaking'. It can levitate, respond to the Doctor's voice commands, and "charge" Ace's baseball bat with enough energy to damage Dalek armour. The bat also proves lethal against a Renegade Dalek blob, but eventually breaks in half when the Doctor smashes apart a Dalek transmat. After destroying Skaro and Davros' mothership on the Doctor's instructions, the Hand of Omega returns to Gallifrey. [Take this as a further sign that the Doctor is operating with the High Council's consent, because otherwise, they might wonder why the most powerful stellar manipulator ever made has just arrived on their doorstep.]

The Non-Humans

The Daleks have now broken into two rival camps, who - owing to their long-running notions of racial purity and xenophobia - now seek to eradicate one another. [Many characteristics of one Dalek camp might well apply to the other, but the technological and biological distinctions are such that we've tried to separate details on the two groups.] One general detail before we begin: we're now told that Dalek armour is 'bonded polycarbide' [and not 'Dalekenium', as in 2.2, "The Dalek Invasion of Earth"].

• *Imperial Daleks*. Davros' forces are now more

When Did Susan Go to School?

...**continued from page 229**

- starts acting oddly (but she has different teachers, so nobody follows her home to Ratcliffe's). In many London schools, the start of the school year would be staggered, so the younger ones begin three or four days before the older ones. Over the weekend, the school is assailed by alien war-machines and the RAF Counter-Insurgency squad, during which time the Headmaster unexpectedly passes away.

Susan returns to school, maybe a week later (possibly after a trip to Brighton on someone's Lambretta, or perhaps a quick trip to Rome after being thrown out of *La Dolce Vita* for complaining about the bad translation). Her grandfather's seventh incarnation therefore decides to skip Mike's funeral and avoid temporal anomalies. (This, conveniently, puts the date of the Shoreditch Incident at what was intended to be the day the first episode aired twenty-five years later, Saturday, 7th of September - assuming that 7th of September *was* a Saturday in the *Doctor Who* world - see 3.10, "The War Machines"; 25.3, "Silver Nemesis" and various UNIT dating quibbles).

Two more months of O-levels by day and Soho coffee-bars by night (and a trip to Eel Pie Island to catch the Rolling Stones before they were famous would have been irresistible). Grandfather returns at some point during this - keeping the pretence of living in a junkyard would have backfired after more than a few weeks, with school secretaries sending out letters that were returned undelivered. Ian and Barbara regard their unearthly pupil with curiousity. The rest you know.

---

upright than before [22.6, "Revelation of the Daleks"]. Their left hand manipulators look less like a sink-plunger than ever, and serve as a manifold connections - the Dalek shuttle pilot is wired directly into the ship's systems, and sits with a slot recessed into the rim, allowing it to operate dials and controls. The Doctor similarly uses a spare "plunger" to tap into the shuttle's astronomical charts, and the Imperial Dalek communications network.

The lights on the side of the Imperials' domes are flatter, and the slats are gold-plated but raised from the main body rather than being pieces of metal attached to it. Whereas the Renegade Daleks within are the blobby Kaled mutants of old, the Imperials have more developed limbs - including a claw-like hand - and electrical implants wired directly into the flesh. As Ace says, they're 'blobs with bits added'.

Most alarming is that a heavy-duty version - the so-called "Special Weapons" Dalek - is basically a big gun on a Dalek base. [The novelisation claims that radiation from the gun has altered this Dalek's DNA and driven it insane. The genetic difference means that even the Imperial Daleks call it 'The Abomination'.] This Dalek has a flatter dome with no eye-stalk [small "windows" are set in the turret, looking like a wartime "pillbox" fort] and it has no "plunger" arm. It's slower and more grimy than its comrades, and the gun mounting is like a hexagonal nut and bolt. The big gun has about thirty degrees of vertical movement, and complete 360 degrees rotation.

The Imperials have a mothership in Earth orbit, and the Doctor estimates that as many as four hundred Daleks are aboard. The mothership has weaponry capable of cracking Earth open 'like an egg', but the Imperials refrain from doing so out of fear of damaging the timeline. The mothership also has surveillance equipment sophisticated enough to detect 'a sparrow fall' at 15,000 km.

The Imperial Dalek transmat seems to have a range of at least 300 km, and an operator usually remains on-station to repair any malfunctions in the device. The Imperials' shuttle first lands at Coal Hill before the story begins, enabling them to set up the transmit system and brainwash the school's Headmaster into their service. The shuttle has massive ground defences, but an unguarded service hatch on top. The Imperials' communications signals are relayed verbally on FM radio, and their Head-Up Displays seem more refined - and display more complicated icons - than the opposing...

• *Renegade Daleks*. Now cast as the outlaws of the Dalek race, despite their taking Davros into custody when last we saw them ["Revelation of the Daleks"]. Renegade Daleks' weapons [and probably those of the Imperials too] cause 'massive internal displacement' and scramble one's insides, yet leave no evidence of tissue damage. One Renegade survives three exploding rifle-grenades with only a bit of charring on its armour.

In most regards, the Renegades are as before: they have grey armour, and the Daleks within are 'almost amoeboid'. They answer to the Black

Dalek. A new development is that the Renegades recognize they have an over-reliance on rationality and logic, so they've captured a young human girl and slaved her to a battle-computer; this puts her ingenuity and creativity at their command. [This is another manifestation of their occasional yearning for creativity and human qualities for tactical ends - see "The Evil of the Daleks"; 17.1, "Destiny of the Daleks" and X3.4, "Daleks in Manhattan".] The child can operate independently of the battle computer, and fire electrical bolts from her fingers.

After the Daleks' total defeat, the remaining Black Dalek becomes "unstable", twirls about and eventually disintegrates when the Doctor points out its total isolation and lack of purpose. The girl is somehow linked to the Black Dalek, and suffers adversely - but appears to survive - when it dies.

Unlike the Imperials, the Renegades seem to communicate via frequencies undetected by humans but - from what we hear - their instructions come verbally. They don't appear to have an orbital platform, and have based themselves in Ratcliffe's yard. The device that enables their time-travel ability - the 'Time Manipulator' globe - seems static-based [as might be expected] and it's a means of their journeying via a crude time-corridor [as per 21.4, "Resurrection of the Daleks"].

Planet Notes

• *Skaro*. The monitor in the Dalek shuttlecraft shows a strange representation of Skaro's solar system - about five circles that we can see, in roughly the same orbit around a yellow one. [This is presumably Skaro's sun, although the Doctor almost implies the yellow thingey is Skaro itself. Skaro is cited as the twelfth planet of its sun in 1.2, "The Daleks", so either this is a *very* big system, or a lot of much smaller worlds there count as "planets", or we can't trust the map at all.

[By the way, we also catch a glimpse of Phebeyus - the planet with three horizontal rings (not impossible but it says a lot about peculiar mass distribution under that gas) - as the Omega device sparkles past. Like the Emperor Dalek, this is a legacy of Whitaker's *TV Century 21* comic strip from the 1960s.]

History

• *Dating*. Obviously, the Earth section is set in 1963. The precise month, though, is a matter for debate and we've devoted this story's essay to it.

Establishing the future era from which the Davros' Imperial Daleks and the Renegades are operating - and the point in which Skaro is apparently annihilated - is much harder to figure out. All we really know for certain is that enough time has elapsed since "Revelation of the Daleks" for Davros to escape captivity, make his Imperial Daleks ascendent and wire what remains of his physical form into an Emperor Dalek shell.

[To recap, the ultimate problem here is that the four stories that compose the "Davros Era" - "Destiny of the Daleks", "Resurrection of the Daleks", "Revelation of the Daleks" and "Remembrance of the Daleks" - give some clues about where they occur in relation to one another, but no year or period is mentioned on screen for any of them. Much of the debate in guidebooks such as this revolves around whether the quartet goes before or after "The Daleks' Master Plan" (3.4), set in the year 4000, and in which the Daleks are a formidable power.

[It's worth considering the Doctor's comment in "Remembrance" to the Wobbly Black Dalek - that it's stranded 'a trillion miles and a thousand years' from its home (presumably Skaro). Well, let's admit that he could just be using demoralizing rhetoric, and we should take it with a pinch of salt. On the other hand, if he *literally* means 'a thousand years', then 2960 or thereabouts is actually a workable guess for the Davros Era's end. Allowing that the dating for "The Evil of the Daleks" will always be something of a wild card. Skaro isn't *definitively* mentioned any later than circa 2540 in "Planet of the Daleks" (there's an oblique line on in "Master Plan" but you have to listen hard) so there's nothing to say it *wasn't* vapourized a few centuries afterward. Also note that some Thals are still based on Skaro in "Planet of the Daleks" - indeed, the Doctor briefly considers letting Jo resettle there with them - but there's none in evidence in "Destiny of the Daleks". A final Thal migration is never mentioned on screen, but it fits what we're shown, and anyways it's near-impossible to imagine the Doctor sanctioning the slaughter of such innocents when Skaro goes ka-blooey.

[Alternatively, placing the Davros Era after "The Daleks' Master Plan" is still feasible for those who prefer, and complicating matters still further is that the Imperial and Renegade Daleks might well hail from different time-zones. It's far easier, of course, to assume they're from the same period, but if the Davros Era *does* stretch into the fifth millennium, then we're approaching that magical date of 5000 AD (14.6, "The Talons of Weng-Chiang"; X1.09, "The Empty Child"; X2.4, "The Girl in the Fireplace"), when time-travel has a brief but spectacular flourishing in human history. So Davros getting such grubby protuberances as he has left on this - and his forces thereby outpacing the Renegades' more crude time-corridor technology - is less implausible than many other Dalek-related Time shenanigans.

[Here we should mention that although Skaro is vapourized, it's been explicitly cited in the new series (X3.4, "Daleks in Manhattan") as a casualty of the Time War - something that Russell T Davies had already established as true in the *Doctor Who 2006 Annual*. Loathe as we are to mention it, this neatly coincides with the retcon in *War of the Daleks* that Skaro wasn't destroyed after all. See *War of the Daleks*: **Should Anyone Believe a Word of It?** under "Destiny of the Daleks" in Volume IV - we'd like to answer this question, "Don't be silly, of course not", but it's starting to look more like, "If you insist, on your own head be it". Of course, this problem goes away if you remember that it's a war between two sets of time-travellers - hence the name 'Time War', and so Skaro could have been destroyed on a weekly basis for centuries.

[As we keep having to say, Dalek chronology arguably only makes sense if you get rid of the idea of one single time-line and pay attention to the plot-line of the Eccleston series where the whole "Bad Wolf" chronology is one that should never have happened. Or, if you're busting a gut trying to make it all fit into one long story, just assume that Dalek Sec is counting the end of "Remembrance" as part of the Time War, which means that the Doctor has even more reason to feel guilty about it.]

Gallifreyan history as the Doctor relates it: 'A long time ago', the stellar engineer Omega created the supernova that was the initial power source for Gallifreyan time travel experiments. [This was first related in 10.1, "The Three Doctors", although it was explicitly said there and in 20.1, "Arc of Infinity" that Omega created a black hole; here it's called a 'supernova'. The one preceded the other, as it would have to.] Omega left behind 'the basis on which Rassilon founded Time Lord society' [see, of course, **Did Rassilon Know Omega?** under 14.3, "The Deadly Assassin" but first **Why All These Black Holes?** under 10.1, "The Three

Doctors" for why you need a big power source to get to the stage where you can harness a black hole.]

In 1963, Professor Rachel Jensen is drafted from her job at Cambridge under the Peacetime Emergency Powers Act. Group Captain Gilmore arranges for a local evacuation under the Peacetime Nuclear Accident Provisions, and the initial stages of this were carried out under the Counter-Intrusion Measures, United Kingdom. A D-Notice and a cover story are prepared in conjunction with this. The Headmaster of the Coal Hill Road Shoreditch Secondary School - which the young Dalek Controller attends - is brainwashed as a Dalek agent and killed by them. Rachel and Allison express regrets that 'Bernard' isn't on-hand, and Allison comments, 'British Rocket Group's got its own problems'. [See "The Christmas Invasion" (X2.0) and **Is This the Quatermass Continuum?** under "Image of the Fendahl" (15.3).]

The Analysis

Where Does This Come From? Before getting onto specific film quotations, it's time for another word about mid-1980s comics. We're in the midst of a rebooting epidemic in the present day, with James Bond, Robin Hood and *Doctor Who* getting rethought from scratch for new audiences, but this is *nothing* to what was going on in the middle of that earnest decade. In comics, the basic assumptions of tights-wearing good-guys and bafflingly unmotivated freakish supervillains were unstitched. This is the era when Batman was rethought as "The Dark Knight", complete with *Dirty Harry* vigilante angst and a killable sidekick. Frank Miller, creator of *The Dark Knight Returns* and "Batman: Year One" was only one extreme of this tendency. In Britain we had Alan Moore who, having buggered up Time Lord history (again, see **Did Rassilon Know Omega?**, and the answer is, of course, "no"), proceeded to revamp the 70s kitsch classic *Swamp Thing* into something very serious. Armed with a load of eco-mystic ley-line stuff, a few books about Louisiana and a willingness to imagine the story from first principles, Moore shifted the story's emphasis from a guy whose body was transformed (sort of) into a swamp creature to the impact of this on his girlfriend. It can be argued that Moore is a one-trick pony, but if so, it's a nifty trick.

One of the reasons for this whole trend was the

rate of change and the collapse of immediate post-war optimism, both of which made all uncynical assumptions of linear progress look naïve and ludicrous. In the late 80s, it was fashionable to laugh at 50s assumptions about what life in the Space Age would be like. This is another symptom of the trend for endless re-runs and allusions to those reruns in films such as *Gremlins* and *Back to the Future*. The reference-games are one thing, but the overall tone of the 80s films was that "we know better now", and that a sardonic sense of deflation is "realistic". As we saw in the notes for "Delta and the Bannermen", the British view was some way ahead of the US in this regard, and our collective memory of the 50s was at odds with that of the Hollywood nostalgia of the 80s.

Now throw into this mix a sense that the "official" account of inter-war Britain was being smoothed out and reduced to cliché by government-inspired guidelines on the teaching of history. Aaronovitch is part of a family who knew from experience what was really going on (as his brother David has repeatedly mentioned in various newspaper columns). Look at the original script's names for the characters, and the antipathy of Professor Rachel "Israel" towards the "Association" of "Mr Gummer" (later Ratcliffe), and it all makes a bit more sense. (And that's "Gummer", as in Trade and Industry Secretary John Selwyn Gummer - a squitty little geek who quit the Church of England when they ordained women.) So Beatlemania and a few leftover supporters of Oswald Mosley (see 7.4, "Inferno") mix more readily here than would even have been possible before. Somewhere along the line, it's occurred to people that 1963 is closer to World War II than to 1988.

Advertisers had cottoned on to this, and were using 1963 as a benchmark for stiffness, wholesomeness and things being shipshape. Often this was done with clips from real ads from that era - complete with someone in colour sneering at them - or lovingly-shot soft-focus footage of a monochrome / pastel idyll, with a hit from the time, reminding us of when life was simple and such-and-such a product was there for us in our childhood. This conveniently suited a government whose party was kicked out of power soon after Kennedy's death, so anyone who criticised this was thought to be doing so for political ends. ("Remembrance" coincided with a number of films set in 1963 - most notably *Scandal* and

Buster - and which painted a more appealing picture of the era than had previously been permitted in the 1980s. The antidote to all this - though set at the end of the 1960s - also arrived in British cinemas at the same time. It was called *Withnail & I*; see much of the Appendix and 27.0, "The TV Movie" for its impact on *Doctor Who*.)

As mentioned before, this generation of scriptwriters think of the early years of *Doctor Who* as a historical period, and are in many ways trying to write to some form of folk-memory of the series. Aaronovitch came to it almost from outside, but with a sensibility formed by paperback SF and - as this is the era of the re-think - we have to acknowledge that SF was going through its own fad of cliché-busting, generally called "Cyberpunk" (but not by the people who were doing it). However, the main influences remain comics and big futuristic action movies where people explode. So whilst the Head-Up Displays allude to flicks like *Terminator* and *Aliens*, this story's visual iconography is more a matter of inserting these anomalous items into 1963, treated with the same attention to detail you'd get in a play set in 1870. Then the Dalek stuff is pilfered from the *TV Century 21* strip (see Volume I for lots more on this), which was reprinted in early *DWMs*. There's also the comparatively late addition of the Hand of Omega (need we even mention *Raiders of the Lost Ark* again?), and the entire approach to the programme's past as just another source among all the rest.

Things That Don't Make Sense   We've got two Dalek factions, both of them bristling with advanced weaponry and targeting systems, yet neither side seems able to hit the side of a barn with a moonbeam. We refer you especially to the first Dalek crossfire in episode four, in which the Imperials and Renegades stand in the open and fire upon one another at almost point-blank range. Literally twenty-five (!) Dalek laser-bolts are exchanged (presuming none of the bolts are duplicates as the camera cuts between the two groups) before either side actually takes a casualty. Never mind that the Imperial Daleks insist on attacking in a pyramid formation, and that the lead Dalek is probably more likely to get hit by friendly fire than anything else.

Meanwhile, Davros' plan with the Hand of Omega... well, it *nearly* makes sense, but it's still rather murky, and one senses we're missing a key nugget of information. Davros says he wants to use it to 'turn Skaro's sun into a source of unimaginable power', which will enable the Daleks to essentially supplant the Gallifreyans and become 'the Lords of Time'. Okay, fine, except that he can't *want* Skaro's sun to go supernova, because he's horrified when this happens against his instructions. So... was the idea to create some sort of star 'of unimaginable power', yet *wasn't* a supernova? It's a bit of a puzzler. Maybe he's attempting to very roughly re-run Omega's original experiment, but if *that's* the case, he's going to wind up with a black hole on Skaro's doorstep, which won't exactly help the local climate either. The issue we're dancing around is that it would *seem* like common sense for Davros to test the Hand on a star other than the one warming the Dalek homeworld, but perhaps he's now too much of a nutter to consider such things.

The Doctor expresses relief after Ace's boom box is destroyed, because it was a dangerous anachronism and could have started the whole microchip revolution twenty years early. True enough, but if it's that dangerous, why the hell did he let her bring it outside the TARDIS in the first place? It's not as if she can hide this in her backpack, along with her illicit stash of Nitro-9. And even though the Daleks now seem equipped with night-vision or possibly infra-red, they can't see through canvas - at least, the Renegades can't. Oh, and a wooden door with bolts stymies the stair-gliding Dalek for longer than it probably should.

At the end of episode three, the Imperial Dalek shuttle shows up on radar and smashes just about every window in the school as it lands. Yet it's clearly been there before, so how did nobody notice this happening the first time around? And while it's feasible that a blind vicar wouldn't notice a floating casket, did absolutely nobody witness five Daleks guiding the Hand through the streets to a space-shuttle that landed and took off *very* noisily? Moreover, this is 1963, when housewives stayed in and cooked or did laundry, and it's a Saturday teatime. In this era television was on VHF frequencies, with lower-power transmissions, meaning that even a car starting up would cause TV interference. [Ian's comments in 1.7, "The Sensorites" about an unsuppressed motor causing interference on a monitor shows how common an experience this was for viewers.] So we have a spaceship landing and transmitting to a larger craft in orbit, and a load of static-powered ray-guns going off, but nobody is heard to com-

plain that they're trying to watch *Bonanza* or *Emerald Soup* and the bleedin' picture looks like a snowstorm. [If you lived in Britain then, this ritual was possibly the most interaction you had with your neighbours outside school hours. An entire way of life has gone. Hooray!]

Talking of 60's vintage tellies, even if we accept that Mrs Smith would have such an unusually large one [although she runs a guest-house, and so having a top-of-the-range set might be a selling-point], it wouldn't - as we're shown - have been off on a Saturday afternoon. Tellies of that era took a while to warm up [even though this one does, it is quicker than most], and would've been left on between programmes - especially as *Grandstand* would have just finished at that time of day, and everyone would have been watching the final football scores for the Pools results [another long-lost ritual - see **September or January?** under 13.1, "Terror of the Zygons"].

Ratcliffe says it's been a 'long and difficult struggle for myself and my men' - not to get all technical, but which "struggle" would that be, exactly? Fair enough that Ratcliffe was imprisoned for sympathizing with the Nazis, but when he makes this statement, his men have only been seen to incapacitate a couple of troopers and load a blown-up Dalek base onto a truck. And cover it with a tarpaulin. Meanwhile, Mike is awfully foolish to expose himself by saying, 'I don't get it - they've got the Hand, why don't they leave?' Why exactly he says this to Gilmore, who knows less and less as the story develops, need not detain us. [Unmotivated infodump conversations are, after all, what make four-part stories possible.] But the problem is that Gilmore reacts as if he understands this after Ace yells at Mike [unless you seriously think that a Group Captain will arrest his own Sergeant just on the say-so of a teenage civilian]. One explanation is that the Doctor explained it all to Ace on the stairs as a whole bunch of Squaddies were within earshot - but if she's the reason that *Gilmore* suddenly knows about the Hand, why is she upset that Mike knows?

In episode four, why does the Doctor let Ace, Gilmore, Rachel and Allison cram inside the Dalek shuttlecraft after him? It seems a little dangerous, and once there, they don't do anything but gawk a bit until the he escorts them out through the bottom. Are we to presume that he's just giving the silly humans something to do [which in this case is feasible]? And either way, did neither the Imperials nor Davros wonder why the Doctor broke into their shuttlecraft and incapacitated the pilot? [We'll presume that the shuttle flies back to the mothership on automatic, unless the pilot comes to.] And it's the last time this special effects oddity happens, so we'll finally allow ourselves to comment on it... when the Dalek mothership explodes, it's certainly curious how smoke curls "upward" in space.

The one that any good and pure-hearted *Doctor Who* fan will spot: the sign to the junkyard here reads 'Forman', but it was 'Foreman' in "An Unearthly Child". [More than one spin-off book has gone out of its way to "explain" this, two of the most notable being *Interference* and *The Algebra of Ice*. This is actually unnecessary, as the essay will show.]

Aldred plays the Headmaster's attack on Ace as if he's just kneed her in the balls. Even to the point of it briefly rendering her unconscious.

Critique On paper, this ought to be the worst idea since "Attack of the Cybermen" (22.1), because it sounds like the very definition of "fanwank". In fact it's almost the exact opposite, as it returns to first principles, explains the basics to a new audience in a new way that means something, and closely examines the underlying assumptions of those early foundations.

It's hardly an original idea; as we've seen, comics were rebooting left, right and centre in this era, and this phase of *Doctor Who* owes so much to comics it's ridiculous. Not that there's anything wrong with this: the most obviously comic-inspired series of the 90s was *Buffy the Vampire Slayer* (which owes a huge debt to the Chris Claremont run on *X-Men*), although it's the spin-off *Angel* that should've paid royalties to Peter Milligan for lifting whole plot strands from *Shade: The Changing Man*[33]. Comics are a visual medium that can use literary devices where appropriate, and thus we have more reason to want *Doctor Who* to be like a comic than like radio. Besides, who these days would claim that *Buffy* is an inappropriate model for *Doctor Who*? (Certainly nobody who wants a job at BBC Wales...) So what this story does is simply to reintroduce the Daleks as a mighty cosmic force, and the Doctor as someone - the *only* one - capable of stopping them. We've not actually seen this since "Planet of the Daleks" in 1973, as each subsequent appearance has wrung the changes with increasing desperation.

Around this, the story has logical mentions of

the programme's past, but not in such a way that it's a tick-box story. The surrounding characters don't just do what's required of them in "traditional" stories. Yes, the Doctor's companion twists her ankle, but it's understandable and happens in such a way that no Who-girl has really done before (Leela came close, but she didn't jump through a window *during* a gunfight). Indeed, Ace gets to beat up Daleks with an energized baseball bat, fire a bazooka and generally take some of the burden of saving the world from the Doctor's shoulders, allowing him to wander off and be cryptic. Mind you, she gets to play the mysterious traveller pretty well herself. We all go on about the scene with John and the Doctor in the café, but the lead-in to this is Ace evading Rachel's questions - and displaying a secretive smile that lifts Sophie Aldred into the list of "Top Five Companions". We'll be expressing misgivings about her in later stories, but here she's utterly assured; flirtatious even, in a way we've not seen since the 70s.

As we said last time the Daleks appeared, there's something about working with them that gets a quality cast to give that little bit extra. We're trying to think of a duff performance in this story, and it's telling that only the extra who stands to attention a split-second late springs to mind. (And even he's been excused, in at least one other publication, as a *homage* to Corporal Jones from *Dad's Army*.) It's invidious to single anyone out - as even apparently clichéd parts such as Gilmore develop nuances as the story unfolds - but Dursley McLinden (as Mike Smith) should've been a star and Jasmine Breaks (as the young girl) still might. (This aspect has lodged in the memory of more than one fan making the new series - see X3.8, "Human Nature" / X3.9, "The Family of Blood" for a really blatant example.)

Where it falls down is in some of the details. We cited a few of the accidental anachronisms - many of which owed to a lack of time to make fixes, or an inability to spot them in the first place. The Daleks on location have inadvertent comedy value (especially the Black Dalek in episode four, wobbling about as if seemingly drunk). The Time Manipulator static ball is something of an embarrassment. And you'll have to take the word of someone who was around in 60s Britain that such errors are more noticeable because so many of the details are spot-on - genuinely looking like bits that were filmed at the time, albeit on VT and with odd music.

Yes... as you might've sensed, we're nitpicking. The basic fact about this story is that after three successive adventures where we were thinking, "It's getting there," *Doctor Who* - the once mighty television institution - is back doing what it does, as well as it ever did. The story's set-up is historical and the premise fantastical, but the emphasis is on the impact this has on the people around the Doctor. In script and acting, it doesn't put a foot wrong. The visuals - with the caveats mentioned above - are at worst competent, at best impressive. Looked at now, it's amazing that so few people saw it on first broadcast. Had the BBC got behind this series, episodes like these would have won it a whole new audience. Like "The Parting of the Ways" (X1.13), it gives us what we'd always wanted to see, *better* than we thought it could look, and resembles our hazy, nostalgic memories of Dalek stories when we were eight or nine (so the title "Remembrance" is entirely apt).

We see them in the school playground, chasing the Doctor around back streets, possessing the Headmaster and landing shuttles in London. We see them knocking lumps out of one another, with the Special Weapons Dalek *and* the Emperor from the comic strip. Unlike the BBC Wales stories, it has no need to use the Daleks' audience drawing-power to heighten another story entirely. The Daleks should never be anyone else's window-dressing. Even with the remote prospect of the lost Troughton stories being rediscovered, and even after seeing Eccleston and Tennant take on vast armies of CGI super-Daleks, "Remembrance of the Daleks" is just about the best Dalek story ever - simply because it *is* a story, and it's *about* Daleks rather than just having them in it.

The Facts

Written by Ben Aaronovitch. Directed by Andrew Morgan. Ratings: 5.5 million, 5.8 million, 5.1 million, 5.0 million. Audience appreciation started at 68% for episode one, climbed steadily upward and peaked at 72% for episode four - a considerable improvement over the high 50s and low 60s scores of last year.

Working Titles "Nemesis of the Doctor"

Supporting Cast Simon Williams (Gilmore), Terry Molloy (Davros), Dursley McLinden (Mike Smith), Pamela Salem (Rachel), Karen Gledhill (Allison), George Sewell (Ratcliffe), Michael Sheard (Headmaster), Harry Fowler (Harry), Jasmine Breaks (the Girl), Peter Halliday (Vicar), Joseph Marcell (John), William Thomas (Martin), John Leeson (Voice, and see **The Lore**); Roy Skelton, Brian Miller, Royce Mills (Dalek Voices).

Oh, Isn't That..?

• *Simon Williams*. As most of you know (and if you don't not, why not?), he was Major James Bellamy in *Upstairs, Downstairs* and spent ages trying to play something else. He was a trendy DJ in *Agony*, a 900-year-old Venusian in *Kinvig* and in a just and fair world would have been in the Southern TV *Dan Dare*.

• *George Sewell*. He started acting fairly late on, under the auspices of Joan Littlewood's radical theatre company based at the Theatre Royal, Stratford. (It's usually called "Stratford East" because it's the one in London, not the Shakespeare Stratford in Warwickshire.) In fact, that's how he had met Sylvester McCoy. However, Sewell's TV work was mainly as cops (e.g. *Special Branch* opposite Derren Nesbitt, or *The Detectives* - a spoof with Robert Powell and Jasper Carrott). In *UFO*, just for a change, he was an ex-cop who was sporadically replaced by Wanda Ventham (see 24.1, "Time and the Rani", among others) without the dialogue changing much. He died just as we were editing this book.

• *Joseph Marcell*. The week in which his big scene in episode two was shown, he was in three other prime-time series, plus on stage in Leicester as *Julius Caesar*. But what everyone now knows is that he went off to become Jeffrey the Butler in *The Fresh Prince of Bel-Air*.

• *Pamela Salem*. In case you'd forgotten, she was Toos, one of the survivors in "The Robots of Death" (14.5). After that, she had lots of roles as temptresses, culminating in a stint in *EastEnders* as Den's replacement.

• *Dursley McLinden*. He'd just been in British gangster-kidflick *The Falcon's Malteser* (it was sadly retitled *Just Ask for Diamond* when it got into cinemas), and later showed up in a TV spinoff. Shortly after "Remembrance of the Daleks", he got a big ad for Twix chocolate bars and thus was all over bus-stops and TV. He died soon after, but people watching this story now still remember the Twix ad and ask us about it.

• *Harry Fowler*. A real veteran. His film career really began with *Hue and Cry* in 1947 (see 6.3, "The Invasion"), continued through the fifties (he was once Joan Collins' love-interest) and then branched into television and radio. He was therefore more famous than anything he'd been in, so calling his character anything other than 'Harry' was a waste of time.

• *Michael Sheard*. Since his previous appearance in *Doctor Who* (19.1, "Castrovalva"), he had become nationally famous as Mr Bronson, the pompous deputy head of *Grange Hill*, and had the most celebrated toupee in Britain.

• *Peter Halliday*. Here he's the blind Vicar in episode two, but we know him from such stories as "The Invasion" (where he was Packer, Vaughn's head stooge), 10.2, "Carnival of Monsters" (as Petrac) and 17.2, "The City of Death" (as Scarloni's soldier, in episode three). He's done loads else, including the original *A For Andromeda*.

• *William Thomas*. He's cropped up in lots of Wales-based films and TV over the years. We mention him here largely because he's the first actor to have credited roles in both the original and relaunched *Doctor Who*. He's here the funeral director in episode two, but gets squished by Margaret Slitheen in the pre-credits sequence of "Boom Town" (X1.11).

Cliffhangers The Doctor is trapped in the Coal Hill School basement, and is horrified as a Dalek chases up the stairs after him; three Daleks surround Ace, and spend ages saying they are going to shoot her; a Dalek space-shuttle unexpectedly lands in the school playground, and the Doctor thinks he might've miscalculated.

The Lore

• With Cartmel's continuing aim of bringing in writers not just new to the series but new to television, other script editors were occasionally alerting him to promising beginners. One such novice, Ben Aaronovitch, had pitched a detective series and sent a few unsolicited scripts to Caroline Oulton, the story editor of *South of the Border*. They were good but not quite right (and anyway the series was about to be pulled, even before a single episode had been shown - if *Border* is remembered at all, it's for being almost comically mid-80s and near self-parodically right-on). Cartmel's version is that Aaronovitch sent a *Doctor Who* script; other sources indicate that Aaronovitch wasn't sure that the series was even still being made, and that "Nightfall" was submit-

ted after Cartmel had read the other script samples that Oulton forwarded. Either way, the point is that Aaronovitch soon found himself being asked for ideas, and would brainstorm with Cartmel, Ian Briggs and others.

So Aaronovitch came up with a neat premise for a script, based on watching old episodes and thinking about how they could be improved upon. Ha! Fooled you... that story wasn't "Remembrance", but instead became "Battlefield". The change owed to the fact that Nathan-Turner announced he wanted a Dalek story. Cartmel seems to have automatically assumed that Aaronovitch was the person to write it (although it also seems that many of the other writers he'd nursed had already got stories in the pipeline, and were nearer to completion than "Storm Over Avallion", Aaronovitch's Arthurian adventure). Precisely who decided that the story should be set in 1963 is unclear, but this seems always to have been intended as the first story of Season Twenty-Five, despite the three subsequent being commissioned (or discussed in detail, in the case of "Silver Nemesis") well before this. Indeed, the scripts for both "Remembrance" and Kevin Clarke's story came in at almost the same time. (This makes the similarities between them more alarming, and Cartmel's failure to spot this until the last minute really odd - more on this two stories hence.) The storyline had to be worked out fairly early on because Terry Nation's agent, Roger Hancock, had to deliver it to his client, and both had to find it satisfactory.

• Aaronovitch's first attempt was broadly similar to what was broadcast, except for name-changes and shifts of emphasis. Originally, the Hand of Rassilon is kept in a lock-up, not a funeral home; the Dalek factions are red and blue; the Blue Daleks (the rebels) are captured, not destroyed (although all remaining Daleks and their technology are zapped to protect the timelines) and the Doctor has a Western-style shootout with the Black Dalek. Ace borrows Mike's jeans (perhaps a reference to the then-famous Levis 501 ads, where another quiffed pretty-boy - Nick Kamen - stripped to his boxer-shorts in a launderette).

• Relations between the new writer and the producer were initially frosty. However, the post-Christmas bash in the production office (held 13th of January, for some reason) began a general trend towards all sides in the making of the series socialising. McCoy and Aldred would go for piz-zas or Greek meals with Cartmel and his boys, and sometimes a director or two. The overall plan of each year's episodes would be worked out, based on what worked so far, what was missing and what the stars wanted to do. (One idea that never reached fruition, however: although motor-bikes kept being written into stories, Aldred never got her wish to ride a big one on screen.) The fol-lowing week or so saw the last two episodes deliv-ered (episode four first), so all the scripts for the season were in (except the last two from Kevin Clarke). At this point, the producer took a long holiday.

• During this time, the Coast to Coast publici-ty machine coughed up another gem. Their *Doctor Who* motion picture was going to be made for an Easter 1989 release, with $14 million to play with and location work in Ireland, Lanzarote and maybe Yugoslavia. Hooray! And it would include former beauty queen and love interest in at least one of those "drilling to the centre of the Earth to find dinosaurs and the North Pole" epics: Caroline Munro. And it would have someone playing the Doctor who wasn't Sylvester McCoy. Every few weeks a different name would be offered to the press, generating a lot more interest than the actu-al series had lately. Those who'd been watching the TV series were not entirely ecstatic that the next name attached to the project was writer Johnny Byrne. (See 18.6, "The Keeper of Traken", 20.1, "Arc of Infinity" and in particular 21.1, "Warriors of the Deep", for why this might not be welcome news.)

• Location recording on "Remembrance" began in April, in various parts of West London. Firmly believing this to be his last year on the series, Nathan-Turner decided to look for new projects and discard the trademark hairdo, beard and shirts. The new-look JN-T still favoured bold colours, but in a style that would soon become pretty mainstream. (Whether anyone told him to his face how much he now resembled Breakfast TV astrologer Russell Grant isn't known.)

The various sites used included the Kew Bridge Steam Museum (Totter's Lane), St John's School (Coal Hill) - this was located on Macbeth Street, which gave the crew pause - and Theed Street Yard (Ratcliffe's HQ) which was owned by London Weekend Television. On the first day of filming, the emergency services were on high alert for IRA bombs as the police believed that it was the sixti-eth anniversary of the Easter Rising. (That this had

actually begun on 24th of April, 1916, and it was now 4th of April, 1988, says a lot about why the British police were held in such low esteem at this time.) Thus, when the Special Weapons Dalek did its stuff, the place was surrounded by fire engines before you could say, "A terrible beauty is born".

• Stop us if you've heard this one before: a stage-direction had Group Captain Gilmore pulling out what was described as a 'chunky serv-ice revolver'. Simon Williams thought that this was possibly the make of gun, not a curious choice of adjective, and referred to it as "my chunky". This got to be a running gag, as you'll see from an out-take included on the DVD, so they ad-libbed the Doctor's comments about the men calling him 'Chunky' Gilmore. Williams' son, Tam, was the boy wearing anachronistic jeans in the opening of the episode proper - the others were the children of the director and the costume designer, and Jasmine Breaks' sister. Breaks was the daughter of a friend of the director, and need-ed to be issued with a permit to work on the series. She's now a researcher for a TV company making Channel 4 "yoof" shows, but has acted recently too.

• The Black Dalek, like the refitted Rebels, had larger wheels to cope with cobbles. Morgan hired dancer Hugh Spight to operate this prop, fearing that it would be slightly too demanding even for the experienced operators. Unfortunately, the over-inflated tyres made the Dalek wobble wildly. Cartmel attended the location shoot, taking time during lulls to amend the script for "The Happiness Patrol".

• With McCoy keen to be more active and physical as the Doctor, it made sense to find a reg-ular stunt-arranger. For the majority of stories from now on, this would be Tip Tipping - he was the right height and build, and came equipped with a wife (Tracey Eddon) who could double for Aldred. McCoy was persuaded not to do the "death-slide" to the top of the Dalek shuttle him-self, eventually. Tipping is also the squaddie who gets zapped so hard he flies back into a sheet of corrigated iron (and the later editions of the DVD do actually have this effect, after everyone pointed out that the quest for high-definition copies had led to BBC engineers leaving this and another less memorable effect off). Now you know what he looks like, keep an eye out for him; he also plays the corporal ('Heinlein' in the script - hmmm) who arrests Mike. Aldred did most of her own stunts, too, but not the one with the window. (Just as well, as Eddon was slightly injured: her insurance covered it, but Aldred's wouldn't have. See "Battlefield".)

• John Leeson, returning to the fold after a few years (see 20.7, "the Five Doctors"), had once been a real BBC Continuity Announcer (back when they weren't people who deserved to be fed to starving mongrels), and so did the spiel about '5.15 pm'. He also redubbed Jasmine Breaks as the Dalek Controller (yes, she did all the dialogue in studio). At one point it was hoped that Terry Molloy would do this as well as Davros, but he wasn't available for that session.

• The Daleks managed stairs the same as any other invalid: with a Stannah Stairlift. Or, at least, it was a modified version of the device advertised on daytime TV, with a bar fed through a slot in the wall of the set. As we've said, the Imperial Daleks were new props, and the Renegades were the old Imperial shells repainted after their last outing in "Revelation of the Daleks". Despite Morgan going over-budget by the total cost of 2.8, "The Chase" (about thirteen grand; this of course doesn't account for inflation), it appears he was still in the running to direct "Battlefield".

• Although Cartmel reports difficulties getting the paperwork done for the old records used in the story, not all of the soundbites used in the pre-credit sequence were difficult. The Palace said that using a recording of the Queen was a no-no, but Prince Philip would be all right at a pinch. Others include JFK (two speeches, including "Ich bin ein berliner"), Dr King's "I Have a Dream" (a big problem if you're trying to date the story from *that*, as it occurred on 28th August, 1963) and Charles de Gaulle. Also permitted, for free (cos he loved the show), was Bob Dylan's "Only A Pawn in the Game". (It was in keeping with the story's theme of prejudice.) Cartmel and Aaronovitch watched the relevant edition of *The Rock 'n' Roll Years* - a nostalgia documentary matching newsreel clips to hits of a given year (the 1963 one even has Ian and Barbara bursting into the Ship as one of its key events).

• We've got to say this, reluctantly: yet another irritating novelty single happened that year, but unlike "I'm Gonna Spend My Christmas With a Dalek" (released during 3.4, "The Daleks' Master Plan"), "Who Is Doctor Who?" (see 6.2, "The Mind Robber"), "I Am the Doctor" (see 9.1, "Day of the Daleks") and *Doctor In Distress* ("Revelation of the Daleks") this one actually charted. In fact,

"Doctorin' the Tardis" (sic) got into the Top Ten for five weeks, one of those at No. 1.

This was actually intended as a scam, to recoup the money lost when a previous single by KLF (Kopyright Liberation Front, which should tell you about their attitude to sampling) were ordered by a court to pay up vast sums to the estates of Rodgers and Hammerstein. Rather than fork out 200% of the proceeds of each copy of the single (which cleverly mixed Stevie Wonder's "Superstition" with "The Lonely Goatherd" - funny how Gwen Stefani avoided a lawsuit, eh), they dumped them over the side of a North Sea Ferry except for one. (Oddly enough, several people claim to have that one remaining copy...)

So as a quick moneyspinner to pay court costs, they sampled the theme and dialogue from the BBC album of "Genesis of the Daleks" (12.4) and hooks from "Blockbuster" by Sweet and "Rock 'n' Roll Part 2" by Gary Glitter. That and a bit of chanting, and you have a glam-rock nostalgia hit that got kids shouting "Doctor Whooo-ooooo HAH! Doctor Who" for months. (This delayed location work for "The Curse of Fenric", as we will see.) Seeing dance-floors filling when this one started - and hip kids bopping to Roy Skelton yelling, 'We obey no-one! We are the superior beings!' - was downright unsettling for fanboys who'd unerringly conditioned themselves to never mention the programme in public. It even caused a brief return to the limelight for Glitter (back when we were allowed to acknowledge his existence).

• Press coverage of the start of recording was mainly enthusiastic, with a resurgency of the notion that the show had been about to get axed again after Season Twenty-Four, and the reports always seemed to dwell on falling ratings and such. Ian Levene was now involved in the proposed film project, and supposedly went on LBC radio to talk about it. Instead he, Saward and Janet Fielding spent the time slagging off on Nathan-Turner. Meanwhile, Daltenreys / Coast to Coast was still approaching the producer to act as a "consultant" to the movie.

• However, within weeks it was the producer who picked up the pieces from an abortive plan that the American stage play *The Inheritors of Time* should be brought to London. Nathan-Turner proposed that Aaronovitch and Cartmel should instead write one, which ideally he would direct. A script involving Daleks, Stonehenge,

Casablanca (the city, if not the film) and a planet called the "War World" (this becoming the title of the play) was devised. In this were new aliens - the Metatraxi - who were obsessed with war but offended by references to food. These might have been recycled for a proposed story to write Ace out of the series (see **What About Season 27?** under 26.4, "Survival"). This play never came about, but the idea persisted - especially with the idea of it starring a former Doctor - to allow a run coinciding with the new series' recording. (See "The Greatest Show in the Galaxy" for more on this.)

• Stop us if... On showing this story to the new Head of Drama, Mark Shivas, Cartmel was irked when the head honcho took a phone call during the 'No Coloureds' scene, and insisted - against usual protocol - on rewinding and showing off this brief moment. Shivas agreed that it was well done, but thought that Ace should have ripped the sign up.

25.2: "The Happiness Patrol"

(Serial 7L, Three Episodes. 2nd - 16th November 1988.)

Which One is This? *Doctor Who*, as Tim Burton might have made it.

Firsts and Lasts Obviously, it's the first time the TARDIS exterior has changed colour (as it's here painted pink). After six stories in three years, director Chris Clough bows out (although he made the next story beforehand).

Three Things to Notice about
"The Happiness Patrol"...

1. Around the time this story was recorded, the tabloid press - who had been cheerfully discussing rave culture and Acid House - suddenly thought that this new and exciting music might, just might, contain some kind of drugs references. So all the garish colours, Smiley logos and lyrics about "Ecstasy" and "Acieeeeeeeeed" became the focus of a manufactured moral panic. Bear this in mind as you watch a tale of "Happifying", "Fun Guns", people being killed with sweets, Smile badges being used to identify potential trouble-makers and a seven-foot Liquorice Allsort serving as the state executioner-cum-spin doctor.

2. And at the heart of this comic-opera Third World fascist Junta, who else but Margaret

Thatcher? Well, all right, not really, but it's obvious who they had in mind. The script may call for a cross between Pinochet, Ceaucescu and Marcos, but then it gives her a husband who's Denis Thatcher without the dodgy (alleged) offshore financial deals and fondness for gin. Except that if this analogy is to be taken seriously, Denis eventually elopes with Marmeduke Hussey, Chairman of the BBC's Board of Governors. It's hard to imagine this reaching our screens if anyone in authority was still paying any attention to *Doctor Who*.

3. This is notorious as the story that bankrupted *Doctor Who*. Made at the end of the season's production, it was intended as the cheap one, but even these frugal costs over-ran considerably. It is, however, impossible to imagine a big-budget version of this looking significantly different. (That said, the car-chases might have risen above walking-speed, but even then OJ Simpson did something similar in real life.) Especially now, with major film directors making movies that strive to look like this story's desperate cost-cutting ploys, this is the one McCoy story that has improved with age. This was helped by the unexpected collapse of several Soviet satellite states in circumstances like the "improbable" sequence of events in episode three, and the overthrow of many Latin American regimes with policies like Helen A's.

The Continuity

The Doctor He's no more capable of ignoring an open microphone than any of us, and croons "As Time Goes By" when he thinks no-one's listening. As with the previous story, the Doctor seems to prefer defeating his opponents just by talking to them - here, he thwarts two rooftop snipers by standing directly in front of a gun barrel, and breaks their resolve by making them confront the idea that guns take life. He adeptly slips out of his bonds in the Kandy Kitchen.

• *Ethics.* The Doctor says he and Ace have travelled to Terra Alpha because he's heard 'disturbing rumours' of 'something evil' there. At an abstract level, this stable but very odd and oppressive society offends the Doctor's sense of fairness and proportion - particularly as he insists that happiness is nothing unless it exists alongside sadness - to such an extent that he helps to overthrow the government in one night. [This is a questionable enterprise at the best of times, especially as the Doctor likely knows the controlling regime has all the guns, so he presumably expected a far higher casualty rate than what we see.

[Starting with "Remembrance of the Daleks" (25.1), continuing into this adventure and going well into the future, the Seventh Doctor's "pro-active" (Andrew Carmel has commented that he despises this term, but seems to admit that it's a fairly apt one) nature has become a sticking-point for many fans. Since the TARDIS now goes wher-ever the Doctor directs, the adventures we see can mainly be classed as "missions" - this sort of thing has been seen before in stories such as "Mindwarp" (23.2), but it reaches critical mass in Seasons Twenty-Five and Twenty-Six. So as the Doctor here says at the start, he's evidently decid-ed to sort out various problems he's heard about - such as the routine disappearances on Terra Alpha or the Gods of Ragnarok (25.4, "The Greatest Show in the Galaxy", where we'll argue that he engineered the "accidental" appearance of the junk-mail robot).

[The more personal issue is what this says about his relationship with Ace. (Although any-one quick with condemnation might want to con-sider that she's *far* better suited to this line of work than - say - Peri was in "Mindwarp", where the seemingly unconcerned Sixth Doctor drags her along as he tries to stop a bunch of gun-happy warlords.) As we mentioned in "Remembrance of the Daleks", the Seventh Doctor only seems to have started his "crusading" now that Mel is gone, and Ace is on-hand as his attack-dog. (Observe his comment on her unfocussed anger in this story: 'you're no use to me like this'.) Revelations in 26.3, "The Curse of Fenric" make it clear that this is also part of a longer-term plan, so is he actually fond of her to begin with or does she grow on him? How much of it is an act? We will return to this, especially in the essays **Did Cartmel Have Any Plan At All?** under 25.3, "Silver Nemesis" and **What Would Season 27 Have Been Like?** under 26.4, "Survival". But it's worth considering that their relationship *does* seem very touching, and the bigger issue isn't so much whether or not he's manipulating her - given Ace's continued approval of his actions, save for exceptions such as "Ghost Light" (26.2) - but whether, at age sixteen, she's got the emotional maturity to comprehend the risks involved.]

The Doctor displays a quiet anger when the political prisoner Harold V is electrocuted, but no real emotion when the Patrol shoots the treacher-ous Silas P. He seems particularly saddened that

Helen A has created an artificial society with no compassion or love.

• *Inventory.* He's packing party-poppers, razzers, spoons and bomb-defusing equipment. And at least one big gold coin.

• *Background.* The Doctor mentions that his nickname at college was Theta Sigma. [Mercifully, this puts to rest the appalling notion in "The Armageddon Factor" (16.6) that 'Theta Sigma' is the Doctor's real name. Mind you, what defines "real" in this context? According to X2.4, "The Girl in the Fireplace" he doesn't remember having *had* a name.]

He's run into a Stigorax predator such as Fifi before, in Birmingham. [At least, it *sounds* like McCoy says Birmingham, but it could be a planet called Birnam; and see **History**. Confounding our attempts to double-check, the novelisation omits this reference.] He's read Dr John Wallace's paper on sympathetic vibrations. [This hails from 1677, and if the Doctor is a Fellow of the Royal Society - see 26.2, "Ghost Light" - he was probably in the audience when it was first delivered.]

The Supporting Cast

• *Ace.* She doesn't like lift music, but seems interested in dinosaurs, especially when the Doctor suggests they might visit the Upper Cretaceous period. He also explains to her that, 'The Brigadier saw one in the London Underground once'. [11.2, "Invasion of the Dinosaurs" episode six; it was a Triceratops. The Doctor says this as if he's mentioned the Brig to her before, in advance of 26.1, "Battlefield".]

She wears a badge in support of Charlton Athletic FC [which in those days was almost as tragically unfashionable as still watching *Doctor Who*]. She can't sing, play an instrument, tell jokes or play the spoons (although she gives the latter an amateur-ish try), but knows the lyrics to "Teen Angel" [if you've lived under a rock all your life, you may need to be told that this is the 'great' song with the girl hit by a train]. She hates smiling when it doesn't mean anything.

Ace looks eager to have a go at disarming explosives, and expresses a desire to engage in willfull destruction of public property. [In a delet-ed scene - and as the Doctor later tells us - she seems very proud of blowing up the attack dog Fifi.]

What are the Gayest Things in *Doctor Who*?

We've been cagey about this subject up until now, as a lot of what people have chosen to see as signs or symbols of homosexuality are simply botched attempts to look "alien" or "futuristic" on a low budget. However, with a lot of gay fans watching with more-than-usual attention, and a lot of gays (out or otherwise) working on the series, it's inevitable that things have been misconstrued - either with seriousness or for comic effect. (See **What's All This Stuff About Anoraks?** under 24.1, "Time and the Rani" for more.)

Although it was illegal until 1967, homosexuality was sort-of accepted in the artistic community, and allowed a lot of coded references to pass into the mainstream almost undetected by the great unwashed. "Naff" is now just another word for "not very good", but it was the Palare word for hetero, like "honky" (see 10.2, "Carnival of Monsters"). In the 90s, anything meant for 70s children was parodied with hints of innuendo. Tired gags about *Captain Pugwash* and *Blue Peter* did the rounds, and records like *The Trumpton Riots* and *Summers' Magic* (a rave-friendly remix of the theme from *The Magic Roundabout*, possibly mentioned in *Nostradamus*) made it fashionable. Victor Lewis-Smith (ahem) milked the joke with a series of sketches about Gay Daleks. (The *Doctor Who* theme mixed with Tom Robinson's "Glad to be Gay" was the only good gag we hadn't already done within fandom. What Lewis-Smith did was make it public knowledge, so that the clip from 21.4, "Resurrection of the Daleks" - the one that shows the unfortunate effect of the Movellan virus - is now routinely accompanied by Dalek voices crying "Ooh! White wee-wee!")

However, bear in mind how long the series had been running before September 1967, when the criminalisation of homosexual acts between consenting adults was repealed. (This only ever applied to male adults, of course; the law didn't do anything about lesbians, because they weren't thought to really exist.) A lot of material had been in code over the past century, and these habits took a long time to die out. Add to this the encryption of *any* sexuality in what was deemed a "family" show, and you'll see why so much of what was shown over the 26 years of the original series was open to multiple interpretations.

We should mention that right from the start, *Doctor Who* had been made with a big gay input - the very first director, Waris Hussain, made no secret of his leanings. (And yet William Hartnell was an enthusiastic supporter. Like many people of that age, Hartnell made a distinction between "them" in the abstract and individuals he knew personally.) In the 1980s, the fact that the producer was out and proud was only significant when anti-Nathan-Turner statements in fanzines became mixed with homophobia (although the main vehicle for such outpourings was *DWB*, with a gay editor). That said, it does *sometimes* affect what we see on screen. About once every three minutes or so.

Now that everything's out in the open, it's a lot less fun finding (or "reclaiming") things in popular TV. So we're excluding the BBC Wales series from this this list, because - as with **Was There Any Hanky-Panky in the TARDIS?** under 6.6, "The Space Pirates" - it'd be like spotting car-chases in *The Dukes of Hazzard*. But then, the whole JN-T era is only marginally less upfront than that. Just look at the accompanying story, where the TARDIS is painted pink, two men elope and the Doctor is - officially - a Friend of Dorothy.

15) Noah (12.2, "The Ark in Space"). The only male character we can legitimately call a queen. (Technically he calls himself 'swarm leader', but how did a hybrid like him get to be boss of all the bugs? The Wirrn want "him" to have lots of well-educated babies, apparently. No other explanation is forthcoming.) Like many middle-aged men who undergo a startling life-change, his biggest problem is keeping it from his fiancée. He then attempts to resolve his inner conflict through the medium of expressionist dance. Noah spends the better part of two episodes trying to get close to his former friends while they sleep, and apparently ends the story pregnant.

14) Peri + Yrcanos 4 Evah (23.4, "The Ultimate Foe"). The 1980s were a grim time for video effects - at least, if your primary concern was some kind of narrative authenticity. Those who love the gaudiness of techno-kitsch from that period - the video equivalent of Old-Skool Chicago House - will find much to enjoy here. From Turlough's disco out-of-body experience (20.3, "Mawdryn Undead") to the moment Sylvester McCoy entered the Daisy Age and crossed to the Dark Circus in the style of an S-Express video (25.4, "The Greatest Show in the Galaxy"), *Doctor Who* was more in touch with club culture than *Top of the Pops*. And this being the

continued on page 245...

ABOUT TIME 1985-1989

The TARDIS Is painted pink in episode one, but repainted blue at the end. [This would appear to contradict the suggested function of the chameleon circuit in "Logopolis" (18.7) - because the pink paint doesn't just slide off when the Ship dematerializes - but not any other stories.]

The Non-Humans

• *Alpidae (AKA The Pipe People).* [The designation 'Alpidae' hails from the novelisation and one version of the script. It's never used on screen - but then neither is the nickname 'Pipe People'.] The indigenous life-forms of Terra Alpha; they're bipedal, short and capable of rudimentary speech [at least, in English]. They have rodent-like three-toed hind feet; large, pointy ears; entirely black eyes and wrinkled grey skin. Some have orange fur - like thinning hair - and beards. They walk upright, often with staves or spears, and wear monk-like habits made of different black-and-white patterned patches. Their teeth look sharp, but since being hounded from the planet's sugar beet fields, they've grown weaker from subsisting in the factory pipes on processed sugar.

They pick-up phrases from other people, and although their voices are abrasive, they're usually easy to comprehend. Once assured that someone is on their side, they're very loyal. Upon infiltrating the Kandy Kitchen, they quickly figure out how to operate the railway-like switching system and flood the pipes with fondant. A couple of them seem to be named after Anglo-Saxon monks: "Wulfric" and "Wences".

Planet Notes

• *Terra Alpha.* When seen from space, it looks almost Earth-like, although yellow clouds swaddle it and there's a purple halo surrounding it. Terra Omega is apparently the nearest inhabited world. [The terminology suggests there's a ring of at least twenty-three populated worlds. Or possibly many more, as we're told about one world - Vasilip - that isn't designated with a Greek letter. However, dialogue struck from the finished cut suggests that Terra Alpha lies in a system of three inhabited planets, the others being Terra Beta and Terra Omega. Half of you will now be thinking about 4.9, "The Evil of the Daleks" - stop it at once.]

The planet seems to be located near Earth, but it's a little out of the way of main space routes. The population are divided into twenty-six castes,

with letters of the alphabet in lieu of surnames - offworlders are given the surname 'Sigma' [although Gilbert M seems to have naturalised, and the Kandy Man is a special case]. The status of each letter doesn't exactly follow alphabetical order, but Helen A is assuredly the colony's leader.

The Galactic Census Bureau previously recommended that Helen A implement controls on population growth, but she ignored the Bureau's suggestions and instead introduced the dreaded social engineering programme that the planet is now wallowing in. Simply put, personal happiness is mandated, and 'displays of public grief' - such as wearing dark clothes, listening to slow music, reading poems (unless they're limericks) or walking alone in the rain without an umbrella - are punishable by death.

Helen A has three main methods of disposing of such people, who are referred to as 'Killjoys'. Her primary enforcers are the Happiness Patrol - squads of gun-totting women who are mostly in their 40s. The patrol sometimes flushes out the Killjoys by employing a covert agent (Silas P) who uses a samisdat newspaper, *The Grief*. Male rooftop snipers are sometimes used to eliminate public protests. Mention is made of Happiness Patrol sections B and F [so there's presumably six sections at least]. Apparently owing to their social conditioning, the Happiness Patrol members are entirely unable to harm those perceived to be happy. They even hand out smiley-face stickers to jolly individuals.

Method No. 2 of execution is 'A Late Show at the Forum', which we're never actually shown, but seems to entail law-breakers or political dissenters engaging in lethal stage performances that involve magic, singing, dancing, juggling, impressions, auditioning for the Happiness Patrol or the Miracle Survival Act (i.e. "If you survive, it's a miracle"). Viewing attendance at the Forum is compulsory.

Finally, Helen A's head executioner is the Kandy Man, a confection-based cyborg who works from his Kandy Kitchen, and who as ordered pumps sweets such as strawberry fondant through pipes to smother the condemned. The ingredients that compose the Kandy Man include caramel, sherbert, toffee, marzipan and gelling agents, but his joints require constant movement to avoid coagulation [so the Kandy Man never sleeps, apparently]. He's honourable in his own way - here thwarting an execution per a bargain with the Doctor -

What are the Gayest Things in *Doctor Who*?

...continued from page 243

1980s, you know what kind of club culture was making the running. "The Trial of a Time Lord" may have affected to join in with big butch blokey SF films of the era, but you have to ask whether strategically-shaven ex-cons could ever have been taken as straight even without names like 'Glitz' and 'Dibber'. And this is a fourteen-part story that ends with a lot of men in frocks ambling out of a room as a whole load of digitally-created triangles (electric blue - not pink, but they might just as well have been) fly around the place.

But right at the very end, we have the most gloriously tasteless thing of the entire Colin Baker era. When the Doctor learns that Peri survived, we have a few seconds of which Liberace would have been proud. There's a slow-motion shot of Peri and Yrcanos, in sepia, and in a fuzzy, pink, heart-shaped border. It's a bit of recycled footage - and indeed, the only one of them exchanging anything like a fond glance in their ninety minutes of screen time - and it's accompanied by recycled music. To be honest, something by Barbra Streisand would have been just as appropriate.

Even with thirteen and a half episodes to brace ourselves for this - episodes which mind you have included the blond boys Tumker and Handril, a planet with a pink sea and (!) the Vervoids - this is still a shock. Out of sequence, it borders on medically dangerous.

13) The Scientific Reform Society (12.1, "Robot"). Yeah, right, *they're* going to repopulate Earth.

12) The Doctor's namedrops (various). Starting with the first (1.3, "Edge of Destruction", in which he cites Sir Arthur Sullivan), the Doctor's claims to have known famous men have been slanted in favour of men believed or known to have had leanings towards other men. We've got Shakespeare (13.2, "Planet of Evil"; 22.3, "The Mark of the Rani", a spectacularly innuendo-riven anecdote in 17.2, "City of Death" and who can possibly forget X3.2, "The Shakespeare Code"?), Alexander the Great ("Robot"), Montgomery (9.3, "The Sea Devils"), Archimedes of Syracuse (22.4, "The Two Doctors") and various other Greeks.

Then there's Leonardo da Vinci. Now, the idea that he was gay was largely Freud's fault (and the Doctor knew *him* too, apparently; see 27.0, "The TV Movie"), but was widely accepted as fact when the various episodes in which the Doctor talks about him were made. We've discussed this in some detail (see **When Did the Doctor Meet Leonardo?** under 17.2, "The City of Death") but one thing remains unclear. Why should such a significant figure never get a story about him in the broadcast series? What could have happened that was deemed unsuitable for children's television? And isn't it odd that Douglas Adams - then a protegé of *Gay News* founder Graham Chapman - should be responsible for this story and "The Pirate Planet"? And let's not forget the scene in 17.6, "Shada" where Skagra, in a big floppy hat and cape, propositions a young man in the street and they leave in the man's car. Was Adams trying to tell us something? Let's see...

11) Mentiads (16.2, "The Pirate Planet"). As every British fan knows, the single most flagrantly queer-themed kid's Science Fiction was *The Tomorrow People*. Not even *Beast Wars* comes close. In its original 1970s manifestation, *The Tomorrow People* smuggled a none-too-subtle subtext into the homes of chip-fed ITV-watching kids. Why they were so circumspect in handling the subject matter, when they overlaid it with so much obvious on-screen homoeroticism, is baffling with hindsight. We watch it now and wonder how anyone missed it.[35]

If you don't know, the premise is that a new generation of psychically-gifted youth have evolved in our midst. They are Homo Superior and pity us poor saps, but are so scared of being treated as freaks that they stay in hiding. However, once one of the TPs "breaks out", he or she is sought by the kids, who live in a space-age pad in a disused tube station. Once assured that s/he is not alone, and that others of their kind are special and there to help, they put on special clothes (notably belts with big buckles) and save the world - but must never let the public know about them. Telling their parents is hard enough. (Come to think of it, maybe calling this a "subtext" was pitching it a little strong.)

So when a *Doctor Who* story uses almost the same premise at around the time that the Thames series finished, you have to wonder. Especially when the cute boy who breaks out in "The Pirate Planet" episode one gets that obvious *Doctor Who* symbol of lost innocence: slicked-back hair. Add in the Captain, a baddie who's worryingly like the

continued on page 247...

245

but remains an intensely dangerous and lethal individual.

The Kandy Man fears heat, and carbonated water and citric acid (i.e. lemonade) can make his feet stick to the floor, but applying water will free him. He's labouring to create sweets that are *so* good and delicious, they kill people because the human physiology can't cope with the pleasure. Eventually the Kandy Man melts while fleeing through a pipe that's filled with fondant goo, leaving only his mechanical components behind.

Most of the dissent against Helen A seems located in Sector Six of the central city [which for all we know is the *only* city on the planet, although 'townships' are mentioned], where two or more "waiting zones" (transient detention centres that contain joke machines capable of delivering a lethal jolt) and a square for formal executions are located close to Helen A's palace and the Kandy Kitchen. The backbone of the planet's economy is sugar - Helen A says she's built 'a thousand' sugar beet factories [although there could well be more, depending on how long she's been in power], most of them located to the east of the main city. They are all heavily guarded, although 112 of them fall to the rebellion that crushes Helen A's regime in its first few hours. Most of the population seems employed in sugar production, and much of the arable land seems given over to it. However, some of the pipes near the Kandy Kitchen don't appear to have been used for decades, if not longer. The 'drone' workers who keep the factories running apparently live in the flatlands, and are forbidden from entering the cities.

The city seems to have piped music twenty-four hours a day [or however many hours they have - they *seem* to be running on Earth time, but the night is extremely long]. The PA system reports disturbances as if they were meteorological features. All statements are topped and tailed with the platitude 'happiness will prevail', and it's a local custom for people to comment on one another's pleasure. (The formula is that someone says he or she is pleased, the second says, "I'm glad you're happy", and the first replies, "I'm happy you're glad" or vice versa.)

Helen A herself seems neurotic in her inability to accept change, opposition or vulnerability in other people. The Doctor views her as a 'schizophrenic obsessive'. She can't tell a joke well - neither can she tell if people are joking with her.

[This looks like borderline Asperger's Syndome, which makes her ability to force an entire planet to fit her perception of the world all the more puzzling. People keep making this diagnosis of *Doctor Who* characters. More plausible is the idea - seemingly confirmed by the story's climax - that she's risen to power on a campaign pledge to bring order and happiness to a hitherto fairly chaotic world, but that she's become so fixated on her public image as "Mrs respectable-family-values" that she's forced herself into an unhealthy pretence of a life. (Never mind Thatcher, the similarity to Indira Gandhi on this score seems remarkable - and see **Where Does This Come From?**.)]

She only seems genuinely affectionate toward her attack dog Fifi, and goes to pieces when the evil mutt is killed. Helen A's favourite method of execution: death by strawberry fondant.

History

• *Dating*. The Doctor cites Terra Alpha as an Earth colony, and says it was settled 'some centuries' into Ace's future. He also says Fifi is a 'Stigorax' - a type of ruthless, intelligent predator that he hasn't met 'since the twenty-fifth century'. [Even if this *isn't* the twenty-fifth century, then, the usual interpretation is that it's at some point in the third millennium, when humanity expands into space and - to judge by stories such as "Colony in Space" (8.4), set in 2472 - many colony worlds become isolated and suffer misfortune of one type or another. Terra Alpha is a bit less cut off from other planets than is sometimes stated - note how Trevor Sigma says he's going to Earth next - but it fits the general pattern.]

Trevor Sigma is a roaming agent for the 'Galactic Census Bureau', and lives at 'Galactic Centre'. [This might suggest Terra Alpha belongs to an alliance of worlds.] He says the 'Constitutional rules of the system' forbid the repeat of an execution that's botched owing to equipment failure - but using an alternative method is permissible - and Helen A acts as if she must obey such rules. Trevor's apparently exempt from Helen A's "happiness" policies, as he's able to walk around in a dark suit. He's also authorized to enter all Alphan property and to interview all Alphans, and by law a full planetary census must be completed every 'six local cycles' [a "cycle" in this case seems to mean a month rather than a year as you'd expect]. Earl Sigma - a medical student from off-world, who's studying fifth year

What are the Gayest Things in *Doctor Who*?

...continued from page 245

Tomorrow People's arch-foe Jedekiah. (The first story was called "The Slaves of Jedekiah", and was about an alien tracking down and abducting young boys to join his "gang". Jedekiah turned out to be a robot disguised as a fat old man, and non-British readers may be amazed to find that it's Francis de Wolfe, who was Agamemnon in 3.3, "The Myth Makers" and more visibly the trapper Vasor in 1.5, "The Keys of Marinus". "Amazed" in that he ever found work again, but also because he's actually better there than he ever was in *The Tomorrow People*.)

Then Adams pops into his devastatingly original script a Juve-lead with a name worryingly like "Timus", the Tomorrow People's ancient Greek chum. By this point, and calling to memory the Doctor's joke regarding the two lab mice in "The Daleks' Master Plan" (3.4), anyone with less-than-total admiration for Douglas Adams might wonder if he ever had an original idea in his life. Certainly, the estate of JM Barrie might have asked if the Mentiads, as telepathic "Lost Boys", had been sprinkled with fairy-dust.

However, unlike Thames' customarily relaxed treatment of Roger Price - the producer / writer / director of *The Tomorrow People* - BBC rules prevented writers directing or directors writing (even Barry Letts had to go through channels to get 11.5, "Planet of the Spiders" made more or less to his own specifications). So where *The Tomorrow People* had casting and camera-angles all down to one man's questionable decisions, "The Pirate Planet" has to be treated as a conspiracy. After all, it's not just the way Pralix starts wearing a pastel muumuu, and starts hanging out with a bunch of forkbenders that gives this story a *frisson*; just look at the Captain and Mr Fibuli. For most of the story it's like watching Burns and Smithers, but when Fibuli dies, we see real emotion from a man who's been playing at being fierce. And this is right after an almost identical scene in the previous story when the general Sholakh dies and his prince, the Graff, kisses him (and not just a peck on the cheek, either). In fact, "The Ribos Operation" (16.1) is a story with a very dodgy sequence involving Unstoffe being lured to Binro's bed. 'I know what it's like when every man's hand is against me', Binro says. However, if we are thinking about queerness in Season Sixteen, there's a far more obvious place to look...

10) Vivian Fay and her Chums (16.3, "The Stones of Blood"). Let's start with Cessair's various *noms de travaille*. "Mrs Trefusis" is just about plausible, it being a Cornish name and all, but the most famous person of that name is Violet Trefusis, who was Virginia Woolf's main squeeze. "Senora Camara" could pass un-noticed, except that there appears never to have been a Senor Camara.

Then it gets silly, with the 'wicked' Lady Montcalm, who murdered her husband on the wedding night. The Mother Superior of the Little Sisters of St Gudula is surely not connected to anything Sapphic. After all, St Gudula is associated with Belgium, also with a cross in Cornwall, but mainly with bad eyesight and a candle. What possible link could there be between a candle, a nun and going blind?

But we're more concerned with Cessair's present identity, Vivian Fay. The man-hating lady who offers Romana a ride on her bike, and says 'it'll be a whole new experience for you' with five times more enthusiasm than the line requires. The very good friend of the truncheon-packing, sausage-sandwich-munching Professor Rumford, who almost immediately spots that Romana's shoes are not going to be comfortable. Even without the hint that Vivian is Morgan le Fay, it seems inevitable that this story will see her chaining Romana up and talking to fairies at the bottom of her garden. (Or to be more specific, in a spaceship in the fifth dimension, but topologically overlaid on the bottom of her garden. Anyway, they aren't fairies really but computer-generated lawyers.)

9) "Planet of Fire" Part One. In which Peri takes off her clothes, and none of the guys in the story seem to notice. Turlough plonks her down on a big bed and then... forgets she's there. His tight shorts cause a stir amongst the tanned, muscular archaeologists. And Peri's step-father Howard and his associate Curt are *so* shagging.

Meanwhile, on Sarn, elderly priest Timanov is taking a close interest in his Chosen One. More young blokes in tight shorts are running around in the sand, looking suspiciously like a Wham! video. In amongst this spaghetti of subplots, we've got Kamelion "submitting" to the Master and a statuette that looks like - of all people - Elton John. The Chosen One also has his flesh embossed with a particular symbol, one identified by Turlough as

continued on page 249...

post-med psychology - says he's vacationing through 'the colonies' and Terra Alpha has designated tourist zones.

Since the introduction of Helen A's "happiness" programme, the population of Terra Alpha has declined by 17%. Many if not all executions are recorded, and Helen A here instigates 'Routine Disappearance No. 500,005'. [Combine the facts, and the initial population of Terra Alpha was presumably somewhere around 2,941,205, and now numbers about 2,441,200. That's almost 94,000 people per letter, if all letters were weighted equally - which they probably aren't, under this system.] Queues at the Post Office are apparently no longer a problem.

Most, if not all, of these deaths seem to have occurred in the six months since Trevor last took a census. However, Priscilla P says she's spent 'five years in the streets' [which could support the notion that Helen A took power on a campaign promise to institute order]. Trevor seems aware of Helen A's brutal methods, and he's even allowed to watch an execution, yet there's no sign that her dictatorship in itself violates the aforementioned 'Constitutional rules'.

Gilbert M, now a resident of Terra Alpha, formerly worked in the state laboratories on the planet Vasilip, and accidentally developed a germ that wiped out half the population. He was consequently exiled [or perhaps *fled*, since exile is an awfully tame punishment for someone guilty of such slaughter, however unintentional], but not before creating the Kandy Man. He was brought to Terra Alpha in Gilbert's suitcase, and born in the Kandy Kitchen, although 'his mind was very much his own'.

Helen A's rooftop snipers are equipped with Mark 3 rifles, but say the prototype for the Mark 4 must be ready - and that women on Terra Alpha [meaning the Patrol] get all the best guns. Fifi here eats chocolate [so it's not toxic to her species, as with Earth dogs].

The Analysis

Where Does This Come From? Needless to say, there's a comic at the heart of it all. *2000 AD* had been running its "Judge Dredd" strip for over a decade, and one of the many menaces therein to a well-ordered society was Umpty Candy - an addictive and lethally-wonderful brand of sweets. Obviously, "umptybagging" was the strip's way of parodying films about drugs cartels. (If you haven't read the strip, bear in mind that "Judge Dredd" was actually a comedy, with slapstick versions of Batman and various cops at loose in a MegaCity where the blocks were named after forgotten character-actors. Layers of obvious satire and slyer jokes were hidden under this. The film version was almost, but not quite, salvaged by the star and the director after studio bosses lobotomised the script.) *Doctor Who* following this trend is hardly surprising, and only right: with the original "Judge Dredd" strips owing so much to stories like "The Sun Makers" (15.4), it was like recovering stolen property.

It's fair to say, though, that this is more a matter of tone than direct influence at a plot level. Even without the apparent overt reference, this story has the overall approach of *2000 AD* circa 1985. Director Graeme Curry didn't need to have read a single edition for this to have soaked into how he - or anyone in Britain under forty - would have written a futuristic satire. Within days of *Doctor Who* vanishing for eighteen months in 1985, Channel 4 showed a 75-minute TV movie called *Max Headroom: Twenty Minutes Into The Future*. This was to launch a show where Max (the allegedly computer-generated DJ) would introduce pop videos, but the film's premise was pure *2000 AD*, whilst the style was an odd mix of *Blade Runner* and *Only Fools and Horses*.

For many, it was axiomatic that the Tory government was made up of the kinds of people who would be villains in a science-fiction dystopia. It was also a given that the big-budget US movies about fascistic regimes or alien invasions weren't anything like how it would happen here. The economic woes of the 70s (see **Why Didn't They Just Spend More Money?** under 12.2, "The Ark in Space") and the assault on civil liberties in the 80s were the result of dogmatic governments being elected half-heartedly by people who just wanted a quiet life. It seemed as if people would let a government vivisect their children, provided they had a manifesto pledge to cut the base rate of income tax. During the eighteen-month Suspension, comedian Lenny Henry did one of the better spoofs of *Doctor Who*, wherein a *Superfly*-style Doctor with a pimped TARDIS runs up and down hundreds of corridors (one with a busker) and is confronted with a Cyber-Thatcher. The audience reaction is telling - they don't hoot with laughter, as it is obvious that she's an evil

What are the Gayest Things in *Doctor Who*?

...continued from page 247

belonging to a 'special' kind of prisoner. The symbol is a triangle - and on Caucasian, slightly sunburned skin, it looks like a pink one.

8) The Rani. Talking of pink triangles, check out the Rani's TARDIS in "Time and the Rani" (24.1). Mind, this should've surprised nobody who paid attention during her first appearance, and we've commented already on the way her Bathhouse was used to turn miners into leather-vested Muscle Marys (22.3, "The Mark of the Rani"). By the time of "Dimensions in Time" (see the Appendix), she's started having such a boy around the Ship, just to tell her how great she is. (The script calls him "Cyrian", but he's generally referred to in fan lore as "Shagg".)

The thing is, as a strong and brittle woman, the Rani is exactly the kind of character who gets a cult following in soaps. There are two classic types of gay-icon female character: the Alexis Carrington type and the mumsy survivor. As Kate O'Mara had just played Alexis' sister on *Dynasty*, she's an obvious candidate for the former. As a character, the Rani is paper-thin but has one key feature that makes her ideal for this: she *claims* to be completely free of emotion but manifestly isn't. In a lot of soaps, this kind of character is the one people root for, especially when she cracks or scores a nasty coup. While she's no Servalan, the Rani is the clearest example out of a great many similar figures in the series.

Funny how Americans are always baffled at how unglamorous our soaps are. American soaps are shown here as kitsch, and Australian ones are our way of sneering at a culture so shallow as to think that sport matters more than human rights. But UK soaps are what we have instead of Country and Western. We love people in proportion to how well they cope with horrible turns of fate; how well they withstand enemy action without becoming bitter; and also how they do what we'd love to be able to do, but are too nice to even contemplate. *Doctor Who* during the phase we shall call "Pip 'n' Jane's Laugh In" was a soap.

And in all British soaps, you have a matriarch who is stoic and practical in a crisis, and is the other pole of gay affection. Which brings us to...

7) Barbara Wright. According to one prominent commentator, she's "*Doctor Who*'s very own Judy Garland". Babs is the woman who Copes With Stuff. From the sheer terror of the first adventure, to the weary resignation as she surrenders yet another piece of knitwear to the cause of stopping the most evil beings in the cosmos, we see this character deal with absolutely everything the same way - by saying, "Let's get on with it". Striding the galaxy in sensible shoes and a Velma jumper, Barbara is still recognisably the same type of character as Pauline Fowler from *EastEnders*, or Meg Mortimer from *Crossroads*.

But there's more. Younger women, it seems, always seem to find excuses to cuddle her. Barbara herself goes from worried Marge Simpson-like matriarch to gun-totin' avenger. (Although, unlike Modesty Blaise or Cathy Gale, she tends to save planets with her cardigans.) That mix of domestic and glamorous, practical and sophisticated, strong and vulnerable, is one with a huge gay appeal. In one moment, during "The Rescue" (2.3), she fires a flare-pistol towards the camera with grim determination, having just seconds before been doing the washing up. In the canon of female characters that get gay fans going "Whoooo", she's easily ahead of the Rani or Mrs Farrell from "Terror of the Autons" (8.1), and only Chancellor Flavia from "The Five Doctors" (20.7) comes close.[36]

6) Thals (various). In the beginning, there was a big long war fought in the trenches (12.4, "Genesis of the Daleks"). Having babies by conventional means seemed like such a non-starter that the Kaleds began playing around with fish-tanks and turkey-basters. This had mixed results: giant clams and a planet where 1/20th of the population looked like Terry Walsh.

So instead, they went for Daleks, a race dedicated to destroying all deviance (starting, we presume, with General Ravon as played by Lieutenant Grueber from '*Allo 'Allo*). Meanwhile, the Thals are striding around in velour and PVC - but, unlike the Kaleds, they have at least one woman. Unfortunately, token female Bettan seems more interested in suicidal acts of revenge than reproducing. She has short hair, big boots and dungarees. Say no more, squire. (The novelisation also claims that the Doctor's attempts to escape the carnage were hampered by men trying to kiss him, but we'll excuse this as VE Day euphoria.)

Fast-forward a few thousand years to "The Daleks" (1.2). The ashen forests of Skaro are home to men in deeply suspect trousers and, again, only

continued on page 251...

alien, and seeing this merely confirmed what everyone in Britain knew. It's the drunk Denis-droid that gets the laughs.

Underneath Helen A's odd policies is a real and grim political fact. In Chile, the dictatorship of Augusto Pinochet was arranging for all opponents or suspected opponents to simply vanish. Sometimes these disappearances took place in the National football stadium, sometimes they went one-by-one on one-way helicopter rides over the ocean. The Nixon government had stood back when the coup that overthrew the democratically-elected Allende government took place (see 4.2, "The Tenth Planet" for an odd sidelight on this). When Thatcher found it convenient to have Pinochet's support during an avoidable war against Argentina, all criticism of Chile's policies was stifled in the UK. It thus became almost routine for anyone who opposed the Tories to bring this up whenever possible.

Of course, Pinochet was not the only dictator, and "The Happiness Patrol" is not directly about Chile. India under Indira Gandhi imposed stern (ruthless, some would say) population control measures to qualify for assistance from the World Bank. Tens of thousands were coerced, bribed or tricked into sterilisation programmes. Romania under Ceaucescu provides even clearer parallels, with public dissent forbidden in ways that would be obvious sources for this story - had anyone in the UK actually known about them before 1989's remarkable events. So the most obvious real-life influence is, of course, Apartheid-era South Africa. This makes it obvious that the outlying areas mentioned in episode three should be designated 'townships' and that the indigenous population should be starving outcasts living like "vermin".

This brings us to a more basic level of allegory. In the original definition of the word, "kitsch" is that form of cultural product that denies the biological, the unpleasant or the awkward. It could be argued that a story that has tunnels that seem like sewers, but are shiny and clean and have sugar in them, is itself kitsch - but then, that's the point. To deny the existence of things like this is unhealthy. South Africa sustained its surreal state by acting as if what it proclaimed was true, and ignoring all evidence to the contrary. People who were of mixed race did not "belong" in such-and-such a township (because that was for blacks only), so a baby born there did not have a box to

be ticked if the father was white. White men do not have sex with black women, so the baby obviously cannot exist.

Similarly, people doped to the eyeballs on anti-depressants do not cope with problems because they don't see them coming: when catastrophe strikes, they just increase the dosage. The increasing resistance in Britain to the "have a nice day" culture - seen as America's bid to take us over - led to many people thinking that happiness was a form of mental illness, or wilful blindness. Certainly the people we saw who were happiest, or at least *told* us they were happy - i.e. all those coke-snorting City types - not only lacked conscience but seemed dead behind the eyes. They listened to the most appallingly bland music. Resistance to this led to things like Goths; all in black and obsessed with death they may have been, but they were more fun to hang out with. (That is, until they started whittering about role-playing games and Cthulhu.)

We forget, though, how close to the mainstream this form of rebellion came in the mid-1980s. Enough of this Indie culture got onto *Top of the Pops* - or the various attempts to remake *The Tube* - for Joe Public to name it and for Goth to be instantly identifiable. (And sporadically revived. American readers will have to take our word for how hilariously retro Marilyn Manson was. Over here, we thought of him as the 90s answer to Tiny Tim.) One of the odd ironies of this story is that by the time it reached our screens, the very same Indie kids had reclaimed the gaudy colours, Smiley logo and love of euphemisms Curry's script associates with the Bad Guys. That shot in the last scene - which shows Priscilla P and Daisy K with washed off pancake make-up and paper overalls - looks exactly like recovering Goths at a rave circa 1988. We also had a rash of media coverage for ex-Butlins staff who had breakdowns from their forcedly acting cheerful morning, noon and night. (See 4.7, "The Macra Terror", and 24.3, "Delta and the Bannermen".) Which brings us back to *Hi-de-Hi*...

To some extent, the Cartmel stories all have a theme of the public "mask" and its consequences. People who devote their lives to an obsession lose sight of what matters. In some cases, it's simply that they have to fake it when dealing with other people, but they usually they're lying to themselves. The one story where this is not overtly mentioned is the next one - "Silver Nemesis" -

What are the Gayest Things in *Doctor Who*?

...continued from page 249

one woman. But even for that, she can't get Alydon to notice her. In a scene that's elicited considerable comment, there's a contrived pun about 'working to the same end' which nobody quite understands. We also have, in Antodus, someone who knows he's afraid of the dark, of heights and of everything else - yet volunteers for this incredibly dangerous mission to the Dalek city just to stay close to another man. It's rather touching, but leads to some incredibly suggestive shots of the Thals crouching as if sitting in each other's laps but stood up. The last three episodes have a lot of shots of half-naked men grabbing each other tight.

(But when they come to make a feature film version of this story, there just isn't time to suggest too much, so they have to go right ahead and have the Thal men wearing eyeliner and crimped hair. The movie also has the menfolk carrying mirrors as basic survival equipment, and is at great pains to point out that Ganatus and Antodus are brothers, really they are. The sequel film has pill-popping, whip-wielding men in leather and PVC landing in a flying saucer that makes planetfall in Chelsea.)

Fast forward another few thousand years to "Planet of the Daleks" (10.4). Taron decides that being involved with a woman is bad news. Shy boy Codal has a big secret he can't reveal, and is too afraid to go against the crowd. Vaber is tough-talking and decisive, overcompensating and fooling nobody. Latep was originally going to be called 'Petal', which speaks volumes.

5) The Ice Warriors (5.3, "The Ice Warriors"; 6.5, "The Seeds of Death"; 9.2, "The Curse of Peladon"; 11.4, "The Monster of Peladon"). The military *camaraderie*, the discipline, the sequins. From the first moment Varga clouted Leader Clent with his handbag, these have been the galaxy's most prominent pooves. Where most commanders of alien forces accept casualties as part of the job, Varga goes to pieces when Zondal is killed, and lunges toward Victoria as if to scratch her eyes out. Never mind the hissing and neck-snaps, these are the only aliens so concerned about interior decor as to shoot down a chandelier, suffer from central heating and be mortally wounded by bad smells. Had they never appeared again, they'd be memorable as nelly aliens - but they kept coming back and confirming everything we'd suspected.

After all, these are aliens who, in their *only* attempt to conquer Earth, get as far as Hampstead Heath and are sidetracked by men in PVC.

(For those unaware, Hampstead Heath after dark is one of the most celebrated cruising spots in Britain. Others include Brighton Pavilion, 15.1, "Horror of Fang Rock", and 18.1, "The Leisure Hive"; and Horsenden Hill, 26.4, "Survival". Recently, with the amusing botched cover-up of a Welsh politician's second "moment of madness" in two years, the euphemism "looking for badgers" has gained currency. This might explain "The Monster of Peladon" and the ill-advised trip down the mines.)

So, the Ice Warriors turn Hampstead Heath into a foam-party and, when the innovative Phipps rigs up his solar projector, they all want a go in the disco-lights. Any doubts about this race were dispelled by the appearance of their supreme leader, the Grand Marshal. Even if we accept the suggestions that a sequined helmet is their version of wearing medals, you don't go into battle dolled up like that.

By the Fifth Millennium, word has got out, even in Third World planets like Peladon. Izlyr and Ssorq have got the honeymoon suite - with a sparkly bedside table, chiffon curtains, a fur rug and (yes, indeed) one double bed between the pair of them.

4) Season Twenty-Two. The six individual stories all seem relatively innocuous if taken separately. If seen in rapid succession, however, the number of young blond men (especially those chained to things), bodies being eyed up like meat, effeminate middle-aged men and examples of botched butchness starts to look like part of a deliberate and premeditated scheme.

Then you see how badly-written the parts for women are, even compared to the parts for men in some of the atrocious scripts. That's the ordinary women, at least: powerful soap-bitch figures like Chessene, the Rani and Kara get a few good lines, but are there to be over-acted into life. "Vengeance on Varos" (22.2) is at least open about it, with muscular men there as eye-candy, and an entire planet kitted out like a night-club. It's when this approach to the visuals creeps into a historical setting ("The Mark of the Rani" and 22.5, "Timelash") that eyebrows were raised.

continued on page 253...

because it's assumed that the public knows all about how the Nazis tried to remove things (usually with either kitsch or gas-chambers) they couldn't deal with, and the Cybermen did something similar (by surgery). Even in something apparently frothy like "Delta and the Bannermen", we see the camp-leader Burton realising, after an exhilarating threat, how bored he'd been with simply looking cheerful.

Perhaps because the available translations were so awful back then, more people talked about Franz Kafka than actually read the books, and certainly few bothered with more than one of the short stories. Thus the allegory of redemption in *The Castle* and *The Trial* was ignored in favour of the basic set-up: someone with a letter for a surname is made to face obscure and baffling bureaucratic ordeals and investigations. Certainly, any attempt to read any significance into the use of one-letter surnames on Terra Alpha had better make a better job than anyone has up until now. The novelisation names the guy executed by strawberry fondant in episode one as "Andrew X", which suggests Malcolm X (and the whole trend in Dance music for names like that, from Jazzy B to Dimples D). Similarly, the enforced jollity of *The Prisoner* resembles how this story ended up looking but isn't really an influence, despite what is often said. But the *idea* of both of these quasi-dystopian worlds is important.

While we're debunking fan lore, the dispatched Andrew X (or Harold L, it hardly matters) isn't wearing a pink triangle badge. Novelist / new series writer Matt Jones' reading of this story as being explicitly and exclusively about gay rights misses the point, although none of his evidence (except mention of the triangle badge) is actually invalid.

It's often pointed out that the title "The Happiness Patrol" is suspiciously similar to the term "Joy Division". This was a) a corps of female concentration camp inmates used by the Nazis as prostitutes and b) a miserable Mancunian band whose leader, Ian Curtis, worked with TV presenter Anthony H Wilson and then hanged himself. The remainder of the band formed New Order (another oddly Nazi name), and were a hip name to drop until they started having hits. A bit like Echo and the Bunnymen (see "Delta and the Bannermen"). Maybe if Season Twenty-Seven had seen daylight, we'd have had stories with titles a bit like "Tallulah Gosh", "Throwing Muses" or

"Hüsker Dü".

Of course, if you're looking for overt "sources" you could do worse than *Monty Python*. In the German TV version, *Monty Python's Fliegender Zirkus*, there's a fairy-tale called "The Princess With the Wooden Teeth" (helpfully rewritten and included in the *Big Red Book* for British fans). In this, we're told of a happy land where everyone is cheerful, because the king rounded up all the unhappy people and had them shot...

Things That Don't Make Sense Once you get past the loopy premise, there's not much to logically take issue with. Well, all right... it's true that Helen A's policy of murdering anyone who isn't happy doesn't seem entirely consistent. Perhaps the sullen Gilbert M is deemed too valuable to have executed (and to such a degree that he survives being sarcastic to the Happiness Patrol in episode three), but there's no reason why the doorman to the Forum - a grumpy git if ever one was born - hasn't 'disappeared' well before now. And even allowing that the Doctor talks down the snipers in episode two, the Killjoy rally seems to continue an *awfully* long time before Helen A or the Patrol bother to move against them.

Are we to genuinely believe that Trevor Sigma completed a planetary census by personally walking around and asking everyone's place of residence? Because that's certainly what it looks like on screen. "Which planet do you come from?" is a question that becomes harder to ask when worlds like this have such strict border controls - why not just ask if their surname is 'Sigma' and save time? Never mind that the top portion of Trevor's enormously long "Missing Persons" scroll just happens to contain the two names that the Doctor stands a chance of actually recognizing, and does.

When the Doctor confronts the floor-stuck Kandy Man, the staging seems odd in that Gilbert M almost seems to magically appear between them. [There's maybe, *possibly* enough time for him to enter from off-camera, but it's a stretch.] It's also convenient for the plot that Gilbert flits off to somewhere-or-other after the Kandy Man is freed, allowing the Doctor to re-glue the tasty villain to the floor. And yes, there's that entertaining bit in episode one, where you can spy one of the Patrol come on set too soon, even as the upside-down Doctor labours to repair the go-cart.

Silas P likes to trick Killjoys with his double-sided calling-card, but he twice hands it over with

What are the Gayest Things in *Doctor Who*?

...continued from page 251

3) Autons (7.1, "Spearhead from Space"; 8.1, "Terror of the Autons"; X1.1, "Rose"). Regardless of whether they were named after Joe Orton deliberately, it's hard to avoid making the comparison. Both were out to disrupt British petit-bourgeois society. Both tried to subvert prominent institutions. Orton's lover, Kenneth Halliwell, even looks like the "Spearhead" design, with scarf, silver boots, shaven head and all.

We'll skate over the obvious limp-wrist comments, and ponder the entire scheme in "Terror of the Autons" to take over the world by dressing up in blazers and handing out daffodils. There are times when *Doctor Who* stories start to seem like *Pinky and the Brain*, and this is one of them. It's not just that they're using lethal plastic devices that *look* like flowers, it's that they're driving from town to town in a small charabanc, passing these daffs to people individually. Aside from being the most laborious way to prepare for an invasion (unless you went door-to-door shooting people and hoped the police wouldn't notice), it's the fact that they're apparently launching their assault against the housewives of Britain - not the armed forces - that makes this so queer-friendly an invasion story. No wonder one of the survivors, Mrs Farrell, has a big camp following within fandom.

With consumer-kitsch firmly in our sights, let's now ponder the use of daytime TV, celeb-goss magazines and tacky bridal dresses in the 2005 rerun of their first invasion. Then look at the publicity photos - in almost all of the ones from the climax, it seems that brawny mannequins are sodomising Christopher Eccleston. But it's their first two attempts that continue to interest us the most: first time around, they have the menacingly quiet and dapper Mr Channing using Madam Tussaud's as the means to destroy civilisation, but who's the PR face for the second assault (the one that culminates in a glitter-ball materialising)? Why, that would be...

2) The Master. Where do we start? The Ainley model, constantly corrupting young men and flouncing about in velvet? The Eric Roberts version, with the implications of oral rape, the attempted grooming of Chang Lee and his Paul Lynde-like delivery of the line 'I always dress for the occasion'? Pratt and Beevers, both constantly looking out for fit male bodies, perhaps?

No, we begin with the camp, witty original. As we saw in Volume II, Camp is a form of performance instead of an essential identity, and the Roger Delgado Master was constantly adopting personae when it suited him. It was a game, right down to the obvious clues in whichever name he chose. He did not take everyday life seriously, and those around him either found themselves joining in, like Rex Farrell ("Terror of the Autons"), or being patronised like Colonel Trenchard (9.3, "The Sea Devils") or the entire population of Devil's End (8.5, "The Daemons"). And as we've said, a propensity for Camp is not absolute proof of homosexuality (but see "The Curse of Fatal Death" in the Appendix), but when even seducing Queen Galleia in "The Time Monster" (9.5) is turned into a game - when hypnosis would have been *so* much quicker - we have to read this alien's trifling with human emotions as non-heterosexual.

Once he starts wearing a stolen body, it gets a little more obvious. Consider "Castrovalva" (19.1). Chaining Adric up in his TARDIS is one thing, but getting the boy to calculate a city full of men in frocks who have little pink triangles on their foreheads is like taking out an ad. "The Mark of the Rani" is a little less obvious, although his handling of Luke Ward would be like corrupting a lad with drugs and gifts, even if the rest of the story wasn't so much like that. About the shape of the Tissue Compression Eliminator, we need say nothing.

By the time we get to 26.4, "Survival", the way the Master gets Midge on side with clothes, gifts and offers of power is absolutely unsurprising. And yet again, Midge gets the standard *Doctor Who* symbol of being lured to the dark side: slicked-back hair. (This story also begins with the Master whisking a young man from Horsenden Hill, shows him stroking a cat for most of the three episodes and has lots of sweaty lads grappling... no surprise that it ends with the Doctor and the Master looking as if they're about to snog.)

In 27.0, "The TV Movie", the Master is put on trial by the Daleks and executed. He worms his way into the controls of the Doctor's TARDIS and guides the Ship to - of all cities - San Francisco. Before you can say "Anna Madrigal", he's in bed with some stud - who promptly kills his wife and starts chatting up teenage boys.

(Actually, to be serious for a moment, this is actually rather unpleasant, especially as the Doctor - who's traditionally off the menu - has discovered girls in the same story. Up until now, the

continued on page 255...

the "surprise" portion (which reads 'Happiness Patrol Undercover') facing up, so his trap rather unduly relies on his victims *first* flipping the card over, rather than just reading what's shoved in front of their faces. And why does Priscilla P, who knows Silas P, shoot him when he's just been "knocked unconscious" and is acting a bit sluggish? If she thinks he's a Killjoy, why not arrest him, expose him to Helen A and get a medal? And what kind of "hit", for that matter, does Earl Sigma give Silas that makes him mutely sit there looking groggy, and with his eyes open? As Earl is a medical student, are we to presume he knows some sort of Vulcan karate chop?

If attendance at the Forum is compulsory, and being out during curfew is a capital offence, why is there *anyone* alive after the Late Show?

The big one... nobody thought to ask Bassetts if they minded having their trade-mark character parodied as a psychotic cyborg. It's not as if the company had never had any dealings with the *Doctor Who* production office. Or that Liquorice Allsorts don't exist in the *Doctor Who* universe. [See, just for example, 13.5, "The Brain of Morbius" where Sarah calls the home-made body 'Mr Allsorts' to avoid copyright infringement, even though we know full well what she means.]

Critique As we've noted, chance and history have been kinder to this story than to many. It looks stagey, and there are a few slightly awkward performances (notably one intensely painful McCoy moment in episode three - 'I can't tell you how HAPPY I am to see you'), but generally the acting's sound. Once again music is woven into the plot, and Dominic Glynn is up to the job. For most of the first episode it can be watched as a relatively clever play, until...

... suddenly *he* appears. Nothing, not even trailers they showed in 1988, nor having seen it a hundred or so times since then, can prepare you for the first shot of the Kandy Man. It comes right out of left-field. Despite what BBC lawyers say, it's blatantly Bertie Bassett, and his wife's played by Harold Innocent. At this point you either accept that this is going to be mental, or you switch off.

But *if* you stick with it, there's a lot to enjoy. Apart from the Kandy Man's appearance, he's one of the wittiest and most grotesquely memorable characters since Shockeye (22.4, "The Two Doctors"), and he's not on his own. There's enough good material for all the main cast, and a lot of incidental delights in the execution. Clough's first idea was to do this as *The Third Man*, then as the 1960s *Batman*, but neither would have worked as well as this. The theatrical nature of the sets is in keeping with a faded Third World dictatorship, but makes us accept the story's allegorical nature. And this is another way the world has caught up with this story: walk through any shopping precinct these days, especially between Christmas and Easter, and you are in Terra Alpha. It's not just the fake emotion and syrupy design of Valentine's Day kitsch, but the way everyone is fervently wishing it'll be over with soon.

Everything in this story, no matter how absurd, has an essential logic and emotional truth to it. There's a sign that people in charge *cared* about what they were doing, making it self-consistent and putting a bit of extra effort in. For cost reasons, the sets are dressed with 1960s teapots and train-station switches; it's a bit fairy-tale ish, but also part of an overall thread running through this season about how the media's peddling of cosy nostalgia and consensus is just a lie to cover up hypocrisy and oppression.

All of that said, a lot of this doesn't quite gel. Those "patrol-cars" are terrible when driven indoors, and should have been ditched. Some of Fifi's shots are abysmal. Still, that's the price you pay for trying something as out-there as this. And whatever this story's downsides, the climax - with the music swelling as we pull back from Helen A mourning Fifi - is worth all of Season Twenty-Three.

It'll sound odd to some, but stories like this - meaning dramas about real people caught up in totally bizarre circumstances - are the reason *Doctor Who* was created in the first place. They always use a clip of this story to illustrate Verity Lambert saying how the series went a bit silly after she left, but "The Happiness Patrol" is almost the most Hartnellish colour story. If this particular adventure isn't to your taste, at least recognize that in this phase of the series, there's going to be something totally different along next week. If it *is* what you like, there's not going to be much like it to follow - but then, there's never been anything *quite* like this story before or since.

What are the Gayest Things in *Doctor Who*?

...continued from page 253

Master's crap efforts at being bad resemble the methodology of a Victorian decadent who prided himself on being "sinful" - i.e. drinking absinthe, having ice-cream for breakfast and eyeing up boys - but was as menacing as the Grinch. So the idea was that the Master was a camp villain and therefore seemed likely to have penned verses celebrating Uranian love. TV's Eric Roberts is now reversing this: the Master is gay and *therefore* evil. Note how the Doctor's efforts to save Earth are entirely so he can get off with Grace.)

By 2007, therefore, nobody familiar with the character could have been wildly surprised when Harold Saxon revealed a love of the Scissor Sisters (X3.13, "Last of the Time Lords") and that his trophy wife was mainly there for show (and, apparently, as a punch-bag). What was surprising was how far John Simm took the phrase 'arch-villain' literally. But then, the Master was written to talk and act pretty much like Russell T Davies (although we assume the much-vaunted 'tone meetings' don't end with writers and directors being gassed like badgers).

1) UNIT. Seriously, did you expect anything else? It goes well beyond any individual character or actor and into a wholesale institutional pinkness.

There was the original high-camp formulation of the organisation as hiding inside car-parks and transporter planes, but going around in beige uniforms and badges with a distinctive logo - but then, that was par for the course in late 60s spy shows. Where it starts getting odd is the Brig's starchiness in the face of increasingly bizarre circumstances. He never lets this professional mask slip, which is automatically suspect. Similarly, once the various Jimmys are replaced by Captain Yates, the chummy blokishness in the lower ranks (i.e. Benton) begins to look like it's for public consumption. Consider "The Mind of Evil" (8.2), which begins with the "sensitive" Benton being relieved of surveillance duty for fainting, and Yates failing to convince anyone that he fancies Chin Lee. Yates and Benton get shot by escaped convicts and split up - Benton withstands getting shot in the head, and is so concerned about Yates as to volunteer to lead an assault on a castle, only hours after a wound that should have invalidated him from Army service. Yates is tied to a chair by the Master (whose backside he manifestly eyed up when the

latter was disguised as a GPO engineer in the previous story). His call-sign is 'Venus', by the way.

By the time Yates and Benton have spent a spectacularly un-laddish boy's night in watching rugby (!) we should not be surprised that "The Daemons" (8.5) ends with Yates inviting the Brig (his *superior officer*) to participate in a fertility dance. Even without the accidental innuendoes of the dialogue in earlier stories, it's starting to look like they're trying to tell us something. Once Benton has ended Season Nine in a nappy, we've got to assume it's deliberate.

But then, so what? It's a military organisation (with lots of near-death experiences), a secret organisation (with inherent deceptions and coverings-up) and it specialises in investigating things that are "odd". And two if not three of the regular members are more fond of one another than the military conventions and chain of command permit ('the love that dare not speak its name'). The point is, though, that instead of acknowledging it (as happens in *Torchwood*) or ignoring it (as happened in World War II), the writers and directors appeared to put so much effort into covering it up, it all seems a lot more prominent than if it'd just been shrugged off. For pity's sake, if you're in a hole, stop digging. So there was a serious attempt to make Mike and Jo a 'will-they-won't-they?' couple in "The Curse of Peladon", which just highlighted the fact that whenever the TARDIS took her away, Jo landed up being proposed to or lusted after. The absence of any of this sort of attention at home just got more noticeable. All efforts to defuse sexuality of any kind in UNIT just rubbed it in further.

In "Invasion of the Dinosaurs" (11.2), Mike switches his allegiance (in the John Le Carre way that's almost always associated with an emotional betrayal), and the novelisation makes Professor Whitaker out to be the most flagrant fag of any *Who* villain who's not from another planet. (This is the story where Benton comes out with the amazingly Kenneth Williams-like line "And pink for yer actual Pterodactyls".) This is the *third* dubious all-male environment Yates has been in, after UNIT and the fun in Llanfairfach (see **What Are the Oddest Romances in the Programme?** under 24.3, "Delta and the Bannermen" for 'Global Kemicals' and their curious workplace practices). When he hangs out in a Dochen and finds out about what the guys do in the cellar ("Planet of

continued on page 257...

The Facts

Written by Graeme Curry. Directed by Chris Clough. Ratings: 5.3 million, 4.6 million, 5.3 million. If you're thinking that vast portions of the viewership couldn't help but recoil in mortal terror at everything on display here, don't... Audience appreciation was a solid 67% for episode one, and 65% each for episodes two and three.

Working Titles "The Crooked Smile" (sort of - see **The Lore**).

Supporting Cast Sheila Hancock (Helen A.), Ronald Fraser (Joseph C.), David John Pope (Kandy Man), Harold Innocent (Gilbert M.), Georgina Hale (Daisy K.), Rachel Bell (Priscilla P.), Lesley Dunlop (Susan Q.), Richard D. Sharp (Earl Sigma), John Normington (Trevor Sigma), Tim Barker (Harold V.), Jonathan Burn (Silas P.).

Oh, Isn't That..?

• *Sheila Hancock.* She sprang to fame in sitcoms like *The Rag Trade.* Inevitably, she's got a *Carry On* under her belt (*Carry On Cleo*, where she played Henghist Pod's nagging wife Senna - presumably Joan Sims was busy). She's recently won plaudits for her memoir of life with John Thaw (her husband for several turbulent years) and her stage work. She is also Chancellor of Portsmouth University.

• *Ronald Frazer.* He was usually crusty officers, like in the original film of *Flight of the Phoenix.* He was playing a pensioner called "Mr C" in a sitcom broadcast at the same time, called *Life Without George.* If you've got *Young Indiana Jones and the Phantom Train of Doom*, you'll see a lot more of him.

• *Georgina Hale.* She made two films with Ken Russell in the 70s: *The Devils* (which looks like a big-budget mash-up of Season Nine, but is a historical drama - it's based on a book by Aldous Huxley and with Russell's own, rather singular, trademarks) and *The Boyfriend* (see 21.6, "The Caves of Androzani").

• *Rachel Bell.* Another Ken Campbell alumnus. She came to this fresh from *Dear John*, the scripts of which will be familiar to American readers. (The BBC sold the sitcom format, but the American version starring Judd Hirsch of *Taxi* fame was so amazingly different - despite only

minor changes to a few lines per episode - that they were able to re-title it *Dear John USA* for UK broadcast, and show it as though it was a different series for a different audience.)

• *Harold Innocent.* He's the hitman who killed Marty Hopkirk at the start of the original version of *Randall and Hopkirk (Deceased).* He was also the villain in the episode of *The Avengers* shown on 23rd of November, 1963. This should give you some idea of the amount of work he's done, and the number of roles he's had in British TV.

• *John Normington.* Shortly before the last time he did this (as the villain Morgus in "The Caves of Androzani"), he'd been in *A Private Function.* This was one of the few times he got to work with Innocent, despite their long friendship. You've possibly seen him again recently, in episode three of *Torchwood* ("Ghost Machine"). He passed away on 26th of July, 2007.

• *Lesley Dunlop.* She'd done this before too (as Norna in 21.3, "Frontios"), and had subsequently carved herself a niche in *Where the Heart Is*, playing a district nurse as unlike Nerys Hughes (Todd in 19.3, "Kinda") as you can get. She was later in a sitcom called *May to December,* which is notable for not-ever being the source of legal action by the then-Labour Party leader, John Smith. (The other lead, played by Anton Rogers, was more like Smith than mimic Rory Bremner's attempt at impersonation.)

Cliffhangers The Doctor and Earl Sigma become trapped in the Kandy Kitchen, and the Kandy Man tells them, 'I like my volunteers to die with smiles on their faces'; Ace is scheduled for the Miracle Survival Act at the Forum.

The Lore

• So Cartmel's found himself another young fresh fellow. Graeme Curry had written a well-received play for BBC Radio 4, after winning an award, and so was asked to contribute to *Doctor Who.* The snag was that he had absolutely no ideas that would work in the format. Not a sausage.

So the idea of a planet where unhappy people are executed was a throwaway notion that Cartmel thought had legs. It was decided that this story would be called something more sensible than their pet-name for it (you guessed it, "The Happiness Patrol") and Curry came up with "The Crooked Smile" - the original name for *The Grief,*

What are the Gayest Things in *Doctor Who*?

...continued from page 255

the Spiders"), we should not be surprised. Doing things in cellars seems to be some kind of euphemism in the *Doctor Who* world (see also "The City of Death"). Yates' last line in the series is 'Ooh! I feel fine!', said in the kind of way Larry Grayson would have done it. (We could explain this reference, but it would take ages. Just watch episode six again and trust us.)

So the Doctor dies and is reborn. In his confusion, he mistakes the Brigadier for a succession of gay soldiers (see item No. 12), while Sarah calls the Brig 'a swinger'. The secret is out. Their new medical officer has been seconded from the Navy, and there's no hint of him fancying Sarah. Within hours of their first meeting, the Doctor can confidently state, 'Harry here is only qualified to operate on sailors'. Benton is promoted, with a new rank that makes everyone sarcastically call him 'Mister'. Last we see him, he's seemingly arranging a date with a girl, but it transpires that he's just taking his kid sister ballroom dancing. The Brig, after his kilt interlude, goes to work in a boy's school (20.3, "Mawdryn Undead") and talks enthusiastically of thrashing Turlough within an inch of his life. Mawdryn's sidekicks identify the Brig as 'a deviant'. When the Brig retires, he gets a nice house with a wife and a garden. He seems to prefer the garden. However, the traditions of the regiment are maintained, an officer more macho than Yates and Benton combined is now leading UNIT. *She* lets us all down by chatting up a cute blonde boy from a

parallel universe, but doesn't mind being called 'sir'.

PLUS
- Harrison Chase (13.6, "The Seeds of Doom") playing in his green cathedral.
- The Member of Parliament with the handlebar moustache (17.5, "The Horns of Nimon") who cries "Skonnos" in a really effete way.
- The Sisterhood of Karn (13.5, "The Brain of Morbius").
- The entire population of Traken (how else do you explain Tremas and Kassia's curious honeymoon?).
- The Skinheads (25.3, "Silver Nemesis").
- Adric (desired by so many middle-aged men, and last seen undoing his belt as a Cyberman kneels in front of him).
- Vogel (22.6, "Revelation of the Daleks"), a self-confessed 'past master of the double entry'.
- Alpha Centauri (9.2, "The Curse of Peladon"; 11.4, "The Monster of Peladon").
- Pretty much everyone on Manussa (20.2, "Snakedance").
- The choreographers (misleadingly billed as 'cheerleaders') in 4.7, "The Macra Terror", who demand that the dancers "make it more gay", and then watch Jamie with unusually keen interest as he dances in a kilt (we'll leave aside Ola's leather gear as a caprice of futuristic costume design).
- Mavic Chen (3.4, "The Daleks' Master Plan"), especially his Edith Piaf moment in Episode Five.

---

the Killjoy newspaper. The idea of armed guards checking that everyone was cheerful became a hook from which Curry hung a number of his peeves about theme-parks, fast-food outlets and lift-music - all of which he decided to depict as fake 1950s Americana. As a professional classical singer, he found the easy listening forced on people in public almost sinister. One idea faded down in the final version was that the Forum's lethal talent shows would have been shown. With another story along these lines - "The Greatest Show in the Galaxy" - already in the works, Cartmel thought better of this. (The irony of this decision, however, will become apparent once we start comparing "Silver Nemesis" to "Remembrance of the Daleks".)

• The Kandy Man was originally to have looked different. The idea was substantially the same, that

the brain and some organs of a scientist (named in the novelisation as 'Seivad' - was his first name "Tllessur"?) had been placed in a confection-based body, but this body was more like a marzipan golem. One version had him as a big doughy body with oversized red glasses, a red bow-tie and a lab-coat. The novelisation restores this, plus a scene that almost made the final broadcast, where he accidentally chops off his thumb and sticks it back on before continuing his work. Curry made a point of not having the BBC's version on the cover of his book, but the video release has the broadcast one painted in over photos. As noted above, the lawyers at Bassetts were not too pleased about their character Bertie Bassett - a man made of the various types of Liquorice Allsorts - parodied as a monster. The company demanded a lot of concessions. The costume was constructed by

Robert Allsopp, re-using the head of the Robot Bus Conductor from "The Greatest Show in the Galaxy" as the humbug-coloured chest.

• Another significant change was that Earl Sigma was to have been a trumpeter, not a harmonica player. Oddly enough, nobody had checked whether Richard D Sharp could actually play one. (Sophie Aldred could, and might have been able to teach him given time.) Instead he mimed playing the harmonica, and Dominic Glynn worked out roughly what he would have been playing, writing the score around it. Adam Burney provided the actual blues harp. Also dubbed on later were Clough himself as Fifi, and his wife - Annie Hulley (then appearing in *Emmerdale Farm*) - as the Public Address voice.

• Clough wanted to soft-pedal the obvious similarities between Helen A and Thatcher. However, Sheila Hancock's initial response to reading the scripts was to copy the Prime Minister's odd way of trying to make everything sound positive. (This was a harder task than it might seem. Sir Tim Bell, Thatcher's communications advisor, recommended that she should change her register and delivery slowly over time, so that any impersonation would be six months out of date. However some of the better ones, such as *Spitting Image*'s Steve Nallon and June Whitfield - yes, really - kept pace with her better than expected.)

Hancock's husband, John Thaw, was starring in *Inspector Morse* at the time. It was a more leisurely production even by the standards of filmed drama, and he doubted that scripts for "The Happiness Patrol" could be made in the time allotted. In fact, despite the heat and the technical difficulties, it was all committed to tape. Indeed, all three episodes *over-ran*, and the first was almost ten minutes over. One snag was that the original idea for the make-up was to look flaked and cracking, so Dorka Nieradzik added Fuller's Earth to the mix. It looked right, but they couldn't get it off in a hurry.

• David John Pope (the Kandy Man) had recently appeared in *Star Cops* as a dodgy Indian software expert, and on the gonzo kid's show *Gilbert's Fridge*. Encasing him in the costume took well over half an hour and, in the August heat, was bad news. The plan was to have all the Kandy Man's scenes done in the one day. Last-minute changes were made to the costume - they concealed the actor's mouth with a metal "moustache", and changed the hands. A microphone

was none-too-carefully hidden in the tin whiskers, which picked up and distorted the actor's words (and some of McCoy's in at least one scene). The day they recorded this batch of scenes was the day that one of the BBC's Board of Governors came a-calling. It was Dame Phyllis James (or PD James when she writes detective books), and against the wishes of her minders, she had a chat with the monster.

• The go-karts were from the same source as Nord's bike in "Greatest Show". Bootsy and Ferrett constructed the patrol car, but the BBC put theatrical masks on them. Both only took one pint of petrol, for Health and Safety reasons.

• This is as good a time as any to clarify the running-order. "Remembrance of the Daleks" was made first, but commissioned last. The scripts came in in mid-January, and shooting took place in April. "The Greatest Show in the Galaxy" was commissioned from Stephen Wyatt before "Paradise Towers" - also by him - was even recorded, and the scripts were in for September. This was shot entirely as an Outside Broadcast (for reasons we won't dwell on here) over May and June. "Silver Nemesis" was commissioned in November and expected in January, but the last script arrived in April. This was shot on location, as planned, in late June and early July. In the last week of July they started recording "The Happiness Patrol", and finished on 11th August with the Kandy Man's scenes.

But then, the BBC timetable for coverage of the Seoul Olympics was announced. *Doctor Who* was delayed and to be shown on Wednesdays from 5th of October. To accommodate this, the broadcast order of the stories was rearranged. "Remembrance" was still first, "Silver Nemesis" had to begin on 23rd of November to coincide as planned with the show's anniversary, so the three-parter had to go in between these. "Greatest Show" could either be dropped until after Christmas, shown over the holidays or made into a 90-minute special. Eventually they went for just putting it out after "Silver Nemesis", beginning on 14th of December.

• Cartmel rewrote the scene where the Doctor has to disarm the snipers. You can tell, somehow. Originally it was a discussion of old movies that got the two boys (named Stan and Sid S - no relation - in the script, but called David and Alex S - no relation - in *Radio Times*) to dump their guns.

• Another well-worn anecdote: Georgina Hale

had wanted to play Helen A, but wound up as Daisy K instead. Nathan-Turner placated her by saying that she was too young to play such a harridan. (Hancock now claims that she was ordered to play Helen A as Thatcher, and complains about anyone having the temerity to remember that she was in it at all.)

25.3: "Silver Nemesis"

(Serial 7K, Three Episodes. 23rd November - 7th December 1988.)

Which One is This? Nazis! Witches! Cybermen! The Queen! ... the same plot as "Remembrance of the Daleks"!

Firsts and Lasts Amazingly for a show that's been running for twenty-five years, this has the first use of captions explaining where and when the first two scenes are taking place. And surprisingly, for anyone coming to the "classic" series after the BBC Wales one, this is the first time that the TARDIS' arrival creates enough wind to blow out candles. It's also the last use of Lime Grove in the series, as the recording studio for the jazz playing on Ace's stereo.

Three Things to Notice about "Silver Nemesis"...

1. There comes a point, in even the most slick and professional *Doctor Who* adventure, when you have to sit back and accept that it's only *Doctor Who*. Inevitably, bathos will set in and some small detail will wreck any chance this has of being like a feature film or serious drama. So here - at the start of episode two - we have Nazis (sorry, we mean to say unspecified paramilitaries with German accents) exchanging gunfire with Cybermen, and a Renaissance witch scoring rather better against the Telosian hordes with her gold-tipped arrows. Within reason it's tense and exciting, and you'll not see that combination of elements done better anywhere on television. But then de Flores, the Nazi (sorry, we mean to say generic elderly Wagnerophile living in South America) war criminal in search of the occult treasure, ducks behind a car. A brown G-registration Ford Granada GXL. With a sickening thud, you realise that it's *Doctor Who*.

2. With all the complications of having three sets of baddies after something the Doctor left behind, you'd think there was no room for any other material. Not so: we have endless complica-

tions with the staff of Windsor Castle; hilarity afoot with Her Majesty (at least, we *assume* that's who it's meant to be); an astonishingly ill-conceived subplot about two skinheads who think that the said Renaissance witch, Lady Peinforte, and her criminal accomplice Richard are social workers; and some interminable padding with a rich American lady. And then, in the 'Special Edition' video of this story, there's *still* some stuff that never reached the screen - including a duck in the TARDIS, a painting of Ace, a chessboard and some more guff with the rich American lady. This being a Cartmel story, the stuff they deleted includes some material we need to follow developments in a later story - or in this case, *two* later stories. The duck wasn't strictly relevant, though, and nobody knows why the rich American lady is there.

3. Yes, even Ace comments on how only two stories ago the Doctor used exactly the same, "oh please don't use this booby-trapped Gallifreyan artefact I've led you to" ploy on the Daleks. In some ways it's just as well that "Shada" (17.6) never made it to the screen, because everyone would compare both Season Twenty-Five versions of the story to that one.

The Continuity

[Note: deleted scenes that were included on the "Silver Nemesis" video - but which didn't appear the broadcast version - have been deemed fair game for the Continuity section. Fandom-at-large tends to accept the added material (such as the portrait of Ace in Windsor Castle) as canon, and Clarke's novelisation reiterates much of it. Besides, these days it's the only copy we have, unless you recorded it at home.]

The Doctor He can imitate birdsong, and repeatedly demonstrates an appreciation of jazz - 'straight blowing' is his favourite kind [although this is pretty much meaningless]. He also shows interest in a chess set in Lady Peinforte's study, and "plays" the game through to the point that the black pieces win. [This will become significant later in 26.3, "The Curse of Fenric", and it's sometimes read that the Doctor is "playing" chess against Fenric, who's moving the pieces through time. On screen this is much harder to justify, for reasons we've spelled out in the accompanying essay. Also, Fenric's attitude in "The Curse of Fenric" suggests he thinks he's been *far* more sneaky than would appear if he and the Doctor were blatantly playing chess against one another. More on this in four stories' time.]

After donning his spectacles, the Doctor can stare at human opponents and "bamboozle" them - meaning they're frozen in place for a few moments after he orders them to not move. [This seems more akin to mental suggestion than the outright hypnotism that the Fourth Doctor employed, and the effect is only temporary; see 26.1, "Battlefield" for more. And who knows? Perhaps the Doctor stole some of those "mental conditioning" glasses from the aliens in 6.7, "The War Games".] The Doctor seems to lose to Ace at chess. [Please... he *must* have been a good sport and let her win.]

• *Ethics*. Continue to be bit dodgy. He seems to spend most of the story piecing together what is happening / has happened, and then it turns out that he was behind it all. [So either he's stringing Ace along in the course of her helping him, or he's genuinely stage-managed some formidable players - the Cybermen, Lady Peinforte, etc - and a scarily powerful weapon (the Nemesis), yet somehow let this endeavour slip his mind.

[It gets worse. Validium is sort of a Gallifreyan anti-mojo - a substance that causes bad luck - and the Doctor arranged for a critical mass of it to be sent into orbit around Earth. But as we're told, the Nemesis statue causes catastrophes every apogee - well, sort of; see **Things That Don't Make Sense** - which means that in *some* fashion, the Doctor's plan to squash the Cyber-Fleet has allegedly helped to facilitate both World Wars and Kennedy's assassination. Fair enough if he didn't have time to plan the rocket-sled's trajectory - although he's meticulous about almost everything *else* in this story - but it's clear that he's playing for high stakes. You might also argue that the Doctor has engineered this crisis specifically to bring de Flores' group of Nazi wanna-bes [see **The Lore**], the Cybermen and Lady Peinforte together and to let them wipe each other out - although to be somewhat fair, Peinforte goes mad and [presumably] chooses to commit suicide, and it's never clear how the "Nazis" figured into the Doctor's plans (or, for that matter, the entire story).

[As with "Remembrance of the Daleks", it's worth wondering why the Doctor didn't just outright order the Nemesis statue to obliterate the Cyber-fleet, unless he first needed to bait them into gathering in one location. Either way, the

argument that he's offering the villains a choice - as with Davros in "Remembrance" - doesn't really apply, since the logic-based Cybermen aren't exactly renowned for changing their minds. Anyways, Ace nearly blows the Cyber-leader to pieces, and it's only by sheer chance that he survives and there's a final confrontation with him at all.]

The Doctor talks sternly to the Nemesis, and apparently told the statue that he would have need of it in future - yet he hopes that won't be the case. He refuses to grant the statue its 'freedom' after this mission is complete, as 'Things are still imperfect'. [See 26.2, "Ghost Light" and practically every other story for why this might seem anomalous. One last thing: one must also wonder how the Doctor is able - at story's end - to resolve Richard's status as gracious host with the fact that the man is a ruthless killer. This assumes that the dead scholar in episode one is Richard's doing and not Peinforte's, but that appears to be the implication.]

• *Inventory*. As programmed, the Doctor's pocket-watch can alert him to change course to another destination, and he says that he might've arranged such a reminder 'centuries' ago [see *Background*]. The watch contains no information about the problem, save for a ratings system - a 'terminal' rating means that a planet somewhere faces imminent destruction. The watch has [for 1988] a sophisticated LCD screen.

The Doctor has built Ace a new portable stereo after her old one was zapped [25.1, "Remembrance of the Daleks"], and it's a very useful piece of kit. Not only can this curious gizmo - which includes the front of a 1930s bakelite set, satellite dish, twin cassette decks and a 3D projector - visually display the planet that's slated for disaster, it can play a music cassette and broadcast a signal strong enough to jam the Cybermen's signals. It also can display 'shrouded' Cyber-warships - provided you you fiddle with the Treble and Bass long enough - and it's also good for relaxing to jazz.

The Doctor carries marbles, helpful for when he needs to give the impression that he's lost his.

• *Background*. Oh dear, you had to ask, didn't you?

The Nemesis apparently related information about the Doctor's past and secrets to Lady Peinforte. [This doesn't seem like part of the Doctor's plan, unless he presumed the informa-

Did Cartmel Have *Any* Plan At All?

We all got so used to hearing fans talk about the "Cartmel Masterplan", few if any active 90s fandom would ever have doubted the existence of such a scheme. It even got a namecheck in *Coronation Street*[38]. Even if you chose to think of the *New Adventures* as "merchandising" rather than "canon", it was hard to ignore. One obvious reason for this obsession is that the bulk of the people who were keen on *New Adventures* were also comics fans, and were measuring *Doctor Who* by the criteria of Cult TV.

And this *was* the era of long-term planning. There are two big names to deal with in this field: Neil Gaiman, author of the revamped DC comic *The Sandman*; and J. Michael Straczynski, executive producer, lead-writer and chief fan of *Babylon 5* (the TV space-opera for people whose lips don't move when they read). Both spoke of their projects as things that were more like novels than the medium in which they were working. Both let it be known that the ending and most of the details were planned long in advance. Both had to adjust their plans along the way because of external circumstances. And these days, it's fashionable in some circles to slag off both.

However, in their pomp (circa 1995), the fact that individual episodes of a sequential narrative were peppered with hints of what was to come - and big secrets that had been kept from before the start - was a novelty. Gaiman pointed out, with growing frustration as dumb interviewers on arts shows found themselves talking to a comic-book author who knew more about literature than they did, that Dickens had worked the same way. (Except, of course, for *Barnaby Rudge* - even Dickens more-or-less admitted that this was nigh-on unreadable.) The main difference between *The Sandman* and any other comic written by someone with a brain was that Gaiman had begun from scratch, with a few details from the 1930s comic of the same name and initially a bit of crossover with some other DC titles then running. Once this had worked, other titles were begun (or rebooted) along similar lines and did it as well or better. Over nine years, this had a cumulative effect that made the story seem more resonant than it finally turned out to be, if read in one go now.

Similarly, *Babylon 5* made good use of the format to set up red-herrings, blind-alleys and genuine shock revelations, with enough clues to get people guessing and attempting to figure it out as it unfolded. The obvious knock-on effect was that Paramount suddenly began *Star Trek: Deep Space Nine*, which was just different enough from the proposal Straczynski had shown them to avoid a lawsuit, but - being *Trek* - it was dumbed down and went for pat answers and feelgood storylines. (At least until a change of producer made it go all moody and conspiracy-minded - but nothing at all like *The X-Files*, gracious no.) *Heroes* has recently made this all seem like a stunningly new idea all over again.

So, people thought, if this is how Cult works, then obviously *Doctor Who* must be like that. And so the scattered clues in Seasons Twenty-Five and Twenty-Six were raked over again and again to provide grounds for any pet theory anyone had. It was obvious that there was something in the Doctor's abrupt change of tactics beyond his just acquiring Ace and getting some kind of sanction from the Time Lords to act on his own authority. Once the Virgin Books' output had settled down with the *New Adventures*, we began to get more pieces for the jigsaw from unimpeachable sources. Platt, Cartmel and Aaronovitch all wrote books for the range in rapid succession. Moreover, it became common knowledge that there was a document in the Virgin offices laying out their secret plan, to which editors referred when sanctioning or vetoing any books including pet theories or flashback scenes about Gallifrey (which at the time was more or less all of them). So the 'Cartmel Masterplan' existed. The question is, *did* it exist while the TV series was being made?

To judge by the actual on-screen evidence, it would appear not. We're told in "Remembrance of the Daleks" (25.1) that Rassilon picked up after Omega, but not even any hint that they were alive at the same time (see **Did Rassilon Know Omega?** under 14.3, "The Deadly Assassin"). Anyway, that came in Aaronovitch's novelisation of "Remembrance", some time later, and not everyone read that. The Doctor deploys a highly ambiguous use of "we" in the same scene (see the Doctor's *Background* under "Remembrance"), but that could be a Time Lord talking to a human, pure and simple. It could even - if he really *was* President (15.6, "The Invasion of Time") - be the Doctor talking about all the dead Time Lords he has kicking around in his head via the Matrix. Then they cut to a scene where the Doctor tells Davros that he's 'more than just a Time Lord" - nothing really substantial there, but then two stories later, Lady Peinforte claims to know all about his dark

continued on page 263...

tion was of no use to Peinforte, and it motivated her to bring the arrow to 1988. But if *that's* true, then everything Peinforte knows might be of the Doctor's invention. We should probably continue, however, as if she genuinely knows something of interest...]

Peinforte refers to the Doctor as 'Doctor Who' [see, of course, **Is His Name 'Who'?** under 3.10, "The War Machines"] and shakes her head a little when Ace refers to him as a Time Lord. Peinforte threatens to reveal secrets about the Doctor that are related to 'Gallifrey, the Old Time, the Time of Chaos', but her knowledge dies with her. [Mention of the Old Time builds upon the Doctor's 'Didn't *we* have trouble with the proto-type...' statement in "Remembrance of the Daleks" - see that story for more. Peinforte's statements don't automatically mean the Doctor is *from* the Dark Times on Gallifrey, however, and could just mean that his 'secrets' relate to them.]

At some point, the Doctor appears to have nipped to Gallifrey and "borrowed" some Validium. [It's probably better to assume that he did this long after leaving his homeworld for the first time, as the idea that the First Doctor left Gallifrey with *both* the Hand of Omega and the Nemesis statue sounds like over-egging the pudding.]

He was present when the Nemesis statue was launched, and encountered Peinforte at that time. [See **History**. Peinforte mentions a desire to have revenge upon 'that predictable little man', and some have construed this to mean that the Second Doctor launched the Nemesis into space. However, Peinforte displays no knowledge of regeneration and seems to readily identify *this* version of the Doctor. So there's nothing to say that No. Seven and Mel didn't have a seventeenth century romp with Peinforte and the Roundheads, save that it makes the Doctor's claims that he's 'forgotten' about his master plan all the more incredible.] The Doctor says that Peinforte's scholar needed 'a little help' in his calculations, and burns a telling piece of evidence from the man's desk. [See **History**.]

The Doctor namedrops Louis Armstrong, and was present when Windsor Castle was built. Yet he seems to have trouble placing Her Majesty as she walks her dogs.

The Supporting Cast

• *Ace*. Likes jazz too, and gets Courtney Pine's autograph [see **Oh, Isn't That..?**]. This time around, she admits to being scared while aiding the Doctor, but declines his offer to return to the TARDIS. She seems perfectly willing to die, if it will prevent the Doctor surrendering to the Cybermen.

She's now a dead shot with a catapult. While Ace was in school, she visited Windsor Castle. Once again ["Remembrance of the Daleks"], the Doctor asks Ace to blow up something with that Nitro-9 that she's obediently *not* carrying. [This is a fundamental shift from stories of old - can you imagine Leela being slyly encouraged to carry Janis thorns?] A backpack of Ace's homemade explosives can wreck a Cyber-ship. The Doctor thinks Ace needs to be spared the sight of a murdered man.

The TARDIS The exterior sometimes looks a lighter shade of blue [because this was intended to follow 25.2, "The Happiness Patrol" in the schedules?]. An arrow somehow embeds itself in the police box woodwork [this an odd idea, in light of the Ship's supposed invulnerability and mathematically-generated 'outer plasmic shell', but it happens again in X3.2, "The Shakespeare Code"], yet the arrow remains in place after the TARDIS has rematerialised somewhere else. [This might be Peinforte's garbled Time Lord knowledge at work, but nothing about these arrows appears to be remarkable, except for their gold heads and poison tips.]

The Non-Humans

• *Cybermen*. Their plan this time: to obtain the Nemesis statue and use it to transform Earth into their base planet, 'the New Mondas'. However, they mention more than once that the entire Cyber-race will become extinct if their plans fail. [This seems an odd assertion, considering they here show up with a massive space-fleet; mind you, *Battlestar Galactica* is based upon almost the same premise - well, one version of it is.]

So it's another invasion of Earth, another makeover. This time they have re-designed chest-units, with tubes connecting the front and back, and these are shorter than before. The heads are bigger and the face-plates more reflective, although the chins are translucent, neither opaque nor transparent. The hands have five fingers - the index finger being more bulbous than before - but all are more robustly armoured. [It's almost like

Did Cartmel Have *Any* Plan At All?

...continued from page 261

'secrets'. Apparently this is to do with the Doctor's true identity and the 'Dark Times' before Rassilon. Significantly, Kevin Clarke had no idea what that might be, but was interested in what kind of guilty secret could blackmail a crusader like the Doctor into letting the villain win. Nathan-Turner was against there being anything too definite that might limit the scope for future stories.

So here's the crux of the matter: having a secret is one thing, but a secret *that* big would inevitably change the fabric of the entire series. Look at the impact the simple revelation of where the Doctor comes from had on his life and the nature of *Doctor Who* (see **Did *Doctor Who* End In 1969?** under 6.7, "The War Games"). Anything *that* important would have to be explained repeatedly for casual viewers. But any big revelation had to be simple enough for viewers to follow, and important enough for it not to have been hinted at before now. (They tried that, as we'll see, in 27.0, "The TV Movie", and made a complete hash of it.) The answer that was finally provided more than seven years after the classic series ended - in the last *New Adventures* book, Marc Platt's *Lungbarrow* - were neither. Not to put too fine a point on it, it was geeky fanboy stuff. The first draft of *Lungbarrow* was the original plan for 26.2, "Ghost Light" - but this was, again, vetoed by the producer for giving too much away. Fan critics have interpreted this action as proof that that the script had some big revelation in it, but in fact it simply meant that Gallifrey's mystique had taken enough knocks lately, thank you (see 20.1, "Arc of Infinity" for what we mean).

Individual stories could mention things as though they were planned, but with the running-order of these two seasons compromised, there's as much reason to take each tale as it comes - and forget continuity - as there is to pore over details. Ace's comment at the end of 25.4, "The Greatest Show in the Galaxy" - 'it was your show all along, wasn't it?' - is to make the ending seem more planned, even though the story seems to begin with the TARDIS wandering into the situation. Remember that *Doctor Who* as a series is still being made to be watched a week at a time, but these days fans with videos subject it to Jesuitical attention in looking for answers which really aren't there. Afer all, Cartmel is less interested in the programme's lore from before he came along, and is focused on making sure people who've only seen the McCoy stories perceive a bigger story underlying it all. Basically, if he was playing the same game as Straczynski or Gaiman, he wouldn't have commissioned two stories with near-identical plots in Season Twenty-Five. Individual writers might play with the series' past for their own purposes, but Cartmel's basic tendency is to go for one-off stories with nothing to do with any other period. Yes, he allowed the Daleks, the Cybermen, the Brigadier and the Master back... to kill each off in turn (although that's not how things panned out, exactly).

But what about Ace? It turns out her storyline is complicated, and there are hints at the end of "The Curse of Fenric" (26.3) that Ian Briggs planned it all along. Except that Ace was intended as a one-off character, to be replaced by "Alf" when the following season started. The two characters were so similar that Ace became the companion and Mel got *her* original ending, travelling with Glitz (unlikely as that sounds). What about the chessboard in Lady Peinforte's room, you might ask? Isn't that proof of a bigger gameplan? Well, apart from the board being laid out totally differently from the alleged "puzzle" in "Fenric", the Doctor's reaction to it is not "oh-oh" but "ooh, someone's losing badly". The point of Fenric's traps is that no move is possible, so moving the pieces would be silly if that were connected. And besides, it forms part of a chess motif in the rest of "Silver Nemesis", and was just as probably included just for that purpose.

Once again, this is opportunistic mentioning of some detail that most people had forgotten, and the conjunction of elements makes it *seem* planned. As far as we can tell, Ace's future would have entailed her being trained for a specific purpose, but again, it's to get rid of continuity dead wood - to end the Time Lords as we have known them - just as the Daleks, Cybermen, UNIT and so on have been. (See **What About Season 27?** under 26.4, "Survival".) Even then, the main object of the exercise was possibly just to use the Metatraxi (see **The Lore** under "Remembrance of the Daleks"), because they seemed kinda neat. All we can say about Cartmel's forward-planning was that he had a list of things to avoid, and a shorter list of things they'd like to try if the resources were available.

So there are a few paradoxes at work here. In order to make the Doctor mysterious again, his

continued on page 265...

they were wearing cricket gloves sprayed silver. Funny, that.] Three Cybermen are capable of lifting the rocket-sled with the Nemesis inside. And they're all looking shinier than normal.

The Cybermen use earmuff-like devices to put humans under their mental control, but on this occasion [as opposed to other "brainwashings" in stories such as 4.6, "The Moonbase"], the Doctor claims that enthralled men are dead and 'no longer human beings'. The Cybermen also seem responsible for the gas-spigots that spring out of the ground and incapacitate the police. [All right, it's never *said* that the Cybermen are responsible, but it makes more sense that their human agents pre-planted the spigots, as the Doctor has no reason to kill the police with lethal clouds, and the Nazis are clueless about this development.] The Cyber-leader remarks on the Doctor's 'new appearance'.

Bullets are essentially useless against these Cybermen [compare with their having the resilience of tissue paper in 22.1, "Attack of the Cybermen"]. On the other hand, the Cyber-guns seem variously capable of small explosions, variously killing people in little puffs of smoke or with weird little energy blips. [Check out the elimination of the human lackeys in episode two, and you'll see what we mean.]

The most significant development is that rather than merely obstructing their breathing as before ["Revenge of the Cybermen" (12.5), "Earthshock" (19.6)], gold is practically lethal on contact. If it penetrates the casing - such as when a gold-tipped arrow or a high-velocity gold coin is used - it causes explosions and instant death. The Cyber-leader *does* survive such an impact and recovers after removing the coin, although he falls unconscious for a bit. Similarly, the Cyber-leader is momentarily staggered when de Flores tosses gold dust on his chest unit. [This looks like a psychosomatic reaction as much as anything else, however - so much for the Cybermen claiming they lack emotions.]

The Cybermen have a probe-like gadget that detects the presence of gold. [Where they keep such a device, considering they lack pockets, is a question best left alone.]

History

• *Dating.* Well, *durr*, it's presently 23rd of November, 1988, as we are told every fifteen seconds in episode one. [Get comfortable for the rest,

because this is going to take a while and get quite choppy...]

The living metal Validium was forged as the ultimate defence for Gallifrey, back in 'the early times', and the Doctor says it was created by Omega and Rassilon [predictably, see **Did Rassilon Know Omega?** under "The Deadly Assassin" (14.3)]. For the substance to become active, it requires a 'critical mass' - hence why the Nemesis statue seen here is incomplete without its bow and arrow. Validium will "awaken" when placed in close proximity to itself, and it feels drawn to its other parts. The lump of Validium that became the Nemesis statue has had many forms - some of which would horrify Ace, it says - and that it changes to become 'whatever [it's] made to be'. About three hundred and fifty years ago, it apparently 'fell out of the sky' in Windsor, whereupon Lady Peinforte dubbed the Validium 'Nemesis' - so it became 'retribution' and fashioned itself as a statue bearing her likeness.

The Doctor says he's 'known' about the mission regarding the Nemesis ever since 23rd of November, 1638, and this is evidently the date he launched the Nemesis statue into space. That occasion coincided with a battle that included some Roundheads. [Go on then, try and guess which section we're going to direct you to now - if you can't, it's right before **The Critique**.]

The Doctor burns a crucial piece of the mathemetician's calculations, but 'someone' steals the remainder [and was considerate enough to clear away the mathemetician's body too, it seems]. The statue's bow became the property of the Crown, but was mysteriously stolen from Windsor Castle in 1788. It eventually came into de Flores' possession. Peinforte kept the arrow.

The Nemesis has circled the Heavens in a decaying orbit since 1638, and drawn close to Earth at 25-year intervals. It's assumed that it's now arriving back in Peinforte's meadow on the very day of year that it was sent away. [It's been argued that an astronomer working in 1638 would not have known about the shift from Julian to Gregorian calendar in 1753. However, if the Doctor *did* secretly aid the astrologer in his work, he could've made adjustment for the missing eleven days. Or if you prefer - especially as the timing of the Nemesis statue's orbit also seems to ignore the absent eleven days - stories such as 3.10, "The War Machines" and 8.5, "The Daemons" seem to prove that *Doctor Who* calendar

Did Cartmel Have *Any* Plan At All?

...continued from page 263

motivation is made obscure, and any certainty we had about his past is challenged. Yet to do this, any revelations we get are negatives, and we're being encouraged to speculate on less information than we *used* to have. It's the *speculation*, not the evidence itself, which suggests powers beyond those we've seen the Doctor display. The last generation of fans embraced this, but those raised on Tom Baker had accepted that the Doctor was a lazy muddler-through who triumphed through literacy, experience and willingness to take risks - things we should all aspire to. For better or worse, making him Omega's granny or Time's Champion removed some of these elements.

As we have seen (**Who Are All These Men in Wigs?** under 13.5, "The Brain of Morbius"), the plot of *Lungbarrow* has the Doctor revealed to be a reincarnation of The Other, someone who hung out with Rassilon and Omega and protested against their wish to use time-travel to impose order on chaos. This was a contrivance to clear up continuity hassles, and knit together ideas about Gallifrey's distant past that owe a lot to Greek myth. (The Pythia, who in Platt's accounts cursed Time Lords to sterility - causing them to develop regeneration - is the name of the Oracle of Apollo, who had a pet snake called a "python", hence the name of the serpent. See the comments on *The Winter's Tale* under "Silver Nemesis".) Like so much of the ingenious piecing together of small anomalies and pet theories in the books, this is impressive as a form of handicraft, like seeing someone

do a crossword. But it couldn't have worked for a mass audience.

(The British Public could have accepted some of the *New Adventures* innovations, and certainly the BBC Wales series has made voice-over narration seem natural in ways that the colour episodes of the "classic" series - by the way, do we *have* to call it that? it's a bit too *Trek*-like for most people - just never felt comfortable doing. See **Who's Narrating This Series?** under 22.1, "Attack of the Cybermen". That said, when the *New Adventures* book "Human Nature" made it to the screen, the Gaiman-lite ending of X3.9, "The Family of Blood" seemed out of synch with everything broadcast over the last three years, however typical it was of the books.)

So Marc Platt had a masterplan, and Ben Aaronovitch had a wish-list, but what of Cartmel? When he inherited the job he had no scripts and no writers, and just Pip and Jane Baker on hand to provide any material at all. Reading between the lines, in his outrageously self-important book *Script Doctor*, it's possible to see some of his motives. He wanted to create a stable of young writers who could put together scripts on time. He wanted to make contacts in the industry, and make a splash with a series for which nobody had high expectations. He wouldn't have minded being asked to edit *2000 AD*. So in some respects, *Doctor Who* was a means to an end. In many ways, this is how it should be, but it remains the case that any "master plan" on Cartmel's part may have been more related to his career, not the series.

---

isn't in synch with ours anyway, so the point might be moot. Maybe *all* the dates in the series are in the Julian calendar.]

It's said that the Nemesis 'generates destruction' [as if it's radiating a "chaos aura" of sorts], and its previous proximity to Earth coincided with the eve of the First World War (1913), Hitler annexing Austria (1938) and Kennedy's assassination (1963). [This twenty-five year cycle will, of course, be given a right good seeing-to in **Things That Don't Make Sense**.]

Lady Peinforte [no first name is given, even on her tomb - see **Where Does This Come From?**] is a seventeenth century megalomaniac of 'noble birth'. She seems fixated on the notion of 'glorious' or 'absolute evil', and keeps insisting that "all things shall be hers" once she obtains the Nemesis statue. She's studied some Latin and a little Greek.

She knows the Remingtons of Remington Graves, especially as Dorothea Remington 'did bribe away' her cook. Dorothea died in 1621, and it's implied that Peinforte killed her. (' 'Twas a slow poison.')

In the present day, the house of the now-'infamous' Lady Peinforte appears to have become a café / restaurant, and the grounds of her estate serve as a safari park (with llamas). She ordered that Richard be buried near her tomb - which is still standing in 1988, even though it doesn't contain her bones - and Richard's grave marker says he died 2nd of November, 1657, age 51. Richard can play the flute, owes someone named Briggs money, and ends this story accompanied by a maiden on a lute. Lady Peinforte herself is apparently disintegrated [as part of an automatic defence mechanism?] when she mentally snaps and leaps atop the horizontal statue.

From the Nemesis, Peinforte learned secrets about the Doctor's buried past, and also some fragments of knowledge that let her accomplish rudimentary time travel. This requires the presence of the Nemesis arrow, a specific potion that Richard prepares, human blood and a target date; the process creates an 'aura' and bumps her and Richard 350 years forward to 1988. [Some commentators (*The Discontinuity Guide* included) have suggested that Fenric from "The Curse of Fenric" helped to facilitate this process, but it's entirely unclear what he hopes to gain by doing so, unless he's so deluded as to think that Peinforte might genuinely be capable of humiliating the Doctor.]

At some time in her near-future (as she doesn't look much older), Ace will have her portrait painted by Thomas Gainsborough [circa 1780]. De Flores is an older German man / former Nazi leader who's presently living in South America. Fifty years ago, he stood at the Fuhrer's side when Hitler 'ordered the first step to greatness'. He's so evil, he's here seen preparing to spatchcock a parrot.

[As for when *this* group of Cybermen come from... well, it's not explicitly stated that they hail from the future, but nothing particularly disproves the notion either. The main reason to think they're from a later era is the current design - but then, the Cybermen aren't particularly known for their linear development, and just because they know about Time Lords, it doesn't automatically mean they're also time travelers. See the Cybermen chronology presented under 4.2, "The Tenth Planet", and consider that this *might* be a last throw of the dice by post-Cyber-War veterans attempting to change history. That doesn't entirely account for the size of the warfleet they've here amassed, but nothing else does either and the framework presented in the chronology - although debatable - will do at a pinch.[37]]

The Analysis

Where Does This Come From? Ever since they first appeared, the Cybermen were deeply implicated with the motions of the planets. Even "Earthshock" had its basis in the asteroid ("or whatever") that was assumed to have wiped out the dinosaurs. Planetary geologist Gene Schumacher was a minor celebrity for a while, and did the rounds of talk-shows explaining how scuba-diving in Mexico was research into astronomy and

palaeontology, really it was. The details of the impact and dust-cloud were still being thrashed out in 1981, when "Earthshock" was written, and a BBC2 *Horizon* documentary on this was a talking-point for weeks after its broadcast. So when *another* such programme speculated that Earth's sun was half of a binary star system with a neutron star (which was long-dead, hence why we never saw it), and that this knocked comets and planets about on a twenty-six million year cycle (hence the odd orbit of Pluto, and Uranus being on its side), we could count the days before this cropped up in *Doctor Who*.

Some of the scientists involved dubbed Sol's twin "Nemesis". If you've read the previous books in this series, you'll no doubt recall our comments on the 1950s bestseller *Worlds in Collision* by Immanuel Velikovski - and will realise that the idea is, in *Doctor Who* terms, almost as corny as "Oops! I started the Great Fire of London" or "That baby's your mother". But Nemesis provided a neat all-encompassing explanation for why all the weird mammals like Baluchitheria vanished thirteen million years ago, other odd mammals went bye-bye twenty-six million years before that, and the dinosaurs twenty-six million years before *that*... right on back through the Devonian, Carboniferous and Cambrian eras.

All of which is a roundabout way of saying: however much "Silver Nemesis" looks like a *Raiders of the Lost Ark* rip-off, there was a solid idea behind the story at one stage. A star of ill-omen, as someone from the 1630s might have termed it, was a big enough idea to make it worth doing as a Big Event Story.

Actually, it *looks* a bit like *Raiders*, but the idea of three components that need to be brought into proximity to activate their magic is from *Indiana Jones and the Temple of Doom*. This is itself a legacy of the idea of critical mass - first theorised in the late 1930s by Hungarian physicist Leo Szilard - as a side-effect of the idea of the chain-reaction. (It was thus an idea that contradicted the Nazis' "racially pure" physics, as they believed that even subatomic particles obeyed the *fuhrerprinzip*. Ergo, it would take fifty years to mine enough Uranium for one atom bomb - see 3.4, "The Daleks' Master Plan".) Writer Kevin Clarke had a basic idea about the "shrinkage" of weapons-grade plutonium from power stations. (It was a topical idea, especially with *Edge of Darkness* winning awards left, right and centre, and Chernobyl reminding everyone of how risky even state-run atomic plants could be.)

Clarke's other big idea was to allude to Jacobean drama. There's a reference to the most famous stage-direction in literature ('Exit, pursued by a bear'). This comes, as you should know by now, from Shakespeare's late fantasy *The Winter's Tale* (which is why we're pretty confident the stage-direction is one the Bard approved, because he'd retired to Stratford and so wrote in more detailed instructions than when he was on-hand in London). For those of you unfamiliar with the play, it's an allegory of renewal and justice set in Bohemia and Sicily. (The "Bohemia" of the play is obviously not the one with Prague as a capital, as it is possible to sail to Sicily and Delos from there, so it's more or less England.) An unjustly accused queen escapes punishment by turning to stone, and once her daughter - now raised as a shep-herdess - marries the son of the man with whom the queen was accused of adultery, balance is restored and she comes back to life.

Done well, this can be an emotionally-charged theatrical experience. The Queen is called "Hermione" (look up the name in a dictionary of classical mythology and this makes sense), so many fans have surmised that it's a good enough first name for Lady P. (But then, we think Kaftan from 5.1, "Tomb of the Cybermen" is called "Betty". Anyway, these days it's fashionable to think that any witch who bosses Richard around must be called "Judy", but you have to be British to get the joke.) As the play has lots of allusions to Hermes and Apollo, and the latter is connected to the goddess of retribution ("Nemesis"), we have another good reason to go with "Hermione". (That said, "Paulina" would work almost as well. As we'll see in this story's essay, the Delphic Oracle - so significant an off-stage presence in the play - connects to Marc Platt's notions of Gallifrey's dis-tant past. As the on-stage agency of Apollonian order is Paulina, this might suggest that the statue has this name, and Lady Hermione Peinforte cre-ated the goddess Pauline. But that just sounds silly to anyone who grew up in Britain. Nevertheless, as an adjective, "Pauline" suggests scales falling from eyes - Road to Damascus and so on - which is almost what happens here. A bit. Maybe.)

The other big allusion here is the name "de Flores", who is the assassin from Middleton and Rowley's play *The Changeling*. This guy has a dis-tinctive scar down his face, and as the name sug-gests he despoils virgins for a hobby - neither of these is exactly applicable to the character in this story. Clarke even tried to get Peinforte's dialogue into iambic pentameter, although this wasn't always appropriate or practical.

Although great pains were taken in the script to avoid the word "Nazi" (such a pity that no-one told the director about this), the connections between the Third Reich and the Occult were pretty well established by 1988. Rudolf Hess, when interrogated by MI5, was so obviously obsessed with the subject that Aleister Crowley was called in (by Ian Fleming - ever wondered why John Dee's cabalistically-inspired code-num-ber was assigned to James Bond?). Even hack hor-ror writers like James Herbert were using this as the Maguffin for thrillers about powerful artefacts, before Indiana Jones even put his hat on for the first time.

Now, one obvious link between Grail symbol-ism (which is what all quests of sacred objects eventually become) and Nazis is Wagner, espe-cially *Parsifal*. (There's an obvious reason why the chief seeker-after-the-Grail can't also be a rapist, as de Flores listens to Wagner but clearly doesn't know the words, but Clarke doesn't seem to have thought it through to that extent.) *Peine Forte a dure* was the mediaeval practice of compressing suspected witches beneath heavy doors. It was made more widely known by Hugh Trevor-Roper's book on the Elizabethan Witch Craze, which analysed the paranoia about suspected witches in the light of more recent political / moral panics about suspected traitors and conspiracies. (Trevor-Roper, later a lord, was also called upon by the Government to analyse the papers of the Third Reich - and was embarrassingly fooled in 1983, when he said that some supposed diaries of Hitler's were genuine.)

Of course, there's one obvious factor we've not mentioned, the need to have some connection between the date 23rd of November, 1988, and the twenty-fifth anniversary of *Doctor Who* on that date. All manner of ludicrous contrivances are needed to connect 'silver' and 23/11/63. Indeed, the stories' running order in Season Twenty-Five was messed up, and all sorts of continuity blun-ders allowed to accumulate, just to have episode one transmitted on the right date.

Things That Don't Make Sense So, to get at the stapled-on symbolism at the heart of this story... the Nemesis' orbit appears to have triggered a major catastrophe precisely every twenty-five years since 1638, right? Well, for a start, 1813 was the one year during that quarter-century when nobody was at war with anyone else (largely because 1812 had been a bit of a let-down for Napoleon). Apart from Kennedy's death (which was damaging to the public psyche, but not really *that* big a problem on the level of bad things happening), 1963 was a comparative golden age that followed the Cuban Missile Crisis. And there wasn't much in 1913 that led to the Great War that hadn't already been started.

So these dates - even the examples the Doctor provides - are hardly cursed. In fact, some would argue that 1688 was the year of one of the great events in British history [see 4.4, "The Highlanders" for more]. 1938 was the year that a seemingly inevitable war was in fact delayed for a time, which gave Britain a vital chance to muster forces, build Spitfires and train pilots. [Curiously, the Doctor specifies "Hitler annexes Austria" as the relevant Bad Thing of 1938, when *krystallnacht* and the Sudetenland crisis might be seen as more obviously ominous signs of what was to come.] Overall, it seems this terrible Nemesis statue causes moments of political and military stability in the middle of otherwise long-brewing conflicts. Ooh, scary.

The bit of history that's *hopelessly* awry, however, is the claim that the Roundheads were present at Peinforte's field in 1638. That's pretty impressive, coming as it does ten years before the Parliamentary forces regrouped into Cromwell's "New Model Army", and five years before the Civil War(s) started. If we can *just* accept that Lady Peinforte has enough stolen knowledge to time-travel, then we *might* also accept that she could pull Roundheads through time to 1638, although good luck to anyone trying to figure out why she might do this. [And why would Puritans want a statue of Nemesis anyway? Not to melt it down, nor to sell it to idolatrous foreigners, surely?] Oh, and a visit from the Spanish Inquisition in an era when even the King's Spanish wife was treated with the utmost suspicion and Catholics were seen as agents of Satan? Nobody should expect that.

Even the timing of the Doctor and Ace's visits to Peinforte's study seems wonky: the Doctor says it's been 'months' since he stepped foot there, but if the Nemesis *was* launched in November, then Peinforte and Richard must leave for the future in 1639, not 1638 as the captioning states and the

Doctor later suggests when he offers to take Richard home. We might try and salvage the captioned date by saying that Peinforte and Richard depart in December 1638, but leaves someone to explain why - if the Doctor and Ace arrive 'months' after *that* - the study fire is still going, and the mathemetician's body seems comparatively fresh.

In fact, it's fortunate that the Doctor seems to have helped the late mathemetician on the side, because the calculations that the man here makes (before his demise, obviously) would require him to deduce Universal Gravitation before Newton's even an embryo, and to place this into Kepler's entirely unpublished calculations, thus devising an Inverse Square Law and rules on Planetary Motions about a generation ahead of time. Compared to this, predicting that we'll change to the Gregorian Calendar in 1753 is child's play. Quite why the Doctor would risk making such a big development get into the public domain ahead of time is only one of the mysteries concerning his behaviour in the backstory here.

Need we ask why people who are obviously intended to be Nazis seem so unfamiliar with the idea of poison gas? Mind you, they have no aversion to using Israeli-manufactured Uzis, so either de Flores' men are mercenaries with no ideological convictions of their own, or de Flores is just a badly informed Wagner enthusiast who thinks the Swastikas are standard set-dressing. Not only does this group somehow fly from South America to Windsor in under a day, but - to judge by what's said in episode one - they appear to check into a hotel in uniform. Or did de Flores go in, wearing *that* suit, and then take time to change into fatigues and a natty scarf whilst lecturing his men on the importance of not wasting time? By the point where de Flores and chums are inept enough to leave their all-important bow just lying about the place in the middle of the gunfight, they're looking so inept that we perhaps shouldn't be surprised.

Onto issues with the Cybermen, who - like the Daleks two stories before them - here display the targeting ability of tofu. The Cyber-spaceship by comparison seems a bit *too* efficient, as nobody notices when it lands right next to Heathrow airport, nor when it wanders down country lanes around Windsor. We're left in the dark about how the Cybermen learned details about Lady Peinforte, although their somewhat spurious ability to target the Doctor and Ace for assassination in episode one is perhaps justified, because they might've just scanned for the TARDIS and a double-heartbeat.

Peinforte and Richard time-travel to 1988, in which her house has become a restaurant, and in which a pair of ladies who lunch look surprised but not really *that* surprised that two such strange-looking people have just "manifested" in front of them. We also refer you to the subsequent scene, in which a waitress is just lounging behind them nonchalantly catching up on the polishing.

The one that everyone seems to notice: how is it possible for a policeman who's been gassed inside the cab of a car to wind up under it? The other one that everyone notices: security at Windsor Castle is such crap that the Doctor and Ace get within a stone's throw of a woman who *must* be Her Majesty by just ignoring a sign and walking inside. And is the Nemesis really wrapped in cobwebs as it appears? Because any spiders along for the ride must've done an *amazing* job before perishing in the depths of space 350 years ago.

During the standoff with Peinforte and Richard in episode two, the Cyber-Leader deduces that Peinforte's supply of gold is limited, and that therefore... his troops must retreat. Uh? Why not just dodge around until their opponents run out of arrows? Also note that the Cybermen all have their backs turned when Richard lets loose his arrow, yet they're all facing Peinforte's tomb when the first Cybermen gets struck, as if they sensed that one of their buddies was a gonner and wanted to watch. Then later, when the Nazis attack, Richard says they've only *one* arrow left - yet he quite clearly had two arrows in his quiver in the previous scene.

The editing butchery needed to get this story down to time (see **The Lore**) meant that the entire sub-plot of Kurt "betraying" de Flores wound up on the cutting room floor - so on broadcast, this created the jolting image of the "escaped" de Flores wearing Cyber-earmuffs for no good reason. The video restored the material before and after this, but even then questions remain, such as why the Cybermen bother to leave de Flores alive *at all* rather than just shooting him, why the Cyber-earmuffs have no effect on him, and why he and Kurt even resorted to the subterfuge in the first place, when they could've just run away. Unless the idea is that de Flores isn't exactly an Olympic sprinter.

Arrows with gold heads would be hard to aim correctly, because even a thin coating of such a heavy metal would affect the balance (and any *less* than a good layer would be unlikely to affect Cybermen so badly). Does Richard, an experienced archer, not notice how odd they feel in his hand? Then de Flores brags that his men have 'no such weakness' to gold, evidently overlooking the downside that an arrow to the throat, head or chest will do his men in readily enough.

As the Nemesis comes to life, we get the jubilant effect of a lightning storm, Peinforte's tomb exploding and everything catching fire. Write your own explanation, however, for why this evident obliteration didn't kill de Flores and Kurt, and [pardon the phrasing] entomb the Cybermen. During the final stand-off, we see Ace run an *awfully* long way into the hanger before she seems to realize, "Oh shite, there's two Cybermen right in front of my face", plus she appears to magically teleport in front of them while the Doctor's chatting. Just prior to that, the "falling" Cybermen look so much like dummies, you're likely to get acid flashbacks to Toberman's twirling dance with one in "The Tomb of the Cybermen". Kurt appears to instantly and without hesitation die from a "mortal" Cyber-shot to the hip.

We can believe that a meteor hitting Earth would be headline news, but that nobody would see it arrive (except a few cops who went oddly silent - and no backup was dispatched). We can believe that you need a magic arrow, human blood and a chicken to travel in time. We can believe that de Flores seriously thinks that these alien machine-men might know Wagner. But Charlton Athletic picking up three points?

Critique Let's get one thing straight: for all we've cited the plot similarities between this story and "Remembrance of the Daleks", even if "Silver Nemesis" *had* been shown first - and "Remembrance" had ended with Ace saying it was just like the trick the Doctor had played on the Cybermen and de Flores - this would *still* be the weaker story by far. On every level, it's an inferior piece of work. It's marred by a lame "comedy" subplot in each of the three episodes (the supposed Royal look-alike, then the skinheads and then Mrs Remington) and an ill-defined purpose for this all-important statue. Why the Doctor is doing what he does - or what he knows about what's going on - is never made clear, and seems to change from episode to episode.

As with quite a few 80s stories - and to some extent those of today as well - more thought has gone into what ingredients can be announced in advance to generate publicity, rather than what any one of these elements actually brings to the story or the experience of watching it. But in one regard, we *have* progressed from a confused piece of work like "The Two Doctors" (22.4), because at least here all the elements mean something to casual viewers. We're now closer to something like "Tooth and Claw" (X2.2), where werewolves, Queen Victoria and kung-fu monks all look exciting in the trailers, but once they arrive it's just running up and down corridors. To fill the two episodes after the Cybermen come along, however, we have Peinforte and Richard being moderately amusing when confronted with llamas and cars, the Cybermen and de Flores trying to trick one another and the Doctor and Ace running between each location and explaining the plot along the way.

Comparison with the BBC Wales series makes one thing much more clear: if a story is intended to be an "event", it should be made as such. This story's main elements could be resolved into an hour-long special with no ill-effects (unless you *really* want to retain the stage-school lads pretending to be working class and talking about 'social workers'). So the bigger question is whether this should have been attempted at all. Nobody in the wider world outside fandom cared about 23rd of November, but the series' silver jubilee was something that the entire year's worth of episodes could have played with - as indeed "Remembrance" had. Underneath all the anniversary malarkey, this is a relatively straightforward story, and the combination of disparate elements is in many ways what makes a story like this worth trying.

You'd *think* that anyway, but in this case it's mainly pointless because they're kept separate. Peinforte is never given a chance to flummox the Cyber-leader. The not-quite-Nazis aren't ever confronted with how pathetic they are compared to *real* supermen, *real* sorcery or a genuinely ruthless opponent. Whilst a present-day adversary is needed to offset the Cybermen and Lady Peinforte, using characters clearly intended to be Nazis unbalances the story. The thankless task of making de Flores work would have been a trial for someone who understood or liked the character and story, and Anton Diffring is clearly not relishing his role. Fiona Walker is considerably more enthusiastic, which brings its own problems. The result is that this isn't an ensemble piece. Everyone is doing what they do almost autonomously.

That said, what we we've got here tells a relatively simple story, entertainingly (with the toe-curling caveats cited above). Once again, if this story had been magically transported back to the dark days of Season Twenty-Two, its virtues would be more apparent. Clarke and director Chris Clough have contrived to produce some amazing moments of pure *Who*. There's Ace, lit from beneath, stalking Cybermen with a catapult; jazz echoing around the cosmos; the Cyber-ship landing (obviously a model) and a real door on location opening and revealing actors in costumes *all in one uncut shot*. Even the notorious 'social workers' scene is preceded with "Shada"-like shots of people in bizarre costumes walking down an English street and hardly anyone noticing.

The main purpose of *Doctor Who* is to entertain the public. Take a look at the audience appreciation figures, and you'll see that this story seems to have done that as well as any this year - even if everyone watching forgot that that it happened almost immediately afterward. Because however much Cartmel seems to have thought he had a higher calling than making watchable television that isn't *quite* like anything else for a large audience, Nathan-Turner has settled for doing it as well as can be expected with the resources.

Still... perhaps the most important consideration here is that we're working within a new paradigm. This new phase of the series is averaging a better quality of episode than at any time since Season Nineteen, even though we have a long way to go before it looks anything like as slick as the mainstream television drama of this era. In fact, consider that "Silver Nemesis" provides a benchmark for the lowest quality of script we can expect from now on, *and yet* it's head and shoulders better than anything by Pip 'n' Jane. Similarly, the next one made, "The Happiness Patrol", is as shoddy-looking as it will get in this period - and yet it's vastly better than "Timelash" (22.5).

The Facts

Written by Kevin Clarke. Directed by Chris Clough. Ratings: 6.1 million, 5.2 million, 5.2 million. Audience appreciation was up again: 71% for episode one, 70% each for episodes two and three.

Working Titles "Nemesis", "The Malopath" (maybe), "The Harbinger".

Supporting Cast Fiona Walker (Lady Peinforte), Anton Diffring (De Flores), Gerard Murphy (Richard), David Banks (Cyber-leader), Mark Hardy (Cyber-lieutenant), Metin Yenal (Karl), Dolores Gray (Mrs Remmington), Leslie French (Mathematician); Chris Chering, Symond Lawes (Skinheads); Courtney Pine, Adrian Reid, Ernest Mothle, Frank Tontoh (Jazz Quartet).

Oh, Isn't That..?

• *Anton Diffring.* He played Nazis. In everything. "Silver Nemesis" was virtually his last screen role, as he died a year later, and his weariness at typecasting is all-too visible. He was also memorable as the book-burning fire chief in Truffaut's film of *Fahrenheit 451*.

• *Gerard Murphy.* Maybe the face isn't instantly recognisable, but the voice was. He's still a prominent radio actor, but in the 80s he was best known as the narrator of the BBC Radio version of *The Lord of the Rings*, which had more influence on Peter Jackson's film than even the original book. You might also have seen him in *Batman Begins* as a judge, and as the pilot of the "Flight into Terror" in *Father Ted*. He was at that stage a member of the Royal Shakespeare Company.

• *Courtney Pine.* One of the most gifted British saxophonists of his generation, and one who got a lot of publicity when the London meeja types decided jazz was 'in' in 1986. Since then the fuss has died down, and he's less in thrall to John Coltrane and Sonny Rollins, so his best work may be ahead of him. Anyway, he was famous enough in 1988 for Ace to plausibly get his autograph.

• *Leslie French.* He was the model for the boy in the statue on the front of Broadcasting House in the 1930s, but in 1963 he'd been in Visconti's *Il Gattopardo* ("The Leopard"), and Verity Lambert thought he'd be good for the new family show she was producing.

• *Dolores Gray.* Not a clue. Sorry. (See **The Lore**.)

Cliffhangers As the standoff between the Doctor and de Flores seems likely to end in gunfire, a spaceship lands and Cybermen emerge; the Doctor realises that the Cyber-fleet must be 'shrouded' and adjusts his scanner, bringing a vast space-armada into view.

The Lore

• One of the first things Andrew Cartmel did on becoming script editor was to ask Alan Moore to write for the series - specifically, for the twenty-fifth anniversary story. We've been hearing a lot about Moore in this volume, but in 1987 he was everywhere (but usually on Channel 4, in his trademark white suit). *Watchmen* - then being serialised by DC, and in case you didn't know, it's considered one of the greatest comic-stories ever made - was at the forefront of the graphic novel boom, when comics were being sold as the new literature. A Moore script for *Doctor Who* at this point would have been a big coup, but would the never-particularly-hip BBC have thought so?

Well, Pat Mills had got a script commissioned in the past, but he'd gone laboriously through regular channels. An inexperienced script editor hiring someone probably unknown to the Beeb hierarchy - and for a high profile slot such as this - would not have been seen as politic. Some fans have speculated that Kevin Clarke as a second choice was a Harry Van Gorkum-like manoeuvre - one that was designed to make Moore seem more attractive - that backfired (see 27.0, "The TV Movie"). The truth is more prosaic, however. Moore said no because a) he was too busy, b) he didn't particularly want to write for series television and c) he didn't like *Doctor Who* much, and felt that all the Doctors after Hartnell gave the impression of being paedophiles. You might recall that Moore *did* write a few comic strips for *Doctor Who Weekly* strips, but it appears that all the series' lore he used came from picking the brains of fans over a few pints.

• So another novice was given a crack at *Doctor Who* - once again, because Caroline Oulton can't think of what else to do with him. Kevin Clarke had a bit of momentum behind his TV writing career, with episodes of *Wish Me Luck* (an ITV drama about wartime bomber pilots) and a commission from *The Bill* coinciding with his decision to take up Cartmel's offer of work. He had, however, very little experience of watching *Who*, and could only devise stories Cartmel found corny.

During the summer of 1987, Cartmel had taken the advice of a fan who had written in, and sat down to watch some of the old stories. Before long he was loaning these out to his "initiates" and getting feedback. Whereas Aaronovitch found himself drawn to the Hinchcliffe / Holmes era (mid-70s Gothic with solid SF logic), Clarke was more taken with Hartnell and the idea that the Doctor was enigmatic and not wholly heroic.

Cartmel was also interested in re-mystifying the character's past, and refined Clarke's ideas into a situation where the Doctor had a dilemma: reveal all, or watch Earth be destroyed. Nathan-Turner suggested that the Cybermen were due for a return, and that this would chime with the 'silver' theme of the magic metal and the twenty-fifth anniversary. (Clarke had asked for Daleks, but it wasn't clear if they could get permission, and Aaronovitch had got the gig by the time they could.)

• Clarke's interests in Jacobean Revenge Drama and the nature of evil did most of the rest. The idea of the impending meteor / comet chimed with the old idea of the "star of ill omen", but allowed a sideswipe at the security issues surrounding nuclear waste. He also gave the Doctor his own enthusiasm for jazz in general, and the then-recent British renaissance specifically. He was delighted when Courtney Pine agreed to appear as himself. (These days, with Andrew Marr and Sharon Osbourne popping up, and cameos from "Peggy Mitchell" and "Davinadroid", we forget that these "real-life" appearances almost never happened. Kenneth Kendall reading a news bulletin in 3.10, "The War Machines" and maybe Alex McIntosh in similar circumstances in 9.1, "Day of the Daleks" were the only precedents.)

• A couple of factors required more re-writes. In making it all on OB, the TARDIS scenes had to go. With no scanner to play with, the role of Ace's souped-up boom box was revised. This was to have had a sign saying 'Please Water Me Daily', but this was vetoed (because children might have copied it). The Cybermen were to have had a scanner-rig that walked after them, or maybe just floated.

• Meanwhile, overseas sales of the series made having all-out Nazis inadvisable, as German-language television had taken the show again. (RTL, although available in Germany and technically subject to the same laws, is Luxembougeois.) The scripts were revised to make it seem that de Flores'

mercenaries held political beliefs that were unrelated to nationality (but then Clough went and cast Germans, and put Swastikas everwhere).

• Finding locations was complicated. Obviously, Windsor Castle was off-limits (as the real Royals would be there), but Arundel Castle was a good substitute. It even had a building in the grounds that could be pressed into service as Lady Peinforte's tomb. (Sound recording at the real Windsor would've been a pain anyway, with Heathrow so close by.) The hangar scenes were done at the soon-to-be-demolished Greenwich Gas Works (which is now the site of the Millennium Dome, or whatever we're supposed to call it now).

Two other possible locations were looked at. When Windsor was still an option, Prince Edward was approached for a cameo with the standard £50 BBC fee, but he was too busy with his Really Useful work. (No, seriously... he worked for Andrew Lloyd-Webber's Really Useful Company, doing something or other.) The Arundel-as-Windsor tourists are a mixed bunch - some were hired extras, and some were just known associates of the series. Clarke and Graeme Curry were there, along with directors Andrew Morgan, Peter Moffatt and Fiona Cumming, plus Cumming's husband Ian Fraser (PA on several stories in this period). Kathleen Bidmead, formerly a PA and later a bit-player (Mrs Smith in 25.1, "Remembrance of the Daleks", and the nosy neighbour in 26.4, "Survival") was also along, with Nicholas Courtney for good measure. (Nathan-Turner had a quiet word with him then - see 26.1, "Battlefield" for why.) The genuine extras weren't alerted to any of this, and spent much of the shoot wondering why they were being treated like human beings for a change.

• Oxygen bottles were on hand for Anton Diffring, who was unwell throughout the shoot and who failed to understand or like the script. He had only accepted the role (Charles Grey had turned it down) because the schedule meant he would be in the UK for Wimbledon.

• With the crisis surrounding "The Greatest Show in the Galaxy" eating up a lot of the rehearsal time, much of the action was done on the hoof, and some scenes almost improvised. Cartmel and the cast re-worked the "confession" scene in the Hangar, and McCoy himself more-or-less directed the "chess" sequence with him and Ace passing around the silver bow in Peinforte's tomb. A lot of the material with the Cyber-controlled "Walkmen" was lost when the actors playing them - Dave and John Ould - were unavailable (as they had been drivers for the Kray brothers, we won't ask why). Ace's catapult malarkey with the Cybermen was intended to be done with a SteadiCam rig, but this was not possible. Clough hired a small helicopter to simulate the effect of the Cyber-ship's passage down country lanes. You can tell, if you look carefully.

• And on top of all their hassles, the production team had a documentary crew under their feet. New Jersey Network had wanted to cover "Greatest Show", but the production of that story had been quite fraught enough. So instead they followed the making of *this* story, and grabbed interviews where and when they could. The BBC chose not to show the finished product, but a version - minus anything connected with Eric Saward (yes, he was *still* sulking) - was appended to the VHS version. This also restored many scenes cut from the broadcast edit and in episode three juggled around the order of certain scenes that - while not making more sense exactly - show how badly the broadcast version was cobbled together. Opinion is divided on whether we needed to see this stuff, but it's less divided on whether the "comedy" with the duck (inserted because of something Noel Edmunds was doing in his new, completely different, Saturday Night show) is actually funnier than the documentary. You certainly get bigger laughs in fandom for impersonating Gary Downie.

• An unforeseen problem with the new-improved non-nose-irritating masks for the Cybermen was that the reflective coating tended to oxidise. This made the Cybermen turn gold, unfortunately. Any other monster and they'd have gone with it.

• Some of the model effects for this and "The Happiness Patrol" had been executed in the Car Park at Elstree during "The Greatest Show in the Galaxy". At around this time, Aldred posed for photos for the poster outside the Forum in "The Happiness Patrol", and the *faux*-Gainsborough painting seen in the extended "Silver Nemesis" VHS version. (The painting confused some visitors to Arundel, as it wasn't in the guidebook.) The newspaper Ace reads crops up again in football-based drama *The Manageress* (can *you* spot the novel twist in the premise?), and the back page was significant in that programme's plot. (Odd that nobody in that episode says to Cherie

Lunghi's character, "We may need to have a pitch inspection if Earth is devastated by a meteor strike".)

• The BBC made a reasonably big deal about the twenty-fifth anniversary, promoting episode one with a special trailer that included both the final shot from the episode's cliffhanger, and... oh, dear... clips of the Zarbi from "The Web Planet" (2.5). Amazingly, this *still* got people tuning in. The series was still running opposite *Coronation Street* (though now on Wednesdays), but the ratings spike noticeably for heavily-trailed episodes such as the first two parts of "Remembrance of the Daleks", or after the Kandy Man was unveiled in all its glucose glory in the trailer for "The Happiness Patrol". (A similar phenomenon is observable for David Tennant's first season, where a steep ratings slump was reversed by a week of trailers promising guest appearances by Peter Kay, Shirley Henderson and Marc Warren.) With this in mind, the following year's promotional decisions look disastrous. Two days after the first episode was broadcast, episodes two and three received their world premiere in a compilation of the entire story shown on TV New Zealand.

One venue where the anniversary *wasn't* promoted was the cover of *Radio Times*, even though several full length promotional shots had been taken in expectation that it was a shoo-in. Suspiciously, the cover that week was given over to *The Chronicles of Narnia* (see "The Greatest Show in the Galaxy"), which had actually begun a week earlier. Nathan-Turner had also negotiated an exclusive photo deal with the *Daily Mail* to cover the scenes with Dolores Gray, but this was apparently wrecked by the unexpected appearance of Gary Leigh and a photographer from *DWB*. One account of these events has the interlopers being escorted away from the shoot at gunpoint. *DWB*'s exclusive duly appeared in their summer special, and included such thrilling images as the back of a wooden screen and Sylvester McCoy standing in a field looking bored.

• Oh, all right: Dolores Gray *was* sort of a star, just not around these parts. The whole thing with Mrs Remington - who becomes Mrs Hackensack in the novelisation (less plausibly, her seventeenth century English ancestors share this surname) - was that the cameo had been written for any well-known American they could get their hands on for an afternoon's work. For example, Kate O'Mara offered to put in a good word with Larry Hagman (TV's J.R. Ewing from *Dallas*, if you're too

ABOUT TIME 1985–1989

young to remember). But as the recording dates got nearer, they became less hopeful of finding a truly big name for a cameo.

Finally, they noticed that Broadway veteran Dolores Gray was in London, doing Sondheim's *Follies*. If you go to musicals a lot, then Dolores Gray is a name - if not, treat her like one anyway, and a lot of the punters at home won't know any different. (British readers will know how easy this is to achieve.) Nathan-Turner made a big deal about her cameo in pre-publicity, but she was hardly the huge Golden Age Hollywood star he claimed. (Actually, Stubby Kaye in 24.3, "Delta and the Bannermen" was considerably more famous, *and* got more screen-time.) Gray had appeared and sung in a few films in the 1950s, and was better known for her stage work. By the way, the car that *doesn't* stop for Richard is driven by Kevin Clarke, who's also the one passer-by to do a double-take as he and Peinforte walk down "Windsor" high street.

25.4: "The Greatest Show in the Galaxy"

(Serial 7J, Four Episodes. 14th December 1988 - 4th January 1989.)

Which One is This? The one with the creepy clowns and the hippy bus.

Firsts and Lasts The only fully-legitimate *Doctor Who* story to be made at Elstree, former home of ATV and thus of all the ITC action shows of the 60s and 70s. Last appearance of the original light-coloured jacket for the McCoy Doctor, and the hatband and bandanna are changed from now on too. Entirely by accident, this is the last time we see the TARDIS walls with proper roundels. (Yes, we see the console room in 26.1, "Battlefield", but its walls are hastily-assembled studio flats with circles cut out of them. And yes, the BBC Wales one has what it pleases them to call 'roundels' for old time's sake, but they're actually hexagons, and thus cannot be considered "round" in any meaningful sense.)

It's the first time Mark Ayres gets to do the music: he's now custodian of the archive as far as sound is concerned, and saviour of the BBC Radiophonic Workshop.

Four Things to Notice about "The Greatest Show in the Galaxy"...

1. In one of those flukes resulting from panic resulting from an unexpected crisis, this story looks a heck of a lot better than if they'd followed the gameplan. For reasons we'll discuss in **The Lore**, they had to abandon Television Centre and make all of this as an Outside Broadcast. Not all of the locations were too far away from base, though: they pitched a tent in the car-park of Elstree studios (where *EastEnders* is made) and lit it as best they could, making the Big Top sequences atmospheric and unlike anything else we'd seen before.

2. Another fluke is that the planned small explosion for the tent in episode four was rethought. The original compressed-air burst of dust fell through when the wrong nozzle was brought to the location, so they rigged up a load of explosives. Nobody remembered to tell McCoy, who at best was informed that he should expect a "large wind". Fortunately, he did the take with as much nonchalance as the script required, *barely* flinched as a sizeable explosion went off behind him, and only reacted once the shot was in the can. Luckily, it was the last shot of the day.

3. We've mentioned the myth of the Anorak Fan (see **What's All This Stuff About Anoraks?** under 24.1, "Time and the Rani"), and a great many people consider Whizzkid - the annoying little twerp who collects Psychic Circus trivia and memorabilia but has no life - to be a parody of this. It's true that some of his dialogue about how it's 'not as good as it used to be' seems a little cutting, but what does that make Captain Cook, *the* famous intergalactic space explorer? He's a pompous bore who tells preposterous anecdotes and is only in it for the money. We could name a few people like that whom you'd also have encountered at conventions, on stage, but it's not for us to name names[39].

4. *Doctor Who* tends not to have much Method Acting (after all, short of going to the supermarket in fetish gear and shooting the checkout girls, there's no way you can really get in touch with your inner Voord - see 1.5, "The Keys of Marinus" for more on this), but we draw your attention to episode one. In this, Aldred and McCoy have to gamely eat Plaup, a fairly revolting fruit sold by the Stallslady. Plaup is made by taking a mango, filling it with a can of Green Giant corn and adding custard. Unfortunately, because of the Stallslady's horse, they required three takes to nail

this scene. Aldred's grimace is clearly not just acting...

The Continuity

The Doctor Has decided to learn juggling from a book. [Whether this is because he knows he's headed for a region where circus skills might be required, or it's a gobsmacking fluke - like developing a taste for jazz the day he encounters a Nazi-Cyberman alliance in the previous story - is left open. To help you decide, see the *Background*. Incidentally, it almost seems, based on the evidence of 19.3, "Kinda", that each new Doctor has to re-learn manual dexterity with each new set of fingers. Here, the Doctor has a book for beginners but is clearly more accomplished a few hours later, so this must only be a form of "brushing up".] He staggers backward under a psychic assault projected by the Gods of Ragnarok [see **The Non-Humans**], as if their power were straining his mental defences.

While performing in the Gods' home dimension, the Doctor knows precisely *when* Kingpin's medallion will travel through from our reality, and where it will appear. [It conveniently materialises at his feet, although it's possible that it was drawn (magnetically or otherwise) to the Doctor's sword - see *Inventory*.] His timing on this score seems both impeccable and impossible, but it lets him goad the Gods into firing power-bolts at just the right moment - and then to reflect those bolts with the all-important, impervious medallion and thereby destroy them. [Look, let's deal with this now... so much of this story feels like we're walking into an adventure that's already in progress - again, see *Background* for why. Hence, the ending relies on a string of movements and decisions that only the Doctor can see properly. We could dump most of the ending - particularly Mags fortuitously kicking the Captain's hand, and the medallion miraculously appearing in the Gods' circus - into **Things That Don't Make Sense**, but the Doctor obviously *is* working to a plan (hence his constantly checking his watch), and it *does* work. Apparently, there's a method to his madness that us mere mortals can't quite comprehend.] After obliterating the Gods, the Doctor is somehow able to cross back to Segonax.

Magic tricks the Doctor here performs, while stalling for the medallion's miraculous arrival: he can sway his body in a circle while his shoes remain firmly planted in place. He can make chicken eggs appear from his mouth; do various stunts with a rope and trick-knots; place said rope in a pan, then make a candle appear from thin air, light the candle with a flame he produces from his other hand, set the rope on fire and turn it into a snake - which can then become his brolly. He can also wriggle out of a straightjacket while hanging upside down. And he can light a match by striking it under his arm. [None of this is out-of-keeping with his previous displays of legerdemain (see, for example, 14.6, "The Talons of Weng Chiang" or 8.4, "Colony in Space").]

• *Ethics.* [If we assume that he merely blunders in to this situation, then his treatment of Ace is fine. But if he's planned it, we're on shakier ground because he's stringing her along - sorry to sound like a broken record, but move along toward the *Background*.] He doesn't attempt to dissuade Bellboy from killing himself - even when it's very clear that's what he intends to do - but is dogged in his pursuit of restoring Kingpin's memories. In the Psychic Circus showring, the Doctor undercuts Captain Cook's authority by calling him a 'crushing bore', but appeals to werewolf-Mags to show mercy, saying he doesn't believe that it's in her nature to destroy everything in her path. As Mags turns her rage upon the Captain, the Doctor hollers for her to stop - even though the Captain has betrayed them all.

He also believes Ace has a moral right to claim a lost earring if the owner isn't present.

• *Inventory.* [Now, this is weird. As you might've gathered, in the end sequences when he's entertaining the Gods, there's suddenly a whole load of conjuring equipment lying around. This possibly implies that the Doctor stores all of this in his pockets, but he doesn't even get as far as rummaging for change when entering the Psychic Circus, so we don't know what *else* he's got about his person. Then again, perhaps the Gods magically supply the items, because one suspects the Doctor didn't haul that stone table in and out of the ring by hand.] He's seen with a 'piece of metal' that turns into a sword [this *could* be one more item the Gods provide for him, but see *Background* for a more detailed explanation]. He appears to purchase fruit from the Stallslady [so it's likely that he's carrying currency that's accepted on Segonax].

• *Background.* The Doctor claims to have fought the Gods of Ragnarok 'all through time'. [This could refer to the beings specifically seen here, or it could be a general term for higher-beings that we've seen in other guises. (If so, 3.7, "The

275

Celestial Toymaker"; 6.2, "The Mind Robber" and 20.5, "Enlightenment" are as good a place to look as any.) It could also be that he's only recently decided to actively *chase* through time fighting them, possibly since his last regeneration.] He says the Gods' memorial stones look 'familiar' to him, and he's knowledgeable enough about the Gods - even though he doesn't appear to have directly confronted them in person until now - to deem their actions 'predictable as ever'.

At the end of his performance in the Gods' arena, the Doctor produces a flat piece of metal that he says was once part of a sword. He tosses the metal into the air, where it flashes and *becomes* a sword, and the Doctor says this item belonged to a gladiator - who fought and died before the Gods in this very ring. [The veiled implication is that the gladiator was a personal friend of the Doctor's, and thus his causing the Gods' downfall is more than a little personal. Note the delight with which he doffs his hat as the Gods and their arena crumble to dust around him. It's possible that mention of the gladiator is just the Doctor's way of showboating, but there's nothing to indicate that he isn't speaking literally. If so, this would doubly suggest that the Doctor arranged for the "junk-mail" robot that "randomly" appeared in the TARDIS and motivated the trip to Segonax - otherwise, his carrying the fallen gladiator's sword, and just *happening* to encounter the Gods, would rank as one of the greatest coincidences in the whole of *Doctor Who*. Lest you still doubt that this is another "mission" of the kind we've been seeing this year, note how the Doctor twice says, 'Things are beginning to get out of control quicker than I expected.' More on his stratagems in **The Non-Humans**.]

He's taken tea from the Groz Valley on Melegathon at least once. He claims to have heard reports of the 'friendliness' of the Segonax natives. [The reports are hideously wrong if the Stallslady is anything to go by, unless the idea is that the locals were more carefree before the Circus arrived.] The Doctor says it must be difficult for the Gods to 'exist concurrently in two different time-spaces', and that he "knows the problem himself" [whatever that means].

The Supporting Cast

• *Ace*. She went to a circus once, but found it naff and boring - especially as there weren't any tigers - and regarded the clowns as creepy. Now she hates both circuses and clowns. She seems to know about motorbike repair and maintenance, and admires the noisy road-bike owned by 'Nord, Vandal of the Road'.

She's clearly at a loss for how to deal with the emotionally-damaged and suicidal Bellboy. Her instincts tell her that Captain Cook is bad news, but that his associate Mags has potential. Ace guns down robot clowns with no compunction, but is unable to stop the Bellboy's giant robot from killing the (human) Chief Clown. [In activating the machine, she gets the definitive Ace line here: 'If this thing doesn't work, I'll kick its head in.'] Her magpie ability to spot shiny things results in her picking out Flowerchild's earring and using it as a badge [see **Things That Don't Make Sense**].

At present, Ace can't find her backpack of explosives. [This is almost played as if the Doctor has hidden it - something of a liability, because she could've made quicker work of the robot clowns. Mind you, that might've spoiled his timing.] She's grown tired of the Doctor's spoon-playing [after having a go herself in 25.2, "The Happiness Patrol"].

The TARDIS A small robot delivering video junk-mail materializes within the console room. The Doctor [again, understanding that he's probably responsible for its appearance] says that its appearnce within the Ship is 'extraordinary'. [We actually count three, maybe four, prior occasions this has happened: "Pyramids of Mars" (13.3), in which the incursion is said to be "impossible", so must be a first; "The Keeper of Traken" (18.6), in which the psychic force of an entire empire lets the Keeper drop by; "The Awakening" (21.2) in which the Malus causes a manifestation of sorts in the Ship - this happens while the TARDIS door is open, however; and most recently Vena in "Timelash" (22.5), who sped through the console room via a Kontron tunnel - mind, the Ship wasn't at its best that year. These days the odd passing ocean-liner can just barge in, apparently - X3.13, "Last of the Time Lords".] The junk-mail robot is able to plug itself into the console and over-ride the scanner. It calls Ace's courage in visiting the Psychic Circus into question, and in such a fashion that she feels compelled to go. [*Still* think the Doctor didn't arrange this in advance?]

There seems to be a cupboard close to the interior door, as Ace is rooting around for her rucksack and finds Mel's costume from "Paradise

Could It Be Magic?

This article is best thought of as matching **Is "Realism" Enough?** under 19.3, "Kinda", and **Is This Really an SF Series?** under 14.4, "The Face of Evil". In the former, we look at the method of presentation by writers and primarily directors, and the degree to which the director takes as read the viewers' "unthinking" assumptions about the meaning of what's happening on screen. (We're talking about things like line-of-sight, as well as the more overt conventions such as Voice-Over or Flashback.) We noted that overt Symbolism can be taken literally or "read" as symbolic. Rarely, but in the case of *Doctor Who* more commonly than in a cop show or soap, you can have both at once. Aliens and robots are icons of "otherness" and remorselessness.

In the latter essay, we're more concerned with how readers read and viewers view, the interpretations and "second-guessing" instead of content. Now, as you might expect, this description of SF isn't what people selling books and movies think is what's important. We wound up with a view of SF as the extreme end of a tendency inherent in anything where a bit of work is needed by the reader to "make" the world in the story work. The "theory-making" about how what is presented to us can fit together as a coherent world is what's important, not the things presented per se. Robots and aliens are just helpful hints.

Precisely where an individual reader / viewer (we're trying to avoid simply plumping for one or the other, and words like "consumer" flatly contradict what we're saying here: the person watching or reading is an active participant) chooses to place any given story is a matter of preference. There are obvious guides, like what the cover-designer has been told to put on the front or the habits formed watching or reading others in the series. But we aren't looking for cut-off points or clearly-defined boundaries.

Consider the following. In Gabriel Garcia Marquez's novel *One Hundred Years of Solitude*, a young girl is so pure that she ascends to Heaven as a cloud of yellow butterflies. In a recent commercial for shampoo, something very similar happens. Obviously, in the advert, it's a symbol. But in the novel it's presented as really happening, and the consequences of this run on for about forty pages. For the author it clearly meant something, possibly many things, and the book is filled with other such events (see 19.1, "Castrovalva"). Virginia Woolf's *To the Lighthouse*, DH Lawrence's *Sons and Lovers* and any number of mid-century classics have items in them which represent complex ideas. (What exactly does throwing stones at the moon's reflection in a puddle signify? Everyone's got an answer.) These, however, are things you might really do or see.

Since Freud, we're all used to trying to interpret dreams. Authors do it: they have ideas of what to put where in a story, and then write the book largely to find out what it means. However, the dime-store Freud in films like Hitchcock's *Spellbound* has it that once you "decode" it, all the problems are magically solved. The books discussed just now don't have "answers" like this. Instead, the books and films with the most alluring symbols linger in the memory. But ordinary audiences who aren't comfortable with terms like "metalepsis" or "Magic Realism" tend to prefer those where the symbols are "managed". Not "explained", not labelled "this is a symbol", but placed in a context where they don't cross whatever metaphorical line the reader or viewer has beyond which a story becomes stupid. Writers might not see it the same way, but if it reaches print or the screen, the chances are that at least one other person finds it interesting enough to avoid this involuntary flinching at sudden shifts in tone or mode.

The paradox here is that in most works, the "irrational" tends to work in very logical ways, whereas things that just seemed like good ideas and have plot justification for being there - often the story is grown around them, like a pearl around grit - can't be simply explained as the author's fear of whatever, and do a lot more symbolic "work". Robots, for Karel Capek (the Czech writer who popularized the word) weren't just the Working Class or Golems or the Id, but at different times they did the job of one or more of these. Similarly, later critics have seen similarities between Isaac Asimov's "Three Laws of Robotics" and how black men in New York were advised to avoid making trouble in the 1940s, but Asimov's robots aren't just a Civil Rights metaphor (even if he took the hint later). So Daleks, to take a well-worn example, got more like the Nazis as they developed, and were nuclear-age fears made flesh and metal, but they are a lot more besides. And nobody, not Terry Nation, not David Whitaker, not even Ben Aaronovitch, knows exactly what - except that they agreed it was not any one thing at one time.

Read Bram Stoker's novel *Dracula*. It's told in let-

continued on page 279...

Towers" (24.2) and the Fourth Doctor's scarf from before Season Eighteen. The console room has a loose panel in its ceiling, and the Doctor lodges a ball up there while juggling.

He also suspends a spring-loaded book-holder from the ceiling.

The Non-Humans

• *The Gods of* [all together now] *Rrrrrrangarrrok*. They're time-shifting super-beings who seek diversions, entertainment and surprises from the lesser races. [Yes, just like just like the Eternals in "Enlightenment".] Within the context of the Psychic Circus, the Gods manifest as a 1950s nuclear family - with a Father, Mother and Daughter - eating crisps and holding up scorecards like those for *Come Dancing* or old ice-skating contests. In their true realm they look like stone, and they're essentially statues that move and have heads like Grecian helmets. Their eyes are like the "eye" symbols used for surveillance around Segonax - this symbol appears on the Circus' kites, at the Gods' Well and on Kingpin's medallion. [The eyes also, it should be noted, look suspiciously like the Eye of Horus ("Pyramids of Mars") - and see **Are All These Gods Related?** under 26.3, "The Curse of Fenric".] They have stentorian voices, can fire thunderbolts from their fingers and make it rain when the mood strikes.

Kingpin's medallion proves impervious to the Gods' powerbolts, but they can sense its presence. [Pause to say that the medallion's origins and connection to the Gods are never stated, and it might've been forged in the mines of Moria for all we're told.] Another oddity is that the Gods can resurrect the dead. [At least, that seems the implication of Captain Cook's revival. Kingpin remarks that the Gods can 'sense' the medallion, then there's a power-discharge between Father and Daughter Ragnarok, and then the Captain's corpse gets up to retrieve the medallion for them.] The newly-walking Captain maintains his personality, but the Gods' final onslaught seems to draw power from his walking cadaver, and eventually he just offers an observation on being dead, collapses and plunges into the Well.

Two entrances exist to the Gods' realm. The Doctor tells them to 'open a pathway' for him, and he then struggles through the doorway to the Psychic Circus showring - pushing his way through a bundle of stringy lights and psychedelic colours - until he enters the Gods' proper arena,

what Kingpin calls the 'Dark Circus'. [The implication is that the Psychic Circus and the Dark Circus occupy the same location, but in different realities or possibly even different timezones - see **History**.] There is also the Well, a rocky chasm with a glowing vortex and the Gods' "Eye" shown dead-centre in it. When Kingpin's medallion is flung into the Well, it appears in the Dark Circus - precisely as the Doctor planned.

• *Vulpanas*. Captain Cook's companion Mags hails from Vulpana, a world where - at the risk of over-simplifying - the inhabitants are akin to werewolves. They undergo physical changes when exposed to particular frequencies of light - in the blue end of the spectrum, it seems [see 13.2, "Planet of Evil" and X2.2, "Tooth and Claw"]. Casting this light into a quarter-moon shape only seems to enhance the effect. When this happens, Mags' nails become talons, her teeth grow large and vicious, and she loses self-control - attempting to kill anyone in her path. The Captain says Mags' people are vulnerable to silver bullets [see 26.1, "Battlefield"].

Planet Notes

• *Segonax*. The planet that presently hosts the Psychic Circus is mainly wasteland, and a larger, ringed planet is seen nearby. Access to Segonax is by 'portable landing bays' (i.e. small teleport terminals) in the desert, rather than by rocket [maybe the ringed planet makes navigation tricky]. Local transport is variously by horse or mid-twentieth-century-style motor vehicles. To judge by the Stallslady - the only native we meet - the inhabitants of Segonax are humanoid.

Monopods from the planet Lelex [presumably nearby] travel have visited the Circus. Vulpana is presumably also close, as the Plaup fruit - according to one of the Stallslady's signs - is grown there. The Stallslady claims that the locals are reluctantly accustomed to the visits from 'infernal extraterrestrials', and resent the Circus being on their patch.

The Whizzkid says he's travelled 'halfway across the Southern Nebula' to reach Segonax, and it appears the Psychic Circus' previous ports of call [see **History**] are in an arc between his world and Segonax. [At least, this is one way to account for the discrepancies between the apparent time the Circus has been stuck on Segonax and the experience of the main performers. From what the Captain says, the Southern Nebula is a big and

Could It Be Magic?

...continued from page 277

ters and diaries (what is termed the "epistolary" form). First Harker has an experience he doesn't immediately believe. Then he has to persuade his fiancée. Then she finds evidence to support her growing conviction. Then Van Helsing pops up and provides answers, such as they are. But consider that Van Helsing's statements, had they come at the start of the book, would have been preposterous. An unsympathetic, critical reading might be that Mina Harker is obsessed with this exotic foreigner and can't bring herself to admit to desire; the "scrapbook" elements of the book we have include pasted-in news accounts of animals going berserk at London Zoo *as if* this is explained by the information in the previous passage that Dracula has arrived. Again, any earlier in the book and this would have been laughable. The "sales pitch" is Stoker's means of managing the symbolism. But who remembers the way the book's written? We're willing to bet that for those of you who've actually read it, this detail escaped you. What people remember is the way these extraordinary moments and images are "like something out of a dream" but presented as really happening, with consequences.

We need to be clear on this. It is possible, as we've hinted, to read *Dracula* as SF. After all, we have Van Helsing providing "explanations" for the symbolic material, and we're given the symptoms first and then a proposed "cause". Nobody really does read it that way. Of course not. So why should the equally spurious explanations given in the average *Doctor Who* romp make it "unmistakably" SF?

We're not saying it does. We're saying that, by-and-large, the fantasy approach is subordinate to the needs of capital-R Realism. Whenever an obviously symbolic story like "Kinda" happens, the next story is presented as unequivocally "real" and yet after-effects of "Kinda" are spoken about as though they had "really" happened. Many woeful books have been written by academics (mainly American) who were told to teach SF without having any enthusiasm for it, and *they* would say that this is the cut-off point: fantasy has closure, and exists in its own "realm" whereas SF overlaps into the everyday world, but on that world's terms. We don't think there is such a "tick-box", because any taxonomy which ignores readers / viewers at the expense of the "creator" is deadening.

So the only difference between SF and Magic Realism is that the former presupposes that the reasons for apparently symbolic things happening are - at least within the story-world - knowable. The latter, however, says it is unavailable to human comprehension. In SF there's a system in place of some kind, and even if the characters or the audience can't quite get a handle on it, someone (or generations of someones) could. All sorts of minor differences can derive from this fundamental distinction, but the majority of what's sold as Fantasy actually works on similar principles (at last as far as authors are concerned) as SF. It's not that there are no rules, just different ones (or cosmetically different ones, anyway). SF tends to be meritocratic, whereas Generic Fantasy - especially the Thud and Blunder / Swords 'n' Sorcery category - works on the principle of Divine Right (i.e. someone born to be king will be, even if raised as a goatherd). Fantasy of this kind is usually a family saga played out on an exaggerated scale. (So all those smart-alec websites pointing out the similarities between *Star Wars* and *Harry Potter* are really stating the obvious. Both could be classified as "mechanically-recovered mythological tropes".)

On the other hand, in SF the person who figures it all out wins. It's about careful observation and testing of theories, however many laser-guns and hydroponic plants there are. "The Truth is Out There", whereas in Magic Realism and some fantasy it is only available to the Chosen - usually as divine revelation or the author arranging for the Chosen to "just know" - rather than to anyone who dares to find it. We're back to doubting the existence of Systems, and that way lies Postmodernism (see **Is Continuity a Pointless Waste of Time?** under 22.1, "Attack of the Cybermen").

And guess what? The quest to find the Answer, whatever it is, usually provides it as part of the journey. This is as true of religious parables (like the Sufi classic *The Parliament of Birds*) as of SF or Sword 'n' Sorcery. This has made a lot of writers very rich, and there has been a long and dishonourable tradition of taking things that used to be symbols (up to and including the Holy Grail) and using them as plot-maguffins for very dull Epics. Within professional SF circles this is called "Plot-Coupon" plotting ("collect the set"), and each item on the Hero's shopping-list corresponds exactly to a challenge that comes about sixty pages later. Yet this is in turn not unlike the "classic" of German

continued on page 281...

complex place, so only a dedicated "stalker" such as the Whizzkid would be able to follow the circus. The ticket-vendor Morgana says they went 'from planet to planet', but this is in reply to the Doctor's comment that, 'You have got around, haven't you?']

• *Cook's Tour*. Captain Cook, *the* intergalactic space-explorer (or so says the Whizzkid), tells a number of anecdotes about his explorations or the Nebula. His encounters are as follows:

- *Anagonia*. Home of the Singing Squids.

- *Boromea*. Can claim bouncing Upas trees.

- *Dioscuros*. Has shrines, which apparently look similar to abandoned vehicles.

- *Fagiros*. Where the Architrave of Batgeld showed the Captain his collection of early Ganglion Pottery.

- *Golobus*. Boasts a Bay of Paranoia.

- *Grolon*. Has Baleful Plains.

- *Iphitus*. Has Galvanic Catastrophods (they're not what they were, though).

- *Katakiki*. Gold mines are there.

- *Leophantos*. Has double-sided coins, and is occupied by Bug-Eyed Monsters [apparently very like the hermaphrodite hexapods of Alpha Centauri - see 9.2, "The Curse of Peladon"; 11.4, "The Monster of Peladon"; 12.1, "Robot"].

- *Melegophon*. Has a Groz Valley, where the tea is rather distinctive.

- *Muscolane*. Has sacred games.

- *Neogorgon*. Notable for a display of electronic dogs, buried in earth up to their necks, as some kind of defence system [some might say this is the only suitable fate for an electric dog].

- *Overod*. Has frozen pits, but these are for tourists.

- *Periboa*. Where the Captain met someone who was walking around after he was dead.

- *Treops*. Has so many odd sights, the Captain doesn't bother to name them.

- *Vulpana*. Where the Captain met Mags - see **The Non-Humans**.

History

• *Dating*. For the Segonax sequences, no clue whatsoever. For the Doctor's performance in the Gods' home dimension, no clue whatsoever. [The Doctor says that the Gods 'exist concurrently in two different time-spaces', and his final performance takes place within their 'true time-space'. All of this *could* mean that the Gods are actually situated thousands or millions of years in the past,

and are powerful enough to interact with Segonax in what's to them a future era. Alternatively - and perhaps more plausibly - their true domain could be a completely separate realm where the normal flow of time doesn't apply at all, similar to that of the Celestial Toymaker.]

The ticket-vendor / fortune teller Morgana implies that she was a founding member of the Psychic Circus, and that the group was formed so those involved could express their one special skill. Bellboy built the Circus' robot clowns [and he orders some of his robots to throttle him to death, so there's no standard-included inhibitor switch, as with 14.5, "The Robots of Death"], as well as a robot bus conductor with laser eyes (along with a "Destroy Robot Now" button on his head), and a blockish robot with even *more* powerful laser eyes.

Bellboy says that the Circus performers were very familial and happy, and would talk through their problems. It appears that the touring Circus previously performed on Othrys, thence Marpesia, Eudamus, the Boreatic Wastes and the Grand Pagoda of Cinethon. Whizzkid says that 'most of [the Circus'] admirers' regard their Boreatic Wastes tour as one of their finest gigs, although this opinion seems to be inferred from the poster advertising the event. [The Boreatic Wastes poster isn't very revealing and just shows some trapeze artists. Whizzkid is probably basing his assessment on what older fans tell him - we've seen that sort of thing in real-life, actually.] Captain Cook is renowned in this era as a famous intergalactic space explorer, and Whizzkid has collected maps of all his journeys, as well as a piece of one of his shoes.

The 'memorial stones' seen in the Psychic Circus ring and the Dark Circus - as well as those that ring the entrance to Well - seem to pre-date the Circus' arrival on Segonax. Mags suspects they've 'always' been there. [The obvious inference is that the Gods already had their hooks into this location, and then the Circus showed up and got corrupted to do the Gods' bidding.] It was Kingpin who persuaded his fellow performers to travel to Segonax [the Doctor implies the Gods 'lured' him there, possibly by mental suggestion], and he - innocently, it seems - used his "Eye" medallion [quite how this powerful object came into Kingpin's possession isn't said] to summon the powers lurking in the Well. The Gods of Ragnarok subsequently dominated the Circus,

Could It Be Magic?

...continued from page 279

folklore, and theorist Vladimir Propp wrote a big book, *The Morphology of the Folk-Tale*, attempting to turn this formula into an equation using Symbolic Logic (see **The Semiotic Thickness of What**? under 24.4, "Dragonfire"). So David Eddings churned out exactly the kind of Heroic Fantasy you'd expect the Cybermen to write, and everyone thought that reading Joseph Campbell's *Hero With A Thousand Faces* was the way to make a corny story mythic.

This doesn't work in *Doctor Who*. If an individual story tries to do this, with another story beginning immediately afterwards, it can either work if the Hero is someone other than the Doctor - someone who accepts the Doctor's help in undergoing a transformation, and passing on this spiritual growth as a societal benefit - or it can have the Doctor learn an important and valuable lesson and die in the process. (That one happens if and only if there's an older, wiser Time Lord around and some handy mad psychic spiders, as in 11.5, "Planet of the Spiders".)

In general, attempts to show the Doctor learning something last for the duration of that story, and then we press the reset button (20.2, "Snakedance"). In the 1980s, when this diet-Jung approach to telefantasy was all-pervading, the companions underwent spiritual refinement via non-realistic plot development (notable near-misses in this were 20.5, "Enlightenment" for Turlough - completed by his reunion with his society and sibling in 21.5, "Planet of Fire" - and the whole Fenric subplot for Ace in the McCoy era). But in general, attempting to have fantasy elements inside a story are subverted or rendered pointless by the story that follows being either rigidly realist or somehow "containing" the fantasy inside more orthodox SF. They can flirt with having things that can't be explained - up to and including the Devil and a black hole with a tradesman's entrance (X2.8, "The Impossible Planet" / X2.9, "The Satan Pit") - but it turns out to have a solution as logical as *Diagnosis Murder* or *Miss Marple*. Every time.

If someone in *Doctor Who* were to turn into a cloud of butterflies, there might be a fig-leaf of technobabble ('Block Transfer Computation' or some other gibberish). Or, they might trust the viewer to either assume that there is one that we're not being told ("I'll explain later") or *maybe* there isn't one. The series' general tenor has been

that everything can be found out, somehow, eventually. "Revealed" truth doesn't tend to work here. The thread that binds all these disparate stories is the character of the Doctor, and he's first and foremost an empiricist. The general assumption among viewers has been that there could be such a fig-leaf if required. In the Garcia Marquez book, as with almost all Magic Realism, the fig-leaf is the residue of Catholicism (or Islam if it's Salman Rushdie), where God micro-manages everything (and we could get really deep into this line of investigation), and where things like family curses are real and transubstantiation goes on regularly. In mainstream SF, there's a similar habit of the empirical, "rational" thought-process. They aren't necessarily mutually exclusive.

Both of these, and many others, are sub-sets (if you want to think of them as overlapping loops) or shadings (if you want to think of them as colours or flavours) of a process that's become known as "fabulism". In the 70s, there was a move to rebrand SF as "Structural Fabulism" (another reason why the contraction "Sci-Fi" is insulting to the professionals), but that would also have to include *Lord of the Rings* and *Dracula*. All take overt symbols and treat them "as though" real. What matters is the effort made to "excuse" symbolism whilst retaining the reasons for its use, and this is really the difference between "hack" fantasy and the genuinely-felt work. The hacks take other people's symbols and shove them around for the sake of it (see 19.6, "Earthshock", for a ripe example). For Bram Stoker, Count Dracula represented fear of foreign manipulators, syphilis, the irrational and probably a dozen other things. For Francis Coppola he represented lust, mesmerism, the cinema itself and a clumsy AIDS metaphor (and lots else). For the board of Hammer Films, he represented bums on seats.

But for Terrance Dicks, the Great Vampire in "State of Decay" (18.4) was ignorance and feudalism incarnate. This icon of the dark tower dwarfing a village, and the slumbering parasite beneath it, were opposed by all the things Dicks' work on *Doctor Who* had been about. Whilst much of the iconography was derived from earlier vampire movies, the other central image of the trashed "truth-telling" machinery and rebels on the border keeping the old ways alive is a classic of 1940s SF. Let's face it, the idea of the Doctor's old mentor - the old man in the hills who remembers how

continued on page 283...

and turned it into a killing-trap for their amusement. Audience members would be encouraged / forced to perform, then judged and eradicated as if by lightning upon receiving a score of 0-0-0.

The "eyeball" was separated from Kingpin's medallion - and this caused his mind to fracture (as he puts it, 'when the mind's divided, the body screams') - and hidden in the Circus' derelict bus. He was re-named Deadbeat and became the Circus' janitor, but affixing the eyeball to the medallion restores his mind. It would appear that a number of the Circus' more benevolent members (Peace Pipe, Juniper Berry, etc) were purged by the Gods, but the more malevolent among them (the Chief Clown, the Ringmaster, etc) carried out the Gods' wishes. Ultimately, Kingpin is the only surviving Circus member, and he shows a desire - along with Mags, reluctantly - to start up a new circus somewhere.

Junk mail is everywhere, according to the Doctor.

The Analysis

Where Does This Come From? It's plundered wholesale from Charles Finney's book *The Circus of Doctor Lao*. This told of how the people of a hick town in Arizona failed to appreciate true marvels in their midst, and were downright bemused by the recreation of the destruction of an ancient city. (Or was it a trip back in time to see it first hand? The book is nicely ambiguous on this and much else.) It's strongly hinted that the city was wiped from the surface of the Earth, in retribution for decadence and lack of reverence. There's a paragraph of downbeat comments about how the circus left, and that's it. Sound familiar? Oh, and there's a werewolf called Maggie Szlosny, to list just one obvious reference. Later, George Pal made a daft adaptation (*The Seven Faces of Doctor Lao*) as a vehicle for Tony Randall with *way* too much claymation - not to mention some half-baked symbolism that embarrassed adults and confused kids.

Stepping away from overt references for a tick, the more astute amongst you will have spotted a bit of a theme through this year's stories concerning repression and spontaneity. It's one of a number of binary oppositions being examined in this season. As is usually the case, such oppositions are generally weighted so that one term is deemed "better" than the other, if only because the Doctor

and Ace choose it over the alternative. Listening is better than pontificating; compassion is better than looking after Number One; being willing to change is better than sticking rigidly to an inappropriate self-image; love is better than money... If you asked anyone at the time to put it in a nutshell, they'd say it came down to the 1960s being better than the 1980s.

However, the stories in this batch aren't entirely sure about that. Notice how the hallmarks of repressive regimes include good manners and nice haircuts, and how retro the equipment used to punish dissent looks. See how 1963 in "Remembrance of the Daleks" (25.1) is full of bigots and people with limited horizons. Observe how the iconography of children's fiction and drug culture is turned into a police state in "The Happiness Patrol" (for best effect compare this with the phenomena described in **Did Sergeant Pepper Know the Doctor?** under 5.1, "The Tomb of the Cybermen"). Then in "The Greatest Show in the Galaxy", writer Stephen Wyatt finally comes out and says it - the hippies had a chance to change things, and they blew it. The worst excesses of 80s selfishness and exploitation were committed by ex-flowerchildren. The generation who went on about love were the people who made porn into an industry. Having fought The System, they were better placed to reinforce it. Richard Branson, Steve Jobs, John Birt, George Lucas and many other evil creatures began as idealistic rebels. Or so they said - many of the most cynical opportunists made the right noises in the 60s and took advantage of people who trusted them. So the calamity of the movement was twofold: it created a whole new breed of megalomaniacs, who knew in advance how the people against them would react, and the majority of those who could have stopped them were too innocent, inert or zonked-out to do anything about it.

Mentioning John Birt brings us back to another strand of the allegory: the BBC itself. Although we are a few years away from Birt getting to be Director General - and inflicting financial procedures on programme-makers that almost crippled the Corporation creatively - his influence is being felt already. If Michael Checkland's term of office was primarily about not upsetting the Government, Birt's moves to run the BBC like a factory - with mindless jargon and targets and obscure management techniques - led to it being more ratings-hungry than ever. Audience-share

Could It Be Magic?

...continued from page 281

things ought to be - is less like the K'Anpo we see and hear about in the Pertwee stories (9.5, "The Time Monster" and again in "Planet of the Spiders") than it is like the traditional Ol'-timer in Robert Heinlein's "juvenile" novels. But the use to which he put this iconography was both symbolic and "realistically" motivated. That's why they're "icons", in both the religious and software senses; images that do a job. The majority of the better *Doctor Who* writers are adept at taking the left-over, "dead" symbols of earlier writers and making them live through their new meanings. The strength of the symbols is what makes it fantasy, the consequences of their apparently literal existence is the SF interpretation. There is no contradiction, unless you are phobic about symbolism. (See **Did *Doctor Who Magazine* Change Everything?** under 18.2, "Meglos" for a definition of "Fanboy", and also 18.7, Logopolis".)

So, to return to "The Greatest Show in the Galaxy"... is that medallion-thingy a Plot Coupon or a genuine Symbol, or both or neither? The Doctor acts as though there were a cohesive logic behind how things work in this domain, but nevertheless he addresses his antagonists as 'Gods'. The completion of the "Eye" activates this bit of metal so that it can reflect the Gods' power back at them, but we're unclear how or how the time-scales of the two zones connect; why is the Doctor looking at his watch, if it's possible that he's thousands of years behind Kingpin? With the Doctor playing at being Moses (turning something into a snake), we're allowed to read the visuals as Fantasy, or indeed Magic Realism, but the dialogue acts like it's SF that got garbled. It only matters if the events in that story had ever been referred to again afterwards (see the essays accompanying "Attack of the Cybermen" and 5.5, "The Web of Fear" for why). For the duration of the story, the distinction really isn't important.

and cost-effectiveness were his concerns when running programming, and even Michael Grade was scared of his remorseless drive for efficiency over the need to make memorable and sellable television. The Ringmaster even uses the words "leaner and fitter", that you'd hear from manager after manager of ailing industries. These were words you would hear from Birt, Checkland and Marmaduke Hussey, the Chairman of the Board of Governors (whose connections with the Government were a little too close for many programme-makers) about the BBC. As we will see (in **What About Season 27?** under 26.4, "Survival"), the whole way programmes were made and commissioned within the Corporation was about to change to suit then-current dogma, and *Doctor Who* was being spoken of as a prime candidate for this experiment.

But outside all of that is a set of images that come from 60s culture, by way of pop videos. We could list clowns who drive hearses or dress as undertakers all day. (So we'll content ourselves with just a quick mention for *Yellow Submarine* and *The Avengers* episode shown on the ideal date - April Fool's Day 1967 - "Epic"; then a cursory mention of Madness' video for "It Must Be Love".) Ken Kesey's Merry Pranksters are obviously a touchstone for the bus. And just in passing... Channel 4 had been filling the afternoon schedules with cheap re-runs and imports, so we'd finally seen *The Gong Show* around the time this was being written.

Things That Don't Make Sense We've covered the ending, although there's a good case for this to need saying on screen. You might have your own theories, but let's press on.

Because there's an overarching problem that we haven't addressed: namely that the Gods of Ragnarok crave entertainment above all else, but they've got a very funny notion of how to obtain it. Piece together events prior to the Doctor and Ace's arrival, and it appears that the Gods killed off some of the benevolent hippies - i.e. people with actual Circus skills (presuming for the moment that performers named things like 'Peace Pipe' and 'Juniper Berry' *had* any useful skills) - in favour of an endless string of members of the public, who are guaranteed to be considerably less entertaining. [Even if Stephen Wyatt was clairvoyantly - and about fifteen years too early - doing a satire on TV companies axing things involving writers to pay for the likes of *Big Brother*, this seems an amazingly dim thing for *soi-disant* "gods" to do. Now that we've said this, try watching *X Factor* or the US equivalent - *American Idol* is the one we know best here - without thinking of Simon Cowell or whoever dressed in 1950s cardigans.]

Moreover, it seems that the audience-members

are *set up* to look foolish, fail miserably and die horribly. Nord scores 9-9-9 for his feat of strength, and then is asked to tell a joke - even though you can tell at a glance that he's spectacularly unsuited for it. The Whizzkid is allowed to just say "hello" and stand there flaccidly until he's zapped. Presuming the Ringmaster isn't a complete nitwit, why does he does he allow such unprepared people into the ring, and why does he seem to deliberately sabotage them? Does he place no value on his own life? Does he lack even the ounce of showbiz nous required to see that even Nord and Whizzkid together would make a better comedy act than either alone? Or maybe he *is* doing his job well until the very end, but that would mean...

We're back at the vexing question of what the hell the Gods want exactly. They *seem* to feed off entertainment, and this is just about plausible - especially if we define "entertainment" as the presentation of things less probable than expected, meaning it's a form of anti-entropy [and that's usually what beings like this are about in *Doctor Who*]. Spinning plates or pulling rabbits out of hats is in defiance of Boltzmann's equations and all the stuff about signal-to-noise ratios that was fashionable in the seventies. Got all that? But in practice the notion doesn't hold up, because anyone who ventures into the Circus ring is killed - which makes them the most probable state of all. So we might instead theorize that the Gods feed on the power of someone dying - but if that's the case, why piddle about with this whole Circus business, when they could just get tickets for a decent-sized war? [Actually, let's not rule this out. The name "Ragnarok" suggests big battles - actually the biggest - as we'll see in "The Curse of Fenric". If the Doctor's been fighting beings who *feed* on war, it would make sense that he's encountered them a lot. But while the idea that the Gods of Ragnarok feast upon circus-related fatalities is an enticing one, it also seems to contradict the generalisations the Doctor makes about them as a race. Arrrrrggggghhh...]

One last desperate gasp at an explanation: what if the Gods feed on the anxiety of the performers waiting to be judged? It's a *psychic* circus, after all. But no, that would make sense if they were creating less finicky circumstances to gain people's worry, and preying on *that*. [Again, reality TV springs to mind, and shows like *The Apprentice*.] The executions are too quick to be nourishing. We've now come full circle, and we can only conclude that the Gods feed on "entertainment". They say so. But unless the deaths that occurred off screen are more entertaining than the ones we *do* see, it looks like the Gods have gone on a diet.

Side Issue No. 1: even accounting for the slain performers, there are nowhere near enough people involved for this Circus to have taken in enough money to run a bus, let alone drive it between planets. If the bus contained all of their kit, including the tents and juggling pins, they can't have had many acts. Perhaps they had a convoy of busses and we only see the one, but that would suppose that the Gods ran through most of the Circus-members like a hot knife through butter, so perhaps they weren't much cop as performers after all. In which case, we'd have to ask why the Circus has any reputation at all, much less one substantial enough for their geeky stalker.

Side Issue No. 2: all right, so some of the "good" Circus members seem to have removed the eyeball from Kingpin's medallion, and hidden it in the bus. We know that the Gods can sense the medallion's power, so perhaps this was done to keep it some distance from the Circus until required. Fine, except that the "bad" Circus members must have programmed the robot bus conductor to kill anyone who comes there. Quite how they accomplished this without help from Bellboy (who doesn't know the conductor has gone evil, or he'd surely have warned Flowerchild about it) is unclear, as is why they would bother when they don't seem to know the eyeball is there. Cumulatively, the robot conductor seems like a confused piece of work, as he's supposedly working for the baddies and murders Flowerchild, then dutifully re-hides the eyeball so the goodies can later retrieve it.

Random concerns, now: the Doctor and Mags incapacitate two *robot* clowns by thumping them a little with juggling clubs. Exactly how does the Stallslady make a living, as she seems to be selling fruit in the middle of nowhere? Why does the Psychic Circus - to judge by the ad boards around the circus ring - use the initials 'PS' instead of "PC"? How exactly is Bellboy punished in the ring at the end of episode one, and how does the Ringmaster's controller mute Mags' screams? And one last note about the ending: it's not that the Gods rain powerbolts upon the medallion-holding Doctor that's the problem, it's that they continue for *so long* after witnessing how the medallion bounces their bolts back at them. Even allowing that the Gods aren't terribly flexible in their thinking, it's a little weird that they don't go "Bugger!" and stop firing.

Oh all right, and there's all the continuity cockups. Ace spends ages looking for a rucksack that we saw her blow up a fortnight earlier [25.3, "Silver Nemesis"], and she picks up and starts wearing an earring she's had on her jacket since they arrived on Terra Alpha ["The Happiness Patrol"]. The errors owe to their changing the running-order of these stories to fit in the Seoul Olympics and the series' silver anniversary, as you'll know if you've been keeping up with **The Lore**.

Critique So here we are in a locale that looks like both a Victorian Circus (the kind you always wanted to run away to, when you were a kid) and an alien planet, with a ringed gas-giant on the horizon behind the big top. And a clapped out alien motorbike is driving towards it. Moments like this are why *Doctor Who* existed. Around that moment is a story with so much going *right,* we hardly dare mention it all for fear of running out of space before we get to Season Twenty-Six. So let's start with what's wrong with it, because that's easier.... The end is garbled. A show in ratings free-fall probably shouldn't ridicule its core audience. The patronising assumption that all black men are great dancers and prone to start rapping at any moment is just made worse by having sinister aliens who disguise themselves as 1950s whitebread; it looks like the production team didn't realise how offensive the Ringmaster would end up being. Mags' werewolf make-up is appallingly inept.

And the moral is... well, the worst thing about Cartmel's right-on moralising is that he's forgotten the basic rule: show, don't tell. Wyatt probably intended the story to illustrate the point without it getting relegated to dialogue from the Captain, and should really have found ways to make the pompous old bully less endearing. Part of the problem is that TP McKenna is just too good in the part. A lot of us were hoping he'd be back for a rematch, like Glitz. The Captain was intended to be a mouthpiece for a nostrum that the writer and editor found odious, but we don't see him suffer as a direct consequence of his beliefs. Instead, Mags kills him because because she has to kill *someone,* and it isn't going to be the Doctor. Then the Captain is reanimated, apparently because he's

the nearest dead body to Ace and Kingpin. So the idea that "survival of the fittest" and "looking after number one" are Bad Things is demonstrated by the Ringmaster and the Chief Clown. Err... except that *they* go along with the majority decision, and the ones who follow self-interest are Bellboy and Kingpin. You see the problem. There's a major discrepancy between what we're told by bad people and what actually causes their undoing in the plot. Another slight rewrite could have clarified this, and linked it to whatever the Doctor did to defeat the Gods. Instead, the bad characters are bad because they're bad, and it just so happens they talk like the government occasionally.

So that's what's wrong with it. On the other hand, what we're seeing in the programme's final phase is a production team and eager young writers revelling in the sheer joy of making *Doctor Who.* This is a series prepared to take risks and just play with the show's potential. They have inherited the single greatest television series in the history of the world, and nobody cares what they do with it. They've got a technical crew who can now make almost anything happen, and do so with no wobbly sets, cardboard spaceships or tinfoil monsters. Better still, they've got an audience who expect wobbly sets, cardboard spaceships and tinfoil monsters, and might very well be impressed by anything better than that.

The end result is something so far beyond what we could have imagined even a year earlier, we hoped that people who we knew who'd scoffed in the past were watching. You might have wanted to accost strangers in the street and make them watch it, yelling *this is what it can be like!* But if you did, the strangers would probably point out that the end doesn't make sense, the rappin' Ringmaster is borderline racist and the werewolf make-up is lamentable. They wouldn't appreciate how much better this is than earlier stories, except in a grudging way. It looks like *Doctor Who* ought to have looked in 1988, and the fact that the series has undergone such an abrupt upsurge in quality so quickly only matters to the few people who sat through it all over the previous five years.

This is a criminal shame, because this is a show being made by people to whom it matters, intensely. The polemic about entertainment being just a job to some people and life-or-death to others seems to have struck a chord with the cast and crew, who - as **The Lore** will demonstrate - put themselves through hell to get this to our screens. Ranged against the corporate whores are a quixotic bunch of misfits. It is surely no coincidence that in this story, the bad guys are turning imagination into a commodity, and it's one of the most oozingly psychedelic things to have hit our screens in ages. It also came just at a point when this attitude and style was again causing the Suits a few sleepless nights (hurrah!). The applicability of the story's premise to BBC policy-changes is obvious, but it is far wider than that. The whole of British culture was due for a big change, and got it.

As when the series championed improvisation and spontaneity against procedure and method - and was made by a team frantically writing the episodes on the hoof and using odds and ends to make the monsters and spaceships - for this story to have been made with anything less than total commitment and love is inconceivable. It would have been obvious to anyone watching. Anyone who denies that Bellboy's death is one of the great moments in the programme's history is lying. Everything around that death - the lighting, the robot design, Ian Reddington's wave and even Aldred's performance wishing him well, knowing full well what's going to happen - is astonishing. This is about what real grief does in a world used to synthetic pleasure. As we said, Bellboy and Kingpin took risks and got damaged, but the alternative is playing safe and that's even more fatal. *Doctor Who* is through with playing safe.

Over the next few pages you're going to read all about the pure hell of making this story. It was worth it. This is everything *Doctor Who* should be. There are real people suffering from or acquiescing to something bizarre, and there are images you'll never see anywhere else - and in combinations that only *this* series can now provide.

The Facts

Written by Stephen Wyatt. Directed by Alan Wareing. Ratings: 5.0 million, 5.3 million, 4.8 million, 6.6 million. (The latter is not just the highest ratings achieved in McCoy's three years, but the highest ratings since 22.6, "Revelation of the Daleks".) Audience appreciation ranged between 66% and 69% for the first three episodes, and slumped to 64% for episode four (when there were more, shall we say, "Not-We" watching).

Working Titles None. (Nathan-Turner suggested the title and asked Wyatt to do something with it.)

Supporting Cast T.P. McKenna (Captain Cook), Ian Reddington (Chief Clown), Ricco Ross (Ringmaster), Jessica Martin (Mags), Chris Jury (Deadbeat / Kingpin), Christopher Guard (Bellboy), Deborah Manship (Morgana), Gian Sammarco (Whizzkid), Daniel Peacock (Nord), Dee Sadler (Flowerchild), Peggy Mount (Stallslady), Dean Hollingsworth (Bus Conductor), David Ashford (Dad), Janet Hargreaves (Mum), Kathryn Ludlow (Little Girl).

Oh, Isn't That..?

• *TP McKenna*. He's been in everything. You might know him as the man with his arm in a sling in *Straw Dogs*, as the double agent Richmond from the final episodes of *Callan*, as a couple of *Avengers* villains, or even for an early *Blake's 7* episode ("Bounty") with the same car used in 20.3, "Mawdryn Undead". He spent time after this story in *Ballykissangel* and the radio comedy *Ballylennon*, as well as all the usual staples of 90s TV drama.

• *Peggy Mount*. It's such an obvious casting, it's amazing that the Stallslady wasn't written with her in mind. She was in early 60s sitcom *George and the Dragon* with Sid James (hint: she didn't play George). Basically, anyone else playing this part would be asked to "play it like Peggy Mount", as she'd cornered the market over the last thirty years.

• *Gian Sammarco*. He was the protagonist of *The Secret Diary of Adrian Mole*, based on a single woman's idea of what teenage boys are like. Like the books, the TV series was set in Leicester, but none of the cast knew what the accent sounded like. Sammarco, from Northampton, came closest. He later did some ads for student bank accounts, playing almost the same character again as he did in *Mole,* or as the Whizzkid. Thus an East Midlands accent became aural shorthand for trainspotters and the like (again, see **What's All This Stuff About Anoraks?**).

• *Daniel Peacock*. He was in the regular cast for *The Comic Strip Presents* (and was thus the toyboy of "Uncle Quentin" in "Five Go Mad In Dorset" - see 7.3, "The Ambassadors of Death" and 6.1, "The Dominators" for why Ronald Allen doing this was funny). More recently, he wrote and occasionally directed dad-friendly kid's show *Cave-Girl* and the curiously-titled *Billie: Girl of the Future*. (One episode of this has a strange girl called Susan starting at her school - is this deliberately to mess with our heads?) He's also had gigs on *Harry and Cosh* and his own creation, *Diary of a Teenage Health Freak*. He wrote a none-too-successful film, *Party Party*, which has a cast you couldn't afford today.

• *Jessica Martin.* She was an impressionist and singer, who specialised in a nasty impersonation of Bonnie Langford. So when she took over Bonnie's role in *Me and My Girl,* we think there may have been some contrition. Martin crops up in Derek Jarman's film *The Garden*, singing "Think Pink" - this may have made sense to someone involved.

• *Chris Jury.* Curiously, he'd auditioned to play the Seventh Doctor, and had been in *Lovejoy*, as Eric Catchpole. That series was given a second chance soon after this, and became a major hit (which is why folks in these parts can't take Ian McShane seriously in *Deadwood*).

• *Ricco Ross.* He did this soon after playing Private Frost in *Aliens*, and before returning to the US, where he pops up as cops or soldiers. He also did a *Babylon 5* along the way.

• *Ian Reddington.* Went on to be one of the more memorable "bastard" characters to run the Queen Vic in *EastEnders*: Richard Cole, AKA "Tricky Dicky". He's currently a regular in *Coronation Street*.

Cliffhangers Everything gets psychedelic inside the Big Top, and the Ringmaster silences Mags' scream with a remote-control device, even as the Doctor asks Ace if they're going inside; the Doctor and Mags find themselves cornered, and Captain Cook announces that the Doctor is the next one due on in the ring; Mags turns into a werewolf and menaces the Doctor (scoring three 9's from the judges in the process).

The Lore

• So let's talk about the Squonk. Wyatt was asked to submit a second story before the first had been committed to tape. Jonathan Powell, on reading the script for Wyatt's "Paradise Towers", asked Cartmel for more along those lines. Nathan-Turner suggested the title, hoping to do something like the abortive "The Nightmare Fair" (see **What Would the *Other* Season 23 Have Been Like?** under 22.6, "Revelation of the Daleks"). Wyatt's first idea was that there were underground beings who came out at night to use the fairground. Then it became about computer games,

and that's where the Whizzkid came from. A collector of alien curios (said to be based on Howard Hughes) was interested in the circus-beneath-the-circus. Even by this stage, the idea of Mum, Dad and Daughter being both judges of a gladiatorial arena and powerful aliens in disguise was worked in.

Next version, the Doctor and Mel (that shows you how early this was) were in a Victorian circus with a black Ringmaster, a body-builder (proto-Nord) and a character called Non-Entity who amplified mental power: it was this that made the Doctor's anger destroy the circus. And there was a punk werewolf-girl, or Macvulpine. Another rewrite had hippies, with something in the ticket-tags that made people oblivious to the real circus (but Mel lost hers, and saw the truth). She adopted an alien pet called the Squonk. This version was more circus-like, but hi-tech (a laser tightrope for example) and Whizzkid began as a slimy rat / fish and became more humanoid as his obsessive nature grew stronger. Later, Squonk became a clown called Honk, who became Deadbeat (and a bit of him was used for Bellboy).

The collector was, after Aaronovitch's input, remodelled as a parody of Indiana Jones. Whizzkid was the galactic games champion, and it was he who died and was brought back (as a cyborg - half human, half scoreboard). The early Captain Cook was to have died unexpectedly in episode one, but Wyatt became fond of the old git, who he saw more as a Colonel Blimp figure. Segonax was like the English countryside circa 1967, with the Stallslady as a member of the townswomen's guild, running a tea-stall and sniffing haughtily at 'riff-raff' like Nord. This version was no longer the three-part studio-bound story of the year.

• Wyatt was working with Nathan-Turner on a project about fanaticism and monomania. This was the latest of many schemes the producer had tried to get a new project off the ground (see Volume V concerning "Impact" and 26.4, "Survival" for *WestEnders* - seriously). Inevitably, one kind of monomaniac sprang to mind. The ITV teletext service Oracle ran a report that the production office referred to fans who wrote in as "barkers" - so obviously, if erroneously, we got the idea that they didn't like us. Hence Whizzkid being regarded as an Anorak Fan parody.

• A final brush-up, and the script we know comes into shape. There's a week's holiday at the start of May, during which McCoy is with his kids (one of whom teaches him conjuring tricks) and Aldred cycles from London to Oxford for charidee. The rest of the team are working pretty much flat out, especially effects wizard Mike Tucker. His biggest task is to make a circus tent model to blow up and use in long-shots, so they don't have to cart a whole marquee to Warmwell. At this stage, McCoy decides that the conjuring stuff at the end could be extended, and the BBC gets in Geoffrey Durham, AKA, the Great Soprendo. His coaching sessions must, by Magic Circle rules, be conducted behind closed doors.

• So off they go to location in - crikey! - a quarry in Dorset. With them they took that coach that had been dropped onto a flowerbed in "Delta and the Bannermen" (24.3), the bits of a circus big-top they would actually need, and the phone number of some motorbike customisers in the area - hefty tattooed blokes called Bootsy and Ferret. The main chassis was from a Triumph with a 1200cc engine and extended front forks, which was welded to a four-wheel flatbed cart. As a five-wheel vehicle, UK law says it's no longer a motorbike, so they could get away without having regulation helmets on while driving. Thus McCoy and Aldred got free rides for the cameras, which in the stifling heat was a big relief. On the front, as you will have seen, are steer's horns.

The same team did the vehicles for "The Happiness Patrol". The motor was tuned perfectly, so the splutters and backfires had to be added later. They hired a hearse per day. The same day as all the motorbike and stuff is the one that ends with Ace eating the dreaded Plaup. Next morning, they finish with the Stallslady, whilst Nathan-Turner takes over second-unit directing for the kites and Flowerchild. (As he has more time to play with, they do three of four takes of her snog with Bellboy.)

• The last couple of days are spent killing Flowerchild and putting Deadbeat back together, i.e. all the bus stuff. The bits with the big buried robot are shot without the expected thunderstorm wrecking the location, and they get away with it all by Thursday night. Only one worry: Aldred has lost her *Blue Peter* badge, and the replacement is a different colour.

By Tuesday, back rehearsing in Acton, they hear that the Government Inspectors have dropped a bombshell. A routine refurbishment of the Rotunda was due to go ahead, and they'd planned it to avoid disruption. Then the Health and Safety

boys, called in as a formality, noticed a problem. Built in 1959, BBC Television Centre has asbestos in every ceiling. This was thought to be a good idea back then, but now it means six weeks of not making any programmes in the studios - or breathing in if you were anywhere near White City.

• Here's where the clever part comes in. Plan B was to go to Bristol, because they're not making *Casualty* at the moment. Someone else has the same idea and is on the phone slightly quicker than JN-T. Plan C, pitch a real tent in a field and do it all on OB. The BBC says no, because it's got to be done on BBC premises, because it's a remount and if they set a precedent for this, all sorts of productions will go to independent studios and put BBC technicians out of work. (Soon, however, there's going to be a complete about-turn on this policy, but John Birt's "Producer Choice" policy will not come into place for some time. See **What About Season 27?** under 26.4, "Survival".) So plan D, suggested by David Laskey (the set designer and creator of Plan C), was to pitch a tent in a BBC-owned facility, like the car-park at Elstree. Laskey's using the new EUCLID computer, so he can redesign the floor-plan in a day.

Sadly, it was not ideal. The production manager had a family crisis and was replaced by Gary Downie. His style of dragooning actors and technicians was new to many on the team, and Aldred in particular took a while to get used to it. A second manager, Ian Fraser, is called in to keep the people outside from revving up their cars during takes, and guiding delivery trucks to the canteen by a different route. The cast had been off for a week, so they took time to get back into the groove, which was not helped by the odd circumstances and the heat. It does give them one advantage: out of the gaze of Health and Safety busybodies, the scene of the Doctor swinging to safety when Mags goes feral can be done by Tipping and McCoy without the lighting manager having to give permission (which he wouldn't have).

The first block of recordings for the "Laskey Studio" is the longest in the programme's history, but - to his credit - it's only at the end that McCoy loses his temper. The PA announcement is dubbed later, but the floor manager had to read in the lines. She had an old script, which didn't match what the Doctor replies to it. All the Big Top material was finished by this stage. The next two days were line-learning and effects, then Captain Cook had to fall down a hole. TP McKenna volunteered and a long-term ankle injury was inflamed. A slight rewrite had the Captain discover Mags and the Doctor, rather than chase after them.

Next, the workshop and TARDIS scenes. Chris Jury finally got a chance to operate the console between takes (see "Time and the Rani"). The robot conductor was played by Dean Hollingsworth, who'd been the Android(s) in "Timelash". He was called back to inhabit the costume when it's in for repair. (He's also the robot junk-mail and the voice-over for the ad.)

It's in the TARDIS scene that Aldred and Downie go head-to-head. This was her last scene (she then had to go off and rehearse "Silver Nemesis", as that had been delayed a week). McCoy had another day, during which he had to escape from a straightjacket, turn an umbrella into a snake and perform the conjuring tricks. One slight problem with the way the story had been written was that Sylvester McCoy is the kind of person everyone assumed could juggle. He never had, hence the scenes of him learning from that book. (It's called *Juggling For the Complete Klutz*, by John Cassidy and BC Rimbeaux, and is very seventies Californian. We regret to note that even this was unable to remedy the innate cackhandedness of this book's author, who was given a copy a year earlier.)

• Under the circumstances, it's entirely understandable that the producer was doing everything short of handcuffing the Head of Drama to the radiators to get another project. Cartmel and Nathan-Turner were looking at some novels to adapt (some sources say Derek Tanguy was their choice). The structure of drama production at the BBC was changing fast, and *Doctor Who* was practically the only series still being made the way that had been standard before the Suspension of 1985. Nevertheless, when the rescheduled Olympic coverage meant that this story had to be swapped with "The Happiness Patrol" Nathan-Turner gave interviews proclaiming it to be the best note on which to leave.

• Nathan-Turner was especially pleased with Christopher Guard's performance as Bellboy. Guard himself was impressed, and suggested to his wife that she might like to have another crack at the show. She's Lesley Dunlop, and you may have just read about her performance in "The Happiness Patrol". One side-effect of the rearranged running-order was that the last line of

the story could have been reinstated. In the end, the Doctor quotes Morgana's line about hanging up her travelling shoes and claims that he never will. With this story supposedly leading into "Silver Nemesis", this was removed.

• Most of Mark Ayres' music was added later, but the background for the Ringmaster's rapping was played live in the tent, for obvious reasons. Ayres based it on *Bad Young Brother* by Derek B, but the scratch sound was a cheat, done by playing the tape back and forth. He'd been busy doing music for some of Keith Barnfather's video productions before this, so stepping up to real *Who* was a dream job. With Christopher Guard and Jessica Martin, Ayres also wrote a song called *The Psychic Circus* that he hoped BBC Records could release commercially to tie in with the broadcast. Given the surprise success of "Doctorin' the Tardis", this was probably a pub conversation that got out of hand, but if it had been done in the style of Siouxsie and the Banshees, they might have got away with it.

• The ratings for the final episode are as good as it gets for post-1985 *Doctor Who* (at least until "Dimensions in Time" comes along; see the Appendix). Once again, it might be because viewers were reminded it was still on. Due to the vagaries of the Christmas schedule, episode three was scheduled five minutes later than usual, so anyone channel-surfing after *Coronation Street* would have caught the tail end of the episode and cliffhanger, and been encouraged to tune in again the following week.

• To help us fill the now-aching nine-month void between the end of this story and "Battlefield", Mark Furness had finally got a *Doctor Who* play off the ground. As we've seen, this came after a number of false starts, including a Chicago-based production called "The Inheritors of Time" by comics scriptwriter John Ostrander (sometimes mooted as writing a Big Finish audio called "Dead Man's Hand", but nothing has surfaced to date) and Aaronovitch and Cartmel's "War World" (see "Remembrance of the Daleks"). The latter was intended to run across the winter of 1988/1989, with Sylvester McCoy playing the Doctor in between production on seasons. Furness rejected this version, and the need for a replacement script pushed the production back to spring 1989 when McCoy would not be available. (McCoy - who, unlike his predecessors and most of his successors, never had to put up with an eight-month production schedule or longer - saw *Doctor Who* very much as his summer job between other work, but still seems to have been up for this. As it was, he spent the winter in a stage production called *The Zoo of Tranquillity*.)

The new script, as with the previous one (*Doctor Who and the Daleks in Seven Keys to Doomsday* - see 13.5, "The Brain of Morbius") was written by Terrance Dicks. But unlike that 1973 play or the 1965 David Whitaker show *The Curse of the Daleks*, it had an honest-to-goodness Doctor: Jon Pertwee. It was written with Colin Baker in mind, but the latter was committed to another production. And it was a musical! The Doctor didn't sing, but nobody who's heard Judith Hibbert belt out "Business Is Business" can doubt that *Doctor Who: The Ultimate Adventure* was utterly unlike anything in the programme's history. Pertwee enjoyed himself but soon became too tired for this sort of thing, so Baker finally took the reins and gave what some claim is his best performance as the Doctor. (When Pertwee was ill, he was replaced by David Banks - who normally played one of the villains - dressed in what looks suspiciously like an Andrew Cartmel-style suit and T-shirt.)

• Wyatt, fearful of being stereotyped as a *Doctor Who* writer, declined to write for the series again (or for the Virgin novels, though he was asked), but he's carved a niche on BBC Radio 4 adapting Russian novels, and at time of writing has just won plaudits for making Fielding's *Tom Jones* work on radio.

26.1: "Battlefield"

(Serial 7N, Four Episodes. 6th - 27th September 1989.)

Which One is This?

We're Knights of the Round Table,
Dimensionally unstable.
UNIT's back - their leader's black -
There's a monster from a fable
And a spaceship under Camelot
(Where Sylvester gets to ham a lot).

Firsts and Lasts

We get our last glimpse of the TARDIS console and a final "proper" appearance of the Brigadier. This is the first sign of a rethought UNIT (echoes of which crop up in X2.0, "The Christmas Invasion" and X3.12, "The Sound of Drums", wherein they've become Spectrum, even though Torchwood got first dibs on Captain Scarlet) and the first time something from the Doctor's long-term future has an impact in the present (as opposed to the *end* of a story affecting the start, as in 18.5, "Warriors' Gate"; 18.7, "Logopolis" or Season Twenty-Three). It's also the last story to have stunts arranged by old Havoc hand Alf Joint.

Four Things to Notice about "Battlefield"...

1. As we have noted, Ace's use of child-friendly swearing has become increasingly irritating, but not as much as Brigadier Winifred Bambera's catch-phrase: 'Shame.' That's 'shame' as in "I've just trodden in some dog-shame". Some scenes are so oddly lip-synched as to make everyone think a ruder word was re-dubbed, but the sound is so patchy, it's more likely they did it to remove people laughing at the ineffective zap-guns and the nelly Knight-Commander. So, that's UNIT, led by a butch woman who doesn't quite swear, versus camp knights from a parallel dimension, led by a butch woman who doesn't quite talk English. The story ought to seem as if it's heading for a confrontation between these two, but it never really gets there. Instead the climax of the final episode is Nick Courtney saying 'I just do the best I can'.

2. Yes, Brigadier Lethbridge Stewart is back, and this is, on balance, a good thing. Even though Season Twenty-Six opens with two old people tottering around a garden-centre talking about UNIT

Season 26 Cast/Crew

- Sylvester McCoy (the Doctor)
- Sophie Aldred (Ace)

- John Nathan-Turner (Producer)
- Andrew Cartmel (Script Editor)

continuity, and even though his presence reminds us of so much else from early seventies stories (stuntmen doing big somersaults near small explosions, limp-wristed extras playing hardened soldiers - check out the Quartermaster Sergeant in particular - and tiresome attempts to make Bessie endearing), the Brig is there to represent the old guard handing on the baton to a new, tough UNIT for the Millennium. Yes, the United Nations Intelligence Taskforce - like the Doctor and the Daleks - is getting a reboot, starting with actual UN uniforms and badges. To imagine how odd the use of Polish and French officers in jobs formerly done by Yates and Benton looked in 1989, try to imagine an episode of *The A-Team* where BA stops shooting in order to pray in the direction of Mecca, and where people actually die from all that gunfire. All attempts to rebrand UNIT are, however, rendered useless when Winifred and Doris drive off in Bessie in the most misconceived scene of the whole of 1980s *Doctor Who*.

3. In keeping with Andrew Cartmel's usual practices, we have a representative of Earth telling a nasty alien "I'm loyal to this planet - clear off", a woman with big fingernails, a polemic about nuclear weapons being bad, and far more material than they could use. Some of the extra material wound up on the BBC Video, and - frankly - it was better lost. In particular, the idea of an organic spaceship is better conveyed by seeing how the onboard computer's innards look like seaweed, as opposed to Sylvester and Sophie walking up a wrought-iron Victorian spiral staircase festooned with Christmas tree lights - apparently in an attempt to make this piece of disco ironmongery seem "organic". Still, what's interesting is how Morgaine's unseen world is more vivid to us than the near-future England, simply through tiny details let slip - it's easier to say a helicopter looks a bit like an ornithopter than it is to build a model ornithopter, for instance. And even the small

pieces of near-future that we *do* have (a voice-operated phone, a five pound coin, a King) are more effective than the Doctor trying to pay for drinks with a Zoid that he keeps in his trouser-pocket.

4. Four episodes is always thought to be the natural length for a *Doctor Who* story. This one has too much material for three, but not enough for five, and hence should never have been made in four parts. Quite simply, the story's natural climax is the final cliffhanger at the end of episode three. There's twenty-five minutes allocated to deal with everything after this, but only ten minutes' worth of material.

So the compromise is that they build up to one of the great moments in the programme's history - the arrival of the Destroyer, a beast that consumes worlds and looks better than anything we've seen in the series so far (and quite a lot since, notably the comparatively disappointing Devil in X2.9, "The Satan Pit"). Then episode four has him saying in effect, "I'm going to destroy the world. Soon. See if I don't. Any time now. I will. Really."... and so forth for something like ten minutes.

The Continuity

The Doctor A small detail, but for some people a significant one: the Doctor volunteers to cook supper. [It comes as the last line in a "tag" scene many would rather forget, but it seems as natural for this Doctor to cook supper as it would have been unthinkable for many of the previous ones. For all his gourmet pretensions (9.1, "Day of the Daleks"; 22.4, "The Two Doctors" and hilariously 19.6, "Earthshock", just for starters), the idea of the Doctor making a meal was only hitherto raised as a joke (mainly in Season Twenty-Two). But once the *New Adventures* got rolling, some of the writers gravitated toward the Seventh Doctor's cooking ability as an important link between him and humanity.]

He's developed a few new skills: he renders Mordred unconscious by simply prodding the man's forehead a little. [But for the dubbed-on sound that makes this sound like a doorbell in the skull, we might consider this an extension of the Doctor's Venusian Aikido.] He seems to date the relative decay and age of concrete just by looking at it, weirdly. Meanwhile, his hypnosis has developed to the level of being a Jedi mind-trick, as he's able to mentally nudge two people into evacuating

when they've obviously got no intention of doing so. [This is a more subtle varient of the 'You will not move' bit from 25.3, "Silver Nemesis", although he's not wearing his glasses this time.] Judge for yourselves if he *really* stops a battle by projecting his voice like a megaphone, or if he's just taking advantage of a natural echo. The Doctor seems to stagger while holding Excalibur's scabbard as Morgaine opens a dimensional doorway, as if her creating 'a rip in the fabric of time and space' is personally affecting him.

This week's bit of astonishing forethought [see any story you like from Season Twenty-Five, barring 25.2, "The Happiness Patrol"]: the Doctor suspects that silver bullets might be useful in this adventure, and knows when Ace has brought him some. However, he falls for the Brigaider's 'Good Lord, is that a spaceship?' ruse, and instantly falls unconscious when the Brig strikes his chest. [Some have interpreted this as a useful technique for knocking out Time Lords, and possibly something the Brig learned while dealing with the Master on a regular basis.]

The Brigadier had Bessie mothballed [presumably after 13.1, "Terror of the Zygons"] after the Doctor left for space, and - in an amazing show of clairvoyance on the Brig's part - Bessie's licence plate now reads WHO 7. Bessie is presently capable of speeds that literally leave burning tire tracks. The Doctor here learns that the Brigadier married Doris. [The spin-off lines make a hash of this, and have the Fifth and Sixth Doctors also learn the news. Nonetheless, each of them is suitably charmed to hear of the development, every time.]

While in the bar of the Gore Crow Hotel, the Doctor sticks to water.

• *Ethics.* In the heat of battle, the Doctor threatens to behead Mordred if his mother doesn't call off the Destroyer from harming Ace and her friend Shou Yuing. Mordred taunts him with: 'Look me in the eye... end my life.' [We're expected to remember this from "The Happiness Patrol" - that time, the Doctor dropped the same argument onto a sniper.] Morgaine and Mordred both know from their experience with the future Doctor/s that he won't kill in cold blood - and predictably but reassuringly, the Doctor backs down. Yet he seems quietly vengeful when he thinks Morgaine has killed Ace and Shou Yuing, and expresses relief to learn that Ace surrendered Excalibur in exchange for their lives.

Where Does "Canon" End?

Now here's a funny thing: if we'd written this essay even a year ago, we would have come to totally different conclusions. Things move fast, and debates that looked settled have a habit of reopening. To begin with yet another attempted definition: we take "canon" to mean what is admissible as being "real" *Doctor Who*, and everything else is "spin-offery" or "fan-fic". In the real world "Canon" is a noun meaning those works that everyone should know about without being told (usually starting with Shakespeare, Cervantes, Borges and Dickens, then the fights start: these days everyone agrees that Harold Bloom's attempt to legislate on this is wrong, but they can't even agree on why). Within our bubble-universe it is an adjective, like "true" or "cool", and used somewhat along the lines of both but with a faint whiff of "local" as used in *The League of Gentlemen*. "That's not canon, this is canon, if this is canon then that has to be too" and so on - the niggling arguments ran almost as long as the similarly grammatically-challenged "Continuity" debate (see 22.1, "Attack of the Cybermen").

It used to be simpler, when there was just one TV show on every Saturday, and a whole slew of second-best options like Target Novelisations, World Distributors' *Annuals*, Nestlé chocolate's *Doctor Who Fights Masterplan Q* and the *TV Comic* and *Countdown* strips. And the Peter Cushing Dalek films. And the Chad Valley *Give-a-show* projector strips. And...

You see the problem. Each of these was dependant on a single Ur-text, the BBC1 series, but that was transient and only a select few stories were ever repeated. By comparison, the spin-offery was tangible, repeatable and capable of being lent to friends to prove a point. If your dad had coughed at a crucial point in "The Deadly Assassin" (14.3), you could borrow the Target book to find out for certain how many regenerations a Time Lord was allotted. The trouble came, of course, when you tried the same trick to find out what Patrick Troughton's first words were, and in which story (see 4.2, "The Tenth Planet").

Once *Doctor Who Monthly* got its act together, and the BBC videos made the stories available to everyone - not just the network of fans with access to friends taping stuff off-air in (say) Australia or Buffalo - the position settled. However, shortly after this the series ended and, as they used to say in the *DWM* comic strips, "all hell broke loose..." Sorry, we don't have a font lurid enough to do it the Steve Parkhouse way.)

Target was an imprint of WH Allen, which was swallowed up by Virgin Books in 1990. The contract with the BBC was still in play, and nobody at the Corporation could be bothered to stop it. So as soon as the series was pronounced dead, they basically stole the corpse and launched the *New Adventures* books. These had the Doctor and Ace going through angsty soul-searching during "adult" adventures with a good amount of swearing (still, at least they weren't all set in Cardiff...). Whilst these were deemed the only game in town (aside from the *DWM* strip, but editor John Freeman was more than happy to play ball), they could do what they liked and could claim to be the definitive account of what happened after "Survival" (26.4). So soon we had exciting new aliens like the Chelonians (jobsworth tortoise-monsters), plucky new characters like Ruby Duvall (a non-copyright Sarah Jane Smith) and, oh dear...

Absalom Daak, Dalek Killer. From the *DWM* strip comes a tragically early-80s breed of hero, who numbs a broken heart by blazing a trail through the badlands whilst attacking Daleks with a chainsaw. (By the looks of him, he was shaving with it too. Pity he couldn't do something about the mullet-and-pony-tail while he was at it.) Daak - or rather, a clone of him - showed up in the *New Adventures* novel *Deceit*, which was written by range editor Peter Darvill-Evans. Now, if Daak could make the transition to novels from the Marvel strip, it potentially meant that any other Marvel copyright character was fair game. Spidey? The Care Bears? Han Solo? Pope John Paul II[43]? It had been hard enough finding excuses to get TV companions into the established continuities of the comic-strips (Peri's meeting with the Sixth Doctor - and Frobisher - was more contrived than Tegan's return in 20.1, "Arc of Infinity"). Now we had characters from the strip popping up in the Virgin (oh dear, sorry to phrase it like this) "Universe".

The strip, meanwhile, had Andrew Cartmel writing for it. Hang on... that's the same Andrew Cartmel who was writing some of the *New Adventures* offerings, and was the script editor in the last phase of the TV series. Here's another problem: for a lot of readers, the *New Adventures* were the authoritative take on what the TV series itself was just about to do when it was culled. Cartmel's alleged "masterplan" seemed to be working its way through the books, and the

continued on page 295...

Later, the Doctor shows no qualms about blowing up Arthur's spaceship, even though it's been described as semi-organic. [Nobody *else* protests about this apparent killing either, though.]

• *Inventory*. Bizarrely, he keeps Liz Shaw's UNIT pass in his hat, as well as his own. [Does it have the publicity still of Jon Pertwee jumping out of a helicopter? See 9.3, "The Sea Devils" for what we mean. But there's a bigger question here: was the pass in the straw hat throughout his third life, and is *that* why he could never find it when questioned by security guards and officious heads of research stations?]

He's carrying a signal-detector with a telescopic antenna, and it isn't like any of the other signal detectors he's carried around over the years. Also appearing from the recesses of his trousers, we see a pair of science-spoons [from 24.1, "Time and the Rani"], Ace's catapult and a cricket ball. In his pocket of loose change, he has a battery-powered Zoid [if you don't remember those, they were like a midway point between Meccano and Transformers], which he assures us is a 'very valuable piece of coinage'. He's also got a small module that fixes onto Bessie's steering wheel, and seems to "ready" the car to travel at high velocities.

• *Background*. Sorry, not much to say here, but...

• *Foreground*. At some stage in his personal future, the Doctor will visit the 'sideways in time' dimension that the sorceress Morgaine and all these knights hail from. Morgaine, her son Mordred and the benevolent knight Ancelyn are all familiar with the Doctor/s of the future - and call him 'Merlin' - but none of them has met *this* incarnation. They each recognize the Doctor has 'worn many faces'. [So it's possible he regenerates in their realm, or simply that they're going to encounter more than one of his future selves. In T.H. White's *The Once and Future King* - see **Where Does This Come From?** - Merlin is characterized as someone who lives his life backward. The idea here - which is substantiated by opening portion of the novelisation - is presumably the same, meaning future Doctors will experience events related to Morgaine and company in reverse order.] Ancelyn also provides a colourful but essentially correct description of the TARDIS.

The Doctor's future self shows no compunction about leaving helpful messages for his seventh incarnation to find. [There's probably all manner of reasons why this sort of thing shouldn't happen

- Laws of Time and that - but the Doctor's relative lack of surprise at this is probably connected to his newfound carte-blanche with regard to the High Council; see 25.1, "Remembrance of the Daleks".]

The Supporting Cast

• *Ace*. Resents the Brigadier treating her as 'the latest one', meaning one of a long line of companions. [For all her resentment, though, we don't get a long fanboy-friendly scene of Ace and the Brig "pulling rank", as in X2.3, "School Reunion".] A glance from the Doctor is enough to warn her off beer and onto lemonade. Ace initially mocks Bessie's retro design, but winds up falling in love with it.

We get a revised version of the "blowing up the Art room" anecdote [see 24.4, "Dragonfire"]: Ace told her teacher, Mrs Parkinson, that her homemade gelignite was a lump of school plasticine. Parkinson asked Ace to put the "plasticine" back in the art room, and Ace - from the corridor - tossed it over her shoulder. It detonated in the middle of Class 1C's prize-winning pottery pig collection.

Ace figures out Morgaine's ploy to make her step out of the protective chalk circle, and later plays into the Doctor's plan by grabbing the silver bullets and jumping through interstitial time, almost as if on cue. She doesn't recognize Liz Shaw's name or photograph. [So this Doctor has eliminated the "companion academy" that enabled Peri to recognize Jo Grant in 22.5, "Timelash" and Mel to know all about regeneration in 24.1, "Time and the Rani".] The fuses for Ace's cans of Nitro-9 are *still* going off early, and the Doctor vows that they're going to have a nice, long talk about acceptable safety standards.

• *UNIT*. Now led by Brigadier Winifred Bambera, although Lethbridge-Stewart seems to outrank her. The two of them act as if they've previously met, although Lethbridge-Stewart only here learns Bambera's first name. [We can charitably assume that the line 'Bambera - good man, is he?' was a joke at pilot Lavel's expense.] Sergeant Zbrigniev formerly served under Lethbridge-Stewart, and learned that their scientific advisor - the Doctor - had a habit of changing his entire physical appearance and personality.

UNIT now seems more multi-cultural than ever [as if there's been a shift in world politics and the make-up of United Nations forces], and its arsenal

Where Does "Canon" End?

...continued from page 293

authors who were most enthusiastically adding to this vision - which entailed examining what they thought this family TV series from the 60s was going to turn into in the 90s - were all convinced that the masterplan would prove to be worth it. That the literary Seventh Doctor's final adventure was Marc Platt's rejected script *Lungbarrow* (see 26.2, "Ghost Light") seemed to make it all worthwhile. Or perhaps not. (See **Who Are All These Men In Wigs?** under 13.5, "The Brain of Morbius".)

It has to be noted how much of what's in the *New Adventures* was introduced in the novelisations of Seasons Twenty-Five and Twenty-Six. The ginger-haired hippy Merlin who's a future Doctor in "Battlefield" (Platt's version of Aaronovitch's screenplay) pops up in the Cyberspace battle at the end of Aaronovitch's *Transit*. (See X2.0, "The Christmas Invasion" for a gag about that - 'Am I ginger?' - although most people think it's a joke about Billie's ex.) Chunky Gilmore's chats with the Brigadier in the "Remembrance of the Daleks" novelisation become part of UNIT's secret history, and that of its WWII precursor 'Longbow'. That the Daleks call the Doctor *Ka Faraq Gatri* (who'da thunk it - Daleks speak Klingon), that Rassilon and Omega knew each other and that a mysterious little bloke called the Other worked with the pair of them crops up throughout. Never mind that this isn't really in synch with what's said on screen, or that the whole "Masterplan" was concocted after the series ended (see **Did Cartmel Have *Any* Plan At All?** under 25.3, "Silver Nemesis"), this is what fans of the books thought.

And look, Ace has been written out and new girl Bernice Summerfield has come in. It transpires that everyone seems to love Benny (she's Indiana Jones played by Emma Thompson), to the point that she gets into the *DWM* strip. The same strip wherein Ace dies[44].

So here's our problem. We have three basic stories, all fiction, and yet somehow the one on TV is more "real" than the strip or the novels. So we must not under any circumstances contradict the TV continuity, but the strip and the novels can borrow from each other *and* have mutually-exclusive continuities of their own. We're saying "strip" singular, but *DWM* was a victim of the Panini Day Massacre, when Marvel UK went belly-up and Italian sticker-book peddlers bought it all up. So the new strip started with a fresh slate, and a new Doctor.

Yes, a new body, at last. Paul McGann's arrival

buggered everything up further. BBC Worldwide thought, "Aha! We can write spin-off books for this new series that's starting", then realised that Virgin did exactly that already. So they ended Virgin's license, but Virgin retained trademark on a lot of "in-house" characters that had been created throughout the *New Adventures*, plus a lot of worlds they'd written into the stories, so they could happily carry on without mentioning any copyright-protected words like 'TARDIS' or 'Dalek'. (Because of a special deal with Terry Nation, only John Peel was allowed to use Daleks, and to make it all more confusing he wrote whole books designed to erase events we'd seen on TV. See **War of the Daleks - Should We Believe a Word of It?** under 17.1, "Destiny of the Daleks".) So Benny carried on in her own series of adventures.

Each of the spin-off series had a self-selecting audience, not necessarily following the other spin-offs and not even guaranteed - depending on which branch we're talking about - to be that bothered about TV *Doctor Who*. Many people abandoned the BBC Books - which were a step back to Target's prose-style to begin with - whilst many more who'd never bothered with the *New Adventures* were motivated to read them because of the McGann movie. That's assuming they could find them in shops. The biggest outlet, WH Smiths, mixed the two series up willy-nilly and kept five-year-old titles on the shelves whilst not stocking newer ones.

Then, in 1999, came the Big Finish audio adventures. These seemed more "real" to some fans, because they had actors from the series, sound-effects, old ideas from TV and - as with the books - BBC sanction. (Though before *they* showed up, BBV had been producing audio plays starring McCoy and Aldred as 'the Professor and Ace'. This attracted the interest of a lot of fans and, eventually, BBC lawyers. The issue of contention seems to have been Aldred's character being named "Ace", so she was hastily relabelled "Alice".)

The thing was, while the audios and the BBC Books both operated within the general property that was *Doctor Who* - and these two branches, at least, bent over backward to acknowledge the TV show continuity, even if only to take a blowtorch to it (*War of the Daleks* again springs to mind) - there wasn't much direct cross-over between them. BBC Video tried to peddle the books as the real thing, to the extent that "Ian Chesterton", when

continued on page 297...

now contains weapons tailored for previously established extra-terrestrial threats. There's armour-piercing rounds with a solid core and a Teflon coating, supposedly capable of going through a Dalek ["Day of the Daleks", "Remembrance of the Daleks"]; high-explosive rounds for Yetis [5.5, "The Web of Fear"]; very efficient armour-piercing rounds for robots [12.1, "Robot"] and gold-tipped bullets for 'you-know-what' [6.3, "The Invasion", although the Doctor must have mentioned this vulnerability at a later point]. They're also packing silver bullets, even though we're never shown a precedent for it.

• *The Brigadier*. Has long since quit teaching [20.3, "Mawdryn Undead"] and married Doris [who was mentioned in 11.5, "Planet of the Spiders"]. He seems comfortable in retirement, contrary to what he said in 1983. [It's possible that Doris' money provides for them, somehow.] Morgaine takes the Brig's threat to kill Mordred very seriously, and senses that the Brigadier is 'steeped in blood'.

Lethbridge-Stewart cheerfully ignores calls from Geneva, even when they're from the Secretary General, until it's mentioned that the Doctor is involved. From then on, he's back into his old life with relish. Despite his protests about having retired, he's up to speed on UNIT's research and development division and their new toys. He seems to resent bureaucracy [odd, as he was a stickler for it in the past] and wants to be in the thick of things. He has a well-developed sense of self-preservation, and seems more anxious when he's *not* being shot at than when he is. Most significantly, the Brigadier's first negotiations with Morgaine show that he comprehends his opponents' world-view fairly quickly, and adapts his strategy to it. In a scene deleted from broadcast, the Brigadier admits to some awkwardness regarding the modern-day attitudes toward women, and their capabilities in battle.

He's now able to second-guess the Doctor on some occasions: not only does he instantly identify the Seventh Doctor [as shown, the idea is that the Brigadier figures it out by a simple process of elimination, but the spin-offs have concluded that he is now *so* familiar with the Doctor, he can recognise him regardless of what body he's wearing], but he gets Bessie out of storage and anticipates that the Doctor will want to shoot the Destroyer. Despite all this, he realises that the time for such adventures is almost past, and formally relinquishes the task of keeping the Doctor alive to Ace.

According to the Doctor, the Brigadier is supposed to die in bed. [It's possible that the Doctor is just speaking metaphorically - as he never mentions how the Brigadier's death here would mean a breach of the timeline - but many fans seem to regard this as the Doctor having some foreknowledge of the Brig's future. The BBC novel *The King of Terror* has the Brigadier passing away in the aforementioned fashion, but almost inexcusably treats this event like a footnote.]

The TARDIS Can receive messages from 'sideways in time', which seems to include a spoken message from either the underwater ship or Excalibur itself. [The message is directed at 'Merlin', and if it's coming from the sword, it might indicate that the Doctor himself constructed it.] As with 20.5, "Enlightenment", receiving weak or distorted signals drains the TARDIS-power normally used for lighting.

The Non-Humans

• *Morgaine*. She introduces herself as 'Morgaine of the Faye, the Sun-Killer, Dominator of the Thirteen Worlds and Battle-Queen of the S'rax'.

[Lots of material for speculation there - the fact that there's 'thirteen' worlds, not nine or fourteen, suggests a lot of changes, especially if they are all owned and run by humans from Earth with low-tech sorcery. 'S'rax' is another of those names in Cartmel stories that sounds like 'Sycorax', which has obvious Shakespearean thaumaturgical overtones, as well as the accidental connection with "The Christmas Invasion" and X3.2, "The Shakespeare Code".] She's ruthless in combat, but has an acutely refined sense of honour. She becomes outraged to discover that her forces fought on hallowed ground without proper respect for the dead, and insists upon a temporary cease-fire, during which her knights hold a ceremony for those who perished in Earth's World Wars. Morgaine mentally (and painfully, for her victim) extracts information from the Brigadier's helicopter pilot [because she's a soldier and ranks as killable] and then disintegrates the woman. [Later, Morgaine extracts the failsafe codes from Bambera's mind without slaying her, so perhaps metally ripping out *one* piece of information is less harmful.] Yet moments after killing the pilot, Morgaine insists upon paying for her son's bar tab

Where Does "Canon" End?

...continued from page 295

narrating the wiped bits of "The Crusade" (2.6), alluded to an unbroadcast adventure in Salem (*The Witch Hunters*, written by Steve Lyons and still available in library sales throughout the country). William Russell looks suitably embarrassed. The videos were part of a cross-promotion campaign, but it's arguable that few people who paid good money for "Time-Flight" (19.7) on VHS were particularly inclined to fork out for (say) *The Taking of Planet 5* as a result. Both Big Finish and BBC Books have included Frobisher as a legitimate companion, and both had Romana as President of Gallifrey. Whether the audios did it because the books had, or vice versa, is almost beside the point. The books had long since had her regenerate into a sort of jazz-age Servalan anyway, although that came at a later point in her Presidency. There is, of course, no excuse for having Frobisher.

(Just to stir the pot a little, the videos themselves were blurring the edges by releasing "adulterated" copies of the old episodes. When 20.7, "The Five Doctors" was rejigged in 1997, the story was now available in three different edits. There were new scenes, old ones went missing and the effects were different. Even the dialogue seems to have been tweaked slightly, as we've found when checking what exactly Troughton says about the Terrible Zodin. The video and DVD of 7.4, "Inferno" are subtly different too. Bonus scenes were interpolated into the VHS releases of 26.1, "Battlefield" and regrettably also "Silver Nemesis". Three variants of "The Curse of Fenric" have now been released in an official capacity. And let's not get into the early videos with cliffhangers hacked out and whole scenes gone - being charged £25 for the one-hour version of "The Brain of Morbius" is still a sore point with many British fans.)

Nevertheless, apart from the Big Finish audio "The Shadow of the Scourge", neither BBC Books nor the audios had much connection to the *New Adventures*, and the *frisson* of the Cartmel / Aaronovitch / Platt "masterplan" had already concluded in 1997. For people who invested a lot in the *New Adventures* because of the connection to what the broadcast series *might* have done, it was now just a bunch of fans making up stories.

Put simply, it was becoming harder to accept these mutually exclusive storylines as equally valid. (Well, you *could*, at the risk of other fans laughing at you - although it must be said that by

now, many of those who favour an all-inclusive approach have developed a thick skin about such things.) Not everyone was even sure that Paul McGann was a real Doctor. Not only did 27.0, "The TV Movie" trample over continuity, but it seemed aesthetically wrong. For some, it was easier to consign it to the same second-division that included Peter Cushing's Doctor, John and Gillian (the Doctor's grandchildren from *TV Comic*) and that sodding penguin.

But there's a snag here, kids: if you try to argue that the books or audios aren't canonical because fewer people read / heard them than saw the "proper" series, then you have to accept that ten million people in Britain watching TV's Eric Roberts 'drezz for the occasion' outweighs three million people watching Ace go "booooom" ("Battlefield"). And when it comes to Cushing, surely the endless reruns of the two colour Dalek films (at least once a year on Channel 4) makes this version of events in twenty-second century Bedfordshire and Skaro in its Gloria Gaynor phase better known than the "canonical" version, shown once a generation ago?

Well, yes, and no. The public may have watched "Grace: 1999" but they didn't inhale. Most of them thought, if asked about it, that Peter Davison was the last Doctor. (Actually, half of them seem to have thought it was his co-star from *All Creatures Great and Small*, Christopher Timothy.) McGann himself claimed to be the George Lazenby of *Doctor Who*, but the sad fact is that he wasn't even that well-recalled. By the Space Year 2000, there was a public collective consciousness of the series, and there was a fanboy's neurotically-detailed knowledge of the minutiae of his or her chosen spin-off. Benny got her own series of CD audio adventures, and appeared in remakes of her post-Doctorate *New Adventures*, and appeared alongside the Doctor and Ace on audio. The continuity strands between different spin-offs became like ribbons on a maypole.

Attempts were made (some as jokes, some much more serious) to sort this out, and one theory even held that McGann is the eighth incarnation of the Cushing Doctor. (This further presumed that the Cushing Doctor had a series of unseen adventures - such as when his next incarnation and Jamie crossed over onto TV continuity, possibly from *TV Comic*, and helped Colin Baker's Doctor in 22.4, "The Two Doctors". In this timeline,

continued on page 299...

by magically bestowing the barkeep's blind wife with sight. Although she seems to have affection for Mordred, she's apparently willing to let him die in battle rather than yield an advantage.

Ultimately, Morgaine finds the Doctor's description of a nuclear war as too dishonourable to be contemplated. Discovering that Arthur - her lover [and half-brother, according to the mythology] - is dead removes her reasons for living, it seems. She fondly recalls their time together in the woods of Celadon, where the air was like honey. It's implied that Morgaine fears the Doctor more than she does the Destroyer.

Morgaine cannot cross a chalk circle if Excalibur is within it ('The sword is protecting you', she tells Ace), but she can try to mentally confuse the minds of those within, and the Destroyer can break this enchantment. Her "sorcery" [see **History**] enables her to catch bullets, down helicopters with bolts of energy, monitor events happening elsewhere (either by looking into an illuminated globe, or by casting her talons across Mordred's eyes and letting *him* watch them), communicate with other people from afar [arguably via telepathy, although it's treated as a normal conversation across great distances]. She can also summon...

• *The Destroyer.* As the name might suggest, the Destroyer claims it can devour whole worlds, and he here appears as a tall, daemonic-looking and blue-skinned being with horns. He can generate energy-streams [green, for a change] from his claws, and claims to consume life energy. [One could *possibly* argue that the Destroyer is a parallel-world avatar of the Fendahl - see 15.3, "Image of the Fendahl".] Even while bound, he can hold open Morgaine's 'interstitial vortex' and allow the Doctor access. He claims he can't destroy the Doctor while chained [but then, he *claimed* he couldn't overpower Ace's chalk circle and does so anyway, the big fibber].

Fortunately for the goodies, silver handcuffs and chains can 'burn' the Destroyer and restrain him. Silver bullets make the creature die in an explosion [or maybe just make it return from whence it came with a release of energy]. Normal bullets are useless against the Destroyer [of course], and he somehow knows how to complete the expression, 'Nothing ventured, nothing gained'. He also seems to generate formidable amounts of saliva.

History

• *Dating.* We're in what's evidently intended as the "near-future" with regards to broadcast in 1989, and the Doctor says it's 'a few years' in Ace's future. [The production team *seems* to be following the 70s aesthetic that UNIT stories take place in the near-future (see **What's the UNIT Dating?** under 7.1, "Spearhead from Space"), but the clues involved are both abundant and confusing.

[On the one hand, we don't see any mobile phones, nobody has a personal computer (although what we'd *now* call a laptop was scripted for the Brigadier to use in the helicopter), Russian soldiers still sport the Hammer and Sickle on their uniforms, and fashions for middle-aged English people seem to have stuck in the mid-1980s. (Perhaps they buy everything from Marks and Spencer.) On the other hand, the Brigadier indicates that England now has a King, commonplace phones have voice-operated software, and inflation has been such that the Gore Crow Hotel charges £5 for a glass of water and a lemonade (although the novelisation revises this to four pounds ninety-five for the water, lemonade, Shou Yuing's half a cider and crisps). None of these details has come to pass, even at the time of writing in 2007. One item which *has* come about, technically: the Doctor pays for drinks with a five-pound coin. There *were* some, in 1990, to commemorate the Queen Mother's 90th Birthday, but they weighed a ton and wore through trousers, so nobody carried them for everyday use. (Anyway, the novelisation says the Doctor has a 1998 'five pound ecuoin'.)

[So... either this is some time in the early twenty-first century (which isn't impossible, certainly now that former Soviet states are queuing up to join NATO and the EU), or it's nearer the time of transmission, and in the same twentieth century that saw Britain land men on Mars in the early 70s (7.3, "The Ambassadors of Death"). That Bambera's aide, Zbrigniev, served with Lethbridge-Stewart and still looks young seems to indicate the latter. (For that matter, so does Shou Yuing being allowed to drive after half a cider.) Whenever it is, Zoids are not legal tender, so eBay hasn't caught on yet.

[Incidentally, the cut scenes provide the intriguing detail that most of UNIT's forces are monitoring the Azanian ceasefire. "Azania", the fictional African state in Evelyn Waugh's *Scoop*, was the proposed name for a post-Apartheid South Africa.

Where Does "Canon" End?

...continued from page 297

the Sixth Doctor was played by Brian Blessed, who had succeeded Martin Jarvis, and so on.) Don't laugh - the reasoning behind this is in the novel *Human Nature*, of which more in a moment.

2005 was Year Zero, because the continuity in the BBC Wales series is so murky as to please almost everyone. Yes, the bits from the mulch of public memory crop up - Cybermen, K9, Daleks - but each is just *there*. There's also a few bits from the Cushing films, including some of the TARDIS design and the use of 'rels' as time units (X2.13, "Doomsday"; X3.5, "Evolution of the Daleks"). Items from the *New Adventures* are included, such as mention of the planet Lucifer (X1.12, "Bad Wolf") and Daleks' name for the Doctor (X2.4, "The Girl in the Fireplace"), although the latter actually came from the "Remembrance of the Daleks" novelisation, which - as we've said - has rather a special place in this debate. At least one episode is, shall we say, a "reconfigured" version of a Big Finish audio (X1.6, "Dalek" is "Jubilee", hence the name of the pizza company, although a similar attempt to adapt Marc Platt's "Spare Parts" ran aground). Two more come direct from a Virgin novel (X3.9 and X3.10 are based upon Paul Cornell's *New Adventures* book *Human Nature*). Notably, nothing in the new series acknowledges the McGann movie (that's the plot and continuity details of the *movie*; please note that this doesn't invalidate the McGann Doctor himself, as we'll discuss). For the majority of the people watching, even televised "classic" *Doctor Who* is an inaccessible and irrelevant piece of background detail.

Which raises the big question: does BBC Wales' version count as being "real" *Doctor Who*? The two are compatible in many ways, but some hardcore fans would answer, "no". It's stated in the dialogue in Series One that the timeline has been tampered with - so, for instance, any effort at resolving the contradictions between "The Ark" (3.6) and "The End of the World" (X1.2) might be deemed pointless, if it's presumed that they're in two mutually-exclusive "universes". Similarly, when the Daleks mess with history in "The Long Game" (X1.7), it means that this series' Dalek chronology is incompatible with the three others in the "proper" series. *Torchwood* and *The Sarah Jane Adventures* acknowledge what's occurred in the Welsh series, but it remains to be seen if they'll drastically contradict the books, the old TV series or even each other. (It has to be noted that the continuity in the pilot for *Sarah Jane* is neurotic, down to the stuffed owl from 14.2, "The Hand of Fear" and photos of the Brigadier and Harry - the latter apparently taken when he was in far-future London in 12.3, "The Sontaran Experiment". This raises all sorts of questions about what else Sarah photographed whilst being tortured by Styre.)

Inevitably, we'll pick this up in **Does Paul McGann Count?** under 27.0, "The TV Movie".

Curiously, nobody seemed to want to change the name in the real (and almost unimaginable, in 1989) Mandela-led multiracial democracy.]

Events as related to the 'sideways in time' reality: Morgaine says she was always able to best the future Doctor/s - whom everyone involved refers to as 'Merlin'- at chess. Ancelyn (who describes himself as a 'Knight General of the Britons') says the Doctor used 'mighty arts' to cast down Morgaine at 'Baden'. [This presumably refers to the Battle of Mons Badonicus - a major victory for Romano-British forces. By the ninth century, it was attributed to Arthur.] Mordred says that Ancelyn cowardly fled the battlefield at Camlann. [In Arthurian mythology, this is cited as the battle where Arthur is fatally wounded. Historians doubt this conflict ever took place, but the earliest account for it appears in the *Annales Cambriae* in 537 AD.]

In 800 AD or thereabouts [the Doctor says that Excalibur's scabbard has been 'waiting' on Earth longer than the eighth century, but the ship's concrete tunnel was built then, so it must be younger than the Sword - logical, as it's the swordbearer's tomb], Arthur - the beloved enemy of Morgaine - died in battle and was buried in "Avallion" (our dimension). It seems that a future Doctor engineered the bio-mechanical ship that carried Arthur to rest in Lake Vortigern at Carbury, but he helpfully left a 'Dig Hole Here' marker in an unknown language for his earlier self, plus a door that responded to his voice commands. The sword Excalibur - apparently capable of opening a dimensional gateway - was left with the dead King. Morgaine's son Mordred has a sword that is 'brother to Excalibur', and which aids her in travelling between realities. He believes that Morgaine sealed Merlin 'into the Ice Caves for all eternity'. [Some accounts have Merlin getting trapped in a crystal cave after lusting after the Lady of the Lake

ABOUT TIME 1985–1989

or, more commonly, annoying his pupil Morgaine le Fay. A version of this underlies 16.3, "The Stones of Blood", and if they returned to the idea, it would keep BBC Wales busy for ages.]

Mordred also claims that his mother has waited 'twelve centuries' to face the Doctor again. [It's claims like this that make the longevity of these dimensional-travellers a bit of a puzzler. Time might flow at different rates between our world and Morgaine's realm - hence the description that it's 'sideways' in time, although something similar was said about the time-concurrent parallel reality in "Inferno" (7.4) - or perhaps Morgaine has used sorcery to extend her lifespan and that of her son. Mordred calls to his mother 'deathless Morgaine', but the Destroyer refers to her as 'this mortal'. There's no sense that Ancelyn is any older than he looks, yet Morgaine expects Arthur to be capable of facing her twelve centuries after their last meeting.]

Technology in Morgaine's realm seems like a curious amalgam of energy fields and mental powers. In a deleted scene, the Doctor attributes Morgaine's use of 'sorcery' to Clarke's Law: "Any advanced form of technology is indistinguishable from magic." [Thus the notion in most of *Doctor Who* - see in particular 8.5, "The Daemons" - that there's no such thing as magic is loosely preserved.] The 'sideways in time' dwellers there have souped-up guns and grenades, but ornithopers instead of aircraft [apparently], and armour capable of traversing dimensions. [Pause to say that the knights in episode one seem to "fall" to Earth, and the manner in which Ancelyn "rises" from the resultant crater is one of the most unexpectedly phallic images in the whole of *Doctor Who*. It's not nearly as bad as the buried Dalek in the first cliffhanger from 2.8, "The Chase" - which even makes grunting noises - but it's certainly in the top twenty, along with the Eye of Axos (8.3, "The Claws of Axos") and the rude flora of Spiridon (10.4, "Planet of the Daleks").]

The Carbury Trust has been excavating a site near Lake Vortigern, with Peter Warmsly serving as site manager, for ten years. Warmsly found Excalibur's scabbard there [how it got outside the bio-ship is a complete mystery], and it came to hang in the Gore Crow Hotel.

The Analysis

Where Does This Come From? Well, we could spend a lot of time talking about comics, and going into detail about Marvel Comics' *Excalibur*: the European contingent of the X-Men. After all, the series had just introduced a new secret military investigation team called 'WHO' (Weird Happenings Organisation), led by Alysande Stuart (a female officer) and her brother and scientific advisor Alasdaire. Their base was under the Tower of London. And we'd have to go into endless nerdy detail about the way Alan Davis and Chris Claremont took the basic idea of Captain Britain and mixed it with Arthurian stuff to make *Knights of Pendragon*, using some of the same *Excalibur* characters and a robot called Gawain[40], and how Captain Britain had lots of dealings with parallel universe versions of himself and...

You get the picture. There was clearly something in the air. Partly it was a realisation that the nation's biggest contribution to mythology deserved better than John Boorman's 1981 flick *Excalibur* and *Monty Python and the Holy Grail*. Partly it was the start of what was being called New Age, and even in 1989 this name was suspiciously like a brand for the real practitioners. Mainly, though, it was that the Arthur story is inherently about loss of innocence, a brief moment of order destroyed by its own contradictions, and is therefore more interesting than ordinary heroism from the past.

Ever since 24.2, "Paradise Towers", we've been dealing with a sense of loss, mainly about 1960s dreams, but also about *Doctor Who*'s own status and past glories. Every century has had different reasons to exploit the elegiac tone of Arthurian romance - from Thomas Mallory's rueful comparison of the virtuous knights to his own experiences in the Wars of the Roses, and to the Tennyson / Walter Scott dismay at Industrialisation and grubby politics. Since the day *Doctor Who* began, the Kennedy Administration has been referred to as "Camelot", and all subsequent presidents were judged (unfavourably) by a standard that nobody considered realistic when Hatless Jack was in the White House.

Obviously, the Arthurian material is influenced by TH White's version. As anyone who reads Ben Aaronovitch's novel *Transit* after White's *Once and Future King* can see, we are more concerned with an overall idea of what being British means. The sheer act of writing about Arthur in the twentieth century sort-of forces that on an author. White made great play of using anachronistic comments about the mediaeval setting, contextualising it with contemporary parallels, and reinvented Merlyn as an Oxbridge don living backwards from the 1930s to the 1400s. This is hardly the only similarity between him and the Doctor: in Robert de Boron's twelfth century account, the wizard evades death by being reborn as a younger man. It's less noticeable for people who came to White from the Disney version of *The Sword in the Stone* and the movie *Camelot*, but White's attempt to create an anti-Wagner - an epic about peace - is immensely influential amongst British fantasy writing. Indeed, a sequence that was cut from "Remembrance of the Daleks" has Davros almost quoting from White. (It's about whether Daleks, made with no conscience, are morally worse than humans - who really ought to know better.) In the "Battlefield" novelisation (written by Marc Platt after Aaronovitch failed to finish it), it's obvious that the Knights' armour is more like *Robocop* or *Terminator* (that business about the Head-Up Displays from "Remembrance" is echoed in the Jesserauntes' visors).

The end of episode three is flagrantly borrowed from the best-remembered *Ace of Wands* episode of the early seventies, "Seven Serpents, Sulphur and Salt". It's the one of the few that was repeated, and it even spawned a spin-off or two. So even though Thames wiped it in a rare moment of BBC-like stupidity, everyone of a certain age remembers it (see 14.5, "The Robots of Death"). In this context, the use of Ley lines and a form of feng shui to travel between dimensions seems less like yet-another Alan Moore knock-off than a very hip reference to the theories doing the rounds concerning crop circles. In the following summer, these would tip over from being something a friend-of-a-friend had heard about to being a national obsession - rather like Uri Geller's fork-bending (see "Planet of the Spiders") or Atlantis (9.5, "The Time Monster", and the essay with 4.5, "The Underwater Menace"). Glyphs kept appearing in the wheatfields of the nation, and evidence emerged that it had been happening for centuries. Was it drunks geometrically trampling the barley, or Satya energy from Pleadeans? More intriguingly, was it the Earth's natural static charges, which had caused certain ancient sites to be associated with hallucinations - thus linking it all back up with Merlin and the Druids? Suddenly, everyone

had an opinion. The precise connection between this and nuclear disarmament - however odd it seems now - is something we'll have to take up under 26.4, "Survival".

Things That Don't Make Sense Even non-discerning viewers seem to ask this question: what exactly happens to Morgaine at the end? She's left alone, grief-stricken, in a caravan with the controls to a nuclear missile. Yes, the Doctor takes the launch keys with him, like that would stop her. And even if she's 'locked up' as the Doctor recommends, are we to presume that a being of eldritch powers - Morgaine of the Faye, Sorceress, Sun-Killer, and Battle-Queen of the S'rax - will do twelve hundred years in Holloway Prison? Like she can bring down a helicopter with a nonchalant wave, but not organise a jailbreak. On the other hand, with her being responsible for so many deaths and so much destruction, is it feasible that she's told to go away and not do it again? [Possibly her honour doesn't allow her to stage an escape. Alternatively, if Ancelyn sticks around, maybe Morgaine and Mordred are just stuck on Earth as well.]

"Vortigern" is emphatically *not* Anglo-Saxon for "High King" - it's the name of the king who asked the Anglos and Saxons in to keep the Vikings out, and in the Arthurian stories, he's the one who replaces Uther Pendragon when the latter is apparently without an heir. So his lake is almost the *last* place to leave Arthur's body. The snake-like "booby trap" within Arthur's spaceship is a bit strange, partly because it never does anything more harmful than smack people around a bit. More oddly, the Doctor knows that the ship responds to his voice commands, yet he never tries the obvious approach of just telling the snake-thing, 'It's me, knock it off'. The result is that the episode two cliffhanger relies on the Doctor being struck unconscious by a booby-trap that he'll set in future. How undignified. [More forgivably, in the same scene you can actually see how the glass door that traps Ace is cracked - that's odd in continuity terms, but see **The Lore** for the real-world explanation.]

Morgaine's knights wear armour that stops bullets, except when the plot requies that it doesn't. Notice how Bambera's gun seems useless during the exchange in episode one, and fails to harm Mordred at almost point-blank range [all right, *he* might have magical protection courtesy of his mother], but despite this seeming invincibility, the knights get liberally shot dead and fall in battle to the UNIT soldiers in episode four. Mind, this might owe to the knights' impressive ability to shoot stuff without actually hitting someone. During the initial exchange with Anceyln, their accuracy isn't *quite* as woeful as the Daleks in "Remembrance of the Daleks", but it's close.

Bambera chastises the Doctor and Ace for using antiquated passes to gain entry to a nuclear missile convoy, but does she respond to this glaring security breach by locking them up and pistol-whipping some answers out of them? No, she just lets them go on their way, and that's *before* Zbrigniev vouches for the Doctor. It's fortunate for Bambera that her UNIT training seems to have included techniques for fighting futurisitic / Medieval knights with a broadsword, and we might also question her sense of priorities toward the end. With who knows how many UNIT troops dead or gravely injured, Bambera bitches for her sergeant to hurry up with the coffee.

And why is a secret military intelligence / alien intrusion countermeasures force apparently doing flood relief and peacekeeping?

Critique Oh, well, it was worth a try. This story is the flipside of the unexpected good luck that's made "The Happiness Patrol" look so much better now. Predicting the near-future is always a mug's game but, even in the spring of 1989, doing an anti-nuclear polemic must have seemed like a reasonably safe bet. Even if betting on the Queen dying or abdicating before 1995 was risky, and positing technological developments is always likely to create hostages to fortune, the only bits of forecasting they got *right* now seem so obvious that nobody notices any more.

Some commentators have wanted to examine this story's disjunction between the script and what finally materialized on screen, but the visual flaws aren't entirely the director's fault. Luckily, the advent of DVD affords the possibility to do for "Battlefield" what was done for 26.3, "The Curse of Fenric" - remodel it with better effects, scenes in a slightly different order and no cliffhangers. This might reveal a classic. The script has a lot of faults, but most of them come down to pacing. There are scenes that could go, and some that no amount of redubbing, re-scoring or digital effects can salvage. But there are some *amazing* moments, including a few that the director has made out of unpromising material. He uses shadows ingen-

iously on at least two occasions, both leading up to cliffhangers.

In general, though, this looks like children's television (from a director who struggles to make *Basil Brush* watchable). It's cast well, and everyone does what they do well, but - and it's another problem of the pacing - half of them vanish before they've done all they should. Where it *really* falls apart, though, is in the action sequences. The guns are terrible, the fights are lamentable and there are long-shots that ought to be close-ups and vice versa. Quite why this should be is another matter. Part of it is the time allotted for location shooting, but - despite being hit by a BBC strike - this is no shorter than usual (and the weather held for a lot longer than normal).

Yet all of this is frustrating, as this story is the start of three or four exciting directions the series could have explored. The *New Adventures* later explored time paradoxes and the idea of the Doctor leaving hints for his younger self (even if they annoyingly overplayed these ideas), and the rethought UNIT could have come off as a spin-off at any time. Incoming beings from alternate universes are a whole new avenue for invasions of Earth, and allow the *frisson* of parallel worlds without the inherent silliness and tedium that they usually entail. Old UNIT needs to be left to one side, and the Brigadier is there specifically to be written out once and for all. On which topic, the *most* frustrating thing is that they bottle out of the obvious ending, with his funeral. Not that we were sad to see the Brig again, but it turns into too much of a nostalgia-fest.

So if "Battlefield" is unsatisfying overall, let's celebrate the moments of real charm and potential greatness: Morgaine's way of 'picking up the tab', the Doctor's way of waking up Ancelyn and Winifred, the Brigadier facing down a being that can eat worlds, the third cliffhanger. Let's give thanks for another almost flawlessly cast story. Then let's all read the novelisation instead.

The Facts

Written by Ben Aaronovitch. Directed by Michael Kerrigan. Ratings: 3.1 million (the absolute worst-ever ratings for an episode's premiere broadcast), 3.9 million, 3.6 million, 4.0 million. Audience appreciation was a respectable 69% for episode one, and slowly whittled down to 65% by episode four.

Working Titles "Storm Over Avallion" (and numerous permutations of this).

Supporting Cast Nicholas Courtney (Brigadier Lethbridge-Stewart), Jean Marsh (Morgaine), Marcus Gilbert (Ancelyn), Angela Bruce (Brigadier Winifred Bambera), Christopher Bowen (Mordred), Ling Tai (Shou Yuing), Angela Douglas (Doris), James Ellis (Peter Warmsly), Noel Collins (Pat Rowlinson), June Bland (Elizabeth Rowlinson), Robert Jezek (Sergeant Zbrigniev), Stefan Schwartz (Knight Commander), Marek Anton (The Destroyer).

Oh, Isn't That...?

• *Angela Bruce.* She usually played social-workers or nurses (yes, she's another *Angels* alumnus). Ms Bruce was at this stage known for two odd roles: she'd just been Lister's female parallel-universe alter ego / girlfriend in *Red Dwarf,* and was between series as the authority-figure in Greatest Kids Show Ever, *Press Gang.*

• *James Ellis.* The only major star of *Z Cars* not to have been in *Doctor Who* to date. In those days (1962), a Belfast accent was unheard in mainstream drama, and was certainly never used for good guys. PC Lynch was the only character to remain right through all incarnations of the series (see 2.1, "Planet of Giants" and accompanying essay).

• *Noel Collins.* Yet another fugitive from *Juliet Bravo.* He was the seen-it-all Sergeant that all British cop-shows have (a function Bert Lynch had eventually assumed after starting off on patrol-car duties in *Z Cars*).

• *Angela Douglas.* Yet another *Carry On* alumnus, usually playing dippy public-school totty. (Even when she's ostensibly an Indian princess ; y'know, we thought of asking the publisher of this series if we could give out DVDs of *Carry On Up The Khyber* with Volume I, as it would've saved time on explanations.)

• *Jean Marsh.* You *did* read Volume I, right? She's the star / co-creator of *Upstairs, Downstairs,* the former Mrs Jon Pertwee, the companion-that-wasn't in 3.4, "The Daleks' Master Plan", and - as noted in Volume I - the go-to-girl for incest subplots in *Doctor Who.* At the time they made "Battlefield", she was fresh from the unfairly-neglected *Return to Oz* (where she played a witch-queen) and the fairly-neglected *Willow* (where she played a witch-queen). How could they *possibly* have anyone else in mind for Morgaine?

• *Stefan Schwartz* The erstwhile Knight Commander went on to a directing career, working on Britflicks like *Shooting Fish* and *The Abduction Club,* and episodes of *Hustle.* We assume he wore less lipgloss and eyeliner on these. On which note, we ought to mention...

• *Marc Warren.* Look very carefully at the scene with the camp Quartermaster Sergeant. As far as we can tell, the future star of *Hustle* and X2.10, "Love and Monsters" is unloading stuff from the UNIT lorry.

• *Ling Tai.* She's been a hostess in the last gasp of *Crackerjack* (no, please... let's give it a rest) and has popped up elsewhere since (see **The Lore** for her previous form).

Cliffhangers Enemy knights corner the Doctor and his allies in a barn, and Mordred orders his men to 'Kill them, kill them now!'; a booby-trap knocks the Doctor unconscious, whilst Ace is shut in a chamber filling with water; the Destroyer arrives, and Morgaine threatens that Ace and Shou Yuing will become 'his handmaidens innn Hellllllll'.

The Lore

• Aaronovitch devised this story soon after meeting Cartmel, if not before. A lot of the story you will know from "Remembrance of the Daleks", but it's unclear if this or the idea that eventually became the *New Adventures* novel *Transit* is the story they ditched when Nathan-Turner secured the use of the Daleks. (Cartmel recalls that Aaronovitch's unsolicited script was called "Knight Fall", but historian Andrew Pixley calls this account into question. Given that the other Cartmel anecdotes we've been able to check seem to be a bit - how shall we put this? - ben trovato, and that the revisions to Pixley's "Archive" feature were in a *DWM* special published after Cartmel's *Script Doctor* - but had nothing new to say on this - we'll veer towards Pixley's version. According to him, "Nightfall" was a satire on privatisation and nothing to do with falling knights.)

• Seeing the way the stories were being made, Aaronovitch conceived his "Avalon" story as a three-parter to be made on location, as per "Delta and the Bannermen" (24.3) and "Silver Nemesis". By this time, Cartmel had taken on Aaronovitch as a special project, narrowly failing to get him onto the Writers' Course. The writers brought onto the *Doctor Who* team were now almost a gang, but

Cartmel and Aaronovitch seemed to be the leaders. Cartmel introduced his padawan around, and took him along on a visit the model shop where the Biomechanoid head for 24.4, "Dragonfire" was in the final stages of construction. (Those of you who've recently read Volume II will recall something similar happening with Terrance Dicks and Robert Holmes. The comparison is more pointed when it's recalled that Holmes was fortuitously around when the Sherwin / Bryant team were swapping jobs and Dicks was alternating between writing and editing - and that Holmes was thus as involved as anyone in re-formatting the series for colour and Earth-based stories. See **What About Season 27?** under "Survival" for our speculation on how much more exact the parallel might have been.)

• In proposing a story where modern soldiers confront mythical beings, Aaronovitch made plans to include a multi-ethnic cast to cover a range of belief-systems (and, of course, to look cool). One idea was an early version of Bambera, but this time a USAF captain, as a possible latter-day version of the beloved Brigadier Lethbridge-Stewart from the author's childhood. Nathan-Turner thought it might as well include the Brigadier himself, and checked with both Nicholas Courtney and the agents for Mervyn Haisman and Henry Lincoln (as they'd created the character in 5.5, "The Web of Fear"). Contrary to what is sometimes said, there seems not to have been a plan for Shou Yuing to become a semi-regular character, but a previous character called 'Thai' was given more detail.

• Courtney wanted this to be the Brig's last hurrah. He agreed to appear one last time, and was prepared to give up a part in the West End to do it. It was decided that this story should come second in production to allow him to do both (as it was, he had to give up the stage play anyway). Even when the character was reprieved, Courtney accidentally-on-purpose let slip that they had more than one ending planned, and one was the death of "Greyhound". During the writing of this story, Aaronovitch got drunk and spilled the ending to a bunch of fans at a pub, and so it's rumoured that a number of dummy endings had to be written to avoid spoilers. Other, less plausible stories from the music press had Kate Bush in the running to play Morgaine, and 70s rockers Hawkwind performing the music. (On the latter score, we can only say, "If only...")

• Director Michael Kerrigan came to the project late: Courtney's availability meant that the filming had to be rescheduled. We've been told that Andrew Morgan was originally assigned to the story, but he wasn't free. (There's also the problem of his £13,000 overspend on "Remembrance of the Daleks", which may have debarred him from working on the series. However, Nathan-Turner was convinced that had he been producer of Season Twenty-Seven, Morgan, Wareing and Mallett would have served as directors.) Morgan and Kerrigan worked on *Knights of God* together, so the former suggested the latter. Kerrigan was puzzled by much of the script.

• With Aaronovitch believing that the story was set in Cornwall, and the producer for some reason thinking it was in the Lake District, the logical place to go for location work was Leicestershire. In fact, Rutland Water was only technically in that county, as the boundaries changed - controversially - in 1974 and have since changed back. Rutland, Britain's smallest county, is between Leicestershire and Northamptonshire, which is why the location details seem to be spread over a vast area - Corby, in Northamptonshire, is right next to Rutland Water, in Rutland now but officially Leicestershire in the 80s, and the woodland locations were all done around this ghastly town. It's only a five-mile radius, but the paperwork makes it seem like it spread over three whole counties. With 1989 shaping up to be hotter and drier than the previous year, there were health worries about the scenes with Ace in the water. (As we will see in "The Curse of Fenric", Aldred had overcome her reluctance to go into water - we'll pick up on this in a moment.) The weather seemed likely to hold, so the title "Storm Over Avallion" was dropped to cover themselves if it remained bright and sunny (as it did).

• With lots of advance warning about an impending strike, the recording schedule allowed for time off. Rather than go half a mile into Corby[41], the team went 120 miles to Skegness, a traditional seaside resort. Some real archaeologists were perplexed by the fake "dig". The local press arrived to see the explosions, and a feature made it into the Leicester *Mercury*. Being close to where he grew up, Nathan-Turner was keen to stress how picturesque and hospitable this area was.

• Ling Tai (Shou Yuing) had briefly co-hosted *Crackerjack*. (All right... one last time. CRACKERJACK!) Video evidence exists of her with a ten-year-old boy called Jonathan Morris, who would grow up and write *Doctor Who* for BBC Books. She's been spotted in the background of *Doctor Who* stories before. (Check out 18.1, "The Leisure Hive" and 21.1, "Warriors of the Deep". No, don't get them out just to look for her.) June Bland (as the landlord's blind wife) is more visible as Berger in 19.6, "Earthshock". She'd been sporting the same hairstyle since *The Newcomers* in 1967. The contact lenses she had to wear here caused a few problems at first. Marek Anton (the Destroyer) had just been in "The Curse of Fenric" as Vershinin, and Robert Jezek is now better known (comparatively speaking) as the voice of Frobisher in the Big Finish audios.

• As you may know from the novelisation - by Marc Platt but based on Aaronovitch's notes after the scriptwriter got intense writer's block - the original idea was that the Destroyer should begin by looking like an Armani-suited human, and develop into a daemonic form after the chains were broken. Mike Tucker had originally designed a way to do this, but he was moved onto "The Curse of Fenric", and so Sue Moore and Stephen Mansfield took over.

• You may already have heard this one, too. In the cliffhanger for episode two, the tube that Ace was in cracked as the water was added for the close-ups. The version the *News of the World* printed says that she was seconds from drowning. In fact the main worry was electrocution if the water got onto the camera or lighting leads. Some claim you can hear McCoy shouting the word we think "Shame!" was a euphemism for in the broadcast version. Anyway, the contractor had got the specs wrong, and Aldred got a slightly cut hand - and the BBC got a training video on what to do in a potential flooding emergency.

• As noted, episode one scored the worst ratings of any episode on its first broadcast in the UK. (Some repeats had rated lower, and the absolute nadir was achieved by 10.5, "The Green Death" and 13.3, "Pyramids of Mars", when they were shown on Sundays at noon on BBC2 in 1994.) Episode one faced stiffer than usual competition, however - not just *Coronation Street*, but also one of England's World Cup qualifier football matches live on BBC2.

Just as significantly, the new season received virtually no publicity, especially compared to the previous year. Various production factors had left the promotional budget depleted, and Nathan-Turner decided to hold much of this in reserve for

"The Curse of Fenric" - by which time all the newspapers could talk about, in relation to *Doctor Who*, was just how poorly it was doing...

26.2: "Ghost Light"

(Serial 7Q, Three Episodes. 4th - 18th October 1989.)

Which One is This? In which Ace goes down a rabbit-hole, through a looking glass and to a mad tea-party (can you see where we're going with this?). Monsters in evening-dress and pistol-packin' housemaids occupy a Victorian mansion that's creepy and kooky, mysterious and spooky et cetera. Don't have the soup.

Firsts and Lasts Starting with the most obvious: owing to the jumbled running-order, it's the last story to be made as part of "proper" *Doctor Who* pre-2005 (even if you count 27.0, the McGann abomination, as "real", it wasn't made in the same way as part of the same series). It's definitely the last story to be made at Television Centre. It's also (perhaps more significantly than anyone realised) the first time a *Doctor Who* writer had cut his teeth in fanzines, then wrote other, non-*Who* stuff to hone his craft (as opposed to Andrew Smith's meteoric career - see 18.3, "Full Circle").

Three Things to Notice about "Ghost Light"...

1. The music. There's so much music in this story it seems to spill out into whatever you watch next. And good stuff it is too, if you don't mind being more-or-less ordered to think or feel a particular way about a specific scene or character. That said, compared to Murray Gold's strongarm tactics in the BBC Wales stuff, it's almost subliminal. There's even an honest-to-goodness Victorian Music Hall ditty (Gwendoline's 'That's the way to the zooooo, *that's* the way to the zooooo...') that's so apt, some people thought it must have been a pastiche written for the story. Almost a decade since he dumped Dudley Simpson, Nathan-Turner has started to think that maybe an orchestral score might be worth doing again. So, like most of this year's output, this story's score reached an equilibrium between cheap synths and dull "conventional" scores, and most of British television in the coming decade will sound like late 80s *Who*, unless it tries really hard not to.

2. The dialogue. Practically every line is a reference to something else, be it a Victorian novel, old

television, earlier *Doctor Who* adventures or even the works of Douglas Adams (see Volume IV if you don't know why Adams is relevant). Those few lines that aren't include a few sick jokes and nonchalant references to history and biology. The result is a curious hybrid, rather as though someone had taken an episode of *Upstairs, Downstairs* and dubbed the soundtrack of *Animaniacs* onto it.

3. The politics. We're still in the late 80s, and Ben Elton is still doing his stand-up routines, turning the phrase "Oops! Bit of politics yes indeed ladies and gentlemen" into one word. (It's odd nobody notices how much his delivery resembles Anthony Ainley's contributions to some of the Davison stories.) Here we have a lengthy dig at people who mis-use Darwin for their own rapacious ends (not even slightly like the ones in 25.4, "The Greatest Show in the Galaxy" or 26.4, "Survival", then) and those who refuse to accept that anything can change (which is, of course, completely unlike 25.2, "The Happiness Patrol" and 24.4, "Dragonfire"). So what are we to make of the way Control becomes a "Ladylike" by learning to speak with an RP accent?

The Continuity

The Doctor After he's assessed that Josiah is a threat to the Crown and all within Gabriel Chase, and that Light is an extremely powerful being that demands further investigation, the Doctor achieves his goals by manipulating various parties present and negotiating with the more lucid among them [see *Ethics*]. He's sarcastic to rigid-minded priests and pseudo-scientists alike, but indulges the clearly deranged explorer Redvers in order to find out more [and to facilitate a cure, as with Kingpin in "The Greatest Show in the Galaxy"]. He evidently thinks of himself as a master strategist, at one stage wailing, 'Even I can't play this many games at once!' Like his earlier incarnations, the Seventh Doctor is unimpressed by money, but he makes a joke of it when Josiah attempts to purchase his services as an assassin [compare to 16.4, "The Androids of Tara"].

He offers to get Ace - if she likes - a badge for the Royal Flying Corps. Things the Doctor doesn't like: burnt toast, bus stations, unrequited love, tyranny and cruelty. Control says the Doctor won't ever appear in Light's revised catalog.

• *Ethics.* [This is another one of those instances where you have to wonder whether he's putting

Ace through sheer hell for *her* benefit or his. It's fairly certain that this story is initiated by the Doctor coming to suspect an alien influence in the tale that Ace relates about the creepy haunted house she found in Perivale, but it's *also* possible that he's decided to set her an "initiative test", and in so doing has taken her to the scene of her worst nightmares. Either way, none of this was written as part of the Doctor's ongoing game with Fenric (see "Dragonfire", but only once you've seen 26.3, "The Curse of Fenric"), as the season's running order was swapped, and if anything "Fenric" was meant to foreshadow this story. Also, Fenric himself seems to check off instances where he *was* in conflict with the Doctor ("Dragonfire", and 25.3, "Silver Nemesis") but fails to mention anything pertinent to Gabriel Chase.

[All of that taken into account, is the Doctor healing Ace, training her up for something, or just dealing with an alien menace? Your answer may depend on how you read the next story, but it may be worth noting that some of the other people he "cures" in this story do benefit. Redvers Fenn-Cooper is given focus and a new purpose in life and Control is in charge of her destiny. Balanced against that, Lady Pritchard and her daughter are turned to stone and Inspector Mackenzie is made into soup - although one could certainly argue that they'd already fallen prey to Josiah. Light himself / itself cannot be saved, or at least not before he / it destroys all life on Earth.]

Although the Doctor's actions ultimately help Control, he facilitates a meeting with Light by promising her freedom that clearly isn't his to give.

• *Inventory.* With him on this jaunt is a small radiation detector [but see **Things That Don't Make Sense**]. He seems to have whatever tools are required to fix a broken lift overnight. [The dialogue seems to suggest that the fault is more than just a broken handle, otherwise those surprisingly proficient housemaids could have done it.] He's got a little medical hammer, and - somewhat against the odds - is carrying the the fang of a cave-bear, which he uses as a calling-card to gain the Neanderthal Nimrod's trust. [This might suggest that the Doctor has been initiated into some Neanderthal tribe.]

• *Background.* At one point the Doctor comments, 'Who was it that said, "Earthmen never invite their ancestors round to dinner"?' [This would weirdly imply that the Doctor has has

What Were Josiah's "Blasphemous" Theories?

The only criticism of "Ghost Light" which holds any water is that the date 1883 is a bit arbitrary. Charles Darwin died in 1882, and *The Descent of Man* was published in 1871. The book which lit the blue touchpaper, *On The Origin of Species*, was published in 1859. Almost a quarter of a century later, the Rev Matthews is seen fulminating against Josiah. This is not unknown, and proponents and apologists for the theory of evolution were still having to fight their corner (witness the "Monkey Trials" in 1925 and the mid-1980s attempts to get "equal time" for Creationism in American schools, and please let's not even venture into discussion about the "Intelligent Design" debate). Yet a question remains: why should Matthews have singled out Josiah for his condemnation?

The battle-lines were drawn in 1860 with T.H. Huxley's debates with "Soapy Sam" Wilberforce - Matthews' spiritual precursor and looky-likey. Both sides gained support as the years went by, but the substance of the arguments remained pretty constant after 1871. (Just to fill in the blanks, the first Neanderthal specimen was found in 1825, the Brixham Caves dig proved that humans had been coeval with extinct mammals in 1859, Java man [Pithecanthropus] was unearthed in 1891 and the Piltdown man hoax was 1912.) There were refinements and modifications, and what's broadly termed Darwinism had debates within the framework of the basic theory, just as it has now. Yet, just as now, the differences over details were tiny compared to the differences between people who accepted the broad idea and people who wholly rejected it. No refinement could single any one evolutionist out from the rest as especially deserving of clerical condemnation.

In fact, the main "heresies" within the pro-Darwin camp concerned Man's relationship with Nature. If, as Darwin said, species did not arise out of nowhere, separately created, how do we account for human intelligence and compassion? Alfred Wallace, who almost pipped Darwin to the post with his own version of Natural Selection, held that this was the only avenue for Divine Intervention, otherwise we'd only be a tiny step away from apes. A review in the *Spectator* (12th of March, 1871) maintained the strong hint that intelligence has removed humanity from the innate morality - in its own terms - of beasts "as is indicated by many foul customs, especially as to marriage, of savage tribes". This was basically a rewrite in scientific jargon of Jewish tradition (and

therefore bad, presumably). Any evolutionist who took this notion any further would, if anything, find himself gaining support from the church. So this cannot be the basis of Josiah's vile blasphemy.

The singular nature of Josiah himself may have afforded him a different perspective on the issue. He was, as is stated, the probe for Light's examination and catalogue, and he'd spent some time forcing himself to evolve into a Victorian gentleman. His consciousness had resided in at least two earlier, ungainly bipeds, which could move under Control's volition. That anyone 35,000 years ago would have made the decision to change into something out of Burne-Jones is clearly daft. (This is *still* what the story seems to indicate, though, because it's never really clear how long Josiah has been in charge. One reading - that the spaceship's been there since Nimrod's time - is still put forward as an account of the plot.)

Yet even today, people think of humans as "more evolved" than fruit-flies or hedgehogs, despite the fact that these have undergone more changes recently than we have, *and* have adapted themselves to fit the world, rather than altering the world by making houses and lightbulbs. (Hedgehogs have, on average, longer legs than they did a century ago because the ones that could run faster lived to have babies. This made a rapid and significant difference after lorries were invented.) This does seem to accord with what little Rev Matthews actually says when he's not huffing and ending every sentence with 'is it not?' in an attempt to sound Victorian. If Josiah was arguing that the process of Natural Selection was teleological - i.e. that there was a definite goal behind it all along, namely us - he would have been closer to the clergy than the Darwinians. In fact, his development(s) resemble nothing so much as the Rev Charles Kingsley's novel *The Water Babies* (1863), in which it's stated that "your soul makes your body, just as a snail makes its shell". Josiah didn't evolve in the conventional sense - he shows no interest in breeding with Gwendoline, Mrs Pritchard or the lorryload of serving-girls milling around, and his bodies seem to be extruded from his consciousness somehow. As we saw in Volume V, this is how things "really" work in *Doctor Who's* version of development (see **How Does Evolution Work?** under 18.3, "Full Circle").

This opens up the possibility that he might have been arguing for a bizarre version of

continued on page 309...

heard / read / seen *The Hitchhiker's Guide to the Galaxy* (and thus all the press commentary on how its author worked for the hit TV show *Doctor Who*), although the perplexing conversation about Arthur Dent in X2.0, "The Christmas Invasion" - not to mention Douglas Adams' own inclusion of *The Origins of the Universe* by Oolon Colluphid into 17.1, "Destiny of the Daleks" - seems to indicate that the *Hitchhiker's* characters are "real" in the *Doctor Who* universe. In which case, Earth is doomed, and all stories set in this planet's future are invalid.]

The Doctor is a Fellow of the Royal Society 'several' times over [so he re-registers in each incarnation?]. He can recognize a Zulu assagai spear on sight, and knows a good Indian takeaway in the Khyber Pass [see 5.2, "The Abominable Snowmen"]. He says that Nimrod is the finest example of a Neanderthal that he's seen 'this side of the Stone Age'. [Incidentally, in one of the deleted scenes, the Doctor mentions getting incarcerated in Newgate Prison, and that it took him 'three weeks' to 'try to get out' of there.]

The Supporting Cast

• *Ace*. Says she was age 13 when she ventured into Gabriel Chase in 1983. [Depending on when her birthday falls, this means she was born in either 1969 or 1970; the spin-off books have gone for the latter. It's worth repeating, though, that Ace's mannerisms aren't really consistent with her hailing from 1987 - see "Dragonfire" for more. The novelisation says Ace was 'nearly 14' on p8, and 'only 14' on p131.] As before ["Silver Nemesis"], when things get tough, the Doctor offers that Ace can return to the TARDIS, but she deems it 'the easy way out'.

In 1983, Ace was friends with a girl named Manisha, but 'white kids' [as Ace puts it] burned out Manisha's flat. [We're never told if Manisha died, but it seems likely given the on-screen account and Ace's very deep-rooted emotional scars. The novelisation to "Remembrance of the Daleks" is confusingly worded, but seems to suggest that Manisha was whisked off to Birmingham. See also "Survival".] After this, Ace climbed over the wall of Gabriel Chase. [Ace apparently told the Doctor she did this 'on a dare', but it seems that she didn't mention Manisha in her first account, and it's here implied that she ventured into house while angry over her friend's plight.] The house was falling down, and the 'evil' and 'hate' that Ace

sensed there [probably the lingering after-effect of Light's dispersed energy, and perhaps also left-over energy from its ship] - when coupled with the trauma Ace felt from the firebombing of Manisha's home - pushed her over the edge and made her set fire to the ruined mansion. Understandably, Ace now has 'a thing' about haunted houses.

It's implied, but by no means certain, that Ace had a probation officer. [Her blowing up the school art room ("Dragonfire" and 26.1, "Battlefield") seems the sort of thing that might warrant this. Sgt. Paterson in "Survival" mentions that Ace was once 'let off with a warning', but whether or not he's talking about Gabriel Chase depends on whether you think the authorities would give her a light slap on the wrist for torching abandoned mansions.]

Ace encourages Gwendoline to wear male evening-dress [some imaginations have run wild about exactly what the girls are doing while changing behind that curtain], and later, she's momentarily aghast to find that the Doctor has got a dress for her to wear. [Contrary to what's in other guidebooks, it is most definitely *not* the dress seen in the Gainsborough painting in the extended version of "Silver Nemesis". Anyone with the patience to pause both of these at once - one story's on DVD, one's only on video at time of writing - can check this, but we can understand any reluctance to go near the extended "Silver Nemesis" unless you're being paid. Besides, a Victorian would have considered the earlier lilac-trimmed dress too scandalously *decolletée*.]

Apparently, Ace has amended her diet since the bacon and egg sandwiches that she ordered in "Remembrance of the Daleks", as she's casually appalled at what Victorians have for breakfast ('Cor! Cholesterol city!').

The TARDIS Within moments of the Ship's arrival, Ace is making jokes and teasing the Doctor about his TARDIS navigation. [This is curious, because in all the time we've known her, the Doctor has got his Ship to *exactly* where he wanted it to go, save for a small spot of trouble when Excalibur was calling through the dimensional ether in "Battlefield". Are we to assume there have been a bundle of unseen adventures, or did obsessive-fan-turned-pro Marc Platt somehow miss two years' worth of episodes?]

This time around, the Ship has landed in a fairly awkward place, with not much clearance left

What Were Josiah's "Blasphemous" Theories?

...continued from page 307

Schopenhauer's Immanent Will, a consciousness which occupies a body but has no say in what it does, a sort of backseat driver. (That's summarising very, very crudely, so Philosophy graduates should please cut us some slack.) The most extreme version of this to be still recognisably philosophy is that of Nietzsche, who of course said "God Is Dead". That would annoy the clergy. He also proposed that the world is in an extreme form of "Carnival of Monsters" (10.2) - that everything which has happened will keep being repeated, and we won't realise because our perceptions are part of it. (See also **Can You Rewrite History, Even One Line?** under 1.6, "The Aztecs" for more on Willpower and History, and 26.4, "Survival" for another side to Nietzsche's take on humanity's need for challenges.) His alternative is that Man is "a rope across the abyss" between ape and angel, and that if our consciousness evolves, we might be able to wrest control of this cycle. Josiah does think of himself as the Superman, with a morality higher than church and law and able to bring order to the Empire. He's the self-made man taken to ridiculous extremes.

This looks like a pretty good fit, but we're obliged to propose alternatives. One is that, as an extraterrestrial himself, he was proposing a Von Daniken account of our development. It does make one wonder how much Light had to do with the Daemons (in many stories we could ignore safely this angle, but Marc Platt shows enough familiarity with the show's past to have at least thought about it), to say nothing of the Fendahl, the Silurians, Scaroth and so on. The mere existence of life on other worlds raises theological problems by the shedload (was each planet redeemed at once, or was there a separate Christ for each one?) and removing God from creation in the one area where there was room for manoeuvre would be a tough sell. Matthews doesn't mention aliens, just that it's blasphemous and it's about evolution. The theories of palaeontologist and Jesuit Pierre Teilhard de Chardin (alleged to have been in on the Piltdown scam) might also have been involved, but that's way too complicated to explain here (a quick version is in the next essay).

Piltdown Man raises one final possibility. As you probably know, this was a faked specimen (actually two, found three years apart) of the "Missing Link", a notional species midway between human and ape based on a misreading of Darwin's suggestion of common ancestry. Has Josiah been experimenting on the samples Light took? Was he planning to exhibit Nimrod as a living Piltdown, possibly to justify his claim to be a Superman and replace the Crowned Saxe-Coburg?

---

between the exterior door and a wall. [If this kind of thing can happen, it's astonishing that we don't see it more often. See X2.11, "Fear Her" for an example of a gag so obvious, nobody dared do it until now.]

The Non-Humans

• *Light*. An alien being of unknown origin, evidently composed of energy, and who's conducting a survey of all life in the Cosmos. [One curiosity is that Light asks Control, 'How many more millennia must I suffer your company?', as if someone has tasked Light and his assistants with this duty.]

Light can 'move at the speed of thought' but travels - along with its Survey and Control agents - in a stone spaceship that can transport / teleport itself instantly and silently. [The Doctor's line that the ship 'doesn't want' Josiah to have his Empire almost suggests the ship is alive, but nothing further is said.] Despite Light's resistance to change - for the sake of keeping its catalog of information current - its form is variable. Somewhat debatably, it seems to innately shape itself in accordance with the dominant lifeform on any given planet, and it here 'naturalises' as a male humanoid with gold skin and silken robes. [See 9.4, "The Mutants" for a similar being, and imagine the fan theories that have followed.] Light has, perhaps appropriately, a Pre-Raphaelite look. It - or "he" [as we will henceforth call it] - is initially suffused with a warm glow and speaks in a high voice. This later develops gravitas as he becomes less perplexed and more resolute.

Light can kill with a glance, sense microbes evolving, effortlessly render handguns useless and turn people into stone so they won't undergo change. [In one of the deleted scenes, he can also lock doors as if by telekinesis.] Josiah estimates that an energy loss from Light's ship, if left unchecked, could obliterate most of southern England. Light finally decides to stop *all* change on Earth with a 'firestorm programme' initiated from its spaceship, but upon the Doctor convincingly arguing that Light himself undergoes change, Light disperses and the 'firestorm' energy is redirected for the ship's departure.

Light seems able to call up data displays onto any nearby flat vertical surface in Gabriel Chase. [Either that, or the house was built to accommodate a spaceship in the cellar and a readout on its stained-glass windows. We don't know much about the former owner, Sir George Pritchard, but this seems rather improbable.]

• *Josiah* and *Control*. The other members of Light's survey party. Effectively, they're twins. [The novelisation blatantly says that they're 'linked', which probably explains why Josiah has locked Control up rather than just killing her, and why Control can direct Josiah's husks. It's a little strange, though, that Josiah didn't stop to think that Control might be capable of manipulating his cast-offs, and that she hasn't directed them to free her before now.]

The overall idea with [as they're here called] Josiah and Control seems to be that Light sends one of them out into a biome as a Survey Agent, to undergo whatever changes the environment makes beneficial to a life-form. To put it another way, the Survey Agent's job is to seek out the creature at the top of any hierarchy and mimic it. The other one (the control for the experiment) is kept pristine for comparison. [However, as we'll see in a bit, there's every reason to think that the two of them can swap roles for any given survey. This might occur after Light "blanks" or "resets" their biology, but the story seems to indicate that evolution is a one-way process for them too.]

The Survey Agent's consciousness develops in a succession of new bodies, with each previous form being cast off but retaining rudimentary motor function. Both Control and Josiah can direct the actions of these creatures. However, if one or more of the previous forms gets damaged, the Survey's consciousness reverts to a previous state. [This is briefly shown and very odd, but it suggests that the information gleaned by the Survey remains intact, whereas the mind using that information is in an earlier state, like trying to open a file made with Windows NT on Windows 95.

[To further explain the ending... Josiah is the Survey Agent and Control is the Control Agent throughout the story, but they swap places in the finale. Control has become the dominant partner through exposure to beings more complex than

herself (such as Ace, the Doctor, Redvers and Josiah himself), and damage to Josiah's former bodies makes him devolve to take Control's former post. The novelisation substantiates this by referring to Control as 'the original Control' once the switch takes place, and Josiah jibbers in Control-speak in both the book and the TV version.]

Josiah's penultimate form is described as 'lucifugous', meaning he's very sensitive to light [more technically, it would mean he shuns or *avoids* light], but his final body has no such vulnerability.

History

• *Dating*. We're told that the story takes place in 1883. [Nobody makes any reference to Krakatoa, but under the circumstances this isn't necessarily significant (as the people who would have brought it up in conversation are either under hypnosis or imprisoned). In sending people to "Java", Gwendoline fails to mention how hazardous it would be for shipping after such a devastating eruption, so we can probably play safe and say it was before August - although the novelisation says it's September. Late summer allows for the thunderstorms, but it's dark just before 6.00 pm, so we could surmise late spring or early autumn.] In 1883, Perivale has only seven houses, and no blacksmith on the village green [this blacksmith thing is a throwaway line from "Dragonfire", one that Ace takes at face-value despite not being present when the Doctor says it].

Light says he previously spent 'centuries' cataloguing all life on Earth, from the smallest bacteria to the largest ichthyosaur. [Icthyosaurus was the fossil that the teenage Mary Anning found in Lyme Regis - "she sells sea shell on the sea-shore" and all that - and was the first complete skeleton found in the UK. This is one of the first things to get dinosaurs into the Victorian consciousness. That happened a generation before Darwin, and was part of the whole mid-ninteenth century fad for amateur palaeontology. [See the inaccurate but memorable statues near where Crystal Palace used to be - the ones Carole Ann Ford posed by for the 1973 *Radio Times* special. If Light picked this species-name to impress a Victorian audience he's adapting faster than we thought.] However, the Icthyosaria - because there was a whole class of these aquatic reptiles discovered thereafter - were

Jurassic, so had been extinct for ninety million years.

Nimrod, a Neanderthal, says his people worshipped Light as 'The Burning One'. [It's troublesome to determine exactly how many journeys Light's crew has made to Earth, and in some respects it's easier to think that Light has been sleeping since Nimrod's era. After all, if Light has been cataloguing life throughout the cosmos in the intervening millennia, it seems unbelievable that he's only now getting outraged about 'changes' occurring to planetary biomes. Surely, if he's been at his job for *that* long, he's witnessed evolution taking place before now?

[But, much more likely, it seems as if Light has catalogued life here three times at least. One visit entailed his placing Nimrod into a 'quarantine cubicle' as the last surviving member of the 'extinct' Homo Neanderthalis, and a prior visit seems to have been in the Jurassic era, unless Ichthyosauria lasted longer than anyone now thinks. The Doctor's reaction to a Pleisiosaurus - from the same period - popping up in 10.2, "Carnival of Monsters", indicates that this is not the case. Then two or three years before the story begins, Light arrived back on Earth...]

Light's survey ship arrived under the building called Gabriel Chase, which was owned by Sir George Pritchard. Whilst Light slept in its chamber, the Survey Agent ran amok. The Survey locked up the Control Agent, mentally enthralled Pritchard's wife and daughter, had Gwendolyn Pritchard murder her father and established himself as the gentleman 'Josiah Samuel Smith'. Sir George Pritchard officially disappeared in 1881. When Inspector McKenzie was assigned to look into the affair, he was somehow made to sleep and kept in one of Josiah's drawer-cases.

Josiah now deems the British Empire to be 'an anarchic mess', and he's presently scheming to assassinate Queen Victoria - a plot that entails his gaining access to Buckingham Palace through an invitation extended to the explorer Redvers Fenn-Cooper. [It would appear that Josiah's acting on a desire to find and supplant the most powerful being on Earth, hence his plan to kill the woman who owns a quarter of the planet and use her Empire to conquer all else.] Redvers came to see Light's energy and was driven mad as a result, thinking that *he* was searching for the lost explorer Redvers Fenn-Cooper.

Stories from Redvers' travels [if they can be believed]: the pygmies from the Oluti Forest led him blindfoled for three days through uncharted territory, and he saw a swamp-full of lizards who looked like dinosaurs. 'Young Conan Doyle', he says, just laughed at his claims. Redvers also faced rampaging buffalo in the Congo, and was acquainted with the daughter of an N'tamba chief - but she had a bone through her nose and ate a cousin for breakfast.

The Analysis

Where Does This Come From? We suggest that you read, if you haven't already, the essay **Did Sergeant Pepper Know The Doctor?** (which you'll find under 5.1, "The Tomb of the Cybermen") and possibly the two essays either side of this. To cite absolutely all the references would take a much bigger entry, and would spoil your fun in finding them. Instead, we'll concentrate on the cultural context and the really big clues.

So let's start with Lewis Carroll. There are overt allusions, such as the reference to Ace as "Alice" and calling the lift a 'rabbit-hole'. More sly is Josiah's mention of calves brains, but we glossed over that in Volume II. (Although the DVD commentary missed it. This wasn't in the script, though, but was Ian Hogg's ad-lib.) But at the bottom of most of Carroll's work is a fear of change, of transience and impermanence - he couldn't face this as a priest-in-training, but he accepted it as a mathematician. Everything in Wonderland is in a state of flux when it should be certain, or kept in a holding pattern when it should be progressing. Worse for Alice and Carroll, nobody seems to care. Alice herself notes that the baby is much happier as a pig.

If we refer the reader once again to Jonathan Miller's 1966 film version for the BBC (music by Ravi Shankar and a cast that defies description), it's with the observation that it had only its second showing during the BBC's week-long fiftieth birthday celebrations for television. (It was the week of episode one of 23.3, "Terror of the Vervoids" just to make the contrast more poignant.) Miller sardonically uses the hymn "Immortal, Invisible, God Only Wise" to denote the absurdity of the Queen's attempts to regulate and control this. The attentive reader will have noticed already that, to many in Britain, the government of the day seemed similarly obsessed with categories and control in matters that seemed hitherto out of the purlieu of the State. It might be thought, therefore, that Light was yet another of Cartmel's broadsides against the Tories.

However, this is not the case. As we will see in a moment, the government made a fuss about a return to what they called "Victorian Values", but the *real* start is Marc Platt's job. He was cataloguing the BBC's radio archive, a job which not only got bigger the longer it went on, but called for increasingly fine distinctions. (We might also allude to a well-known paradox, most clearly cited by Russell and Whitehead in *Principia Mathematica* - see "Tomb of the Cybermen" again and 19.2, "Four to Doomsday" - about a catalogue of books, some of which are themselves catalogues. Where do you list "those catalogues that don't list themselves"? This connects to Gödel's Incompleteness Theorem, which we encountered in Season Eighteen and will again in "The Curse of Fenric".) The Doctor's taunting of Light about the incomplete catalogue (his mention of 'Bandersnatches' and 'Slithy Toves' should not need explaining) is flagrantly the same gag as used by Edmund Blackadder against Doctor Samuel Johnson's Dictionary in *Blackadder the Third*. (And before you all write in, yes, the Doctor tells this as an anecdote in the Big Finish audio ...*Ish*.)

As a well-connected fanboy, Platt cannot fail to have known about the subplot in 4.9, "The Evil of the Daleks" involving Og the Neanderthal roaming around in Maxtible's house. We have to say once again that the writers of this period were working from a folk-memory of the programme's past, but in Platt's case it was far more detailed a recall. Hence the Doctor's question about a Chinese fowling-piece (as per 14.6, "The Talons of Weng-Chiang") and a paraphrase of something-or-other that Douglas Adams wrote in between his scripting episodes of 16.2, "The Pirate Planet" [but see **Things That Don't Make Sense**]. The choice of a Victorian house was largely a compromise between Platt's Mervyn Peake-inspired earlier submissions and the need for an entirely studio-bound production (see **The Lore**). Yet it was also a knowing nod to the fact that BBC Costume Dramas were on their way out, at least in the successful form of the 1970s and early 80s. Managerial practices made it obligatory to commission these from independent companies, without the in-house costumes and sets, thus pushing up the overheads and making each one a one-off - an "event" - and thus needing an overseas deal ahead of production (see **What About Season**

27? under 26.4, "Survival"). Platt consciously conceived this story as a fond pastiche of such bygone glories.

Thus the names of characters are all allusive and playful. "Mrs Grose" was the housekeeper in Henry James' *The Turn of the Screw*; the author of *The Last of the Mohicans*, James Fenimore Cooper, lent his name to Redvers; Gwendoline, aside from being Platt's mum (his dad was called "Ernest") is the cunning ingenue in *The Importance of Being Earnest*; and Nimrod is in the Book of Genesis, as all Bugs Bunny fans know. (It's also the make of AWACs plane used by the RAF and soon to be scrapped, but this may be tangential.) In those days, the beer sold at the Fitzroy Tavern was "Samuel Smith's", and "Josiah" was another of Platt's relatives.

Literary allusions abound, from throwaways like Josiah's 'I'm a man of property' (the title of the first book in Galsworthy's *The Forsyte Saga*, and we refer you again to "The Evil of the Daleks") and references to Reading Gaol (more Oscar Wilde) to Conrad's *Heart of Darkness* (which Platt studied at O-Level, apparently). The Reverend being Dean of "Mortarhouse College, Oxford" is more complicated. There's a Peterhouse, which was parodied by Tom Sharpe in his novel *Porterhouse Blue* (conflating it with the "porterhouse steak" to suggest excess and stodginess; both establishments are in Cambridge). This was adapted for television in the mid-80s. ('Mortar-house' as in bricks and mortar? It's unlikely to be yet-another dig at the Redbrick universities, as this would be anachronistic and at odds with Matthews' character and beliefs. But there's a public school called Charterhouse that provides us with stodgy politicians and civil servants to this day. Many of its alumni go to Magdalen College, pronounced "maudlin". Magdalen+ Charterhouse = Mortarhouse.) Oxford in this era was still having theological ructions, although nothing like as violent as in the 1840s with the rise of the "Oxford Movement". In the essay with this entry, we will discuss what an earlier Bishop of Oxford had done about this evolution stuff.

Josiah Samuel Smith is a literal "self-made man". In this, he is at least partly a parody of Samuel Smiles, a Victorian author (and that was his real name) who wrote a guidebook to advancement in life called *Self Help*. This advocated a rigorous and vigorous programme of entrepreneurship, plus ruthless cultivating of useful friends and remorseless hard work, to achieve material wealth. No concessions were made to aiding others, taking time off to ask why you were doing this, or worrying about the effect of this on your health.

These were the "Victorian Values" that Margaret Thatcher espoused. Not everyone agreed, even in Smiles' time (read your Dickens if you don't believe us). Another form of self-remodelling was elocution, to remove the "taint" of regional upbringing or lower class. In books such as Hardy's *The Mayor of Casterbridge*, the efforts of self-made men to re-mould their daughters into "ladies" are ridiculed (look up Chapter 20 and watch out for the dialect words that JK Rowling pilfered). George Bernard Shaw had a look at this in his play *Pygmalion* (mutilated into *My Fair Lady*), which is the source of at least three gags in this story but also the whole subplot of Control becoming a "Ladylike". We will return to this in the essay too.

Visual cues would similarly take months to go through one-by-one, but the main source is Pre-Raphaelite paintings. Light resembles both a Rosetti angel and more specifically Arthur Hughes' painting *The Annunciation* in Birmingham's Art Museum. The poet / painter Dante Gabriel Rossetti is also a touchstone for the red-haired, velvet-jacketed Josiah, with the round sunglasses perhaps a nod to GK Chesterton's *The Man Who Was Thursday*. Ace and more specifically Gwendoline dress in white tie and tails like George Sand or Vesta Tilley (although twenty years too late for the former and ten too early for the latter). Nimrod is markedly similar to the ads for Monkey Brand Soap, used for cleaning kitchenware. Any edition of *Punch* from this era, or more especially a decade later, would have had one of these.

To broaden things out further, it's worth examining Dennis Potter's influence. After the success of *The Singing Detective* and its riling of Mrs Whitehouse (see Volume IV) a number of Potter's early works were re-screened, now that he was officially a 'genius'. Platt cites one of these - *Where Adam Stood* (1976) - as an influence, but let us not forget the then-recent film *Dreamchild*, in which the elderly Alice Liddell is feted in 1930s New York and reconciled to her embarrassing past. (This film combines the talents of Potter and Jim Henson - how much more like *Doctor Who* do you want? Well, the Gryphon has the voice of Fulton Mackay - see 7.2, "Doctor Who and the Silurians"

and 5.6, "Fury From The Deep".) They had wiped the 1965 play Potter based on *Alice*, which had starred Deborah Watling (see "The Evil of the Daleks", as if you needed to be told). We will return to Potter in the next story.

Also worth a look is John Fowles' novel *The French Lieutenant's Woman*, a novel made famous by a film only loosely like it, and which took the metaphor of evolution as far as developing its own plot in mutually-exclusive directions, and riffing on the story of Mary Anning (see our comments on Ichthyosaurs, above) whilst examining the impact of the theory on the characters' behaviour. Josiah's disquisition on moths changing colour because of pollution was one familiar to children subjected to BBC Schools Radio in the 60s, even though the paper describing the process was only published in the 1950s.

Two more theories, occasionally advanced, need to be mentioned here. One is that it looks suspiciously like *The Rocky Horror Picture Show,* especially the dinner-party scene where it turns out they've been eating one of the guests. Another is that all those stuffed birds, a Victorian house and something in the cellar making people kill is all very *Psycho*.

Things That Don't Make Sense You will see it solemnly reported in other guidebooks that Neanderthals (in this case, Nimrod) couldn't speak because their larynxes were inadequately formed. This is, it turns out, not true. It was likely that the squeakings they made would not have travelled very far (not much cop for hunters), but theoretically they could have spoken as well as a child. However, the neural set-up might not have supported syntax or the level of abstraction to get beyond mimesis (representing a cow by making "moo" noises, for instance). More alarming from this point of view is Nimrod's depiction as a hunched-up, shambling figure. This is what Neanderthals were thought to be like for ages, but it turns out that the most complete skeleton anyone had was an arthritic old man. [Still, it's better than 1.1, "An Unearthly Child" on that score.]

The density of allusions here isn't much of a problem (indeed, some might say it's part of the fun), but it is an issue that they're all much more topical for the 1850s than the 1880s, when this story is apparently set. We've somewhat addressed this disharmony in **Where Does This Come From?**, and more on the trouble it causes in the accompanying essay, but let's bluntly ask the question: was it *really* necessary to move the time-frame forward thirty years? [An earlier date was mooted when the story was in development, but Nathan-Turner insisted on the 1880s, as it would allow the cast to wear nicer costumes. Possibly, it also seemed appealing to make place the story an exact century before Ace set the house alight.] And even in the 1880s, it's unlikely that Matthews would have encountered telephones.

We could list absurdities and inconsistencies for ages: why does Mrs Pritchard bring Control copies of *The Times* if Josiah doesn't want Control to adapt? Why is does it seem as if the sleeping Light is inside Redvers' snuff-box? Why does the candle shoot a jet of flame near Josiah's face? Why does a being who can fly around the world in a second need a functioning lift? How did Ace get undressed and into a big nightie? [Should we presume that Mrs Grose redressed her, and that she slept through the experience?] Even allowing that energy from Light's spaceship seems to be animating various objects [and also accounts for the stuffed animals' eyes glowing in episode one], how do insects that were presumably cyanosed and covered in lacquer come back to life?

Would a clergyman in 1883 even know the phrase 'mumbo-jumbo', as Matthews does? How can it be dawn at 4.30 am and dusk at 5.00 pm on the same day? It's conceivable that Gwendoline would mistake the name 'Ace' for 'Alice' if it were printed on the page, but she's heard it spoken aloud. That said, this is the least of Gwendoline's delusions - all the business with her attacking people and sending them to "Java" aside, she seems to wear a locket with pictures of herself and Mrs Pritchard no matter what she her attire, yet she's apparently never looked at the item or wondered what it meant in the last two or three years.

Larger concerns now: why and how, exactly, does the Reverend Matthews devolve into a gibbering monkey? If the idea is that something was done to him to throw evolution into reverse, shouldn't he have become a baby? If he was being "restored" to a hominid state akin to our ancestors, could his brain have had the necessary convolutions for language and recall? [Ignoring the lack of anything looking like 'Homo Victorianus Ineptus' in the known fossil record, the actual condition of Rev Matthews is more akin to the hapless protagonist of Aldous Huxley's satire *After Many A Summer*, in which longevity has allowed the 200-year-old millionaire to "mature", ceasing

to be the neotenous ape all humans actually remain because of our normal lifespan keeping us like baby chimps. There was a BBC adaptation of this novel directed by Douglas Camfield. However, this would take both gene-manipulation and a time-machine to make it happen overnight. See also X3.6, "The Lazarus Experiment" for a similar mistake about evolution and X3.13 for a riff on this neoteny idea.]

And what, we might ask, is the problem with Josiah's evening maids? If they've been hired to work when he's conscious and hide in cupboards when he isn't, why have Mrs Grose and the day staff not come across them when cleaning? And if they're kept hypnotised - as their blank demeanour seems to suggest - why can't they work in the day? And if these dazed women are real people under a spell, didn't the agency that sent them to Gabriel Chase wonder why they never spent their wages, or emerged on alternate Tuesdays or whenever the contracted day off was?

But we're dancing around the central question here: why does Josiah employ Mrs Grose and the daytime maids *at all*? There's nobody to cook for, as the occupants are asleep all day. Never mind that Mrs Grose keep insisting that 'nobody in their right mind' would stay in Gabriel Chase after dark - as if she's witnessed or knows something *really* interesting - making it a mystery why she's stayed at her post for so long. Perhaps she's been retained to "humanize" the staff and stop the outside world getting too suspicious about Gabriel Chase, but if *that's* the case, then letting her leave and gossip around the town is probably a lot riskier than just sacking her.

So all right... on the strength of Light's comment about 'seeing how it works', the Night Maids might be automata, but *that* just makes their non-functioning by day and Mrs Grose's presence all the more puzzling. Worse, when all's said and done, a couple of the evening maids are unaccounted for. There's at least four that we can see, and Light kills two of them, so the other pair seem to have vanished from the narrative when the Doctor and Ace have their final conversation in the "empty" house. Also, Heaven knows what anyone who investigates Gabriel Chase in the next hundred years will make of Josiah's latest cast-off, which by all signs is left to rot in the attic. [Mind you, it's decomposing pretty fast even when alive.]

Why did Light, a being of seemingly inexhaustible energy, go to sleep in the first place?

Josiah's desire to seize control of the British Empire seems clear enough, but how exactly he intends to deal with the awakened Light in episode three is entirely left dangling. He says he expects that Light will accept his invitation to dinner, but what he plans to do once Light shows up... well, who knows? At the same dinner, Josiah seems surprised that the Doctor knows about his plan to assassinate the Queen, and asks him, 'Who have you been talking to?' Whom does he *think* the Doctor has been talking to, if not the only other person who knows Josiah's plans, namely Redvers? [One small detail that *does* make sense, once you've seen the deleted scenes, is that Redvers is in the upper observatory in episode three to chat with Josiah. The edits made to the broadcast version resulted in his solemnly being there for no evident reason.]

The *biggest* worry, however, is that this story uses evolution as a metaphor for self-determination and mental health - as set against insanity and rigidity - but it has absolutely no understanding of Darwin. Humans are *not* the most evolved species: if anything, the ability to shape our environment has stopped us developing. So if Josiah is really measuring himself against the most perfectly-adapted life-forms, he would be a beetle or a shark. The definition of "success" that puts humans at the top is one we developed, not perhaps one that a visitor to this world would recognise.

Critique Throughout these books we've faced a communications problem. Americans and other non-UK folks don't get some basic British idioms, and need simple things like "beans on toast" and "Gordon Bennett" explained. Approximately half the sales of *About Time* are in the US, very nearly half are in the UK, and the likes of Canada, New Zealand and Australia account for the remainder. (This is a rough guess, because - for instance - it's hard to establish how many international customers order from Amazon US. But it nonetheless surprised us to hear, as we expected the American portion to be a lot more. There's also one regular customer in Madrid, apparently, and we hope he's following all of this without our catering solely for his benefit, although we'd like to take this opportunity to apologise once again for 22.4, "The Two Doctors".)

One idiom that's caught on here lately is so handy, it's amazing we got by without it for six centuries: 'Marmite.' It's a yeast extract, high in Vitamin B complexes and - when spread on buttered toast - it's the flavour of a British childhood. Foreigners and some particularly strange locals don't like it, and cannot comprehend anyone who does. The adverts celebrating the product's centenary made a big play of this, depicting people voluntarily eating it under circumstances that resemble nightmares (one was a pastiche of *The Elephant Man*, another referenced *The Blob* and so on), and with the simple slogan "You either love it or you hate it".

That's it. The word now expresses clearly any matter on which there is no middle-ground. We thought of trying a suitable American equivalent, but there just aren't any. It occurred to us to try *Yentl*, except that even hardcore Barbra Streisand lovers (of whom there are many in UK fandom, as you might imagine) find this film a bit of an ordeal. So "Ghost Light" is the Marmitest of all Marmite stories, in that there is no possibility of either side comprehending the other's position. People who don't like it will never get it, and those who adore it cannot think down to the level of the others without a major blunt-force trauma to the skull.

... sorry about that, didn't mean to show our hand so soon, but now you know. So if you happen to be one of those unfortunates who can't watch this story, forget the rest of this review and go watch a Streisand movie or something.

We'll assume you're watching these in order of transmission. What you'll have seen is that the base-level of professionalism, of watchability, of not-being-as-crap-as-Season-Twenty-Two-ness has risen to the point where embarrassing lapses like "Silver Nemesis" or "Battlefield" are the exceptions. A story like "The Greatest Show in the Galaxy" now looks like normal service being resumed, not a freak example of things going right that's floating around bemusedly in a sea of mediocrity and ineptitude. Unless you're one of those strange people who can't see past the Kandy Man to the merits of "The Happiness Patrol" (the *third* most Marmite story ever, with No. 2 being 2.5, "The Web Planet"), you'll also see how each story since Cartmel took over as script editor has been a fresh look at an old topic, or a previous style of the programme.

What you'll *also* see, if you watch the stories in the order they were made, is that each new adventure is bolder than the last. Each takes the series' format further from invasions of the Home Counties, monsters attacking humans because that's what monsters *do*, and all the tired old chestnuts of the recent past. We're getting steadily further from the idea that aliens and space-humans talk in a stilted version of English with no apostrophes or wit, and in an interchangeable vocabulary. The last two proper script editors had tin ears for dialogue (we can't speak for Antony Root), and Cartmel seems to have had some deficiencies in this regard, but he knew when his writers could do the job and usually opted not to rewrite everything in his own idiom.

Marc Platt writes *some* lines that aren't quotes, and they're generally as spot-on as anything else. There's a few odd Ace lines (not that every story doesn't afflict some curious dialogue on this bizarre teenager, our favourite being "Silver Nemesis" and 'nice rocket technology' - which is so wrong it's perfect). But to the script's credit, there's also a few lines that actually sound like 1989 teen-speak ('well safe'). The Doctor casually mentions burnt toast (a liberal coating of Marmite can fix that, incidentally) and "bust asians" (actually 'bus stations', as you'd probably deduced) and *sounds* like a real person again, not someone there to trick gods and explain the plot. With this performance, McCoy is in the unenviable position of having to make the Doctor the most normal person in this world, and he pulls it all together. For once, he's on the receiving end of physical comedy from other characters, and has to say lines of such astonishing complexity *and* make them sound like he's thinking aloud. The result is that - arguably for the first time since 17.2, "City of Death" - the Doctor seems as intelligent as we're always being told he is, as well-read and able to step into any situation and outwit people. The rearranged running order puts episode one of this *tour de force* right after episode four of "Battlefield", and the contrast is so stark as to be almost hilarious.

So "Ghost Light" is the pinnacle of this phase of the series. Well, in most regards. The one thing many people say is that, unlike the next two stories to hit our screens, you need to have your *Doctor Who* head on to watch it. This is a curious criticism. It assumes that you don't need it to watch, for example, "Colony in Space" (8.4). A member of the general public stumbling across an episode in 1971 had just as much work to do - making sense of a glove-puppet in a motorised throne, or Roger Delgado explaining supernovae to someone who already knew about them - as anyone encountering Inspector Mackenzie asleep in a bottom drawer in 1989. If anything, the resemblance between this and so many other Victorian dramas makes it possible they might not even know what series they were watching - which isn't something you can say about "Colony in Space". The problem (if such it is) with "Ghost Light" is in fact the exact opposite: if you watch it as though it were orthodox *Doctor Who*, you're going to make the most awful mess of working out what's what.

One of the key differences between *fans* and *fanboys* is that the former might have read the books alluded to in this story beforehand, just because they read everything. Fanboys will only be seen reading, watching or listening to something once they have been told that it is a "source". So non-fans made sense of this far quicker than fanboys. We know this from our long experience of house-shares. Watched as orthodox television, without making the assumptions one makes when exposed to "cult" stuff over a number of years, this all makes perfect sense if you pay attention. "Cult" fans are used to being spoon-fed. *Doctor Who* only became "cult" posthumously, but throughout the 1980s, the script-logic (such as it was at times) became increasingly like that of comics and American blockbuster space films. "Ghost Light" is a story that has the logic of a three-act play, the reference-games of a good novel and the aesthetic of a Merchant-Ivory film. It's playful and makes concessions to the general viewer, but it doesn't signpost the plot-points, nor make a distinction between these and "mere" wordplay. It is unmistakably the work of a *Doctor Who* fan of some years' standing, but not in the same depressing way that 22.1, "Attack of the Cybermen" shows signs of fannish instigation. The one thing that really makes this story *Doctor Who*-ish is that all the other elements, however much they have been "sampled" with no intervention or reworking, are in the same story interacting with one another. There is nowhere else that these characters and this situation could exist all at once.

And if you *do* watch Season Twenty-Six in production order, apart from "Battlefield" seeming more out-of-place than ever, the thing you see is how far the series is walking a tightrope between making stories out of ideas and making dramas out of characters. This might seem like an artificial distinction, but when you see this and "Survival" as a matched pair, it will become clearer. In

"Survival", the various figures are exposed to the planet's effect and respond in different ways. Although they move in a milieu that has signs and throwaway dialogue all around hinting at this being a story with a moral, this is mainly about how the people cope (or don't) and what the different reactions and their consequences tell us. In "Ghost Light", the different ways that people adapt (or don't) are simply different ways to adapt. It is not-adapting that is bad, not that any one adaptation is any worse than any other. And so the fun of the story is seeing how these assorted characters interact and develop, shut inside a house that is one big laboratory. We are not being preached at, we're simply invited to examine our own preconceptions while everyone else does likewise (or fails to and dies).

After polemics like "Greatest Show", being allowed to make up our own mind(s) is an enormous relief. Being congratulated for spotting where the story is going, rather than waiting for it to catch up with us, is welcome too. The dialogue isn't quite as clever as it thinks it is, and Matthews ending every sentence with 'is it not?' in his first scene simply sounds like a bad impression of chat-show host Russell Harty, not a real Victorian prelate. The characters are given in broad strokes, but with only three episodes, this isn't a story with time to hang around being subtle. As we said, the viewers are expected to be about half a page ahead of the characters, and able to mull over the implications of what's being said or shown to us. If any viewer is in trouble, there's always the chance to watch it again. Because, unlike a lot of *Doctor Who*, this is a story made in the certainty that a lot of people watching are recording it to re-watch. If not, there's a lot else to enjoy, like the sets, costumes, music and overall atmosphere.

This is a self-confident series, assured that the bright ones watching will either take notes and look it all up later, or in fact already know what everyone's talking about. So much else on television in the late 80s was painful for bright kids to watch without six layers of irony. Now, even bad late 80s *Doctor Who* seems like Tom Stoppard compared to most things made lately. Watching "Ghost Light" now is like looking back at a lost world when mainstream TV could do things like this and follow it with *Bergerac*. Indeed, the next time *Doctor Who* tried anything set in a big Victorian house (X2.2, "Tooth and Claw"), it was the crassest cliché imaginable: Queen Victoria and a werewolf, with soldiers, kung-fu monks and lots

of running around corridors. Making a story where people sit around and talk philosophy that is more exciting and funnier than a Russell T Davies script is a big achievement. Celebrate its mere existence - or better yet, just watch it again, ideally whilst eating Marmite on toast.

The Facts

Written by Marc Platt. Directed by Alan Wareing. Ratings: 4.2 million, 4.0 million, 4.0 million. Audience appreciation was a solid 68% for episodes one and two, and 64% for the last episode.

Working Titles "The Bestiary", "Not the Bestiary" (basically a joke after Nathan-Turner said he didn't like "The Bestiary" and wanted a different title), "Life-Cycle".

Supporting Cast Ian Hogg (Josiah), Katharine Schlesinger (Gwendoline), Sylvia Syms (Mrs Pritchard), Michael Cochrane (Redvers Fenn-Cooper), Sharon Duce (Control), John Nettleton (Reverend Ernest Matthews), Carl Forgione (Nimrod), John Hallam (Light), Frank Windsor (Inspector Mackenzie), Brenda Kempner (Mrs Grose).

Oh, Isn't That..?

• *Sylvia Syms.* In the 1950s, America had two basic icons of female allure: Marilyn Monroe and Lauren Bacall. We had Diana Dors and, um, a number of frightfully nice ladies, most of whom were signed to J Arthur Rank. The nearest we got to a Bacall was when Sylvia Syms played the only woman in World War II (or at least, if you believed the version in 1950s British films) in *Ice-Cold in Alex*. After smouldering terribly decently, obscurity beckoned until the 1970s, when she became a kind of female Richard Briers (24.2, "Paradise Towers") in sitcoms on ITV.

• *Ian Hogg.* He came to this fresh from his very own cop-show. Two, actually, as *Rockliffe's Babies* (old cop given raw trainees) engendered *Rockliffe's Folly* (ex-cop does something else, but keeps helping former colleagues. Not a bit like *Bulman*, then). Like all Scots actors of his generation, he spent most of the 90s in chainmail.

• *Frank Windsor.* By this time, he was almost free of the type-casting that had dogged him since *Z Cars*, which had caused him to take parts in things like Ranulf in "The King's Demons" (20.6) and some dreadful ITV dramas. Now he's completely free of it, by virtue of a series of ads for a funeral plan. (The accidental catch-phrase, "This charming carriage-clock could be yours", is now a far bigger career albatross than anything he'd done before.) He was also in *A For Andromeda*, but you'll have to take our word for it, cos the BBC wiped the tapes. More importantly, he was the Scoutfinder General in *The Goodies*.

• *Michael Cochrane*. He'd also done this before, as Lord Cranleigh in 19.5, "Black Orchid". Under that story, we discussed *Wings* and *The Archers*.

• *John Nettleton*. He was Sir Arnold in *Yes Minister* and narrated drawings of historical events in early 70s *Blue Peter* (see **The Lore**).

• *Katharine Schlesinger*. She'd previously played Catherine Morland, Jane Austen's only baseball-playing heroine, in a 1986 version of *Northanger Abbey* (it was a a a gothic spoof, as you probably knew).

• *John Hallam*. He was Brian Blessed's - sorry - wingman in *Flash Gordon*, Dirty Den's cell-mate in *EastEnders* and Sir Wilfred De'ath in the last episode of *The Black Adder*. His other TV credits would go on for ages, but he was the first person in an ITC film series of the late 60s to be seen to drive a white Mk II Jaguar over a cliff. (Of course, he didn't *really*, but the clip of a Jag exploding was filmed for his death scene in *Randall and Hopkirk (Deceased)* and then re-used in every such series on almost a weekly basis.) His big starring role was in *The Mallens* (see 22.3, "The Mark of the Rani").

Cliffhangers Bug-eyed monsters in wing-collars and tail-coats menace Ace; the being in the cellar, identified as 'Light', comes up the lift to meet with the Doctor.

The Lore

• Marc Platt had been submitting stories since 1975. He'd sent one ("Fires of the Star Mind") in to Robert Holmes - this was set on Gallifrey, would you believe. He'd also, with Jeremy Bentham, worked on a Sontaran-Rutan yarn ("Warmongers") in the continuity-heavy early 80s. (This seems to have been set in the Blitz, and may be connected to his proposed Ice Warrior story for Season Twenty-Seven.) Once Andrew Cartmel became script editor, a version of what was to become Platt's *New Adventures* book *Time's*

Crucible was resubmitted. Cartmel rejected this but was intrigued, and asked Platt in for a chat. By this time, Platt had been involved in fandom for over a decade, and written for many of the high-end fanzines (such as *The Frame* and the "Making of the Five Doctors", a precursor to this) and *DWM*.

Platt developed two ideas with Cartmel. One ("Shrine") was about Tsarist Russia and a reincarnated god, the other was a reworking of his Colin Baker story "Cat's Cradle" (the aforementioned "TARDIS Inside Out" idea that became *Time's Crucible*) and was set in the Doctor's worst nightmare, the place he'd been trying to leave all along. (If you don't know, this is what eventually became *Lungbarrow*, the last *New Adventures* book, which we discuss in **Who Are All These Men in Wigs?** under 13.5, "The Brain of Morbius" and **What About Season 27?** under 26.4, "Survival".) With such an intricate gothic setting, it seemed entirely in keeping with what Cartmel wanted, but Nathan-Turner thought that this was risking yet more big revelations about the Doctor's past (see "Silver Nemesis"). So it became Ace's worst nightmare and a Victorian house.

• Alan Wareing was given this and "Survival" to direct in one block, with this coming last. His initial idea for Light was of a Victorian preacher (he took the notion from the otherwise unremarkable film *Poltergeist II*). The exteriors for Gabriel Chase were shot whilst in Dorset on location for the other story, and Paintbox changed the weather and added an observatory. Another film idea Wareing kept was the sliding of the maids out from the walls, inspired by "the Penguin" in *The Blues Brothers*. The maids were all dancers, and were recruited by Gary Downie.

• Nick Somerville, the set designer, put in a lot of work. Very little of the set was from stock, although some of the dressings were used in more than one section of the set. Some of the upstairs sections were in fact raised, so that actors could ascend stairs to get there. This also helped when setting up the snuff-box scene in Redvers' cell. Although the furniture was sometimes authentic Victoriana, the lift was a small hydraulic one adapted to look period. Getting into the spirit of the story, Somerville furnished the Lower Observatory with a raven and a writing-desk, and liaised with the effects and lighting teams to create the membranous screen onto which the readouts were projected.

• In casting Redvers, Wareing looked into the availability of Harry Enfield. Given that his earliest TV appearances had been on *The Tube* as "Sir Harry Stocracy", this isn't as unlikely as many commentators have thought. *DWM*'s usually infallible archives claim that they also enquired about Michael Caine for one part - Josiah would be the most likely candidate, but the casting of Light seems to have caused trouble. Blimey! Michael Caine in *Doctor Who*. It is just, ju-u-ust conceivable, as he was doing a series on screen acting for the BBC at the right time. Had this happened, it's improbable that the Doctor's "Did you know?" joke in the cut scene in the Nursery would have happened. (As anyone hereabouts knows, Peter Sellers started the fad for impersonating Caine by reeling off odd facts in a halting half-cockney accent, and Mike Yarwood turned it into a cliché. Sir Michael bowed to the inevitable and published a book called *Not A Lot of People Know That*, which Yarwood used as Caine's catch-phrase).

• Nathan-Turner's other contribution to this script was that a token monster was required for the small kids without A-Levels. Thus, the Husks were brought forward in the mix. The original idea was to re-use the Frog and Fish masks from Barry Letts' then-recent version of *Alice's Adventures in Wonderland* (which provided work for Michael Wisher and Lis Sladen, if nothing else). This didn't quite work, so the new masks were devised. These were based on moulds from Ian Hogg's head (although you'd be hard-pressed to tell), and one looks suspiciously like the head of Omega from "Arc of Infinity" (20.1). That dress Ace wears is one Ken Trew had made for an episode of *The Onedin Line*. Aldred hated it, especially the corset.

• Platt asked for a suitable song, something about birds in cages or zoo visits. It's possible he was recalling a ditty used in a 1971 *Blue Peter* feature about London Zoo ("Walking in the Zoo is the OK Thing to Do"). A trawl through the BBC's formidable files found JF Mitchell's "That's the Way to the Zoo". Katharine Schlesinger (as Gwendoline) took a few singing lessons just in case, but she couldn't play piano. So Alasdair Nicholson recorded the song twice - once with his guide vocal and once not (the one to which Schlesinger mimes - her voice was pre-recorded too). McCoy was also to have mimed playing a Meade Lux Lewis boogie-woogie piece sequeing to the *Moonlight Sonata* when Josiah enters, but there wasn't time for a better take, and McCoy was

unhappy with his "performance". John Hallam, an early choice to play Light, turned out to be double-booked on *The Chronicles of Narnia* (where he was Captain Drinian) but ended up doing both. The curious vocal delivery was his idea, to show Light adapting involuntarily to the social norms around him.

• Katharine Schlesinger's name was spelled 'Katherine' in the end credits for the first two episodes, although Nathan-Turner saw that this was fixed for episode three, and retrospectively amended the master tapes so all subsequent airings and the 1994 VHS release had the correct spelling. The *Doctor Who* Restoration Team that handles the DVD material judged that switching it back - in the sole interest of presenting the story as originally broadcast - would be a bit rude, and let the correct spelling stand for the commercial release. The error is mentioned in the DVD's information text, though. (You really care about this, don't you?)

• A quick update on the schedule. This was the last story to be committed to tape, and was shot between 18th of July and 3rd of August. Aldred has been contracted to stay for another four episodes, and McCoy for another year. Nathan-Turner has now quit three times, and so has arranged to go on leave once editing and publicity for this season is out of the way. He'll stay in touch with BBC Enterprises to supervise merchandising, but not make any more episodes. Cartmel is being offered work by other BBC drama productions.

The launch of BBC1's Autumn season had Jean Marsh and Aldred join Nathan-Turner and Jonathan Powell in a screening of some clips from "The Curse of Fenric". This is 16th of August (Aldred was shooting *Corners* that day and was still in costume as a native American, so it must have been really confusing). Cartmel leaves on 15th of September, after being headhunted by *Casualty*. On the 19th, Nathan-Turner has to have "Battlefield" episode four ready to show bosses before going on holiday. That holiday ends with him recording a five-minute introduction to the series for German-speaking viewers who were to see forty-two episodes on RTL. (These were dubbed into German, with the Seventh Doctor being dubbed by the same actor who did Tom Baker's voice. The result is worth seeing just once, like 2.5, "The Web Planet" with episode six in Spanish.) By the time Nathan-Turner gets back, it's clear that the ratings for "Battlefield" are a disaster, so they do a relaunch in which Peter Cregeen - of whom much more later - allays fears that the series is ending. But, he says, it might be a while before any new episodes are made...

26.3: "The Curse of Fenric"

(Serial 7M, Four Episodes. 25th October - 15th November 1989.)

Which One is This? It's the one in 1943 - with a thinly-disguised Alan Turing character, some John Carpenter riffs and Nicholas Parsons.

Firsts and Lasts Here we are, seven episodes from the end and a month before the fall of the Berlin Wall, and *Doctor Who* finally does a story set in World War Two. For the second and final time (the first being eighteen years previous in 8.2, "The Mind of Evil"), we have a scene with people talking foreign in subtitles on screen.

Four-and-a-half Things to Notice about "The Curse of Fenric"...

1. Even *before* re-editing, re-grading and remixing, this story looked a lot more like TV in the 1990s than what we had been seeing in the 1980s. Largely to cut down on screen-time (of *course* it over-ran), we have dialogue dubbed over visual events happening in another part of the story. This moves things along briskly, but even so they find time to do a still, slow scene of the Reverend Wainwright reading from the New Testament (1 Corinthians 13). Not only does this provide justification for his inability to withstand the Haemovores, not only does it hint at the key code-word in Millington's plan (but see **Things That Don't Make Sense**), but it gives us a chance to watch an experienced actor give a good performance, and forget that we're watching Nicholas Parsons. For a few moments, at least, his sins are forgiven (see **Oh, Isn't That..?**).

2. The Doctor finds a way to scare off Haemovores with a psychic defence founded on faith. We know what the others find to believe in (or not, in one case), but what of the Doctor himself? He mutters something and this seems to do the trick. Close examination (and the rather curious novelisation) reveals that it's... the "official" list of companions. What a let-down! And yet, what a clever way to get this in, almost as an afterthought. Certainly, those of us who sat through

through X2.9, "The Satan Pit" have no cause to complain, as that story - in so many ways a dumbed-down version of this one - makes it seem like a huge revelation that the Doctor believes in his companion.

3. Ace's extraordinary chat-up lines are made to serve a number of functions. Her dialogue is a statement of her feelings of being displaced in time, a suggestion that burgeoning teenage sexuality and time-travel are similar, a hint of the oncoming thunderstorm and a prosaic plot device to allow the Doctor to free Captain Sorin. At least, that's the theory. What actually happens is that children's TV presenter Sophie Aldred (pushing thirty by this point) coos gibberish to a British soldier (Marcus Hutton) who looks rightly embarrassed, and at any moment we expect one or the other to start singing "Windmills of Your Mind". Ace even announces this ingenious strategy to him by saying, 'I'm not a little girl'. No, dear, you're not.

4. It's a history of post-war lit-crit. Ian Briggs, as the author of "Dragonfire" (24.4), must be assumed to know what he's doing when he has things so remarkably similar to theories of reading, in the right sequence. We start off with dime-store Freud (things under the surface threatening to come up). Then we go through American "close reading" (getting inside the author's head by trying to be him), Structuralism ('It's a flip-flop thingy'), Russian Formalism (literally decoding it with a computer, using glyphs and diagrams), Semiotics (it's recognisably like *Dracula*), misapplied Saussurean Linguistics (the arbitrary nature of the sign, so a Soviet badge works like a crucifix) and so on.

There's a lot more we could cite, in almost ludicrous detail. Then, right at the end, after Game Theory's been tried, what's the solution? Go back to the basic assumption of a binary opposition at the heart of the text and try removing it (black and white pawns team up). In other words, it's Derridean Deconstruction. Note that his discussion with Rev Wainwright mentions Nietzsche's *Beyond Good and Evil*, a book that was being "rediscovered" in the mid-80s by people trying to get out of the trap that all those Parisian 60s guys had found themselves bogged down in. So did the Doctor arrange for World War II to happen just to teach Ace about "Free play of the text"?

4a. As always, Cartmel got the story to fit into the allotted number of episodes by cutting out a lot, and the director - finding that it *still* over-ran - had to hack out more. Some of this extra material is available on the BBC video, added in the appropriate places but still in episode form. There was talk of doing this as five episodes, but the Powers-That-Be wanted rid of the show ASAP, with Christmas coming[44]. So now, with the broadcast mix on the DVD, the video revamp and the feature-length "complete" version on the DVD with redone music and effects, there are three commercially-available versions of this story.

The Continuity

The Doctor When asked if he has a family, the Doctor replies that he "doesn't know", and agrees that it's terrible not knowing. [Compare for a start with 5.1, "Tomb of the Cybermen", in which the Doctor says his family sleeps in his mind, and the passing references to his family in the Welsh series.] He says the Prisoner's Dilemma [see **Where Did This Come From?**] is based on a false premise, 'like all zero-sum games', but that it's a neat algorithm, nevertheless.

He's not only ambidextrous, but can forge Churchill's signature with his right hand whilst forging the chief of secret service's signature with his left. Of course he can read Russian, and he enjoys debating philosophy with Rev Wainwright. He's knowledgeable about Viking runes, but refrains from directly translating the ones seen here. [Naturally, we must now ask if he *could* have done so if he wished. Intentionally or otherwise, text in classic *Doctor Who* is often translated like speech, and certainly the writers for the BBC Wales version seem to believe that the TARDIS' translation ability covers the printed as well as the spoken language. See especially X2.08, "The Impossible Planet", in which the Ship's inability to translate an ancient language is cause for alarm.

[This is something of a revised idea, however, as classic *Doctor Who* isn't clear on the point and the *New Adventures* - published in the interim between the two shows - held that a written text doesn't have a mind for the Ship's telepathic circuits to interface with. So we should perhaps assume that he's never seen this particular runic alphabet, or spent much time around any of its native speakers. That might seem unlikely, but then he didn't hang around when the Vikings came calling in 1066 - see 2.9, "The Time Meddler". Actually, the more curious point is that *this* Doctor - the one who tends to make massive

preparations before confronting an adversary - didn't brush up on his Viking history and languages while readying to deal with Fenric. But the fact that Ace can't translate the runes either - and the TARDIS seems to equally facilitate translation among the Doctor and his companions - suggests he didn't.]

The Doctor calms a traumatised Russian soldier just by touching the man's forehead. [This is the second of three uses of the "psychic doorbell" this year.] And he deduces that having faith in something can create a psychic defence against Haemovores. [He appears to work this out on the fly during the assault on the church, or he'd probably have used it sooner.]

• *Ethics*. Gives us another one of *those* options with regards to the Seventh Doctor's manipulations. [Some might argue that he's a real ratbag this time, forcing Ace into yet another traumatic situation and letting innocent bystanders get mown down in the process. Alternatively, if you look at what's actually broadcast, he's decided to remove the *real* manipulator behind Ace's life and free her (plus her entire stretch of the gene-pool as well) from the genuinely ruthless malignancy that's been trying to trap him. It's also feasible that - almost as an afterthought - he's removing a toxic possible timeline where Earth is destroyed in its own effluent, but see **History** for more.]

The Doctor seems very concerned about the suffering of others - he's outraged when Millington shuts the benevolent Russian soldiers in with the murderous Haemovores, gets upset when two doves are gassed to death just to prove a point, deems Hitler a 'dreadful man' and expresses disdain upon seeing pictures of cities and 'innocent people' being bombed. Upon threat of execution, he doesn't beg for his own life, but instead exhorts the soldiers to let Ace go. He also sends her to reassure Wainwright that there *is* a future.

• *Inventory*. Despite having taken so many pens with him in 1963 [25.1, "Remembrance of the Daleks"], he needs to borrow two fountain-pens to forge his own documents. He doesn't return these, either. He's still got that clothes-brush, and a copy of *Doctor Zhivago* that mysteriously turns from the English edition to one in Cyrillic.

• *Background*. Two obvious things to state here. One is that he describes the Universe's creation [the Big Bang, Event One or whatever you prefer to call it] as though he's speaking from first-hand experience. And somehow, the decision to even say this much - and to explain how the 'evil force' created in the fires of creation survived - is painful for him. [Given all the hints of "Dark, Mysterious" stuff in his newly-revamped past, this might be significant. He was much more casual about the creation of the Milky Way (19.1, "Castrovalva") and the Fifth Galaxy (17.1, "Destiny of the Daleks"), and - threat to his Ship aside - he was rather elated, not horrified, about the creation of a solar system in 1.3, "The Edge of Destruction". So either the Doctor's latest incarnation has learned something about the beginning of the universe, or maybe this is just a bit of self-mythologising. This of course ignores the contradictory evidence from X2.9, "The Satan Pit" and X3.0, "The Runaway Bride" that the TARDIS has never been further back than the creation of our Solar System, and there is no such thing as 'before time'.]

The other main point is that circa 200 AD, the Doctor bested Fenric and trapped him like a genie in a jar. [See **The Non-Humans**. Even the novelisation is unclear as to whether *this* Doctor pickled Fenric the first time around. It certainly fits the Seventh Doctor's *modus operandi*, but it could equally be a random adventure undertaken by almost any incarnation. Mind, if it *is* Seven, then we've the same problem as 25.3, "Silver Nemesis" as to working out precisely when he found the time to instigate these secret plots.]

Intriguingly, he's familiar with the German Naval Cypher room in Berlin - even down to the files - and can spot anomalies such as Millington's school picture (the big one is a sign on the desk saying 'Commander AH Millington', which he studiously ignores). He also seems to know about Dr Judson. [The novelisation claims that Judson is renowned as a mathematical genius across Europe and America.] To judge by the on-screen evidence, it doesn't appear that the Doctor knew in advance that baby Audrey was Ace's mum. [He's hard to read in the final confrontation, but he perks up just a little, as if the revelation of the baby's identity is new information to him; see **Things That Don't Make Sense**, though.]

The Doctor says he's personally seen the future that the Haemovores hail from [see **History**].

The Supporting Cast
• *Ace*. By now, she and the Doctor have their "act like you own the place" routine down pat.

Ace has issues with her mum, to the extent that she claims to hate the woman, yet bawls 'Mum, I'm sorry!' when she thinks she's seconds away

from death by firing squad. She's outraged to find the Doctor keeping secrets from her, but remains loyal and understanding once he explains the nature of the enemy they're facing. Despite her tough-as-nails exterior, Ace seems to go uncharacteristically gooey when confronted with a baby, and she's fiercely protective of the child. She used to think she'd never get married, but now seems more unsure.

It's here revealed that Ace's mum Audrey was an infant in 1943. Ace's paternal grandmother was Kathleen Dudman - she worked for the British military during Wartime, listening to coded German radio messages. At story's end, Ace tells Kathleen and her infant daughter to head for London and stay with 'her nan' at 17 Old Terrace, Streatham. [Go straight to **Things That Don't Make Sense**, but please don't waste your time looking for this locale. It's as real as the Powell Estate or Hillview Road, Croydon.] Still no mention of Ace's Dad, and she naturally assumes that Kathleen is a single mum by choice. [Even the 2005 series fought shy of having illegitimacy mentioned, although a pregnant bride is permissible these days.]

Ace is friendly with the evacuated teens Phyllis and Jean, and - having gear in her rucksack as always - goes rock-climbing with them. She deems swimming as 'stupid', but later seems to overcome a fear of undercurrents. Ace thinks her Computer Studies teacher, Miss Birkitt [for whatever reason, the novelisation names her as Miss Sydenham], was 'well good'. [So Ace thinks kindly of a teacher and seems to have enjoyed the course. She's ruining her reputation as a troublemaker.] She displays an understanding of the lessons presented in that class, including logic diagrams and bi-stable arrays (flip-flop thingies) rather than the O-level syllabus of the mid-80s. [It's possible, then, that this was an after-school club of some kind. Most of these in her time would have been about BASIC and how to play Elite on the BBC Micro, not really her sort of thing. The more they try to make Ace a hooligan, the worse these revelations of previous Lisa Simpson activity sound.] Ace only did French O-level, not Russian. [Yet again, then, it looks as if she isn't from 1987, because she'd've done GCSE, not O-Level. Plus it makes her sound like a closet nerd who overcompensates by blowing things up.]

She says she's from London, and implies she

Are All These "gods" Related?

If you've been out of the loop concerning BBC Wales' version of *Doctor Who*, it may have escaped your notice that Gabriel Woolf has recently played a second terribly-powerful entity in X2.8, "The Impossible Planet" / X2.9, "The Satan Pit". (If you're *really* out of things, his first was as Sutekh the Destroyer in 13.3, "Pyramids of Mars".) On seeing Woolf's name in that week's *Radio Times*, many fans made up their own theories, most of which - it must be said - were considerably more interesting than what we got.

With the overall sense that the BBC Wales team were suffering from "Anoraknophobia", such a piece of casting must have been done in the full knowledge of what effect it would have had, and would have been vetoed by the Big Guy if they wanted to stop fans drawing such a conclusion. However, the anticipation of some link between Sutekh and whatever-that-thing-was is curious for anyone who recalls the programme from the 1970s or earlier. Are we to try to make links between Mavic Chen and Tobias Vaughn because both "The Daleks' Master Plan" (3.4) and "The Invasion" (6.3) cast Kevin Stoney as a suave master-criminal? Are Morbius (13.5, "The Brain of Morbius") and Magnus Greel the product of some occult link between evil Time Lords and the botched time-experiments of 5000 AD (14.6, "The Talons of Weng Chiang", which also has Michael Spice as a faceless villain)? Was Richard Coeur de Lion one of Scaroth's twelve facets (2.6, "The Crusade"; 17.2, "City of Death"), what with Julian Glover playing both parts? We offered a frivolous suggestion for some of this duplication business in the essay with 20.1, "Arc of Infinity", but some people *still* take things at face value and to a ludicrous extent, even when reason says, "Hang on a sec..."

Beings of immense power offer viewer-interpretations the possibility of influence beyond any one world or time, but we have to be careful. Mere casting decisions are not evidence. What we *can* surmise is that writers who collaborate might be aware of one another's plans. Even then, we can't really make assumptions beyond what was broadcast. (Similar thoughts have been expressed about the number of minor deities and aliens with names a bit like Shakespeare's unseen witch "Sycorax": the planet "Segonax" in 25.4, "The Greatest Show in the Galaxy", Fifi the Stigorax in 25.2, "The Happiness Patrol", the Battle-queen of the S'rax in 26.1, "Battlefield" and so on - especially now that we've actually had aliens called "Sycorax" in X2.0, "The Christmas Invasion" who do voodoo with blood. And yes, the Doctor might be responsible for the getting the name into circulation in X3.2, "The Shakespeare Code", but his loose lips can't account for all similar groups of names.)

We *do* however, have a large number of beings in *Doctor Who* with amazing powers - some are called "gods", and some are just acting like them. On the surface, it *is* tempting to put all such superhuman beings into one bracket, rather than there being a hierarchy. In one way, we have a clue from a refusal to acknowledge just such a link. Andrew Cartmel decided that, having used the name "the Gods of Ragnarok" in "The Greatest Show in the Galaxy", he would not permit it in "The Curse of Fenric" (26.3). In a story based on some of the apocalyptic elements of Norse mythology, the absence of any reference to Ragnarok is highly peculiar. It's the name of the final battle, when the giant wolf Fenris attacks Odin, and the Tree of the World (Yggdrassil) is blighted at the roots. What's the link between this and the Judges seen in the previous season in a trans-temporal talent show? Not much, except that the "Gods" have a vague Viking look. (Actually, they're a *bit* like the pieces in the Lewis chess-set at the British Museum, but not as much as all that.) But more intriguingly, they have visual links to the Eye of Horus from "Pyramids of Mars". They also behave like other similar beings, such as the Eternals (20.5, "Enlightenment", apparently the same ones mentioned in X2.12, "Army of Ghosts" and "The Shakespeare Code") and the Toymaker (3.7, "The Celestial Toymaker"). These might be connected or related, but nothing in any of their habits connects to the whole unleashing-chaos thing. If anything, the *modus operandi* of the Gods of Ragnarok is to *restrict* the potential for chaos or anything unexpected.

Of course, this wasn't nearly obsessive enough for the *New Adventures* kids. They found ways to link everything to everything else and bring it all under the umbrella of HP Lovecraft's "Cthulhu" stories. (The irony being that the overarching "Mythos" was itself posthumously imposed on Lovecraft's stories by his own obsessive fans.) The basic idea is fiendishly stupid. The Universe is one of a sequence of "concertina" Big Bangs and implosions, with each one ending in the event that creates the next (not quite in synch with the suggestion from 20.4, "Terminus", then). The image of the

continued on page 325...

once got into Greenford disco without a ticket. She once again uses the rolled-up metal ladder that she carries in her backpack ["Dragonfire"] and implies that she can mix up a fresh batch of Nitro-9 in a jar. [So... does she carry the base components around in her backpack with her? That would, admittedly, be more safe than carrying loads of primed explosives everywhere.] Just for a change, her 'five-second' fuses run over and here last about seven or eight seconds.

Ace once bought a Soviet hammer-and-sickle emblem cheap in a market, and somehow hears concealed machinery noises that the Doctor fails to notice.

The Non-Humans

• *Fenric.* It's described, loosely, as a remnant of the Big Bang. The Doctor deems it a force of 'pure evil'. 'Fenric' is but one possible name for this force, and the similarities between its apparent motives and the End of the World in Norse mythology is just one of its cunning plans [see the essay accompanying this story]. Fenric seems to revel in the deaths of others, claiming that quantity is preferable to quality.

As has been stated, Fenric has encountered the Doctor once before. On that occasion, the Doctor pulled bones from the desert sands, carved them into chess pieces, and challenged Fenric with an apparently insoluable chess problem. Fenric failed to find the solution, whereupon the Doctor trapped its weakened essence in the 'Shadow Dimensions' for seventeen centuries. [The jar that "holds" Fenric is apparently an interface to these realms. Fenric here says it has 'found a body again', but it's never clear what form its previous body took.

[By way of further explanation, the novelisation retells the story of Fenric's capture as an Arabian Nights pastiche, where El-Dok'Tar traps the djinni Aboo Fenran with the aid of a bottle containing the Seven Shadows from the time before Time. As a reward, he gains a slave-girl called Zeleekha as his new companion. That the story describes the journey across the "Central Way" from the White City to the Isle of Dhogs as arduous - when anyone familiar with the London Underground will confirm that it's much easier than using the Northern Line - suggests that we take all of this with a pinch of salt.]

Although imprisoned with no physical form, Fenric has been able to manoeuvre people and objects through time. It seems to have particular influence over the DNA of the Viking who buried the flask in Northumbria. [We'll track the flask's journey before it arrived there in **History**.] The result is that there's now an entire bloodline of people who seem more capable of providing Fenric with a body should he escape. Among these so-called 'Wolves of Fenric' are Ace, her grandmother Kathleen Dudman, Dr Judson, Commander Millington, the Rev Wainwright, Captain Sorin, and the Haemovore named Ingiger (AKA "The Ancient One") - all of whom are apparently descended from Joseph Sundvik (1809-1872). [Again, more on his lineage in **History**.]

Much of Fenric's actions have been concentrated toward obtaining his freedom and - just as important, it seems - getting the Doctor to allow a rematch. Part of Fenric's elaborate invitation, it appears, was in the form of a teenage girl who got whisked across the cosmos in a time-storm for the Doctor to adopt. [See "Dragonfire", as if you didn't know what we were talking about.] Fenric also takes credit for the chess game that was played out in Lady Peinforte's study. [See "Silver Nemesis", although the actual on-screen evidence in that story is highly suspect. Yes, we've checked. No, we don't have girlfriends.]

"Wolves" possessed by Fenric get a green or red glow in their eyes, but seem to retain their personality traits - so Fenric-Judson is sardonic and Fenric-Sorin is arrogant. Fenric-Judson displays the ability to teleport from place to place, and seems greatly weakened - as during the first chess match, presumably - while trying to find a solution to the Doctor's puzzle. He only regains his strength after leaping into Captain Sorin and Ace blabs the solution. Eventually, Fenric-Sorin seems to die when the Ancient One betrays him and kills them both with toxic chemicals. [We might wonder if an energy being such as Fenric can perish in such a fashion, though. You'd think the odds would've been ripe for a rematch in one of the *Doctor Who* spin-off works - especially as the novels broke a Guinness World Record for longevity - but to date it hasn't happened.]

• *Haemovores.* Here appear in two forms. On the one hand we have blue-skinned, nobbly, marine monstrosities - the sort that represent a form humanity will evolve into in future. [See **History**, but beware that this gets confusing.] However, persons freshly "turned" into

Are All These "gods" Related?

...continued from page 323

year Ten Trillion seems to put the kibosh on this (X3.11,"Utopia") as the Universe has expanded out so thin that all the stars have gone cold and we're into Heat Death, which suggests a lack of Dark Matter in sufficient quantities to pull it all together again into a Big Crunch and start all over again. So as well as nixing parallel universes, BBC Wales seem to have ruled out anything "before" or "after" this one. Nonetheless, in the *New Adventures* framework, the end of the universe prior to ours ended with various powerful beings hanging around and popping into the new-born cosmos, where they found themselves much more powerful and having more scope. The thing is, they still follow the laws of physics from the previous cosmos, and these don't quite fit our local conditions.

Still reading? Well, these beings got themselves worshipped by the most ancient indigenous races (under the names Lovecraft gave them, once his work was out of copyright), and some of the matter they brought with them was not only strangely potent, but corrupted any autochthonous lifeforms (words like "native" or "aboriginal" aren't nearly strong enough, and "local" just won't do). Some of the side-effects of this are described by the writers of these books, and other apparent inconsistencies and anomalies in broadcast stories are "explained" by this. Hence, apparently, Stahlman's Gas (7.4,"Inferno") and the Animus and its connection with the gravity-defying Menoptra (see 2.5, "The Web Planet", and Christopher Bulis' inadvertently ribtickling novel *Twilight of the Gods*).

Most intriguing - in some ways at least - was Paul Cornell's attempt at resolving all the vampire material (primarily 18.4,"State of Decay", but connected to 20.7,"The Five Doctors" and "The Curse of Fenric"). At its heart, his puzzlingly-titled *Goth Opera* has a clever speculation. If the Guardians of Time were present at the Big Bang, before the laws of Physics have settled down, they - by which we mean the Black Guardian - could cause exemptions. The Great Vampire and his hordes, who beset the Gallifreyans in the Dark Times, might exhibit abilities not only contrary to accepted science, but antithetical to all life that evolves here. So far so good, but then Cornell goes into detail about how Rassilon's gifts to his people - regeneration especially - are a legacy of a near-fatal vampire bite, which is apparently why he has gone into a perpetual sleep rather than jeopardise the lives of his people. Again, this isn't out of keeping with what we've seen on screen. However, the next step - in which the psychic defence that shields people from Haemovores is connected to the hypothalamus, and is thus stimulated by garlic - takes us over the edge. Hilariously, Cornell has the Doctor using garlic bread against the blood-sucking Australians, and Tegan resisting them through her faith in the novels of Primo Levi.

If you need the inscrutable behaviour of powerful aliens to make sense, this is probably your best bet. Especially after both "The Satan Pit" and "The Runaway Bride" (X3.0) took great pains to rule out Cthulhu-lite as a possibility in the new-improved post-Time Wars continuity. In this version of events, some vast battle took place before our solar system formed, and in the process Huon particles were removed (except for a few at the heart of the TARDIS and some at the centre of the Earth) - but, crucially, there ain't no such thing as "before" time. Now, it may be that this new version, in which the Doctor weirdly says he's never been any further back in time than 4.6 billion BC, will supplant Haemovores and the Great Vampire with plasmovores and Dalek Sec, but so far the changes have been fairly conservative. (*The Sarah Jane Adventures* seems to take place in both continuities, so they *are* probably the same unless this is inconvenient, just like always.) That is, aside from the whole issue of how a fundamental particle can be removed from creation without unbalancing everything else. (Unless Huons were inverse gravity particles, and they were making everything expand too fast - we've discussed this before through these books, so we're not going to dismiss the idea just yet.)

But the question remains: are the various god-like beings in *Doctor Who* all connected? Do the Daemons (8.5,"The Daemons") work for the White Guardian (16.1, "The Ribos Operation" and more), for instance? This would explain Azal's odd behaviour, nudging lesser beings towards a higher state of consciousness. (If, as we've been finding along the way, there is a link between consciousness and time, there are beings who'd have a vested interest in breeding and training other beings.) The majority of such beings fall into the broad categories of "Order" and "Chaos", but often within species. This looks suspiciously like Guardian influence, so that Sutekh and Horus started a war that wiped out a race of immensely powerful individuals. Was this

continued on page 327...

Haemovores - notably the young girls Jean and Phyllis - mostly look human save for their extended talons, fangs and extremely scary hair. [The conversion into the blue-skinned creatures probably takes some time to achieve, and arguably entails a corruption of the brain cells. The Ancient One seems intelligent enough, but it's at the top of the food chain, and none of the other blue-skinned creatures is heard to speak.]

Haemovores - or the mostly-human looking ones, at least - seem to have a hypnotic effect over their intended victims, able to either freeze them in place or lure them in closer for a kill. Conversion into a Haemovore can happen extremely fast, as the radio room girls are seemingly "turned" within minutes. Haemovores can 'weld' metal beneath the sea with their bare hands.

The best defense against a Haemovore is to concentrate on an object or concept of faith (such as faith in God, one's companions, the Soviet Revolution, etc) - this creates a psychic barrier that holds the Haemovores at bay and causes them great pain. Bullets at best slow Haemovores, but they seem vulnerable to a stake through the heart. The Ancient One can emit a telepathic signal that kills the other Haemovores, and Jean and Phyllis are seen turning to dust when this happens. Otherwise, the Ancient One and two other Haemovores become a green sludge upon death. [This occurs in some of the re-inserted material, but it's canonical enough for our taste.]

History

• *Dating.* We're constantly told that the story takes place in 1943, although there's very little on-screen evidence for this specific date. [It's definitely World War II, and the absence of any Americans might be a clue - few if any would have been seen this far north until after D-Day, which occurred on 6th of June, 1944. If this *is* 1943, however, we have to dismiss the oft-made suggestion that it's the Allied bombing of Dresden that has shaken Wainwright's faith. Even if he somehow knew about the scale of the firestorms well in advance of the public's understanding of the event, this didn't actually occur for another two years.

[It seems that Jean and Phyllis have only recently been evacuated, which if anything indicates that the story takes place slightly earlier than we're told. The Soviets only became Allies after Operation Barbarossa - Hitler's assault on a nation

with whom he had signed a non-aggression pact - which would suggest this story probably occurs no earlier than the Summer of 1942, after the Siege of Leningrad. Either way, there's no attempt to explain how Sorin's team crossed the North Sea without running into anti-U-boat defences, or the U-boats themselves. We see small dinghies, so presumably they were evading ASDIIC (even though we've little indication that this base actually has radar).

[We could of course *try* to date these events off Judson's Ultima machine, but then matters really get complicated. The original Enigma system had been pretty much cracked in 1940, thanks to a combination of number crunching and various people thinking themselves into the shoes of the coders - Millington's attempts to "think like the Nazis" did most of the work in the early stages - plus having detailed plans and operating manuals. The legend that it was all down to Alan Turing and his Colossus machine is mainly to do with the later development of a four-wheel encryption system, after Montgomery's victory in Egypt tipped the Germans off to the fact that their security was compromised. That was spring 1943, and Colossus came into service on 8th of December that year. (It was aided by an earlier machine called "Robinson", so-named after artist W. Heath Robinson, who drew lash-up gadgetry odder than Rube Goldberg's devices. The BBC Wales TARDIS has an element of his style.)

All of which is to say... this story has to be set no less than two months after Monty's triumph (again, spring 1943), as the cogs and "bombes" required for such a machine would need to be hand-made to very fine tolerances. However, as Ultima is faster than Colossus and a generation better than Robinson, the decision *not* to use Judson's device has to occur a similar amount of time before December, to allow Turing's comparatively cruder machine to be built.

[Incidententally, we *could* assume, in light of the BBC Books Eighth Doctor novel *The Turing Test*, that Colossus was needed after all when the Naval Intelligence bods gave up on Ultima. Or we could make the leap of faith that some kind of "son of Ultima" was later built, and that this is how the Post Office came close to controlling the minds of all puny humans in 1966 (see 3.10, "The War Machines").]

If the Doctor's rather colourful description of the Dawn of Time can be believed, two 'forces' -

Are All These "gods" Related?

...continued from page 325

some kind of pruning, to give the lesser species a chance? Well, we could ask rhetorical questions for ages, but this just runs us up against a bigger question. If we could comprehend their motives, would they be *really* be higher-beings?

It's a tradition of most religions that our efforts to get our heads around the behaviour of gods is pointless, and that all rationality eventually becomes futile. If we can understand their ways, they can't be gods. Zen koans and Erasmus' *In Praise of Folly* are just the most famous examples. The obvious counter to this is that a made-up deity falls into the category of "plot", and each must conform to the needs of satisfying story-telling. Any sufficiently advanced technology is indistinguishable from a *deus ex machina*. Generically, each godlike being is the engine of a story, and has to be treated as the one and only - if the Doctor used Fenric to destroy the Gods of Ragnarok, we would rightly accuse the author of cheating. So in essence, every individual story is monotheistic.

But we can't help noticing that there is a regular sequence of development of beings from broadly humanoid to psychically-gifted to incorporeal - from ape to angel - almost as if all conscious being are pre-destined to follow the same path towards godhood. It's remarkably like the theories of the philospher Pierre Teilhard de Chardin (see **What Were Josiah's "Blasphemous" Theories?** under 26.2, "Ghost Light"). He posited that we would ultimately evolve to a point ("Time Omega") where humanity's capacities are indistinguishable from those of God. As a Jesuit and palaeontologist, he was concerned to try to square a theological circle. However, the one instance we see this happen on screen as a natural, unmediated process is "The Mutants" (9.4), and it is part of a cycle. Eventually, we must presume, they will revert to the humanoid state, and then become 'Mutts' again.

But if we take the idea that *all* races who keep developing eventually become able to manipulate matter by sheer will, and that by following this path all beings will participate in the state of grace (or whatever you call it), we have a big cop-out. Even the Time Lords don't know what happened after a certain point. Some might suggest that the whole of evolution was being stage-managed by forces from *after* that time for a particular end. Perhaps the more powerful beings are later stages of the races they influence, a self-directed intervention to make sure that the later ones come into being. (This is not just random theorising on our part. "The Daemons" is at least partly derived from Arthur C Clarke's parable *Childhood's End*, in which the stern but benign beings who force humanity to evolve cause a psychic trauma reverberating back through time, so that our ancestors think of tall beings with horns and a smell of sulphur as bad news.)

Of course, this being a Mad Norwegian book, we probably ought to mention in passing the last *New Adventures* theory from *Christmas on a Rational Planet*. In Lawrence Miles' account, there is no Universe prior to this one, and all that the Time Lords know is wrong. As this comes after all the Cthulu-lite books, it has to be taken seriously. The idea is that the Time Lords invented nasty masculine logic and order, and Rassilon exiled all madness / chaos / fantasy to a small pocket-universe (see **Where Does This Come From?** in 26.4, "Survival" and **Is Continuity a Pointless Waste of Time?** under 22.1, "Attack of the Cybermen"). The Old Spaces aren't from a different previous universe but a different, previous state of this one before harmony was imposed. A side-effect of this imposition of universal laws is that the Time Lords themselves don't know that anything else was ever possible. But nobody in any version of *Doctor Who* really developed this, unless you count the "Obverse" from *The Blue Angel* by Paul Magrs and Jeremy Hoad. And even this is unsatisfactory: all it does is shove all the disorder into part of a nice neat category, with a designated area for things not otherwise categorised.

'good and evil' - were present at the 'beginning of all beginnings'. Chaos followed as time, matter and space were all born. The forces were 'shattered' as the universe exploded outward, until only echoes of them remained, yet somehow the evil force (here manifesting as Fenric) survived.

The Doctor's first encounter with Fenric took place 'seventeen centuries' ago [so circa 200 AD];

what became of Fenric's flask immediately after that isn't said. [Nor is it stated why, if the Doctor was responsible for bottling Fenric in the first place, he didn't just stash the flask away somewhere secure rather than letting it wander about Europe for so many centuries.] Although imprisoned, Fenric pulled the last intelligent life-form of a dying future Earth - 'the Ancient One', AKA

Ingiger [it's a female name, so we'll call the Ancient One "she"] - back to ninth century Transylvania. The Ancient One was unable to return home, and dutifully followed the flask for centuries. Along the way, she appears to have been responsible for all the vampire lore that followed her path through Transylvania to Whitby, and infected a small army of humans with the Haemovore taint.

A [ninth century, it seems] merchant bought the flask in Constantinople and took it with him through Europe, but Viking pirates stole it. They tried to return to Norway, but came to take shelter at Maiden's Bay - now Maiden's Point, a notorious make-out spot - in Northumbria. A mysterious black fog killed off the Vikings, but one of them (married to a woman named Astrid) survived long enough to bury Fenric's flask and carve runestones as a memorial to his fallen comrades. Through the curious coincidence of runic characters resembling symbolic logic junctions in a flow-diagram, it's these runes that provide Dr Judson with a program that - when run through a computer - unleash Fenric from its bottle. In addition to the runes previously carved, Fenric scorches a fresh set that makes the Ultima machine rattle off the names of the Wolves, and the phrase 'Let the chains of Fenric shatter'. [Incidentally, it's presumably the flask's presence that's given rise to the toxic green sludge in the area, and Fenric also presumably had some influence on where the naval base was sited and who got seconded there. Yes, this stretches the plot to the breaking point. Fortunately, we can assume that Fenric simply has foreknowledge of World War II, and didn't orchestrate seventeen centuries of European history just to set all of this up.]

The descendents of the Viking who buried the flask after his fellows settled in Northumbria [if you can't see the glaring contradiction here, make all due speed to **Things That Don't Make Sense**] gave rise to the bloodline of 'the Wolves of Fenric'. One of them was Joseph Sundvik, who was born 8th of April, 1809, and died 3rd of February, 1872. His wife Florence lived 3rd of July, 1820, to 12th of January, 1898. Their daughters were Sarah, Martha, Jane, Clara and Annie, and a granddaughter - Mary Eliza Millington - only lived 13 days, from 4th to 17th of March, 1898. [If the grandmother and granddaughter died within two months of one another, it was a hell of a year for that family.] Another of Joseph's granddaughters

was Emily Wilson, who became the grandmother of Captain Sorin.

St. Jude's Church was built upon some of the Viking graves. The Rev Wainwright - who studied at St. Andrews - is presently the Vicar there, as was his father and grandfather before him (the latter at the end of the last century).

Base Commander Millington and Dr Judson went to school together, and knew each other before the accident that put Judson in a wheelchair. [It's here implied - and confirmed in the novelisation - that this occurred twenty years ago, and that Millington was responsible.] When Millington served as Chief Petty Officer aboard a Navy vessel, an explosion in the engine room forced the crew to seal off the section and restrict the flames, even though this trapped some crewmen within and signed their death warrants. Kathleen Dudman's husband - Frank William Dudman - presently serves in the Merchant Navy, Atlantic Convoys, but is here reported missing, presumed dead, after an enemy torpedo strikes his ship.

'Six months ago', a Russian sabotage team went into German-occupied Romania, but only one member of the group survived. He talked about dead men coming out of a black fog. [This initially sounds relevant, but ultimately the report doesn't seem to have anything to do with Fenric. It's probable that the Ancient One spread the Haemovore taint in the course of her travels, which accounts for these random instances of bloodsucking activity in Transylvania.]

Captain Sorin is here leading a team of Russian soldiers who have orders to steal Dr Judson's code-breaking masterpiece of engineering - the Ultima machine, which is capable of running more than 1,000 combinations per hour, and has 'automatic negative checking'. The Soviets hope to use the machine to crack the British ciphers, but Whitehall is aware of this plan, and has issued orders that Sorin's mission be allowed to succeed. The Ultima machine has been fitted with a jar of the green toxin, and when the political climate is deemed appropriate, the British will include the word 'Love' into one of their ciphers. This will cause the pre-programmed Ultima machine to self-destruct, and the resultant toxin cloud will destroy the Kremlin, if not all of Moscow.

We've saved the most contentious historical issue for last: it's first said that the Haemovores originate from 'thousands of years' in the future, but the Doctor later specifies that their time occurs after 'half a million years' of industrial progress. Earth in this era is said to lie dying, its surface a chemical slime. The pollution has caused humanity to evolve into the bloodthirsty Haemovores, and the Ancient One claims to have watched her Earth 'die' in the chemicals.

[The aforementioned bone of contention is that some guides (The Discontinuity Guide included) are of the opinion that the Haemovores hail from a *possible* future - one that's erased when the Ancient One turns on Fenric and fails to poison the world. Little of the on-screen evidence substantiates this view, however. Again, the Doctor attributes the rise of the Haemovores to 'half a million years of industrial progress', not to something as sudden and cataclysmic as the chemical release that the Ancient One plans to cause. Ingiger's suicidal move doesn't automatically "save" those she loved, but this is no more daft than Greg and Petra sacrificing their lives to let the Doctor return to "our" world in 7.4, "Inferno".

[The good news is that it's pretty obvious that either Fenric or the Doctor is lying to the Ancient One. The bad news is that no matter whom you pick, *both* interpretations are rather paradoxical. If the Haemovores came about through industrial pollution, then it appears that Fenric has asked the Ancient One to cause Earth's ruin many millennia ahead of schedule - an act that would paradoxically prevent her own creation. This would surely entail a massive amount of damage to the timeline, although it's debatable if a nihilist being such as Fenric would refrain from causing such historical havoc. On the other hand, if the Doctor is lying in the interest of eliminating the Haemovore future altogether - which fair enough, he might do - then we're back to the problem that the Ancient One is paradoxically preventing her own creation.

[All things considered, we should perhaps decide that Fenric is lying and the Doctor is telling the truth, because lying on Fenric's part would only *threaten* a paradox, whereas fibbing on the Doctor's part would actually trigger one. Plus, generally speaking, it's much easier to assume that the Ancient One's restraint preserves the genuine future, rather than wiping out a timeline that's nonetheless influenced our "real" history for more than a millennium, and is only feasible if Earth had been overwhelmingly poisoned in the 1940s. Either way, Earth's timeline is vast enough to accommodate the possibility of the Haemovore

era and a subsequent clean-up. In fact, the next story to occur chronologically after this era would be "The Mysterious Planet" (23.1) - set in 2,000,000 AD, and allowing for a recovery time of 1.5 million years.]

The Analysis

Where Does This Come From? In 1979, the BBC did a documentary series, The Secret War, which told the technological side of wartime espionage. The true stories of the gadgets and research we'd seen in umpteen British films of the 1950s, such as The Dambusters, was at least as interesting as the fiction. But the real shock was something the series advisor, Professor RV Jones, was only allowed to tell now that thirty years had passed: Britain had computers before anyone else, but this had been classified. So it was that Alan Turing began to creep from being a footnote in technical journals and a one-off mention in articles about AI research to being - posthumously - a complex and tortured figure worthy of having plays written about him. A hefty and technical biography, Alan Turing, The Enigma by Andrew Hodges, left people convinced that they could follow the maths and emotional turmoil equally well, even if only the former was published in the author's lifetime. The apparent need for a gay martyr (and Turing's death, either a highly symbolic suicide lacking any note or a grimly ironic accident - the ambiguity allowing all sorts of speculation) made him a touchstone figure in the 80s and early 90s.

This documentary nearly coincided with the boom in domestic computing - or at least the reports of such a boom, as the real sales didn't start until a couple of years later. People were interested in logic junctions back then, trying to program for themselves in BASIC or Machine Code (see **LOAD: "What Did The Computer People Think"?** under 21.6, "The Caves of Androzani".) Whereas Computer Studies lessons in the 70s had seen kids forced to learn to read punched paper-tape and write essays about Charles Babbage, in schools there was now as much interest in Hilbert and Gödel's efforts to see which questions could actually be answered (mathematically speaking) as in hacking their own snooker programs or cutting the sleeves off their Rush T-shirts. This all came back to Turing's paper on "Computable Numbers", which sought to pick up where Gödel left off.

For those of you who've not read Volume IV, we

ought to explain again the role of mathematics and chess in Cold War strategic thinking. Following the work of John von Neumann, a Santa Monica think-tank - the RAND Corporation - sold successive American governments on the idea that Game Theory could allow a for a rational war in which everyone could predict what their opponents would do, so nobody would ever start anything. One of the game-plans they developed was the Prisoner's Dilemma[45]. In formulating strict and calculable values for things, they were able to make computers that could play chess, and indeed could work out an opponent's optimum move without seeing the pieces move. In particular, this allowed previously imponderable political and tactical factors to be calibrated in ones and zeroes. On this basis, the importance of flowcharts and circuits - both amenable to binary states - crept from the rarefied world of electronics into military and economic planning.

It's customary at this stage to mention John Carpenter's 1980 flick *The Fog*. Ian Briggs himself claims that the film version of *The Man Who Fell To Earth* (1973) was a buried influence on the Ancient One's plight in "Fenric". However, a later Carpenter, *Prince of Darkness*, is at least as big an influence (this would have been in cinemas around the time that Briggs was thinking to do a second story for Cartmel). It has computerised decoding, ancient lettering and a satanic force being released thereby (we bet "The Satan Pit" author Matt Jones saw it too). The most obvious antecedent is *Dracula*, and most especially John Badham's 1979 version of this, which at least attempts to make it itself look like Whitby, North Yorkshire. People connected with *Doctor Who* would be more likely than most to have seen this, as the part of "Walter" was played by Sylveste McCoy, as he spelled it then. Colour supplements in the mid-80s reprinted the evocative Victorian photos of the Yorkshire coast by Frank Meadow Sutcliffe, then being exhibited. Briggs is from that neck of the woods himself, but also reasoned there was more chance of Vikings settling in Yorkshire than in Kent (Cartmel's preferred option).

The Viking element was one Briggs had decided upon after a holiday in Sweden. The similarity between runes and flow-charts was obvious - once it's been pointed out. In the book *Gödel Escher Bach: An Eternal Golden Braid* (we mention a lot at the start of Volume V, and in the aforementioned

bits of Volume IV), this is pointed out by Achilles and a Tortoise. This book (we'll assume that the majority of you, like the majority of people who've bought it over the years, have never *quite* got around to finishing it just yet) refers back to Lewis Carroll's work in Symbolic Logic and the bits of his oeuvre most people skip. In his novelisation to "Fenric", Briggs makes play with Carroll's paradoxes, so we can't dismiss this. Vikings and chess, to anyone in Britain watching *The Saga of Noggin the Nog* (from the same stable as *Bagpuss* and *The Clangers*) is an obvious connection, as the Lewis chess-set in the British Museum, an inspiration for the cartoon, became terribly fashionable thereafter. This Hebridean archeological find has endearingly long-faced kings and knights, and facsimiles were a popular gift. (And if you *do* know your *Noggin*, stories with Davison and Ainley in become just that bit funnier.)

Similarly, we shouldn't lightly dismiss the similarity between this story and the first of the four *Timeslip* adventures from 1970. (It was one of the many ITV attempts to clone *Doctor Who*, this one specifically being ATV's Sunday afternoon effort, and worthy-but-dull until Victor Pemberton came in and made it trashy and dull. In this, the Germans were after a prototype computer, one of the annoying kids let slip how much he knew about radar and the father of the *other* kid was the equivalent of Private Perkins in "Fenric".)

However, the main reason to bring this up is to show how much *Doctor Who* was out of step with the clichés of children's TV. Until now, World War II was off-limits, despite some efforts in the Troughton era (see 5.4, "Enemy of the World" and 5.5, "The Web of Fear" for more on "Operation Werewolf", and 4.5, "The Underwater Menace" for Brian Hayles' "Doctor Who and the Nazis"). The reasons why the topic was avoided can get complicated, although no less than Barry Letts - who served aboard a World War II submarine - has suggested that the veterans for a long while found it a particularly difficult topic to discuss, and didn't believe that anyone could relate to what they'd experienced.

Even in "Fenric", perhaps as part of the RTL deal, the Nazis are noises-off (see "Silver Nemesis"), and it's the Soviets that are shown invading England in the 1940s. And this being the "right-on" Cartmel era, they aren't *automatically* baddies. Indeed, Ace gets another romance with a doomed blond soldier. *Doctor Who* had always played with the iconography of war movies, and often equated invasion threats with the real fears of Nazi occupation (see **Is This *Really* About the Blitz?** under 2.2, "The Dalek Invasion of Earth"). Roger Delgado's Master was effectively Von Gelb from *Freewheelers* (see 5.7, "The Wheel in Space"), an ex-Nazi attempting to overthrow Britain with some devious ploy, and just escaping at the end to start again next time. This story finally had a wartime setting, but even so, the Nazis couldn't be given unmediated screen-time. Even today, no actual Germans appeared in X1.09, "The Empty Child" / X1.10, "The Doctor Dances", although one - Jamie's father - was significantly written out of the script in an earlier draft. More short-lived family adventure shows could do this, but somehow it was like a series that had a "will-they-won't-they" romance at its heart; once Nazis appear in *Doctor Who* and World War II is a subject and not a backdrop, the game is over.

But there's a more thematic reason: namely, that the Germans (and indeed the Americans) are virtually irrelevant here. From about a hundred years prior to the Second World War, Russia displaced France as Britain's arch-enemy on the stage of European politics. Crucial to this rivalry was the impression that both nations saw the resulting wars and intrigue in the same terms as "The Great Game", with whole nations - principally in the Middle East, the source of Fenric's jar - as the board (see **Is *Doctor Who* Camp?** under 6.5, "The Seeds of Death"). Millington here is effectively a critique of this worldview, in which the Second World War (and indeed the First World War and the Cold War) are distractions from this ongoing conflict. The ploy with the Ultima gambit isn't as much an anticipation of the Cold War as an expectation that normal service will be resumed shortly (this was hardly a foregone conclusion in 1943). There is an unspoken assumption to this attitude that the British and Russian secret services "understand each other", in a way that the Nazis or the Americans don't get. We note that the novelisation (though none of the variants of the televised version) fingers Nurse Crane as secretly working for Moscow - just like anyone who was anyone in British counter-intelligence in this period... After the film-theory in-joke names of characters in "Dragonfire", it will come as no surprise that all the Soviets are named after characters in the plays of Anton Chekov (see also 13.4, "The Android Invasion" for a Chekovian gag). The novelisation carries it on, giving the un-named

soldier who's lured into the sea by Jean and Phyllis as 'Trofimov' (as in *The Cherry Orchard*).

We ought to mention the influence of Norse mythology here, but the proper place for this is in the essay accompanying this story. There's also, as you might have guessed, a *2000 AD* strip "Fiends of the Eastern Front", wherein likeable German soldiers notice that their Romanian colleagues are late risers who don't like garlic and so on. We could even mention the sub-aqua vampire thing from *Swamp Thing*, but we'd rather people think that Cartmel had at least one original idea in his head.

Things That Don't Make Sense By and large, the story presumes that the Viking pirates (variously called the 'Viking settlers') who took Fenric's flask came to reside in Northumbria and started banging out babies. That would be the same Vikings who - not that long after arrival, it would seem - died horribly in a black fog, would it? Maybe some of them *did* survive to reproduce, but the Viking runes in the church basement indicate they all got stuck in Northumbria and were brutally killed to a man, case closed.

Either way, the key phrase here is 'Viking settlers', which - from what we know of the Scandinavian menace - is bit of a contradiction in terms. We might imagine that the Vikings did some pillaging and raping before the black fog came along, and that the babies' mothers weren't cursed but were instead allowed to escape, but if so, how did the children wind up with Nordic surnames? Anyway, why would a fog that killed rampaging Vikings - but allowed defiled local maidens to escape and raise fatherless children - not make a bigger impact on local folklore than 'Maiden's Point'?

More troublingly, the specific Viking who carved the runes and buried the flask is touted as the progenitor of the Wolves of Fenric, but he writes that *he's* going to die that evening. So again - unless we're to implausibly presume that his wife Astrid came along to cheer the pirates as they went about their plundering, how did the man's descendents wind up living in Yorkshire? [Mind, the rune-carver asks his wife to "forgive his sin", so perhaps - as we've just suggested - he inseminated one of the local wenches before the evil fog caught up with him. It's certainly possible that the Wolves are the product of an adulterous act, which is in keeping with the gothic roots of the tale, although this would potentially drain away some of the narrative's drama. "Tonight, I shall die, but at least I got off with the farmer's daughter."]

How dense is Ace - who's normally smarter than this - to *not* realize what's up with that baby before Fenric spills the beans? If she can rattle off her grandmother's address in the middle of a crisis, then one presumes she's been told her mother's maiden name, her grandmother's name period and her grandfather's fate at *some* point. Yet she fails to connect the dots and realize that gee, Audrey has the same name as her mother, and Kathleen Dudman and her husband Frank Dudman - who dies while serving in the Merchant Navy, just like her granddad - have the same name as her grandparents. Does Kathleen need to drop a comment like, "It's my fondest hope to have a grandchild named Dorothy, and that she will love explosives and Charlton Athletic FC..." before Ace takes the hint?

About this whole business about Ace sending Kathleen and child to stay with 'her nan', who lives at 17 Old Terrace, Streatham. Not only is it a bit questionable to recommend that Kathleen and child stay in Streatham, considering Jean and Phyllis were evacuated from London, but it's a bit mind-boggling to presume - as seems to be the implication - that Kathleen arrives to find an empty flat and winds up staying there for years. [A solution offers itself if we assume that "Ace's nan" in this instance is actually her paternal grandmother, but then it's starting to make *too much* sense, as it would suggest that Kathleen meets the family already in residence at 17, Old Terrace, and that their kids one day get married. So Ace has just doubly facilitated her own conception. We can overlook the paradox this seems to cause - as there's potentially enough of that already, thank you, see **History** - but you still have to wonder how awkward Kathleen must feel to meet "Ace's nan" while the woman's far too young to have any grandchildren. The trump card here is that Kathleen never learns Ace's real name, and that - given Ace's unstable household - one presumes Kathleen died in the decades to follow, meaning the Ace of the 1980s never knew her well, if at all.]

So... Sorin's boys were going to take the Ultima machine across the North Sea in a dinghy, were they? Or if the plan was for them to get hold of the British codes, why take the machine with them and let everyone know that the code had been broken? Or if they simply intended to take a few

photos of Ultima, why make such a song-and-dance about it, with commandos and all? We also can't help but wonder how the British know the Soviets' plan in such detail, yet have kept their own elaborate double-bluff so secret. Or, more to the point, how they achieved such stealth in 1943 but not 1947, when MI5 was thoroughly riddled with Cambridge-educated "moles" who'd been there since the 1930s. Plus, even if Sorin's mission succeeds, one wonders if the Soviets won't bother to examine the Ultima machine and get curious about what purpose that jar of mysterious green liquid is meant to serve.

Wainwright's reading of the Biblical text has him speak of the three graces, Faith, Hope and... well, the Authorised King James Bible of 1608 (as used in churches until the 1970s) translates *caritas* as "Charity", but later editions (and a few much earlier ones) go for the more literal "Love". As does Wainwright. Not a big problem compared to the anachronisms in X1.9, "The Empty Child" (and let's not get started on *Torchwood*), but unfortunately the script makes a big deal about the word "Love" in two other scenes. We're a few years away from the Prisoner's Dilemma too, but that's a minor detail, as it's one of a whole load in a tradition beginning in 1920s Germany.

One that's frequently noticed: signposts are up in wartime. In real-life, they were removed to befuddle German troops in case of invasion. [We'd better say this while we're here: another oft-alleged anachronism simply isn't. The teddy little Audrey has is a 1940s pattern, the very one this book's author had in 1963, and not really that much like a 1980s "SuperTed" doll at all.[46]] But, still on this tack, would 1943 teenagers have heard of Jane Russell? Her first film (*The Outlaw*) got a limited showing in that year, but she didn't really become famous until 1946. Ace has a nylon bomber-jacket, and nobody minds. She also has a lightweight rucksack - quite handy in Wartime - and the Doctor allows her to risk this anachronism, even though her having a ghetto-blaster in 1963 was tantamount to strangling Churchill at birth or something ["Remembrance of the Daleks"]. And none of these soldiers looks in her rucksack, as would be standard procedure in Wartime (the fact that she's even *got* a rucksack would constitute a big security blunder), to find a highly-suspicious rope-ladder and explosives.

Two bits of foreshadowing that aren't really resolved: why are the first Russians to be attacked left holding bits of Haemovore-twisted metal? Did the Haemovores put them there, and if so, why? And which particular bit of symbolism from Norse mythology motivates Millington to order that all chess sets in the camp should be destroyed?

Then there's the church battle near the start of episode three... it's very dramatic, isn't it? But you have to wonder *how* sopping wet the Haemovores are, if a water trail preceeds their entrance by about fifteen seconds, especially as most (if not all) of this group has just risen from the graveyard and not the sea. It's unclear why the Doctor's trio isn't overrun (as the Haemovores are coming in through more entrances than they can feasibly cover) and no explanation is offered for why Ace thinks ditching the Doctor and Wainwright and abseiling down the church tower is a good idea. Perhaps she's intending to get behind the Haemovores and lob deodorant cans of Nitro-9 at them - but no, that can't be right, as she leaves her explosives-loaded backpack on the roof. The novelisation claims that she's running out to "get help" - reasonable enough at this point in the story, although she might've done better to suggest they retreat to the bell tower, board up the door and then *all three* of them abseil down her handy ladder. The resolution of this has two Haemovores grab Ace and spend an awful long time just looking at her and lightly touching her skin (as if they're preparing to give her a facial) before Sorin's group arrives to save her.

Dr Judson is presumably one of the greatest mathematicians ever born, yet he's happy enough to copy down and decrypt "ancient" Viking runes that Fenric carved that evening, and which weren't present the previous day. [A case of "being unable to see the forest for the trees", that one.] We could also be unkind and mention the way Dinsdale Landen has to wheel back Judson's chair as he's "struck by lightning" in episode three, but one suspects the production team is doing the best they can. Nurse Crane observes the Doctor faking credentials and forging the signatures of high-ranking British officials, yet only regards this with puzzlement, and doesn't tell anyone about the probable security breach. And in one of the added scenes, watch in amusement as Sorin briefly panics and clutches at his chest for his missing Soviet emblem, failing to remember that there's another one dead-centre atop his cap.

Commander Millington is paranoid enough to booby-trap his chess set with explosives, but instead of going for direct detonation and killing everyone in the room, he's apparently considerate enough to rig up a timer so interlopers have time to get clear. [The novelisation puts this handiwork down to Fenric, not Millington, but that makes even *less* sense if Fenric wants to confront the Doctor at chess again.] And why exactly Fenric and the Ancient One bother to eliminate their own lackeys - beyond the need to not litter 1940s England with bloodsucking Haemovores - is anyone's guess. The Haemovore kill-off is also a bit contradictory, if we're eventually meant to believe that the Ancient One is *so* concerned about her kind, she's willing to betray Fenric in a bid to save her future.

Then we come to the finale, in which Ace [look, we're sorry to keep picking on the girl, but she's so prominent in this story, she can't help but cause the majority of the errors] brashly feels the need to dash back to the weapons depot and get the winning move to the Doctor's chess puzzle off her chest. She's just left Fenric-Judson there, not Sorin, yet her common sense doesn't seem to dictate that he's probably still there and she should avoid the place unless the Doctor tells her otherwise. And how would it help to tell Sorin the solution anyway? All in all, Ace is acting as if she's just found out the crucial piece of information that will let the heroes *defeat* Fenric, when it's obvious that she's stumbled upon the strategem that the Doctor is desperate to keep secret.

But then, Fenric, the *Evil!*-evil-since-the-dawn-of-time, makes a couple of errors too. He's correctly guessed that Ace's faith would be in her new best friend, the baby, but if he / it is capable of such insight - and if he's been observing the Doctor and Ace's behaviour at *all*, as the reference to "Silver Nemesis" seems to imply - why does the Doctor's ploy of saying "waste the brat" confound him? Then as events reach a fever pitch, Ace's faith in the Doctor prevents the Ancient One from confronting Sorin / Fenric. Does it occur to the Doctor simply to say "Ace, would you step over here, please?" It does not. Instead he goes through all the palaver of listing her character deficiencies in detail - probably giving the kid a complex to replace the one he took her to Gabriel Chase to resolve - and then "cures" her by telling her to jump off a cliff. [Actually, that's a fib for the sake of a cheap gag. He doesn't tell her to jump at all; he takes her to a dangerous cliff where she jumps of her own volition, for some reason.] Ultimately, Fenric-Sorin seems to die in a toxic cloud after failing to teleport to safety - which Fenric-Judson could do, at least.

Oh, and after the weapons depot explodes [and why this destroys rather than *releases* vast amounts of toxic chemicals is another mystery], watch the Doctor's left hand. It's accidentally covered in mud as he and Ace hit the ground. McCoy seems to realize this problem and looks toward his hand in a brief moment of, "Oh shite, what do I do now?" before getting back into character and finishing the scene. But then in close-up seconds later, the Doctor's hand is perfectly clean as he tweaks Ace's nose. [Side note to comment that, for all we know, this might be akin to the "doorbells in people's foreheads" treatment from 26.1, "Battlefield" and 26.4, "Survival". Is he really using some kind of mind-altering shiatsu on Ace every time he appears to be demonstrating affection?]

Inevitably, we end with Ace's "seduction" of the Sergeant in episode three; honestly, what *is* that dialogue about? Contrary to what the Sergeant says, the second hand on a clock barely moves at all. As for the abrupt shifts into the third person... it's like a really bad early 1990s perfume ad. And this is 1943, so "Oi! Wanna see me pants?" would have been enough.

Critique By now, we're in danger of making this story seem like a rag-bag of influences and references, but what's impressive on a first viewing is how cohesive it all is. The overall sense of a situation where nothing has been left to chance, and every element suits someone's purpose, is what gives the latter episodes a sense of foreboding. The Doctor, supposedly so good at engineering situations, has been ensnared in someone else's game - one that's been set up over centuries.

Watched a *second* time, this level of contrivance (either by Fenric or his real-life surrogate, Ian Briggs) seems almost to get in the way of the story. It makes Ace's adventures up to that point retrospectively seem more like tests, and everything about this Doctor's relationship with the first genuinely likeable companion since Romana ring false. Once again, the belief that this was all planned out in detail from Day One has affected how we see this story. And once again, it falls apart on closer analysis. The Doctor was *not* using Ace to lure Fenric into a trap, he was using Fenric to undo a knot of angst in Ace.

What setting the story in Wartime does,

though, is raise the stakes. It also grounds all of the emotional bonds that Ace forms in a world where split-second decisions of who to love and how deeply to get involved are normal coping strategies. It also gives directors and actors a vast repertoire of off-the-shelf reactions, which are available for viewers and programme-makers to judge this story against. What we're trying to say is that the only implausible thing about Millington is his moustache. (It's against Navy regulations, but scripted as part of his method of thinking himself into Hitler's shoes.) All of the man's plans, responses, and obsession with Nordic myth are in keeping with known fact. Whereas Steven Moffatt took his Blitz-era details from third-hand sources for "The Empty Child" / "The Doctor Dances" (X1.09-1.10), Ian Briggs has done his homework. As far as we can tell, this is how people in 1943 *actually* behaved, give or take a few lines from Jean and Phyllis.

Yet it was a curious move to do a Wartime setting. They had got far further without ever doing one of these than anyone making a series like *Doctor Who* would have managed anywhere else or in any other time. The longer it went on, the more would have been resting on the first attempt. In this regard, maybe "Silver Nemesis" was a good move, because it warmed us up for it. Yes, a few anachronisms slipped in - although nowhere near as many as were lying in wait - but the characters' attitudes serve a wider purpose, as we've seen. That said, the *bigger* achievement here is making the maths and runes seem to make sense to non-specialist viewers and those who knew this stuff alike.

McCoy seems more natural, more "right" than in almost any story. Sure, there's his famous ranting, and every fan can do "Eeevilevilsince-thedawnof Tiiieeeeme" as a party piece. We get comedic stuff just to reassure the kids that this is the same show they know, but nothing here seems out of place in a story as serious as this. Similar misgivings concerning Aldred, and that scene with the Sergeant, are more grave. Is she doing a very good performance of a very confused kid, or a lame rendering of teen-angst? Your response may vary if you know real British teenagers, but on the whole she deserves the benefit of the doubt.

No such caveats apply to the older guest cast. Everyone was amazed at Nicholas Parsons as Rev. Wainwright, but the real surprise is Dinsdale

Landen, often a one-note performer. He's good while playing Dr Judson, but as Fenric he's genuinely classy. The proof is that the *New Adventures* kept trying to give the Doctor opponents like him. Everyone else in this story is similarly rounded - at least, everyone over thirty. The soldier-boys are worryingly like the Season Twenty-Two eye-candy, but Anne Reid (Nurse Crane) and Janet Henfrey (Miss Hardaker) make their potentially flat characters seem to have lives outside the story. This is another adventure where women get all the big dramatic scenes, and we have to wonder why Cory Pullman (Kathleen Dudman) never got as high-profile a role as this again. With everyone so well suited to their roles, there come a few moments when the Doctor and Ace enter a scene and you suddenly remember that this is *Doctor Who*, and not a more-respectable-yet-supposedly-"adult" drama.

That brings up a bigger point. Too often over the previous quarter-century, *Doctor Who* required special allowances to be made. You had to accept certain conventions - such as three to six men in rubber suits constituting a mass invasion by an entirely alien species, a quarry was actually another planet and everyone in the cosmos speaks BBC English except comedy characters. When actors well-versed in playing period characters found themselves in that mongrel demi-genre, the "pseudo-historical", they were there as backdrop, almost moving scenery, with dialogue more by way of being sound-effects than speech. But here we have a story where 1943 is vital to the nature of it all, and everyone does their bit to maintain this, whilst the Doctor, Ace and Fenric distort this around them. It's a story that can only work as *Doctor Who*, but requires no overblown "*Doctor Who* acting" as distinct from any other kind. It's possible, especially with the DVD's feature-length edit, to sit with non-fans and watch this as just a routine TV play about vampires and Soviet marines in Yorkshire. You miss a lot doing that, but it doesn't need you to apply other standards.

The Facts

Written by Ian Briggs. Directed by Nicholas Mallett. Ratings: 4.3 million, 4.0 million, 4.0 million, 4.2 million. Audience appreciation was 67% for episode one and consistently 68% for the rest.

Working Titles "Wolf Time", "The Wolves of Fenric".

Supporting Cast Dinsdale Landen (Dr. Judson), Alfred Lynch (Commander Millington), Tomek Bork (Captain Sorin), Nicholas Parsons (Rev. Wainwright), Cory Pulman (Kathleen Dudman), Joann Kenny (Jean), Joanne Bell (Phyllis), Janet Henfrey (Miss Hardaker), Peter Czajkowski (Sgt. Prozorov), Marek Anton (Vershinin), Anne Reid (Nurse Crane), Aaron Hanley (Baby), Stevan Rimkus (Captain Bates), Raymond Trickett (Ancient Haemovore).

Oh, Isn't That..?

• *Nicholas Parsons*. His lengthy career is like a test of how old you are. If you're under thirty, he's the host of Radio 4's *Just a Minute*, a somewhat harried referee of conniving contestants. Any older than that, and you recall him from the legendarily cheap 70s gameshow *Sale of the Century*. (This was made by Anglia - the most ambitious second-league ITV station - whose usual output was charmingly bucolic. The phrase "And now, from Norwich, it's the quiz of the week" tells you more about the endemic sense of futility in British culture in the Tom Baker years than anything we said in Volume IV - but only if you've ever seen Norwich.)

If you're older than that, you might know him as the straight man to comedian Arthur Haines, back in the era of two-channel television. *Earlier* than that even, he was a Martian in an ad directed by Gerry Anderson before the latter decided to work with puppets instead - Parsons voiced the hero in Anderson's puppet western *Four Feather Falls* as well. The point is, as you might have figured out, nobody expected anything like as good a performance out of him as we got.

• *Janet Henfrey*. She was most well-remembered for playing the stern schoolmarm in Dennis Potter's *The Singing Detective* and earlier *Stand Up Nigel Barton*. Briggs wrote the part of Miss Hardaker along these lines, and asked for Henfrey (or the closest reasonable fit) to play her.

• *Anne Reid*. Since this, she's been in *dinnerladies* and more recently *The Mother*. (She was Daniel Craig's love-interest. The age-difference was the plot.) You might've seen her playing housemaid to Gillian Anderson in *Bleak House*, and by now you'll *definitely* have seen her in X3.1, "Smith and Jones", playing the straw-sucking Florence.

• *Dinsdale Landen*. He'd been in a sitcom called *Devenish* (a big ratings hit and with a spin-off novel, but you'll not find anyone else who remembers it). He was a character-actor of some distinction, and had recently been in a prestigious BBC production of Joe Orton's *What the Butler Saw*.

Cliffhangers Russian commandos surround the Doctor and Ace; the Doctor's party arrives too late to stop Millington and Judson running the Viking runes as a computer programme; lightning leaps from the mysterious jar into the crippled Dr Judson - he stands, opens his glowing eyes and says to the Doctor, 'We play the contest again, Time Lord'.

The Lore

• After writing what he thought was the comedy story of Season Twenty-Four, "Dragonfire", Ian Briggs wanted to try a straight horror story with a historical setting. Cartmel suggested the Blitz (figuring that the 1970s wasn't "historical" enough, although Briggs and most viewers in the 1990s would have disagreed). The various elements of the story came together quickly, especially after the holiday in Sweden mentioned above, and Briggs got a first draft together in two months. Rewrites were rapid, due to the story being brought forward in production order, but Briggs found time between these and his day job to write a pamphlet called "Futharks and Flip-Flops" explaining the technicalities to Cartmel. (As you may know - all right, perhaps you don't - the runic alphabets of however many characters were termed "Futhark" after the equivalent sounds of their first six letters.) Although changes to the script after this draft were minimal, Briggs' involvement in the rest of the story's production was to be fairly hands-on.

• The first attempt at a Haemovore mask looked like a lamprey, but Nathan-Turner thought it looked too rude for children's telly. (He kept it for himself, though). Mk II was another Moore and Allsopp design - like many of the recent monsters, it was blue rather than green. Effects designer Graham Brown built the Ultima computer from the innards of the old television set on which he was watched *Doctor Who* as a boy.

• This story was first into production, but early on Nathan-Turner decided it would be shown around Hallowe'en. In part, this was due to uncertainty as to whether Nicholas Courtney would be available that early for "Battlefield". For Nicholas Mallett's plan to come off, the recording would

have to be executed in under a fortnight, working around the school holidays. With the Forty-Mile rule in place, the locations would all have had to have been in Kent or Sussex (which was Cartmel's idea of where this should have been set). In fact, the underwater scenes and much of the coastline required safer waters, so cameraman Alan Jessop - a diver himself - suggested Lulworth Cove. This is in Dorset, so right at the farthest edge of what the BBC beancounters would have allowed. The bulk of the story was shot at an almost empty MoD training camp in Kent, which had the right look (and a Nissen hut, which could double or treble up as the script required). It also had a firing range right next to the stretch of coast they were using, so everyone stayed exactly where they were told to be.

• However, this story suffered from the weirdest weather since "The Claws of Axos" (8.3). When they needed calm and mist, they got a blizzard. When they needed a lowering sky turning to thunder, the sun shone. And when they thought the tide would be in their favour, the waves were huge.

(If you try reading these Lore entries in production order rather than broadcast order, something you will spot is that the weather in the late 1980s was just ludicrous. Hurricanes, snow in April, prolonged droughts causing reservoirs to shrink and brilliant blue skies lasting until November got global warming onto the political agenda here while Al Gore was still a senator with a fleet of chauffeur-driven limos. This is worth bearing in mind when looking at the abysmal ratings for "Battlefield" episode one - it was shown on a beautiful sunny evening when people were having picnics before the school term began - and when watching the stories made in summer. Ian Reddington, as the Chief Clown in 25.4, "The Greatest Show in the Galaxy", had to ride around in a black hearse with the windows up - and while wearing a top hat, a thick coat and clown make-up - but at least he was outside. By contrast, David John Pope - the Kandy Man in 25.2, "The Happiness Patrol" - was in a studio with the air-conditioning off during takes. We'll return to this when considering the origins of 26.4, "Survival".)

• As well as the new, darker costume, McCoy elected to wear the duffel-coat he usually wore between takes on cold days. This was agreed to work with the ensemble. Aldred had decided to wear period costume, including stockings and suspenders (as she had asked for in "Remembrance of the Daleks"), but for most takes had thermal long-johns. In fact, the one time Ace is seen to wear the stockings is when Tracey Eddon is doubling for Aldred on the church roof.

• So the material shot at Crowborough (the Ministry of Defence base) was blighted by skies that were never the same for two takes running, and by thick, sloppy mud. The fake mine-head sank into the earth. Aldred almost did likewise during the Doctor's apology for breaking her faith. The hoses used to wash away the remaining snow were later used to fake torrential rain during the firing-squad scene - the one sunny day of the shoot. They had already revised the dialogue for Ace and the object of her "seduction" - Sergeant Leigh - and it originally alluded to the heat making her clothes stick to her (a scenario known to devotees of premium-rate phone-lines the world over). Jean and Phyllis' death scene was done twice - once here, rather hurriedly and for the benefit of a "behind-the-scenes" show for children (*Take Two*), and later again in a more careful, if less scary, fashion. The second take was one of the many items Nathan-Turner undertook as second-unit director. He supervised much of the underwater material, as the tides at Lulworth delayed Mallett, but that's getting ahead of ourselves. Some scenes were more-or-less directed by Ian Briggs, who was on hand for last-minute rewrites like the one mentioned just now, and who had been a lecturer in drama.

• The church selected as "St Jude's" was St Lawrence's Parish Church in the Moor, in Hawkhurst. You'll be relieved to hear that this fine example of ecclesiastical architecture was undamaged, as the wall the Haemovores knock down was specially built. (A couple of days later, in the same village, a wall built for a similar purpose in the school that doubled as the cellar needed hefty BBC-issue crowbars to remove. The school caretaker had done a good job building it.) The graveyard scenes were the first to have help from Nathan-Turner as second-unit director, and that day - Friday, 14th of April - was also the one Marvel chose to descend from nearby Tonbridge Wells, with a Dalek in tow, to do publicity shots. The producer had banned all unauthorised press.

Next day, they had other visitors. Pepsi the Wonder Dog (see 24.3, "Delta and the Bannermen") came back for Miss Hardaker's death-scene. McCoy's wife and two sons came around (whereupon Sam and Joe Kent-Smith were pressed into service as rather short Haemovores for the scene in the tunnel). Aldred's mum turned up, and chatted with old school chum Janet Henfrey (who had presumably washed the latex scars off her face by then). Parsons had two interesting visitors. One was the Vicar of Billingshurst - near to where they were shooting - who lent his blue, ermine-lined robe (so at least *one* of the cast was warm and in character). Then a couple of visiting Norwegians mistook him for a real vicar (as had some locals, until they looked more closely). Asked how long he had been rector, Parsons replied, "Only a short time".

• A day off, then on to Lulworth, AKA "Maiden's Point". A strong wind made the fog-machine almost unusable, and delayed the arrival of the Royal Marines with the dinghies. Aldred, never fond of water, had asked to do a big jump and to do her own underwater stunt. On seeing the broadcast scene, none of her friends believed that it was her. (She'd have worse luck with water in the next story to be made: "Battlefield".) The delays meant that effects engineer and diver Graham Brown - who was to have played the Russian soldier who comes back to life under the sea - was with Mallett's crew recording the Haemovores rising from the waves when the second unit were able to dive. Effects operator John van der Pool took the role, and was larded with pancake make-up. (Yes, there *were* some Russians who were black, notably Pushkin, but not so many as all that. If we followed the convention and said "make him seem Caucasian", some smartarse would write in and point out that the Caucasus was part of the Soviet Union.)

Back on the beach, the various Haemovores had to be weighed down with rocks until they arose. The crew called the various character-faces by jokey names ("Biograph Girl", "Mrs Bridges", "Claire Rayner", "Demis Roussos"...) The masks had been dotted with seeds to speed up the drying of the latex, and these had sprouted, making a curious texture. All the costumes had to have ruffs or high collars. A persistent rumour claims that one of the masks was previously seen in the *Eagle's* fumetti strip "Doomlord", but to check that would involve caring. Another rumour is that future Channel 4 newsreader Sue Turton is one of the Haemovores, but we can't find any proof of this.

• Mark Ayres was asked to put together a score for this, and he leaned heavily on Russian composers (you'll spot a lot of Stravinsky's *Firebird* in

ABOUT TIME 1985–1989

there). The revised version used settings more like specific instruments, and removed the gag reference to Glenn Miller in episode one. Ayres supervised much of the re-working for the DVD, as Mallett had died after leaving a proposed running-order of scenes. One problem in editing the original version was that many short close-up shots from the climax had been wiped. The editing of this story was mainly to keep it to the right length, and about a quarter of an hour was lost. Some of this was restored in the video release - after a letter-writing campaign by fans - and the DVD has almost all of it, with the sequence amended to remove cliffhangers and build up pace logically. It's also digitally re-graded to make the rain look like it's falling from clouds, rather than being a hosepipe on a sunny day.

26.4: "Survival"

(Serial 7P, Three Episodes. 22nd November - 6th December 1989.)

Which One is This? The triumphant anti-climax, in which the Dark, Mysterious Doctor™ takes on his ultimate adversary in a parable about menstruation and the Cold War. Or it's the one in which Sylvester and Anthony Ainley roll about in a quarry, while Sophie and her teen-pals redo *Planet of the Apes* in the style of *Grange Hill*. Special guest-star Salem the cat (or a close relative). And this time, it's the Doctor who hides behind a sofa.

Firsts and Lasts It's absolutely the last *Doctor Who* story. Except for all the others.

Three Things to Notice about "Survival"...

1. *Doctor Who* leaves as it began, with the curious juxtaposition of a grotty London street and a savage wilderness full of skulls and bones. The difference is that they keep switching from one to the other, and varying the tone within these two zones. So in some respects, this is the most wildly inconsistent story ever - but in other ways, it's precisely controlled and thought out. Apparently random details in the street were all considered in detail, even the junk on sale on Ange's stall, the posters at the Youth Club (see **The Lore**) and the cat-food labels.

2. After the Doctor faced down Fenric last week, the revelation that the "evil force" operating a robot cat called "Shomi" (which is what a lot of

people seriously thought was happening, based on the cat-master's garbled words 'Show me') was only the Master initially seemed a bit of a let-down. But for people who didn't remember as far back as 22.3, "The Mark of the Rani" or 23.4, "The Ultimate Foe", this story re-introduces the character in a curious manner. The first cliffhanger makes great play out of revealing that the person with the electronically-disguised voice (what the BBC news was legally obliged to do for Sinn Fein spokesmen in those days, so we could all tell) is... some fat bloke with a silk waistcoat (with lapels, for heaven's sake). For anyone who didn't recognise him, Ace asks on our behalf and even *before* she's met the villain seems to know that he's a bit of a lightweight, cosmic villain-wise.

But for the *rest* of the story, the Master is there as the "control" sample - a specimen of what could happen to even the Doctor if the protagonists don't get away from the Cheetah Planet. And guess what... with almost nothing to do and barely any dialogue, Anthony Ainley's as good here as we ever see him, and far more plausible a threat to the Doctor than he ever was faffing about stealing Concorde or dressing as a scarecrow. (Although, concerning the way the Master grooms Midge, see **What Are the Gayest Things in *Doctor Who*?** under 25.2, "The Happiness Patrol".) Shame he lands up looking like Cat from *Red Dwarf*.

3. Yes, Midge. Whilst a lot of Ace's old gang seem to have come straight from the less intense sections of Children's BBC, such as *Chucklevision* or *Rentaghost*, actor Will Barton is clearly thinking more of *A Clockwork Orange* or *Scum*. (And this is the same story that has Hale and Pace as comedy storekeepers. Like we said, wildly inconsistent.) A lot of the press coverage of this story - there was some - were geared to "watch out for a star in the making". And while he's done all right for himself, it's the tiny mite who plays his kid sister who's the famous one now (see **Oh, Isn't That..?**).

The Continuity

The Doctor One last time with the mental tricks: the Doctor incapacitates Sgt. Paterson by touching a finger to the man's forehead, whereupon there's a "doorbell inside the mind" sound again. [See 26.1, "Battlefield" and a corollary in the last story.] In a bizarre oversight for this incarnation, the Doctor gets roped as part of Ace's tripwire trap.

The Doctor thinks that he and the Master are an explosive combination, and allows for the possibility that one day, one of them might blot the other out. He again demonstrates skill at driving a motorcycle [24.3, "Delta and the Bannermen"], and also the ability to dodge / escape / teleport from a head-on motorcycle collision. [We're probably meant to infer that the Doctor's bike collides with Midge's cycle in an impressive explosion, but that Midge fares worse and dies while the Doctor is merely thrown clear into a convenient rubbish pile. As filmed this looks a lot more awkward, as if the Doctor has vanished using magic, and reappeared face down on some rubbish bags and a discarded sofa cushion.]

He comprehends some facets of the nature of the hunt, and resolutely says he's not afraid of the feral power that's taking hold of the Master. In grappling with the Master on the Cheetah Planet, the Doctor [who, forgive us for saying, doesn't exactly look like a powerhouse] rallies enough strength to overpower his foe. [Whether this owes to his physical strength or stronger willpower isn't clear.] To nobody's surprise, he deems the TARDIS to be his home.

• *Ethics*. Notably, he seems willing to let Ace volunteer to become *enough* of a Cheetah that she can teleport them and the kidnapped Perivale residents home, even though this risks her permanently losing her own identity. In most regards, the Doctor stands back and lets Ace make her own decisions, and find her way out of a moral and emotional mess. He keeps a close eye on her - just in case - but doesn't forbid her consorting with the Cheetah named Karra. His innate wisdom seems to overcome comparatively low-level blood-lust that the planet engenders in him. Nevertheless, he leaves the Master mentally incapacitated on a planet that's about to explode.

• *Inventory*. His pocket-watch seems to aid him in tracking Ace's movements - almost as if it's a scanner of sorts - and it also allows him to make calculatations and determine the most stable part of the Cheetah Planet as it breaks up. Actually, this story is more notable for the things he *isn't* carrying, such as contemporary money and a tin-opener [both of which Ace provides].

• *Background*. Like the Master, he's heard of the Cheetah People and their Kitlings, and seems familiar with *some* of their characteristics [see **The Non-Humans**], but there's a lot he doesn't know about them.

The Supporting Cast

• *Ace*. Has asked the Doctor to take her back to Perivale so she can see what her old gang is up to. [The oddest thing about this visit - and it's easier to deal with it here rather than **Things That Don't Make Sense** - is that it's hard to get a grip on the status of Ace's family. Fair enough that she doesn't want to call her mother - despite her apparent soul-searching about her mum in the last adventure - and she doesn't even ask her friend Ange about her. Yet neither does she show the slightest anxiety about turning a corner and bumping into her at the local grocers or wherever. Other people Ace apparently doesn't show a desire to look up, tellingly: her granny Kathleen (26.3, "The Curse of Fenric", so she probably lives away or is deceased) and her friend Manisha (26.2, "Ghost Light", so she probably died after her flat was burned, then.) Yet Ange asks if Ace is back in town to visit her family, so you'd think she's still got *some* relations about the place.]

Everyone calls her "Ace". Her mum had her listed as a missing person, and Ange thought Ace had died or gone to Birmingham. [This is usually quoted as an anti-Brum gag, but it's just as likely a dig at Aaronovitch and the garbled version of Manisha's fate in the novelisation of 25.1, "Remembrance of the Daleks".]

Ace's contemporaries in Perivale include: Ange, here seen accepting change in a can labelled 'Hunt Saboteurs'; Jay, who's reportedly moved over west and is doing window cleaning or something; Stevie, who's killed by the Cheetahs prior to this story; Flo, who married Darth Vader 'the braindead plumber' [we doubt that it's *that* Darth Vader, unless he was missing Padme and killing time waiting for the Death Star to be finished]; Shreela, who survives events on the Cheetah Planet; and Midge, who's corrupted by the Master, has a little sister named Squeak and also a gran who lives upstairs. In the past, Ace and her friends used to hang out on scrubland around Horsenden Hill and start bonfires, or go to the local youth club.

Sgt Paterson recalls that the police let Ace off for something-or-other [possibly the Gabriel Chase arson from "Ghost Light", but it's unclear] with a warning, and he advises her that it doesn't cost much to phone home. [Paterson's interest in Ace doing so is curious, and *almost* makes you wonder if he's shagging Audrey. Post-Jackie Tyler, these things seem far more plausible, but as his first words to Ace are 'Don't I know you?', it's very unlikely.] U2 were "practically drawing their pensions" when Ace went clubbing, and the album *War* seems to be a new one on her. [It's yet-another piece of incidental evidence that suggests she left Earth in 1983, the main stumbling block still being that she says she was 13 in 1983 in "Ghost Light", and is 16 when she meets the Doctor in "Dragonfire".]

She doesn't know who the Master is before the Doctor tells her. Unlike the other abductees, Ace becomes very attuned to the Cheetah alpha-female Karra, and comprehends the ways of the Cheetah People without losing her identity. Under the Cheetah Planet's influence, she's able to teleport the Doctor's stranded party back to Earth, and can catch glimpses of the Master's activities and location through her "cat's eyes". She disobeys the Doctor's blatant and direct instructions - something of a rarity in this season - and takes part in the brawl against the Cheetahs in episode two. Yet she clearly trusts the Doctor enough to risk succumbing to the Cheetah Planet entirely.

Ace is wearing the Soviet emblem that Captain Sorin gave her ["The Curse of Fenric"]. She's pretty good at throwing rocks, can ride horseback and considers the TARDIS to be her home. [Here we should add that, on screen, nothing is said about Ace's fate after "Survival", and she's not mentioned when we next encounter the McCoy Doctor in 27.0, "The TV Movie". Paul Cornell's *New Adventures* book *Love and War* has Ace leaving the TARDIS, but she then ages about three years and returns again - only to depart the Doctor's company (barring the odd guest apperance) in the Kate Orman book *Set Piece*. Meanwhile, the *Doctor Who Magazine* strip settled for killing Ace off entirely, and we've yet to see if Big Finish will concoct a third account.]

The Supporting Cast (Evil)

• *The Master*. He's presently trapped on the Cheetah Planet and his plan this time around entails luring the Doctor there so *he* can find a way out. [The novelisation suggests that prior to this, the Master triggered a bloody war in the Antari System and was forced to follow a Kitling back to the Cheetah Planet when his scheme went awry. One snag is that the Master's directing the Kitlings and the Cheetah People to hunt in Perivale - on the presumption that the Doctor and Ace will eventually turn up - relies upon his knowing details about the Doctor's current companion, whom he's never met that we can tell.]

The Master's sheer willpower has enabled him to take on some of the Cheetah People's aspects without his fully becoming an animal, and maintaining control and his sense of identity are of utmost importance to him. The Master doesn't want to live as an animal, but declares that if he *does* lose his battle of wills with the Cheetah Planet, then he will hunt, trap and destroy the Doctor.

As a pseudo-Cheetah person, the Master has bright yellow eyes, fangs and the occasional tendency to howl at the moon. He has some control over the Kitlings, being both able to see through their eyes and dispatch one to track the Doctor. The Master's hypnotism seems more powerful than ever when used on those corrupted by the Cheetah Planet's influence. Midge's identity is erased to the point that the Master can mentally speak through his lips, and the youth centre teens are snared by the Master's mental power as exerted through his head flunky. [He seems to want the self-defence class as a private army for its own sake as much as to bait the Doctor.] The link between the Master and Midge becomes so strong, Midge appears to die as much from the Master's rejection as from his motorcycle injuries.

Ultimately, the Master claims the collapsing Cheetah Planet as his home, and is last seen there before the Doctor teleports away. The Master also has a go [whether he seriously expects it to work or not] at breaking into the Doctor's TARDIS with a lock-pick, but is interrupted before we can learn if he's capable of succeeding.

The TARDIS It arrives on a suburban street corner, once it appears that nobody is looking. [The delay in the Ship's arrival thus fails to prevent the abduction of Stuart, the car-washing bloke from the opening scene. Things like this keep happening, don't they? It must be part of the TARDIS' programming to avoid being seen, but if the Ship can detect such things, it should demonstrate better judgment than it often does about whether it's going to land in a war-zone or whatever. [See X3.12, "The Sound of Drums" for the idea that the TARDIS has a 'perception filter', which would logically make this feature redundant (but which itself would make that business on Logopolis a total and terminal waste of time), and also 5.7, "The Wheel in Space" and 1.3, "Edge of Destruction" for proof that one former story editor had already thought of this.]

What About Season 27?

Just because one Season Twenty-Six episode got 3.1 million viewers, it didn't mean that John Birt's BBC had no place for *Doctor Who*. If anything, the programme's potential made it *so* appealing to *so* many interested parties that the Corporation bosses had a hard time choosing which route to follow - and that is what delayed the series' return for the first few years of its absence.

In the new BBC regime, it had been decided (mainly by the Government - who had got it into their heads that competition was always a good thing, and that if they couldn't sell off the BBC, they might as well make it play by their institutional rules) that the Corporation best served the public as a sort of video "publisher". Namely, it should distribute items made by other people - so long as the programme quality remained at the level and within the guidelines of stuff they had hitherto made in-house. Obviously, or so it was thought (particularly by Birt), the BBC's function was to provide news and lots of it, with entertainment, drama and sport serving to kill time between bulletins and current-affairs programmes. So it was announced that from 1990, at least 25% of television output had to be made for the BBC by others (as opposed to being imported, like *Star Trek* or *Neighbours*).

It was like the Klondike! Suddenly anyone who'd worked in telly - in whatever capacity - got a few rich chums and well-connected buddies together. They'd hire an office somewhere near Tottenham Court Road tube station, get a logo and a two-second screen ident made, and - lo! - they were a production company. Some of these had been going a while (as Channel 4 had run this way since 1982) and some were set up with the impending ITV franchise auction. Some others were made up of people who unexpectedly lost out when the results of this were announced, notably Thames. All of them had their eye on getting a slice of mainstream credibility via the BBC.

Imagine, then, the amount of interest when it became obvious that the BBC themselves weren't going to make *Doctor Who* any more. Here we have a series that, by 1989, made almost twice as much in overseas rights and merchandising as the Corporation spent on it. It had international brand-recognition. There was also that whole issue of the forthcoming feature film. Although the BBC's official line was that they were hanging on to the rights to see if they couldn't reboot it themselves, and that no discussions with anyone about co-production would be happening any

time soon, the vultures began to circle. The obvious candidate would seem to be Daltenreys, parent company of Coast to Coast, who were already holding the film rights (they were going to start filming any day now, honest!).

First off the mark - while the BBC series was still in production - was Millennium Productions, who shot a pilot titled "The Monsters of Ness" in Venice in 1988. (This starred one David Burton, whose car was proudly emblazoned with the announcement that he was "the new Doctor Who" for several years afterwards.) Victor Pemberton - whose Wartime family sagas already claimed that he had been producer of the series - had a company called Saffron Productions, and he let it be known at conventions that he thought he could do a better job than anyone. Even better than Verity Lambert, who had a company (called Cinema Verity, of course), but was pointedly not saying anything on the subject when asked (for reasons that should become obvious during the Appendix).

Meanwhile, Terry Nation (who, according to Trivial Pursuit and some of the lazier press, created *Doctor Who*) now put his hat into the ring, in concert with Gerry Davis. They promised a back-to-basics approach, with an older Doctor and a pilot episode re-starting the story from scratch. We'll hear a lot of that during the 90s. One obvious trump-card they held was that they owned the rights to the monsters the public actually knew.[48] And *all* of these people stressed how they would retain the "Britishness" of the series and the "behind-the-sofas" thrills, but not be crap like everyone "knew" it was these days. We should also mention one other major player in the co-production bidding, CBS Television. Obviously, compared to a few old sixties relics in Dean Street, they had a bargaining chip like a tactical nuke: guaranteed US distribution and big bucks. However, the BBC were cautious about how the integrity of the "franchise" - as we now have to call it - would withstand US input.

The Head of Series and Serials, Peter Cregeen, had every reason to hesitate before deciding between any or none of these options. The main reason *Doctor Who* was ending had less to do with ratings per se as the relative size of the audience compared to the resources (not just money) put in. That was largely down to Michael Grade thinking that nobody would want to watch both this and *Coronation Street*. Grade was long gone.

continued on page 343...

341

The Non-Humans

• *The Cheetah People*. They're essentially a fun-loving species, although their definition of "fun" is generally carnal. They bite, scratch, are attracted to shiny juggling balls and make an awful fuss, but hunting is mainly an expression of their self-image, not a desperate search for meat. They'll generally leave people alone, unless they're hungry. Nobody - not Time Lords such as the Doctor and the Master, it would appear - knows much about the Cheetahs, because nobody's survived long enough to find out.

It cannot be understated that the Cheetahs are tightly linked to their planet's life-force. When they fight one another, the planet reflects the conflict and explosions are triggered, hastening its demise. They're still bipedal and ride horses, but their senses are sharper and they have tawny fur all over. They seem to live entirely in the moment, with no memory or ability to conjecture. They have vestiges of clothing and a tendency to wear necklaces (made from the teeth of their opponents). Their retractable claws can cut steel wire, and they wear boots, unsurprisingly.

Humans and Time Lords can also fall sway to the planet's influence and take on the Cheetah People's attributes, although attacking a Cheetah seems to greatly hasten this process, and killing one seems to tip Midge's mind over the edge. The Doctor keeps insisting that standing still - even amid a brawl - is the best way to avoid undue attention from the Cheetahs. He also indicates that he's never heard of them hunting so far from home. [So they seem to have preferred hunting grounds, and Earth is off their beaten path.]

Cheetahs can sense tripwires and see in the dark. They sometimes hunt at night, but always in the open. Their fate of the Cheetahs is left open-ended - as their homeworld breaks up, the Cheetahs near the Doctor and the Master are seen to vanish. [It's possible that - linked as they are to the planet's lifeforce - they're simply "extinguished" as it dies. However, the Doctor's comment that 'They've gone' seems to indicate that they've used their teleportation abilities to flee, and the fact that one of them returns for Karra and Midge's bodies indicates that at least some of them reach a safer locale.]

• *Kitlings*. Described as 'feline vultures', but effectively look like sinister, hissing black cats. They can scavenge across the cosmos, teleporting theselves to any suitable hunting-ground and tele-porting suitable prey back to their homeworld for the Cheetah People to hunt [again, see **History**]. They *seem* to be responsible for killing and eating a grocery store owner's cat.

Planet Notes

• *The Planet of the Cheetah People*. [Look, if it had a better name, we'd've used it.] It's a desert world, with one visible moon. We've previously noted how the life-force of this "extremely old world" interacts with humans, Time Lords and the Cheetah People alike, so...

People affected by the planet begin by developing a yellow taint to their eyes, then a dissociation with their past selves, rapid growth of their canines and accelerated appetite. [The symptoms are predictably like lycanthropy, but also - most noticeably - like the side-effects of Stahlman's gas. There are more than a few similarities to the overall situation from 7.4, "Inferno", which might suggest that the inhabitants tried to penetrate the core of their world.]

Some pools of water on the Cheetah Planet contain a kind of life-energy that both heals a Cheetah and reinforces their savagery. Once Ace drinks some, she's able to hear Karra's words and feels a kinship with her, but gets put in greater danger of losing control completely.

History

• *Dating*. The setting is clearly contemporary, and the Doctor tells Ace she's been 'away as long as you think you have'. [We might imagine that Ace has been gone for two years - the same duration as her on-screen tenure - although it *feels* like a bit less than that. A few of her friends have left town, but most are still hanging around to become Cheetah food. She's been filed as a missing person, but not for so long that her homecoming seems like a virtual return from the dead.] Ace specifies that it's a Sunday.

Perivale is described as a boring suburb where nothing happens. The youth club used to have a coffee bar but now doesn't, and Sgt. Paterson teaches self-defence classes there every Sunday afternoon.

The Planet of the Cheetah People was once home to an advanced civilisation, but it seems they mistakenly believed they could control their planet's life-force. They bred [or rather, genetically engineered] the Kitlings to serve as 'minds they could talk to, eyes they could see through', but

What About Season 27?

...continued from page 341

Another reason was that the style of production was an anachronism. The set-up we laboriously described in the essay for "An Unearthly Child" (1.1) was long gone in any other drama series: having an in-house production team, with a series producer who'd come up through the ranks, was not how things were done any more. Also, there were no obvious candidates to replace Nathan-Turner. Anyone remotely suitable was being poached for *EastEnders* or the few remaining BBC dramas from the old school. Andrew Cartmel's move to *Casualty* was one of the most obvious examples of head-hunting in this era.

Cartmel is occasionally mentioned as a potential producer himself. It's clear he thought he was capable of doing the job. (His book on those years, *Script Doctor*, ought to have been called *Damn! I'm Good.*) It's also clear that enough stories were in the pipeline, and that some idea of what was going to happen to Ace and the Doctor had been thrashed out in detail. Lots of fun can be had piecing this together and concocting a plausible Season Twenty-Seven as the BBC could have made it. Obviously a good place to start is the "Endgame" documentary on the "Survival" DVD, but *DWM* #255 made an entertaining and convincing feature of this issue long beforehand, albeit with a few leaps of faith along the way. We'll pitch in with a revised version later, but before that we'll indulge in a bit of hindsight Dave Owen understandably lacked when he wrote that article in 1997.

Between the 1989 and 2005 series of *Doctor Who*, the only really successful British-made science fiction was *Red Dwarf*. How did such an unpromising set-up flourish? There was a loyal fan-base, eventually, but the key factors in its success were that it was written by people who paid attention to details and made by BBC Manchester. To summarise crudely, the writers - Rob Grant and Doug Naylor - had worked on *Spitting Image* as script editors, and thus knew about effects budgeting. Once their series had got a third six-episode run, they effectively staged a coup. Because they were in a regional BBC studio complex, they had autonomy that those in Television Centre lacked. With the aid of a sympathetic lead director, Ed Bye, they managed to make the next few years' worth of the show look more expensive whilst costing less, mainly through economies of scale. Instead of dismantling the sets after each recording to make

way for local news or *The 8:15 From Manchester*, they had a dedicated *Red Dwarf* unit. You have as long as it takes to remember how the theme from *The Sarah Jane Adventures* goes to figure out what we're going to say next.

The BBC Wales *Doctor Who* is a success - at least, in part - because it's made somewhere other than London, where they don't really do much else. Now that they've got Upper Boat to play with, they can make *Who* and three spin-off series (yes, three... we mustn't forget *Totally Doctor Who*). So if *Red Dwarf* could pull it off in the early 90s, and to an extent *Casualty* did it in the late 80s (being primarily a Bristol-based production, thus the only thing they make that isn't narrated by David Attenborough), why couldn't the BBC make *Doctor Who* elsewhere then? The one precedent was "Horror of Fang Rock" (15.1), and everyone was impressed by the technical support they had in 1977. With their Charter pledging that they serve all of the UK, and a commitment made every so often to broaden out the production-base of its programming, this would be a tactful move.

So let's assume that they decided to make Season Twenty-Seven in-house - just to keep the rights active whilst they negotiated with various interested parties - and made a big fuss of moving a flagship drama and British television institution to Birmingham's Pebble Mill studios (home of *The Archers* and *Top Gear*). The Owen piece in *DWM* assumes that Ian Fraser would be producer. He was an experienced production associate, was married to Fiona Cumming and was a friend of Nathan-Turner. (He was also among the visitors to mock-Windsor in 25.3, "Silver Nemesis.") Good call, but he might have known slightly too much about the backstage crises to want such a poisoned chalice.

If we go with Cartmel, who is assumed to stay put in the *DWM* piece, we have a problem of finding a new script editor. Ben Aaronovitch is obvious choice in many ways, but he's a potential liability in many others. He was already slipping with regard to deadlines, and this would later cause trouble. It's more likely, then, that his semi-official role as consultant would be made a paid job, if only to fund his move to Moseley. Pebble Mill was blessed with many talented editors and a track-record of dealing with obsessive fans who quibbled on minutiae (if you've seen the website for *The Archers*, you'll see what we mean), so any

continued on page 345...

this only led to their own corruption. As they devolved into savagery and became the Cheetahs, it affected the world's ecology and geology. All that remains of their culture is a handful of ruins, and the strange abilities they now enjoy.

At story's end, the planet is physically destroyed, but the Doctor implies that its life-force - which seems to exist as a state of mind as much as anything else - will, to some degree, live on within those it influenced.

The Analysis

Where Does This Come From? You'd have to be blind not to spot that there's some kind of subtext, although precisely *what* might evade anyone who doesn't know any women who were at university between 1985 and 1995. Yep! We're in "drawing-down-the-moon" / pendulum-dowsing / princesses saving dragons from St George territory. This is almost a compendium of folklore about women drawing strength from natural forces and turning into cats. (It's traditionally the No. 2 option after snakes, just as men turn into wolves or apes: we've seen all the rest recently.) Writer Rona Munro had been in this zone before: her stage-play *Piper's Cave* taps into the Hebridean stories about "Selkies". (It sounds more sensible than "were-seals", but that's what these women are - love-lorn lasses who swim away from their old identities and become undines.)

Look at the key scene in "Survival". A big blood-red moon is reflected in the water, and seems to make the water energised with some kind of life-essence. Ace takes a sip and starts learning to commune with her "sister". Now, if the links between the moon and blood need explaining, there are any number of helpful books about what happens to girls when they reach thirteen or so, or you could ask your mum. If you need the link between a full moon and suddenly going all hairy and killing people explained, you really *have* been out of things for a while. The connections between this and the apparent switch at the end of the story to a parable about disarmament might require a quick gloss, though.

Back in the 80s, we were being told on a fairly regular basis that "objectivity is masculine subjectivity", and that reason and logic and science were a fiendish conspiracy by men to devalue female power (because, apparently, women can't "do" science or logic). The most obscene and dangerous

expression of phallocratic folly was the Arms Race, which entailed old men boasting about whose was bigger. This resulted in a concerted effort to resist such dangerous patriarchs as Reagan, Andropov and, um, Thatcher. Never mind that rather a lot of men thought the Yanks using East Anglia as a glorified aircraft-carrier was a bad thing, the protest movement was wimmin only. Or at least, the hardcore camp outside RAF Greenham Common was made so. The RAF themselves weren't entirely keen on the Yanks, but got pelted with used sanitary towels all the same. So with focal groups like this acting as seminaries (sorry, but any other word has connotations of battery hens, and anyway, female plants produce seeds too), the previously discarded, repressed or neglected versions of old stories were deployed as means to overcome centuries of "brainwashing". It was presented as a direct linear connection. Retell *Cinderella* as a tale of female emancipation and stop a war.

The people who had been doing this for decades before were slightly embarrassed about this. Angela Carter, whose retold fairy-tales were filmed as *Company of Wolves* (directed by a bloke, but he was Irish and so another oppressed minority - although any film Neil Jordan made thereafter that didn't have the English as bad guys was slated by critics) found herself feted as a mystic. Marina Warner was safe from this, because she was an academic so couldn't quite "get" it, but she wrote books that re-examined folklore and fairy-tales. (Her insights were crucial in the small industry that formed around theoretical responses to the *Alien* films, and indeed Tim Burton's *Batman Returns* looks like it was written after reading one of her essays.)

One of the old stories had been retold much, much earlier. In 1941, to recoup the losses made by the Hearst newspapers' fatwa against *Citizen Kane,* RKO studios set about making sure-fire money-spinners. Producer Val Lewton was given a list of market-researched titles of films people would want to see, and he set to adapting the Russian folk-tales he heard as a kid so that they could use old sets and a small cast. *Cat People* (1942) reworks an older idea of women who turn into leopards when jealous or aroused, and has a young art-student marrying quickly but unhappily. An older woman from the same region (Serbia, which is interesting with hindsight), and who looks decidedly feline, addresses her as "sister".

What About Season 27?

...continued from page 343

number of them could have been seconded as proper script editor, leaving Aaronovitch as story editor and free-floating agent of chaos. Alternatively, Colin Brake - then working on *EastEnders* and later to be more overtly involved in *Doctor Who* - was a good bet. By his own admission, Brake was angling to take over from Cartmel at this time. Even Marc Platt might been asked.

The thing is, before any of this kicked off, Cartmel was in his new job at *Casualty*. It's possible that this might have removed him from contention, or perhaps he was being groomed. It's known that any new series of *Doctor Who* would not enter production until 1991 at the earliest, so that gave him eighteen months to get experience of mainstream drama and some different contacts.

However, *Casualty* looks even *more* studio-bound than *Doctor Who*, even with the set-piece helicopter crashes and whatever. One thing Cregeen said in his press-release about how he wasn't axeing *Doctor Who* at all, gracious no, was that he wanted it to look less cramped. This gives us a clue as to one possible way the BBC might have used their "Swiss Army Series" for another experiment. With the BBC's track-record of using the series to pioneer new techniques, they might plausibly have tried out the "Frame Removed" technique that is now standard for all TV drama except *Casualty* and *EastEnders* - shooting on VT, but processing it to make it look sort-of like film. A bit. This allows all the video trickery of the last few years, but a more export-friendly end product. BBC Birmingham (they knocked down Pebble Mill years ago) churns out daytime drama *Doctors* in industrial quantities, and most other soaps - including the one made in Cardiff about Rose Tyler and some bloke - are manufactured this way now. The Corporation was experimenting with this in 1992, trying it out live on *Top of the Pops*, so had *Doctor Who* been going they might have used it for that purpose alone (see "Dimensions in Time" in the Appendix). We can't help but notice that the last two years of *Doctor Who* had seen a move towards using one-camera OB set-ups rather than three-camera studio, as had been the norm. This was an innovation from *Brookside* and had crept into the other major soaps after *EastEnders* had taken up the idea and pushed more resources at it. Now, only sitcoms are made the three-camera way.

Broadly speaking, a Cartmel-produced series would have kept more of a toe-hold in Earth's recent past. Although we know that the script he had ready and waiting, Robin Mukherjee's "Alixion" (see **What *Else* Wasn't Made?** under 17.6, "Shada") was set in an asteroid full of insect monks, the real trail-blazer for this phase would have been "Remembrance of the Daleks" (25.1), exploring "issues" within a recognisable place and time. One plan often discussed is the idea of the semi-dodgy businessman from 1960s London who would return in the 1990s as well-connected associate, a sort of anti-UNIT. Ace's replacement, according to many sources, was to have been his daughter, delivered as a baby by the Doctor at the end of one story and "collected" as an adult at the start of the next. (The scene we keep hearing about is her introduction, wherein the lady is at an elegant party in a country house, sneaks off to open a safe and finds the Doctor inside it saying, 'What kept you?')

We also know that Marc Platt had a notion for the 60s story to involve Ice Warriors, and that the plan had been for Ace to join the Prydon Academy of Gallifrey. (Look, just because "Death Comes to Time" made the idea of the Time Lords working just like the Jedi Knights seem crap, it doesn't mean a decent writer couldn't have pulled it off.) Nathan-Turner had been in negotiations with the London Dungeon at Tooley Street for use in a possible future story (which is why the press launch for "Silver Nemesis" happened there), and this is usually assumed to be connected with the Ice Warrior story. Prior to this, somewhere, would have been a story where she's set some tricky task and the Doctor is forbidden to interfere, or something. That task may or may not have been connected with the notion to use the Metatraxi from the proposed stage-play Cartmel and Aaronovitch had devised in 1988 (see "Remembrance of the Daleks"). We also know that at least three other *New Adventures* authors had (or claim to have had) script proposals that were being looked at favourably.

One final consideration is that McCoy's tenure would have ended at the end of Season Twenty-Seven. Owen makes some interesting guesses about replacement casting (and his favoured Eighth Doctor, Richard Griffiths, had been asked to replace Tom Baker and would just have been looking for a role about then). However, a cliffhanger to

continued on page 347...

ABOUT TIME 1985–1989

Thereafter it is implied that Irena, the bride, is stalking her supposed rival and turning into a savage animal in the process. Finally we get proof that she is a were-cat, but she dies in the process[47].

"So what?", you might ask. Well, in 1982 Paul Schrader remade it with Nastassja Kinski, and David Bowie did a song for it, which is on the album *Let's Dance* - the T-shirt for which is what one of the kidnapped locals, Derek, is here seen wearing. Like we said, the details are significant. But more importantly, the 1942 film was rediscovered by the lecturers who were trying to keep up with all the feminist critiques flying around in the 80s, and reappraised in "Cult" film mags, so it's almost inconceivable that nobody involved in making "Survival" had seen it. Those same mags might also mention Harlan Ellison's *Outer Limits* segment "Soldier", with a future warrior saluting a cat because in his time they are telepathically imprinted with orders and are thus superior officers. But if we go down that path, we'll start off about Cordwainer Smith's "Instrumentality" stories and this book's already quite long.

As we've mentioned in earlier McCoy stories, the new batch of writers seem to be working from a folk-memory of their own of earlier *Doctor Who* as an overall genre, not in any detail. In this light, the apparent similarities between the end of this and the climax (meaning the last cliffhanger) of 7.4, "Inferno" are striking. We should also formally mention what we've joked about before, that the iconography of hominid animals in horseback hunting humans is right out of *Planet of the Apes*, but with an overlay of Sergio Leone Spaghetti Westerns. The sequence with Ace cupping water in her hands while Karra immerses her entire head is like the Biblical story of Gideon recruiting soldiers. It's also a bit like *Tron*.

What's also worth noting is how the theme of Social Darwinism - the crass assumption that "Survival of the Fittest" meant "most fit" and not "best fit" - is taken to extremes here. The end of the story was to have had the Youth Club lads kick Midge to death. The notion that things that cannot adapt to change are doomed is also referenced, from the annuals for defunct hit shows of the 60s on Ange's stall to the debate over Sunday trading. (We still have the compromise that was reached on the statute books, which perplexes both visitors from countries where "twenty-four hour opening" means all day, and from nations where even walking the dog on Sunday will get

you ostracised - but you won't know this until Monday morning.) Do you think Andrew Cartmel was perhaps riding a hobby-horse? This story's token Nietzsche reference is the oft-cited line from *The Joyous Science* (there are other translations of the title) about "magnificent blond beasts". People have erroneously got it into their heads that he was talking Aryan supremacy, when he was actually thinking about lions. The idea was that it could be possible to live with no fear of consequences and entirely in the present, and that animals who do this don't worry about death - but death nonetheless comes to them sooner. Happiness through lobotomy might be preferable to a life of anxiety caused by intelligence and memory. As we've said, this was now being discussed again, after decades of don't-mention-the-War furtiveness.

If you didn't know, hunt saboteurs were (and are) people opposed to the bizarre form of pest control practiced by people whose parents were cousins, wherein the slower, stupider foxes are weeded from the gene-pool by toffs dressed like Romana in "The Horns of Nimon" (17.5). This alleged "sport" is now illegal, but still carries on in areas where the police are too busy investigating corruption and incompetence amongst their urban counterparts to arrest fellow Freemasons. The foxes, meanwhile, have moved into the cities.

Things That Don't Make Sense Not much to report here, now that we've dealt with the ambiguities of Ace's family, the oddities of the motorcycle crash and what happens [or what we *think* happens] to the Cheetahs who menace the Doctor and then just fade away. Another reason we've less to talk about: the programme-makers seem to have finally got the hang of this "plot-logic" thing.

One visual goof worth noting: Ace runs away from the Doctor's side, yet she's back there in long shot as the Master spies upon them. We might also question how *none* of the Perivale residents happen to look out a window and spot the horse-mounted Cheetahs abducting people in the middle of the street, but perhaps they're just timid folk and don't feel inclined to report it. The Doctor, knowing that the Master longs to find a means of escaping the Cheetah Planet, doesn't seem to anticipate that his rival will follow and overhear him telling Ace how this can be accomplished. It's also a little weird to watch the Master command one of his Kitlings to 'Hurry', where-

What About Season 27?

...continued from page 345

lead into a new production regime might have appealed to the BBC, as it had in 1969 (see 6.7, "The War Games"). Assuming - as Owen does - a season of fourteen twenty-five minute episodes, we could be looking at "Alixion" as a regeneration story. However, those of you who've read BBC Books' *Illegal Alien* by Mike Tucker (yes, the one who did special effects) and Robert Perry might surmise that a 1940s Cyberman story would make a more enticing match to kill off this seemingly invincible Doctor. It happens that this was submitted at just the wrong time (during pre-production on 26.3, "The Curse of Fenric"), but they took a rain-check even when the true identity of one of the pseudonymous authors was known.

Owen's guesses for Season Twenty-Eight look suspiciously like an attempt to do Season Twenty-Two again, properly. The Daleks, the Rani, the Cybermen and two stories set in graveyards - to say nothing of a sideswipe at TV violence. We doubt this would have happened.

Our earlier hunches about the way the BBC would have deployed *Doctor Who* strategically rely on the other bidders not having their acts together in time. With the CBS proposal removed from the table, we still have Pemberton, Nation 'n' Davis and Daltenreys in the running. Any bid by Pemberton would have wound up having the same sort of strings attached as an in-house series: a regional base, film-look and longer episodes (probably more of them per annum). Daltenreys might have grabbed the tax-breaks available to make big productions in Ireland, or might have based production in Pinewood studios. But first they had to make that feature film, and that wasn't going at all well. CBS's agency, Philip Segal, remained interested in the series, but wasn't too crazy about the Coast to Coast script (with hindsight, this is really worrying). But then he left Columbia and the project seemingly died with his departure. (Naturally that wasn't the case; see 27.0.)

Of course, there was one other production company in the bidding, although not seriously. It was called Teyburn, and they seem to have made a bid in conjunction with the music publishers-turned-TV quiz-show makers Noel Gay. The head honcho at Teyburn - who was interested in making a soap but kept a hand in just on the off-chance - was John Nathan-Turner. It's possible that he was the only head of a production company in Britain who didn't want to be producer of *Doctor Who*. He stayed around to manage the merchandising rights, which is why he'll be back in the Appendix.

Let's end with a wild-card. What if the BBC decided to give the rights to the series to an experienced and proficient production company who hadn't asked for it? Two obvious choices spring to mind. One is Talkback, originally makers of comic adverts, then of comedy shows starring founders Mel Smith and Griff Rhys Jones, then of other things once they were made part of the Pearson empire. Pearson took over Thames, who didn't stop making television just because they no longer had a franchise to transmit it themselves. Thames / Pearson brought back *The Tomorrow People* in a slick, film-look international way, with glossy effects and an all-star cast (but still the same innuendoes).

Ponder this combination for a moment: state-of-the-art effects, location-work in Australia and guaranteed international sales. Zenith, mentioned in passing in some comments on possible bids, were riding high with *The Paradise Club*, a curious series which echoed 30s Warner Bros films by having Leslie Grantham (Kiston in 21.4, "Resurrection of the Daleks", and a lot else that wasn't *Doctor Who*) and Don Henderson (Gavrok in 24.3, "Delta and the Bannermen") as brothers - one a gangster and the other a priest. The third such company was Cinema Verity, and they had made a couple of hit shows. *May to December* (see 25.2, "The Happiness Patrol") scored highly with viewers, but *So Haunt Me* (about a family coping with the ghost of their new home's former resident - and if the title hasn't given you the hint as to her ethnicity, you're a nebbisch) didn't quite catch fire. However, the negotiations between the BBC and CBS had included Lambert as a representative of the Corporation, so there would have been a conflict of interest if she'd asked her company to prepare a pitch.

---

upon the cat casually saunters away its own damn good time, thank you very much. And, um... well, it's a bit strange that the Master - evil fiend that he is - doesn't take the opportunity to kick the Doctor's posterior when it's presented to him atop the rubbish pile in episode three.

Clutching at straws now, but it's odd that the producer objected to the music for this story.

Critique So that was *Doctor Who*, that was. It's been a long, weird journey: from Kennedy's assassination to the fall of the Berlin Wall, from Gerry and the Pacemakers to New Kids on the Block, and from howlround and a pen-torch to a computer-generated purple galaxy. It's worth pondering that length of screen-time for a moment, because it highlights something a lot of us forget about "Survival". It's the first time we've had the TARDIS arriving on a suburban street-corner since "Attack of the Cybermen" (22.1), and that was hardly Yeti-in-the-loo territory. Five years, give or take three weeks, have elapsed since that episode. Aside from the unscreened "Shada" (17.6) and various jaunts to manor houses in the countryside or well-known tourist destinations, the last time there was a scene like this was the end of 14.2, "The Hand of Fear", in 1976. The majority of the target audience hadn't been born when *Doctor Who* last routinely did what many older fans assumed was the "natural" set-up of a story. As a result, Sunday morning domesticity has never been portrayed in the Outside Broadcast / Paintbox / "Dark, Mysterious Doctor" configuration of the series.

Seeing this after the BBC Wales version makes several things clear. Whilst what we hear and spot in this story's background is a complex web of allusions and metaphors, what's up front is a form of television drama that would be unthinkable today, with tentative steps towards what stories set in the Powell Estate would be doing unselfconsciously. Ace's gang have families who miss them, even if she's still the street-tuff quasi-orphan previous stories needed. No effort is made to show these families, though. Only Midge's little sister Squeak and a couple of nosy neighbours represent community. More damagingly, Ange's update of where the old gang are now has such corny dialogue, and such a bad sitcom performance, that any effort at subtlety in later scenes is contaminated. No one who'd not lived in mid-80s Britain could imagine the routine use of such scenes in dire kid-vid fare as *Woofer* and *Graham's Gang*, or - the best approximation we can think of for good intentions undone by producers bottling out - *Tucker's Luck*. Rona Munro is trying to write something attacking a whole trend in contemporary society and - like the post-*Grange Hill* adventures of Tucker Jenkins that we were told would "tell it like it is" about youth unemployment - it has its claws clipped.

But look at the details. Everything is tilted towards the same point, all the clues there for subsequent re-watching. They've made their own cat-food labels, chosen the posters and T-shirts, made their own graffiti and even told us that the cornershop is "Under New Management" (geddit?), so we have to assume that we're being Told Something. And in the process they've turned streets in Perivale into a studio-set, as self-consistent and controlled as Terra Alpha ("The Happiness Patrol") and just as rhetorical. So knowing what the original script wanted - wasteland instead of Horsenden Hill, Midge's former followers kicking him to death once he's no longer top cat, and knowing how overtly symbolic the Planet scenes were intended to be - we can still see a complicated allegory under what's a fairly routine-looking *Doctor Who* adventure for the handful of children still watching. It was visible on first broadcast, before we found out all this background, but hidden inside a kid's show.

Is this a good thing or not? The basic level of competence needed to make a decent *Doctor Who* story is present - barring a few child-actors and a wonky cat-robot - but if the hefty symbolism and allegory had been brought to the fore, made more of and waved in our faces, would this have been any more watchable? Yes and no. Yes, because that's what a small but voluble proportion of the viewing public said they liked. The late 80s and early 90s were a golden age for a certain kind of drama where strict mimetic realism was eschewed in favour of dense, playful and highly-worked pieces. Terms like "ludic autonomy" were bandied about, and people came away from these feeling clever: if they were lucky, they actually benefited long-term and realised what else can be done when you step outside soaps or action-movies. Comics did it too, and these were seized upon by trend-mongers as a blinding revelation (this is when the term "graphic novel" could be used in public without anyone sniggering). See Paul Cornell's first TV play (the ten-minute "Kingdom Come") for a benchmark of what was permissible back in those days.

And there's the rub. This was a false dawn, and before too long the IQ of the assumed audience sank below room-temperature. In the longer term, Wareing's decision to keep these details present for anyone paying attention (but down in the mix behind 'Perishin' cats, it's the owners I blame') and do a *Doctor Who* story set in a suburb and a quarry-like planet with amusingly feline monsters was a better strategy. The story *looks* quite old-fashioned now, but what's in it is more modern-seeming than routine TV from 1989.

In fact, compared to the remarkably similar "Fear Her" (X2.11), this seems like a far *more* contemporary endeavour. Munro's diatribe against a now-extinct political dogma has become a more subtle and intriguing analysis of something inherent in *Doctor Who*, the assumption that evil (if that's the right word here) can be fought without that fight becoming part of its effect. "Survival of the Fittest" isn't really the issue here, it's the assumed corollary "look after Number One". The Cheetah People are linked to their planet and, in some ways, to one another. Yet they fight amongst themselves (destroying the world - not *all* the symbols here are subtle) and hunt one another in a selfish desire for sport.

The Master's usual self-control is undone by his other gift, hypnosis, as his own psychic abilities destabilise his identity. And yet, the Doctor is immune so long as he realises that he's *not* just someone who opposes malign forces because he's the Doctor, but someone who's in a situation where the community is being damaged by... people who've got fixed ideas about their role in the world. That's why Sgt Patterson is in this story, and again director Alan Wareing and Cartmel have sounder instincts than Munro. Patterson was originally to have been the local cop. Making him a self-important, pompous wannabe (he isn't even regular army, but TA - see Volume I, page 87) consolidates this. He wants the local community to conform to his rules, but has no real mandate to do this, any more than the Master does. Although - like the teenagers - the character of Patterson seems to have been drawn more from other dramas set in "the real world" than from genuine observation, Julian Holloway makes this a more interesting character than it could have been. (In fact, read the novelisation for how trite the original portrait of him was.)

There's very little in the way of a suggested mechanism by which the planet infests people and their fighting destroys the world. This is, in itself, not a problem: any technobabble or form of words in the place where an explanation might have been would sound silly. We're teetering on the absurdity at the heart of 4.8, "The Faceless Ones" (in which the Chameleon-People lost their identities in "a gigantic explosion") or, more cogently, the modulation of light-frequencies that turns kung-fu monks into werewolves and is somehow contagious (X2.2, "Tooth and Claw"). We're left to accept that experienced scientists from Gallifrey can figure out a connection, whereas a girl from Perivale can know it.

In case it's not obvious, what we're saying is that this story is "Kinda" (19.3), but done in a less "look-at-me" manner. The Doctor is at risk if he simply lives up to his character notes and opposes the Master on principle, follows his "scripted" agenda and is a literal "idiot", bound to an illusory self-image. Ace becomes acquainted with a socially-unacceptable but equally real alter-ego. Wareing knows when to play with being a bit more dream-like than normal television practice, but does not ring-fence it from the narrative as Peter Grimwade did. "Survival" risks bathos, and much in these three episodes falls flat by being routine *Doctor Who* stuff (the Master does that to stories) after threatening to be more. As always, the Nathan-Turner era's idea of "normality" is almost unrecognisable in places, owing more to other TV than anyone's actual life.

We're duty-bound to continue onward and consider events In 1996 and some extra tidbits (in the Appendix), but here in 1989 - in the last adventure of the classic series' twenty-six-year run - there's a pioneering feel, and a sense that they've found a new way to discuss matters without the "either-or" of polemic or adventure. The surface features are like orthodox *Doctor Who* but better, with a really exotic locale in that same old quarry, impressive music and suburban streets made to look sinister. McCoy's figured out how to use his comedic and theatrical gifts within drama. Ainley is never better. This series can now do anything, and knows it. New doors have been opened and the embarrassments of the recent past are long-gone. What better time to stop?

The Facts

Written by Rona Munro. Directed by Alan Wareing. Ratings: 5.0 million, 4.8 million, 5.0 million. Audience appreciation was 69% for the first two episodes, and 71% for the finale. Both sets of figures represent the show's best performance in Season Twenty-Six, so things were looking up a little as the series took a bow.

Working Titles "Blood Hunt", "Catflap".

Supporting Cast Anthony Ainley (The Master), William Barton (Midge), Julian Holloway (Paterson), Lisa Bowerman (Karra), Norman Pace (Harvey), Gareth Hale (Len), Sakuntala Ramanee (Shreela), David John (Derek), Kate Eaton (Ange), Adele Silva (Squeak).

Oh, Isn't That...?

• *Julian Holloway*. He was usually the keen underling in *Carry On* films. For example, he was Major Shorthouse in *Carry On Up The Khyber*, alongside a cast who've almost all been in *Doctor Who* (except Sid James and Kenneth Williams, alas). His dad was Stanley Holloway (already famous in these parts long before *My Fair Lady*). He's not a real Glaswegian, you know.

• *Gareth Hale* and *Norman Pace*. Two former schoolteachers who'd been slowly making a reputation as comedians, and finally cracked it with their characters "The Management". So now that sight-gag in the shop-window makes sense (not that it's funny or anything). These were dim-but-violent night-club bouncers, both called Ron. Oh, how we laughed. A sketch-show followed, some of it amusing (they've wrecked *Play School* and *Rainbow* finally and for good with the phrase "we know a song about that" applied to inappropriate subjects). However, "a double act with two straight-men" summed them up for many.

What's often forgotten was that they did a straight drama in which they played the "chalk and cheese" detectives Dalziel and Pascoe. With other people playing the roles it was - and is - a major hit. With Hale and Pace, it, er... wasn't. Oh yes, and for 1991's *Comic Relief* they did a terrible novelty record, *The Stonk*, that got to Number One - and so we can add two more names to the dishonourable list of people who did that and *Doctor Who*. (We'll exclude Billie, since "Because We Want To" was committed before she turned sixteen, so she's not legally culpable.)

• *Adele Silva*. Look her up online, and only the *Doctor Who* sites neglect to show her as an adult, not wearing much. For the rest of the world, she's the *Emmerdale* sex-bomb and star of photo-shoots for endless lad-mags. For us, she's the kid who said 'bad cat man'. And they call us "sad"...

Cliffhangers The Kitlings' operator is revealed in his tent, and we find that it's the Master; Ace turns around, and her eyes betray that she too is succumbing to the planet's influence and going feral.

The Lore

• Despite a reasonably good track record in her short career, with four plays making it to TV, Rona Munro was still eligible for the BBC's training course for new writers. Inevitably, Cartmel asked her to work for *Doctor Who*. The only addition to the original proposal she submitted was the Master's unexpected return. The finished script was amended slightly, with Patterson originally planned as a cop, Ace burning Karra's body, Midge getting kicked to death and the climax happening in a patch of waste ground.

More was made of the Master's perplexity at what the Doctor had become. This time, instead of a dark secret from his past, the Doctor was to have alluded to having 'evolved'. Again, this was vetoed as giving too much away, although it was hardly noticeable to begin with. The other main change to the Master's part was that all the scenes with him up trees or looking over the balcony at West London were removed because of Ainley's fear of heights.

• The animatronic kitling was less useable than everyone had hoped, even with an extra day of work on it. The prop, called "Sooty", was awkward because the motors had to be smaller than in previous animal robots. The same mould was used to make the various dead cats found in the story. Three real cats ended up being hired, and given gel "ruffs". Location work started on 10th of June, with the vanishing milkman and Squeak's scenes.

• The strike that also affected recording of the two previous stories in production was at its height here. This was a remarkably well-mannered dispute, with the BBC hierarchy on the one side, and members of the Journalist's union and those of the associated technical staff on the other. It mainly affected news broadcast (and news and current-affairs shows were replaced by repeated comedies and old films, to the delight of many). *Doctor Who* was included in the affair because the series was using Outside Broadcast equipment officially designated for sports coverage, but the dates of the walk-outs were known in advance - hence the jolly day out to Skegness mentioned in "Battlefield". Wimbledon had first dibs on the OB rigs, though, so a lot of the Perivale scenes were first takes.

(By the way, this strike also gave rise to what is widely regarded as the best *Doctor Who*-related comedy sketch, in Radio One's series *The Mary Whitehouse Experience*. This purported to be a retrospective to the notorious 1973 walk-out by the Monsters' Union, demanding an end to restrictive practices such as running the end credits the moment one of their members gets a close-up. If you can find a copy, give it a listen, just to get some idea of how fondly-remembered *Doctor Who* was even though nobody was watching it at the time. And then ask someone to explain who Bobby Davro was, because we're not going to do *all* the work for you.)

• Hey look, it's Pepsi again, eating cat-food. This was her last screen appearance, and she died soon afterwards. This sequence also had the use of a local boy's cat, after the professional pussies proved uncooperative and licked off their gel. Aldred braved her allergies to do the cat-handling scene here. A more widespread medical worry was the heat, not just for those in fur body-stocking but with all that cat food left lying about. This would get worse when they got to the Warmwell quarry.

• Some of you might wonder why Lisa Bowerman wasn't covered in the **Oh, Isn't That..?** section, but even though *some* fans now watch her scenes as Karra a bit more closely now than they did in 1989, the simple truth is that the public doesn't regard her as anyone special.

Bowerman had earlier been a semi-regular in *Casualty* - she'd played the paramedic Sandra Mute, and Wareing had directed the episode where the character died (there as here, from a stab-wound). She had experience with horses, but had not ridden in over five years after a bad fall. So she was coached for three days by the trainer who had taught Faye Dunaway for the remake of *The Wicked Lady*. However, in rehearsals it was the riding scenes that caused the most laughs, as Bowerman ran around the "Acton Hilton" going "Neigh". On location, her worst problem was that - unlike the others - she had to take some of her glued-on fur and whiskers off in a hurry to do the death scene. The contact lenses had irritated Bowerman's eyes too much for Karra to die with her eyes open, and there were only minutes remaining that day to shoot in such light as was left. And they decided that her own hair was too neat, so a wig was added. (The delays meant that they missed a nice sunset which Wareing had hoped to use for the Doctor and Ace walking off, darn it.) So Bowerman, as the last alien and the last character to die in the classic run of *Doctor Who*, had a special place and got interviewed a few times. And each time, she said she'd love to come back, in whatever form the series returned, and ideally as a goodie.

Once Virgin had lost the book rights in 1996, they continued the *New Adventures*, now Doctorless and based around their own companion and all-purpose heroine: Professor Bernice Summerfield. Virgin eventually produced twenty-three *New Adventures* books starring Benny (and it's perhaps telling that many fans - even some of the professional ones - think the series didn't last near as long as that), before the range ended and Big Finish audio came to her rescue. They remade the earlier, audience-friendly adventures on CD as a precursor to their getting the full-blown *Doctor Who* license - and it was Lisa Bowerman who got to play Benny. Big Finish producer Gary Russell had sized her up as the best person for the job, but BF owner Jason Haigh-Ellery insisted they should do things properly and hold auditions. Bowerman won the part anyway. So that's her career, now, trying to sound natural using made-up swear-words and saying, 'Oh my goddess'.

• The motorbike stunt caused problems, but not practical ones. Former champion racer Eddie Kidd had decided that he knew how to choreograph the scene, and so Tip Tipping took a bow after the day's shooting ended and Paul Heasman took over the stunt arranging. Kidd doubled for Will Barton, Tipping for McCoy as usual, and the scene was done mainly through fast editing. Tipping died in 1993, in a parachute stunt that went wrong, and the BBC revised its policy accordingly.

• Off to the Warmwell quarry, again, and with temperatures of 110, the running and wearing fur was beginning to be a problem. One of the Cheetahs removed her costume and stormed off (one of McCoy's fondest memories of the story, as it happens) but Aldred got cramp from salt loss and the effect of the sky needed a rethink. (Wareing wanted overcast conditions, and assumed that he'd get those in August in Britain.) This is when the strike had its worst effects, so a lot of time was spent simply lying in the sun recuperating from the morning's work. In the conditions, the working day ending at 3.00 pm suited everyone. Impromptu barbecues and swimsuits were the order of the day. (Only one thing needed a later shoot - the second-unit stuff for "Ghost Light", completed on the Thursday). Indeed, the last day's shooting was narrowly completed ahead of a walk-out. This was a scene with the Doctor and the Master (the one originally envisioned as Ainley hanging from a tree and dropping a kitling onto his foe).

• After four attempts to quit the series, Nathan-Turner had made it known that he would remain as a caretaker, looking after the exploitation rights and supervising BBC Enterprise's video releases. This was another "short-term job" that he stayed with for ten years, more or less. Of course, he had other irons in the fire. Every so often, he would go to the various Heads of Department with proposals for drama series. It seems that the department was humouring him, as the suggested series become more out-of-synch with what passed for mainstream drama in the 1990s. We have already mentioned *Impact*, an attempted revamp of Peter Ling's *Compact* (see 6.2, "The Mind Robber" and 20.5, "Enlightenment"), and *WestEnders*, a Chelsea-based counterpart to *EastEnders*. Other potential flops included *Vili the Clown*, about a Soviet-era circus; and *The Captain's Table* (apparently an up-market *Triangle*). There was also *National Champion* - a possible winner here, as it was the true-life story of Bob Champion, who overcame cancer and won the Grand National on a horse which had also overcome a life-threatening illness. It's a great story - just a shame that someone else made a movie about it with John Hurt. A pilot for *Pub Talk* - a series of fifteen-minute chats - was shot and featured Nicholas Courtney and Tony Selby. Nothing came of that, nor of *Rye Spy*, a gentle comedy about espionage in the Sussex town of that name. Concerning *The Little Jean Little Show*, it's perhaps best to say nothing.

• The decision was taken to finish the last episode with at least a potential ending for the entire series. Cartmel wrote the 'cities made of song' speech to be dubbed over the shot of the Doctor and Ace walking off toward the TARDIS. McCoy recorded the cypher-dub session on - of all days - 23rd of November.

• After years of being the stalwart of semi-pro fan videos and audio projects, Sophie Aldred ceased even trying to make it as a "presenter" (she had a gig on a Noel Edmunds Christmas special and a religious talk-show) and settled into a lucrative career doing ad voice-overs. She's now making more doing Hovis and TravelSupermarket.com ads than she ever did when we could see her. Sylvester McCoy had a few last goes as the Doctor (see 27.0, "Starring Paul McGann", and the Appendix for "Dimensions in Time"). By now you may have seen *Search Out Science* (on the DVD of this story) and he's rounded out as a character-actor. Notable work includes: a heartbreaking episode of *Rab C Nesbitt*, a brutal comedy show in Glaswegian dialect; playing a one-legged serial killer in a true-life crime film on the opening night of Channel 5; and a vicar who looked like a beaver. At time of writing he's the Fool in a controversial production of *King Lear* starring Sir Ian McKellan. However, in the months after the last "official" episode of *Doctor Who*, he read *Charlie and the Chocolate Factory* on *Jackanory*, and did a special series for them improvising stories from phoned-in suggestions by children. The nation's eight-year-olds all wanted to have him exploring other planets, even if the BBC suits didn't.

the tv movie

27.0, "The TV Movie"

Produced by Peter V Ware, Executive Producer Philip David Segal, Screenplay by Matthew Jacobs, Directed by Geoffrey Sax. BBC Worldwide Ltd and MCA Television Ltd, distributed through BBC Worldwide and Universal Television (an MCA Company), 85 minutes, May 1996.

Which One Is This? If you're the type of fan who's read an Eighth Doctor BBC novel - or experienced an Eighth Doctor audio from Big Finish - and generally regarded either of them as "real", then it's the brief debut of the Eighth Doctor. For everyone else who remembers this at all, it's that abysmal American rip-off. (You know the one, it had a McGann in it - not Joe, one of the others.)

Firsts and Lasts For our purposes, it's the first and only televised outing for Paul McGann - the so-called Eighth Doctor (see the accompanying essay) - and the only form of *Doctor Who* completely made outside the UK, apart from fan videos. It's also the only appearance of Eric Roberts as the Master, and the final TV appearance of Sylvester McCoy as the Doctor. (Mind, he dies *again* in a webcast story also made under the aegis of the BBC - again, see this story's essay.)

Apart from the repeat of "The Evil of the Daleks" (4.9), it's the first story to have the Doctor retrospectively narrating it. (We'll ignore 14.3, "The Deadly Assassin", as we can't tell when the Doctor might have read those lines, or indeed if it's just the actor Tom Baker reading the scroll.) Indeed, this opening spiel by McGann's character is dubbed over both a pre-credit scene and a sequence where McCoy is flying his time machine. (Incidentally, this is the only occasion that McCoy gets to use a sonic screwdriver.)

Regrettably, this is the only time a version of the theme tune begins with the "middle-eight", and it's the only fully orchestral effort used on TV (as opposed to various lamentable efforts by Geoff Love and his Orchestra in the 70s).

This is the first story since 7.1, "Spearhead from Space" to be executed entirely on film, and the first since 20.7, "The Five Doctors" to be conceived as a feature-length TV movie from the outset. Thus, it's the first form of televised *Doctor Who* not to be part of an ongoing series, -ish, sort of.

"The TV Movie" Main Cast

- Paul McGann (the Doctor)
- Daphne Ashbrook (Grace Holloway)
- Eric Roberts (the Master)
- Yee Jee Tso (Chang Lee)
- Sylvester McCoy (the Doctor)

(This is us being tactful about its questionable canonical status, although some might count McCoy's inclusion as a continuation of the story that ended with 26.4, "Survival".) It's the first since 10.5, "The Green Death" to have the Pertwee-era logo (a decision made more poignant by that actor's death the week before transmission in the UK). This is also the first story not to have a proper title - fans have devised *many* names for this story (some printable, some not), but partly owing to the VHS and DVD releases calling this "Doctor Who: The Movie", it's more popularly designated as "The TV Movie" because... well... it is a TV movie. And the *Doctor Who* movies had Peter Cushing in them, as any fule kno.

This was the first time *Doctor Who*, in any form, made the cover of the *TV Times*.

Ten Things to Notice in "Grace: 1999"...

1. The TARDIS has been made over by Bela Lugosi. It's lit by sodding candles! It looks, indeed, like the set for the Meat Loaf video "I Would Do Anything For Love...", and only lacks cobwebs and a ready supply of peasant girls in dirndl dresses to have their necks bitten. This is the ideal setting for the adventures of a time-travelling anti-hero, played by Eric Roberts, or of a nomadic outsider with pretentions towards that gothic / romantic self-pitying consumptive poet look. What's really odd is that we first see this when the incumbent Doctor is Sylvester McCoy, now in tweeds and a waistcoat, and generally looking jollier than we've seen him since Mel left. It's as if he knows he's going to die soon and turn into a cut-price Percy Bysshe Shelley. Still, we get a nice long look at the new set, and linger over a recorder, jelly-babies, the sonic screwdriver and shedloads more fanwanky props, most bearing the Seal of the Prydonian Chapter ("The Deadly Assassin"), during which time a casual viewer would switch over, and the few people who'd recognise this stuff

would have some memories flooding back. Unfortunately for some, these would mainly be horrible recollections along the lines of "Arc of Infinity" / "Attack of the Cybermen" (see 20.1 and 22.1, and weep).

2. Behold, the most gobsmackingly awful info-dump line since 22.5, "Timelash". American viewers - who'd apparently forgotten the programme's premise, a mere decade after *Doctor Who* was popular in the States - had to digest the following, and Paul McGann had to find a way to make this sound like natural dialogue: 'I'm closing my eyes so he can't see you, Grace, but it may be too late... (the Eye of Harmony is) the power-source at the heart of the TARDIS... the TARDIS is my ship which carries me through time and space - T.A.R.D.I.S., it stands for Time and Relative Dimension in Space... The Master is a rival Time Lord - pure evil! I was bringing home his remains from Skaro where his final incarnation had been exterminated by the Daleks - *or so we thought*!' And you wonder why even advocates of this project deem it a miserable introduction to *Doctor Who*.

3. Furthermore, this line marks the point at which a committee starts rewriting Matthew Jacobs' original screenplay. Until that point it had a few annoying additions, such as the last-minute voice-over by McGann to explain the set-up in similarly grating detail, but most of the idiocy was visual, not verbal. There was even - yes, it's true - some real sparkle, culminating at exactly the mid-point of this movie with the near-perfect Doctoresque non-sequitur 'These shoes - they fit perfectly!' But a minute or two later, he's spouting the garbage quoted in item No. 2. And before this we have what's possibly the single most stupid scene in the programme's history, where we discover that humans can operate Time Lord technology better than the Time Lords themselves.

4. Jacobs' salvage-job on a project beset by various scenarios and script-bibles written by halfwits still bears the taint of this long gestation. It would seem that John Leekley wrote what was briefly the most breathtakingly silly material ever committed to paper, but then Robert DeLaurentis set about trying to take the record from him. We'll cite some of this later, just so you'll know - in the analysis to come - how lightly we got off with Jacobs' work.

In fact, it's all too easy to see how a story about the Millennium and a fight between Good and Evil aliens both reborn that day has Biblical over-tones - so when McGann is shrouded and looking abandoned, everyone thinks "Jesus". The Master appears first as a big red eye, then as a serpent, then as a zombie. The Doctor is made to wear a crown of thorns (yes, they deny it was deliberate *now*, but surely *someone* noticed) and Grace - get that name - is brought back from Heaven (or so she says). Furthermore, look at the picture she has on her wall: Leonardo's sketch for St Anne, mother of Mary. St Anne is the one who had The Immaculate Conception. So is the Doctor suddenly becoming half-human meant to suggest that she's his granny? (Well, as we'll see, that pseudonym 'Bowman' isn't accidental.) 'I know who I am now' Grace says, and declines to get involved with this cute alien. And she's the one who makes the obvious comment about the Doctor's resurrection and the date...

All of that said, with the motif of Puccini's *Madame Butterfly* running through this story, perhaps we are meant to think that Grace will follow *that* story's unhappy end. In which case she'll immolate herself after the Doctor leaves her alone, unemployed and pregnant. (Look, the evidence is all there, and once you've seen the Leekley scripts, the idea of the Doctor being his own grandfather will seem imaginative and tasteful by comparison.)

5. Any notion of the Cartmel era's Doctor as a wily manipulator who's six steps ahead of the game can be discarded as McCoy - apparently without sparing a look at the souped-up scanner to see that it's safe - walks straight out of the TARDIS into a hail of bullets. His eventual death scene on Grace's operating table was slightly marred for British viewers back in 1996, partly because of some odd editing (apparently the scene as shot was "disturbing", but see **The Lore**), but *mainly* because of its resemblance to a TV ad of the time. We half-expected him to wake up and lip-synch to Nat King Cole singing, "Let's Face the Music and Dance". (If you're British but didn't view it this way, we bet you will now that we've pointed it out.) What's *really* disturbing is that the gurning performed as the Doctor's face morphs is mainly McGann, the supposedly "serious" actor. (Incidentally, one thing to look for very closely is the effort that goes into making it seem that McGann is taller than McCoy or Ashbrook. That publicity photo of the Seventh Doctor handing off the TARDIS keys to Eight entailed the latter standing on a box. Arguably, this trickery altered the

Does Paul McGann Count?

As most people in Britain, and those of you who read the essay with "Time and the Rani" (24.1), will know, the authentic voice of British *Doctor Who* fandom was Vince Tyler from *Queer as Folk*. This is someone who was upset when the series was put on opposite *Coronation Street*, meaning that he had to choose between his two favourite programmes. This is someone who is more excited by colour copies of "Planet of the Daleks" episode three than by drugs. This is someone who, in trying to catch out someone who claimed to love him for to the extent of learning about his peculiar ways, asked for a list of the actors who'd played the Doctor. When the person being asked stopped at McCoy, Vince put in the trick question: 'What about Paul McGann?' The entire nation held its breath, as the key moment to which the series had been building hinged on whether Stuart would fall for it. 'Paul McGann doesn't count!' came the reply. See, it *was* love.

Obviously, when two characters created by Russell T Davies say something like this, we're inclined to think that maybe he agrees. Davies himself has twice publicly cited incidents in "The TV Movie" as part of the Doctor's past, and in the interviews for the 2005 launch, he was mutedly enthusiastic about McGann's performance and the entire Universal / BBC co-production. But then, he *would*, wouldn't he? The BBC had just entrusted him with their biggest gamble, so he had to be publicly upbeat about all of it - Whomobile, Venom Grubs and all. Two years on though, this Movie - and its rather momentous revelations - seems to be the only portion of the programme's back-catalogue that the BBC Wales series hasn't mentioned[50].

Ponder that for a moment. In every way that matters, the BBC Wales Doctor is wholeheartedly a Time Lord. He's been given several chances to admit to being half-human (up to and including X3.8, "Human Nature" - more on this in a bit), and it's never come up. At times he's vaguely hinted at having a family, but - unlike the McGann Doctor - he's never mentioned having a father. It's not as if there were no circumstances under which a mention of any of the Movie's shock disclosures would have been germane. Conversations about the Daleks and their relations with the Time Lords have been quite significant and abundant. The idea that other Time Lords aren't anywhere to be found might lead to mention of other possible fugitives. Time Lord DNA, which can magically transduct itself down wires by use of gamma rays,

might have been less effective as an anti-Dalek measure if the Doctor were a half-human hybrid (see, X3.5, Evolution of the Daleks" *could* have made less sense - we've chosen to think of it as Whitaker-Science). Now that he's travelling with a female doctor (or at least, a medical student), the name 'Grace' might come up. (Then again, to be fair, we know the Doctor tends to go for closure where possible - see X2.3, "School Reunion".)

So consider how the BBC Wales series writers - and its head honcho in particular - seem more than happy to embrace old elements such as the Macra (4.7, "The Macra Terror"; X3.3, "Gridlock"), the Isop Galaxy (2.5, "The Web Planet"; X1.12, "Bad Wolf") and even little bits of the Cushing films (the inside of the console room door, the Daleks marking time by 'rels' in their countdowns) but *not* the fairly glaring revelations of "The TV Movie". They've even brought the Master back (X3.11, "Utopia") without bothering to account for his escape from the TARDIS' innards - although to be fair, the Master's claim in X3.12, "The Sound of Drums" that the Time Lords 'resurrected' him for the Time War probably covers all contingencies. Besides, this would hardly be the first time that the Master pulled off an unexplained escape (see 19.7, "Time-Flight"; 22.3, "The Mark of the Rani"; 26.4, "Survival").

There is no attempt to connect the unseen helium-breathing Dalek lawyers with a crazed Dalek Emperor who loves *The Weakest Link*. Indeed, while considerable time and work has gone into jury-rigging the latter end of BBC Books' Eighth Doctor range to avoid contradicting the new series, this has been a one-sided affair, with the Welsh series making no overt attempt to embrace the Movie or the published sequels. And if we're being *really* technical, it's never even been said on screen that Eccleston is the Ninth Doctor and Tennant the Tenth. (The closest we've come is Tennant telling Sarah Jane in "School Reunion" that he's regenerated 'half a dozen' times since she last saw him as Tom Baker, but this isn't the place to parse the potential meaning of 'half a dozen', as some fans seem to insist on doing.)

Aesthetically, at least, quite a few odd little touches from the Movie seem to have persisted. The TARDIS interior in the BBC Wales series is not as influenced by the Vancouver model as some have claimed, but the floor of the Eye chamber - a raised metal mesh - looks similar. Likewise, the use

continued on page 357...

perception of the new Doctor's character - moving forward, the book writers would regard him as a tall, "resolute" Doctor when he's probably better suited as a short, weird one.)

6. Shortly after this aired, Britain acquired a fifth terrestrial TV channel - it was imaginatively called "Channel 5", then rebranded as "Five". McCoy graced its first night with his portrayal of serial killer Michael Sams, but hardly anyone noticed. In its earlier incarnation, the channel filled its Friday nights with cheap imported TV movies, and introduced the UK's lovers of kitsch to Shannon Tweed and umpteen showings of *Street Fighter* (see 24.2, "Paradise Towers"). The point is that even before *South Park* and *The Onion* made TV's Eric Roberts a figure of fun, we knew that he and his agent must've sounded like Meg Ryan during her infamous café scene in *When Harry Met Sally* - yelling "Yes!" upon being offered any acting work at all. In 1996, Roberts was known mainly for one thing that wasn't his fault (being Julia Roberts' half-brother, obviously) and was vaguely remembered for a few others that *were* his doing. We're trying to say that you can't choose your family, but you *can* avoid doing more than one Fox Movie of the Week. So what you will observe when Roberts plays the Master is that he's clearly taking the proverbial; even before he flounces down the TARDIS' musical staircase wearing a Punch and Judy tent ('Ah always drezzz for the occasion', he Scarletts), this is a villain you really want to win. He's Basil Fawlty-ish when paired with Chang Lee, but against McGann, it's clear to see which would be better equipped to play the Doctor in a series. Clue: it ain't the scouse ponce[49].

7. John Debney gets the blame for the music score, but in fact apprentices Louis Febre and John Sponsler did a lot of it. Debney, whose other credits include the *Justice League of America* TV movie (another of Five's regular re-runs), is now doing real films such as *The Passion of the Christ* (2004) and - an amusing juxtaposition, this - *Sin City* (2005). Sponsler adapted the Ron Grainer theme tune into a horribly bombastic march, although it was only by last-minute negotiations with Warner-Chappel that they got to use it. Gee, thanks.

8. As is so often the case, the default value for the original conception of Gallifrey was Krypton as seen at the start of *Superman: The Movie*. Although producer Philip Segal rejected this idea,

we note that the end of this story is basically the "fly really fast the wrong way around the Earth and make time go backwards, so she doesn't die" option from that same film - a strategy that's now routinely derided in bad High School sitcoms on Nickelodeon. (And now they've retroactively affixed this very same ending onto the *Superman II: The Richard Donner Cut* DVD - will we never be free of it? Not if X3.13, "Last of the Time Lords" is any indication.) At least, in the fine tradition of Terrance Dicks-edited *Doctor Who*, Grace asks the same question we're all asking - 'What the hell is a Temporal Orbit?' - even if none of us gets an answer.

9. Like all fantasy television set in 1990s America, this was filmed in Vancouver. You'll probably recognise at least one location, the hospital, from umpteen episodes of *The X-Files*. You might even recognise Yee Jee Tso, as Chang Lee, from *Sliders* and *Stargate SG-1*, as well as lots of other hit shows filmed in Canada. Most of the rest of the cast have similar form. Obviously, being ostensibly set in San Francisco, there's a lot of stock footage (which, amongst other things, makes it seem like Bruce the paramedic is paid way more than Grace the heart surgeon, because he apparently lives in the tourist areas and not Sausalito). The use of different stock footage also adds the curious notion that one effect of the TARDIS landing is that it's night all around the world at the same time. This may also be a freak side effect of the strange idea to move the International Date Line to San Francisco, seven hours after Britain had its New Year's Eve bash at the Millennium Dome on the Greenwich Meridian.

10. And like all fantasy television of the 1990s, it comes in two basic colours: blue and orange. There's the occasional greenish glow - like the skeleton visible under the Doctor's shroud as he regenerates, or the Master's eyes - but, by and large, it's the same lighting and dry-ice fog as everything else on television back then. So even though it's 35mm film, it looks like cheap frame-removed VT like the BBC Wales series. For those of us used to the cost-cutting measures of the classic series, however, this one seems insanely extravagant. There are *some* economies made, as the director's commentary on the DVD makes clear, but then you get stupid things like one shot, only half a second long, that features a hundred chickens running around on a freeway.

Does Paul McGann Count?

...continued from page 355

of a *Star Trek* style time-vortex that's blue when travelling backwards and orange when travelling forwards might be influenced by the Movie (and not, say, by *Star Trek*). The orange fairy-dust that emerges from the TARDIS power-source to reanimate Grace and Chang Lee is not entirely unlike that which was used to provide *deus ex machina* moments around the time of Eccleston's regeneration. (Once again, this is a pretty generic effect, and so both "The TV Movie" and the BBC Wales series could be said to have lifted it from the same basic sources. A recent documentary about the Romantic poets had this effect for when Jean-Jacques Rousseau, played by Tennant, was inspired to write *The Social Contract*.)

Still, once you take *all* of this into account, it's starting to look like confirmation of what some British fans have long concluded: that the TV Movie belongs in the same apocryphal category as *TV Comic* and the stage-plays. The alternative - accepting that the damage the Movie causes to well-established continuity *and* to the spirit of the series was both permanent and what the BBC desired - was too painful for a lot of people who'd been children in the 60s and 70s. Indeed the BBC themselves sanctioned the radio / online oddity "Death Comes to Time", which ended with the McCoy Doctor dying *all over again*, as if to efface the Movie's existence. (See A2, "The Curse of Fatal Death" for more detail than this turkey warrants.) At least, that's what it looks like with regards to the Movie and possibly the spinoff books - conversely, the BBC seems to regard the BBC7 Big Finish material starring McGann as entirely kosher. They've even been using the relaunched TV series to promote the digital channel's audio dramas.

Further complicating matters is that if you consider McGann's Doctorate as one large body of work, and of equal weight in the BBC Wales scheme of things, you may tie yourself into knots when watching "Human Nature". This is an adaptation of a Virgin *New Adventures* book of the same name by Paul Cornell, but done as though it had never happened before (thus ruling these books out of the "canon" according to some fans, but not others). Tellingly, in Mr Smith's notebook - along with the half-remembered versions of the Eccleston and Tennant adventures - we see sketches of the Hartnell Doctor, the McCoy Doctor and someone who is *probably* meant to be the McGann Doctor. Most of the pictures are well exe-

cuted, except the one that's supposed to be Rose, so we'll allow a small amount of room for doubt for the real die-hards who refuse to countenance the idea. That said, the BBC website has released a full-blown version of the journal pages in question, and it clearly displays the ten Doctors from Hartnell up through Tennant, McGann included. (By the way, that's the top of Colin Baker's head - not Tom Baker's noggin, as some viewers thought - down there by Davison's brow. Tom is in the top row, by Troughton and Pertwee.) Fair enough that the website graphic is supplemental and hardly definitive, but it *does* affirm what many were thinking from the slice of the Doctors' faces as seen on screen.

You see what we're suggesting. For anyone unprepared to admit that the Movie's hopelessly asinine assertions are a legitimate part of the ongoing *Doctor Who* story in the same way as - for example - 1.5, "The Keys of Marinus"; 22.5, "Timelash" or 17.5, "The Horns of Nimon" (because everyone's prepared to include these, for some reason), it's *possible*, if you hold your breath, screw your eyes up really tight and bunch your fists, to have an Eighth Doctor played by Paul McGann[51], but whose debut took place under different circumstances than those we see in "Grace: 1999". Throw out the bathwater, as many of the books themselves later did, but keep the baby.

There are some practical considerations for this, not the least of which being the sheer volume of official releases that tout McGann as the Eighth Doctor. At time of writing, there are seventy-six (!) original novels, three novellas and thirty-four audio stories featuring the character as based upon McGann. Indeed, the fact that BBC Books has an entire range that's *named* 'The Eighth Doctor Adventures' is a bit of a no-brainer, never mind that the some of the *DWM* comic strip collections have 'The Complete Eighth Doctor Comic Strips' prominently displayed on the cover. True, the majority of fans ignore the spin-offery and only accept the TV stories (whilst the British public only know of the latter anyway) - but let's try to be fair and admit that some *do* accept them. The BBC has a lot invested in McGann's having been in the series for more than 53 minutes in the Movie and 1/6th of a second in "Human Nature", and deep down many people like the *idea* of an actor of his calibre being in the fold, regardless of the unpalatable circumstances. However, something similar

continued on page 359...

The Continuity

The Doctor(s) Both of the Doctors sit down to read *The Time Machine* by H.G. Wells [compare with 22.5, "Timelash", if you must], and both like to listen to jazz [see 25.3, "Silver Nemesis"] on vinyl.

• *The Seventh Doctor.* [Named in the script and on dressing-room doors simply as 'The Old Doctor'.] It's explicitly said that he's 'nearing the end of his seventh life'.

He's got the same hat and face since we last saw him ["Survival"], but he seems to have physically aged a bit, and he acts rather less in control. He's now a little portly, has longer hair, and has taken to wearing a tweed suit and a silk waistcoat. We don't actually see him that much, so we can't gauge how much he differs from - or is similar to - his previous appearances. [He never gets to make a joke or mentally bamboozle an opponent, for example. Nor does he juggle or play the spoons.]

He's apparently had a fit of nostalgia, having acquired a new sonic screwdriver and a large number of jelly-babies, and littering his bachelor-pad time machine with objects from his past. This version of the Doctor becomes a casualty of gang warfare, when he accidentally walks into a volley of gunfire. Whereas he's taken to hospital and the bullets are removed easily enough, he's mis-diagnosed as having something wrong with his heart (which is actually fine, albeit non-human, plus he's got two of them), and perishes on the operating table when cardiologist Grace Holloway lodges a medical probe somewhere in his chest that it isn't meant to go. This incarnation's final words: 'Aaaaaaaaaaaaaaaaaaaaaaaaaaaaa!!!' [Or, if you prefer, his last actual *comment* is one that's directed at Grace: 'You've got to stop!']

• *The Eighth Doctor.* [See **Does Paul McGann Count?** for the inevitable argument about what to properly call this character.] He's got a more vulpine look than his previous self, and uses a Scouse accent [lots of planets have Liverpools, presumably]. He's not much taller, but he's essentially got the same hair-colour, blue eyes and two hearts as his previous self. Regeneration temporarily gifts him with enhanced strength - enough to knock a reinforced morgue freezer door off its hinges - and he's at first stricken with amnesia. [The latter being - alas - *the* defining characteristic of this incarnation, if you've read the spin-off books.]

This Doctor clothes himself in a fancy-dress outfit that a hospital worker intends to wear as 'Wild Bill Hickock' to a New Year's Eve costume party. He later acquires a pair of shoes that belong to Grace's boyfriend Brian. [He doesn't wear socks, though. So does he blister at all, or do these magically heal in the first fifteen hours after his regeneration, as with the wound caused when he pulls the fibre-optic probe out of his chest? See X2.0, "The Christmas Invasion" for more on this miraculous ability.] He claims to be afraid of heights [possibly owing to his "death" in 18.7, "Logopolis", or maybe it's just something that he says to reassure Grace.]

It *seems* as if this Doctor instinctively knows the futures of various people whom he encounters. [Some fans have gone through mental gymnastics trying to account for the new Doctor's foreknowledge, even positing earlier visits to early twenty-first century San Francisco where he flukily met all these same people. On screen, however, this seems to be presented as a psychic gift of sorts.] Weirdly, the Doctor shows little restraint in showing off this ability, and doesn't seem to fear that revealing such foreknowledge might damage the timeline. [Let's hope that he's just giving away information that's already part of established history - otherwise, his advice to Gareth might result in *millions* of people being alive who wouldn't have been otherwise. See **History** for more.]

The most troublesome development of all: the new Doctor says he's half-human on his 'mother's side'. [If he'd *only* made this comment to Professor Wagg, we could write this off as his merely distracting the man with whimsical nonsense, in order to nab his security pass. Unfortunately, the Master *also* proclaims that the Doctor is half-human after staring into a visual representation of the new Doctor's retina. We have no way of knowing if the Seventh Doctor's eyes in any way differed from those of a pure-bred Time Lord.

[The Doctor later claims that regeneration can cause him to 'transform into another species' when he "dies", so one theory holds that this Doctor was "infected" (after a fashion) with humanity partly because the anaesthetic applied during his operation left him "dead" for longer than the customary period, and partly because he "changed" whilst in a morgue full of dead humans. That might allow us to conclude that the McGann Doctor is half-human, but that *none of*

Does Paul McGann Count?

...continued from page 357

was true of Peter Cushing (for those of us who'd been watching since the 1960s) and later Sir Derek Jacobi's appearances as both the creator of Doctor Who in a parallel universe (in a Big Finish audio) *and* the Master's robot avatar to enable the Richard E Doctor to consult his old friend from within the Eye of Harmony. Now that Jacobi has been 'legitimised' as Professor Yaffle, sorry, Yana, "Scream of the Shalka" starring Richard E seems to have been demoted. Perhaps the only way to settle this is for McGann to pop up in the BBC Wales series as either the Doctor who destroyed Gallifrey or an alternate-universe Doctor. There is, alas, more chance of Frobisher the Penguin popping up in Series Four than of this happening.

The overall point remains that even if you view "The TV Movie" as the sort of stuff that makes people bleed from the eyes, the McGann Doctor has become extremely hard to ignore. The veritable tsunami of material put out in relation to the Welsh series (the "official" list of Doctors on the BBC website included) counts McGann as the Eighth Doctor, and even if we speculated that Davies has set aside his private belief that McGann doesn't count in the understandable interest of touting the party line (and the McGann rendering in "Human Nature" seems strange in that light, because it's hard to imagine BBC officials putting a gun to Davies' head over such a minor detail), that *is* - whether we like it or not - the party line. Yes, a lot of material (and the TV show itself) labels both Eccleston and Tennant as just 'the Doctor', and doesn't specify that the former is Nine and the later is Ten, but that same ambiguity hardly invalidates McGann. And c'mon - even the staunchest of hold-outs would have to concede that they will probably never see a BBC-related *Doctor Who* item of any sort that skips McGann, and claims that Eccleston is Eight and Tennant is Nine. Suffice it to say that when producer Julie Gardner and BBC Head of Drama Jane Tranter rattle off McGann in the official roster of Doctors during their interview for "Do You Remember the First Time?" (the *Doctor Who Confidential* instalment for X3.10, "Blink"), you can tell which way the winds are blowing. Mind you, they did have to be helped...

the other Doctors are. The last few moments of Christopher Eccleston's Doctor includes dialogue that seems to confirm this as a possibility. Along those lines, we can write off the 'on my mother's side' line as being completely facetious and entirely improvised. Unless you believe that this Doctor is *really* so brazen as to go about proclaiming his until-now secret family history (for a start, see 5.1, "The Tomb of the Cybermen" and 26.3, "The Curse of Fenric") to complete strangers. See *Background* for talk about his father, though.] Despite the suggestion that the Doctor is half-human, Grace determines that his blood isn't like human blood at all. [See also "Spearhead from Space"; 22.4, "The Two Doctors"; 18.4, "State of Decay".]

He also seems prone to sudden bouts of kissing.

• *Background*. The Doctor's homeworld is still called 'Gallifrey'. He recalls spending time there with his father, pleasantly lying back in the grass on a 'warm Gallifreyan night' while a meteor storm lit up the sky. [No mention is made of the Doctor's father in the Welsh series - then again, the Doctor *himself* talks about being a father (X2.11, "Fear Her"), getting married (X3.10, "Blink") and so forth. The idea might seem peculiar to some,

but in truth there's nothing on television to rule *against* the Doctor having Time Lord parents, and X3.12, "The Sound of Drums" (even as it flagrantly ignores the assertion of books such as *Lungbarrow* that Time Lords are 'loomed' fully grown) seems to substantiate the idea.]

The Doctor claims to have been with Puccini when he died. [This occurred in Brussels, 1924, and wasn't the serene bedside passing that you might almost infer from the Doctor's account. Puccini was a chain smoker and developed throat cancer, although he technically died from a heart attack after a less-than-successful radiation therapy.] The Doctor says he also knew Leonardo [apparently while the man had a cold - and the Doctor calls him 'Da Vinci', stupidly], Freud and Marie Curie.

• *Inventory*. Remarkably, the contents of the "dead" Doctor's pockets only fill a small paper bag. [See stories such as 12.1, "Robot" for why this seems so atypical.] The Doctor also owns a Gladstone bag full of tools, of which the Neutron Ram [19.6, "Earthshock"] and the sonic screwdriver are the most prominent. He's carrying a pocket-watch and a yo-yo, and owns a 900-Year Diary. [This is actually smaller than the 500-Year diary of the Troughton stories - are we to presume that the book is dimensionally transcendental or something?] The jelly-baby thing is getting out of hand [see **Things That Don't Make Sense**].

• *Ethics*. He seems to avoid using violence if possible, and threatens to shoot *himself* to coerce a policeman into yielding his motorcycle. The new Doctor is still adept at motorcycling [see "Survival", 8.5, "The Daemons" and many others], and such is his nobility that he offers a hand to save the Master - even after all the trouble he's caused - from the Eye of Harmony's pull. [Is it *just* nobility? Even before Rassilon as good as gave away a big secret about the Master's future in 20.7, "The Five Doctors", the Doctor has always acted as though killing the Master would cause more damage to the time-lines than anything his rival ever did. (Indeed, given the lunacy of many of the Master's schemes, it almost seems as though the Doctor is trying to prevent his fated friend from doing himself a mischief in whatever scam he's pulling.) With hindsight, it's hard not to think that the Master's role in the Time War was somehow foreseen, but "The Sound of Drums" indicates that involved the Time Lords 'resurrecting' him. Even then, the gambit apparently came to nothing because the Master - supposedly the 'perfect warrior' for such a conflict - crapped his pants and ran away, leaving the Doctor to end it.]

The Supporting Cast

• *Dr Grace Holloway*. She's presently living with a man named Brian, but he finally loses patience with their relationship, and moves out after she abandons him during a *Madame Butterfly* performance to go and perform some heart surgery. Grace operates with Puccini playing in the background, has a reproduction Leonardo sketch on her living-room wall, and also owns what might be an Edward Hopper in her office.

As a child, Grace dreamt she could hold back death - it was this dream that motivated her to become a physician. Yet she sticks to her principles even in the face of managerial attempts to solve problems by burning evidence, and consequently quits her job. She's remarkably apt at improvising excuses for the Doctor [she even names him 'Bowman', which suggests she's read both the Leekley "bible" and the *Odyssey*], and she gets into this "companion of the Doctor" gig enough to threaten a cop at gunpoint, although it seems she can't shoot straight. She suddenly gains the ability to hotwire the TARDIS console, which

is - to judge from the dialogue - how she re-sets her alarm clock too.

Grace drives a blue Range Rover, and a clock she owns has Westminster chimes [so Anglophilia seems to be her thing]. Rather conveniently for the plot, she's on the board of the Institute for Technological Advancement and Research (ITAR).

• *Chang Lee*. A street-urchin, gang member or whatever you'd like to call it. Not only does he seem to hang around so he can poach the belongings of the "killed" bystander that he takes to Grace's hospital, but he displays no remourse after two of his fellow gang members are gunned down before his eyes. It looks as if he's initially lured into the Master's service by greed as much as hypnosis. Yet despite all of these personality handicaps, he comes good in the end. Lee can drive an ambulance [a rather unexpected skill]. The Doctor finally allows the no-longer-doomed Lee to keep his bags of gold dust.

The Supporting Cast (Evil)

• *The Master*. When the story opens, he's in custody, in his 'final incarnation' [as when we last saw him, technically], and gets handed a death sentence by the Daleks. Electrical bolts seem to blow him to pieces [if not atomize him entirely], whereupon his remains are put in a box and given to the Doctor for - in accordance with the Master's last request - transport back to Gallifrey.

However, it turns out that the Master isn't dead, and his remains somehow congeal into a caustic, gelatinous goo. This Master-slime is amazingly malleable - he can sabotage the TARDIS Console after wriggling into it like a large worm, *or* take on the appearance of a King Cobra *or* become thin enough to "spittle" himself through the TARDIS keyhole *or* emulate a puddle of water. Eventually the slime gel shoves itself down the throat of a paramedic named Bruce and thereafter the Master controls the man's body. In such a form, the Master remains capable of hypnotism, but he can also spew vast amounts of goo - enabling him to either kill [or so it would seem with the Institute guards, unless they're just frozen in place] or slowly bring anyone thus "slimed" under his mental influence. Oddly, the Bruce-Master seems helpless when the Doctor sprays him with a fire extinguisher [the implication - well, probably - being that he's vulnerable to cold]. This new body is decaying, however [Tremas' form (18.6, "The Keeper of Traken") was a lot more stable], hence the Master's urgency to steal the Doctor's remaining 'lives' [see **The Time Lords**].

As with his last appearance ["Survival"], the Master's eyes both pre- and post-execution seem feline or even ophidian. [By the way, if Time Lords *can* become hybridized with other species, that might, at a pinch, cover how the Master has apparently become a jelly-snake: see **What Were Josiah's "Blasphemous" Theories?** under 26.2, "Ghost Light" and **How Does "Evolution" Work?** under 18.3, "Full Circle" for more. Terrance Dicks' novel *The Eight Doctors* offers a far more mundane explanation, claiming this is all a secret plot on the Master's part - one that entails his having already ingested a 'deathworm'. Prior to X3.13, "Last of the Time Lords", this seemed like the crassest cliché ever, but then they went and nicked every early 80s science fiction movie except *Tron* in the last ten minutes, including the last shot of *Flash Gordon*.]

This new version of the Master is unfamiliar with idiomatic 1990s English, but he's increasingly confident with his use of rather arch comedy. He's also ruthless, killing Bruce's wife with one hand while using the other to tell her to be quiet. [We've never seen any version of the Master kill someone quite so cold-bloodedly. In the past, he's generally disposed of people using futuristic guns.]

He initially dresses sensibly, then dons some shockingly ghastly red-and-black variation of the traditional Time Lord robes, which he finds somewhere in the TARDIS. Eventually the Master gets pulled as if by gravitational force into the TARDIS' Eye of Harmony, a process that seems to simultaneously elongate him out of shape, disintegrate his form and blow him up. [And yet the bugger *still* survives, after a fashion; see X3.11, "Utopia"; "The Sound of Drums" and this story's accompanying essay.]

The TARDIS Still stands for 'Time and Relative Dimension in Space', and still looks [roughly] like a police box on the outside. Once you get past the door, though, everything's different from the last time we saw the Ship's interior [26.1, "Battlefield"]. The interior doors are great stone slabs with carving on them, and over their lintel is the Seal of the Prydonian Chapter [see "The Deadly Assassin" but also 12.5, "Revenge of the Cybermen"]. That seal will be bloody everywhere, so get used to it.

The current TARDIS key is a mid-70s model

[see 11.1, "The Time Monster" to 13.3, "Pyramids of Mars"], and a spare is kept in a compartment on the exterior, right over the 'P' in 'police'. [So the Chameleon circuit - or 'cloaking device' as the Doctor crassly terms it now, as if Romulans installed it - had better not start working again.]

The roundels are now gone from the Ship's interior, which is [as we've said] mainly illuminated by candles - either normal-sized and in candelabrae, or huge great candles that would need two strong blokes to lift them. [The TARDIS itself must be maintaining this look, else the Doctor would be spending all his time replentishing the candles and cleaning up great globs of melted wax. This also seems like a shocking fire hazard, what with the leaves, dirty great blazing torches set into the walls and strong winds from nowhere that seem to characterize the rest of the Ship.]

The console room now has a lounge with an overstuffed armchair and footstool, a Dansette record-player, a vast wall made up of files and drawers and a lot of accoutrements associated with earlier Doctors. [Annoyingly, the camera dwells on these as if expecting rounds of applause for each one we recognise.] There's a chess board with a match [against whom?] *in media res*. The Console itself is now made of wood and attached to the ceiling - with a Time Rotor shaft rising to the top - but in every other way it's more cumbersome than before. It also has a hand-brake. The scanner now looks like a 1950s TV set, but on a pantograph, and it's pulled down from the ceiling by a toilet-chain. The readouts appear on this, as navigation now uses a different display. The controls are very basic, with rollers that contain preset time and location options such as 'Humanian Era' and 'Rassilon Era'. [See **History**.]

Around one wall is a big bookcase, and set into another is a vast filing cabinet with drawers full of useful things. In one drawer [filed under "G", one supposes] is a brace of velvet sacks that contain gold dust. [These would've been handy in 19.6, "Earthshock" or 22.1, "Attack of the Cybermen".] A control makes the console room ceiling turn into a hologram projecting a representation of the outside universe - either as it stands now, or would appear in a potential future if matters are left unresolved. [This feature would've saved some bother in 13.3, "Pyramids of Mars".]

One corridor contains a large mantelpiece with dozens of clocks, and it's unto this that the Doctor places a casket with the Master's remains. A distorting mirror is set over the mantle. Leading from this room is another pair of big doors, which open abruptly when touched lightly by a human. These doors lead into what the Master calls 'the cloister room' [although this suggests that he doesn't know what the word actually means - cf 18.7, "Logopolis"]. There's a pair of bats living in this so-called cloister, which has leaves on the floor even though there's nowhere from which they could have fallen.

In the floor of this room is a raised catwalk - made of metallic mesh a *bit* like the present TARDIS floor - in the centre of which is a hemisphere of stone. It's boxed in with four staves, each bearing a carved head and a circular mirror on the top. This, we are told, is the Eye of Harmony, the power source at the heart of the TARDIS. The Eye can be opened if a human looks into a shaft of light that's caused when one of the staves is removed. While open, the Eye can display a representation of the Doctor's current and previous self, or a representation of the Doctor's eye, *or* allow those present to view whatever the Doctor looking at. He can stop this just by closing his eyes, however. The light beams that emanate from the Eye can also, it seems, facilitate the transfer of 'lives' from a Time Lord to another being [see **The Time Lords**].

If the Eye isn't closed, then eventually its emanations will change the molecular structure of whichever planet the Ship is on - to the point that the planet will be 'pulled inside out' (or something like that) and a destructive wave will obliterate a lot of other worlds. A chip taken from the ITAR beryllium atomic clock enables the Doctor to repair the Console and close the Eye, but it's been left open too long by that point, so Earth is still in danger of getting turned into a pretzel. What eventually solves the problem [and it's genuinely painful to type this next bit] is that some rewiring on Grace's part puts the TARDIS into a 'Temporal Orbit', which takes the Ship back in time from 31st December to the 29th. This retroactively nullifies the effect of the Eye being open, somehow. Once that's done, a glowing mist escapes from the Eye and [eeessh] brings Grace and Lee - who've been variously killed by the Master - back to life. [Go straight to **Things That Don't Make Sense**. No, wait a minute... the only *possible* explanation for this absurdity is that Grace and Lee were murdered while the TARDIS was in its Temporal Orbit, so perhaps they were somehow outside time and their deaths weren't "fixed" in history,

meaning the TARDIS' energies could jump-start their corpses. This is, presumably, what was meant by the 'state of temporal grace' in 14.2, "The Hand of Fear", making the clunking line about repairing the 'temporal grace circuit' in 20.1, "Arc of Infinity" all the more wrong.

[If this is a natural side-effect of being in a TARDIS, we have several dead characters and a couple of regenerations to account for - hell, there's three corpses in 19.6 "Earthshock" alone - unless regeneration is in itself an aspect of this atemporal flux, as was originally implied (see 4.3, "The Power of the Daleks"). It might, *might*, also account for Cap'n Jack turning into Captain Scarlet after Rose-as-Bad-Wolf fixed his mortality good and proper (X1.13, "The Parting of the Ways", although this wouldn't account for his allegedly turning into a big face in a fishtank later on). If this is normal in the TARDIS, it *just* about provides a sensible solution for the Doctor's antics at the end of 15.6, "The Invasion of Time": he can't actually kill the Sontarans, so he's got to incapacitate them and slow their progress with increasingly baroque booby-traps. And that's as good an explanation as you're going to get, without us claiming that the Eye uses technology plundered from the Genesis Torpedo in *Star Trek*.

[As for the TARDIS having its own 'Eye of Harmony', let's assume for a moment that it isn't the *true* Eye of Harmony, which we were assured in "The Deadly Assassin" and "The Invasion of Time" was the source of the Time Lords' power: a bottled black hole that's been 'set in an eternally dynamic equation against the mass of' Gallifrey, and hardwired into the quantum force-field so that the planet would evaporate if it were to be removed. The books have tried to reconcile all of this by claiming that *every* TARDIS has a little Eye of Harmony, and that they all somehow tap the main Eye on Gallifrey for power. None less than Fanwank Cardinal Gary Russell tried to sell us that idea in his novelisation to the Movie, and as entirely concocted explanations go, it works as well as any. This *still* leaves a big flaw in "The TV Movie" at the narrative level - and pardon if we address this here, because **Things That Don't Make Sense** is already pushing 2,600 words - in that if you take this story on its own terms, it only functions if you pretend that no other *Doctor Who* ever happened, and that *there's only one TARDIS in the Universe*. For instance, one might quibble with the notion that the TARDIS is capable of destroying a planet if you but remove the covering from its engine, meaning that if other TARDISes *are* in operation, it's miraculous this hasn't happened several times over.]

The TARDIS now seems strangely receptive to human beings; it seems to give Lee access to the alleged Cloister Room because it 'likes' him, and human eyes are required to open the Ship's Eye of Harmony. [See **The Doctor** for what this suggests. The Big Finish audio "The Apocalypse Element" attempts to suture this by calibrating Gallifreyan tech to respond to a human retina - initially that of the Doctor's companion Evelyn Smythe. Well, *someone* had to do it. See also **Who Decides Who Becomes A Companion?** under 21.5, "Planet of Fire".]

The Doctor remarks that from Earth, the TARDIS can reach his homeworld in about 'ten minutes'. [Maybe he's just speaking figuratively, unless TARDISes can somehow reach their native Gallifrey quicker than other worlds. This is contradicted in every other story where the Doctor goes there voluntarily.]

The Time Lords It's reiterated [after the likes of "The Deadly Assassin"; 20.3, "Mawdryn Undead" and so forth] that Time Lords have a total of 'thirteen lives'. [Nobody told McGann this, however, so watch out for redubbing.] Here the process of regeneration is more closely compared with "death and rebirth" than on previous occasions, and the Doctor implies that this "change" was atypical owing to the surgery anaesthetic keeping him "dead" for too long. [We've already covered the possibility that Time Lords can hybridize with other races under **The Doctor**, save for speculating what would happen if a Time Lord regenerated on Zolpha Thura, the home of a race of giant cacti - see 18.2, "Meglos" - and then became Lord President. Where would they put the Coronet?] Regardless of the death allusions, though, the Doctor claims that Grace and Lee have 'been somewhere' he never has when they're killed and brought back to life.

Using light-beams from the Eye of Harmony as a conduit, the Doctor's remaining 'lives' [regenerations] can be transferred into the Master, and back again once Grace takes the Ship into its Temporal Orbit. [Idiotic as this might sound, there's a precedent for it - if the Valeyard in Season Twenty-Three and the mutants in "Mawdryn Undead" *both* think they can make use of the Doctor's remaining regenerations, then a transfer

of such 'lives' is possible. We might even speculate that it's down to the muddling over the years of whether artron energy ("The Deadly Assassin") powers Time Lord tech or is inherent in Time Lord bodies. However, this still doesn't account for the claim that if the Doctor looks into the Eye, his 'soul' will be destroyed, and the Master will claim his body.]

People on the Doctor's home planet have a saying about size not being important, apparently. [Ponder that when next watching "The Five Doctors".]

Planet Notes
• *Gallifrey*. It's a lot further away than we've been led to believe up until now [see **Where (And When) Is Gallifrey?** under 13.3, "Pyramids of Mars"], stipulated as being 250 million light-years away from Earth [which would put it in another galaxy entirely]. The holo-screen shows it as being blue-ish in colour rather than the traditional orange ["The Invasion of Time" again, plus 1.4, "Marco Polo", X3.3, "Gridlock" and most spectacularly "The Sound of Drums"]. It has warm nights, and rather lurid meteor showers every so often.

The Non-Humans
• *The Daleks*. Here unseen, and rendered as having unintelligible voices that sound very much like Smurfs.

Evidently, they've got a legal system that not only allows them to put the Master on trial, but permits the accused to make a last request. [Hints of such a Dalek legal system crop up in 22.6, "Revelation of the Daleks", but this still seems odd. Regarding the last request, go straight to **Things That Don't Make Sense**.]

The Dalek homeworld of Skaro is represented as being deep orange when seen from afar. It seems to be located a very long way from Gallifrey. [That's if we take the Doctor's comment that Gallifrey is situated from Earth a mere 'ten minutes in this old thing' somewhat literally, yet the trip from Skaro takes long enough that he settles down to read a book.] Skaro now seems to have two similarly rugose moons.

History
• *Dating*. The story's climax coincides with 31st of December, 1999, although the TARDIS arrives on Earth on the evening of 30th of December. The shift from 1999 to 2000 is meant to hail the launch of San Francisco Mean Time, a strangely

unannounced change in the world's navigational system [see **Things That Don't Make Sense**] that's to be marked with the activation of the world's most accurate clock: a vast mechanism based around a tiny beryllium chip, housed at ITAR.

As the year 2000 dawns, medical science has developed a more sophisticated form of endoscopy for use in complex cardio-vascular operations. Dr Grace Holloway is going to do something amazing one day, or so the Doctor claims. Meanwhile, he also "intuits" that Gareth [no surname given, but he's 'Gareth Fitzpatrick' in the novelisation] - here seen as a staffer at the ITAR - will ten years from now head a seismology task force as UCLA. Gareth's work will lead to a new means of accurately predicting earthquakes, and his inventions will thus save the human race 'several times', but first he must graduate in poetry. To this end, the Doctor advises that he answer the *second* question on his mid-term exam, not the third. [Curiously, this *does* match with established *Doctor Who* history - not the poetry or exams bit, but it happens that the world is about a dozen years away from successful prediction of earthquakes (see 5.4, "Enemy of the World").]

Gallifrey is stated on the bargain-basement scanner to be 'local dateline 5725.2 Rassilon Era'. [Although the home-made course coordinates also say 'December 30th 22.40' before the Master exudes into the works - in one shot before this, it's apparently 24th of February.]

The Doctor warns Lee to avoid San Francisco a year hence. No clue exists as to when the Master's trial on Skaro occurs [although it must logically happen before the Hand of Omega vaporizes the planet in 25.1, "Remembrance of the Daleks"].

The Analysis

Where Does This Come From? As you're doubtless aware, Hollywood has a long and disgraceful track record of finding old TV properties and turning them into dreadful films. For instance, whatever your opinion of the TV series *The Avengers*, virtually nobody who's seen it can consider the 1998 motion picture remake with Ralph Fiennes and Uma Thurman as anything less than a travesty. Of the various big-screen attempts to refresh the appeal of a lucrative franchise, only the ones that use the opportunity to satirise the attitudes of the original (*The Brady Bunch*, for example), say what

couldn't *quite* be said then (*The Addams Family*, and once again the sequel was better) or make fun of the whole re-launching of franchises process (*Josie and the Pussycats*) remain watchable.

So to deny that the executives who green-lit this project were mainly motivated to get a pilot for a frothy show combining the two biggest comparable series of the time - *Star Trek* and its various spin-offs, and *The X-Files* - would be utterly pointless. Most of this film's key concepts are done in the most familiar ways an American show *could* do it. The TARDIS travels through a cone of swirly orange stuff that's midway between the warp-drive of the *Enterprise* and the eponymous *Stargate*, like it was a mere hyperspace tunnel such as the hundred or so we saw in 80s / 90s shows. The theme tune is made as Jerry Goldsmith-ish as possible, apparently so as not to scare the viewers with anything unusual or imaginative. The Master's intermediate form is the kind of CGI parasite that was wheeled out in the *Babylon 5* episode "Exogenesis", and he's then made into a surrogate Trill symbiont from *Deep Space Nine* / a Goa'uld worm from *Stargate SG-1* (delete according to personal show loyalty).

But the *big* one is the way that Grace, a sceptical medic, is won over by the enthusiastic "believer" - in a will-they-won't-they romantic way, just like Mulder and Scully. In a lot of ways, the idea of a female identification-figure stepping into a world she didn't know existed is traditional Hitchcock (think of *The Birds*), but in the majority of his films, it's men making the big step. One interesting attempt to make this work as a TV series was when Ian Fleming was called in to devise a sort-of *North by Northwest*, but which entailed a series of ordinary housewives and secretaries caught up in Cold War stuff with an enigmatic and suave stranger. This became *The Man from UNCLE* (see 3.4, "The Daleks' Master Plan"; 7.1, "Spearhead from Space"), and a later attempt to make this work led to the show most critics compared "The TV Movie" to: *Scarecrow and Mrs King*.

However, in attempting to render *Doctor Who* as we had always understood it into a format suitable for US mainstream audiences, the execs went for the usual ploy in adapting comics and old TV shows: the "origin" story. Basically, they attempted to explain and rationalise twenty-six years' worth of improvised solutions to practical problems into a manageable set-up for a new series, and in so doing opted to give the Doctor a "first mission" connected with his "family", during which time he meets new friends slated to become the series cast. The consequence is the same mess and sense of futility - albeit punctuated by good performances and nice moments - that's found in works such as Russell Mulcahey's attempt at *The Shadow*, the 1998 *Lost in Space* film, the John Goodman *Flintstones*, Sean Connery's career-ending *League of Extraordinary Gentlemen* and dozens of others. Appallingly, this is how studio executives think it should be done.

Meanwhile, as we'll examine in detail in **The Lore**, the influence of books on script-writing that emphasises "journey" and "growth" was at its height in this period. The idea is that the Doctor is the identification-figure once he's introduced, but that the female lead is the investigator who takes us to him. Once Grace became the protagonist this was downplayed, still lurking in the Jacobs script, although the decision to make the "old Doctor" more prominent and give a voice over at the top of the story altered this balance again.

Things That Don't Make Sense   The Master's attire, the fact that the Seventh Doctor doesn't bother to check the TARDIS scanner before walking out into a hail of gunfire, the fact that there's a TARDIS-sized Eye of Harmony [see **The TARDIS**], Grace's ability to rewire the Console sans any technical skill, and - oh yes - the TARDIS' miraculous ability to resurrect the dead. If only we could stop there...

As we've mentioned, the Daleks now put their war criminals on trial. All right, this seemed to previously occur with their creator Davros, but in this case they're arraigning the Master. Setting aside that the Time Lords don't seem to take issue with the Daleks putting one of their number on trial [at last we get a "trial of a Time Lord" worth seeing - if just for comedy value - but then they cut straight to the sentence], what *really* complicates matters is that the person carrying out the Master's last request is the Doctor. That's The One They Call Doc-Tor [or, in Skaroese, *Ka Faraq Gatri*, 'The Oncoming Storm', etc] - their greatest enemy. He's apparently allowed to watch the trial without fear of extermination, and to peacefully depart with the Master's remains afterward. So... do they put him up in the Skaro Hilton when he arrives? Imagine the awkward small talk in the lobby. [The scene in *The Empire Strikes Back* where Darth Vader invites Han and Leia to join him for a pre-torture finger-buffet has nothing on this.] As you might imagine, this entire scenario was laughed at even *before* the 2005 series went to great lengths to shoot it down in flames. [The novelisation, at least, has the decency to claim that the Doctor somehow snuck onto Skaro and collected the Master's remains unannounced. Then again, of all the people to have an APB on, you'd think the Daleks would be on alert in case of visits from *him*.]

So... the unnamed gang members gun down two of Chang Lee's associates, and they then have him dead to rights. They cock their pistols and mention his name. It's clearly personal. Yet instead of following through on this, they run away like girls when they mistakenly shoot a short Scotsman. Are they of the opinion that the sound of gunfire only attracts attention if the victim is white? Come to think of it, why did they stay perfectly calm when a police box materialised out of nowhere, with a sound of a hundred elephants [a perfectly normal event in Chinatown, obviously], and only panic when Sylvester McCoy arrives? Were they scared that the risk of spoon-playing had reached critical?

For that matter, Chang Lee shoots five bullets and then sticks his pistol into the waist of his jeans - he'll have a blister in an unfortunate place in the morning. And it doesn't seem to have occurred to him beforehand that it's - wow! - only two days until the year 2000! My, he's been sleeping soundly.

Almost everyone at Grace's hospital is an imbecile, or at the very least acting very strangely. The Doctor's chest X-ray reveals that he's got two hearts, but all common sense goes out the window when this occurs, as nobody thinks about - oh, say - *trying again* or fetching a stethoscope. Come on! If this was "real" *Doctor Who*, the first thing anyone with even the vaguest medical background would do is whip out a stethoscope, to comic effect. But no, so they measure John Doe's fibrillation and send him into surgery without the vaguest of routine checks - like whether he's got AmEx - and start carving him up. Does nobody in this hospital know how to take a pulse?

Grace then sashays in and performs surgery, after just donning her scrubs over her ballgown (hardly a textbook procedure, that), and takes an emotionally charged personal phone call while scrubbing up. Overall we'd accord her with some intelligence, but gaze in astonishment as Grace - a *senior* cardiologist - declares she's 'going to try something' and gives her fibre-optic probe a tug while it's in the Doctor's chest, thus killing him. *That's* what they taught when Grace was at medical school? "If in doubt about where you're located in the patient's heart, give it a tug and hope for the best?"

Tellingly, Bruce comments that the Doctor will have to be rich 'where he's going', i.e. Grace's hospital. Yet Grace and her cohorts have no problem using pioneering (translation: very expensive) surgery on a John Doe who was found in the street after a gang shooting. Hospital financeers are observing this procedure, even though it's rather late at night for such a formal visit, and even though the hospital officials know in advance that this man's cardiovascular system is verkakte. As a means of impressing important people, this is highly dubious, don't you think? Moreover, despite the aforementioned signs that Grace works at a lucrative hospital, an entire wing of it is rendered as being post-apocalyptic - shattered windows, a leaky roof and a row of *very* conveniently placed mirrors included - once McGann is up and walking about. We might also mention the nurse who sticks her face in front of the delirious Doctor yet does nothing to help him, and the morgue that's evidently staffed by idiots who fail to recognize the name 'Wild Bill Hickock', sit about watching *Frankenstein* and joke with the stiffs. [Perhaps the idea is that they can't do the patients any further harm.] Ultimately, one thing becomes clear from all of this: if you're going to San Francisco, wear flowers in your hair if you wish, but at all costs avoid Walker General.

Oh, and a lingering bit about the hospital: it would appear that someone there is going to the New Year's Eve costume party dressed as TV's *Doctor Who*, as evidenced when McGann pulls Tom Baker's scarf out of a locker. [Eureka! Proof that this adventure isn't canon - *Doctor Who* is the only British TV show that doesn't exist in the *Doctor Who* universe. That must be why Grace is so upset to find that her boyfriend has taken the sofa...]

So for the first time in *ever*, we're meant to care [as much as one *can* care under these circumstances] about the possibility of romance between the Doctor and his companion. Such a pity that their kissing is among the most spurious on network TV, and that Grace's relationship with her live-in boyfriend isn't the least bit credible. If any-

thing Brian looks incredibly bored as Grace dashes out of the *Madame Butterfly* performance, and - to judge by his subsequent phone call to her - it's only *now* occurred to him that he's living with a heart surgeon who's got little time to spare for her personal life. Then Brian decides to end their relationship, but apparently doesn't even bother to tell Grace that he's leaving, and he moves out with *amazing* speed. Please note that he's cleared out the very next day when Grace and the Doctor arrive home, and to judge by the sofa comment, he's even managed to take some of the heavy furniture with him. It's also something of a plot device that Grace sleeps over on a hospital couch rather than just going home, although we might imagine that she's more sick of her boyfriend than she lets on [or - who knows? - the film-makers are establishing a 'sofa' motif].

Much of this story's time-frame seems out of kilter. It's 11.57am when the grinning nurse towers over the Doctor, then Grace is asked to cover up the Doctor's death, whereupon she quits and packs her goodies into a box and the clock reads 3.41pm when she finally tries to leave. (Side note to say that the burnt X-rays are *still* alight when Grace finishes the confrontation with her boss, even though they should've been extinguished by that point.) Then the Doctor and Grace return to her pad, and it's back to 3.20pm. Two minutes and some dodgy lip-synch later ('twelve' redubbed as 'thirteen'), the clock strikes the half-hour. And sorry to be pedantic, but even if 31st of December, 1999, *was* the eve of the Millennium [which was a year later, as you know], why is everyone ignoring the big celebration in Greenwich? Nobody's even mentioned the Millennium Bug.

Assuming that the product-placement for jelly-babies wasn't some kind of legal requirement to placate Bassetts' after "The Happiness Patrol" (25.2), we have to pause to wonder where the new Doctor gets them from. He has to steal clothes and is left with *none* of his predecessor's accoutrements, remember, yet later he magically produces jelly-babies from somewhere. Now, it *does* look as if the old Doctor's bag of jelly-babies is left behind on Grace's desk when Lee steals his other possessions, and we might speculate that the McGann Doctor later retrieves them from her off screen. This presumes, however, that Grace felt compelled to take a dead man's sweets home with her after quitting her job.

We're also obliged to wonder about the totally nonsensical circumstances behind the policeman with the bad motorcycle brakes - you know, the one who through *astonishing* coincidence has a quick zoom in and out of the console room - but doing so runs the risk of our losing the will to live.

The shoddy new TARDIS console has hand-written preset historical periods and planet coordinates. All right, but there's only room on each roller for four of these - even the Earth-centric BBC Wales series has taken the Ship to more times and planets than this. And one of these is to get the TARDIS to Gallifrey in the 'Rassilon' era. Cute, but imagine the potential for time-paradoxes including the TARDIS preventing its own construction, and then stop and count all the times we've been told that this is something even the Doctor can't do. [Eek! An ethical dilemma: sure, the Movie's crap, but this detail makes it and "Silver Nemesis" incompatible. One of them has to be ruled out, so which would *you* rather was removed from the canon?]

Owing to the side effects from the Eye of Harmony being open, the Doctor announces that he's lost twenty pounds in twenty minutes. He's in a new body, though, so how does he know? It would also appear that, just for a giggle, it's been decided to move the Greenwich Meridian from the line where it's been since the 1700s - and by which all maps and charts the world over are calibrated - to San Francisco. Presumably they moved its antipode (the International Date Line) at the same time, just to wreck everyone's New Year parties by sending the clocks nine hours out of whack. This might explain why it seems to be midnight at the same time in Moscow, New York, San Francisco and Paris, and only sunset in London and Wiltshire. It *doesn't* explain, though, why the newsreaders mention this abrupt change in the planet's navigation system in passing, as if it's no big deal.

Even if we *were* to grudgingly accept the 'half human' line as true [and does anybody?], it makes little sense in the context of the story. If the Doctor's semi-human eyes are somehow more compatible with Time Lord technology than those of Time Lords, as we're lead to believe, then for what possible reason did the ancient Time Lords install this as standard? And it *must* be a standard, because the Master recruits Lee to open the Eye even *before* he has reason to think that the Doctor is half-human. Or if humans are now the *only* species capable of manipulating Time Lord tech,

doesn't this rather invalidate the claims about time travel in 22.4 "The Two Doctors"? Isn't it also a bit of a security hazard, if the Doctor's TARDIS responds to *anyone* who's human? [But it *almost* makes 19.2, "Four to Doomsday" make some kind of sense, so maybe this is a keeper.]

It seems the destructive energy radiating from the Eye of Harmony has a sense of occasion, because Earth's doom is set for precisely midnight on New Year's. It's therefore very fortunate that San Francisco just happens to be home to the world's most advanced beryllium clock, and which helpfully (*overly* helpfully) happens to contain the vital component that the Doctor needs to repair his Ship. We might also wonder how the Master thinks that acquiring the Doctor's remaining lives is going to help him, if the Eye of Harmony being open will destroy Earth - and one would imagine the TARDIS as well - as the clock strikes twelve. [Shame on him, in fact, for failing to recognize this very problem a *second* time, after events in "The Deadly Assassin".]

Then again, perhaps the Master's confusion owes to the fact that he seems to be written by three different people. One minute he's unable to speak naturally ('the Asian child'), then he's using phases like 'Yes way', then still later he corrects Grace's grammar - despite the fact that he has three times ended a sentence with a preposition. In spite of the triggered fire alarm and the ongoing security situation at the Institute, a custodian is seen causally hoovering, and nobody looks out of the window to see the Doctor and Grace slowly descending on a fire hose. Grace knows what a Neutron Ram is, somehow. The Master correctly divines that she knows how to put on the *Clockwork Orange* eyewear. She's also able to come up with convincing technobabble for explaining dimensional transcendentalism, despite her supposed inability to set an alarm clock. As the New Year arrives, even if we could ignore the countdown and the music's getting louder, the Master's decision to (all together now) 'dresszzz for the occasion' is a bit silly when you remember his ultimate goal (sometimes, at least) is to take over the Doctor's body. What does it matter how Bruce's corpse is dressed?

Real stupidity, though, comes in the closing scenes. Not just the resurrection bit, but the result of the Doctor suggesting that Grace - whose 'amazing' future he seems to already know - should throw it all away and travel with him. She's already said 'I finally meet the right guy and he's

ABOUT TIME 1996

from another planet'. She's literally had the time of her life. He offers her a ride in a palatial space-time vehicle moments after apparently bringing her back from the dead, and mere hours after her boyfriend has dumped her and she's quit her job. Yet she refuses, on the grounds that she "knows who she is". Compared to this sort of fickleness, some of the relationships on *Torchwood* look sophisticated and Martha's departure at the end of Series Three is dramatically justified.

Finally, a bit of off-screen idiocy: Philip Segal tells everyone that he was a huge fan of Pertwee, then *in the next breath* says that he put in the chase sequence in because he wanted to show that this Doctor was totally unlike his predecessors. You couldn't imagine any previous Doctor on a motorbike, he claimed. Setting aside the small matter of Sylvester McCoy doing it three times, there's the issue of the mighty and vehicle-loving Jon Pertwee riding one in 8.5, "The Daemons", and also a Honda trike in 9.1, "Day of the Daleks". Later, Segal claimed that he wanted to avoid using a logo that carried associations with any one era of the programme's past. So he used the one from Seasons Seven to Ten.

Critique   PLEASE please *please* **please** please please please please PLEASE please puh-*lease* PLEASE please in the name of sanity PLEASE please please please please *please* please for pity's sake *PLEASE* please por favor please please please please PLEASE please please bitte schon PLEASE please please please please make it stop make it stop make it stop make it stop make it stop make it stop make it stop make it stop make it stop make it stop make it stop (etc)

Critique (Second Attempt)   All right, we'll do it properly. For all that we might deride this project, there are two major problems that almost - *almost* - cancel each other out. One is that Segal kept chucking in more and more of what he called "kisses to the past", the other is that studio executives with no feeling whatsoever for the programme's past wanted a generic "Cult" show in line with all the others. So it looks like a knock-off of *Lois and Clark*, and has dialogue and a protagonist wrenched from *Star Trek*. (Oh, come on... who's half-human and travelled back in time to San Francisco, after returning from the dead?) The Jerry-Goldsmith-in-a-basket arrangement of the theme is a dead giveaway, but this isn't *necessarily*

a disaster.

No, really. Provided you're lucky and judicious, a hardcore fan-professional can use his or her deep knowledge of *Doctor Who's* faults and potential to guide new writers through something that's consciously modelled on a hit US fantasy show. Yes, it can work - after all, that's what we've got now. We'll leave it for someone writing a book like this ten years in the future to decide whether the issue is simply that ripping off *Buffy the Vampire Slayer* is intrinsically smarter than ripping off *The X-Files*, *Star Trek* or *Quatermass* - or whether a fan who follows the spirit of *Doctor Who* but ignores the letter is any worse than a non-fan who simply tries to make something completely unlike anything else on TV at the time. The fact remains that producer Philip Segal's ability to get the wrong things onto the screen is more obvious than his efforts to keep them off it, but this movie *does* exist, and it wouldn't have done without him. As much as one can criticize the final effort, a great many potentially worse movies were forestalled by his veto. Sadly, we're not here to review those.

Segal's best moves, in fact, were in hiring the right people for the central jobs. As Big Finish fans know, Paul McGann is a natural Doctor by virtue of his being slightly reluctant to become identified with the part. His mannerisms don't seem to have been thought up in a script conference, but come from unselfconscious empathy from an actor figuring out the character on the hoof. Matthew Jacobs might have included a shedload of continuity references that make some of the script creak, but he too has the right instincts. Completing this line-up are director Geoffrey Sax, who fought studio heads to inject a slightly offbeat taste for visual puns and odd moments, and Eric Roberts. Like many of the best actors in the BBC Wales series, he has a vague half-memory of the show's 1970s habits without being enslaved by a need to copy it precisely.

The overall look is very much standard-issue mid-90s US television. A lot of the credit for this looking as good as it did goes to editor Patrick Lussier, who took Sax's idea of intercutting between the Master's rebirth and the Doctor's - plus a few other similar bravura touches - and made them work. Incredibly, Sax came from a background in studio-based comedy. The most effect-heavy show in the UK in the 1980s, *Spitting Image*, was his main qualification for this, but nothing in that series could have prepared him for motorbike chases and gunfights. The worst that can be said about these scenes is that they look interchangeable with the bulk of US prime time of the period. And into this the Doctor is inserted, to distort it all around him. This is what *Doctor Who* does. It *could* have worked.

In fact, consider that before this effort, the idea that creaky old *Doctor Who* could be made to look like it belongs in the modern TV environment was laughable. Constructing a standing set for the TARDIS and getting a high-profile "serious" actor to play the Doctor was, pre-1996, unthinkable. Conversely, the main way in which this movie is visibly influential on the current episodes is as a warning. Moments in "Rose" (X1.1) look like they were inspired by a need to dodge this film's errors. We aren't privy to any BBC Wales "bible", but we suspect it would consist of a list of mistakes to avoid - all of them from the first half of this movie. Most of those mistakes were a long list of things that really "must" be in the story "for the fans", or "for the US audience". Ignoring both of these led to the enormous success of the 2005 series, which should tell you something about where "The TV Movie" goes awry.

Because here, we're witness to the worst excesses of mid-80s *Who* (and a smidgeon of '70s *Who*'s self-confident oddness), but with big-budget routine television forced inside and distorting it. Maybe with less riding on it, financially and institutionally, the more idiosyncratic talents on display could have made something special. Certainly, Segal seems to have shown the drive and instincts that the good people at BBC Wales have demonstrated is vital. But as the sheer effort of getting this made and making it not seem *too* out of place on US television took a lot of energy, why not a *touch* more to make something that would matter to people as a story, rather than merely because it exists?

Ten years ago this looked like someone desecrating the corpse of a much-loved childhood friend. Now, for obvious reasons, it looks like a rather peculiar blind alley. For British viewers of a certain age, the obvious comparison is *The Comic Strip Presents...* feature film *The Strike* (also known as *Strike!*), in which a drama about the 1984 miners' strike is adapted for Hollywood, cast amazingly wrongly and rewritten to suit American audiences. The difference is that *The Strike* and "The TV Movie" is that the former was deliberately done as a comedy. (So much so, in fact, that Arthur Scargill - in reality a fat, balding demagogue with a Yorkshire accent - is played by Al Pacino, or rather Peter Richardson portraying "Al Pacino", with Jennifer Saunders playing "Meryl Streep" playing Scargill's wife. He races to Parliament on a borrowed Harley Davidson, pausing to save orphans from a collapsing mineshaft.)

We rather hope that, after reading all of these books, the average American reader doesn't need to come and live in Britain for five years to see how gratingly wrong so much of "The TV Movie" is. After seeing "Rose", an object lesson in how to relaunch it for a new audience and get away with it, British readers can forgive Segal for making compromises with BBC's clueless Jo Wright and a hundred or so faceless Universal and Fox drones. It got to the screen without any really inept visuals, so it proved one point - that this project is less entertaining and less like *Doctor Who* than the Cushing Dalek films is an object lesson in how many cooks it takes to spoil a broth.

What this looks like, more than it looks like a botched *Beauty and the Beast* or any of the other shows it apes, is one of those awful board-games where they've just stuck a picture of the TARDIS on the box and made a generic space game. It's got cut-and-paste items wrenched from any of the many guide books doing the rounds in the 80s, but with no real idea what *Doctor Who* is about, what it's for, who might be watching. There's no reason for any of the "kisses to the past" to be there, and their presence makes a silly story sillier.

Even at the base level of making just any old TV movie rom-com with aliens, it fails on the basics. There's no chemistry between the leads. There's no suspense in the baffling and garbled climax. There's nothing we've not seen done better in other shows. The final line of the movie is a supposedly comic 'Oh, no - not again!' For this alone, the entire production team should have been burned at the stake.

The Facts

TV Movie Ratings 9.08 million (UK broadcast).

Working Titles Actually, none; Segal suggested to fans that if they need a name for the specific episode (as opposed to calling it *Doctor Who*, which is confusing even if you accept it), perhaps "Enemy Within" would do. This doesn't appear on any paperwork, and nobody took up the offer.

Supporting Cast John Novak (Salinger), Michael David Simms (Dr Swift), Catherine Lough (Wheeler), Delores Drake (Curtis), William Sasko (Pete), Jeremy Radick (Gareth), Eliza Roberts (Miranda), Dave Hurtubise (Professor Wagg); Mi-Jung Lee, Joanna Piros (News Anchors).

Oh, Isn't That..?

• *Eric Roberts.* Some of us in Britain knew him from *The Pope of Greenwich Village* ("Charlie! They took ma thumbs!"), but for a lot of us he was the-one-who-wasn't-Jon-Voight in *Runaway Train*. Around the time that this was made, it did look like he might be on the verge of breaking out of TV typecasting with big roles in proper films like *Heaven's Prisoners*, *It's My Party* (both of which saw the inside of cinemas) and *Power 98* (which didn't). He also had a small part in John Waters' little-seen *Cecil B. Demented*. Now, with *The Dark Knight* on the blocks, a regular spot in dire sitcom *Less Than Perfect*, a semi-regular post in *Heroes* (as "Mr Thompson", leading to a geek meltdown where he shares a screen with George Takai and Chris Eccleston - none of whom is the most interesting person in that shot!) and retaining his dignity in a video for the Eminem / Akon tag-team, he looks like finally cracking the big time. Again.

• *Daphne Ashbrook.* We're legally obliged to mention that she was in an episode of *Star Trek: Deep Space Nine* ("Melora"), but had most recently been in an episode of *Murder, She Wrote* (she dunnit, thus making her officially the most famous person in the guest cast). In the 90s, she spent a lot of time in TV movies of varying quality - some have been shown on Channel 5, but we're sure there were some good ones too. More recently she was in early episodes of *The OC*, which is already filed under "remember that?"

• *Sylvester McCoy* We imagine that by now you have some idea who he was, but imagine being Joe Shmoe from Idaho seeing him listed in the credits as 'Special Guest Star'.

The Lore

• If you really want to know, there are two books and a *DWM* special just about the making of this story and all the backstage dramas leading up to it. We've also covered a lot of it in the Appendix entry on "Dimensions in Time" and the essay with "Survival", so we'll skip a lot of the Story So Far. Basically, Philip Segal had been pressing for a big budget co-production version of *Doctor Who* since he got his first big job in TV, but had wanted to be involved in making the series for a lot longer. He grew up in Essex, but his family moved to the US in the late 1970s. Just as Season Twenty-Six was ending production, Segal - then working for Columbia Pictures - called BBC Enterprises to propose talks on co-production. A working honeymoon in London saw him having promising talks with Peter Cregeen (op cit) and Roger Laughton, Enterprises' co-production supremo. All sorts of other companies were in the bidding, so nobody could promise Segal anything, but Columbia was easily the front-runner. Segal got to talk to the good people at Daltenreys, whose film project was getting the headlines and thought that their script (which he hated) was sufficiently unlike anything he wanted to do as a series to leave room for both projects. All looked well, but as soon as the BBC had agreed to his demands, Segal quit Columbia and took a bigger job at ABC. Meanwhile, the Daltenreys project died on the vine, or so it seemed. After a year - during which Segal supervised the transmission of *Twin Peaks* and *thirtysomething* (but came on board too late to be instrumental in their creation, as is sometimes claimed), he moved again - this time to Amblin Entertainment.

Yes, Amblin. Having that nice Mr Spielberg's name to throw around gave Segal a lot more leverage with the BBC. By now Mark Shivas was fielding calls at the BBC, although Cregeen was still involved. Segal's main job was getting *seaQuest DSV* and *Earth 2* off the ground, which is how Universal come into the story. Cregeen was still dragging his feet, as by now (we're in early 1992) the Corporation was starting to think that making *Doctor Who* itself might be cost-effective. All this talk of films and big-budget co-productions had kept the series in the public eye, with no actual episodes to embarrass anyone and the BBC2 re-runs doing quite well. Segal, now also involved with The *Young Indiana Jones Chronicles* - in which both Jon Pertwee and Colin Baker would appear - now had Peter Wagg as a possible co-producer. Wagg had been contacted by Green Light (formerly Coast to Coast, who were the subdivision of Daltenreys actually making the film - do keep up) and used their interest to get some motion with the BBC and Amblin. Wagg talked to Shivas and used his own production company, Yertez, to do the paperwork, including a first draft show "bible". (Yertez was set up by Wagg after his first big hit, *Max Headroom;* see 24.2, "Paradise Towers". Make-up for the character Max Headroom was by Coast to Coast, now trading - as we've said - as Green Light.)

The horse-trading continued. Then in February 1993, there was a new Controller of BBC1. Alan Yentob was rather more enthusiastic about the project. When a lot of British TV execs came to Universal to be given the works tour with a view to buying *seaQuest DSV*, the Amblin executive in charge - Philip Segal - took "Yo" Yentob aside for a little chat. The project was back on track and the BBC and Amblin had resolved a lot of their differences. What could possibly go wrong?

Adrian Rigelsford, that's what. You may know that part of the story already (see "Dimensions in Time" if you don't) so fast forward to Autumn, and Segal and Wagg have had a chat with Lumiere Films. They're now in with the Daltenreys project, and want to amalgamate with Amblin on this. Segal isn't keen. By now things are so weird, there's nothing the British tabloids can't claim that doesn't seem plausible. This is where the rapping TARDIS console reports, the David Hasselhoff rumour, the Ridley Scott story and all the rest began.

In reality, Segal had sounded out Michael Crawford, but that was about it. Of far greater importance was getting a decent script. Enter John Leekley, a Universal staff writer with a reasonable previous form, and whose brother was a fan of the series. Like most of the worst fantasy scriptwriters, he had got it into his head that you should begin with an "origin" story and should base it squarely in Joseph Campbell's theories. Because films based on *Hero With a Thousand Faces* always work, don't they? (That was sarcasm, if you hadn't guessed. We direct the unconvinced reader to rent out *Willow* or *Howard: A New Breed of Hero* for films sticking doggedly to the template and falling flat. Then see 23.4, "The Ultimate Foe" for more on how fashionable half-digested mythopoaeia was after Lucas had a go.) The "Leekley bible" has a special place in fan lore as the most comprehensive misunderstanding of the series ever, as well as providing the hilarious suggested catch-phrase 'power up the crystals, Cardinal'. You may need a stiff drink before, during or after reading the next two paragraphs.

The Doctor and the Master are, of course, half-brothers. The Master is trying to become President of Gallifrey but the Doctor, a keen explorer, is too busy investigating caves on his home planet (infested with spider-Daleks, as you'd expect) to bother until he finds ancient scrolls prophesying a saviour. Cardinal Barusa (sic) is the ailing President (and, conveniently, the Doctor's grandfather), who dies telling him to find Ulysses, the Doctor's missing father. Barusa's spirit enters the power source of Ulysses' old TARDIS, which the Doctor now takes over, with Barusa appearing as a hologram when the plot needs explaining. The TARDIS lands in London in the Blitz, where the Doctor meets an American girl who thinks he's a Nazi, and that's the first ad break.

From then on, various different versions exist, but they all seem to find ways for the Doctor and Lizzie to wind up in Egypt. Pharoah Cheops was Ulysses, apparently. There, they are attacked by either robot dogs or 'Cybs' (from Telos if they can get the rights cleared, or completely new aliens, a bit, if not). Then there's a trip to the Renaissance, and the Master pops up and takes them to Skaro for some reason. Another version has Ulysses regenerate and become a pirate whilst the Doctor sees Cheops' (human) wife and realises that she was his mother. Oh, and there are two Swords of Rassilon conveniently placed for a duel to the death between the half-brothers. But the Doctor is forbidden to kill the Master because if one Time Lord kills another, it removes his powers. And Ulysses can become Lizzie's father from Kansas when necessary. And the Kaleds are spared when Davros and his creations get space flight and leave Skaro. And the Doctor's eyes being inherited from his mum is somehow important (as it would later *be* somehow important, if completely at odds with the logic of the story, in the Jacobs script). The follow-up series would revolve largely around the Doctor's quest to find his father, who as it turns out spends most of his time impersonating figures from human history. (Most intriguing is the suggestion that he was "Bluebeard", alias fifteenth century proto-serial killer Gilles de Rais, but sadly this is a typo in a story about pirates.) The episodes would largely be remakes of BBC serials, often relocated to new American settings, including a new version of "The Gunfighters" (3.8) to be called "Don't Shoot, I'm the Doctor".

• Amazingly, Leekley's script generated a lot of positive feedback from the BBC, and a sample of dialogue about what the Doctor said to Napoleon before a battle was used as the audition-piece for potential Doctors. With Peter O'Toole apparently enthusiastic about playing the Cardinal, they started making long lists of actors to approach. The BBC were keen to have a reasonable-sized star, but were more insistent on whoever they got being British. The people they actively sought and weren't told to go away by include several big names, at least big in Britain. Here's a sample: Tony Slattery, Harry Enfield, Peter Capaldi, John Sessions, Hugh Laurie, Robert Lindsay, Mark McGann, Tim Curry, Anthony Head, Rowan Atkinson, Roger Rees and Jonathan Pryce. Of the less-than-household names, the front-runner was Liam Cunningham, but another part came up at a crucial juncture.

But a dark horse candidate had been on the back-up list. The McGann brothers are sort of a British equivalent of the Baldwins. Two of them get lots of work, the others pop up from time to time, and once in a while you get all four. Paul, the shortest of them, was making fairly sizeable movies and was now spending a lot of time in Los Angeles. Segal saw one of the films (*Dealers*, about the London Stock Exchange) and was impressed. In the middle of shooting a drama series with the rest of the clan (*The Hanging Gale*), Paul took leave of his brothers and did an audition in September, six months after brother Mark had had a go. If you've seen *The Hanging Gale*, you'll have some idea where the Doctor's costume came from. And that wig makes sense, sort of.

• Although they'd already scouted locations in Utah, the team still hadn't had final confirmation. Spielberg, fresh from doing *Schindler's List*, found the proposal insufficiently invigorating (the stuff with the snakes and mummies looked a little familiar, too). Segal was worried about it, and Leekley was replaced by Robert DeLaurentis, a veteran of *St Elsewhere*. His first idea was to give the Doctor a bulldog called Winston as a companion. (Sometimes, there just aren't words.)

• Meanwhile, Sylvester McCoy mentioned at a convention that his old mate Paul McGann had been approached, but had cold feet about the project. DeLaurentis produced a story with Borusa dying completely at the start, and with the Master also leaving Gallifrey, chasing Borusa's ring (bequeathed to the Doctor) and charming his way across time and space to stop their father returning and reclaiming the Presidency. Somehow Daleks can disguise themselves as humans, and Lizzie gets several name changes, but it's still Leekley's quest-story. But it's got more humour and energy, as Segal wanted. (He's subsequently said that of the three scripts, Leekley's was his favourite.) Leekley was still developing story treatments for the proposed series including his new tale about Doc Holliday.

• Which brings us to Matthew Jacobs, whose dad played the Doc in "The Gunfighters" as we're sure you remembered. Jacobs had written a very well-received script based on the book *Marianne Dreams*, filmed as *Paperhouse*. (If you've not seen it, imagine if X2.11, "Fear Her" made sense.) He'd moved to San Francisco after this, and worked on *The Young Indiana Jones Chronicles*. It's starting to make sense now, isn't it? Of course, the DeLaurentis document was still in play, and Franco-American couple Jean-Marc and Randy Lofficier were acting in an Ian Levine-ish capacity as "fan liaisons" to Segal, something the executive producer would later come to regret. (They suggested changing from "Borusa" to "Pandak" - see "The Deadly Assassin" - and swapping the Daleks for the Ogrons.) They also proposed a future episode, based on their rejected *New Adventures* proposal "The Terrible Zodin". Seriously.

Anyway, they had *another* idea for an origin story, this time with an amnesiac "Dr Smith" on Earth - see 1.1, "An Unearthly Child" - and set in the present day. Jacobs was also keen to remove complications and started off with three simple ideas. One was that the story should pick up where the BBC series left off in 1989, but with a new character finding out about the Doctor as we do. Another was that the Master should be the only villain. The third was that there was a good reason for the Doctor always coming here, but he himself wasn't sure whether it was genetic or not. Segal was intrigued by this.

Other elements were less clear. In which city should it be set? Jacobs knew San Francisco, but favoured New Orleans, especially as his idea included the Master trying to become worshipped as a god by raising the dead using the stolen TARDIS. It was set on Hallowe'en 1999, so the voodoo theme could have looked impressive (see 22.4, "The Two Doctors" for a counter-example). The newly-reborn Doctor, hazy after regeneration, is befriended by a street-kid called Jack - who goes over to the Master's side after seeing his own father brought back to life - and the cardiologist Dr Kelly Grace. Yes, really. Later tweaks moved it to New Year's Eve 1999, and involving a "millennium star". The Doctor's memory is prodded by an opera that Kelly sees: *Turandot*. (It's about guessing a stranger's name to save someone's life... do you see what he did there? By the way, it's mentioned in the finished product as the work that Puccini left unfinished at his death, and which Franco Alfano finished on his behalf.) Segal changed the setting to San Francisco, and this made changing Jack to (as the Master eventually puts it) 'The Asian Child' a logical next step. The Master-morphant invades the body of an ambulance driver who's described as being like Bruce Willis, hence the name.

• Quite how we got from this promising set-up to the mess they broadcast isn't entirely clear. The BBC were concerned that McCoy was to be involved at all, that McGann might not be and that the Chinatown stuff wasn't right. There were comments about how the story was too linear. (Wagg had by now left the project, but had a minor character named after him.) Casting was still underway, even for the main role. So here's where Harry Van Gorkum enters the story. These days Segal says he was okay, but was mainly there to make a reluctant studio accept McGann. By this stage, Fox were going to show this as their "Movie of the Week", a one-off that might go to a series (the so-called "back-door pilot" strategy that gave rise to so many innuendoes). Segal had taken the project with him when he left Amblin (a present from Spielberg, apparently). Fox wanted a rethink on the casting (i.e. an American if possible). Van Gorkum, British-born but US based, tested well and incoming director Sax thought he was promising.

Whatever Segal's real motives, for the BBC McGann was non-negotiable. McGann himself was less adamant, but agreed to do it if Fox wanted him. Segal did a trade-off with Universal that if he got to choose a Doctor, they could pick the Master. He wanted Christopher Lloyd, but they suggested the ubiquitous Eric Roberts and Fox agreed. Roberts got all sorts of concessions - one of which, his wife getting a part, solved the casting of Bruce's wife Miranda. All of this meant that Roberts ended up costing more than Christopher Lloyd would have done, and the Master ended up as the focus of Fox's advertising for the film. Universal being happy with Roberts meant that McGann was finally announced as the new Doctor in early January. Ten days later they started shooting in Vancouver. (Incidentally, *Babylon 5* fans will doubtless have tried to suppress all memories of the hapless spin-off *Crusade*, but especially the one where Van Gorkum appears as an alien version of Agent Mulder. We're sure he's got some work since then).

• McGann's head had been shaved while he was filming *The One That Got Away*, an inadvertently hilarious adaptation of ex-SAS man Chris Ryan's Gulf memoirs (watch out for the Trojan Goat). So some hasty wig-fitting was arranged. They use two different styles, neither terribly convincing. With twenty-five weeks of production, Sax opted not to watch any old episodes, but instead to rely on instinct and a feeling for what it had been like. He'd directed a spoof Season Seventeen clip for *End of Part One*, a series which had required him to pastiche many other styles. McCoy arrived, both with his hat and Mark Gatiss - who had been sent to help the outgoing Doctor record a video diary. (The contracts had made a "making of" documentary difficult to arrange.)

• But what of Daltenreys / Green Light in all this? The film whose development we've been following throughout the course of this volume finally sputtered to a halt in the spring of 1994, and the rights reverted back to the BBC. As we've mentioned, Daltenreys had brought Lumiere aboard as co-production partners. The first thing incoming producer Felicity Arden did was throw out the latest Johnny Byrne draft and commission a new script from Denny Martin Flinn, co-writer of *Star Trek VI: The Undiscovered Country* (1991). Lumiere saw the possibility of a *Trek*-style film franchise in *Doctor Who* and recovering ex-Spock Leonard Nimoy was brought aboard to direct. Nimoy saw Pierce Brosnan (then pre-Bond) as his ideal Doctor, though later reports indicate that Alan Rickman was the favoured candidate. Casting the Doctor would inevitably involve protracted negotiations. To ensure that principal photography could begin before the rights expired, Flinn's script included flashbacks to an earlier incarnation of the Doctor, which could be shot first with a less famous actor. Quite why this didn't happen is a mystery and possibly still sub judice, but when it became clear that filming wouldn't start in time, Lumiere walked and the project collapsed. In February 1997, Peter Litten and George Dugdale filed legal action alleging that the BBC - now favouring the Amblin project - had consciously obstructed production on the film until it was too late. The case never reached court. Back to Segal's love story.

• As we said, the precise details of the production are explored in ludicrous detail elsewhere. The shoot became increasingly frantic and some days went on into the next with no break. Sax negotiated three extra days, and it went $170,000 over budget. But it went to air in the US on 14th of May, 1996 (two days after its TV premiere in its spiritual homeland, Canada). It's a bit of an exaggeration to say that it vanished without trace - 9% audience share and 8.3 million viewers against a much-hyped episode of *Roseanne* isn't bad, but it wasn't what the enterprise needed to go to a series. (Irony, something we're told Americans can't do, strikes here. On the same night, in the same slot, NBC showed an early episode of *3rd Rock from the Sun* - a series around which a word-of-mouth "buzz" was growing. It followed *Frasier*, a sitcom made by anglophiles along the lines of *Fawlty Towers*. If Segal had been able to pitch his series as Fox's "answer" to these shows, and not *The X-Files*, he would have been able to make a genuinely *Who*-ish American show a reality...)

• A week before the UK debut, the movie was upstaged. Jon Pertwee died and the entire nation seemed to grieve. The following day the *Radio Times* did a big special issue, with lots of opportunities to buy merchandising. The smart thing, however, to get was the rival listings *TV Times*, which gave its front cover to the movie. (This was the ITV guide, so it had only been allowed to cover BBC programmes since 1993, meaning this was a real first.) The day after that (Wednesday 22nd), the video of the movie was in the shops, including some midnight openings of HMV especially for the occasion. BBC1's plan had originally been to show "The TV Movie" in the autumn (or even at Christmas) following the video release in the spring, but various factors ruled this out. The video release was delayed for a week for re-editing. There had been another horrific shooting incident (see 24.1, "Time and the Rani") in the weeks beforehand, and in the sensitive climate the BBC made various cuts, particularly to the sequence where the Doctor is shot. However, this clashed with the video classification policy of the BBFC, who insisted that the sell-through version would have to be as broadcast. The video was recalled for editing, the certificate was bumped from a 15 down to a 12, and various shops had to hastily reschedule planned signings.

• In the UK the ratings and audience share were much healthier, especially for a Bank Holiday - oddly enough, anecdotal evidence suggests that only hardcore fans refused to watch. The reviews were mixed. The consensus was oddly like that of fandom: they loved McGann, enjoyed Roberts and kinda liked Ashbrook, but everyone involved with the script should be fed to hyenas. A year on, unsold copies of the video were clogging up retail outlets' bargain bins, providing the British Public with the only clue that this had ever happened. On 13th of November, 1999, it was shown again as part of a theme night on BBC 2, mostly uncut this time. The early sections of *Doctor Who Night* went well, and Mark Gatiss' spoofs were well-received (except for one line in the first one), but showing an edit of the last two episodes of "The Daleks" (1.2) killed the momentum, and people had gone to bed or switched over for the football when the Movie started. It got 1.4 million viewers this time. A proposed second showing by Fox on New Year's Eve 1996 was unexpectedly replaced by *Revenge of the Nerds IV*. We have no record of how many people complained or even noticed.

• Sax has worked again, and has now made two honest-to-goodness feature films. Reviewers savaged the first of these, *White Noise*, but they admitted that he made a suitably spooky atmosphere that the stars failed to use. (Indeed, it's No. 88 in the *Rotten Tomatoes* website's list of 100 worst films - *Elektra* is 89 and *Catwoman* is 100, if that helps.) The next film, last year's adaptation of Adam Horowitz's bestseller *Stormbreaker*, is rather better.

appendix a

A1: "Dimensions in Time"

(BBC Worldwide 1993. Produced by John Nathan-Turner. Written by Nathan-Turner and David Roden (pen-name for David Mansell). Directed by Stuart McDonald. Two episodes, seven minutes and five minutes.)

Provenance This was broadcast once, in two eight-minute episodes. The first was on Friday, 26th of November as part of BBC1's *Children in Need* appeal telethon (see 20.7, "The Five Doctors"). The second was transmitted the following day as part of *Noel's House Party*. Both were shown in a format allowing viewers who'd bought that week's *Radio Times* with the special glasses (proceeds to the charity) to watch the action unfold in 3D.

And if that were not exciting enough, the story had the five surviving Doctors, and a host of companions. They were splintered across time in Albert Square, and meeting the *EastEnders* regulars as they fought the dreaded Rani in 1973, 1993 and 2013. Wow! Sounds great!

Things To Watch Out For in "Dimensions in Time"...

1. On Christmas Day 2006, viewers to BBC 1 had two reasons to celebrate (apart from the Baby Jesus thing, naturally): the Doctor and his companion Donna in "The Runaway Bride" (X3.0) and the death of Pauline Fowler in the traditional wrist-slittingly depressing *EastEnders* yuletide episode. (See X2.8, "The Impossible Planet" for the Doctor's take on this.) We thought the miserable cow would never go. Yet here she is, in November 2013, looking a lot healthier than she did in 2006 and talking to her late sister-in-law Kathy Beale. Albert Square hasn't changed much since the early 90s. The same posters for indie bands and DJ compilation CDs are stuck on the same corrugated iron walls, and the same people are wandering about in the background. (If you're wondering, berets and pashminas will be back in that season.) Yet they've installed a hover-train link over that abandoned railway-bridge, even though Albert Square is almost certainly going to be demolished for the 2012 Olympics.

2. The Rani has a humanoid servant to be obsequious to her this time. This guy is apparently called 'Cyrian' - not "Shagg" as is often reported - and is the regulation Season Twenty-Two-style bleached-blond in a leather waistcoat, but with earrings. And - oh, look - playing Cyrian is that nice Sam West who narrates all those wildlife documentaries when David Attenborough's having a lie down. His mother must be so proud. So here is a man who'd later be a leading RSC player and Artistic Director of the Sheffield Crucible Theatre, getting a baptism of fire in his first TV appearance. He deserves a BAFTA for keeping a straight face when Kate O'Mara struts in and says (all together now): 'Pickled in time, like gherkins in a jar'.

3. In many ways this "adventure" (although calling it that is almost an insult to adventure stories as a collective) is the *Rocky Horror Picture Show* of fandom, an audience-participation party. If you get to see it soon, wait for the first cliffhanger, when Peter Davison and his almost-unrecognisable sidekicks Nyssa and Peri (uh?) see Her Kateness step out of the Queen Vic. We defy you not to join in, thus:

The Rani: You're all going on a journey...
Us: How long, Kate?
The Rani: ... A verrrry long jourrrrney.

Other lines to join in with include 'Who was that terrible woman'? 'Good luck, my dears', 'Two fousind an' fir-eeen' and responding to Leela's baffling line 'I was Romana' with the football terrace chant 'You wot? You wot? Youwotyouwotyouwot?' What you say when Liz Shaw goes to duff up the evil renegade is up to you, but this is when everyone watching perks up.

4. Anyone watching this without the special glasses might get a bit nauseous. Admittedly these days, *everything* on telly has shaky hand-held cameras going round and round the actors, but there are rarely big and peculiar objects in the foreground to make the 3D look spectacular. Fifi (25.2, "The Happiness Patrol") and Kiv's corpse (23.2, "Mindwarp") are strange enough things to see on a fruit and veg stall in any case, but by that stage we've seen a Tractator (21.3, "Frontios") hanging out of the window of the pub and the Fourth Doctor in a virtual reality world where CGI jelly-babies orbit him. That the Rani's TARDIS has the Hartnell and Troughton's disembodied heads floating about for no good reason is

almost sensible by comparison. So's the ghastly rave mix of the theme tune, by the way, but with the glasses on, the titles don't look quite so naff.

5. So there's Jon Pertwee, in Albert Square with Bonnie Langford, walking past a poster for Nine Inch Nails. He tells her that someone's been rummaging around in his memories. Lo, in the foreground, someone's got a box of old cabbages and is rummaging about in them. There's so much more... the Mitchell brothers walking in on Romana like the set-up from a bad porn movie; Andrew Beech, dressed as a Time Lord and trying not to cry; an entire scene so that Colin Baker's Doctor can share some screen-time with the Brigadier (at last, we can all sleep easy); Sylvester and K9 given the thankless task of explaining the increasingly ludicrous plot, and managing to seem enthusiastic, whilst leaving us in no doubt what they think of the script...

The Doctor(s) Have started wearing each other's hairstyles. The Third Doctor seems to know who Mel is, and has encountered something called a 'megaluthian slime-skimmer'. The Fifth has changed his hat but not the rest of his clothes, and seems to be calling the shots. The Seventh wanted to take Ace to the Great Wall of China.

Fellow Travellers There's someone purporting to be Susan who can't believe that the fat bloke in the lurid coat is her grandfather. There's someone called Leela wearing a dog-blanket who is really au fait with regeneration and mind-transference. A lady we think may be Victoria has just stopped selling flowers in Trumpton long enough to shriek *who was that terrible woman*?

A portly Brigadier is weighing down a helicopter, Mike Yates is driving Bessie, Ace is atypically annoying, Mel is pert, Liz Shaw is prepared to shoulder-charge a heavily-armed alien, and *yet* Sarah is still dressing like she did in 1976. She's clearly her old self, though - unlike Nyssa and Romana, who have lost all dress-sense and seem to be played by ladies who think it's a rehearsal. Peri's dress-sense has improved, and K9 is still the voice of doom.

Of the more recognisable guest characters, Pauline Fowler knows where she was when Kennedy was shot [but don't tell Arthur], and seems to be pestered every twenty years or so by oddly-dressed men who demand to know what year it is. Arthur Fowler died some time before

2012 [actually 1996 in the series] but Pauline and Kathy didn't. [As it turns out, Pauline was done to death by Ray Brooks, alias David Archer from *Daleks' Invasion Earth 2150A.D.* Kathy moved to Leicester and was reported dead about two years before her sister-in-law.] Frank Butcher has never seen people being dragged into a pub, but apparently can see the aliens invisible to everyone else. Phil and Grant Mitchell were on speaking-terms and had seen Doctor Legge [unlike regular viewers, who'd not set eyes on him since about 1988].

Baddies The Rani has started using the Season Fifteen console. As we will see, this is a tried and true model [see A2, "The Curse of Fatal Death"]. She's got Cyrian with her as an adoring acolyte, and a nearby time vortex in which to dump any floating heads that might be cluttering up her workspace. The specimens in her menagerie are kept behind the roundels on the wall [so much cheaper than cavity-foam insulation].

Status
• *Canonicity*. John Nathan-Turner thought it was echt canon, and even gave it the Production Code that would have followed 26.2, "Ghost Light". As far as he was concerned, it was the start of Season Twenty-Seven. Opinion is divided on the matter - or at least it was while Nathan-Turner was among the living, and thus at least one person thought this undertaking might not be best forgotten. The thoughts of his co-author - David Mansell - are known only to himself. He appears to have gone into hiding. His last sighting was submitting a short sequel [officially called "Rescue", but more affectionately known as "Shagg's Story"] for Marvel's *Doctor Who Yearbook* the following year. Even attempts to explain the bewildering dialogue and apparent black hole where a plot ought to be founder. If this is a "lost" Season Eighteen story as is sometimes claimed - allegedly owing to K9's presence - why is the McCoy era title sequence used? [Answer: it's got a galaxy spinning in the right direction for the 3D effect.]

• *Deviation*. Massive. Any attempt to explain the nature of the character-swaps - such as the notion that the companions are telepathically conjoined, or are somehow the same person - invariably proves ludicrous. There's a Time Lord lumbering around like any other monster, in full Prydonian ceremonial drag.

Plot Oh dear, you had to ask. Well, one version of this is that the Fourth Doctor and Romana and K9 are subjected to hallucinations caused by a time-rift, and that the Rani is making them see Albert Square filled with monsters. The side-effect is that the Doctor flips between past and future incarnations and Romana sees herself as Victoria, Leela-in-a-tent, Mike Yates and so on. (This would be fine if there was ever only one companion with him at any time, but this does not always happen. Still, it's preferable to the other idea - that the companions are in fact all interchangeable segments of one gestalt being through time. Seriously, we've seen this proposed. This isn't any more tenable than the gibberish this was devised to explain, so we'll start again with just what we can see.)

Brace yourselves... The Fourth Doctor sends an SOS to his other selves saying that the Rani has started plotting to capture them. She is putting together a menagerie of all life-forms and generating a time-vortex. The Seventh Doctor and Ace are drawn off course to Greenwich, 1973, and land at the Cutty Sark. Thereafter, a series of time-slips send the Doctor across a thirty-year period, wandering around the market at Albert Square, E20, in November 1973, 1993 and 2013. There he encounters a mixed-bag of his former companions, some of whom recognise him.

Soon the Doctor realises that the Rani is behind it and, in his fifth body, sends a summons to his other selves to unite. The Rani steps out of the local pub and unleashes her menagerie, but only the time-travellers can see these beasts and antagonists. Flitting from life to life, and with companion after companion accompanying him, he's able to elude the Rani, but Romana is captured. Due to the time-slips, it's Leela that the Seventh Doctor rescues, and yet because it was another Time Lord (Romana) that was placed into the mental "pool", the Doctor is able to invert the Rani's warp-field. Returning to the TARDIS, he rigs up a device using Ace's ghetto-blaster (25.3, "Silver Nemesis") and K9's sensors, and consigns his arch foe to her own technicolor vortex, freeing the severed heads of his first two incarnations from her console room as he does. [You'll have to believe that it took several viewings to sort that out. We demand some kind of award for sitting through it so often.

[Incidentally, perhaps the most sensible gloss on all this comes from the 1994 *New Adventures* novel *First Frontier*, in which the Doctor claims to have a recurring nightmare where all his old enemies chase him round a soap opera.]

Review Everyone knows that this is a disgrace, an abomination, liable to cause internal haemorrhaging and the single worst thing ever palmed off on the public as *Doctor Who*. Everyone is right, but most of them ignore how funny it is.

What we have here is the daftest thing on British television in the 1990s. It's a classic of misjudged enthusiasm, up there with the *Star Wars* 1977 Holiday Special, except with Mike Read and Pam St Clements instead of Itchy and Lumpy[52]. That misfire, however, was the result of people trying to wring money from an unexpectedly lucrative film, and is therefore entirely to be expected. This - even allowing that *Children in Need* relies upon familiar faces doing pointless and embarrassing things, and only works if the gobsmacking *wrongness* of it increases exponentially each year - is right out of left field. The end result besmirches the good intentions of all the people who gave up their time to participate, and it loses a lot of the potential charm a strange one-off like this might have had.

If, however, you get into it with 3D glasses and popcorn, you will know some of the siege mentality that *Doctor Who* fans had to develop in those days. Embrace it, because it's as much a part of the whole package as Fluid Neutralisers, *TV Comic* strips with giant metal wasps and Zebedee University, Dapol's two-armed Davros doll, "K9 and Company", Roberta Tovey and *Totally Doctor Who*. We can't be snobbish. That would mean either rejecting the "classic" series for not having the production values of the McGann movie or the BBC Wales series, or discarding everything after "Survival" as fraudulent and a betrayal of the "spirit" of the series. (Actually, we might accept that as an argument *if* it wasn't at least as true of anything after 3.10, "The War Machines", or 6.7, "The War Games" or 21.6, "The Caves of Androzani" or...)

In other words, this turd of a story may not be canon, but it really happened. This misbegotten gibberish got more viewers than anything "officially" part of *Doctor Who* had since 1985 - and for the public, it was almost exactly like they thought the series always had been. If you can get hold of a copy at all, try to find one with all the other stuff around it: Andi Peters enthusing unconvincingly, Noel Edmonds and his terrible comedy patter with Pertwee, the Pet Shop Boys and the truly amazing part-CGI routine with go-go girls *and* 3D spirals apparently in the same studio and Terry Wogan looking completely bewildered. Better yet, try watching it after a few episodes of *EastEnders*.

It was designed to do a job, and it did it. Kids were helped off drugs and into sheltered accommodation with the money raised. The BBC got a high-profile work-out for an experimental 3D technique, in a context where nobody expected much and a few duff effects were almost obligatory. *Doctor Who* got a *Radio Times* cover for the first time in ten years, and everyone managed to crawl from the wreckage of the debacle over "The Dark Dimension" (see **Background and Stuff**) It's a one-off, a freak and could only have happened in that brief spell when 3D "Magic Eye" posters were "in" and *Doctor Who* was back on the agenda. We shall never look upon its like again. Thank goodness.

Ratings 13.8 million, 13.6 million. These figures are for the overall programme (or in Children in Need's case, the 15-minute segment of the programme) rather than just the "Dimensions in Time" bits.

Cast No one was actually credited for this (they should be so lucky) but the main players were: Jon Pertwee, Tom Baker, Peter Davison, Colin Baker, Sylvester McCoy (the Doctor); Kate O'Mara (the Rani), Sam West (Shagg... er, Cyrian), Sophie Aldred (Ace), Deepak Verma (Sanjay Kapoor), Shobu Kapoor (Gita Kapoor), Bonnie Langford (Melanie), Wendy Richard (Pauline Fowler), Gillian Taylforth (Kathy Beale), Carole Ann Ford (Susan Foreman), Letitia Dean (Sharon Mitchell), Elisabeth Sladen (Sarah Jane Smith), Nicola Bryant (Peri), Sarah Sutton (Nyssa), Pam St Clement (Pat Butcher), Caroline John (Liz Shaw), Nicola Stapleton (Mandy Salter), Richard Franklin (Captain Mike Yates), Nicholas Courtney (Brigadier Lethbridge-Stewart), Adam Woodyatt (Ian Beale), Steve McFadden (Phil Mitchell), Ross Kemp (Grant Mitchell), Lalla Ward (Romana), Mike Reid (Frank Butcher), Deborah Watling (Victoria Waterfield), Louise Jameson (Leela), John Leeson (voice of K9).

Background and Stuff

• First, a word about this version of 3D. Every ten years or so, someone comes up with a new twist on this. Around the time of *Spacehunter: Adventures in the Forbidden Zone*, there was a trial of a system for broadcasting television in the same

system, with offset blue-tinted and red-tinted pictures transmitted on the same screen. It was unwatchable to anyone without the goggles, and in monochrome even if you *did* have some handy, so it was not a hit.

The new process was a massive cheat. Essentially, the brain processes colour and shape differently. It takes fractionally longer for the lobe at the back of the brain to "decode" blue pictures than red pictures. So if you've got a blue lens on your right eye and a red one on the left - or just something on your right eye (half a pair of sunglasses can do it) - then anything moving left-to-right will appear to be in front of anything right to left. So you can show colour TV images that, with the right lenses, get depth so long as everything is going round and round and round anti-clockwise (if it were seen from above). The rest of the picture is unchanged from what would normally be on any programme. (So if they'd persisted, shows like *This Life*, with the hand-held camera revolving around the emoting self-obsessed lawyers, would have been a 3D show. In fact it might have been, but nobody can be bothered to try it.)

So as with SteadiCam (17.1, "Destiny of the Daleks"), Scene-Synch (18.2, "Meglos") and Nicam stereo (25.1, "Remembrance of the Daleks"), the BBC has let *Doctor Who* be a guinea-pig for an experimental process.

• We've got to talk about Adrian Rigelsford. We're so used to having him down as the arch-fibber of fandom (keep reading) that it comes as a shock to find that "The Dark Dimension" was really honestly going to happen. Sort of.

The gist of it is this. BBC Enterprises decided it had been doing so well out of the video releases, they took up the opportunity to make a special for the show's anniversary in 1993. Rigelsford, whose reputation then was fairly good, co-wrote a screenplay and asked his chum Graeme Harper (21.6, "The Caves of Androzani"; 22.6, "Revelation of the Daleks", some episodes of the Welsh series) to direct. With Harper's name attached, there was genuine momentum behind this. And to try to keep it secret, they gave it the code-name "The Environmental Roadshow".

However, rumours started to emerge. At first these were intriguing. It was being shot on a digital system that could look like film, but be as cheap as video. (Actually it wasn't; the proposal was to use super 16mm film and transfer to video for editing and effects.) It was about a powerful force from the Dark Dimension, which was causing the Doctor to be 'unravelled', so the opening scene would have been a coffin with the Seventh Doctor's hat and umbrella on it. This meant they could have Tom Baker as the star, and Sophie Aldred as a science teacher called Dorothy who was suffering memory-losses. The official reason for Baker's prominence was that Peter Davison, Colin Baker and Jon Pertwee would all have too much other work at this stage. Brian Blessed was contacted to play the villain, probably called "Hawkspur" but other names have been mooted. He appears to have shot some test footage, wearing a monk's cowl and pawing the TARDIS in a warehouse. This caused fresh rumours that he was to be the movie Doctor. (There was also talk of David Bowie - but then, there usually is, in this sort of thing.) A production team consisting of many BBC staffers who had worked on the series was being put together, with Kevin Davies (of whom more later) handling post-production and Tony Harding on visual effects. His team included Mike Tucker,who worked on designs for a Special Weapons Dalek and a revised Cyberman, the latter being circulated to DWM and various fanzines.

The storyline has since come into the public domain, and bears many similarities to later Virgin New Adventures (including an archeologist from 2525 called "Summerfield" - they asked k d lang to play her, though possibly only in the writer's imagination) and some BBC Books. It had Ice Warriors, Daleks, Cybermen and the Brigadier, and at the heart of it was a time-paradox and a situation engineered by the Seventh Doctor as a trap (there's a surprise). The more details have emerged, the more tantalising the prospect of this story - especially given its possible status as a 1990s Doctor Who free from 3D gimmicks or TV's Eric Roberts.

So what went wrong? The usual reason given is that Pertwee, Davison and Baker (C) saw scripts that relegated them to bit parts and got their agents to complain. The whole casting procedure had been botched, in fact, but not insuperably. This is certainly true, but isn't the main reason. As we now know, Philip Segal was in negotiations with the BBC on behalf of Amblin and saw the scripts. He thought that it was both too ambitious for the paltry budget and liable to damage any long-term co-production series he could get off the ground. And the budget was pretty puny. £80,000 for pre-production would have been laughable for a mundane show, let alone one with complex effects and extravagant sets. Moreover, when John Nathan-Turner - still in charge of Enterprise's Doctor Who output - was approached to be a consultant, he saw it as a less-good version of something he had wanted to launch. This job was almost non-existent, with himself there as a "fig-leaf", adding his name but with no real input. He refused to become involved. For many observers, Nathan-Turner walking away from a project because he didn't think it was workable was like the canary in the mine-shaft coughing up blood. By July 1993, the BBC had lost confidence.

Rigelsford returned to his previous employment of writing behind-the-scenes books about the old stories (we refuse to call them "non-fiction", as it would appear that his earlier works included made-up interviews with William Hartnell et al). He achieved brief national fame for selling the TV Times an interview with Stanley Kubrick that is now widely regarded as bogus. And he recently spent some time in prison for selling photos he'd "borrowed" from stills archives in national newspapers and the British Library. So when all is said and done, the high-point of Rigelsford's career - unless you count his writing the Big Finish audio "The Roof of the World" - is him sticking his tongue out at Don Henderson (24.3, "Delta and the Bannermen").

• Into the gaping void in the anniversary celebrations came Nathan-Turner. He'd been asked to come up with something for Children in Need and had suggested the multi-Doctor Albert Square romp as a throwaway idea. With the BBC backpedalling on whether the Rigelsford script was ever really a goer (although they'd briefed the press that it was to be shown on Sunday, 28th of November), this took on a wholly different character. The 3D theme, the crossover with Noel's House Party and the "interactive" component all added their own complexities.

• Meanwhile, Kevin Davies got to work on drama clips for the documentary the Late Show team had been asked to make. He had very different ideas to those of the BBC2 Arts strand. He also made brief films for the repeat of "Planet of the Daleks". One, a spoof UNIT recruitment film, was written by Cartmel and Aaronovitch. (It's on the DVD of "Spearhead from Space".) He had previously directed The Making of the Hitchhiker's Guide to the Galaxy for BBC Video, and developed several ideas for documentaries to mark Doctor Who's thirtieth anniversary. These included the Dalek-centric Nation's Creations - proposed for the ITV arts slot *The South Bank Show* - and compilations *Tomb of the Time Lords*, *Doctor Who: The Phenomenon* and *Eulogy for a Doctor*, all of which would feature copious new material with former companion actors reprising their old roles.

Unsurprisingly, the BBC thought that the potential audience for this would be negligible, and the *Late Show* team set about recycling their earlier *Resistance is Useless* piece as items inside Davies' curtailed documentary. Davies was bitterly disappointed with the re-edited version, which was seen by only 4.3 million viewers in a peak time slot. In part, this was because a finished copy was not available for BBC Scotland in time, and in that country it was hastily rescheduled for a later slot on BBC2 the same evening. The following year, BBC Enterprises commissioned Davies to rework the documentary into something closer to his original intentions. This version was released on video in November 1994 as *More Than 30 Years in the TARDIS*, and it sold well and set off a mini-boom in direct-to-video *Doctor Who* documentaries such as *I Was a Doctor Who Monster*, *Doctor Who's Lust in Space* (less fun than it sounds) and Davies' own *Dalekmania* (see B2, *Daleks Invasion Earth 2150 A.D.*).

• The phone-in vote between episodes allowed viewers to chose which *EastEnders* character would aid the Doctor's escape from the Rani in the second episode. The choice was between Mandy (a prominent regular character on the series) and Big Ron (basically a long-standing extra). Unsurprisingly, the former eased out the latter and the version with Ron Tarr has never been seen (Tarr himself had previously done *Doctor Who* as an extra in 17.1, "Destiny of the Daleks".) Also unseen were a Dalek and Dalek trooper among the Rani's menagerie. This was on the instructions of Terry Nation's agents, who presumably weren't fazed by cries of "but it's for charideeee". Additionally, roughly two minutes of material were cut from the second episode on the instructions of Noel Edmonds. *Noel's House Party* revolved around minor celebrities getting gunged and the antics of Mr. Blobby (a giant pink gibbering slapstick goon played by Barry Killerby, also the arch-villain in a well-known series of fan-produced audios), but it's nice to know that its host was not completely unembarrasable.

• The negotiations for all this would have been a quagmire if not for the charitable aspect, but were waived on condition that after "Dimensions in Time" was shown, it would never be broadcast or made available to the public in any form whatsoever again. Nevertheless, Nathan-Turner managed to get it shown at a convention in the USA, for the benefit of all those unlucky Americans who might otherwise never have seen it.

• The 3D gimmick was decided upon for 1993's *Children in Need* before anyone thought of bringing in *Doctor Who*. Nathan-Turner was originally approached about producing a five-minute 3D sketch in April 1993. He had recently left BBC Enterprises, where he had largely been concerned with supervising special releases (such as the reconstruction of 17.6, "Shada", and the release of episodes from incomplete 1960s stories). Enterprises had shelved many of Nathan-Turner's plans for thirtieth anniversary videos, and he was personally aggrieved to be offered a script consultancy on "The Dark Dimension" after having a similar project of his own rejected. He accepted the *Children in Need* job as his (latest) farewell performance on *Doctor Who*.

• The exact name of Nathan-Turner's collaborator on the script has sometimes caused confusion: David Roden Mansell was an actor and had been obliged to adopt the name David Roden under Equity rules. He had been submitting scripts to Nathan-Turner after seeing him lecture on writing for television, and was the first name the producer thought of when he realised that he would need a co-writer for the sketch. Roden's initial idea was "Destination: Holocaust", in which the Seventh Doctor and the Brigadier battled Cybermen in the English countryside, but Nathan-Turner felt this was too ambitious and effects-heavy. Roden later reworked it as "A Quiet Day in the Country", a sketch performed live at a *Doctor Who* at Longleat House on Sunday, 18th of August, 1996. This featured Nicholas Courtney, Roden himself as 'Sergeant Fenton', Cybermen and lots of pyrotechnics. (Less than a month later, the *Doctor Who* exhibition at Longleat burned down, but we don't believe this was in any way suspicious and fully accept the official account that a faulty replica K9 was to blame.)

Ideally the sketch would be made entirely on location and feature a single distinctive antagonist (which meant that old and often tatty monster costumes in BBC stock would not be needed). Initially this would have been the Master, but Anthony Ainley proved unavailable and so the Rani was substituted. Her henchman was named

Cyrian after the actor the team wanted for the role: Sir Ian McKellan. Ponder this for a moment.

• It was Nathan-Turner who suggested the *EastEnders* connection. The suggestion of featuring all the surviving Doctors came from Michael Leggo, producer of *Noel's House Party*; by now "The Dark Dimension" had been cancelled, so this was no longer a logistical problem. Roden hoped to direct the sketch himself, but was overruled by *Children in Need*. Stuart McDonald would handle the pre-recorded sketch as well as supervising the live event on the night. Nathan-Turner and Roden developed a second storyline featuring the Celestial Toymaker - "The Endgame" - as a back-up if the *EastEnders* scenario failed to work out. This would have been made at Chessington World of Adventure, and Roden hoped to persuade Michael Gough, with whom he'd recently appeared in Derek Jarman's *Wittgenstein* (a film oddly more like *Doctor Who* than this mess) to reprise his role as the Toymaker.

• The large cast proved difficult to co-ordinate, and it was the disparate *Doctor Who* contingent rather than the *EastEnders* regulars who were the problem. Peter Davison, Kate O'Mara and Bonnie Langford all had prior commitments that needed to be juggled, Tom Baker was (as always) unhappy with the script, while Louise Jameson just had reservations. Frazer Hines had to pull out at the last minute due to an unexpected overrun on *Emmerdale*, and was replaced by Carole Ann Ford. A lot of the story was dictated by cast availability, with McDonald's crew only having the run of the Albert Square backlot for two days in September.

In the confusion following the cancellation of "The Dark Dimension", reports of former companions being touted to reprise their roles (e.g. Katy Manning, who was unavailable) were misinterpreted by fans as a sign that the special might be salvageable after all. Once reports of "Dimensions in Time" began to leak out, the BBC moved swiftly to dispel the impression that this was a disappointing substitute for "The Dark Dimension" or a serious revival of *Doctor Who*. Against Nathan-Turner's wishes, the sketch wasn't assigned a formal production code and was described in BBC publicity material as a 'pantomime'.

• Tom Baker was required only on the first of the four-day production, Tuesday, 21st of September, at Fountain TV Studios where the TARDIS interiors were taped. The original TARDIS set had been destroyed after "The Greatest Show in the Galaxy" (25.4), but a new version had been built for PanoptiCon 93 just over a fortnight earlier and was supplied by Andrew Beech. Before this became available, the plan had been to CSO the actors into a model. Baker made some very eccentric suggestions - which were completely ignored - for playing his brief scene as the Doctor, and he had to wear the Season Eighteen version of his costume (which he described as "the shitty one"). This day also saw the TV debut of one-time *Doctor Who* Appreciation Society member Sam West, who may still harbour the ambition of playing the Doctor (and may yet get the chance). The next two days were devoted to Albert Square scenes, during which Jon Pertwee was appalled to discover how ill his old friend Wendy Richard looked, not realising she'd been made up as an old woman for the 2013 sequence.

• From the point of view of *EastEnders* producer Leonard Lewis, the main logistical problem with the shoot was that most of his cast wanted to be in it. As *EastEnders* was being made for twice-weekly broadcasts at the time, this would have been impractical. Long-term *Who* fan Adam Woodyatt made a very brief appearance in the special despite being busy with his regular role. According to Gary Downie's account, the attention his regulars paid to "Dimensions in Time" annoyed Lewis, leading to friction between the two. Downie would later single out three other groups who caused problems for the production: fans, who were playing monsters or supplying props and costumes by request (Downie suspected they were bitching about the show behind his back); the BBC (who allegedly insisted that their facilities be paid for, while everyone else was chipping in free of charge); and *Children in Need* itself (no reason given, but he claimed he never again donated so much as a penny to them).

• Aside from the *EastEnders* backlot, the principal locations were in Greenwich, including the Cutty Sark and the Maritime Museum for the final day of recording. Louise Jameson's scenes were among the last to be taped, and she appeared only on condition that she wouldn't be forced to wear Leela's costume from the original series. Eventually she appeared in a modified Hiawatha costume that was improvised on the day. It shows.

• Keff McCulloch returned to provide incidental music for the sketch, but not the revised version of the theme tune. Plans to commission a new interpretation from the Pet Shop Boys or

ABOUT TIME

Erasure fell through (both were "too busy", though *Children in Need* vetoed an interim plan to use the former's *Forever in Love* with the McCoy title sequence). The "rave" version was eventually the work of a duo called Cybertech, who had submitted a demo tape to Nathan-Turner, and who later released a CD of music inspired by Virgin's *New Adventures* (which mysteriously failed to chart). Early reports indicated that a variation of the *EastEnders* titles would be used, with additional animation of the TARDIS zooming towards London, E18, but ultimately a hyperactive take on the McCoy titles were used instead. This featured the only credit on the entire production - for Nathan-Turner and Roden as writers.

• The other *Doctor Who* event for the thirtieth anniversary was a new radio serial, "The Paradise of Death", broadcast on Radio 5 over the summer. This reunited Jon Pertwee, Elisabeth Sladen and Nicholas Courtney in a script by Barry Letts, and was deemed successful enough to be worth repeating. The following year, a second Letts script was recorded with the same cast. "Doctor Who and the Ghosts of N-Space" was intended to air early in 1995 (now on Radio 2, since the fifth channel had since converted to a rolling news / sport programme) but vanished from the schedule. It was finally aired early in 1996 on the back of the announcement of 27.0, "The TV Movie". The BBC's lacklustre response to the second serial - combined with Pertwee's death later the same year - killed off *Doctor Who* on radio, at least for a time (but see A2, "The Curse of Fatal Death" for a further twist).

• Perhaps surprisingly, this piece of car-crash television *was* John Nathan-Turner's final substantial contribution to a series that he'd found impossible to put behind him. He continued to organise and supervise *Doctor Who* exhibitions, and also wrote a long account of his time on the series that was serialised in *DWM* between 1995 and 1997, and later released as an audiobook by Big Finish. He died in 2002.

Influence   Well, 3D TV never really caught on. *Children in Need* continues, and still finds ways to incorporate *Doctor Who*, as the so-called "Pudsey Cutaway" from 2005 demonstrates. Moreover, the Comic Relief charity took up the baton in 1999, as we will see.

It must be borne in mind, however, that this was part of a wider re-think of the series' status.

That autumn, the Friday night schedule was a throwback to Saturdays in 1973 - arguably *Doctor Who*'s annus mirabilis - as re-runs of "Planet of the Daleks" (with Kevin Davies' five-minute documentaries preceding each) were followed by a surprise hit, a revived *Generation Game* with original host Bruce Forsythe showing he still had "it". BBC1 head Alan Yentob was clearly thinking beyond the category of "Cult" and looking to broader appeal. Yentob was interviewed in the original transmitted version of *Thirty Years in the TARDIS*, shown a week before the anniversary. This was a curious beast; partly a sneering retrospective by the *Late Show* team, and partly a nostalgic evocation of how it felt to grow up with the series by indulgent celebrities. Re-staged famous moments were used to introduce interviews with former personnel, but the narrative device of a small boy running around the streets and seeing post-boxes turn into Daleks allowed a glimpse of what the series could look like with 1990s effects and a budget. Yentob was deliberately very cagey about future plans. With hindsight we can see why, but also why this the Pertwee repeat and "Dimensions in Time" were deployed to re-introduce the series to a new generation on BBC1, not shoved into the ghetto of kitsch reruns on BBC 2.

A2: "Doctor Who and the Curse of Fatal Death"

Produced by Sue Vertue, Written by Steven Moffat, Directed by John Henderson. BBC, Four Episodes, all five minutes (except part four, seven minutes), 12th of March 1999.

Provenance   Since 1985, when comedy stars did their bit for African famine aid by doing a *Live Aid*-style concert, the Comic Relief charity has done a telethon every two years - raising millions for good causes here and abroad. One regular telethon strand was spoofing popular drama series, often with the original stars as part of the draw. People across the country do silly things (usually themed around clowns' noses), or simply buy special tie-in products. *Doctor Who* was suggested by *Red Nose Day 1999* producer Sue Vertue. One of her two *Doctor Who* connections is that she's the daughter of Beryl Vertue (Terry Nation's one-time agent, which might explain how the Daleks were finally able to make their charidee debut). Her other connection with the series? We'll explain later.

Things to Watch Out For in
"Doctor Who and the Curse of Fatal Death"...

1. Part of the point of this enterprise is to have all the things we've secretly thought we'd like to see happen - or asked why they didn't - all in one go. So the Doctor arranges pre-emptive escapes through time-paradoxes, becomes romantically involved with his assistant, retires from saving the universe and flatly refuses to take the Master seriously. Oh, and he farts a lot. The Master is, in this version, unable even to gloat coherently. An entire episode is built around the cop-out 'I'll explain later' (as in when the Doctor's companion Emma asks why Dalek spaceships have chairs). Another is given over to the Doctor regenerating four times in ten minutes.

But the thing is, it's our fond memories of the series that make it funny. Not once is there a "Daleks can't climb stairs" gag or anything about wobbly sets or naff effects. Some might argue that if the 1980s series had achieved the production values of this one - and the same light touch with the dialogue - there would have been no need to do this as a one-off fundraiser, as *Doctor Who* would still have been going. One cliffhanger relies on us expecting there to only be three Daleks and seeing thirty.

2. The people involved mainly had similar affection for the project (one didn't, having grown up overseas, but oddly he seems to have got the hang of it very quickly). The music is all sourced from old episodes, and there are about thirty different cues. Roy Skelton is called back in to do Dalek voices one last time.

The Doctor(s) Is now in his ninth life, and is stylish but still recognisably dressed as a Doctor [the clothes all came from high-street stores, but were combined oddly]. He's softly-spoken, has collar-length hair and a calm - if not downright smug - manner. [His later incarnations will be dealt with in due course.]

The Master states there is no limit to how many lives the Doctor can have.

Fellow Travellers

• *Emma*. No surname is given, and she's perhaps slightly too plump to get away with that mini, but she has a neat line in put-downs and smart come-backs. We don't make her acquaintance long enough to see if she lives up to the Doctor's description of her, although we've no reason to doubt that she's "more exciting than any sand-quarry".

Baddies

• *The Master*. Begins by wearing a high-collared cloak like the one modelled by TV's Eric Roberts [see 27.0, "The TV Movie"]. He is a ranting, borderline-hysterical egoist, whose frustration with the Doctor's effortless superiority makes him deliver infantile threats and add the suffix "of doom" to things. He begins as a hybrid of Delgado and Ainley, but the later remodelling (after 936 years of crawling around sewers) is pure Season Eight. [Except for his, um, Etheric Beam Locators, which are Dalek baubles on his chest... there's two of them, like a bikini top.] The Doctor's noble sacrifice towards the end has him renouncing villainy and seeking to emulate the Doctor's example. [Yes, it sounds implausible, but the Daleks also give the Doctor a free pardon after his decision to end his career saving his arch-enemies, and only something like this can begin to account for the odd set-up at the beginning of "The TV Movie".]

Ratings 9.8 million, 9.4 million, 5.8 million, 8.7 million.

Cast Rowan Atkinson, Richard E. Grant, Jim Broadbent, Hugh Grant, Joanna Lumley (the Doctor); Julia Sawalha (Emma); Jonathan Pryce (the Master); Roy Skelton, David Sargent (Daleks' Voices). [n.b. The video release credits Dave Chapman (alias Otis the Aardvark; please don't ask!), not Sargent, as doing Dalek voices. Historian Andrew Pixley follows suit, but there was fallout about this in the *DWM* lettercol. Since there weren't any credits in the broadcast version, we've gone with what *seems* like the accurate version.]

Plot The Master gloats that he has set a trap for his arch-nemesis, the Doctor, on Zaston IV. The Doctor, who can hear this over the TARDIS communication rig, suggests instead that they meet on Tersurus, as he has an announcement to make. On arriving at the castle, the Doctor explains that the Tersurons were a wise and benign race shunned by the rest of the cosmos merely because they communicated via flatulence. They have been extinct for a century. The Master arrives and rants for a bit, but then the Doctor announces that as he has now saved every planet an average of twenty-seven times, he's retiring to marry his traveling companion Emma. The Master is a bit put out by this, and states that he went back in time a century to discuss the building of the castle they're in with its architect, and has put a death trap exactly where the Doctor and Emma are standing. He springs this, only to find that the Doctor had a similar chat and 'The Spikes of Doom' were replaced by 'The Sofa of Reasonable Comfort'. The Master resorts to Plan B, a trap-door leading to the legendarily filthy sewers of this planet, and announces, 'Farewell, Mr and Mrs Doctor...'

Episode two begins with the Master realising that the Doctor had *another* visit with the architect, and had the trap-door moved to right under the lever that the Master is pulling. The Master plummets into the depths, only to return moments later - aged and smelly - after spending three hundred and twelve years crawling through sewage, and another ten minutes finding his TARDIS and returning to this time. Seconds later, he falls down the open manhole *again*. He returns 624 years older than at the start of the adventure. With him are a contingent of Daleks, who don't mind the smell because they lack noses, but one of them accidentally knocks the Master back down again. A now-seriously aged Master, with a Zimmer frame, joins the chase after our heroes. The Doctor leads Emma through the tunnels to what he thinks is a safe exit, but behind the doors he opens are thirty Daleks...

So Episode Three begins with them tied to chairs on a Dalek spaceship. The rejuvenated Master is helping the Daleks conquer space and time with a Zectronic energy beam. They plan to exterminate the Master when his usefulness is ended. The Doctor, knowing that the Master can speak Tersuron well enough to bribe architects, and that the Daleks can't smell anything, warns his arch-rival. A skirmish breaks out and the Doctor is caught by a stray energy-bolt. He begins to regenerate...

... into an arrogant, Byronic figure (Richard E Grant) who loves himself and who is amused to find that the Daleks ('these metal gits') need his help. Zectronic energy will cause a massive implosion, destabilising the cosmos, and the Doctor is the only one who can stop it. Just as he has almost finished, and whilst Emma is fetching champagne, he fuses the controls. Emma steps out of

the TARDIS to find a new Doctor, a bumbling, gauche chap (Jim Broadbent) who is girl-shy and clumsy enough to die again seconds later. The next Doctor calmly suggests that he should've unplugged it before trying to fix it. He emerges from the smoke to reveal a charming, dashing Doctor who looks uncannily like Hugh Grant (to which Emma adds, 'Result!').

As the celebrations begin, a surge of Zectronic energy hits the Doctor. The Master says that this would be powerful enough to remove the power of regeneration. He renounces evil as a mark of respect for his fallen comrade. The Daleks also honour their greatest enemy's sacrifice. Emma refuses to believe that the Universe would let the Doctor die. Her faith is proved right as, against all the odds, his features glow and shift into those of Joanna Lumley. This new Doctor is confused as to how etheric beam locators have been grafted onto "his" chest, but soon works out that the engagement is off. However, she is now strangely drawn to her former adversary. 'Why do they call you "the Master"?' she asks. 'I'll explain later' he replies, laughing evilly...

Status

• *Canonicity.* None at all, but that didn't stop avenging spods writing it to complain that this was a BBC plot to use up the Doctor's remaining lives and prevent a new series. (If they'd paid attention, though, they might have heard the Master proclaim that Time Lords have 'many, many' lives. Sometimes, even *we* think that the trainspotter cliché is unduly generous to these creeps.)

• *Deviation.* The pronunciation of Tersurus has shifted since Chancellor Goth was there (14.3, "The Deadly Assassin"). Obviously, with hindsight, the timeline that unfolds here is antithetical to that of the BBC Wales series, but at the time there was nothing to stop it. With the Daleks appealing to the Doctor for help, the Master in yet-another new body and several regenerations taking us from the Ninth to the Thirteenth Doctor (assuming Atkinson was playing No. Nine), we're not in the same situation that has emerged since X1.1, "Rose". Even so, subsequent developments in the "official" series have vindicated several of the ideas first hinted at here. The main one that remains a no-no is the Doctor using time-paradoxes to pre-emptively get himself out of bother. Another is that he's vulnerable after regeneration, and makes mistakes that cause another death and another and so on. The new and unexpected "fifteen hours" trick that the Doctor uses to grow a new hand (X2.0, "The Christmas Invasion") means that the last three Doctors in "The Curse of Fatal Death" would probably have been unnecessary.

Review   We've talked a lot about the "spirit" and "letter" of *Doctor Who*, and this is another example. The makers of "The TV Movie" made an episode of a bog-standard US series, and stuffed it with references to things that had happened in *Doctor Who*. Here we've got a deliberate attempt to wreck continuity, but if you can measure "*Who*ness" and correlate it to minutes of screen-time, this wins over anything you'll see in this volume, even "The Greatest Show in the Galaxy" (25.4).

Comparison with McCoy is apt: Atkinson's low-key performance here is closer to the Seventh Doctor than any of the others, and his musing over the cruelty and injustice of the Universe is at times unnervingly close to Season Twenty-Six. The willingness to engage with the supposed glory days of the 1970s is here too. There's a key difference between this and even 26.4, "Survival", though. Whilst the Daleks are taken seriously (even if they get to deliver one good joke), the Master is the butt of all the jokes. This script takes the concept out into a back alley and gives it the good kicking it deserves. Richard E Grant, as the newly-regenerated Tenth Doctor, remembers the Master as 'ah yes, the camp one'. Jonathan Pryce has nailed the character in one go: this is a man who realises that he is a pretty useless villain, and has wasted his life trying to be bad - something for which he has no aptitude - but can't stop now.

The thing about parody is that it's a form of criticism, based on laying bare the things behind the production. "The Runaway Bride" (X3.0) factored in the fictional public's collective amnesia about repeated invasions and the need to run up and down lots of corridors, but only after spoofs had made both untenable. Parodies say the unsayable, and so we have time-paradox *deus ex machina* escapes that would render almost all previous stories devoid of any tension, open mocking of the Master's rants and ambitions, admission that the Doctor only rushes around saving planets because he's not met the right girl, and an ungushing statement that the BBC was blitheringly stupid to end the series.

Nobody puts a foot wrong, but the real surprise is how much it looks like Hugh Grant is living out a childhood dream to play the Doctor. Atkinson is comfortable in the role too, but he should be: at least two episodes of *Blackadder* had him this calm and in control when confronting ranting villains. (*Blackadder's Christmas Carol* has several other *Doctor Who* connections, and the final episode of *Blackadder II* sees him effectively play the Doctor to Hugh Laurie's Master.) Richard E Grant spends ninety seconds in the role, but makes more of an impression that his *Withnail* costar Paul McGann did in an hour. McGann and Grant were later given second chances to play the Doctor on audio, and in Grant's case - "The Scream of the Shalka" webcast - the Doctor gets to be animated (so he deserves more than a footnote, but not a whole entry here). It's often said that his performance here is how Colin Baker's should have gone; that's not fair on either of them, but it's certainly more promising than his online attempt. Jim Broadbent, who'd been a parody Doctor before, plays a completely different character to the one he did in the Victoria Wood skit where he defeated Crayola - either could easily have worked in the series proper. Joanna Lumley defies the expectation that she'd be a slinky mystic like she was in *Sapphire & Steel*, and plays the Doctor as a jolly-hockey-sticks keener, wanting to go off and have adventures.

Within the context of *Children in Need*, we forgave "Dimensions in Time" a great deal. Within the context of *Comic Relief*, we have to admit that this story went as far as it could. We'd all rather have this in the canon than the McGann Movie.

Background and Stuff

• *Comic Relief* had been around since 1986, with the *Red Nose Day* telethons beginning on BBC1 in 1988. (Viewers were exhorted to buy and wear uncomfortable plastic noses to wear on the day.) "The Curse of Fatal Death" wasn't the first big *Doctor Who* connection. In 1991, two pages of *The Totally Stonking, Surprisingly Educational and Utterly Mindboggling... Comic Relief Comic* had been devoted to a crossover between (on the one hand) all seven Doctors, various companions and monsters and (on the other) Dan Dare, Digby, the Mekon and the Treens. [See **What Kind of Future Did We Expect?** under 2.3, "The Rescue".] This historic meeting was marred by Terry Nation withholding the rights to the Daleks (two years later, he did it again - see A1, "Dimensions in Time"), who are implied purely by off-panel cries of 'Exterminate! Exterminate!' and (later) 'Donate! Donate!'

• Rowan Atkinson was the first choice to play the Doctor in the proposed sketch, and the actor was keen. (Atkinson had previously expressed an interest in playing the Doctor, but then so has everyone in Equity. More interestingly, he went from "Doctor Who and the Curse of Fatal Death" to a time-travelling special edition of his most famous role, in *Blackadder Back & Forth*, AKA The One Good Thing About the Millennium Experience[53]). Compared to "Dimensions in Time", putting the *Comic Relief* special together seems to have been comparatively straightforward.

• Steven Moffat was an obvious choice to write the sketch, as he was a) a *Doctor Who* fan and b) Mr Sue Vertue. Moffat had written the definitive kids' show of the previous decade, *Press Gang*, but was then known as a writer of sitcom / farces *Joking Apart* and *Chalk*. He'd previously authored what's sometimes regarded as the best *Doctor Who* short story ever made ("Continuity Errors", for Virgin's *Decalog* series in the mid-1990s), and he was (and is) a regular presence at the Fitzroy Tavern. (Newcomers will be able to identify him by the inevitable crowd of adoring women clustered around his person.) As we've seen, Moffat set out to write a comic version of the series based around recognisable icons that could, at a pinch, be seen as an authentic part of the series rather than another spoof. In the meantime, enthusiasm for the idea at *Comic Relief* meant that the production escalated from a two-minute sketch into one of the major elements of the telethon.

• The idea of ending the sketch with multiple regenerations meant that high profile actors could cameo in the role. Moffat's script suggested Colin Firth (as 'the New Doctor'), Mel Smith ('the Plump Doctor', later 'the Bashful Doctor'), Lee Evans ('the Geeky Doctor', later dropped) and Robson Green ('the Gorgeous Doctor'). It appears that the production team had very little trouble finding the stars they wanted, even those - like Jonathan Pryce - who were expected to turn it down. Julia Sawalha had previously auditioned to play a companion (Ace or the Season Twenty-Seven girl Kate Tollinger, depending on who you ask) before becoming famous in *Press Gang*.

• Recording took place over three days in February 1999 at Pinewood Studios, the use of the stage being donated free of charge. Fans sup-

plied the TARDIS set and various Daleks; ultimately, more working Dalek props were used in this than had appeared in much of the series proper. Recording was covered by a documentary crew, *Doctor Who Magazine* and the *Radio Times* (though Victoria Wood got the cover slot). The Master and Emma's costumes were later auctioned - along with other props and items from the production - via *Doctor Who Magazine*, thus granting the world the sadly unforgettable image of *DWM* deputy editor Alan Barnes dressed in Sawalha's skirt and tights.

• Apart from Richard E. Grant, who we'll deal with shortly, the Doctor cameos were all recorded on the final day. At this point, Jim Broadbent was as familiar a face on British TV as any, but was still a couple of years away from winning an Oscar for *Iris*; Joanna Lumley was fresh (if that's the word) from playing Patsy in hit sitcom *Absolutely Fabulous* (which also starred Sawalha); and Hugh Grant was ... oh, you know about him. (Russell T. Davies later offered Grant the role of the Ninth Doctor in the 2005 series, but he turned it down - a decision the actor has since said he regrets.)

• By the end of recording, it was clear that the finished story was going to be longer than expected. The plan had been to show the sketch in two parts, but these would have been longer than ten minutes each, which might stall the overall pace of the telethon. One solution was to cut it further into three segments, beginning with a ten-minute episode one (which is how it was billed in *Radio Times*), but ultimately it would be shown in four parts. The video release - which followed in September - reverts to two longer episodes and rejigs the title sequence (dropping the 'and' from the title in the process). With a total running time somewhere under twenty-five minutes, the official video release was bulked out with what we'd now call "extras", including the making-of documentary *Doctor Who Uncovered*, but also three other BBC-produced *Who* spoofs from the mid-1980s. Of these, the most familiar was from *The Lenny Henry Show*, the most relevant was Jim Broadbent's confrontation with Crayola in *Victoria Wood: As Seen on TV Special*, and the longest was *French & Saunders'* unbroadcast attempt to wring humour from "The Trial of a Time Lord". (This was less funny than the original, so deserved to have been "lost".)

• Richard E. Grant had grown up in Swaziland and had barely heard of *Doctor Who* before. His best known role (then and now) was alongside Paul McGann in the cultiest of cult films, *Withnail & I* (1986), which - since the third lead is Richard Griffiths, made an honorary Doctor by *Doctor Who Magazine* (see the essay with 26.4, "Surivival") - could be regarded as a kind of alternate version of "The Three Doctors" (10.1). As we've mentioned, Grant would play the Doctor again and in a rather more serious capacity than this, but how we get there is a long story...

• After the Barry Letts serials of the mid-1990s (see A1, "Dimensions in Time"), there were various half-hearted attempts to relaunch *Doctor Who* on radio. One of these, called "Death Comes to Time", made it as far as a pilot recording that reunited Sylvester McCoy and Sophie Aldred, but was promptly rejected by BBC Radio. Unperturbed, producer Dan Freedman convinced BBC Online to release the pilot via the Internet in 2001. This proved frustratingly popular, and the rest of the serial was commissioned for webcast the following year.

Freedman was now confident enough to announce that this was all part of his grand plan to return *Doctor Who* to the telly. However, the finished serial was incoherent and a more shameless grafting of *Doctor Who* onto sub-*Star Wars* bibble than even John Leekley could have imagined (see 27.0, "The TV Movie") and bizarrely ended with the McCoy Doctor's death. Script editor Nev Fountain was the first to leave the sinking ship, claiming he had no idea that the script - attributed to the elusive "Colin Meek" - was actually by Freedman himself.

Nevertheless, BBC Online felt they were onto a winner with webcasts and turned to Big Finish - purveyors of licensed direct-to-CD audio plays since 1999 - for the next two serials: "Real Time" (starring Colin Baker) in 2002 and a leaden adaptation of 17.6, "Shada" (starring Paul McGann and an all-star cast) in 2003. Plans for a fourth serial, to be produced in-house, were considerably more ambitious...

"Scream of the Shalka", by Paul Cornell, was going to be the fortieth anniversary story, and the first of many featuring the new, genuine, 100% official Ninth Doctor as played by Richard E. Grant. He had two new companions: Alison (Sophie Okenedo) and, er, a robot version of the Master played by Sir Derek Jacobi (see X3.11, "Utopia"). Odd though this sounds, "Shalka" was a serious deal. The three earlier webcasts had fea-

tured very crude flash animation that looked rather less dynamic than *Bleep & Booster* (but without Peter Hawkins or the Radiophonic Workshop as backup). This time, the UK's foremost animation studio, Cosgrove Hall, were hired to provide something classier (as they had done for another BBC web serial, "Ghosts of Albion", earlier the same year). "Scream of the Shalka" was trailed heavily on television when it appeared over November / December 2003, but by now events had already been outstripped it. Announcements about a new TV series from BBC Wales made the webcasts redundant, and Grant's rather humourless and self-proclaimedly eccentric "Ninth Doctor" has not been heard since. Cosgrove Hall, however, won several industry plaudits for the animation, and got the gig to reconstitute the missing episodes of "The Invasion" (6.3) with funding left-over from the proposed "Shalka" sequel. A far cry from the late 70s, when they were being sued for re-using tracks from the album *Doctor Who Sound Effects in Danger Mouse*.

Comic Relief cemented its links with *Doctor Who* in the 2007 telethon, wherein Catherine Tate and David Tennant were reunited (see "The Runaway Bride") and Tennant played himself in an elaborate sight-gag with Billie Piper's estranged husband Chris Evans. A tie-in edition of *The Beano* went further and united two of Britain's most beloved institutions, as the Bash Street Kids saw off a Dalek and the Doctor had to face the far more daunting menace of School Dinner. If you don't understand that last sentence, it really isn't worth our while trying to explain it.

Influence Well the obvious thing is that the best episodes of the BBC Wales series (so far) have been by Moffatt. In these and others, the Doctor is far more confident about his effect on girls, and seems not to mind being desired.

appendix b

B1: "Dr. Who and the Daleks"

(Aaru Productions 1965, Directed by Gordon Flemyng, Screenplay by Milton Subotsky from a story by Terry Nation, Produced by Milton Subotsky and Max J. Rosenberg. Eighty-two minutes, colour)

Provenance The first film version of the series, and one made in an era before video - so they could remake a transmitted story bigger, louder and in colour. The screenplay is derived from the script of "The Daleks" (1.2) but tweaked somewhat. It was made by Aaru productions, but has so many similarities with the cheap British-made early sixties Amicus films that it's usually bracketed in with them. Producer / writer Milton Subotsky was also guilty for perpetrating perplexing teen flicks like *It's Trad, Dad!*, and inflicting the notorious 1980 TV miniseries of Ray Bradbury's *The Martian Chronicles* on us. You might remember him from such Doug McClure films as *The Land That Time Forgot* and *At the Earth's Core* (which were made a decade later than the Dalek flicks but show that, for Subotsky at least, very little had changed in the interim). He redeemed himself partially with 1980s *The Monster Club*.

We're in an era when the British film industry was almost perpetually turning out fantasy adventure romps, either set in the late nineteenth century or - in the case of Hammer studios - in a mittel-European nation that might as well be in the late nineteenth century. One of these was Jacques Tourneur's last feature, *City Beneath the Sea*, from the Poe poem but adapted by David Whitaker. This has more in common with *Dr. Who and the Daleks* than might seem obvious, especially all the malarkey in tunnels and caves. The 1960 George Pal version of *The Time Machine* cannot be overlooked as an influence, not just visually and rhetorically, but in making this look like a sure-fire winner at the box-office. We're also in the era of portmanteau films, four or five chilling tales linked by a narrative gimmick (Subotsky did a lot of these as well). In these, Peter Cushing was increasingly getting away from typecasting as Baron Frankenstein or Van Helsing, and was instead playing character parts.

Things to Watch Out For in "Dr. Who and the Daleks"...

1. The Daleks are post-synched. Nobody told the actors inside the shells that the dialogue would be spoken in time to the lights on their heads, and so some of them are flashing at random and the voice artistes are hes I tatingtofit all the dia logue totheflashes (in a vocal technique later developed by Captain Kirk and Tony Blair).

2. Ian Chesterton is played by entertainer Roy Castle. We know him best for children's television, such as the curious show *Record Breakers* (in which he and the editors of the Guinness book, notorious twins Ross and Norris McWhirter, set about investigating record holders and setting some new ones). He was also a jazz trumpeter and played several other instruments, could tap-dance, sing and probably levitate objects by mental power. Yes, he was *that* gifted. So why did his agent keep trying to make him appear in bad films as the comic stooge?

At least one other film has him and Peter Cushing together - Cushing as a mysterious doctor and Castle as a doofus. (This is the almost-legendary *Doctor Terror's House of Horrors*, which really *was* made by Amicus, and also has Alan Freeman menaced by couchgrass - unconvincing? Not 'arf! - and Donald Sutherland marrying a vampire. Castle plays a character whose troubles begin when he buys a packet of cigarettes - tragically, this is a little ironic, as he died in 1994 from lung cancer.) For the first half of the film, Castle is playing the juve lead as Norman Wisdom might have done. Thereafter he keeps it real and is much better. (We're reminded of his best screen role, in *Carry On Up the Khyber* - yes, again - where he's the straight man and thus an awful lot funnier, especially in drag in a harem.)

3. Everyone calls the protagonist 'Doctor Who'. To his face. He uses the name himself. It's odd the first few times, but soon gets to be almost charmingly daft. It must be in the phone book under "W", and we presume the house is in his name.

4. There comes a moment when the Thals have to be persuaded to take up arms. On television, this took Ian and Barbara the better part of an episode to debate and organise, but here it's a quick trick pulled by the Doctor. *This* Ian is

appalled by the Doctor's suggestion that they hand Dyoni over to the Daleks. Some viewers were amazed to hear Ian be so outspoken in his criticism, and to see the Doctor merrily wink at him in reply. In fact it's Roy Castle's residual northern accent at fault: the line, as written, is "Doctor, you can't!"

5. In similar vein, the assault on the Dalek citadel is detected and the Thal party is apprehended in the lifts. One Dalek, on recognising the star of *Record Breakers*, appears to shout "Stay where you are - you are crap!" It even looks as though they paralysed his legs to stop him tap-dancing.

It's alleged that a young Donald Sutherland is one of the Thals. We've never spotted him, but with all that make-up it's hardly surprising. They do look like they've gone clubbing in 1981. In fact, the majority of the extras were Covent Garden porters - big macho chaps whose objections to make-up were assuaged by extra payments and having the make-up girls shave their chests and arms. Nevertheless, some of the "blond giants" look a little uncomfortable.

6. The Dalek City seems to be made mainly from shower-curtains. Charmingly, the hi-tech scanners dotted around the place have rabbit-ears TV aerials. The predominant colour scheme is beige and salmon-pink. This reminds us of the fact that when this was made, prawn cocktail was considered the height of sophistication.

The Doctor Doctor Who lives in a nice little cottage with his granddaughters, and potters around inventing. He's devised a time machine, which he shows to his elder grandchild's new boyfriend on their first date. For reasons best known to himself, he's disguised his device as a police box and keeps it at the bottom of his garden. It's bigger on the inside than on the outside, but has no central control panel, yet he keeps it primed for use. Nevertheless he lives in this cottage, and reads *The Eagle*.

Uniquely, this Doctor has a moustache [though see 18.1, "The Leisure Hive"]. He has slight arthritis, and walks with a stoop. He has pince nez glasses on a blue ribbon, and wears Edwardian velveteen jacket and waistcoat. Unlike his supposedly callous TV counterpart, this Doctor shows no remorse at having to choose the Thals to live and the Daleks to die. He doesn't even offer any sympathy [although this time, the Daleks don't plead with him for help]. He tends to wink at people.

Fellow Travellers Doctor Who's grandchildren, Susan Who and Barbara Who, live with him. Barbara has a new boyfriend, Ian Chesterton, who is eager to please. He's also clumsy.

Susie Who [sorry, but that's probably her surname] is an eight-year-old girl who finds fault with technical books of relativity. She's seen reading Eric Rogers' *Physics for the Inquiring Mind* [it's a real book, by a Princeton professor, and is highly recommended]. She wears a short gingham skirt and an anorak. Apparently she helped build *Tardis* [not *the* Tardis or upper case TARDIS, as in the TV series] and this took several years.

Barbara Who works nearby. She has just met a nice young man, but is understandably anxious about bringing him home to meet the family. She wears a sensible twinset and sensible shoes, and has early 60s-style big hair. For some reason, she thinks orange ski-pants are the thing to wear on a date. She seems to know how to operate some of the Ship's systems.

Baddies

• *Daleks*. Come in red, blue and black varieites. They talk more haltingly than those on TV, but are just as selfish. They're inordinately fond of lava-lamps. These Daleks have bigger lights on the sides of their domes, almost as if someone had stuck jam jars on there. They shoot gas-guns, but only as a last resort. As with their comic-strip counterparts, they measure time in Greek-style characters, and have ball-point pens with big spheres on the other end. Some have pincers instead of suckers.

Plot Barbara brings her new boyfriend Ian to meet her kid sister Susie and their guardian, the eccentric scientist Doctor Who. He proudly shows off his new invention to the clumsy but affable Ian. It's a time machine, built into a police box. Ian stumbles and sets the ship off on a random journey. *Tardis* lands in a forest that has been devastated by an atomic war. Keen to explore, the Doctor removes a component of his machine, and they look over the abandoned city. They're soon trapped by the citizens, called Daleks, who live on radiation and inhabit metal cones. Ian tries to escape and is shot, losing feeling in his legs for some hours.

On finding that the radiation is affecting them, the humans ask the Daleks for permission to fetch some vials of liquid that they suspect the Thals - residents of the jungle, and thought to have been wiped out - left for them as remedies. Susie is sent, and makes brief contact with a Thal. The drugs work and the humans escape, only to find that the part the Doctor took from the time machine is lost. The Thals are persuaded to help them return, as Susie has heard the Daleks plot genocide.

A two-pronged attack is planned, with the Doctor and Susie helping the Thal women to swamp the Dalek sensor array with light from a hundred mirrors, and Ian and Barbara going with the men on a dangerous mission through the aqueducts to the Dalek generators. As the crisis point approaches, the Doctor leads a frontal raid on the city and overcomes the Dalek defences. He is, however, captured. A full-scale battle ensues and the Daleks are prevented from detonating their warhead with seconds to spare. The Doctor is confident that he can return the family home, but Ian is shocked to see Roman Centurions when he opens the *Tardis* door.

Status

• *Canonicity*. For the public, it's just as canonical as the televised version. The films have been shown on terrestrial television more than any form of *Doctor Who* in the UK. Since the big TV debut on a Saturday night in 1972, they were shown on BBC1 half a dozen times up to 1987, usually in the Saturday mornings in the summer when Test Match cricket was not on. (Tests take place on alternate weeks in the summer, so they arranged family films for the "off" weeks, and these two Dalek flicks went into a pool with Cliff Richard musicals, Norman Wisdom "comedies", bad American stuff like *Megaforce* and even - on one occasion - *Devil Girl from Mars*. This gives you some idea of what the BBC thought of *Doctor Who* in the mid-80s.) Since 1994, Channel 4 has shown it at least as often, only on weekend afternoons, sometimes in bills with *Forbidden Planet* and, lately, during the same weekend as the BBC Wales series starts.

For the hardcore fans this film is a mild embarrassment, mixed with fond memories of seeing it as a kid. The key factor is that we were already used to multiple versions of this story through the Whitaker novelisation *Doctor Who in an Exciting Adventure with the Daleks* and the *TV Century 21* comic strip. For a lot of people - including the Big Finish scriptwriters and (it would seem) the BBC Wales series producers - it's part of the collective memory of the series, and as we'll see in the

Influence section.

• *Deviation*. There's no effort to suggest that the Doctor and his family are anything other than British. As with many of the spin-offs, the slow accretion of background details and explication is abandoned in place of a quick info-dump to bring anyone who'd not seen the series up-to-speed. The result is an involuntary gag-reaction, as even hardened fans have to swallow this film's version of the donnée in seconds. Once on Skaro, the story develops as it had on television but with a more pro-active Doctor. Even the matter of sabotaging the fluid link is handled as a dotty old grandad playing a silly prank.

The operation of *Tardis* is explained as a glorified teleport, rather than as a mystery connected with other dimensions. Similarly there's a technobabble explanation of the Ship's inner dimensions that shows why Whitaker was wise not to have any such scene in the broadcast stories.

A more significant change is that the Daleks are obviously bad right from the start. They are colour-coded for status, and have strange voices. Instead of a devastating ray, their weapons fire out toxic gas. This can make metal melt or explode. Unlike their monochrome counterparts, the Daleks have learned the secret of countdowns that don't peter out when it is obvious that action sequences are over-running.

Another thing to spot is that the film Daleks are credited with having operators, and photos were taken of them getting into the shells. Compare this to the way the BBC tried to preserve the myth that the TV machines were radio-controlled, right up until "The Power of the Daleks" (4.3).

Review   Seen as a specimen of *Doctor Who*, this is joyless, mechanical and trite. Seen as a Saturday Morning movie - possibly as a programme of shorts, cartoons and games organised by your local cinema as a sort of kid's club (this was common in the 60s, the most celebrated club being the ABC Minors) - it makes sense. If your experience of *Doctor Who* was of a sixteen-inch black and white 405-line image rationed to twenty-five minutes per week, this would be like eating a laundry-bag full of Skittles in one sitting. Actually, not Skittles, but rather the supermarket own-brand equivalent with more tartrazine and a strange tinny flavour. Our notional child cineaste would be bouncing off the ceiling, but still think that something wasn't quite right.

These days, with colour television pretty well established even in parts of Northamptonshire, the film looks a bit shopworn. We've seen it on telly so often, we don't even know when it's going to be on. We know what colour Daleks are, and why they look better in monochrome. We've seen them flying around Greenwich, zapping Cybermen. Nowadays, there's no point in having a film that was designed simply to say "Look, kids - Daleks in colour! And in Widescreen! With money spent on the sets!" Watching this film on a TV screen is like listening to the radio version of *Return of the Jedi*, but not as funny.

But nostalgia's never like it was. These days we recall with slight disbelief an era when *Doctor Who* was a national joke, and fondly look back on the BBC screenings of this as a guilty pleasure. When we were watching it, we might have been embarrassed if anyone else mistook this for "our" series, but we remembered back further. There had *also* been a time when film-makers, TV schedulers and other strange grown-ups thought that anything that had a police box and a Dalek in was somehow as good as any other thing called *Doctor Who*. We took what we could get back then. Most of us saw it first in 1972, right after "The Time Monster" (9.5). It was so unlike what we were used to, it looked like some cobwebbed oddity. Now, for most people in Britain, it's more familiar and reassuring than any other form of *Doctor Who*. There's room to debate the point, but this movie and its sequel are better known than anything with Tom Baker or David Tennant in it.

But we have to be objective. We can't measure it against the *New Adventures* or BBC Wales' show or "City of Death" (17.2), but rather against Doug McClure drilling to the centre of the Earth or Todd Armstrong looking for the Golden Fleece. They're all staples of Saturday afternoon filler films on Channel 4 whenever there's no horse races or *Big Brother*. There's no killer pterodactyls or animated skeleton-warriors, but one thing that strikes the viewer now is that it's Bond for kids. We all think it's pretty self-evident that the Daleks are Nazis-in-drag, but the simplified version of the story has brave commandos, drawn from blond pacifists (like Swedes), who sabotage a power-station to save their village. All very Alistair McLean, but look at the Dalek citadel again. The Daleks are Bond villains. We've stepped out of Nazi iconography and into big-scale megalomaniacal technophilia. Whilst Skaro's forests are rather 1950s mauve and lilac filigee, we've got chunky metallic doors that would be impressive in a model for *Thunderbirds*, but with real actors running up to them. Cleverly, we first see the city through branches and across the length of the studio, rather than as a clear shot of an obvious model.

Now, imagine you've not seen it before, and are in the third row sipping Kia-Ora and munching Toffee Poppets. Watch the scene when the cliff-wall bisects and the Thals plummet past a huge illuminated wall as Daleks pour out from the city, guns fuming.

Working Title None.

Background and Stuff

• Strangely it wasn't the Daleks that first brought *Doctor Who* to a filmmaker's attention - it was "Marco Polo" (1.4), which caught the eye of the Walt Disney company. Disney had a track record of making live-action films (such as *Doctor Syn, Alias the Scarecrow*) in the UK, usually to be shown as part of *The Wonderful World of Disney* on TV in the States but released theatrically in Britain. Whether this is what they had in mind for "Marco Polo" isn't clear, as their interest doesn't seem to have extended beyond an initial enquiry.

• The prime mover behind the Dalek films was Joe Vegoda, the managing director of distributors Regal International, which in turn owned Aaru. Milton Subotsky agreed to produce *Dr. Who and the Daleks* for Aaru as his own outfit Amicus specialised in lower budget horror films. (This is where the Amicus / Aaru confusion comes from. Basically, this is as Amicus as it gets with regards to content, but the money makes it an Aaru production.) Subotsky, who had yet to see the Daleks on television when the deal was made in December 1964, had just finished work on *Dr Terror's House of Horrors* for Vegoda. As we have noted, this supplied *Dr. Who and the Daleks* with its two leads.

• Cushing was cast as the lead, as the TV series was still largely an unknown quantity overseas and a "name" star was required to guarantee international sales; William Hartnell wasn't considered, not the least reason being he was tied to the punishing BBC production schedule. Terry Nation was also too busy to adapt his own script, so Subotsky handled this himself with some basic uncredited input from David Whitaker. His job involved pruning down the introductions for

Doctor Who, his family and *Tardis* to a bare minimum, while generally toning down the violence and suspense in favour of humour and action. The aim was to make the film in time for release over the summer of 1965 (mission accomplished), get a U certificate (check) and initiate a series of science-fiction comedy films that would be as successful as James Bond, released at the rate of one per year (er...)

• Gordon Flemyng replaced Hammer veteran Freddie Francis (who'd also handled *Dr Terror's House of Horrors*) as director before shooting began. Around the same time, Jennie Linden took over the role of Barbara from the originally cast Ann Bell (she'd been in - guess what - *Dr Terror's House of Horrors*). Linden, like Roy Castle, would later be too busy to appear in the second film and is better known to a later generation as a narrator on compilations of *The Word*. Cast as Susan, Roberta Tovey was daughter of actor George Tovey, who would later play the poacher in "Pyramids of Mars" (13.3). Other members of the cast would go on to roles in the TV series, notably Barrie Ingham (Paris in 3.3, "The Myth Makers") and Geoffrey Toone (the high priest Hepesh in 9.2, "The Curse of Peladon"). The Thal artistes were generally plastered in make-up and fitted with gold wigs, but if you've seen the film you've probably spotted that already. (Cushing's wig and makeup is rather more naturalistic and harder to spot.) Minimum height restrictions applied, and the male Thals were required to shave their chests and arms.

• A batch of eight new, larger and more colourful Daleks were commissioned from Shawcraft for the film (and subsequently poached by director Richard Martin to bulk out the numbers in 2.8, "The Chase"). Their appendages were generally more practical than the sucker arm seen on TV, while the fire extinguisher guns (which fired bursts of carbon dioxide) were adopted when John Trevelyan advised that the originally mooted flame-throwers would rule out a U certificate. (Trevelyan was secretary of the British Board of Film Censors at this time; alas his fascinating career is too tangential to relate here, beyond mentioning that he's possibly the only censor in history to have helped a cinema owner pay off his fines for breaching public decency laws by cadging the money out of Andy Warhol.)

• Experienced TV Daleks Robert Jewell, Kevin Manser and Gerald Taylor were hired to train additional operators, though they had to be released for pre-filming on "The Chase", which overlapped the film schedule. Reportedly there was friction between the Daleks, especially as Jewell negotiated himself an extra fee as the "chief" Dalek. David Graham and Peter Hawkins provided the voices uncredited after filming had wrapped.

• Filming began Friday, 12th of March, 1965, on the forest set, which was built on the huge Stage H at Shepperton. For some shots, Gordon Flemyng elected to leave the anamorphic lens on the camera, as he found this created a quite disorientating otherworldly effect. The Daleks were largely confined to the Dalek city sets which were constructed on a separate stage. The shoot lasted six weeks, ending just before studio work began on "The Chase". By this time, the publicity machine was in full swing and the volume of new Dalek-related merchandise was enough to fill an eighteen-page brochure. *TV Century 21* - at this point serialising the Daleks' comic strip adventures - ran features and competitions adorned with colour photos from the shoot. In May, several Dalek props were sent to the Cannes Film Festival, where they were photographed with John Lennon (who was busy promoting *Help!* and not appearing in "The Chase"). The film premiered at Studio One in Oxford Street on Thursday, 24th of June. On the whole reviews were mixed. Barry Norman liked it. (For American readers: imagine if Leonard Maltin had ever read a book that wasn't movie-related, or a chilled-out Joe Queenan.)

• Film-specific merchandise included a single of the theme music, "The Eccentric Dr Who" by Malcolm Lockyer and His Orchestra. (This had been commissioned specifically to sound nothing like the Grainer / Derbyshire music from the TV series, just as the *Tardis* set for the film was unrecognisable as Peter Brachacki's design. It sounds almost exactly like the theme for the TV show *The Human Jungle*, or indeed a close cousin of *Perry Mason*.) Lockyer also released another tie-in single, "Who's Who", with vocals by Roberta Tovey in-character as Susie. If you're not sure which of the various *Doctor Who*-related novelty songs this is, it's the one that features the line: 'He's always been a friend of mine / Who? / Doctor Who!' Shudder quietly and move on.

• The merchandise blitz *didn't* include a novelisation that Subotsky planned to write; the BBC vetoed it since David Whitaker's *Doctor Who in an Exciting Adventure with the Daleks* was still in print. (This would be issued in paperback in the US in 1967 to tie in with the film's North American release. It sported a photographic cover deriving from neither the BBC nor Aaru, depicting human weaklings cowering before the alien might of giant squeezy detergent bottles.)

• Readers who grew up after the triple-whammy of *The Godfather*, *Jaws* and *Star Wars* may not be aware that the smash-and-grab model of movie exhibition - where a new film is bundled into as many cinemas as possible on opening weekend, and lives and dies by how well it does in those three days - didn't always dominate the industry. *Dr. Who and the Daleks* spread slowly across the nation and was still arriving in new parts of the UK in September. It was generally shown in a double bill with Disney's *The Tattooed Police Horse*, but quickly established itself as one of the year's big hits. (We assume that people weren't turning up to see the horse.) It was in circulation at around the same time as *Those Magnificent Men in their Flying Machines*, as visitors to Southgate tube station prior to 1994 would have known from the posters still up. A second film had been on the cards during production, and the box office receipts only confirmed this.

In the US, however, *Dr. Who and the Daleks* wasn't a success. It was released without much fanfare by Crown International in 1966 and treated largely as juvenile filler. Dell Publishing, at this time trying to break the DC / Marvel duopoly on the mainstream US comics market, issued a one-off adaptation of the film at the end of the year. This soon acquired the distinction of being one of the rarest and most sought after pieces of *Doctor Who* merchandise... until Marvel reprinted it in *Doctor Who Classic Comics* in 1993, and the value of extant copies went through the floor.

Ratings 9.9 million people saw the film's TV debut in 1972. At the cinema, *Kinematograph Weekly* ranked it as one of the Top 20 moneymakers of 1965.

Cast Peter Cushing (Dr. Who), Roy Castle (Ian), Jennie Linden (Barbara), Roberta Tovey (Susan), Barrie Ingham (Alydon), Michael Coles (Ganatus), Yvonne Antrobus (Dyoni), Geoffrey Toone (Temmosus), John Bown (Antodus), Mark Petersen (Elyon).

Influence As we said in Volume I, this is the first time someone other than William Hartnell had been seen as the Doctor (even the stage-play came later). This reading of the role takes elements of Hartnell performances and inserts them into a script written for the first conception of the character. The result is odd, but Cushing pulls it off by playing for laughs. When it came to rethinking the part for Patrick Troughton, this was crucial. Similarly, we can't ignore the fact that soon after the film's TV premiere in 1972, the character of Harry Sullivan was conceived almost as a clone of Roy Castle's Ian.

In "Planet of the Daleks" (10.4), they re-used a prop shell from the film for the Dalek Supreme. Dudley Simpson's score included a synth rendering of the film's main theme as a sort of fanfare for its arrival. The Daleks on film had to use fire-extinguishers instead of the electronic over-exposure effect for exterminations. Soon after this film opened, we had "The War Machines" (3.10), in which large lumbering robot killers did exactly the same on location in London.

Roy Castle's campaign to raise money for people who contracted lung cancer through passive smoking (as he had) lifted him from fondly-remembered TV star to national hero. He helped get the law changed, and set a precedent for court cases against tobacco companies. Several British *Doctor Who* conventions have raised money for the appeal run by his widow.

B2: "Daleks Invasion Earth 2150 AD"

(Aaru Productions, 1966. Directed by Gordon Flemyng, Screenplay by Milton Subtosky from a story by Terry Nation with additional material by David Whitaker, Produced by Milton Subotsky and Max J. Rosenberg, eighty-four minutes, colour)

Provenance Subotsky tries again, this time with an adaptation of "The Dalek Invasion of Earth" (2.2) and with the same crew. Cushing and Tovey are back.

Things to Watch Out
For in "Daleks Invasion Earth 2150 AD" ...

1. If the first attempt was a strangely watered-down version of the TV serial, this is a tighter, less shoddily-executed version of its television coun-

terpart. For those coming to the Richard Martin six-part serial after seeing this film, the Hartnell story is a major let-down. This account has Ray Brooks as the David figure, and he's far more convincing as a guerrilla leader. (One scene has him shooting a Roboman in a manner that suggests Jedi training, but we'll forgive that.) We've got a flying saucer that still looks pretty impressive, Robomen with a distinctive (and kinky) look (not to mention a memorable theme tune) and lots more exterminations, by public demand.

2. Into all this we fling a new character: PC Tom Campbell, played by Bernard Cribbins. He's almost as odd a choice as Roy Castle, but marginally better at slapstick. After his two novelty hit singles about digging a hole and shifting furniture, it's apt that he saves the world by digging a hole and shifting furniture. (Few who grew up in these parts can resist putting on a Dalek voice at the climax and yelling "Don't dig there, dig it elsewhere, you're digging it round and it oughta be square".) Cribbins has also been Cushing's comic foil (the version of *She* with Ursula Andress) and was a regular on *Jackanory* (for some of us, he's the definitive Bilbo Baggins).

3. One feature where this film really scores over the serial is in the depiction of those who chose to collaborate with the Daleks. We aren't given time to sympathise, but instead have to accept them straight off as morally compromised. In particular, Ashton is turned from a minor spiv to a thoroughly cynical Harry Lime figure. Fortunately they cast Philip Madoc in the role, so he's plausible for the brief moments he's on screen, and his explosive death never fails to get kids cheering.

4. The pre-credit sequence ends with a close-up of a man with a carrier bag looking bemused because the police box has vanished. That's Bernard Spear, a noted comic actor of the era who's been completely forgotten.

The Doctor   Doctor Who, his granddaughter Susie Who and niece Louise now live in a police box that pops up in different times in Earth's history. He's always eager to help, which is why he arranges a time-paradox to get his new friend Tom a promotion. He knows the layout of central London very well. He's still a bit muddle-headed, and his arthritis is easing.

Fellow Travellers   Louise is said to be Doctor Who's niece and we learn nothing else about her.

She calls the Doctor 'Doctor' rather than "Uncle". Publicity photos show her mixing chemicals in a lab and flirting with Daleks, but nothing as interesting happens here. She's got a weird tweed mini-Ulster, but very groovy boots. Susan is much the same as in *Dr. Who and the Daleks*, though less precocious and know-it-all than before. She has big handwriting and appears to be in a very brightly-coloured school uniform (Zebedee University?). The versions of Ian and Barbara from the first film neither appear nor are mentioned.

At the start of the film, P.C. Tom Campbell of K Division seems to be planning to take a holiday in the sun, but by the end he's more excited about the prospects of promotion. After apprehending the gang, he drives off in their getaway car, which we don't think can be normal police practice in such situations. [We assume that Doctor Who has told him to do this, as they already know the car leaves the scene of the crime, and this is the only way to avoid a complete paradox.]

Baddies   The Daleks are just as colourful as in the first film, though this time we see gold and black models who seem to be at the top of the hierarchy. They are highly susceptible to magnetism and end up being sucked into the Earth's core. They measure time in 'rels'. These are fractional divisions of time almost exactly like our Earth "seconds", except when the plot requires them to be spaced anything up to fifteen seconds apart. They have a big 'Rel Counter' conveniently marked in English, with lots of flashing lights and a big switch with 'Total Power' (also conveniently marked in English). One of these Daleks can move very fast under water.

Robomen are processed humans in shiny black jump suits and crash helmets. Unlike the TV version, there's no initiative test qualifying humans for conversion, and the process seems to be reversible [or at least, they can remove their helmets with no ill effects].

Plot   P.C. Tom Campbell of K Division stumbles into *Tardis*, believing it to be a real police box, after being coshed by a gang of thieves while out on patrol. *Tardis* takes off, transporting Tom, Doctor Who, Susan and Louise to London in the year 2150 AD. The city is in ruins and a falling girder blocks the entrance to the police box. The Doctor and Tom set off to find a crowbar; in the meantime, Susan and Louise are captured by rebels who have a subterranean base off Embankment tube station. Doctor Who and Tom are apprehended by Robomen and their masters, the Daleks, who have invaded Earth in a flashy new flying saucer.

The rebels are planning a counterattack, using special bombs devised by the scientist Dortmun. This comes just in time to save the Doctor and Tom from being converted into Robomen, but the bombs don't work and the attack turns into a rout. Tom and Louise are trapped aboard the saucer as it takes off and heads for the slave mines in Bedfordshire. Susan and the Doctor separately follow them. At the mines, Doctor Who learns that the Daleks are planning to drop a bomb into the Earth's magnetic core, but may be susceptible to the magnetic forces this will unleash. The Doctor is soon recaptured but manages to turn the Robomen against the Daleks and set off a general uprising / escape among the slaves. Meanwhile, Tom has blocked the shaft to divert the Dalek bomb. When it goes off, the Daleks and their saucer are sucked down into the mines. With the Dalek invasion defeated, *Tardis* returns Tom back to the point just before he was attacked and he overpowers the thieves.

Status

• *Canonicity*. It's substantially the same story they told in the run-up to Christmas 1964, but with the rough edges smoothed away. If you ask a member of the public (or at least, one who could reasonably be expected to know about any of this), he or she will know dimly about a story where the Daleks took over London, and a resistance movement stopped them by doing something with the Earth's magnetic core. It's been referred to a few times in the televised series since, so anyone not neurotic about the series will have a vague idea. And the chances are it's this film, not the broadcast six-part serial, which they remember. Nation himself seems to have remembered the film rather than the original when writing 12.4, "Genesis of the Daleks".

• *Deviation*. Neither David nor Tom tries to chat up Susie. But then, they don't really seem to notice Louise either. (Neither do most viewers, it has to be said.) The removal of this subplot from the teleplay makes a lot of other changes necessary, especially with regard to who goes to Bedfordshire with whom. One effect of this is that the Doctor isn't removed from the story for an episode. (He and David travel together, Tyler's surrogate takes Susie and Louise and Tom flies in the spaceship - but he also disguises himself as a Roboman, leading to some relatively amusing comedy schtick.) The Robomen are more Gestapo than zombies. Perhaps sensibly, the Slyther is removed from the story and a lot of the material about Larry, his brother and Wells' resistance efforts are streamlined away.

Basically, this has all the plot-beats from the original but reallocated. Susie and Wyler do what Barbara and Jenny do on telly, Larry and Craddock are merged and some of Larry's functions go to Louise.

Review This film's afterlife on the small-screen has been rather more successful. It is, after all, less reliant on knock-'em-dead spectacle and more on action. The comic interludes of Cribbins trying to pass for a Roboman are funny, but have been placed in a tense situation. It's not exactly *Sleeper,* but it's a situation in an action movie, not part of a comedy overall. The Daleks are better, and don't look ridiculous on London backstreets. Their ship is a classic of its kind. Very little in this film goes wrong.

What we should bear in mind is that Peter Cushing is easily the most experienced and famous actor to have played the Doctor. He has screen experience going back to Laurel and Hardy, and fell into horror-movie typecasting after playing Hamlet on the West End stage. His star quality keeps everything else in this film in place. Although he does less than before, the scenes where he's absent are that little bit flatter. As a result, actors in relatively minor parts make an effort not to be swamped. Philip Madoc almost steals the movie in under three minutes.

The difference between the two Dalek films is the difference between a kids' movie and a movie for kids. The former has no real ambition beyond making a film that children will enjoy, and that looks like what they imagined *Doctor Who* stories "really" looked like. The latter is a film that works on its own rules, and whilst children can watch it, they don't ever suspect that they are the sole audience. Nobody, from the cast to the effect crew, is making it "for kids" - but everyone knows that kids will love it. That's why, for all its plot shortcomings and logical lapses (all there in the original, so we can't blame them), this is the one today's young audiences will voluntarily watch.

Ratings This did less well at the box office than the first film, but reliable figures are hard to come by. 10.7 million saw it on BBC1 in 1972.

Cast Peter Cushing (Dr. Who), Bernard Cribbins (Tom Campbell), Ray Brooks (David), Andrew Keir (Wyler), Roberta Tovey (Susan), Jill Curzon (Louise), Roger Avon (Wells), Geoffrey Cheshire (Roboman), Keith Marsh (Conway), Philip Madoc (Brockley), Steve Peters (Leader Roboman), Eddie Powell (Thompson), Godfrey Quigley (Dortmun), Sheila Steafel (Young Woman), Eileen Way (Old Woman), Kenneth Watson (Craddock).

Working Titles "The Daleks Invade Earth", "Daleks Invade Earth 2150 A.D."

Background and Stuff

• As we've seen, the first film was a hit and by mid-December 1965, much the same team had re-assembled to work on the sequel. It was clear from the start that Roy Castle and Jennie Linden wouldn't be available for the rematch, and part of Subotsky's brief for the new script was to introduce similar characters to replace them. By now, Regal International was in the process of being absorbed into British Lion, who would distribute the new film. While *Dr. Who and the Daleks* had a reasonably large budget of £180,000, the new one would be more expensive and a sponsorship deal was arranged with Quaker Oats to promote one of their breakfast serials through product placement. So the finished film is dotted with hoardings advertising Sugar Puffs and they also appear to be the staple diet of the resistance. (We're lucky that the film doesn't end with the Daleks being driven from the Earth by the Honey Monster...) In return, Sugar Puffs promoted the film with a competition to "Win a Real Dalek" (not literally, we hope). However, it looks to the uninitiated that Thomas Cook holidays and Del Monte tinned fruit were also in on the deal (note the lingering shot of the Travel Agents' when Tom is waiting for the robbery to start).

• This time round, David Whitaker's contribution to the scripts were acknowledged with an additional material credit (long-standing fan lore generally assumes that he wrote the top and tail sequences set in the present day). Bernard Cribbins was brought on board to replace Roy Castle - he was later one of many actors to be

offered the role of the Doctor by Barry Letts in 1974 - while Jill Curzon would play Louise instead of Linden as Barbara. Other reasonably well-known cast members include Ray Brooks (who had just been in *The Knack* and would later provide the voice of *Mr. Benn* and murder Pauline Fowler in *EastEnders* - see A1, "Dimensions in Time") and Andrew Keir (who would appear in the lead role of Hammer's version of *Quatermass and the Pit* the following year).

• André Morell (who'd taken the lead role in the BBC's version of *Quatermass and the Pit* in 1958/9) was offered a part but was committed to another role on the relevant dates (see 3.5, "The Massacre" to find out what). TV series bit players like Roger Avon and Geoffrey Cheshire also crop up but the most noticeable is Eileen Way (she's the Old Mother in 1.1, "An Unearthly Child" and Karela in 17.3, "The Creature from the Pit") as the old woman who betrays Susan and Wyler to the Daleks. (In the same scenes, Sheila Steafel was redubbed by another actress as the younger woman, for reasons that are now lost in the mists of time.) Robert Jewell was the only returning Dalek operator from the first film (though this time, filming would begin just in time to avoid a clash with 3.4, "The Daleks' Master Plan"). He was hired to play the lead Dalek and also to train regular extras to fill the remaining casings.

• Shooting began at Shepperton on Monday, 31st of January, 1966. The James Bond spoof *Casino Royale* was already spiralling out of control at the same studios, and the teams from both films mixed freely. (If you don't already know, *Casino Royale* is the only film to bring together the talents of Orson Welles, Woody Allen, Richard O'Brien, John Huston and Ronnie Corbett. Its ostensible star, Peter Sellers, had already stormed off set by this time, never to return. Sometime later, Bernard Cribbins ended up in this legendary oddity.) This time, Stage H was given over to the 150-foot long Dalek spaceship ramp set. The bigger budget meant some exterior shooting could be carried out this time, including the action scene of Wyler and Susan driving through a horde of Daleks on the Shepperton backlot. (Curiously, Keir seems to have had a stunt double for this sequence, but Roberta Tovey didn't...) Other location work was carried out at nearby Littleton Park and later in London (for the sequence of the Dalek emerging from the Thames, and the preceding scenes in the abandoned warehouses), though the exterior of the mine was the same backlot, saving anyone the bother of having to find a suitable quarry.

The shoot was far from smooth, leaving many involved with the production dissatisfied (especially Subotsky, who felt that the finished film had to be salvaged on the cutting room floor). Production wrapped on Tuesday, 22nd of March, and at this point the producers still expected to be making a third film - probably based on "The Chase" - the following year. A persistent rumour suggests that Subotsky's initial instinct was to adapt 1.5, "The Keys of Marinus" next, until someone alerted him to the fact that it didn't have any Daleks in it.

• Publicity for the film included a special photoshoot for *Titbits* - a Victorian leftover, so not what you're thinking - of Jill Curzon posing with a Dalek and stripping. Unlike Katy Manning, she kept her bikini on. There was no meeting with John Lennon this time, though one Dalek was brought to New York to do a photocall outside the Empire State Building (though this might have been to promote the release of the first film in America). Back in Shepperton, Daleks were also meeting with members of a Soviet cultural mission to the UK, who - unlike Lennon - needed an explanation of what they were looking at. Curiously, much of the publicity concentrated on the Robomen at the expense of the Daleks and the *Doctor Who* connection. The UK poster was emblazoned with a huge image of a Roboman, and the first word of the title was almost invisible (indeed some reference books go as far as to claim that *Invasion Earth 2150 A.D.* is an official alternative title). The music this time round - rather more dynamic than in the first film - was by jazz pianist Bill McGuffie but wasn't released as a single, despite some interest from Fontana Records.

• The film opened at Studio One on Oxford Street on Friday, 22nd of July, paired up with the western *Indian Paint*. (In other parts of the country, it was released in conjunction with the thriller *Hide and Seek* or the adventure film *Queen of the Pirates*.) Remember our comments in the review of the last one: the Saturday Morning clubs were the obvious audience for this film, and probably ran competitions of their own in most cases. Reviews were still mixed, and after a promising start, the box office fell short of *Dr. Who and the Daleks*' take in 1965. An abridged version of the soundtrack was broadcast on the BBC Light Programme's *Movietime* on Friday, 18th of November, but by now the film was being seen by its producers as a big disappointment. The US distribution rights were sold to Walter Reade, whose company promptly collapsed. It was clear that the Dalekmania boom was petering out and plans for a third film were suspended.

Nevertheless it was felt there was still mileage in Cushing's version of Doctor Who. During 1966, Stanmark Productions approached the BBC about the possibility of making a fifty-two-episode radio version of *Doctor Who*. The intention was that Cushing would reprise his role as Doctor Who, alongside new companions Susan and Mike. A fifteen-minute pilot was rejected, as various BBC departments deemed this unbroadcastable (except, apparently, for unsophisticated listeners in Australia and "some parts" of the United States). This is now lost, so it's unclear whether Cushing was involved, but Stanmark was still hopefully touting publicity material with groovy mid-1960s graphics at the start of 1967. Cushing, as you surely knew, continued to appear in films into the mid-1980s, his last being *Biggles: Adventures in Time* (don't ask). His Doctor and associated companions have only subsequently reappeared briefly in comic strips ("Daleks versus the Martians", *DWM Spring Special*, 1996) and short stories ("Dr. Who and the House on Oldark Moor", *Short Trips and Side Steps*, 2000) by fans with too much time on their hands.

• As noted, both films made their TV debuts in the summer of 1972 as part of the *High Adventure* season that filled the gap left by *Doctor Who* Season Nine. During the late 1970s, both were commercially available as 8mm cinefilms for home projectors, but since 1982 have been more readily available on video and (later) DVD. The *Dr. Who Movie Collection* DVD set from Studio Canal in 2002 also included the Aaru-orientated documentary *Dalekmania*, which had been directed by Kevin Davies (see A1, "Dimensions in Time") for video release in 1995.

• For the decade after *Daleks Invasion Earth 2150 A.D.*, little interest was shown in bringing *Doctor Who* back to the silver screen. The next big film project was Tom Baker and Ian Marter's ill-fated *Doctor Who Meets Scratchman* (see 13.6, "The Seeds of Doom"), licensed in 1978. Around the same time, Douglas Adams developed a treatment for *Doctor Who and the Krikkitmen*, which eventually formed the basis of his novel *Life, the Universe, and Everything*. *Scratchman* was effectively killed off by the realisation that it would have to compete with *Star Wars*, but the long-term effect of the skiffy-cinema boom was to alert lots of companies to the sort of money that an internationally-recognised property like *Doctor Who* could bring in. Numerous bids were made for the screen rights to *Doctor Who* through the first half of the 1980s before they were awarded to Coast to Coast. (See **The Lore** throughout this volume for this seemingly never-ending story.)

One of these unsucessful approaches was from Milton Subotsky. He alleged that he still had a valid option on a third film and now planned to make *Doctor Who's Greatest Adventure*, in which two Doctors have to team up to deal with a threat too big for the Time Lords. The BBC quickly established that his rights to *Doctor Who* had long since expired. Subotsky died in 1991, but plans to revive *Doctor Who's Greatest Adventure* - with Michael Sheard as one of the Doctors - were announced in the late 1990s. This was alleged to be "The Keys of Marinus", remade with a budget. Again this came to nothing, and seems to have been designed to ride the coat-tails of publicity for (yet) another big budget blockbuster *Doctor Who* movie that didn't happen.

• "The TV Movie" (27.0) finally killed off the Daltenreys / Lumiere movie, and in 1997 it vanished in a flurry of writs, never to be mentioned again. This left the field clear for another company to take over and a new *Doctor Who* film was announced at the Cannes Film Festival in 1998. This seems to have been intended as a co-production between BBC Worldwide and HAL Films, the London-based subsidiary of US super-indie Miramax. Over the next two years, fandom and the tabloid press was abuzz with speculation and the usual list of unlikely would-be Doctors (including Denzel Washington and Dudley Moore, the only time they've both been up for the same part as far as we know) was trotted out. By 1999, it appeared that producer-director team Jeremy Bolt and Paul Anderson were developing the film for the BBC. (To clarify, that's Paul *W.S.* Anderson who had directed *Mortal Kombat* and *Event Horizon*, and not Paul *Thomas* Anderson who directed *Boogie Nights* and *Magnolia*.) Then - just as things were getting interesting, the BBC got cold feet and the film was abandoned, leaving Bolt and Anderson deeply disappointed. Still, while the film was in development, it effectively blocked any new BBC TV production, so the "Doctor Who 2000" revival planned by up-and-coming producer Russell T. Davies had to be put on hold.

Influence For better or worse, this is the real start of the "Yeti-in-the-loo" theory (see **Is "Yeti-in-a-Loo" the Worst Idea Ever?** under 5.5, "The Web of Fear"). However much it purports to be in "the future", this film avoids even the TV version's efforts to seem like anything other than present-day London under the yoke. The audiences responded to this better than to the chintzy alien world of the first film, and the producers of the TV series drew a conclusion that they thought would suit their budget and need for gimmicks. 1968 saw the start of a trend towards stories like this, to the exclusion of much else.

This is also the film that emboldened Tom Baker and Ian Marter to write their *Doctor Who Meets Scratchman* script, on the grounds that they couldn't do any worse.

The BBC Wales series knowingly references the *Tardis* design, with the inner door made as the white-painted police box with the phone in a metal cage. The Welsh series Daleks even mark time in "rels" (X2.13, "Doomsday" and X3.5, "Evolution of the Daleks").

the end notes

1 Watch those stories with this in mind, and it becomes obvious that the Doctor only needs a light squeeze on his shoulders to be incapacitated in agony. Once or twice would be funny, but every single time... well, it looks like a deliberate policy. We know that *isn't* the case, but we might imagine that if nothing else, this explains Tom Baker's scarf.

2 For reasons never properly investigated, these individuals tend to wear shirts with vertical stripes, always the same one for each person, every time. Forget the cliché of the "Anorak", the Stripes were the true face of geek-fandom until other, more socially-gifted fans began to wear them as a form of semi-ironic solidarity.

3 We'd hate to think that this useful vulgarism was the only thing for which Craig Hinton would be remembered, but he *was* rather proud of coining it.

4 This will need some gesture towards explanation. In 1973, *Last of the Summer Wine* was a gentle comedy about three elderly men who'd been at school together, and lived in a Yorkshire village causing low-level mischief. It was Norman Clegg (Peter Sallis, see 5.3, "The Ice Warriors" and 20.5, "Enlightenment") and Compo Simmonite (Bill Owen), plus one or other ex-military types. By 1983, it was about Compo getting into jet-propelled bathtubs or frogman outfits and letching Nora Batty (Kathy Staff). Every week, for about fifteen years, Compo would roll out of control down a steep hill, or be in something that exploded. Then, when Owen died, the series found its feet again as a retirement home for any actor who can do a Yorkshire accent, including Bert Kwouk (Lin Futu in 19.2, "Four to Doomsday") and the stars of many 70s sitcoms you might have seen. It's an ensemble piece, with Sallis wheeled on for a cameo once a week, and is now actually funny (provided you can follow the dialect). Not, we would imagine, a series that would travel well.

5 Except that the 2005-model Ship has hexagons instead of roundels that are actually round, and thus resembles Dalek technology as depicted in the BBC Wales version - but not as much as it looks like the Teletubbies' house.

6 Harry Hill's various odd programmes have shown a consistent willingness to allude to the series, up to and including guest-spots for Pertwee and Davison, and with Burt Kwouk (19.2, "Four to Doomsday") as a semi-regular. Then there was a whole episode where the Brigadier (played by Nicholas Courtney) was allegedly welcoming former Cabinet Minister Claire Short as the new Doctor. Hill bought her a vase, but the Cyberleader dropped it. He also has "Stouffer" a singularly unconvincing puppet black cat (so now you know why people expect him to turn up in 26.4, "Survival") and his recent series *TV Burp* - in which he ridicules clips from that week's broadcasts - seems to be where BBC Wales get their ideas. Just before the ad break, he ritually ponders which of two oddly-matched characters is "better" (for example, off the top of our heads, Queen Victoria and a werewolf) and yells "There's only one way to find out - FIGHT!!" Then actors dressed as these duke it out as they go into the break. Once it's been pointed out, nobody can avoid thinking of this when watching X2.13, "Doomsday" or the *Torchwood* episode "Cyberwoman" (which, if you missed it, has the supposedly "adult" spin-off build an episode around a pterodactyl and a cyber-bikini-babe knocking lumps out of each other).

7 Long-standing readers of *About Time* will, by now, have detected a certain cynicism on the authors' part with regards to *Blake's 7*. Yet if we're being entirely honest, there are points where something should be *more* like *Blake's*, not less. For instance, the saving grace (so to speak) of "The TV Movie" is TV's Eric Roberts playing Servalan - if McGann had treated Chang Lee like Avon treats Vila, everyone would have loved this project. And series such as *Friends* and *Happy Days*, to name but a couple, would have been bearable had we suspected they'd copy the manner in which *Blake's* concluded.

8 That includes people we know who were going to *Doctor Who* conventions and writing for fanzines. Part of the issue is that ratings didn't reflect people who recorded one channel and watched another - most *Doctor Who* fans with video access were dutifully recording BBC1 out of habit, but actually sat in front of ITV on Saturdays

at teatimes. And quite right too: *Robin of Sherwood* was the regulation mid-80s fantasy staple of half-digested Jung, and was delivered by John Abineri - he wore antlers on his head with the stoic dignity of a man who'd been painted green and given a Bo Derek wig (16.5, "The Power of Kroll"). *Robin* had people in smocks and buskins running around Welsh hills and woodland, and fun could be had watching for Terry Walsh in the fight scenes. It was all done on 35mm film in various castles, like 16.4, "The Androids of Tara"; 9.3, "The Sea Devils" or 11.1, "The Time Warrior", and had a theme-tune that was distinctive without being embarrassing.

9   Fan lore claims that these are Italians who've never seen the series, but it's a myth. We know a fair bit about the major World Distributors artists for *Doctor Who,* and they all seem to have been British (or at least not noticeably foreign: Walter Howarth, Edgar Hodges, Paul J. Crompton et al don't sound particularly Italian). So quite why they showed the Fourth Doctor in a business suit on an airline is a bigger puzzle than ever. However, the TARDIS seatbelts seen here are an innovation that first appears in the 1970s annuals.)

10   A uniquely British concept, hence the American pronunciation. "Charity" is from the Latin *caritas,* meaning love for others without having necessarily met them. "Charidee" - pronounced "chyeaarridee" - is the ostentatious use of a charitable pretext for self-promotion and irritating stunts. As we will see when discussing "Dimensions in Time", the annual *Children in Need* telethon results in celebrities behaving in really excruciatingly unwatchable "fun" stunts. This isn't exclusive to Britain, we know, but the mockery of it - originally in a sketch by Harry Enfield and Paul Whitehouse as DJs Smashie and Nicey - is curiously specific to these shores. We give, whilst hating ourselves for condoning these activities, and then the next day slag off the smarmy celebs who probably spent more on drugs that night than was actually raised. At least with American PBS telethons, the money is being raised by events connected to the cause. *Comic Relief* and *Children in Need* have mood-puncturing "Let's take a moment to remember why we're doing this..." heartstring-tugging films. Emotional blackmail so soon after a custard pie fight is just counter-productive.

In the mid-80s, after Live Aid, the fad for sing-along singles with celebs all taking a turn at doing a line (of the song, stupid), got out of hand really fast. As with the Elton John Diana Funeral Dirge, individuals who didn't like the record were bullied into forking out for it, which explains why so many of the comedy actors appearing later in this book had UK Number One hits (see 23.2, "Mindwarp"; 26.4, "Survival" and many others). It's also why the abject failure of "Doctor in Distress" caused so much glee among those who resented this "hijacking" of the issue. See 22.6, "Revelation of the Daleks" for more on this - shall we say - extraordinary project.

11   If you're British and were around then, you'll know at least one story about Matt Bianco and *Saturday Superstore*, but we won't repeat it here.

12   At last something that needs explanation for both Americans *and* Britons! *Fortycoats* was an Irish children's TV series of the early 1980s spun off from an earlier series called *Wanderley Wagon.* Magic tramp Fortycoats travelled through all time and space - but mainly Ireland - in a dimensionally transcendental shop accompanied by a stroppy girl who'd wandered in by mistake and an uptight young man dressed as a schoolboy. This was shown around the same time as Season Twenty-One, and were it not for RTE's much lower budget and the substitution of the Whirligig Witch for Ainley's Master, some viewers might have found the resemblance overwhelming.

13   Damn! We got through Volume V without mentioning her, which is pretty amazing really. When Punk happened in 1977, local TV companies needed to look like they knew what the Youth of the Nation wanted, and Birmingham's BBC opt-out slot ran a series called *Look Hear.* It was presented by a short, plump, lisping actress called Toyah Willcox, who got noticed and spent the next couple of years as punkette-in-residence in Derek Jarman's entourage. She even appeared in his breakthrough film *Jubilee* (as a teenage pyromaniac called Mad) and as Miranda in his *Tempest,* but then someone gave her a recording contract.

Between 1981 and 1983, she was unavoidable with dayglo hair bigger than she was, and a string of raucous hits with her unmistakable pronunciations of words like "mystery". (A vicious impersonation of Toyah - first name only in those days - launched Tracey Ullman's career.) Toyah was, briefly, the love-goddess of the sort of people who bought magazines with columns by Mat Irvine and Patrick Moore (you know... geeks). But then it all ended. She married Robert Fripp, the *least* likely rock icon for someone like her, went into daytime TV presenting and binned the lime-green lycra.

We mention this for two reasons. One is to help set the context in which Davison-era *Doctor Who* has to be seen. The other, concomitant on this, is that she is *exactly* the kind of person who should have appeared in 1980s *Doctor Who* yet never did. We repeat: Toyah Willcox was *never* in *Doctor Who*. So, for all the people who were dimly aware that the series came back after the Suspension and who keep asking us about it, the person you're thinking of is Sophie Aldred, who played a teenage pyromaniac called Ace for the last two years.

14   The only one that Pincher's book omitted was that no satisfactory way existed to open an envelope undetectably once it had been sealed with sellotape. They could have built a hospital with the money it cost to try to stop us finding this out.

15   In Alan Clarke's notoriously salacious *Diaries*, the lecherous junior minister describes watching an episode being filmed on his estate. His rather confused account of what he's told the story *is* would make a much better series than we got. It also makes for a bittersweet read, as the teenage actress after whom he is lusting died tragically young soon after.

16   Not *the* oddest, though. Several candidates for this title spring to mind: *The Perfect Pickle Programme*, *Five to Eleven*, *Live into 85* and *Artemis 81* - and that's just in as much time as it's taken to type this. However, the weirdest one taken for granted was the live coverage, over hours of prime-time, of darts matches. Obese men with mullets standing on one leg as Sid Waddell delivered commentary that had little to do with the match, or indeed anything in this dimension, in a broad geordie accent. This was "normal" for Michael Grade's BBC1.

17   The Free Will, creativity and democracy-at-all-costs agenda seems to be part of the whole Entropy thing (and we could go into a lengthy discussion of Claude Shannon's work on signal-to-noise rations and their similarities to Ludwig Boltzmann's equations for Entropy, but it wouldn't kill you to do *some* of the reading for yourselves, would it?). All the Doctors have admired humans for taking risks and investigating for themselves, and in recent years this has become the definition of "human" (see, for example, X2.8, "The Impossible Planet"), even if David Tennant pronounces it "chooomin".

18   Assume for a moment that the display of strange faces in the mind-bending contest with Morbius were all earlier Doctors (except the one that's obviously Morbius). This would mean that the Doctor's final incarnation wore cricket gear, and whoever this person is that's travelling around with Peri and Mel, he's someone else entirely. And what happened between the Doctor's twelfth and final incarnation? It's the Watcher from 18.7, "Logopolis".

19   We only needed one more name, so "and so on" seemed a bit clunky. Anyway, let's start a rumour that Keith Chegwin, 70s kids' show presenter and now professional has-been self-parody, has been approached by BBC Wales. What do you bet the *News of the World* would believe that Cheggers was to be the Eleventh Doctor if enough of us said it?

20   At least in the television series proper. Thirteen years later, producer Bill Baggs reunited all three - and the Tetraps - for an audio story called "The Rani Reaps the Whirlwind". We wouldn't like to speculate on Ms O'Mara's fee for the production, but we can't help but notice that a lot of BBV's other plays of the same tax year are monologues or two-handers. And we suggest a look at A1, "Dimensions in Time" too. The Bakers were upset at their character being used without them writing for it. So "Dimensions" really *could* have been worse...)

21   Environmentally-minded, RTD is recycling names. Do a drama about a gay man falling in love with a woman, call her "Rose" (*Bob and Rose*, 2001). Have another Rose and give her the name of the family in "Image of the Fendahl", then give

Ma Tyler's first name to her successor. Martha Jones may be related to Stuart Jones, whose best mate was Vince Tyler (*Queer as Folk*). And you start the sequel with an abortive threesome between Stuart, Vince and a black guy called 'Mickey Smith'.

Now, the sheer number of Joneses in Wales makes it slightly more plausible that the new companion's got the same surname as the Prime Minister (X2.0, "The Christmas Invasion") and *Torchwood*'s Mr Fixit, but when a totally unrelated series - *Life on Mars* - has a time-travelling cop called Sam Tyler, named by the author after Rose and his own son, it's starting to get like the Terry Nation "Tarrant" obsession. And then the author of *Life on Mars* was invited to write X2.11, "Fear Her".

22   The one bright spot in mid-80s rock-music television was *The Tube*, a shambolic series on Friday evenings that had an impressive record for launching stars. It mixed music, comedy and style features apparently at random. In many ways, it seemed the natural heir to *Tiswas* as much as it was consciously an 80s *Ready, Steady Go!* Unfortunately, people with Clever Ideas about how the younger generation "consume" television tried their own versions, and there was a torrent of smug, pretentious, irritatingly-presented music and current-affairs shows - which entailed wonky hand-held cameras, fast-editing for no good reason and bite-sized items of no use to man or beast. Most of these were the fault of Janet Street-Porter, who quit presenting when everyone started imitating her garbled, gurgling delivery and began producing shite like *Def II* and *Network 7*. TV bosses watched these avidly and thought them "hip" and "edgy", but nobody under 30 would be seen dead with such stuff on in the room.

The worst excess of "Yoof" TV, as the style became known, was *Club X*, which was a pretentious arts show inside a night-club with terrible acoustics. So you saw trendy people wandering about from fire-eaters to painters, doing that jabbing towards the camera that rappers do, but nobody - including the people being interviewed - could follow what they were saying. Paul Cornell apparently wrote for this, but luckily they didn't sully his reputation by using any of his work.

23   In the early days of Channel Five in the UK, when picture quality and the number of films not starring TV's Eric Roberts were at a minimum, it was actually possible to wait for an ad break - when the flatmates went for coffee - and put on "Paradise Towers" while they weren't looking. It's amazing how often they got to the cliffhanger and end credits before realising.

24   Those of you who can't read Welsh'd better learn, as they're making another series of *Torchwood*. A double-l is pronounced like a spanish "c", midway between "h" and "l". Two "d"s make a "th", "u" and "y" swap and "w" is a vowel. So "Heddlu" - pronounced "hethleo" - is "police", "Pobol Y Cwm" means "Switch off the television" and "Ffalabalam" means "You will not understand the next ten minutes of this conversation".

25   It bombed because we'd had the Twist and the Madison, but when the single "There Ain't Nothin' Like A Shag" came out, no British radio station would play it (for reasons that should, post-*Austin Powers*, be obvious). So the dance craze passed us by, therefore nobody here was nostalgic for it in 1987.

26   Before the War, the Tavern was where George Orwell and Dylan Thomas would hang out and complain that people kept pestering them for autographs. Thomas stopped coming when Aleister Crowley became a regular. For a large chunk of its history, the Tavern was the heart of Fitzrovia - and therefore the focus of the capital's cultural life.

Since 1984, it's been adopted by *Doctor Who* fans, but not in such numbers as to stop the place being swamped with students and ghastly media types. At designated times of the year, the ritual has been for us to walk into a jam-packed pub and decide "nobody's here yet", then wait to spot a familiar face. About half of these faces are people you'd wanted to talk to for ages; the others are people you'd like to avoid if possible. Later, you'll be introduced to someone you've been chatting to online for years, who was actually the first person you saw when you walked in. If you're lucky, you can chat to the writers of the new series and the authors of your favourite spin-off books. If not, you can have Nev Fountain tell you how funny he is.

Mostly, though, you have access to a vast reservoir of information from all walks of life, including barristers and medics (increasingly useful as we "classic" series fans get older). By 9.00 pm, the Not-We thin out and we get a chance to sit down. (Usually, the fans start forming breakaway cells on the street outside, so if you prefer, you can spend the entire night without going in.) By this time, anyone who's been wearing a long stripey scarf or an anorak has drifted away, because everyone's ignored them and denied any knowledge of being "those *Doctor Who* people" when asked by journalists or geeks. As we keep saying, fandom is an ice-breaker, but not the sole reason we hang out together afterwards. Until recently, one would accept cheaply-made freebie fanzines as the only mention of the series permitted, whilst we meet to talk about our lives, interests and problems and hire each other to write or produce some commercial gubbins. (*About Time* began as a chat at the Tavern, as did *Dreamwatch* and Big Finish.)

The absolute height of the Tavern was, paradoxically, when the series ended in 1989 and we found we liked having our own agenda more now there were no distractions like new episodes. The lowest ebb was in 1995 to 1996, as the impending TV Movie killed first *DWM* as it had been, then Virgin's *New Adventures,* and then a lot of the fun of being fans of a forgotten show. Now, we all bitch about each other's spin-off projects, gripe about how bad *Torchwood* is and spit in the pints we buy Nev Fountain.

Then, come closing time, we run the gauntlet of the truculent Australian Oompa-Loompas hired as bar-staff and either go home, or to each other's homes, or to exciting night-spots we can't really afford. If, at the latter, we meet anyone we know from the Tavern, we pretend not to recognise each other.

27   Incidentally, that episode aired the week that Brad Pitt ran off with Angelina Jolie.

28   A slightly more feasible hobby than you might think. The publisher of this book went to a high school where students in the late 60s blew up the chemistry lab, in an ambitious / inventive / foolhardy attempt to make homemade rocket fuel. However, in Britain at that time, after-school chemistry was more associated with recreational pharmacology and bicycle theft.

29   No surname is ever given on screen, so when Paul Cornell wrote his Virgin *New Adventures* book *No Future* he asked Briggs, who said, "It's whatever it was in *The Wizard of Oz*." Cornell asked someone else who - muddling it up with *Charlie and the Chocolate Factory* - pronounced that Dorothy's surname was "Bucket" (and not pronounced "Bouquet", either). So Cornell - in conjunction with Kate Orman when she wrote the novel *Set Piece* - saddled the character with the surname "McShane", and thus it has been across three mutually-exclusive spin-off continuities, to the extent that Mike Tucker and Robert Perry contrived to kill one Ace and introduce her parallel universe avatar to cover the name-change.

30   Slash is assuredly a minority hobby, and British fans just don't do it... well, we should clarify that. Fans of the pre-2005 stuff generally don't. Fans of the Welsh series sometimes do, but they're usually part of the British Public, and not what we commonly regard as *Doctor Who* fandom. Most of us hadn't *heard* the term "slash" until the Jenkins / Tulloch Tag-Team of Terror casually informed us that this was what we spent our waking hours doing. Actually, most of us were busily writing professionally by that stage, even getting original *Who* fiction into print by way of Virgin Books or the BBC or getting proper novels published. (We shouldn't get too snobbish or elitist about all of this, however, because - and here's a whole new dimension to the debate - some of the *New Adventures* authors wrote gay erotica for Virgin under pseudonyms.) But even now, with people coming to *Who* from other "Cult" TV fandoms within the UK, slash numerically remains a minority interest, however much of it is swilling around online.

If you're among the uninitiated, slash is a kind of fan-fiction where the male protagonists of butch shows such as *The A-Team* discover how they really feel about one another, in maladroitly-written gay porn by people who often have no clue what gay men actually do with one another. The classic example is Spock and Kirk, doing all sorts of *ponn-farr*-related rudeness. The most worrying recent example - not so far discovered by academics, so we offer this to anyone looking for a thesis - is slash about the three presenters of blokey auto-review show *Top Gear*, which may cause British readers to feel slightly ill. *Doctor Who* is its own slash, as a glance at **What Are The Gayest Things In *Doctor Who*?** under 25.2, "The Happiness Patrol" will amply demonstrate.

To be frank, the idea that *Who* slash was even *needed* was part of an overall misconception that *Doctor Who* was somehow just *Star Trek* with different accents. British *Doctor Who* fandom started from rock music fan activities: not three-day conventions but pub-quizzes; not merchandise tables but sarcastic fanzines modelled on Punk handouts.

31   One of the best British introductions to Bakhtin's work is by Simon Dentith, whose dad played Major General Rutlidge in 6.3, "The Invasion". Imagine how discovering this the day after writing a piece on the Rabelaisean tropes associated with UNIT, and IE turning London into their own playground and the literally gutless Cybermen using sewers and pop music to take over the world, can freak you out.

32   Look, this is Shoreditch, not Alabama. The simple and sad fact is that anyone in the Bed and Breakfast business had to be careful not to alienate existing customers, and to avoid the prejudices of the neighbours. Recent events have shown that the British Working Class might mouth off about minorities they don't know much about, but also are statistically more inclined to have babies with people from ethnic groups other than their own. People here are scared of being thought racist, but also lapse into stereotypes. Back then it was slightly different, but the ignorance combined with the fear of consequences in unpredictable ways.

In early 1960s London, it was rare for "coloureds" who weren't in long-term jobs with the NHS or London Transport - with automatic accommodation - to have guaranteed rent anyway. Many landlords would happily have taken on immigrants as tenants (they had lower expectations and were less likely to cause trouble), if only people would refrain from lobbing bricks through their windows or refusing to serve them in the shops. That bit of London had a long track-record of adopting and adapting to immigrants, and Mrs Smith is very likely descended from Irish labourers and Huguenots, if she but knew it. Mrs Smith had probably not actually met any "coloureds", except maybe John at the café, but Mr Smith might well have served with Jamaicans in the War and had other ideas. But he apparently died, so his widow presumably had to raise a son the best way she could, with complete strangers taking over her home.

Yes, she should have taken a stand, and people like her too. Yes, a character like this might be expected to if this were *Doctor Who* and *not* real life - if you see what we mean. Yes, in real life she would have been part of the problem. And yes, her son turned out to be a monster. But this doesn't automatically mean she's a bad person - she's just a symptom of what happens if everyone waits for someone else to do the right thing. That sort of thing happens a lot in Season Twenty-Five.

33   Consider this an addendum to *Redeemed*, Mad Norwegian's *Angel* guide: there's the entire notion of taking over a derelict hotel after removing a previous malignant force that occupied it; and a big thread where the tortured hero unexpectedly becomes a father and the kid vanishes into a parallel dimension, only to return as a sulky teen some weeks later in accordance with a prophesy. More broadly, the entire tone of *Shade* seems to have informed *Angel* (angsty demonic force and impossible relationships with mortals, punctuated by pop-culture references and shafts of pure camp). There's also time-travel and flashback malarkey, including Our Hero, his airhead not-quite girlfriend, *her* girlfriend and John Constantine getting put on trial in Salem, 1692, plus - in 'case you're curious - a whole thing with Hemingway and Joyce coming to stay at his pad and reading their own futures.

34   The 5th of November was what England did instead of Hallowe'en. Guy Fawkes was a York-born mercenary who fought in the Thirty Years' War on the Catholic side. A conspiracy by well-placed English Catholics to assassinate the King and all lords and bishops at the State opening of Parliament was narrowly averted, and Fawkes - who was caught placing the explosives under the Palace of Westminster - was the patsy. Catholics were made pariahs for centuries, only permitted to vote in 1838, and Royalty are still forbidden to marry them, hence Prince Charles' prolonged bachelor status. With Puritans soon after coming to power and banning any quasi-pagan festivities - such as Christmas and All Souls Day - Guy Fawkes' execution was an excuse to have a feast with bonfires, fireworks and burning effigies in mid-Autumn.

Two centuries later, Christmas became more of a big deal, with Dickens and Prince Albert rebranding it as the family event of the year. The

Scottish version of Hallowe'en - still celebrated in a largely Catholic nation - was later sold back to us by the Americans. "Guising", wearing soot on your face and going from house to house performing, was the Scots equivalent of the pre-Puritan Mummers' plays and became part of the origins of Minstrel shows. (See earlier volumes for comments on Mummers and "Mummerset". Lots of them.) So these days, the tradition of making a Guy Fawkes out of old clothes and lumbering it around in a pram to ask for a penny with which to buy fireworks (even if you couldn't buy them until you were sixteen) has almost been replaced by the loathsome "trick or treat". As most cultures have a winter solstice festival of some kind, Britain today has fireworks for Divali and Eid at around the start of November. So the rabidly anti-Catholic pretext for reviving the pre-Christian fire and freshly-slaughtered roast beast knees-up has been largely forgotten.

35   The pre-credit sequence from "A Man for Emily" (the single most bizarre and high-camp *Tomorrow People* story) has a lingering shot that slowly pans, from feet to head, of a young, near-naked Peter Davison lolling about wearing boxer-boots, tight lamé shorts, a Harpo wig and a dazed expression. This is the only clip many people have seen since broadcast - it was his first TV appearance, so it gets trotted out sporadically but oddly *doesn't* convey a distorted impression of the series as a whole. This is a series wherein young men would wear kilts or wet shirts in almost every second episode, after all.

36   The Cult of Flavia is loyal out of all proportion to her screen-time. Dinah Sheridan's performance in "The Five Doctors" is all right, even if she looks bored most of the time, but through a combination of the silly hairdo, the delivery of her name by Anthony Ainley in *that* scene and her being the only remotely sensible person in the Gallifrey section of the story, she's lodged herself in the memory.
There is a party game where you have to keep a straight face whilst answering any question with "Chancellor Flavia" - which is practically impossible if you remember her. Gay-themed Fanzine *Cottage Under Siege* made great use of the character's intrinsic camp appeal, but more recently it has emerged that Murray Gold and Russell T Davies refer to the vocal music used to denote a

deus ex machina plot development as "The Chancellor Flavia Theme". The idea is that it's her singing whenever the Doctor magically grows his hand back (X2.0, "The Christmas Invasion") or Margaret Slitheen turns into a turnip (X1.11, "Boom Town"). The BBC: this is what they do.

37   The headline in the *Guardian* for 17th of May, 2007, proclaims that Russia began the Cyber-War by disabling Estonia's e-government. This may radically affect attempts to date 12.5, "Revenge of the Cybermen". At the very least, the use of this phrase in all seriousness by a respected newspaper is mildly alarming.

38   Mavis Riley even used the words, in a script by Gareth Roberts. Mavis, by then the widow of Derek Wilton, who'd died of a heart-attack brought on by road-rage (doncha just love it when *Corrie* tackles social issues? Makes 'White kids firebombed it' look like David Mamet) secretly planned to move back to Cumbria and open a Bed and Breakfast guesthouse in Cartmel-in-Furness. In 1997 she finally achieved this, but not before referring to it as her 'Cartmel Masterplan'. Mavis Riley's catch-phrase, "Well, I don't really know" provided Les Dennis with years of material: we could explain his contribution to the sum of human happiness, but just watch that episode of *Extras* and try not to think of him dating Sophie Aldred. Mavis was played by Thelma Barlow, later of *dinnerladies* (see 26.3, "The Curse of Fenric") and X3.6, "The Lazarus Experiment").

39   Although you can surely make some good guesses, if you've ever played Anecdote Bingo.

40   Paul Cornell, whose farewell BBC Eighth Doctor novel *The Shadows of Avalon* reads like an attempt to redo "Battlefield" only less imaginatively, is at time of writing rumoured to be about to helm a relaunch of *eXcalibur* (sic). But then, Kylie Minogue was widely rumoured to be the villain in the forthcoming Christmas episode.

41   Take it from a former resident of that grotesque town: Corby is not a place to visit voluntarily.

42   Yes indeed, True Believers, Marvel did a comic-book biography of Karel Wojtiwa in the late 80s. It had the Pontiff with his red cape and

arms aloft where the Spider-Man logo should be on the front cover, top left, as if about to fly to the rescue. The penultimate page, set just after he was shot, has someone in St Peter's Square point into the sky and say "Look! It's John Paul II!" He even gets to quip, "It's a dirty job, but someone's got to do it" cleaning up after Nazis use the seminary as a latrine. It was a one-off (or "origin story" as they call it in comic circles), which is a shame. If they'd done a series, he'd probably have met the X-Men or Spider-Man in Ish 5. Excelsior!

Curiously, in all the online discussions of Marvel "Universes" this is never mentioned, although the possible links between *Death's Head*, the adaptation of *Transformers* and one or more Captain Britain comics are the subject of heated debate until someone over sixteen comes in and tells them off.

43   The exact sequence of events is even more complicated than this. John Freeman moved on and was replaced by Gary Russell - who dropped the ongoing strip in favour of new stories with older Doctors. Then Russell was replaced by Gary Gillatt, who waxed lyrical in his editorials about how much he hated the books. The Seventh Doctor and Ace reappeared in a story that negated two years' worth of their earlier strip adventures. Ace then died in a bid to show that the strip could not only contradict the books, but was the true and only inheritor of the new canon laid down by 27.0, "The TV Movie".

44   Though, as in 1986 and 1987, the fourteen-week run from September left a week's gap before the Christmas schedule. It was filled this year by a repeat of *Perfect Strangers*, a US sitcom with the high concept, "What if someone like Latka from *Taxi* had his own show, but it was rubbish?"

45   You and a friend have committed a crime. The investigating officer places you in separate cells, incommunicado. He offers you a deal. Confess and you get two years. Grass your friend and you get six months. Get grassed by your friend, seven years. The cop is gambling that each of you will grass the other, or each confess. The assumption that the optimum strategy is to betray your friends was - it emerged - a result of the originator, John Nash, being a misanthropic paranoid schizophrenic. By the way, Nash - who has appar-

ently seen the error of his ways - is said to be a *Doctor Who* fan. The biopic *A Beautiful Mind* neglected to show this.

46   BBC Wales' first venture into big-budget fantasy for kids, *Superted*, was a cartoon about a rejected teddy who got superpowers and hung out with a Spotty Man from a Spotty Planet. The voice for the latter was Jon Pertwee, the narrator was Peter Hawkins and Superted was Derek Griffiths, *Play School* presenter and so much more. Add to this Melvyn Hayes as a cowardly skeleton, and it's easy to see why it's so fondly remembered, lousy though the scripts were. All together now: "Gweat Moonth of Thpot!")

47   Well, not as finally as all that. The film is rare in that the sequel is not a remake, but a totally new story about Irena's spirit protecting her husband's child; he married the other woman afterwards. *Curse of the Cat People* has no connection with cats except that Irena, Alice and Olly are in it. Incidentally, for *Doctor Who* fans the confusing part is an actor called "Kent Smith" playing "Oliver Reed".

48   The Daleks and the Cybermen. Honestly.

49   That's a more serious point that you might think. If you've bought this book, odds are good you have some idea of what *Doctor Who* is like, but try looking at "The TV Movie" through the eyes of an average American viewer. You would see an ordinary joe - a paramedic - forced into a nightmarish situation and the loss of his wife. He's played by the one cast-member you've seen in anything else. Situated against him is a goofy little Scotsman who turns into a tricky, fast-taking sexy guy with long hair and a British accent. In American viewership terms, this is about like having a neon signs saying "Do Not Approach".

In fact, watching almost any US blockbuster movie in Britain in the mid-90s, it felt that we were the only group it was acceptable to hate. From Hannibal Lecter down, if you want a classy bad guy, you get a Brit. Bruce Willis went through all but the most recent *Die Hard* dealing with the adverse consequences of letting people who talk properly though customs. Hugh Laurie has to do a bad Tom Waits impression to get any work now. Evidently, Christopher Eccleston was offered the part of serial killer Sylar on *Heroes*, but turned it down on the grounds that he didn't want the villain portrayed as yet-another evil British / European-type (so he wound up playing a homeless invisible man instead). Even the supposedly "astute" twenty-first century refit of *Battlestar Galactica* has committed the same ethnic slur. So even if you somehow slogged through the tiresome info-dumps in the TV Movie's first half hour, it would've seemed out-of-kilter.

50   There might be legal reasons for this, with the joint-ownership of the rights to the Movie complicating matters. This is the official reason we hear Ainley going 'heh-heh-heh' and Delgado yelling at Azal - 8.5, "The Daemons" - from inside Professor Yana's watch in X3.11, "Utopia" but not any soundbites of 'This. Is. An. Ambulance!' or 'Ah always drezz for the occasion'. Few people believe it, but it gives RTD a fig-leaf.

51   In trying to distance himself from the film, McGann did a lot of other work, especially in voice-overs for mildly tittilating documentaries on Channel 4 - the same "I'm a legitimate actor, go away you anorak-wearing non-entity" ploy adopted by Eccleston in the immediate aftermath of his jumping ship. One of these, The Sperminator, told of a medic who ran a sperm-donation service with himself as the only donor. With the Oprah / Springer-style captions identifying those people doing talking-head pieces in capital letters, this gave us the memorable conjunction of McGann's voice and the words DOCTOR WHO FATHERED 73 CHILDREN. It's worth accepting McGann as the Eighth Doctor just for *that*, surely?)

52   Chewbacca's cute nephews in this TV masterpiece. If you didn't know that, or that it even existed, look it up on YouTube: it will make your nose bleed.

53   The Millenium Dome. John Major's government had decided they would honour the turn of the millennium a year early by, among other things, building an enormous white dome on the Greenwich Meridian and filling it with unspecified "precious things". That bit of Greenwich can be seen in its previous state in 25.3, "Silver Nemesis", but Birmingham put in a better bid and had transport links already. (This scheme was settled upon around the time that 27.0, "Grace: 1999", was in development, so there must have been something in the air.) The notion of aiding deprived areas with crappy theme-parks was Trade Minister Michael Hestletine's all-purpose Big Idea - he had suggested something similar for Liverpool after riots, and it was launched in 1984 with a record of two Beatles classics by Jon Pertwee. He'd also been behind a plan to have Corby, Northants (26.1, "Battlefield") made over from a Third World cesspit into a *Dan Dare* Experience.

In 1997, Major's government was voted out, but the Dome had secured the enthusiastic backing of incoming prime minister Tony Blair, who unwisely decided that it should be the centrepiece of the millennium celebrations, a showcase for corporate sponsorship and a veritable carnival of whimsy. The result wasn't quite as tedious as painted - it had a TARDIS in it and film of John Scott Martin reminiscing about his childhood, so we liked it - but it quickly turned into an expensive folly and national joke. The Dome was enlivened by exactly three things: a) the day it was ram-raided by international jewel thieves; b) the amusing *Blackadder* film running regularly at its cinema complex; and c) the fact that Michael Grade was in charge and receiving a salutory lesson in what "unpopular" really means.

ABOUT TIME

1970-1974

SEASONS 7 TO 11 (SECOND EDITION)

ABOUT TIME

THE UNAUTHORIZED GUIDE TO **DOCTOR WHO**

1970-1974
SEASONS 7 TO 11
(SECOND EDITION)

TAT WOOD

Coming in 2008... In the *About Time 3* second edition, Tat Wood vastly expands upon the Jon Pertwee Era, bringing this installment of the *About Time* series up to the size and elaborate depth of its fellows.

New essays in this second edition will include "What the Hell Were the Daemons Doing?", "Where Were Torchwood When All This Was Happening?" and "Is This Any Way to Run a Galactic Empire?"

Many existing essays and entries have been greatly retooled, and evidence from the new *Doctor Who* series (unbroadcast when this book first published) has been taken into account. In every regard, this book displays the eye-popping complexity readers expect from the *About Time* range.

(At present, Mad Norwegian has no plans to do second editions of the other *About Time* volumes.)

ISBN: 0-9759446-7-3
MSRP: $19.95

www.madnorwegian.com

*1150 46th St
Des Moines, IA
madnorwegian@gmail.com*

mad norwegian press

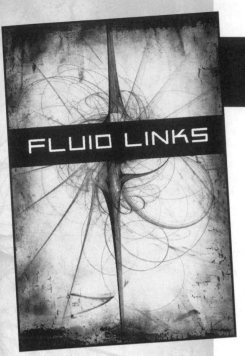

who made all this ?

Since the heady days of *About Time 3*, when 'Judoon' was just the noise a mattress made when you threw it down stairs and 'Captain Jack' was just a bad Billy Joel record, **Tat Wood** has: left Ilford to live in an attic overlooking Alexandra Palace, which he later left to go out on the open road; run a school for a year; quit teaching - twice; been the public face of the Bangladeshi Women's Society (despite two obvious drawbacks); written for a forthcoming academic publication whilst reviewing odd television for *TV Zone*; and been proved right about a lot of the stuff in the earlier books. This is all the more impressive when you realise that he is really in a hospital bed in the year 2041, in a coma and hallucinating about being in 2007 after being hit by a hover-car.

Only one of these facts is untrue.

His favourite story in this volume is (quickly tosses coin, "Greatest Show" loses) "Ghost Light". His least favourite would have been the Paul McGann TV Movie, but that doesn't actually count as *Doctor Who*, so it has to be "The Two Doctors". Well, there's a surprise!

Mad Norwegian Press

Publisher/Series Editor
Lars Pearson

Copy Editor
Dave Gartner

Interior & Cover Design
Christa Dickson

Cover Art
Jim Calafiore

Cover Colors
Richard Martinez (artthug.com)

Associate Editors
For AT6: Robert Smith?, Michael Thomas. *For MNP:* Joshua Wilson.

Technical Support
Marc Eby

The publisher thanks... Lawrence Miles (without whom, there would be no *About Time*); Rob Shearman, who stepped up to the plate when "The Two Doctors" needed a defence; Bill Albert, Jeremy Bement and everyone at the Iowa *Doctor Who* fan club; Shawne Kleckner; Lynne Thomas; and that nice lady who sends me newspaper articles.

1150 46th Street
Des Moines, Iowa 50311
madnorwegian@gmail.com
www.madnorwegian.com